Born in N..e author
of Gabriel'..Pride of
Carthage. Acacia: The War with the Mein marked his first foray
into fantasy literature and was greeted with universal acclaim
winning the 2009 John W. Cambell Award for Best New
Write..ne and
his wife and children are now based in Massachusetts, where
he is working on the concluding volume of the Acacia Trilogy.

For more information on David Anthony Durham and his
books, see his website at www.davidanthonydurham.com

'Entertaining and engaging . . . If *War with the Mein* is an indication of what is to come in this epic saga, Durham could be making a very big name for himself . . . an accomplished novelist and storyteller'
SFFWorld

'The reader is transported and transfixed . . . full of wonders, brought to us by a masterful writer, a wizard of mind and place'
Jeffrey Lent

'Vastly entertaining . . . Will good win out over evil? In Durham's morally ambiguous world, the uncertainty is part of the thrill'
StrangeHorizons

'A big, fat, rich piece of history-flavoured fantasy . . . imagined with remarkable thoroughness'
Time

'A novel of large impact, as radical a rewriting of George R. R. Martin as Martin himself has performed on Tolkien'
Locus

'Thrilling . . . Durham's new world – like our old one – is crawling with wickedly fascinating characters'
Entertainment Weekly

'A fascinating world . . . the characters are gratifyingly multidimensional, flawed, gifted, and conflicted in their makeup and motivations, and capable of change'
USA Today

'A truly epic fantasy – or rather the beginning of one – with a rich world and nuanced characters. Superbly written'
Fantasy magazine

'Durham has pulled off something remarkable: a huge, sprawling epic that manages to weave together history, politics, intrigue and thunderous action scenes without ever losing track of the multitudes of finely-drawn characters'
RevolutionSF

Also by David Anthony Durham

GABRIEL'S STORY
WALK THROUGH DARKNESS
HANNIBAL: PRIDE OF CARTHAGE
ACACIA: THE WAR WITH THE MEIN

The Other Lands

David Anthony Durham

BANTAM BOOKS

LONDON • TORONTO • SYDNEY • AUCKLAND • JOHANNESBURG

TRANSWORLD PUBLISHERS
61–63 Uxbridge Road, London W5 5SA
A Random House Group Company
www.rbooks.co.uk

**THE OTHER LANDS
A BANTAM BOOK: 9780553819687**

First published in the United States in 2009 by Doubleday, a division of
Random House, Inc., New York, and in Canada by
Random House of Canada Limited, Toronto.

First published in Great Britain
in 2009 by Doubleday
an imprint of Transworld Publishers
Bantam edition published 2010

Copyright © David Anthony Durham 2009

Book design by Maria Carella
Map illustration by David Cain

Addresses for Random House Group Ltd companies outside the UK
can be found at: www.randomhouse.co.uk
The Random House Group Ltd Reg. No. 954009

The Random House Group Limited supports The Forest Stewardship Council
(FSC), the leading international forest certification organisation. All our titles that
are printed on Greenpeace approved FSC certified paper carry the FSC logo.
Our paper procurement policy can be found at www.rbooks.co.uk/environment

Typeset in 11/13pt Goudy by Falcon Oast Graphic Art Ltd.
Printed in the UK by CPI Cox & Wyman, Reading, RG1 8EX.

2 4 6 8 10 9 7 5 3 1

For Maya and Dolphino,
without whom there would be no
Mena and Elya

Contents

The Story So Far
15

Prologue
23

Book One
The Gray Slopes
35

Book Two
On Love and Dragons
229

Book Three
Song of Souls
415

Acknowledgements 603

USHEN BRAE

←WESTLANDS
AND
SKY ISLE

AGRICULTURAL
REGION

AVINA

LEAGUE
PLATFORMS

Gray
Slopes

SOUTHERN
DISTRICT

FUDEL
ANCESTRAL
LANDS

THE
THOUSANDS

Lithram
Len

THE RANGE

THRAIN

SUMERLED

The
Bleeding
Road

Soul Catchar

OUTER ISLE

Sheeven Lek

PALISHDOCK

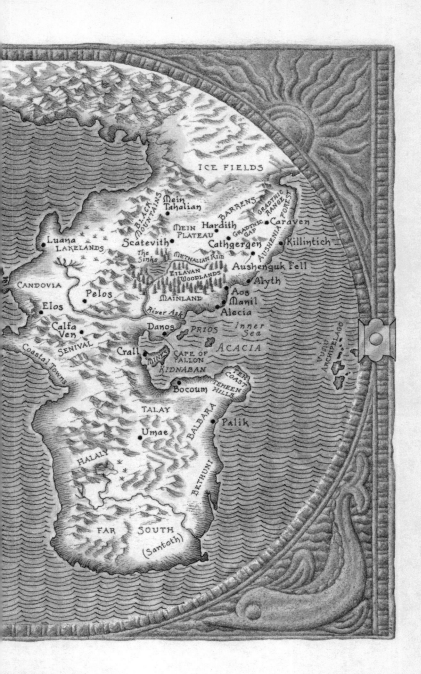

The
Other Lands

The Story So Far

Thasren Mein, an assassin, journeys from the far north. He is the youngest brother of Hanish Mein, chieftain of the exiled northern people from which they take their surname. Thasren bears with him the anger of a defeated people, and he carries a weapon meant to strike at the heart of the ruling Acacian Empire and to announce a long-planned war.

As Thasren moves south into the milder climate of the central empire, the family he is targeting lives an idyllic life, oblivious of the danger creeping toward them. The Akarans, led by King Leodan, have lived for generations at the center of a prosperous empire. The land has been relatively peaceful for years, although the nation's early rise was the result of chaotic warfare. It had been mythologized in tales of the first king, Edifus, his son, Tinhadin, and the legendary band of sorcerers, the Santoth, who were supposed to have helped them win power.

King Leodan rules from the beautiful isle of Acacia, at the center of an inland sea. He is a widower who dotes on his four children: Aliver, a head-strong boy of sixteen; Corinn, the family beauty; Mena, an insightful adolescent; and nine-year-old Dariel, a boy with an adventuresome spirit. Leodan knows that the empire is held together by a number of long-standing crimes. In addition to keeping an iron military grip on the provinces, for years the Acacians have traded with faraway foreigners known as the Lothan Aklun. A naval trading conglomerate, the League of Vessels, handles all the details, so that the two sides never interact. The Acacians send a regular quota of children into some unknown slavery, receiving riches and a drug called mist in return. The empire then distributes mist among the populace, keeping them dull and obedient.

Leodan shelters his children from this, wanting them to have happy childhoods full of love. But in his solitary moments Leodan temporarily forgets his guilt over the empire's crimes—and his longing for his dead wife—by inhaling mist himself.

The king's closest friend and confidant, his chancellor, Thaddeus Clegg, was raised with Leodan. Thaddeus has a secret, one that has turned him against his old friend. He has recently learned—with Hanish Mein's scheming assistance—that the Akaran family was responsible for the death of his beloved wife and infant child years earlier. It was not a crime Leodan had any part in, but learning of it bitterly twists Thaddeus against the king. When a soldier arrives to warn the king of troop movements in the far north, Thaddeus kills the messenger, thereby buying his distant ally Hanish crucial time to unleash his surprise attack.

And what a multi-pronged attack it is! Thasren stabs King Leodan with a poisoned blade during a banquet. Hanish's other brother, Maeander, leads one army sweeping down from the northwest. To the northeast an alien race, the Numrek, fight savagely on the Mein side. All around the Known World, Meinish soldiers conscripted into the Acacian army rebel. Hanish himself drags a navy across the frozen tundra so that he can launch the boats on spring-flooded rivers and appear suddenly in the Inner Sea, in the heart of the Acacian Empire. In addition to all this, Hanish unleashes a contagion that sends the vulnerable Acacians into writhing agony. And he slaughters them without mercy.

Caught off guard by the sudden fury of the attack, Acacian authority collapses. On his deathbed, Leodan calls on his old friend Thaddeus to enact a plan they had discussed years earlier. Despite everything, Thaddeus agrees. His love of the children is too great for him to hand them over to Hanish Mein. Instead, he sends the children out into the far reaches of the empire, escorted by lone guardians, to be hidden. The hope is that they will grow to maturity in safety and one day reunite and win back the empire.

Very little goes as planned. Only Aliver makes it to his intended destination. He is raised among the Talayan people of the south, in a tribal culture of warriors and hunters, runners who roam the arid plains of their vast continent. He even comes to learn that the mythical sorcerers, the Santoth, are real. He meets them and discovers they would very much like to return from their banishment and aid him but feel their magic has been too corrupted by time. They ask him if he has *The Song of Elenet*, the text in which the Giver's magical language was written. He does not, so they remain in exile. Aliver grows to manhood in this challenging environment and learns a great many things that build his character and leadership potential. His siblings do not fare quite as well.

Corinn is betrayed by her guardian. She is delivered into Hanish's hands and forced to live among the new Meinish court that has taken over her father's palace. For years she chafes against the luxurious bondage she is kept in, but slowly Hanish's charisma and charm begin to win her over. Much against her will, she falls in love with her captor.

Mena does not reach her planned destination either. Her guardian is killed, leaving her adrift in a small boat at sea. She drifts until she comes ashore on the remote, primitive Vumu Archipelago. There she is greeted as the earthly embodiment of one of the island's main deities, Maeben, the eagle goddess of wrath. Mena is raised in the temple in a position of privilege, although bound by the religion's strict rituals and formalities. For years this is her life, until Melio Sharratt—a childhood friend of Aliver's—discovers her. He assures her that the Akaran story is not over and secretly trains her in sword craft.

When Dariel's guardian cannot find the person he is supposed to deliver the young boy to, he abandons him amid the chaos of human migration happening in the mountain passes of Senival. By chance, the prince is found by Val, a giant of a man whom Dariel had met while exploring the servants' regions of the palace. Val had always told the prince tales of his earlier life as a pirate on the Gray Slopes. He proves the truth of it when he takes Dariel with him, raising the boy as a brigand and sea captain.

Thus the four Akaran children grow to adulthood in vastly different environments, completely out of touch with one another for years. They are brought together through the work of Thaddeus Clegg. The former chancellor, still living with the guilt of having betrayed his king, works among a network of agents to find and bring the Akarans back together.

Hanish Mein steps into the role the Akarans had occupied. He increases the slave quota and continues to suppress the people. It is not long before the varied peoples of the Known World, who had once chafed against Acacian rule, find themselves in even more dire straits under Hanish Mein.

And they don't know the worst of it. One of the early Acacian kings, Tinhadin, had put a curse on them. They are not allowed to pass out of life. Their bodies mummify and they remain trapped in them—not alive, not dead. It was a vindictive act of a mad tyrant, and Tinhadin could not have foreseen that the collective souls of all these Meinish ancestors would band together in a group called the Tunishnevre. They speak to Hanish and demand that they be transported to Acacia for a ceremony that will finally free them back into life with all the power and rage they've gained from centuries as the undead. The ceremony requires elaborate preparation and the blood of one of the Akaran line to succeed.

Aliver begins to rally the vast tribes of Talay. He speaks of a new dawn for the world, with a rule that will be just and fair, with power spread among the various peoples. He swears he will abolish the trade in child slaves, and with the distant help of the Santoth he helps the people defeat the mist addiction that has plagued them for so long. Dariel, fresh from skirmishes with the league, joins him. Mena, having broken with her adoptive religion, reunites with them also. Together, they drive an ever-growing army toward Hanish's forces.

Having helped orchestrate the reunion, Thaddeus takes some solace in seeing the children grown, healthy, and strong. He leaves them and sets off on a mission of his own. He realizes he knows where *The Song of Elenet* is hidden in the palace of Acacia, and he knows a secret way to enter and get to it. He manages this and plans to return the book to Aliver so that he can fully call on the Santoth. Before he leaves, he sees Corinn and makes contact with her, hoping she will flee with him.

What he doesn't know is that Corinn has undergone considerable changes. Unlike her siblings, she has never experienced life among the people. She knows only the palace, the court, wealth, and the shrewd manipulation of power. She has finally given her heart to Hanish, but one evening she overhears her lover communicating with the Tunishnevre. She hears him swear that he will kill her to release them. This is the last of many disappointments, and it makes her believe she can rely only on herself.

Thaddeus shows her *The Song of Elenet*. Feeling its power, Corinn makes up her mind. Instead of fleeing with Thaddeus, she poisons him. She hides the book and quickly works behind the scenes to secure her own power. She makes a deal with the league, convincing them to sit out the coming war, and she forms an alliance with Hanish's old allies, the Numrek, promising them the status Hanish never granted them. She brings in Rialus Neptos, a former Acacian governor with a duplicitous nature, to help her. She never exactly works against her siblings. Indeed, her actions aid them by taking the league and the Numrek away as threats, but neither is she working in concert with them. Her sights are set on Hanish, and she carefully arranges the pieces to strike him, even as he puts the finishing touches on his plan to resurrect the Tunishnevre.

Meanwhile, Aliver's army meets the Meinish forces, led by Maeander, on the plains of northern Talay. The clash lasts for several days, the advantage veering back and forth. Maeander unleashes savage beasts called antoks that do great damage to the rebellious forces, but so does Aliver's connection with the Santoth aid his cause and protect his people.

Then Maeander approaches the Acacians personally. He offers, invoking ancient customs, to fight Aliver in single combat. Aliver can't resist this chance of ending the contest between them, instead of letting so many of the common people he's grown to love die. Against Mena and Dariel's protests, he agrees. For a time it seems he might prevail, but all too suddenly Maeander strikes a fatal blow. Aliver falls dead.

In a moment of rage, Dariel orders the troops to attack Maeander, thus breaking the oaths given prior to the duel. Fighting resumes between both armies in earnest, and the Meinish forces appear to be winning. Waking on the morning that looks to be the end for the Acacian forces, Mena and Dariel are both stunned to see enormous, shadowy shapes approaching from the south. The shapes shrink to human size as they grow near and reveal themselves to be the Santoth. They've come out of exile, troubled and angry because they sensed Aliver's death. They know now that their banishment will not be lifted, and in rage they unleash their anger against the Meinish army. They rip apart the land and tear whole groups of soldiers to shreds with their songs and spells. Once the Santoth withdraw to the far south, it becomes clear the Acacians have won the battle.

Back on Acacia, Corinn has sprung her surprise attack on

Hanish, using her new Numrek allies, whom she has smuggled into the palace via the same route Thaddeus used. They attack and kill the Mein, eventually capturing Hanish. Corinn orders his execution on the very altar on which he had planned to sacrifice her. Rialus performs the act.

As the book ends, a sort of peace has returned to the Known World. Corinn steps unchallenged into the role of queen, receiving her two living siblings with gracious but somewhat cold hospitality. It seems her vision of the future might be very different from the idealistic notions Aliver had espoused. Also, she is pregnant with Hanish's child.

Prologue

In Luana, during the ninth year of Hanish Mein's rule

It should have been him. Just him. Ravi shouted this again and again. He jumped to be seen above the crowd. He pushed through the other children and grabbed at any of the red-cloaked soldiers he got near enough to reach. They ignored him or shoved him back into place or brought a crop down on his head and shoulders. Ravi would not stop shouting. They were making a mistake! He would go with them wherever they wished to take him. He would behave. He would do whatever they asked, but Mór should be no part of this! She was their parents' only other child. They needed her. Their mother could not live without her. He had heard her say so more than once.

"Please," he shouted, "let her go! Let her go home!"

A squat soldier rounded on him. He was shorter than most of the men, thick around the waist, with leathery skin and hair that bristled like a spiny rodent's. His crimson shirt stretched tight across his belly. He grabbed Ravi by the chin and spoke close to his face, the man's onion-scented words hot on his skin. "You're both quota," he said, his accent strange to Ravi's ears. "You understand? You've both been given. Two peas from the same pod, two pups from the same litter. That's just the way it is, lad. Accept it, and your life won't be so bad."

The man tried to push the boy away. When Ravi clung to his arm, the man growled that he had been patient enough. He balled his hand into a fist and smashed the boy on his nose.

Ravi saw black for a moment. When his eyes cleared he stood sputtering, stunned, his lips and chin and chest splattered with blood.

"Ravi . . ." His sister's voice finally reached him. Her voice was part of why he had been yelling. He feared to hear it. He began to move toward another red-cloaked man, but Mór threw her arms around him and would not be shaken off. "Please, Ravi, stop it! This helps nothing. You'll make them angrier."

Angrier? Ravi thought. Angrier? What did it matter if they were angry? He came near to whirling on her with harsh words, but her grip on him was tight and, in truth, he did not really want to break free from her. He knew that she was right. She was always calmer than he was. She never wasted actions, as he often did. On the farm, she worked each day steadily and slowly. She moved like an old woman, he used to think. But somehow she always finished her chores before him, no matter that he was faster and stronger than she. Even now, she was more self-assured than he was. Acknowledging this stilled him more than her grip on him and more than his fatigue and his battered face.

"Good, Ravi, come," she whispered, starting to pull him back into the mass of children. "Better they don't see you. They're not going to let me go. You know that, and they might separate us if you keep drawing attention to yourself. I don't want to be alone, Ravi."

Neither did he. He let her pull him into the group, sliding between the others until they were two among many. Now that he had ceased his commotion, he and his sister were little different from the rest. He saw a few faces from the neighboring village. The rest were strangers, but judging by their clothing, demeanor, and fear-filled eyes they were much the same as he and Mór. They were farm children, too, from the fertile but isolated territory north of the Lakelands. They had been gathered together near a town he had never been to.

24

They were like so many sheep brought into one corral and kept in place by wolves in red garments.

How many of them were there? Hundreds, Ravi thought. Children as young as seven or eight, some as old as he and his twin sister at thirteen. They all had frightened eyes and often whispered to those nearby, trying to gain some understanding of what was happening. Many had tear-streaked faces, smudged and dirty. Their hair was mostly silver blond, their complexions smooth and pale, eyes narrow and deep set in a way that foreigners sometimes laughed at, thinking them a dim, passive people. They weren't dim, though, or passive. They were far enough north that they had often gone unnoticed by those of the Known World. That had changed suddenly, Ravi realized, and the change already felt irrevocable.

The siblings sat down knee to knee among the others. Mór wiped Ravi's face with her sleeve, instructing him to raise his head. He did so sullenly, accepting her attentions but not able to look her in the eyes, as he knew she wished him to do. He had not cried once yet. He feared that looking into her face might change that: her face was too clear a reminder of things lost.

A few days ago the world Ravi knew had been measured by the rolling miles of farmland and moor around his village north of Luana. His family's cottage sat on a hill surrounded by fields of the sweet red potatoes that were one of the area's main crops. The houses of their nearest neighbors rimmed the horizon, spaced out by a half mile or so. A lonely landscape, damp each morning and cool throughout most days, no matter the season. It was a simple life he had led, daily toil at the tasks that modestly sustained their family of four.

His father was a quiet man with big hands; he limped from some injury of his youth. His mother had absurdly crooked teeth, which she showed often as laughter peppered all the words that came from her mouth. He knew that his mother

25

had lost two children in childbirth before having him and Mór. This was not unusual. Perhaps she was sad beneath all those smiles, but she made sure that Ravi never saw signs of it.

He had dreamed of escaping to something more exciting: sailing on a trading vessel, joining the guards that occasionally patrolled the provinces, or stealing a neighbor's horse and riding out into the world. He had found excitement, but not in the way he had imagined.

The red-cloaked men had arrived in the dark hours far from either dusk or sun return. Ravi heard the knock on the door. He heard his father grumbling a moment later, and he listened to the creak of the door and to the mumbled exchange that followed. Probably one of the neighboring farmers, Ravi thought, come to ask help for some midnight mishap. The farm over by the marshes had been having a problem with sheep thieves. Perhaps they were organizing a chase.

"Ravi," Mór had whispered from her cot on the other side of the room, "who is it?"

He shushed her. He had started to pull off his sheet, planning to tiptoe across the floor and listen through the crack in the door, but he got no farther than plucking the cloth between his fingertips.

A shout came from the main room, the sound of something—a chair, he thought—knocked over, the scrabble of feet on the packed-earth floor. He froze. Another shout and whispered curses and then sounds he couldn't place for a moment and then he could: the dull thuds of fists against flesh. He swung his legs free from the bed and set them on the floor. The light shining around the door frame shifted and danced and grew brighter. He watched it, hearing Mór's sharp inhalation of breath.

The door to their room flew open, kicked by a booted foot. Torches lit the room, cruel in their intensity. Through the torchlight the bodies of men emerged, burly, garbed in crimson. The first strode across the room and slammed a hand down on Ravi's neck. He leaned in close, studying the boy, the torch so close to his head that his features were a motley of distorted highlight and shadow. A second figure went to Mór. He was gentler. He placed a finger under Mór's chin and turned her so that the first man could see her face.

"Yes," he said, glancing between them, "you're two sides of the same coin. You two are one, together in the womb, together in your fate. Your councilmen told us true. Come on. On your feet, both of you. We'll not harm you if you come quiet."

He was so matter-of-fact, so casually intimidating that before he knew what he was doing Ravi was standing. He and Mór were pushed through the doorway into the main room. What Ravi saw there stayed in his memory only in fragments, disjointed images captured between the jolting motion of being shoved, stumbling. He saw his mother's face, open-mouthed, her teeth looking like the fangs of a wolf or bear. His eyes shot around to find his father. He couldn't find him. He saw a commotion of men near the cookstove, their arms and legs moving like those of some monster. He never did see him or pick out his body from among the motion, but Ravi knew that his father was at the center of it.

Ravi was roughly conveyed through it toward the door. His foot caught the side of the doorjamb, and he sprawled out into the night. He hit the ground hard on his forearms and elbows, rolled, and had a clear moment of thought as he watched the figures striding out after him. Red cloaks. They wore red cloaks! And that meant he and Mór were to be taken by the eaters! Older boys had told stories about such things, saying that from time to time the king to the south sent hunters through Candovia in search of the children his god loved to devour. Ravi had never believed it. It had never happened in his lifetime, and he knew older boys were cruel and liars. But now a man was reaching down for him; his father was pinned beneath a seething mass of limbs; his mother wore

27

a wolf's face; his sister was crying out at some roughness.

The anger was in him complete and instant, like oil on a fire. He kicked at the man reaching for him, a glancing blow off his shin. This made him angrier and he kicked again and again, his legs churning as he squirmed on the hard-packed ground. The man cursed and jumped back, then came in again, his entire bulk trailing behind the point of his boot toe. Ravi tried to wrap himself around it and pull the man off balance, but the boot tore free and came on again. In a moment others joined it.

That was the first time they beat him senseless. Because Ravi was unconscious he remembered nothing of how they were bundled into a wagon waiting by the road. He did not hear his mother's wail or see her appear in the doorway, held back by a soldier's arm. Nor did Mór ever tell him of it. Yet somehow he knew. He knew as certainly as if she had lent him her eyes and her ears.

Two days after the soldier squashed his nose—two days of travel, of beatings, of sleepless nights and numbing days—the children were herded with other groups from other villages near the coast. Many of them had been gathered in the coastal towns to celebrate the return of spring. Perhaps that was why they could be harvested in such great numbers. How the red-cloaked soldiers dealt with the children's parents Ravi was not sure. They could not beat them all, could they? Perhaps this was why they marched the children so mercilessly. Perhaps, but Ravi also felt certain there was more to it. Sometimes he could smell the pungent scent of mist carried on the breeze coming from the towns they skirted. It struck him with the melancholy that smoke from burned ruins would have. But the towns were not in ruins; not, at least, in the physical sense that was easiest to envision.

None of the children understood what was happening. Yes, they all knew the stories of the red-cloaked men, of the vanishings, but the stories had never been like this. They had heard of a child or two going missing every few years. Nothing more. And the tales had always said it was young children who were taken, none as old as Ravi and Mór. Whatever was happening now was a thing beyond even the nightmares that the older boys tried to weave into younger minds.

They were marched through the morning and into the afternoon. Around dusk they came down through sea bluffs and got their first view of the great league vessels. Their size was hard to gauge. At first Ravi thought them no large craft, but then he realized they were quite far out. They were, possibly, massive. They lay on a shimmering expanse of azure. The twins walked hand in hand near the front of the column. Ravi felt the swish of the tall, damp grass against his legs and thought he was lucky to be up front instead of behind, where the grass would be trodden down and could not be felt. Then he thought himself unkind or a fool or both. This is not possible, he thought. Not possible. But they continued to move forward, the world denying his claim without the slightest hesitation.

Ravi squeezed his sister's hand tighter and watched the ships.

They slept on a narrow ribbon of sand that night, hemmed in by crumbly cliffs guarded by watchers. Some of the children feared the ocean and cried. Ravi wanted to shout at them to stop, but he knew that would be unkind. He did not wish to be unkind. That would be making a bad thing worse and doing it to others as innocent as he. He was angry, and he did not want to let that anger fade or be replaced by fear or docility. He wanted to do something with it.

"Swear to me that you'll never give in to them," he said. These were the first words he had spoken in some time. He did not look at his sister but instead gazed unfocused. He raked his hands through the damp sand, feeling the texture in his fingers.

When Mór did not answer, Ravi faced her and studied her in the yellowish light of the fires that rimmed the encampment. He took her by both wrists and held tightly enough that he knew his grip pained her. "Don't go quiet. Swear that you won't!"

Mór looked miserable. "Ravi, how can I? You see them."

He drew close to her face. "Swear it! Don't give yourself to them. Don't."

She began to protest again, arguing that she would have to obey, alluding to the things they would do to her if she did not. Ravi cut her off.

"You're not listening," he said. "What I mean is don't ever believe that you are a slave, no matter what they make you do. The red cloaks say that we belong to some others now. They say we're not our own masters and that we have no parents. But they're liars. That's what I'm telling you to remember. You believe that they're liars?"

He waited until Mór nodded, then he continued, "Don't forget that. Don't let them make their lies into truths. Never forget that you are Mór, sister of Ravi, child of the parents we share. Promise me that."

She promised, and he finally let go of her wrists. "Why do you say these things?" Mór asked. "You act as if we are separated, but we're not. Just be quiet and don't draw attention and they will leave us with each other."

Ravi said nothing, and was glad when she did not ask him to swear, as he had done.

Sometime in the middle of the night he decided what he would do. And it was the opposite of not drawing attention. Mór would not understand it, but if he managed what he thought he could, she would come to understand later. He did not know exactly how he would do it, but he resolved to try. He felt he would know the moment when it showed itself.

Second to the league vessels themselves, the barges that approached the shore the next morning to transport the

30

children were the largest human-made structures Ravi had ever seen. Squat rectangular rafts, they stretched wide along the shore, flattening the waves beneath them. They were made of a slate-gray material, dull in a manner that seemed to capture the light of the risen sun. Ravi could not say what made them move, but something did, slowly, inexorably. And there were people aboard them. Not many, and not near enough to make them out clearly. But on one of the closer barges a cluster of five figures stood atop a raised platform. They did not move and were nothing more than outlines at first, but Ravi felt certain that each stared directly at him.

The children on the beach stared as if these silent things and those aboard them were more frightening than anything they had yet faced. They began to murmur and whisper. A boy near the twins said, "This is sorcery." Nobody denied it.

"Don't wet your trousers," one of the soldiers nearby said, guffawing. "Look at the lot of you. Gape mouthed like so many carp!"

Another added a remark about the smell of soiled undergarments. Still another—a bit farther away and moving forward with his arms outstretched to push the children in—made a joke about the enormous chopping block approaching them.

"Why are they doing that?" Ravi wondered aloud. "Why frighten us still more?"

His sister, holding his hand, did not respond.

The barges came on. The figures standing on the raised platform were more visible now. They were cloaked in hooded garments of the same dead gray as the vessels. The surf struggling beneath the crafts billowed out, grasping at the children's feet. They began to draw back, felt the pressure of others behind them, and began to panic. It spread as quick as touch. Over the rising confusion, Ravi heard the soldiers increasing their taunts. They knew this would happen. They were enjoying it!

This realization brought a shout to his mouth. "We are not slaves!" Without knowing he was doing so, he yanked his hand free of his sister's. He spun around, calling out over the heads of the mostly smaller children in all directions. "Do you hear? We are not slaves!"

His voice must have carried well, for many faces turned and stared at him—round faces, gaunt ones, sunken eyed and grime caked. In their eyes he thought he saw hunger, agreement. He thought he could stir that into certainty. "Just because they say we are doesn't make it true. We are not slaves just because they say we are!" His voice grew stronger. He asked them to look around. See how many they were. They were hundreds. Down the beach were thousands! The soldiers were few. How could they enslave so many?

He answered himself: "Because we let them!"

The soldiers noticed. They shouted to one another, to him. He saw two converging on him from different directions. The nearest was a bull, his shoulders bulbous and enormous, as if all his anger were gathering atop his frame.

Ravi grabbed Mór and pulled her away, both of them agile as anchovies. He slipped through the crowd, repeating again and again that they were not slaves. He told the others to fight, to run, to do anything but not give in. He couldn't tell if they were really understanding, or if the chaos had crashed over them, but all around the children jostled and scurried. They punched at the men who grabbed them and wrenched themselves free. A tide of them had pushed over a fallen man, and many small feet were trampling him as they surged down the beach.

Toward freedom, Ravi thought. He knew that Mór was beseeching him, but it didn't matter. He had her by the wrist and he was doing what he had to. He was changing everything.

"They cannot stop us all! Run to your homes!"

He had just spun around once more, mouth open, ready to

flee if the soldier was too near. He was thinking it was time to join the others escaping down the beach. That's what Mór wanted, he was sure, and they would do it now.

He turned just in time to receive the full force of a soldier's tossed baton across his forehead. It had been thrown from a distance with great force and uncanny accuracy. It knocked Ravi's head back and turned his eyes to the cloud-heavy sky. Suddenly he had no legs. His body fell so that the back of his head was the first part of him to hit the hard sand. It left him stunned, breathless, one arm upstretched, his hand, which had just held Mór's, empty.

And then a fist closed over his hand, and a shape blocked the sky. The soldier yanked Ravi upward, spinning him in the air, then drove him face-first into the sand. He pressed his knee into Ravi's back, the full weight of him. Ravi's mouth formed an oval as the air inside him escaped. He gasped for more, but the man pressed him like he wanted to drive his knee through him into the ground.

"What to do with him?" he asked.

"End him," another of the soldiers answered, his voice calm. "It's a waste, but we'll still have her. The numbers will be right anyway."

Ravi, his head to the side on the damp sand, his lungs pressed at, and his eyes rimmed with tears, watched a knife cut into view. And past it, he saw his sister, watching him, her face heartbreaking, desolate. A soldier had her by the shoulder, though it was clear there was no fight in her. Ravi wanted to tell her not to look, but he could not. And he did not have to. Something else caught her attention, someone whom Ravi could not see but whom she stared at with no lessening of her distress.

"Wait," another voice called. Ravi did not know whose it was, but the voice carried authority. It was a strange voice, inflected with sharp edges even though the speaker was unhurried.

33

The blade hung above him, waiting.

"He's got the spirit that eats death in him," the voice said. The speaker paused for a few moments. "He's got life in greater measure than most. I see another use for him. I think the Auldek will like this one."

Book One

The Gray Slopes

Chapter One

When the Balbara lookout shouted the alarm, Princess Mena Akaran was up from her campstool in an instant. She broke from the circle where she had been sitting with her officers and climbed the ridge at a run. She drew close to the sharp-eyed young man, sighting down his slim, brown arm and out from his pointing finger across the arid expanse that was central Talay. It took her a moment to see what he did. Even then, it was neither the creature itself she saw nor the party who hunted it. They were too far away. What marked their progress were the billows of smoke from the torches the runners carried—that and a yellow smudge at the rim of the world that must have been dust kicked up by their feet. They seemed to be as far off as the horizon, but the princess knew they would close that distance quickly.

She half slid down the sandy slope and regrouped with her officers. One captain, Melio Sharratt, she assigned to the farthest southern beacon; to the other, Kelis of Umae, went the northern beacon. They already knew what to do, she told them. It was only a matter of seeing it accomplished, timing it perfectly, and having luck on their side. She left it to them to get the others in position and remind them of their instructions, but before she dismissed them she urged them both to act with caution.

"Do you hear me?" she asked, leaning close to the small group. She took Melio by the wrist to remind him of this but did not look in his face. She knew his grin would hold constant, dismissive of the danger moving across the plain toward them. He may have become the head of the Elite, but the role had done nothing to alter him. His longish hair would be cast casually across an eye, often swept aside only to fall in place again. They had wed five years earlier. She had never hidden her love of him from others, but neither did she let it distract her at moments like this. She spoke as if her words were meant for all the hunting party, as, in truth, they were.

"I want nobody dead. Only the foulthing dies today," she said.

"Those words coming from you?" Melio asked. "Will you abide by them yourself, or will this be like last time, with that—"

Mena spoke as if she had not heard him. "Nobody else. That order falls on each of you personally. We've lost too many already."

Her eyes settled on Kelis. The Talayan's gaze was as calm as ever, his skin dark and smooth, his eyes slow moving. It was a face she had grown to deeply care for. In a strange way this Talayan was a living reminder of her eldest brother. Aliver had grown to manhood with him as his companion. Kelis had known her brother during the years that she had been separated from him. Even now, after all the evenings they had spent talking about what her brother had been like then, she still did not feel they had conversed enough. She hoped they would have many evenings more.

She made a point of not meeting Melio's eyes as he moved away. If they were together again, whole, at the end of the day, she would show him just how much she felt for him with all her body. That was the way it had been with them lately: distant as they faced danger, enraptured with each other in the short reprieves afterward.

The next half hour was a whirl of preparations. Moving among soldiers, shouting instructions, checking everything personally, Mena was as slim and leanly muscled and sun burnished as she had been during the war with Hanish Mein. She still wore the sword with which she had swum ashore on Vumu as a girl, but she was far from being that girl. Only an unobservant eye could fail to see that her lithe form contained within it a coiled energy hardened by loss, by war, and by an inner struggle with the deadly gifts that seemed to define her. There was love within her, too, but she kept that on a short tether. It was a softness that was difficult to spot within the Maeben fierceness she so often had to rely upon. Had she the time and the quiet, she would have chosen to settle into the kinder aspects of her nature and come to know them again, but the peace that followed the end of the war with Hanish Mein had hardly allowed it. Maybe when this work was done she could lay down her sword and rest.

She caught her breath only when all the preparations that could be made had been. She climbed back upon the ridge and stood where the lookout had. The chapped skin of Talay spread out before her, miles upon miles baking under a flawless blue sky. She watched the creature take on shape and proportion as it closed the miles, the smoke of its pursuers driving it toward the trap Mena had laid for it.

This was not the first of these foulthings she had faced. Indeed, she had been at the work of hunting them for almost four years now. She had seen eight of them killed, but she'd also lost hundreds of her soldiers in the process. And each time was different. Each creature was its own atrocity and had to be dealt with accordingly. Each trap was an elaborate construction that, if it failed, needed to be abandoned to prepare for some other opportunity.

It began not long after the Santoth had unleashed their twisted magic upon the Mein army. Nobody could say for sure just how the foulthings came to be, but it had something to do with ribbons of the Santoth's song unleashed on the natural creatures of the world, spells that drifted until they lighted

39

upon some living creature. In most cases, the animals were so corrupted by the touch of the Giver's tongue that they died: lamed, malformed, burned or battered or torn one part from another. Many got caught in rips in the fabric of the world that passed through them and left them melded with other objects, joined with trees or stuck fast in rocks or half submerged in the earth. Their carcasses dotted the damaged ground, a feast for vultures.

At first they had believed any creatures touched by the sorcery died because of it. And because many human beings were so touched, many were led mercifully out of this life and on to the next. Nobody wished to see their loved ones live with that sort of corruption on them. The people of Talay, in particular, had always told tales of the lasting damage left by the Santoth during their first angry march into banishment. They took it upon themselves to ensure that their people did not spread any contagion among them.

Most of the burden, however, fell upon the Mein, as they had received the brunt of the sorcerers' fury. As the vanquished enemy, they had little say in their fate. Those who showed signs of contamination were killed, culled just as one might cull sick animals from a herd of livestock. Queen Corinn was firm in her orders on this; and from the first days of her reign few chose to disobey her—not outright, at least.

Dariel might have asserted his rights as a male heir, but he did not. A year after Corinn released their father's ashes and ascended to the throne of Acacia, she gave birth to the nation's heir. Soon after, they began to receive troubling reports. At first Corinn dismissed them as the nightmares of a frightened, fatigued populace. The Antoks had stirred all sorts of fears in people's minds, she explained, and the strange appearance of the Santoth had woken old superstitions. Magic had been unleashed upon the world for the first time in twenty-two generations. Of course, the people again trembled at night and concocted stories of beasts that hunted them. Time would heal, Corinn said. The earth would come to rest again and the natural order would sew creation back into its tight weave.

But the reports did not fade as time passed. The sightings, which were sporadic for the first few years, grew more frequent, the witnesses more reliable. What they said differed in the particulars, but all their descriptions had made Mena's skin crawl with growing trepidation. In the hills near Halaly a herd of goatlike creatures cut a swath of devastation. Goatlike, the people said, but in truth only their heads resembled gargantuan likenesses of those animals. Their bodies were squat with numerous, malformed limbs jointed at random places, more like a spider's legs than those of any mammal. They were each as large as an elephant and insatiable. Fortunately, they ate only vegetation and were near as easy to slaughter as domesticated ruminants.

Other creatures had different tastes and were not so easy to kill.

The Bethuni spread stories of many-footed serpents that could both slither and run. At first the people thought them amusing, until they began to grow at a rate that frightened them into action. There was a lion with a row of blue eyes along its back, doglike creatures large enough to send laryx scurrying in fright, vultures so mutated by the bounty they had consumed that many of them could no longer fly. Instead they waddled, following their great beaked noses like bands of the plagued.

The people came to understand that these beings had been warped rather than killed by the Santoth. These they called the foulthings. Once Corinn acknowledged them, she ordered them hunted and destroyed. She charged Mena with this mission, giving her a small army and presenting the task as yet another way that her younger sister might carve her name into the pantheon of the Akaran greats.

Mena suspected that Corinn intentionally wished her to be kept busy and kept away from other affairs of the empire. But she could not put the unease she felt into enough order to decide what to do about it. Instead, Mena had set to the hunt. The beasts were real, after all, and who better than Maeben on earth to face them? She and her army ranged far and wide across Talay, from its shores, across its grasslands and deserts, into its hills and mountain reaches, through marshland and even to the great river that marked the boundary with the far south. That dry watercourse she did not cross. She had no desire to awaken the Santoth again. Nobody wished for that.

She faced the creatures one at a time as much as possible. She fought with the help of those in whose territory the hunt took her. It was with Bethuni huntsmen that she had set the fires that consumed the writhing, many-legged aggregation of snake creatures that had grown large enough to swallow dogs and sheep and even children whole. Balbara warriors marched beside her as they cleaned the land of vultures so fat their wings were useless. And with Talayan runners she had tracked the blue-eyed lion across the grasslands, running it to exhaustion before she killed it herself with an overhand thrust of a long pike. It was that act Melio had referred to earlier. Even exhausted and panting, the lion had been a fierce thing, its mouth a great cavern of fanged fury when it roared, its claws five scimitars as they slashed out.

Mena had risked her life to plant the killing blow. She had not truly needed to do it herself, but sometimes she could not control the impulse to. Sometimes she needed to offer her life for the one taken, just to see if her bill was due. Somewhere lurking in the back of her mind was the feeling that the many lives she had ended would someday ask for her own to balance the scales. She did not run from this. Indeed, at times she wanted to embrace it and accept whatever reckoning the spirits offered her. So far, they had offered none. Nine years had passed since the new violence that Corinn called peace had begun. So many times Mena could have died, and yet throughout it all she had rarely suffered more than minor cuts and deep bruises and sprained joints. Perhaps the Giver was saving her for something. Perhaps, but if so, why was he so completely silent, ever absent?

This thing they hunted now—this they had put off as long as they could. It was the third to the last of the giants. She knew of only two others, although she did not want to think of them just now. She had her hands more than full. Watching it approach filled her with fear as great as any she had experienced. It was not just the brute force of it; rather, it was the twisting of the natural order, the possibilities it suggested about what monsters could exist or might come into existence to plague the future. And it was the fact that it had been set upon the world by the very same sorcerers who had twice secured her family's throne. Because of that she felt she owed it to the world to see the foulthings extinguished.

What roared toward her, driven into her trap by torch-carrying Talayan runners, was a monstrosity that came with a shrieking entourage of hundreds of other creatures. Those in the horde were not themselves warped. They were what the Talayans called tentens, primates with long snouts and a carnivore's jaws. They were fierce and dangerous in their own way, but they had long lived on the plains. They ran mostly on all fours and were normally as content to eat groundnuts as they were to hunt smaller monkeys and rodents. No danger to humans as long as they were left alone.

The huge beast they followed ran on two legs in a waddling gait that was fast, humanlike, and more grotesque because of the similarity. Occasionally, it corrected its balance and expressed its outrage by bashing the earth with its knuckled fists. It was woolly-haired with a great brown-red mane about its neck, an ocher and blue snout, and a predator's forward-facing eyes. It stood three times a man's height at the crown of its head. Above this rose two circular horns that added yet another man's height. These horns were the only part of the creature of true beauty, a ridged perfection of form. Beautiful, yes, but not when worn as the headdress on the bellowing thing now closing to within a few hundred yards. Likely, the creature had once been a tenten—explaining why the troop followed it. Some speculated that it had eaten a corrupted corpse of a horned animal and had thus grown horns itself. However it had been created, it was not natural and could not be left alive.

Melio and Kelis had reached their assigned posts. Earlier, they had established a series of piles of brushwood that were spaced in a widemouthed cone shape meant to funnel the foulthing toward a chosen area. As soon as the creature passed between the first of these outposts, the men touched fire to the pyres. Instantly they combusted in audible whooshes of flame and black smoke. The runners pressed on, near enough now that Mena could hear their shouts, bursts of sound peppered throughout the group, meant to further confuse the animals. She knew Melio and Kelis would be joining the runners, taking up their torches, adding their voices to the din. A little closer and another pyre went up, and another after that. Each successive explosion narrowed the pathway the creatures had and directed them toward Mena and the fifty crossbowmen she commanded, each of them with a second who stood just beside him.

"Ready yourselves!" she called, her voice as stern and confident as she could make it.

The crossbowmen began to extend their line, forming a widening U shape. They moved gradually as if they were not watching the animals speeding toward them. The bowmen walked with their weapons strapped to their bodies over their shoulders and around their waists. The bows were heavy, meant to fire a single, powerful shot. A second shot was unlikely since the bolts had to be loaded and the crossbows cranked slowly back to the ready position. On the bottom end of the U shape, the pairs positioned themselves behind metal rings that had been secured to the earth by long stakes.

It was into this area that the foulthing and its troop arrived in a cloud of snarling, dusty hair and teeth and anger. The giant itself was enraged. It danced about, smacking the ground, tearing up clods of dry earth and tossing them in the air. It bared its teeth, snapping at the sky. Its yellowed eyes shot rage out of them like a physical force. Standing on two legs, it spread its arms wide and thumped its chest. Around it hundreds of the tenten followed its lead. The cacophony of it, the turmoil, the nearness of such animal fury was almost too much to stand calmly facing.

But Mena made sure she did. She held them there for a few minutes, letting them settle into the space, asking her soldiers to be calm before they acted. Now that the animals were inside the U shape, the bowmen at the far ends slowly closed the open portion, making a great circle with the creatures in the center. The men took up positions around the rings nailed in place for them. The runners and the rest of the force spread out around the bowmen's circle, thickening the ranks. Only when all were in position did Mena lift her arm. It was nearly time, and if they all did as they had planned, it would be over in—

It happened before she had any chance to stop it. One of the bowmen shot prematurely. The bolt flew dead straight and with all the released energy of its slowly cranked, twisted cable work. The force of its leaving would have knocked the bowman off his feet, except that a second man clasped him about the waist and stood with his feet planted firmly. The missile trailed a thin rope. It spooled out with a hiss. The bolt slammed into the foulthing's chest, impacting its rib cage, and did not sink far. The force of it tossed the creature back in a sudden, rolling confusion of limbs and horns. When the tumble stopped, the thing was on its feet once more. It stood for a moment, confused and breathless, tenten bodies all around. Most of them still howled and bared their teeth; a few lay crumpled and broken from its rolling over them.

The foulthing grasped the bolt by the protruding shaft and yanked it out. The barbs tore through its flesh, but if it felt that particular pain it gave no sign. It focused on the bolt as if it were a living thing that might still harm it, and then its eyes played out along the rope that connected it to the cross bowman. With a roar it jerked the two men toward it, yanking them off their feet and dragging them on their bellies into the raging tentens.

The fools! Mena thought. They had forgotten what they were supposed to do. Who were these two? What she did then she did with instinctual quickness. She ran forward, drawing her Marah sword, yelling as she did so, hoping to draw the beast's attention. As she neared the first of the tentens she swung her sword in wide arcs that cut clean through fur and skin and bone. The animals jumped back from her, all teeth and snarls. She hacked her way at a dead run toward the fallen men. She found them writhing and screaming, entangled together beneath a biting, scratching mound of tentens. The animals did not notice her until she had hacked the heads from two, limbs from even more, split another down through the skull, and spilled the guts of another in a gush that coated the two men.

A wave of soldiers rushed to help her. She stopped them all with a slash of her palm. "No!" she yelled. She knew that if they continued it would break the formation. There would be no order and they would not be able to carry out the rest of the plan. It would be chaos and many more than just she would die in it. "No!"

They stopped, tripped over each other, stood stunned and unsure until she motioned them back. She had barely managed to do so before another tenten leaped at her. She ducked beneath it and sliced its leg clean off.

"Come on!" she hissed. "Get loose of it!" She smacked the bowman with the palm of her free hand and then stood upright. With the same hand she drew her short sword.

The foulthing was some thirty or so strides away. It had paused to watch her. For a moment it was a statue amid a whirlwind of motion. Mena saw something like intelligent curiosity on its face. Its eyebrows seemed to lift slightly; the corners of its mouth twitched. She had not noticed how human its hands were, long-fingered and delicate as they caressed the rope. She experienced the moment as one of shared silence. She almost felt the creature was going to say something, do something. But the moment was short-lived, and the foulthing spoke no words. It seemed to grow tired of studying her. Those humanlike hands yanked on the cord again.

When the line went taut, Mena caught it between her two blades and sliced through the rope. The beast was thrown off balance and went down again. Mena turned and pushed, dragged, and shouted the two men to their feet and back to the safety of the circle.

"Remember your rings!" she shouted. "Every second, tie the ropes down!"

With that, the princess raised her arm, then immediately let it drop. Before it even reached her side, her generals had shouted in answer. In the next instant a confusion of bolts and ropes flew at the foulthing from all directions. Many hit it—in the chest and groin, deep in its calf and punching right through its other ankle, in its lower back and just above, in the muscled flesh of its upper torso, in the neck. Several passed through the curve of its horns, the ropes tangling in them as the creature spun. A few took out the lesser apes, skewering three or four at a time before losing momentum. And the bolts that missed sped straight toward the opposing bowmen and troops. This was when the seconds came into play again. They shifted from pressing forward on the bowmen to pulling back against them. The ropes snapped taut before reaching the other side, and the crossbows, even if yanked out of their wielders' hands, were held fast by the sling straps.

Once the ropes were secured, archers stepped between them and lofted ropes attached to blunted arrows over the creature. Others retrieved them on the opposite side and anchored each end, further tightening a web of bonds on the foulthing, catching many tentens in the process. Mena watched until the injured and bound foulthing was pressed tight to the dry ground. She turned away as Halaly spearmen began to move into the circle, their long, narrow pikes able to impale the tentens at a distance. The auditory chaos was no less than before, but she knew the difficult task was over.

Melio found her walking slowly back toward the rock outcropping from which she wished to take in the horizon again, to see the largeness of the world and marvel at it. "You really must let others risk their necks on occasion," he said, grinning. "You're lucky your men fear you as much as they fear your death. If they didn't, they might have stormed in and messed everything up. But you know that. You managed to pull it off, and it still gives you no joy."

"How are the two?" she asked.

"The two you rescued?" He tossed his hair out of his face and studied her. "I believe they are injured but will both live to tell of it."

"Any others?"

"Nothing but minor injuries, some bites." Melio touched her arm, turned her toward him, and pulled her close. "Mena, this went well. You should be pleased. Let's dance tonight as the Halaly do and be glad that there's one less foulthing walking the world. Think of it that way."

Mena accepted his embrace, welcomed it, and wanted to be folded into it for much longer than she allowed herself in public. But she did not think as he suggested. Not completely, at least. She would never forget the look in the beast's eyes.

That night, after the celebrations, she dreamed of the creature's stare. She woke unsure where waking events ended and dreaming began. She told herself that it was the dream that made her so uneasy, not the reality. It was not possible that she had seen intelligence in the creature's eyes. She had not heard its thoughts, not with her waking mind. It had not expressed a hatred for her and her kind that, in its reasoned, simmering potency, went far beyond that of any simple beast. That had been only in her dreams. Of course. Only in her dreams. Strange, though, that so soon after the event she could not easily separate the truth of it from her imaginings.

She decided to send a letter to the queen, declaring that they had one less foulthing to worry about. That's all she would say. She would keep moving. Keep believing.

Chapter Two

In the offices that had once been her father's, Queen Corinn Akaran bent over her desk, arms spread wide and palms pressed against the smooth grain of the polished hardwood. The flared sleeves of her gown formed an enclosure of sorts, a screen that shielded the document from view on two sides. She was alone in her offices, but she knew—better than anyone else in the palace—that until she had eyes in the back of her head she could not trust that she was ever as unaccompanied as she believed herself to be. She favored this posture when she wished to focus her attention on a particular document, above which she would hang like a falcon poised to drop on a field mouse far below.

Nine years had passed since she had wrested the Acacian Empire from Hanish Mein's grasp. Nine years of wearing the title of queen. Nine years of bearing the nation's burdens on her shoulders. Nine years in which she confided fully in no one single person. Nine years of showing only glimpses of herself to different people, never the whole to anybody. Nine years as a mother. Nine years of secret study. Nine years of learning to speak like a god.

Her beauty was such that few noticed the effects of the passing seasons on her. She was slim enough to be the envy of women ten years her junior; youthful enough to be the ideal for girls who did not yet have to measure themselves against her; shapely enough in her carefully tailored gowns that men's eyes followed her of their own accord, whether the man himself wished them to or not. No man who was attracted to women failed to see beauty in her full mouth, in her olive complexion, in her rounded shoulders and bosom, and in the curve of her hips. When had such a form ever embodied so much power and been driven by a mind as calculating? When had such a sensuous face ever been so latent with danger? She had surprised everyone with her sudden emergence to power, and all who had known her in her youth remained shocked by it.

Corinn knew these things as well as anyone. She made a point of knowing things. She knew that in the lower town the people called her the Fanged Rose. She rather liked the name. She knew which nobles were still fool enough to think they might bed her. She knew that a movement was afoot in the Senate to force her to marry. If they had their way, she would produce a legitimate heir to displace the son Hanish had fathered. They would not have their way. She knew which senators most hated her for curtailing their power and which clans and tribes most chafed against her recent decision to establish one national currency—the hadin—that the royal reserve exclusively minted. She knew which nobles needed to be played against one another during the intricate work of pushing her plans forward. She was glad to know all these things. Added together and weighed one against another, the balance always tipped in her favor. She was secure in rule, and she had plans to become even more so soon.

If all the scheming complexity of her position had etched fine wrinkles at the corners of her eyes, so be it. If she was fuller in the hips and chest than she had been before childbirth, what did that matter? If she walked more on her heels and less on the eager balls of her feet, that was as it should be. She had been lovely as a girl, but she knew that there were other ways to be lovely as a woman. She was not yet the age her mother was in her memories, which meant she had not reached the age to measure herself against her understanding of beauty. And of mortality. That day would come, she knew, but not just yet.

For the time being, her physical appearance was a gift to be used as readily as skill with a sword. The core of her power now resided in her mind, her thoughts, and her capacity to outflank others from a place of intellect hidden behind her pleasing façade. She had never been the vacuous vessel so many had assumed. It just took a great deal of anger to finally awaken the talents she had long let lie dormant. For that anger she had Hanish Mein to thank. In her own way, she remembered that daily.

At one corner of her desk sat a letter from the winery of Prios. Their vines were ready, it declared. They would happily begin the mass production the queen charged them with. Just as soon as the additive reached them, they would begin bottling. Good, she thought. The people had been clear-eyed too long already. She knew they were starting to grumble, and with good reason, too.

The document she now studied was the last of the reports she had commissioned on the state of agriculture in northern Talay. It told a dire story. While central Talay had always been arid, the north had been somewhat more temperate. The sea currents and the wind that drove them had brought moisture enough to keep the land fertile, well suited to producing grains and fruits and vegetables that could be traded with the floating merchants for goods from throughout the Inland Sea and from as far away as the Vumu Archipelago. These goods, in turn, were sent south into central Talay, which had its own goods to offer in the form of livestock and mineral wealth. Thus, there had been a balance of farming and trade for generations.

Not so any longer. The damage done to the plains of Talay by the war and by the Santoth magic had left them parched. Something in this had changed the flow of the winds. Now a scorching breeze swept up from the plains and evaporated the sea moisture before it ever reached land. What fog there was, they said in Bocoum, hung offshore, temptingly haunting them like a mirage that appeared each morning but would come no nearer. Northern crops had withered more year by year, and this summer looked to be the driest yet. Even the wheatgrass—usually so hearty—had silvered to straw. It combusted and fed wildfires that blackened the sky.

The last time the merchants docked at Bocoum they found the Talayans had little to trade. Instead of engaging in commerce, the merchants found themselves fighting off assaults from the famished, desperate farmers and townspeople. Considering the way the sea currents whirled trade around the heart of the empire, this break in the chain of commerce had far-reaching consequences.

Who would have thought that a lack of water in one place would affect the prosperity of nations hundreds of miles away? It was, Corinn knew, a threat more formidable than any of the foulthings her sister hunted. It required her focused attention, and she was now ready to offer it. Her answer was a simple thing, really, rooted in a basic need and in her newfound ability to deliver gifts no other living being could. If what she had planned worked as she believed it would, they would surely find another name for her in Talay. A name of praise. Perhaps she would decide upon the name herself and have it whispered among the people until they took it up. She would make them think the name was of their own devising. There was a power in naming, she had come to believe, a great power.

The bone whistle by which her door guards alerted her of arrivals 'came to her, two notes that identified the person entering as her secretary, Rhrenna, a relative of Hanish Mein's who had been something of a friend to her during her captivity in the Meinish court. Corinn chose her over Rialus Neptos, the other nonfamilial holdover from her previous life. He was her confidant in many areas, yes, but she could not stand having him around too often. It suited her much better that such an intimate position be filled by a woman, and a woman decidedly indebted to her.

For a time after her sudden rise to power Corinn thought Rhrenna had been killed during the massacre of Mein she had orchestrated with Numrek aid. It was not until a number of weeks later that the young woman was found hiding aboard a trading vessel off the Aushenian coast along with several of her maids. When Rhrenna was brought back to Acacia, Corinn had welcomed her with something between honest affection and relief. It was good to know that not all those she had sentenced to death were lost forever. It gave her the opportunity to provide amnesty, and she needed that.

Rhrenna entered. She was pale and slim, attractive in a fine-boned way, but she looked as if the bounty of Acacia never quite nourished her as completely as one might hope. She spoke in a pleasant voice, one suited to song and often called for late on banquet evenings. "Excuse me, Your Majesty, but you have visitors. Sire Dagon and Sire Neen of the league wish a brief audience with you."

"Dagon and Neen? I didn't even know they were on the island."

"Yes, they just arrived. They beg your forgiveness but swear the matter is urgent."

By custom, the leaguemen should have petitioned her officially for a meeting at least three days ahead of time. As much as she would have liked to turn them away, Corinn knew that if she did she would wonder what had brought them so urgently. She would spend her time trying to figure it out. Better to hear them and know from their mouths. Then she would search out the truth behind what they said.

She greeted them in the meeting room adjacent to her main balcony, one large chamber open to the air down its whole length. Instead of enjoying the view, however, she sat at ease in a high-backed chair, the brightness of the day at her back. Her fingers curled around the knobbed fists of the armrests.

"To what do I owe this unexpected pleasure?" she asked, crossing her legs as Dagon and Neen approached. "Two sires calling on me at once. A rare treat."

"The pleasure is all ours," Sire Dagon said, bowing his head in the slow manner of leaguemen.

"We beg forgiveness for the intrusion," Sire Neen added. "The matter is of considerable import, Your Majesty. We could not but bring it to you immediately."

Both men fell into ritual greeting, spreading platitudes like rose petals they hoped would scent the room. They were dressed in the silken, luxurious robes of their sect and moved with a monklike air of reverence. They were not from a religious organization—indeed, their main doctrine centered on the insatiable appetite for wealth—but they were a closed group with mysterious ways that few outsiders understood. Outwardly, they were always gaunt, most often tall, with necks elongated by a lifelong stretching process. Their heads were bound in infancy and squeezed into a conical shape that eventually hardened to permanence. It was said they smoked their own distillation of mist—one so potent it would kill normal folk—that lengthened their life spans. But as no one outside the league knew when any of them was born or when most of them died, it was impossible to verify this rumor.

Though they talked as if this visit had no purpose other than social interaction, Corinn noticed that neither man fingered a mist pipe. This, more than anything else, was an indication they were anxious to get to the point. She obliged them. "Sires," she broke in, "sit down, please. I know your time is valuable. I trust you haven't had problems with the additive? You assured me it was perfected."

"It is!" Sire Dagon exclaimed. "It is. Even as we speak it is being delivered to Prios with careful instructions. No, it's another matter . . ." He paused a moment, cleared his throat, and began, "We have always been direct with each other, you and I. Direct and completely honest. I will be exactly that way with this matter."

Mentally Corinn rolled her eyes. League directness had a lot in common with the knotted brambles that choked the hills along the rivers in Senival. One could get tangled in that "directness," pricked a thousand times by barbs that dug deeper if you fought them. It was true that she had known Sire Dagon longer than Sire Neen. She felt vaguely more comfortable with him. It was he with whom she had brokered the arrangement that withdrew league support from Hanish's war effort and with whom she had drawn up the basic details of their continued commerce. They were not details she was proud of, but such were the realities of rule.

Chief among the concessions she had made was deeding the league ownership of the Outer Isles. The chain of white sand islands that had once been Dariel's haven as a brigand was now a series of plantations for the breeding and raising of quota. They deemed it necessary for the entire system to be self-enclosed. There could be no outside influence whatsoever. Nobody could trade or interact with the breeding population. What's more, the breeders themselves could have no memories of anything other than their life on the islands. For this reason, they had acquired infant children for several years now.

It would be some time yet before they were truly producing quota as Sire Dagon and the others envisioned, but it would lead to complete self-sufficiency. The slaves themselves would plant and harvest their own food. They would trade for goods among themselves within an enclosed system that cost the empire nothing. They would know nothing other than the existence the league engineered for them—and that, Sire Dagon had promised the queen personally, would be an existence of stability and even some measure of comfort. Once the league set in place a system of apparent self-governance for them, along with a religious doctrine shaped to the situation, the slaves need not even feel themselves slaves at all.

The result of this all was that they would offer their children up without question. Different islands would host them at different ages, so that parents would not grow to love children. Children would never know their parents. The exact details the league never disclosed to her, and she never asked. Just the fact that she had allowed it was a close enough bond between them. It would hold, she believed, for generations, perhaps for another twenty-two, as had been the case with the original agreement Tinhadin had brokered. Did it ever trouble her conscience? Yes, but such, as she often reminded herself, was the burden of rule.

"I would expect nothing less from you, dear Dagon," she said, making sure her courteous tone had a bite to it, "and you will get nothing less from me. Proceed."

Sire Dagon nodded, his eyes half closed as if the words were music to him. "Queen Corinn, you must know by now that the league holds you in the highest regard. In truth, we haven't held such complete faith in an Akaran for several generations. No insult to your ancestors intended, of course. It's just that we find yours a remarkable reign, young though it is."

"So full of promise," Sire Neen slipped in, grinning. His teeth had been led, not to points, but to roundness, each of them a gentle curve of measured uniformity. When Corinn looked at him she kept her gaze pinned to his forehead. His eyes had a dead quality to them, a reptilian flatness that she could not—and to some degree did not wish to—penetrate. She was not sure which of the leaguemen held greater rank, nor did she know where or how Sire Neen had served the league before taking over management of the Outer Isles project. They never offered the information, and she never asked.

Despite their claim of directness, a few minutes more passed with both men praising the peace she had brought, both of them sure that the empire would soon be more prosperous than ever in its history. Eventually, Corinn lifted her finger.

"Please, you digress again. What are you really here to tell me or ask of me?"

The two leaguemen conferred with their eyes and seemed to conclude that the time had come. Sire Neen said, "There has been an unfortunate development. Recently, last fall to be precise, we sought intelligence about the Auldek."

"Sought intelligence?"

"There has never been a more closed, maddeningly secretive people than the Lothan Aklun," Sire Dagon said with no hint that his listener might find this complaint ironic coming from him. "As you know, the Lothan Aklun are to the Auldek what we are to you. They are not the market you trade with; they are simply the merchants who hold sway in the Other Lands."

Corinn interrupted. "This was a detail the league was slow in divulging."

"If we were cautious in divulging our information, it was largely because we knew and still know so little ourselves. Bad information is no better than information. Surely you agree?" He paused, but not long enough for Corinn to answer. "We know the Other Lands are vast. We know the Auldek are powerful. But that is all we know. As you will understand, that is no knowledge at all. So we concluded that now as we are entering a new age under your leadership it was essential that we learn more of this nation we are so dependent on."

"You sent spies among them?"

"Just so."

"But before we learned much of anything," Sire Neen proceeded, "one of our agents was found out and captured. He, in turn, was convinced to betray other agents. Several were captured and . . . questioned."

"How many?" Corinn asked.

"Oh . . ." Dagon pursed his lips as if the exact number were of no consequence, but then he produced it. "Twenty-seven."

"Twenty-seven? Are you mad?"

Neen fondled his gold neck collar, fingering the dolphin shape embossed there. "It is a large territory. One or two spies would have told us nothing. It would have been a waste and still a risk at that. Our spies were finely trained, disciplined, and looked perfectly the part of grown slaves. We were all shocked when one was caught and shocked that he gave up the others so thoroughly."

"It seems," the other leagueman said, "that the Lothan Aklun took possession of them. They have very persuasive forms of torture."

Corinn tapped her fingernails against the hard wood of the armrests, waiting for more. "So you've been caught spying? How have the Lothan Aklun responded?"

"Put simply," Sire Neen said, "this has placed us in an awkward position. What we believe will help is a direct entreaty from yourself. We will make our own apologies directly to both parties, but if you could stand strong with us, while avowing complete innocence in the matter, it will strengthen our position. The Lothan Aklun need to know that the league and the Acacian crown are two fingers of the same hand."

"You want me to tell them you're my preferred middlemen, is that it? But what if they can offer better terms?"

Both men looked aghast, though she knew it was a show. Nothing surprised men like these. Sire Dagon said, "Majesty, you can have no idea what sort of mistake that would be."

Corinn smiled. "Why don't you tell me, then?"

Sire Dagon showed her the palms of his hands, his long fingers crooked. It was a rather odd gesture that she had yet to understand fully. "You and the next several generations of Akarans would waste your lives trying to learn all the many branches of Lothan Aklun duplicity. They are vile, completely without conscience; and they would seek to cheat you in every way possible. They huddle on the isles of the Barrier Ridge, scheming new treacheries. It is only because we—the league—

have dealt with their every scheme over the centuries that you are spared such things. They would love nothing better than feasting on your ignorance of their ways."

"And," Sire Neen added, once more showing his ghastly teeth, "the league owns the Gray Slopes. Without us you can no more get to the Aklun than they can get to you. Only we have successfully navigated that great ocean and all its dangers."

"So I've been told time and again."

"If you like," Sire Dagon said, "you could see for yourself, with your own eyes. We have permission from the League Council to offer you transport across to meet with them. Nothing would impress upon the Lothan Aklun the strength of our partnership like seeing you stand beside us."

Corinn looked between both men, trying to read them while not betraying how shocked she was by the proposal. In all the years of the quota trade, no Akaran had met with the Lothan Aklun. The league had guarded their exclusivity jealously. If this offer was genuine, they must really be worried. "I cannot leave Acacia right now," she eventually said, "but I will send my brother, Prince Dariel, with a message from me to the Lothan Aklun. He should be returning to Acacia in a few days. He will appease them and then get on with business."

She could not read whether or not they were happy with this pronouncement, but for them being hard to read was as essential to life as breathing. Rising, she dismissed them formally, promising to sort out the details with them in the coming days.

Alone once more a few minutes later, the queen again stood over her desk, trying to recall each word spoken and the gestures that accompanied them. Of course, the leaguemen had not told her everything. They would never do so anyway, but they likely hid some aspects of the affair that she would do better to know about. She would have Rialus send out his ears, his rats, to see what more they could learn. As for her brother, perhaps he really should accompany them. There were surely things to be gained. It was an opportunity best grasped before the league found a way to squirm out of it.

She heard somebody enter the room. She felt a flare of annoyance, but it vanished just as quickly. She knew—from the rapidity of his steps and the lack of a whistle to announce him—exactly who it was before he had begun speaking.

"Mother, watch this," a child's voice said. "See what I've learned."

Corinn straightened, looked up, and watched her son, Aaden, dash into the room. He carried a wooden training sword, a small, light version designed for children. Appropriate, for a child of eight was what he was.

"Watch," he ordered. "I'll do the first part of the First Form."

Without waiting for affirmation, he set his legs and brought the sword to ready position. He focused on the imagined foe standing before him. Corinn grinned. Her little Edifus at Carni, already imagining carnage. He had never known a day of hardship in his life, and yet he already hungered for conflict.

The boy moved with the awkward, intense concentration of the young. He stepped and swung, parried and turned on the balls of his feet. He wobbled a few times and corrected missteps on occasion, seeming so focused that he barely breathed through his tight lips. Watching him, his mother paid little attention to the Form itself or to his performance of it. She simply stared at him, amazed at the act of creation that had brought him to life. She had made this child! This complete, exquisite human being. How was it possible that she possessed the power to draw that small mouth and fill it with those perfect, tiny teeth? And his eyes . . . well, they were gray flecked with brown, almost too large for his face. But he would grow into them, and when he did, they would melt all whom he set them upon.

Had she done all this?

The boy spun in a sudden flourish, his long wavy hair

sweeping around him. Corinn always felt she should have it cut short, keep it trim and close to his scalp, neat. But she never had the heart to order it done. In his infancy, she had held this boy and stroked the hairless crown of his head and run her fingers around the soft indentations in his skull and pressed her palm over the spots. He had seemed so vulnerable then. He had remained so for nearly a year before his hair began to thicken and lengthen. Part of her had feared the prospect of his having straw-blond Meinish hair, but as it grew in she loved the look and touch of it. How could she help but adore it? It was her son's hair.

True, he was Hanish Mein's son as well. The proof was there in the gold highlights of his brown hair, in the already sharp line of his jaw, and in the shape of his mouth. His features often had something of Hanish's dreamy quality, a mirthful expression that had often disguised his true thoughts and intentions. Yes, he was Hanish's son. Corinn lived with awareness of that fact every day. But he would not bear that traitor's name. He was officially all Akaran; Corinn was all the parent he needed. If one sought to name his father—she had once snapped at an ambassador impertinent enough to question her on the child's parentage—look no further than the line of Akaran itself. That's what Aaden was! The child of Edifus and Tinhadin and every other Akaran who had ever walked across the Known World. He was named after Tinhadin's firstborn son. Corinn thought that appropriate and, hopefully, prophetic.

Corinn found it disturbing that there were no words to adequately describe the love a parent feels for a child. Before she'd become a mother she'd known so little. All those years she had understood nothing of what her mother and her father must have gone through raising four children. It rankled her to think how foolish she had once been. It was a strange, unpleasant emotion to follow so quickly on her adoration. It concerned her that she might, at some point in the future, look back from a place of greater wisdom and again find that the self she now was—at thirty-three, the mother of a single child, the widow to a lover who had planned her murder, a sister to two living siblings and one dead, an orphan who could no longer look to her parents—had been ignorant on some matter of import.

She kept such thoughts exclusively to herself, of course. To the outside world she was a display of statuesque certainty. And why shouldn't she be?

She was the queen of a vast empire and the keeper of the most powerful knowledge the world had ever known. She owed it to her people to be certain in all her actions. Hesitation, deliberation, second thoughts: these were signs of weakness, the kind of flaws that kept her father from being a truly great king. The failings that temporarily lost the empire.

No matter, she thought. Acacia now had a great queen. The nation would thrive because of it; she promised it would. A queen to stand strong, a mother to raise the nation's next king. That was what Aaden was to be, even if the world was not yet as sure of it as she was. Born outside of an official marriage, Aaden was not guaranteed the throne. He could succeed her, but not without challenges and protests from other Agnate families, those who would rather she marry among them and bear a legitimate child. Also, any child of a marriage of her siblings—like Mena and Melio's—would step before Aaden in the line of succession. But there was no such child yet, and before long Corinn would surprise them all.

As focused as the young swordsman had been, when he reached the end of his memorized routine he dropped his role completely. His sword arm went limp at his side and he strolled toward his mother's desk, a look of sudden boredom on his face. "That's about all I've learned. I wanted to learn the end bit, but Thotan said I had to begin at the beginning."

"Aaden," the queen said, "that's wonderful. You'll be a fine swordsman someday. Better than Dariel, I'd wager. Better even than Mena!"

The child accepted the praise with a curt nod. He assured her that he already was a fine swordsman. No someday needed to qualify it. Still, something about the compliment rekindled his focus. He turned his attention back to the Form, determination etched in the lines of his forehead, the tip of his tongue pinched between his front teeth.

"I enjoyed watching that," Corinn said, "but you should go. I have matters to consider."

"All right," the boy said, and then he lowered his voice, went conspiratorial. "But show me something first. An animal. Make something I've never seen before. No! Make something that nobody has ever seen before."

Glancing around, Corinn said, "Aaden, you know I don't like to do such things here with so many eyes around."

"But there's nobody here," Aaden said, incongruously leaning in and whispering.

"Wait until we're back at Calfa Ven."

"Mother! Just one thing and then I'll go. It's been ages since you've shown me something. We're alone. Look."

Corinn took a moment to verify that the room was empty, that no eyes watched, and no one was within hearing. She rarely indulged any living person anything not completely to her liking, but Aaden was difficult to refuse. Or, in truth, with him she did not want to refuse. Seeing pleasure on his face was a joy like none she'd known before.

She said, "Go make sure the door is pulled tight, then."

Stepping from around her desk, she withdrew into the small alcove in the corner of the room, out of sight lest somebody barge in unannounced. Such an act was strictly forbidden, of course, but she still chose caution. Certain that they would not be disturbed—and with a portion of her senses able to detect the movement of persons in the hallways nearby—Corinn began to sing. She did so softly, as if she wished to push the words out and into a shallow bowl on the floor before her, directing them carefully and so as not to spill over some imagined rim. She sang words that were not words, sounds that carried in them the ingredients of existence, the threads that wove together life. She felt Aaden return and knew him to be standing wide-eyed just beside her. She did not shift her gaze from the area above the floor that she sang to.

If she had been asked to explain just how the Giver's tongue worked she could not truly have done so. It was not a practice that led logically from one point to another. It was a language that never held still, that changed before her eyes and in her ears. There was an order to it, yes, a manner in which one moved toward greater and greater mastery. Yes, there was learning involved. She had labored for years over *The Song of Elenet*, especially when sheltered away with Aaden and a small staff at the hunting lodge of Calfa Ven. Countless times the text on those ancient pages had risen to speak to her, like spirits trapped on the parchment and unleashed by the touch of her eyes. They spoke to her of the Giver's true language. They put her through exercises, twisted her tongue around words made of sounds she had never heard uttered.

Despite all this, the act of singing remained something of an improvisation that leaped from all those hours of study and took on a life of its own. Though this frightened her—sometimes waking her from dreams in which her song had suddenly turned to nightmare—the act itself was a thing of such enraptured beauty that she could no longer be away from it long. Aaden wanted her to sing; truth be known, she hungered for it even more than he.

And sing she did. Her words—unintelligible, beautiful, and infused with an almost physical power—filled the alcove. Sound danced in the air as if the small chamber were laced with invisible ribbons, like snakes airborne and slithering, circling. As Corinn continued, the circle grew ever smaller. She pulled the spell in, drew it tighter, filled that invisible bowl with sounds that shrank into greater substance. Soon the words of her song swam like hundreds of sparkling minnows, a seething globe of them getting denser and denser. Within this, a form began to take shape.

Something that nobody has ever seen before: that's what Aaden asked for. And that was what she was singing into being. She would let it live there before them for a few moments, and then she would sing its unmaking.

Chapter Three

The guards at the lower steps of the palace grounds made the mistake of barring the young man's passage. One of them asked him what he was about; the other hit the stranger's chest with the flat of his palm, his knife hand ready to pull his dagger from his waist sheath; a third sounded a whistle of alarm. They all expressed indignation that a laborer, a peasant—whatever the new arrival was in his tattered clothing, with unkempt hair, calloused hands, and bare feet—would dare try to gain entry to the royal residence. He could be executed on the spot for it. They held this fate off, the first guard said, only because they wished to know the nature of his insanity before doing the deed.

In answer, the intruder took a step back. He set his hands on his hips and stood smiling. He knew his garments were worn thin, grimed by what looked like years of wearing, patched in places and shredded in others. His toenails were black crescents; and the creases of his elbows, neck, and forehead were drawn with thin lines of dirt. He stood with easy confidence, however. His white-toothed smile asked them to see the person behind these outward trappings. See the mirth in his eyes and wonder at it. See the etched musculature beneath the rags. See his face for what it was, not what it appeared to be. It was a tense moment, although everyone but the young man seemed aware of this.

Responding to a blown whistle, several other Marah

approached, menacing, sword hands ready. Among them was a face the man knew well but did not much care for. Rialus Neptos hung at the back of the new arrivals—no fighter he, but as usual eager to observe anything he could report to the queen. He was not her chancellor, as he was rumored to think himself, but everyone knew that he shared a closeness with Corinn Akaran that none could fathom. He was a councillor she seemed to grant as much access to as she offered her siblings.

Rialus was quicker than the rest to recognize the young man. For a moment he looked just as perplexed as the guards. "Draw no swords!" he shouted, pushing forward. "Draw no swords, you fools! Do you not see this is Prince Dariel?"

The second guard—the one who had touched him but not yet spoken—sputtered, "Prince—Prince Dariel?" He glanced at the others, his face twisted in puzzlement. He moved his hand away from his dagger as if shocked that he had ever gripped it. "Your Highness, I don't understand."

"Ah, you've pegged me," the young man said, holding his mirthful expression a moment longer before breaking into laughter. "And your lack of comprehension is clear, friend! Your partners here are the more confused. Have I really been away for so long? I thought it just a few months!" He paused, but nobody had a ready response. "None of you has ever seen a prince in pauper's clothing, I take it. It's the man who makes the clothes, you know, not the other way around." He danced in, suddenly light on his feet as if fencing. Nodding toward the councillor, he added, "Rialus Neptos, it seems, understands this better than most."

The second guard continued to sputter, while his two companions begged forgiveness. Several of the newly arrived Marah bowed low to the ground. Rialus tried to form a question about his garb; seemed to sense the question was fraught with insult; and instead posed a series of queries, after none of which he kept quiet long enough to hear the answers to. Dariel mentioned casually that he was here to see the queen on matters of state. He should probably be on his way, but should Rialus prefer to interrogate him first . . . He sketched his indifference in the air with his hand. For that matter, he did not mind being delayed by each Marah who wished to question him. Of course, the queen might not like to be kept waiting . . .

A moment later Dariel was striding along. Rialus shuffled a half step behind him, signaling furiously with his hands and arms and face at any soldier or guard that might possibly think to intercept them. By the confused looks the men and women sent him, it was clear few understood his antics. Not, at least, until they recognized Dariel's face and bearing. Despite his garb the prince walked with assurance and obvious military fitness. All who might have questioned him instead stepped to the side.

"Is it true what I hear said about you, Rialus?" Dariel asked.

"What's that, sir?"

Dariel did not slacken his pace, but looked at the councillor askance, one corner of his mouth lifted. "That you've found love, Rialus. That you found marital harmony in the arms of a woman who was once your servant. I'd no idea you were so liberally minded, though I had heard you were on something of a diligent search for a . . . well, for a wife to complete you."

This had been a running joke for the last few years. Rialus, once he had his quarters set up in what had been a Meinish compound during Hanish's rule, had set about staffing it almost entirely with attractive young women. It was rumored that not all of them knew much about keeping an official's house in order, but most of them made up for it with a propensity toward buxomness. A few, it was said, came directly from houses of prostitution and served entirely to satisfy Rialus's considerable carnal appetite. Who could blame him— pent up as he had been in Cathgergen for so many of his prime years? Dariel really felt no superiority to him in this regard. He did not even condemn Rialus for marrying a servant girl. Truth be known, he envied him the freedom to marry whomever he chose. This was not a freedom he himself had, as Corinn had made abundantly clear.

"No need to explain yourself to me," Dariel said, cutting him off before he got fully up to speed in his sputtering explanation. He slapped a hand down on the man's thin shoulder, feeling him wince beneath it. "Be a happy man, Rialus. Plant a child in her. Become immortal . . ."

The prince's voice trailed off. He had just mounted one of the upper stairs and turned on the patio to take in the view. As ever, the terraced descent of Acacia to the sea was a wonder to behold. Beneath him, the land cascaded down, level on level, merging together like a maze cut by stairways and fortifying walls, with great houses in the higher reaches and smaller structures lower. Corinn had ordered new paint colors mixed to announce the return of Akaran rule and to represent the new age she believed they were entering. So the rooftops and spires and globes below him flashed in brilliant hues of sky blue and crimson and orange, of brown and silver that shimmered like sun on water.

Dariel found it somewhat garish, really. He almost remarked once that the colors suited the amboyant tastes of a Sea Isle brigand outpost, but he had held his tongue, sure that Corinn would not care for the comparison. Still, garishly clothed or not, Acacia had weathered the changes of human fortune with quiet resilience. He wondered if the island itself would outlive all empires and go on in its beauty long after humans ceased clamoring over it. The sea would surround it then just as now. The sun would rise from one horizon and set in the other, just as now. In a way this notion of a lonely Acacia was a pleasing thought, though Dariel was not sure why that should be so. He should want his people to rule here without end. He did, of course. But a person, he had come to believe, can want two conflicting things at the same time.

After the councillor had vouched for his identity, Dariel left Rialus at the entrance to Corinn's offices. Entering the inner chambers, the prince was aware of a scent in the air that he often detected around his sister. It was something other than the fragrant concoctions that bubbled quietly in small pots throughout the room, something other than the blossoms from the flowering bushes kept in great basins on her balcony. He thought it an essential oil she must wear dabbed somewhere on her person, a scent all her own. Strange that, because he did not exactly find it a pleasant smell, sharp and dry as it was.

Corinn waited for him. She was alone, standing with her arms clasped at her waist, her face composed as if she had anticipated the exact moment of his arrival. She had developed a tendency toward always seeming completely ready, never surprised. It was yet another small thing about his sister that left him uneasy. The grin that lifted her cheeks could not have been anything but genuine, though, spontaneous. That was another characteristic he had become more aware of in the last few years. She could shift from her aloof composure to girlish familiarity and back again so completely that when she was in one state it was impossible to imagine her in the other.

"What a sight you are, Dariel!" she exclaimed. "You come to poke fun at me. Is that it? Look at you!"

"You sent me out to work among the people like a slave," Dariel said, raising his arms and spinning so that she could take his clothing in, "and so I return to you looking the part."

"Aaden is desperate to see you, you know? But if you walked in like that, he'd likely draw his sword and challenge you." She moved forward, stepped into the embrace of his uplifted arms, and hugged him briefly. Pulling back, she studied him. "Let us sit and talk."

A moment later, the two reclined in soft leather chairs, sitting across from each other, a carved stone table between them. In the center of it a small fire glowed, giving off considerable heat. A servant set two tumblers of mulled wine on the table and then retired.

"Tell me," Corinn said, taking up a tumbler and warming her hands around it. "Did you accomplish what you wished?"

He nodded. He had his own question to ask and felt it should be dealt with first. "What word from Mena?"

"Mena is well. She has nearly completed the work I asked of her. Melio is well also, and Kelis. They have performed admirably at their tasks. I know part of you wished to be with them, hunting the foulthings, perhaps protecting your sister— but Mena needs no protection. You were right when you brought this charity work proposal to me. Now tell me of it."

Dariel reached for the wine, inhaled the spicy scent, and fell into a detailed response to her query. For the past year he had found a sort of joy in daily labor that he had never known before. It came about because he was so very fatigued with war, with piracy, with violence, with seeing his loved ones die. For several years after the war with Hanish Mein, Dariel had led forces to hunt down the surviving Mein—the ones still in any sort of rebellion, at least. And he had squashed the flare-ups of rebellion all over the empire, each people trying to find some way to grab more of the Known World's map before things settled again. It had amazed him that the peace seemed just as violent as the war. It was always this way after wars, advisers told him, but still it troubled him. This hadn't been just any war. It was Aliver's war! The war to set the world to rights so that there need be no future wars. Everyone said they believed this; few, it seemed to him, also acted as if they did.

When the peace was finally established, he found himself just as ill at ease. He did not want the throne, though he could have claimed it as the male heir. That sort of power did not appeal to him. He had no desire to loaf about the palace court-ing noblewomen, as Corinn seemed to wish him to do. Nor could he return to the Outer Isles and again sail those gray slopes of water. The isles had been handed over entirely to the league in a deal Corinn had struck with it on her own authority. The league owned them now, their own separate state within the empire. It was recompense, Corinn made it clear, for Dariel's stunt on the League Platforms. He did not understand until later, but she was actually quite angry with him when she fully understood his role in the attack. It had crippled the league's capacity to trade across the Gray Slopes. It had cost them thousands of quota lives and hundreds of their own kind. It was such a monstrous success that Corinn had to acquiesce to giving them more than she would have liked. And, she hinted, she had needed to give away even more to get them to promise that Dariel would not end up dead in some mysterious way: poison or accident or mysterious disappearance. The fact that she clearly considered them capable of all these things had set his skin crawling.

Also, as soon as the quiet settled upon him, he began to have dreams—nightmares, really—about the day Aliver was killed. At first Dariel thought it was some belated way of mourning his brother, but as the dreams grew more intense he realized it was not just that. He dreamed more and more of the aftermath of the duel, more and more about his murder of Maeander Mein. He had ordered it, even though Aliver had granted Maeander protection and agreed to the particulars of the duel. Dariel could not be sure that his blade had even touched the man, but he had whispered for his death and made all his people accomplices to the murder. It was a foul way to stain the sacred moments after his brother's passing. The shame of it grew within him as time passed. More and more fervently, he wanted to find a way to live without regret, to do enough with the life he still had before him so that he would feel he had been a force for good in the world.

It was Wren who suggested he again find work to occupy him. Not murderous work, though, not military. "Why not build?" she had asked. "Likely, you'd be as good at that as you were at piracy and sabotage." She actually had to suggest it several times before the seed split within him and took root. Wonderful, quiet Wren, sharp as a razor in more ways than one.

When he took the proposal of rebuilding to Corinn, he found her amiable enough. With her blessing, he set out on the work that had occupied him body and soul. As Wren had suggested, he built. He arrived in Killintich with a small army of surveyors, engineers, architects, historians, and laborers. Once proud, the capital of Aushenia had suffered neglect and abuse since the Numrek invasion. Dariel set about rebuilding that damaged city brick by brick. He worked right beside laborers, digging ditches, slopping through canals, hefting loads on his back. It was toil unlike any he had known before, and he loved it. The work may have been nothing more than an attempt to busy himself, but he hoped it was more and that he was doing good for the right reasons. It was important to him that this be true.

He described for Corinn the small moments he felt he would never forget. How he enjoyed sitting at fires with villagers and eating stew from wooden bowls, talking about such things as the weather and the growth of crops. He welcomed the fatigue with which he lay down each night, pleased that he had stolen nothing, killed no one, planned no destruction. He loved sleeping on straw mattresses and watching barn cats hunt mice and listening—as he once had in a village near the Gradthic Range—to two owls converse through the night. On the road outside Careven a blond-haired boy had presented him with a crown woven of grass. At a commemorative ceremony at Aushenguk Fell an old woman had approached him silently from behind. Without a word, she pressed her flat chest against his back and wrapped her stick arms around his torso and clung there. "She had no weight at all," he said, "light as a bird." She never said a thing, but he was sure the gesture was one of thanks.

"As it should be," Corinn said. "I don't know that there was any similar venture done by an Akaran in all our generations of rule. Word is, you've done us a great service. The people speak well of you. I've learned from you, brother."

Dariel took a long draft of wine, enough to wash down the first thoughts he had on hearing this. She always thought foremost of rule and reputation and of the empire's fortunes. Perhaps she had to, as queen, but he wanted to remember the good he did for the people he served, not for the Akaran name.

"There is still so much to do," he said. "I barely know what to attend to next. There must be some way we can fight the drought in Talay. And I know it will seem a strange idea, but we must convince the Mainlanders to begin planting new trees to replace the ones they cut from the Eilavan Woodlands. I passed along the edge of it on the way to Aos and I saw miles of stumps and bracken, hardly a forest at all anymore." He paused, for no reason other than something in the patient way Corinn watched him indicated that she was humoring him, that she had something to say but was letting him ramble on first. "What?"

"I heard something that doesn't please me, Dariel. You have been critical of my policies."

Just like that, he felt a cold hand grip his heart. He felt the pulse in his palms, suddenly strong. It was absurd. She was his sister! There was no danger here, no matter that his body seemed to think there was. "I haven't," he said. "I don't know what you mean."

"King Grae complained to you about our tax levees on Aushenian ports. You, I've heard, said— Do you recall what you said?"

He did, but he shook his head, shrugged.

"You said, 'You may have a point.' How could you say that? Do you understand how that undermines me?"

"I didn't mean that. It's just that they pay us for—"

"Don't question me! They pay us for the very possibility of the prosperity—the peace to trade. That's what we give them;

what we take is no more than our due. If we give them their commerce, we're giving them the first piece of their independence."

Would that be so bad? Dariel thought but did not dare say.

"We cannot do that. We cannot even suggest that it's possible. Grae doesn't know what's good for him. He's like a child who would eat only sweets. He may be happy—until his teeth drop out. No, the only way to prosperity in the Known World is my way, the Akaran way. Never show doubt about that, certainly not before others' eyes."

She inhaled, ran her hand over her face, and changed her demeanor. With warmer, more complacent tones in her voice, she said, "It's fine that you have already given so much and that you wish to continue with such work. Father would have been proud. Aliver would have been proud. The delay between now and when you may return to such work will be a small thing, I'm sure." She set down her tumbler, untasted as far as he could tell, and leaned forward in her seat. "I am proud of you, too, Brother, but I have an important assignment for you. There has been a mishap in the Other Lands. I will need your help to mend it."

As he listened, Dariel teetered between dread and excitement. The league had been in contact with the Auldek, those mystery people to whom so many children had been sent. It had not gone well, and now the league needed help. It was hard for him to fathom.

Corinn was telling him he would travel across the Gray Slopes! He would ride waves as large as mountains—if the tales were true—and see the massive schools of sea wolves, the dreaded creatures that only the league had found a way to evade. He would set his eyes on the Other Lands. Amazing, something no known Acacian had ever done.

"You will be my ambassador," Corinn said, smiling as if there were something more ironic about this than he knew. "You will represent me and carry all my authority with you.

You, Dariel, are charged with the most important mission I've yet asked of anyone. The collapse of this foreign trade is a greater threat to us than Hanish Mein ever was. I don't exaggerate. Hanish could be killed outright and moved beyond. Easy. But if we don't resume the mist trade—"

"You don't mean to start that again?"

"I do. Stop! I know what you think about it. I know what Aliver promised. But he's not here. We cannot go on indefinitely trading quota for gems and metals and trinkets. The trade has been pathetic, unsustainable. We need a return to the stability that kept this nation together for twenty-two generations."

Dariel started to protest, but she spoke over him.

"And I mean that in two different ways. One, we have partners—the league, the Lothan Aklun, even the Auldek—who expect things of us, are invested in us, have so much in place. Do you want them all as enemies?"

Again, Dariel would have spoken, but Corinn did not pause.

"No, of course not. Two, the people of the provinces are growing disgruntled. Tell me you don't know this is true. They gripe and plot and scheme to cause mischief. It's only a matter of time, Dariel, until they rebel. And that would do no one any good. It would be chaos. Suffering."

This time she did give him leave to speak. Words failed him, though. She was not wrong. There was discontent out there. He had felt it thinly veiled behind men's eyes. Even as he worked to help the people, he knew they did not accept him or his work as completely as he wished.

"And know this," the queen said. "I will not drug them as we did before. It won't be the same, Dariel. I promise that."

Do you promise it won't be worse? Dariel thought. In new ways?

Corinn stood up, smoothed her gown, and waited for Dariel to rise. When he did, she extended her arms, palms down but fingers reaching to clasp his. "Go to them, brother, and do not fail to assuage them and negotiate a continuation of the peace. Without it, we are truly in jeopardy. We are blameless. All you have to do is convince them of that and then charm them."

Dariel took a moment to respond. Part of him wanted to refuse her, but that was not easily done. And surely he could be a better emissary than anyone else she might send. Perhaps, in seeing the Lothan Aklun and Auldek in the flesh, he would learn things about them and find ways to alter the nature of their trade. She wished him to go for her reasons, but perhaps he could find a way to trade in something other than quota and mist. She wouldn't fault him for that—not if he brought a new arrangement to her that would replace the old. Perhaps this was a first step toward that. He tried to believe he heard these possibilities behind her words, but something kept him from mentioning them directly.

"When will I leave?" he asked, surprised that the first thing he uttered indicated acceptance of the mission.

"You sail with Sire Neen in two days' time. He began preparations as soon as he knew of your safe arrival here. Take no distractions with you. Understand? Wren does not go with you." Dariel must have registered his disappointment on his face, though he was not aware of doing so. "Very little of what falls on us as leaders is easy. You know that. Much of it challenges us. I've no doubt you won't love your time with Sire Neen, but for now we have no choice but to stay allied with the league."

For a moment, Dariel felt himself a boy again, as confused and helpless as when his guardian spirited him from Kidnaban and into years of hiding. This, in turn, made him think of Val, his protector during those years, as much his father as Leodan. "Is this the real Corinn?" he asked, measuring his voice to keep it even. "You'll send me off again before I've even caught my breath? You're a hard taskmaster, Sister."

Corinn found something about this amusing. A smile played

across her lips and vanished only when she spoke. "I have to be, Brother. I am queen."

"And what of my work?"

"Oh, it will go on. I'll see to it myself."

Dariel, despite his disquiet, laughed. "You, Sister, will do charity work among the common people?"

"I will," Corinn said, releasing on him the full radiance of her smile. "Not in quite the same way as you. But I have things planned. I have to. As I said, I am the queen."

A little later, Dariel padded barefoot through his chambers. The rooms were fragrant with the heavy incense Wren favored. The lamps burned low flames, not actually lighting the room at all but just allowing the outlines for him to navigate toward the inner rooms. He felt a deep need to talk with her, to explain what had been presented to him and to plot ways that she could come with him, even though he knew she couldn't. Wren was not a talker, not sentimental either, but that did not stop him from trying to talk to her, from wanting to wring emotion out of her to match with his.

He found her sitting on the bed, waiting for him. He cleared his throat to announce himself and she looked up. Wren stood. She wore a satin robe, long and intricately embroidered. As she walked toward him, he prepared several phrases of greeting, but the sensuous placement of her feet and the rocking of her hips took the words from his mouth. She loosened her belt and shrugged the robe from her shoulders and continued forward, slim and marvelously formed. She smiled, and Dariel did, too. Neither spoke.

Chapter Four

The man had spent too many years working in the mines of Kidnaban to easily stand straight now. Knowing he had a few moments more of solitude, he did not try. He leaned against the warehouse wall, hearing the muffled discussion going on beyond it. He had been tall even as a boy, a head above almost anyone he had ever stood near since adolescence. But that was when he stood upright at full height. He had few opportunities to do that during the years he worked in the mines. He had either crouched low as he shuffled down subterranean corridors or had strained beneath backbreaking loads he had to balance on his shoulders as he climbed the countless ladders that crept from the depths to the surface. After twenty years of that, his spine crooked in places it had not done in his youth. He was comfortable only in one position, curled on his side in the moments before sleep found him. Other than that, his physical life was measured in degrees of discomfort. He told himself it was better that way; this way he would never forget why his work mattered to him above all other things.

A door nearby swung open abruptly and a thin man appeared, blinking in the daylight and casting around with a hand shading his eyes. "Barad! There you are. Come in, they will hear you now." He motioned for the large man to approach. When Barad neared, the other man grasped him by the elbow and spoke enthusiastically. "It is safe, my friend. Have no fear while in Nesreh. We are friends here!"

Barad the Lesser let himself be led. "I know that," he said. His voice was boulder deep and rumbling. "Yours are good people, Elaz. I wouldn't be here if they were not."

On entering the chamber, Barad could see little. It was lit dimly by high slots in the ceiling and by lamps of smoke-blacked glass. He could tell immediately—by the moist heat, the scent of bodies, and the muffled layer of sound in the air—that the warehouse was filled with people. They were waiting, silent now that he was finally among them.

With a great effort to keep his face placid, Barad drew himself up. He raised his chin, flaring his nostrils as he took the calming breath he needed to stand at his full height. Perhaps because it was such an effort, the effect of his doing so was considerable. He was a tall man, with long legs and arms, big handed with knuckles that any street brawler would have envied. He felt the people's eyes upon him, impressed, perhaps wary. He had always had this effect on people. That was why he did not rush to begin speaking. Let them see him for a moment. Let them note the strained purpose on his rough-cut features, the way his heavy eyes suggested a tranquil, melancholy strength within. He was never sure that he truly felt this in himself, but he knew others saw it there and it suited him that they did.

After a few words of introduction from Elaz, he began. "If you will listen," he said, "I will tell you a story."

A few voices responded, saying they would listen. Some others clapped their hands against their chests, a sign of affirmation. Barad could pick out individual faces now. Tired faces. Overworked faces with the characteristics that marked the relatively isolated coastal people of Talay. In many ways their flushed faces, wide cheekbones, and short noses distinguished them among the Known World's races. But the curiosity, the faint hunger in their eyes was no different from what he had seen in others' eyes across the empire. That was what he was here to speak to.

"I will tell you my story, hoping that in it you will hear your story as well. Hoping you will understand that we many share the same story, and a tragic one it is."

He explained that he had been born in the camps outside the mines of Kidnaban. He had been raised in the knowledge that his life was committed to pulling precious metals from the earth. That was all there was ever to be of it: labor. Whatever living he was to do would be done in the pauses between labor. Loving, raising children, learning of the world: all of these things happened only in stolen moments. He was a water bearer at five years of age, a rubble sifter at seven, a wagon helper at eight. By ten he was tall and strong enough to haul small sacks. At twelve he was a digger, taking out any anger he had on the tunnels in the earth. And he did so for more years than he liked to count. He knew nothing about the outside world but lived day and night under the supervision of guards in great towers; whipped by drivers; scowled at; chained often. He did not know why he worked this way. Did not understand the economics of the world and how the nuggets of metal that he dug up would enrich men a world away.

How was such a life livable? Two things made it so. One, the drug called mist. "You've heard of that, I'm sure. I think you know it well." Each night—or each day, depending on the shift he worked—he could inhale the green smoke into his lungs and dream of a world of real life. The other thing that made his labor livable was that he somehow did find the moments to be a man. He loved a woman and put a child inside her. He saw that child born and live a few precious years, stealing moments to feel himself a father.

"I lost this child, though," Barad said. "Lost him and his mother." He cleared his throat and held to silence for a moment. He always thought beforehand that the next time he spoke he would explain just how he lost them, but—as had happened a hundred times before—his throat clenched tight on the words. It did not open again until he resolved to move on, leaving this one thing unsaid.

In the months leading up to the second war between the Akarans and the Mein he began to hear a voice in his dreams. He would not have known the war was coming, except that word of it came to him like a whisper carried far by a breeze. It drifted into his mist-sodden mind. Right there within his own head, drugged on the floor of the mines, he heard the returning prince's words. He was miles and miles away, yes, but Aliver had found a way to speak to him. What did he say?

"He said the world was set for change. He said he was returning from his long exile and that with the power of the empire's people behind him and with help from the ancients he was going to not only overthrow Hanish Mein but also overturn the entire order of the world. He would blow away mist like the wind disperses morning fog. He would put fire to league ships and drive out the Numrek, and, most important, he would never again sell our children into whatever slavery awaits them across the Gray Slopes. I was not the only one who heard such things. Many came off mist at that time, but"—he smiled, tapping his temple—"this head of mine is bigger than the norm. It is like a bell that rings louder than others, and so I heard clearly things that others only had inklings of."

And he had swallowed it all, he admitted. He was starved for such possibilities. He hungered to believe it. Why shouldn't he? He remembered everything he heard, and he took to shouting it to the workers around him. At feeding times he spoke to gathered groups as they ate, heads down, trying to ignore him. He bellowed inside tunnels and railed from ladders as he climbed. At first nobody paid attention to him. Guards sometimes punished him, but they thought him harmlessly mad. Slowly, though, slowly, more and more found their mist dreams turning into nightmares. Eyes began to follow him. Grimy faces lifted from their food when he spoke. Eventually, the masses came to him, hungry for Aliver's message. He gave it to them, and felt the hope grow in them. Thousands and thousands of them, opening their eyes with new clarity, eager for the future.

"My first mistake was in shouting too loud. The people heard me, yes, but so did the ears of Hanish Mein. The minute we rose in anger, he clapped his hand down on us with a rain of arrows and fire, with steel blades and unbending anger. What were we—who had only hope as a weapon—to do against the might of an empire? That was my first mistake. It would have been my last, as well, if Aliver hadn't launched his war."

When the prince did, Hanish had to turn his attention to that greater horde of humanity marching toward him through Talay. Barad escaped the mines during the chaos but was too far away to join Aliver before he died. He never saw his prince, but he did know the moment his voice was silenced.

"That was a tragic day, friends," Barad said, exhaling as he did so. He let the pain tug at his features. He knew this was an orator's trick, but in this case it was an honest action. It did pain him to recall the moment those whispers died in his ears. He had never felt a greater loss since. Oft-times he was still reminded of it, enough so that he sometimes froze in place with his head cocked, listening.

He moved on with his speech, talking through the aftermath of the war. Communication was irregular for the common people then, and Barad was a-wandering, staying far from the mines, finding some joy in the freedom to travel but unsure of his purpose anymore. Like everyone else, he took a while to know what to make of this new queen. Such a beauty, people said. So clever to outwit Hanish Mein, to use the Numrek against the Mein, and to somehow convince the league to withdraw their support of him. She was, in the first half year of her reign, adored by the entire populace. Aliver became an instant legend; she became his heir, a living, female embodiment of the ideals of her martyred brother. He had not lived, but she had, which meant there was yet hope.

"But that wasn't so, was it?"

A chorus of voices agreed.

"The queen ain't her brother," one man said, "not in any way except in sharing a name, and that's nothing."

A woman added, "She is a viper, that one. Sold us body and soul, the worst of her kind."

Barad let these comments sit, and waited through a few more. These people were finding their confidence enough to add their voices, to grunt affirmation and nod their heads. This was usually the way it went. It never took them long to learn to trust him. Why should it? Everything he said was true. He let them speak among themselves for a few minutes. When they stopped, Barad said, "Now that tale is no tale, is it? It is not make-believe, not a storyteller's fancy. Every word of it is the truth, and I believe you all know that."

Chest claps and shouts indicated that they did.

"And it's no different for you either. The details, yes, but the substance is the same. You coastal folk, you were proud once. You worked the ocean despite its danger. You know this better than I. But with Corinn as queen you've been changed from fishermen of the Gray Slopes to farmers of grain in a single generation. That, truly, is sorcery. Do not mistake me. We must plant and tend and harvest grain as well. It is not that I say the work is beneath you. It's just that each people are born knowing how they are, knowing what they do best, knowing the work of their mothers and fathers, knowing the work that will be their sons' and daughters'. That was what it was like here in Nesreh for generations. But it is not that way anymore. Instead, you pack grain in warehouses and ship it to Islands of the Lost, to that place where they breed our children into slaves to exchange for great wealth in the league's pockets, in the Akaran coffers. In exchange for the drug that they believe makes us ignorant of our own enslavement. Am I correct?"

A few in the audience affirmed that he was, but they were not all sure. How could they know what went on out there?

"I understand that it is hard to be certain of all this. So much is withheld from me as well as from you. But I think we can all agree that Queen Corinn may one day be considered a greater evil than Hanish Mein. Many think her so already. But now I see fear on some of your faces. How can I say such a thing? you wonder. It is a crime, and your hearing it makes you a part of my crime. I say that is not true. If you do not agree, you have done no crime. If you do agree, you have done nothing but acknowledge the truth. And there is no crime in that either."

Barad had stepped from the raised platform on which he had been standing and now moved through the crowd. He was slow, gentle as he pushed between them, a head taller than anyone there. He liked to see their faces at this point and liked them to see his. He dropped his voice slightly as well. The warehouse went silent, heads craning to follow him as he moved.

"I want you to work with me to make the world as Aliver Akaran dreamed it for us. This is treason, I know, but I invite each and every one of you to be traitors with me. How can I trust you? I will be honest with you—I ask that question myself each day. This goal I have—we have, if you are with me—is fraught with peril. Any one of you could be the spy who betrays our cause. One of you . . . it would only take one of you. So how can I trust you?"

He stopped before a middle-aged woman. He took her hand between his massive palms. He could smell the toil on her, the sweat and grime from her labors before coming to this meeting, the almost sour scent of grain dust woven in every thread of her simple garments. He spoke as if to her alone.

"I trust you because I must. Only together can we do this. Only together. If I don't have you with me, I have nothing. I may as well drag myself to Kidnaban and offer my back so that

86

it can be broken once and for all. But if there is no hope for me, there is none for you either. I pray to the Giver that is not the future before us." Still looking at the woman, he said the part of this that was the hardest for him. The only part that felt both true and feigned at the same time. He believed it, yes, but he was never sure whether his belief was founded on its truth, or whether the truth had grown out of his belief. "But I know that is not the future before us. The Giver has chosen us for greater things. We are the Chosen Ones. Aliver whispers that to me nightly. Still, he whispers it. We are the Giver's people, he says. We have only to awaken to it and act."

"What would you have us do, then?" Elaz asked, casting his question from where he stood on the platform.

Barad released the woman's hand and turned back. "Speak the truth each and every day. Speak it to your wives, your husbands. Speak it to your children. Speak it to each other so that you hear it again and again and know it by heart. And to those you doubt, speak only parts of it, test them. If the entire tree is too much for them to gaze on at once, plant seeds of truth in them first. Till the soil of your neighbors with love and with hope for them as well as yourselves. And then be patient. Seeds do not grow until the soil is ready and rains come and the sun promises them life."

"And when will that time come?"

Turning back again, Barad realized it was the middle-aged woman who had asked the question. He smiled, a wide, toothy grin with which he always answered that question. Indeed, he had answered it hundreds of times at meetings like this. He had answered it in the hovels in Candovia and mountain villages in Senival, in Aushenia and among the black-skinned people of Talay. He had even traded messages with the dejected remnants of Hanish Mein's people. Everywhere he found ears hungry to hear him and minds eager to be awakened, hearts ready to be stirred to action. At these moments, he could believe that Aliver had spoken to him for a reason. He could still help see the prince's dreams come true. At these moments, he forgot the pains of his body and again felt as strong as ever.

He answered as he always did, with what he hoped to be the truth. "Soon," he said. "There will come a day when I will shout for all of the Known World to rise up. We are all the Kindred. I will shout, but the sound you hear will be that of your own voice, and it will sweep away the old world and we will make it anew. The queen has no idea what's coming. But we do. Soon, my friends. Soon."

Chapter Five

Rialus Neptos knew he should consider it an honor to be included in the envoy, but he was not very skilled at feeling honored. Actually, he could think of few things more unpleasant than the prospect of weeks aboard a league vessel heading off to the far side of the world. Rialus was a curious man, certainly, but his curiosity had strict boundaries, and he had plenty to occupy him within the confines of the Known World. For that matter, he had a good deal to occupy him within the confines of his own bedchamber.

He suspected Corinn had yet to forgive him for his impromptu wedding to Gurta. Why she should care he could not fathom, but she seemed annoyed by it. Surely, he was not the only man to ever wed a servant! By his accounting it was rather a respectable—honorable, actually—thing to do, especially as he had planted a child within her. An heir to the Neptos fortune. That was something he could not pass up. He had long ago resigned himself to the fact that the Neptos line would end with him. Indeed, in the frozen exile that had been his life in the Mein it seemed a good idea to end the Neptos misery.

But that was then. Now he was Queen Corinn Akaran's councillor, famed for having dispatched Hanish Mein. No other act in his life had changed his fortunes more than the few moments it took to make his hand thrust the knife blade into Hanish's pale flesh. Nobody would ever know how long he hesitated, or that he needed to grasp the knife in both hands to control his trembling. But he had done it. He really had! Hanish was just flesh and blood, like other men. Because of it, Rialus lived at the center of the world. Now he had a position of prominence. Now—thanks to Gurta being made a lady overnight—he would have heirs to pass on his good fortune to. The Giver did reward his worthies! Sometimes it just took a while for him to get around to it.

That was what Rialus kept reminding himself as he nodded to the guards who stood at the gates of the league compound. They were Ishtat Inspectorate, a force that held no real allegiance to the queen. They gave Rialus the shivers, cloaked as they were. That and the halberds they held at the ready. He had heard they could use the weapons for slashing motions that could disembowel or behead a person from eight feet away, or they could break the weapon into two parts—sword and staff both—and thereby crack your skull with one before slicing you open with the other. He could not help feeling they itched to do both, which is why their statue-like stillness caused him to quicken his steps.

Once in the outer chambers of Sire Dagon's offices, Rialus was told to wait. He sat on an iron chair that had a delicate beauty but was amazingly uncomfortable. That was how it always seemed when he was with the league. Their offices were sumptuous, pleasing to the eye, and promising of comfort. But he had never sat on a league couch without finding a ridge that poked him in the back, or fabric that irritated his skin. On the walls hung paintings of their massive ships astride even more massive waves. The angles they tilted at, the dark shapes beneath the water, the way the white fingers of the wave crests reached out for the tiny human figures on deck made Rialus queasy. He hoped that the images were exaggerations meant to impress or tumultuous aberrations that he was unlikely to witness firsthand.

He moved his eyes away. It would be a brief voyage. What

was it? Four weeks across? A few weeks there, and then four weeks back. No more than two and a bit months of his life. He could spare that, considering that Gurta, plump with his heir, would be waiting for him. He did, of course, have Corinn's charges to worry about. She had laid them out for him just the day before.

"I have three charges for you, Rialus," she had said. "First, keep an eye on my brother. I want him safe, and nobody has a better nose than you for sniffling out danger. Whether they come from the league, the Lothan Aklun, the Auldek, or the ocean depths you must spot dangers before they touch him. Second, I want you in the room when the league meets with the Lothan Aklun and the Auldek. You speak the Numrek tongue better than anyone else I know. It just may be you will understand the Auldek language as well. Judge them for yourself and keep your judgement to yourself, understand? Try to find ways to speak with them alone. We may one day deal with them without the league between us, so we might as well know something about them. Third, of course, is that you return to me with a detailed report of everything you witness. My brother will do the same, but I want to hear separately from you. Never in our history of trading with the Lothan Aklun have we had a better opportunity to learn about them. Use it, Rialus. Use it so fully that when you return I don't regret not having gone myself."

She made each assignment sound both simple and laced with threat. She was good at that. He would have to keep his wits about him, make journal notes regularly, and find a way to quell the nausea that roiled in him each time he thought of those ocean waves. And the Auldek . . . Please let them be more refined than the Numrek! Two months, though. Only two months and he would be home again. He could handle that.

When he was finally ushered into Sire Dagon's chambers he found he was late in joining the meeting. Along with Dagon,

Neen, and several league navigators sat the bulky and all too familiar forms of Calrach and his two seconds. The leaguemen sat at repose in their intricate, presumably uncomfortable chairs. The Numrek dwarfed them—all hard-edged muscle and rough features—and yet both parties seemed at ease.

"Ah, Rialus Neptos," Sire Dagon said, speaking through an exhalation of mist, "you join us at last. We've nearly concluded our meeting. Be prompter in future."

Rialus began an explanation that he had been sitting in the outer offices for nearly an hour, but nobody seemed interested. Calrach rose and greeted him with a crushing hug and then stood back, smacking his massive hand down on the frail man's shoulder. "My friend," he said in Numrek, "good to see you. You are not so much a rat anymore. More of a weasel now." He turned to his companions for agreement, which they gave. Each of them in turn inflicted the same chest-crushing embrace on him.

Rialus fumbled through it in terse Numrek. He still hated the language for the barbarity of it and for the contortions it demanded of his tongue and lips. He did speak it well, though, having learned it during his tenure as Hanish Mein's ambassador to the foreign invaders turned allies. Not a thing he liked being reminded of for many reasons. It had been a humiliating period of his life, worse, in some ways, than his exile in Cathgergen. Actually, his wrestling with the Numrek language had helped cure him of his stammer. He now spoke almost as smoothly as he would like.

Once he was seated, rail-thin servants gave him a sweet plum wine in a glass that would not sit straight when he set it down. Nobody else seemed to have the same trouble, which was odd because their glasses looked just like his. It suddenly seemed quite important that he did not spill any of the sugary liquid. He sat back in his chair, small glass held in his lap with what he hoped passed for composure. He wondered what they had discussed before he arrived. The best stuff, he was sure.

Sire Dagon cleared his throat and spoke without a hint of emotion, humor, or irony. "So, good Calrach, you see in Rialus a loyal servant of the queen. He's to shepherd the young prince about; keep him safe from harm, treachery, and such. Just between us, I sometimes suspect the queen thinks we harbor ill intentions toward her brother. I've assured her the league can forgive and forget as well as anyone. Dariel is a prince now, not a brigand, thief, and saboteur. Anyway, Rialus will, no doubt, strive to work in the Akaran interests in every way. But what of the Numrek? Is it at the queen's bidding that you will journey to Ushen Brae? Or have you your own purposes?"

"I believe Queen Corinn demanded that they go," Sire Neen offered, "no doubt to keep an eye on us. The Numrek, too, are loyal to her majesty—"

Calrach stopped him by snapping forth his arm, palm out. He looked for a bare spot on the floor to spit and then did so. "We care nothing about the queen. She is not our queen anyway. She is a bitch who flaunts her tail but doesn't give it up. Instead, she bares her teeth and snaps. We have grown tired of her."

In the silence after this, the two leaguemen exchanged troubled glances. Sire Neen put a hand to his throat as if a cough needed to be soothed down by his fingers. It was a reasonable reaction for any not well acquainted with the Numrek, except that Rialus had spent enough time among these foreigners to know that belligerence was the norm in their speech. They could not be judged by Acacian standards of behavior, even as regarded insulting the queen. He knew this, but so did the leaguemen. There was just slightly too much timidity in their reaction. Noticing it, Rialus figuratively narrowed his eyes.

"But you are still in her service?" Sire Dagon asked.

"We are. There is no reason not to be. If she, through you, allows me to see Ushen Brae again, I am happy to serve her. I will say the words she asks of me." The Numrek leaned back.

"Yes, I will do that. She will not be disappointed. But I don't do it because I love the smell between her legs."

A horrible expression, Rialus thought, one that Numrek men and women both used without embarrassment. It threatened to bring with it a flood of memories, but he pushed them back. Keep your wits, Rialus. He took a sip of the wine and tried to remain as unobtrusive as possible.

Mulat, Calrach's half brother, added, "We do it because what is good for the Akarans is good for the Auldek, and we as their cousins want only what is good for them."

Sire Dagon accepted a pickled plum from a servant, and then dismissed him—or her, it was hard to tell—with a flick of his wrist. He held the soft fruit in his fingers, sniffing it. "Cousins, you say? I've never entirely understood the relationship between the Auldek and the Numrek. Did they not displace you, drive you into the—"

"No, no, no," Calrach said, exasperation flaring. He thumped his palm against Mulat's chest with a force that made Rialus cringe, though it did not really seem to bother the Numrek. "Do not test me again, Leagueman! This thing we don't speak of. It does not concern you. Stop finding ways to ask of it."

Hmm, Rialus thought. So the sires had asked about the connection between the Numrek and Auldek enough times that Calrach had noticed. True, Calrach was sharper than his gruff exterior suggested, but if the league had pressed him on it, they obviously did not know as much about the Auldek as they wished. That was interesting, or troubling, to consider.

"My apologies," Sire Dagon said, bowing his head. "Yours are such an interesting people. You cannot blame me for being curious. In any event, you will be an honored member of our delegation. Invaluable, I'm sure."

Appeased, Calrach let his large frame fall back against his chair.

"Excuse me," Rialus said, "but what was that name you used? Ushebra—"

"Ushen Brae," Mulat corrected. "That is the name of our land."

"Oh, I've not heard that before."

Mulat had a handsome face for a Numrek, cut of features better proportioned for human eyes to appreciate. Still, the slightest displeasure made his face a creviced mask that was hard not to cringe from. "That doesn't mean it's not so. You call our lands the Other Lands, but why should we do so? They are not other to us. This place here is other. Now that we are to see our home again, we will again call it by its proper name."

"Should I—"

"Do what you wish," Calrach said. "It makes no difference. Sires, there are two things more about our going on this ocean voyage. One, I will bring my son. Don't protest. It's no matter of yours. But I'll take him to see Ushen Brae. Two, you must bind us."

Sire Neen's head dipped to one side, birdlike, and straightened again.

That, Rialus thought, was the first genuine show of surprise he had seen yet on a leagueman. He went to set his glass down, fumbling when it wobbled and then reconsidering. He took another sip instead.

"Bind you?"

Instead of answering, Calrach shifted, uneasy suddenly. He thrust his chin at his half brother, and it was Mulat who answered. "We abhor the water. In sight of land, as here in the Inner Sea, it's not bad. But the Gray Slopes . . . these we don't care for."

The sires responded warmly enough. They understood this well. The Auldek did not care for the sea either. They had, in fact, never once seen one of them aboard a ship, a fact that greatly benefited the Lothan Aklun. "This is why you came into the Known World over the Ice Fields. Hardly an easy route."

"It was a feat to make us immortal," Calrach said with a

bravado that, even for him, felt a bit forced. "No other has ever accomplished it. We are not so different from gods, yes?"

Sire Neen nodded but did not answer. Instead, he looped back. "Amazing that you fear the sea so much, and yet—"

"Fear! Fear?" Calrach spat, this time without aiming at all. "I know no fear, but the water will not support us!"

"So you cannot swim? Surely, you could learn. Even the smallest child can—"

For a moment Rialus was sure Calrach was going to smash the leagueman across his too-thin jaw. Indeed, the Numrek half rose from his seat. He grasped Neen's chair at the armrests and pushed his face close, the muscles in his neck quivering, his jaw tight. "We have heavy bones!"

Sire Neen, straight-faced and nonplussed, asked, "Heavy bones? That's a strange ailment."

"I am iron inside," Calrach said. "Drop me in the ocean, and I will sink to the bottom like an anchor. I would not like that. I would have to walk along the bottom to return to land. I could do it, but the very thought of it makes me angry."

Despite the fact that Rialus did imagine Numrek bones to be nearly as hard and heavy as iron, he had to duck his head and clear his throat to keep his amusement from curling his lips. Angry, indeed! Angry like a child lost in the woods. He had not thought the Numrek so adept at manipulating language.

"So you say we must bind you?" Sire Dagon said. "With chains, you mean?"

Calrach loosened his grip and returned to his seat. "Yes, if you wish to live. I cannot promise we'd not go into a rage out of sight of land. You wouldn't want that."

For a moment, as Sire Dagon spoke and Calrach detailed the strength of the bonds that would be needed to contain his great power, Rialus watched the other leagueman. Sire Neen's bland visage did not quite hide the amused interest with which he listened. His eyes were wide and attentive, his cheeks flushed. This might have been from staring into Calrach's shouting face, but he looked pleased. His mouth hung open just slightly, and the tip of his tongue slipped across the round little nubs that were his teeth.

A moment later, one of the navigators began to brief him on preparations being made for the prince, but Rialus only half listened. And then Rialus understood something that had tugged at the edge of his understanding since he arrived at the meeting. He knew, of course, that not even a single word spoken by a leagueman could be taken as truth. He had sensed in every question and glance and pleasantry that the two men were so entangled in deceptions that their spoken words had only the semblance of truth to them. But all of this was standard. Anybody with a working knowledge of the league knew these things. What Rialus saw, however, was there on the tip of Sire Neen's pink tongue as it slid across his teeth. Rialus could not have explained exactly how he knew it, but an uncanny ability to recognize deceit was his chief skill. Who can explain the gifts the Giver bestows on him?

Neen, Rialus realized, was hiding something, plotting something all his own. Rialus turned away from him before Neen noticed him watching, but he kept the image locked in his mind, studying it.

Chapter Six

Do you ever wonder what the world would be like if Aliver had lived?" Melio asked.

"Of course," Mena said. "You know we all do."

"Yeah," Melio agreed. "We all do."

He pulled her closer with the arm he already had wrapped around her shoulders. The two of them lay together in the predawn, touching along the length of their naked bodies. They had just made love, the sort of silent, spontaneous coupling they were often driven to in the quiet hours before facing danger once again. Though they had said nothing since wishing each other a good rest the evening before, Melio's question seemed the continuation of an ongoing conversation.

He continued, "What if he really had abolished the quota trade? What if he had really freed all the races to govern themselves? Can you imagine that? I know it would be a grand confusion in some ways, but it might have been beautiful. Corinn has betrayed it all, though. Your sister, the Fanged Rose. She rather scares me, Mena. You know that?"

"You don't understand her."

"You do?"

Mena shrugged. "I haven't always. And . . . no, I don't completely. But I do know that she tries. She tries harder than you know to do what's right. It may not look like what Aliver would have done, but she is no less devoted to us, to the empire."

"Forgive me, Mena, but she seems mostly devoted to keeping an iron grip on power."

Staying silent for a time, Mena weighed whether she should answer. Talking about her sister—no matter whether she was being critical or speaking praise—always felt like a betrayal of sorts. Certainly, Corinn herself would have thought of it that way. But Melio owned part of her heart as well. He gave her so much and deserved to know how she felt.

"I need you to understand something about her," Mena said. She started slowly, seeking out the right words, testing them first to make sure she was speaking truly. "Corinn is strong. You know that. But she is also very scared."

"The Fanged Rose scared?" Melio laughed. "That I don't believe. I've seen her look warriors in the face as if she were about to bite off their noses."

Mena stayed him with a hand. "I said she was strong as well, but you have to know that strength . . . well, it springs from different sources. It has different roots in different people. In Corinn, it's fear."

"Fear of what?"

"Of being alone. Of being unloved. Of dying. No, don't laugh. I knew some of this about her even as a girl. When our mother died, Corinn felt like part of her died. Everyone had always said she was our mother reborn. Her twin. She was the beautiful one." Melio began to make some jibe, but she cut him off. "No, listen to me. When our mother died, Corinn felt that she lost part of herself. And then . . . well, I don't know how I know this, but I always felt that she believed Father should live for her then. That some of the love he held for Aleera should be transferred to her, just to her. I don't know that I can blame her for that. I was too young to even remember our mother. The loss was different for her. But then Father died, too. She took it as a betrayal. And then there was Igguldan, her first love, I think. He died, too. And then she didn't even manage to escape Acacia like the rest of us. Her

99

guardian, Larken, betrayed her to Hanish Mein. You see, every time she trusted someone . . . every time she put her heart in someone's hands and let him decide her fate . . . And then came Hanish. She fell in love with him."

"Only to find out he was planning on sacrificing her to his ancestors. For all her beauty, she's not lucky in love, is she?"

"You see the pattern, then?"

"I do," he conceded, "and I know all these details. But we all have tragedies in our lives. It's no excuse."

"I know," she said, "and Corinn would never offer it as one. She's the last person who would ever do that."

"But think of the quota! Aliver would have abolished it; Corinn just reentrenched it. It seems so sad that instead of one monarch, we got another. Instead of one future, we—"

"Melio? Shhh. You're making a complicated thing sound simple. Don't."

She wasn't sure that he would believe that. It was easier for him to see the black and white of it. But there was more to the world than black and white. Much more. He did not share blood with both of them, and she could only go so far in explaining her feelings about her siblings at one time. It was complicated, to her at least. "It's easy to see fault, I know. Fault is there, but she's my sister, Melio. I love her. She's part of me beneath the skin. Anyway, I would not want her position. I pray she lives long and that Aaden makes a strong ruler in his time."

Though she did not look at him, Mena could see the crooked smirk Melio likely greeted that thought with. "Never you?"

"Never. I wouldn't want that sort of burden."

"You risk your life—"

"You know that's different. That suits me. What Corinn carries is another thing. I would not accept the crown even if—may it never happen— it was thrust upon me."

"And Dariel? What if rule ever went to him?"

"I don't know," Mena said. She was quiet for a moment. "He did not fight Corinn for the throne when he could have. He has his own demons to wrestle with. He does search for a destiny. I know he wants to do something grand. He's talked about it, but I don't know where or how he'll find it."

The world outside their tent started to gray its way back into being, stirring others into life. Mena sat up, knowing the time had come to take up her role again. Her fingers flexed, wanting to hold her sword. Before that, though, there was something more mundane to take care of. She crawled off the sleeping mat and toward the basin she used to wash Melio's seed from inside her, infusing the water with a concoction of herbs prepared for her by a physician back on Acacia.

"Maybe you shouldn't do that," Melio said. He propped himself on his elbow. "Why not just trust what happens?"

Mena measured the herb powder and swirled it into the water. "Don't be silly. How would I look fighting foulthings while carrying around a fat belly? It would break all sorts of taboos."

"Then stop fighting foulthings," he answered, ignoring her joking tone. "You're not the only one who can do it. Give someone else charge. Not even Corinn could fault you. We've been wed for five years now, Mena. Let's make a child and live like—"

"Like what? Like everybody else? We're not everybody else." I'm Maeben on earth, remember? Wrath in raptor form. What sort of mother would I make? She did not say these things. She only half believed them, and she knew Melio would refute her point by point. He had many times before this. He started to say something else, but Mena had had enough of talking for the time being. She said, "Come. I want to reach Halaly by tonight. There's work to be done."

There was always work to be done. Or so it had felt for months now. Finally, though, it looked as if there might be an end in sight to this war against the foulthings. As far as she knew, there were only two left to face. One in Halaly, one across a large swath of hill region of northwestern Talay. Reports of the latter were scattered and unreliable. The word coming out of Halaly, however, was specific. And dire. It was toward that once powerful interior tribe that she had pushed her band once the tenten creature had been vanquished.

With Melio and Kelis at her side, Mena spent her first evening in Halaly with Oubadal, the chieftain, and his councilmen. They sat on woven mats, beneath the cone-shaped shelter in which the aging leader held court. Mena pushed thoughts of home—or rest and calm and time for reflection—to the back of her mind and focused on the matter most immediately at hand. The tribesmen were impassioned, troubled, and anxious. The waters that had provided them with fish for all their history had been turned into a liquid desert, all because of a foulthing's voracious appetite.

"Tell me of it," Mena said, sitting cross-legged before the chieftain and the few elder councillors still living. She had marched in a few minutes ago, but she came with a purpose and wished the Halaly to know it. Around them, others of all ages rimmed the semiopen shelter; and beyond that, standing in the late day sun, still others—women and children and the many of Mena's own hunting party—craned forward to hear.

Oubadal let others tell the tale through a chorus of voices. At first, they said, the thing had been but a rumor. Two years ago fishermen on the western edge of the lake had started telling tales of large aquatic creatures that would appear to eat the fish they already had on their lines, sometimes shredding their kive nets to get at the small, silvery fish. There had been many of them, they said, but as they grew larger and easier to spot—their back fins cresting the water when they attacked—their numbers began to drop.

Once they found a carcass washed ashore, a hideous thing longer than a man was tall, like a fish but none that they had seen before. It had been bitten nearly in half, something no fish naturally in the lake could have done. They concluded that the monsters had begun to battle one another. That war went unseen by human eyes, except that still other corpses, bits and pieces of malformed piscine body parts, washed ashore as testament to the contest beneath the surface.

Eventually, only one of the creatures remained, but this one fed unchallenged by competitors. It became a massive lump of a monster, all bulbous protrusions on the outside, with one massive, circular mouth at its center. It sucked the life out of their shallow lake. Fishermen could stay on shore and watch it pushing through the shallows, ravenous, too large to be denied.

The tiny fish that had schooled in the warm waters by the millions had dwindled in one area of the lake and then another. It was a collapse of unimagined proportions. Gone were the tiny kive fish, such an important source of protein fried or dried or ground into paste. Gone were the waterfowl that hunted them. Fading was the Halaly vigor—which had been so based on their reliable food sources—and dwindling were the tribute and trade that had made them the beating heart of the continent. If all that wasn't bad enough, the air swarmed with the mosquitoes and biting flies that now gestated in the lake untroubled by the kive fish that had once thrived on their eggs; one of these spread disease, while the other left welts on the skin that easily grew infected.

The dark-skinned men telling all this spoke with voices both angry and incredulous. They seemed to doubt the tale they told even as they spoke it. Mighty Halaly so weakened by a single fish thing? So enfeebled that the bites of an insect laid men low and feverish. They barely seemed able to believe their own words. And yet here they were.

"Has the creature taken any human lives?" Melio asked.

"It has," one of the councillors answered. "It does not hunt us for food, but many men have died trying to kill it."

Another added, "The Halaly have not rolled over and accepted defeat. No."

They had tried time and again to trap the creature, to poison it, to spear it or hook it or something. Thus far, though, they had only smashed boats and seen men broken and drowned. For the last few months they had put their energies into building a fleet of sailing skimmers, light vessels with large sails and compact hulls that could run even through the shallows. With nearly a hundred of such craft now, they had hemmed the beast in to the inlets of the eastern corner of the lake. It had grown so large that it was trapped in the deeper areas, and these they had limited by opening the dams to drain the lake more than usual. It was an extreme measure, but because of it the beast—fat and bloated as it was—had never been more vulnerable. They were ready, he said, to end it.

"Good," Mena said, trying to sound confident and yet respectful of the somber mood of the meeting. "I am glad we will be here to help you do so. I regret it took us so long to aid you, but there were many foulthings. Now, thankfully, there are only two more. One of those we'll kill tomorrow, yes?"

The councilmen answered her with nods, a few grunts—not exactly enthusiasm to match her own. Unsure whether the response was fatalistic or whether it was a comment on her delay in arriving, Mena said, "My family has not forgotten that the Halaly joined us in the fight against Hanish Mein. Truly, you are honored friends in our eyes. All of Talay is so."

Oubadal cleared his throat, the first sound he had yet added to the meeting. He looked quite different from when Mena had first seen him, years before when Aliver had summoned the might of all Talay to his banner. Then he had been in his regal years, slow moving and powerful, heavy and rich and sure of his ownership of his world. He had been insolent to the point of insult in his initial response to Aliver. Mena knew that. Back then, younger men had bowed to his authority, and behind him a chorus of the aged had praised his wisdom. Now the younger men did the talking; the aged were nowhere to be seen. Except, of course, Oubadal himself. His flesh hung limp around him, overripe and flaccid. The skin on his face was still rich and dark, but the eyes that looked out were fatigued, small.

"Your words are kind, Princess," Oubadal said. "You remind me of the Snow King, may he rest forever." He bowed his head at this and then righted. He set his bloodshot gaze on the princess and studied her, as if verifying for himself that he did see the resemblance he had just claimed. "When I first met your brother, I was not as respectful as I should have been. He was a cub in my eyes, a prince without a people to lead. And what is that but delusion? I thought him weak. And then when he died, I thought him unfortunate. Unlucky. I thought he had failed and I felt bad for him."

Though the council shelter was open to the air on all sides, it had grown very quiet within and without. A few crickets held long-distance conversations, but mostly it seemed the night had hushed to listen to the chieftain.

"I know now that I was mistaken on all counts," Oubadal continued. "He left this life in a swirl of noble battle. He left it a man in his prime, lean and strong, a lion whose jaws would yet have grown stronger. He left this life with the fight still in his breast. Many say so. That is how he will be remembered, as a lion. You hear me? Tongues will never tire of his name. Now, Princess Mena, I envy him. Heroes always die young. I should have realized that much earlier."

Mena, understanding the old man better now, rose from her cross-legged position and moved closer to him. She placed a hand on his. "Heroes always die, yes, but they need not be young. I don't believe that. Oubadal, you are a king among your people. You will be remembered as such forever. When I walk from here, I will remind the world how you steered your people through tumultuous times. I will tell them that your people had prepared everything to defeat this monster.

You have already killed it. We are fortunate to be able to help complete what you have already all but accomplished. In a few days, we will hoist it from the water and end it. After that the fish will come back. Prosperity will return to your people."

Oubadal pulled his hand out from under hers and patted her with his fingertips. He smiled, sadly. "Dear girl, you don't understand. Yes, the fish will come back. Halaly will come back. My people may thrive again. But I— I won't see it all. Unlike your brother, I've had many, many days to come to understand this. I've had too many days. It is not easy." He paused, seeming choked by emotion, but he forced the moment to pass quickly. He coughed and then said, "Please, Princess, go with my men and see our new fleet. It is all we have left to fight the beast with."

Mena did as requested. Part of her wanted to stay with the old chieftain, wanted to let the others move away so that she could sit with him in solitude for a time. Here was a man who knew her brother and had sparred with her father when he was a young man. She wanted to comfort him, like a grown daughter might an ailing father. And, perhaps, she wanted to let him comfort her as well. Surely, tales of the past would help her make sense of the present. Wasn't that the way it was supposed to be? Couldn't she talk him through his melancholy and find within his long span of life greater meaning that would be a balm to them both? She believed so, but that was not the tenor of the moment. Instead, she bade him farewell for the time being and followed the younger men out to inspect the new fleet.

It was a sad tour. The Halaly tried hard to demonstrate their resolve, but the toll of the months of suffering and food shortages was palpable in every pause in the conversation, written in the haggard lines of women's faces and in the hunger contained within the ovals of children's eyes. The skimmer ships were interesting, but they looked like vessels meant for youthful recreation, not for battling a monster.

Mena went to her tent aware that there was still much to be prepared physically and much to be repaired in the tribe's morale.

Chapter Seven

On the eve of his departure for the Other Lands, once all the preparations that could be made had been made, Dariel carved out a few afternoon hours to spend with his nephew, Aaden. He buried any appearance of worry about the coming trip under a string of fanciful tales. He was going to sail the Gray Slopes around the curve of the world and right into the great maelstrom through which the Giver had escaped! Yes, that's exactly what he would do. He was going to track the wandering god down and talk his ear off until he changed his mind and came back. And if he could find Elenet along the way, he would give the young man a piece of his mind. Stealing from a god like that? Mucking about with the Giver's tongue? The cheek of it! To do all this, he would have to be slipperier than a snake, smoother of tongue than a floating merchant, more cunning than a Sea Isle brigand.

"Oh, wait," Dariel said, a sly grin growing with his realization. "I am a Sea Isle brigand! That's lucky. Elenet doesn't have a chance!"

Together, uncle and nephew ran through the hallways and up and down the stairs that fed out onto the main courtyard of the upper palace. They sparred with light wooden swords, alternately laughing and threatening. At times like this, Dariel's mind was as nimble and fanciful as a child's. There was nothing linear about their play, no thematic cohesion to it. One minute they were shipmates aboard the *Ballan*, the next they were Edifus and Tinhadin unifying the Known World, and just as quickly they were two laryx fighting for leadership of their pack, or an architect conferring with his worker on a great project. They were, for a few hours, two boys dashing through a palace full of servants who jumped out of their way. Some tutted and scowled. Most of them smiled, for the sight of them was a rare and welcome lightness in a court that Corinn tended with a solemn air.

For his part, Aaden listened to his uncle with an expression that at times said he was humoring the old fellow and at others betrayed rapt interest. He was just a boy, Dariel knew. Though his life had shown him no hardship, he already had a tendency toward seriousness. Corinn's work. There was no doubt that she loved her son deeply, but she had begun molding him some time ago. She would likely do so with greater and greater pressure as he turned toward adolescence. Dariel did not envy the boy.

Dariel tried to lead Aaden down into the subterranean world he had explored as a boy, but the palace walls and passageways deed his memory. He was sure that there was a route from his old nursery into these hidden realms, but he could not find it. He peeked behind wardrobes and reached under wall hangings. He kicked at corners and even got on his hands and knees as if close study of the walls' intersection with the floor would provide some clue. But he found nothing. Before long Aaden grew bored, not to mention skeptical. Another of his uncle's jokes, no doubt, just not an amusing one.

"When I get back we'll have a proper search," Dariel said. The two of them sat munching cheese from a plate on the floor of Aaden's room. "I swear there's a passage to be found here. Your mother knows about it. She had the Numrek use it in the last war."

"So what are you really going to do on this voyage?" Aaden asked, returning to a line of questioning Dariel had fended off earlier. "Does it have to do with the quota?"

Drawing back, Dariel asked, "What do you know of that?"

Aaden held his gaze a moment. "I know enough. Mother said that since I am older than the quota children now, I am old enough to know about them. If they're brave enough to go into the unknown, I should be capable of at least knowing about it."

"Corinn told you that?"

"Yes, but don't tell her I told you," Aaden said. "Sometimes she acts as if I'm too young to know certain things. And at other times you're not supposed to know things that I know. Does that make sense?"

Rising and stepping away from the boy, Dariel picked up his wooden sword and fenced the air with it. The motion was just an excuse for a few moments to think. Of course Corinn had told him some things. She knew as well as he that royal children should not be raised in ignorance of the unpleasant workings of the nation, as he and his siblings had largely been. But he also knew that Corinn considered this aspect of her son's education to be her province. He needed to be careful what he revealed.

"Yes, my trip does have something to do with that," he said. "I mean, it has to do with the Lothan Aklun and our dealings with them. I should not talk about it, though. Ask your mother if you wish to know more."

"Are you so afraid of her? You can't even stand still."

Dariel stopped his nervous sparring dance. "Corinn is my sister," he said. "Why should I be afraid of my sister? Don't be silly, and don't try to trick me. She's my sister, but she's your mother. If she wishes you to know affairs of state, it's up to her to tell you about them."

Aaden pierced a grape with the cheese knife. He lifted it and studied it as if he had not even heard his uncle. "It's just not right. I don't see any way that it's right. Children should not—"

"Wait, Aaden—"

"Be sent off into slavery. Mother told me she knows it's not right, and yet she allows it. Children, Dariel, younger than me. They get taken from their parents! I know you understand what that means. You were sent alone into the world when just a boy, right?"

Dariel lowered himself to his knees, setting the wooden sword to one side. "Yes, I was."

"And it was bad, yes, to be alone like that? On your own, with the whole world around you."

Dariel remembered the aching fear he had felt when alone in that dilapidated hut at the edge of the abandoned village in the Senivalian mountains. A chill, black night, the world like a mouth about to clamp shut and devour him whole. He only said, "Yes, that was not easy."

"So will you stop it? Go and see what it's about, but if it's bad, promise me you'll stop it. Even if Mother gets mad at you for it. I would do it myself, but I'm not old enough yet. Promise me you'll do what's right, and when I'm king I'll remember it." Aaden, still holding the grape on the tip of the knife, slanted his gaze up toward his uncle and waited for an answer.

The response he gave still rang in his ears the next morning, as he made his way through a dock thronging with workers and guards and animals, sailors and Ishtat Inspectorate officers. He had heard of the *Rayfin*, the league clipper that would transport him on the first leg of his journey, but he had seen it only from a distance. On reaching it, he stood a moment, gazing at it, unmoving among the commotion around him.

The ship was a marvel to look at, built for speed with the skill the league had been refining for generations. The body of it was sleek and dangerous looking, covered all over with the shiny, brilliantly white coating that all league vessels wore. He knew it was made with sap from certain trees in Aushenia, but the exact formula they used was a carefully guarded secret. For that matter, just what its function was remained something of

111

a mystery, too. It covered every beam of the hull, the railing, and the deck. It was as if the craft had been dipped in a vat of the stuff and lifted out shiny, slick. Once the ship was at sea, the rows of wide-armed masts would unfurl sail. He had seen that from a distance, and imagined they could set several jibs as well. The ship was likely the fastest Dariel had ever laid eyes on.

Rialus was there to meet him on deck, looking paler than usual. The councillor had proposed that they journey by land across the Tabith Way, reaching the port of Tabith and sailing from there onto the Gray Slopes. The proposal had made Dariel grin. Though it was a reasonable enough suggestion, it was clear from the manner in which Rialus proposed it that he was not comfortable with the idea of being so completely in league hands. Dariel was not either, but they were going to have to get used to that. Sire Neen himself would be traveling by sea, so it would look awkward if they did not as well. Plus Dariel loved the sea. He had loved it when he was hunting league vessels; he was sure he would still love it now, despite the strangeness of being a guest of his old enemies.

"Is that Rialus Neptos?" Dariel asked, grinning. "Or is it his ghost come in his place?"

Rialus did not catch or acknowledge the prince's humor. "The captain says we should leave within the hour to have advantage of the tide. Have you come ready to sail?"

"Yes, yes. All my things were loaded yesterday." He looked down at his new clothing, at the Marah sword at his side, and at the supple leather boots he now wore, as if to say he carried all his possessions on his person. "I'm as ready as I'll manage."

And just like that he was thinking of his last moments with Wren. He knew it would not be the last time. He would smell of her still, and each morning he would awake thinking of her. That was how it had been during his work in Aushenia. He would wonder if he had at last planted a child in her. They had certainly been hoping for one, for years now, it seemed.

Perhaps he would return to find her rubbing a small bump in her belly. He hoped so, but he had decided the trip was worth its perils. The promise he had made Aaden—for he had agreed to the boy's request—convinced him of that. Perhaps he would accomplish greater things than Corinn had planned. He would achieve more on this mission than had been asked of him, and she would later come to thank him for it. That was what happened with his rebuilding projects. It could happen with this, too.

"You said your farewells to the queen—"

"Yesterday," Dariel said, a little sharply.

There had been a small banquet in his honor. Nice enough, Corinn wishing him success at strengthening the empire's bond with the league, as if that were his only mission. More than one person had asked veiled questions about his feelings about the league, considering his conflicts with them during his youth. He had joked in answer, his grin and humor seeing him through it. Inside, he harbored the same unease himself.

For her part, Corinn seemed completely unconcerned. Perhaps she was concerned, but how to read that possibility Dariel was not sure. She had embraced him in parting, looking into his eyes and saying the kind things one expects a sister to say to her only brother. It had felt wonderful at the time, as if he were still a boy and her affection for him a balm. In the bright light of morning—and with Aaden's request still on his mind—he saw her face but no longer felt the warmth he wished he could.

"I can't wait to get outward bound," he said, to himself as much as to Rialus. "Ocean air: that's what I need."

"Finally!" Rialus said. "Calrach. I was starting to doubt he'd come."

But come he did, and he did not seem too happy about it. He strode at the front of a small band of Numrek. His feet smacked audibly on the stone dock. His arms swung about him as if they wanted to batter somebody, as if he was just hoping an offender would be fool enough to get in his way. He snapped his head from side to side, looking for an insult that the backing-away crowd did not offer. His hair, long and black as a courtesan's, swirled about him as he moved. It was an odd display, full of agitation. That was something Dariel had witnessed often enough on Numrek faces, but this was different. Whatever had insulted Calrach was not to be found in any of the cowering folks around him.

"What's he in a huff about?" Dariel asked.

"That's not anger. That's the Numrek version of fear."

The Numrek entourage mounted the gangplank like invaders. They were up in a few moments. Calrach shouldered through the Ishtat guards who awaited him. They milled about, several with their hands at their sword hilts. But the Numrek were no martial threat. They carried no weapons, and whatever angered Calrach had no human form. He roared something to his companions. They answered back just as belligerently. A moment later they had all vanished into one of the hatches leading belowdecks.

Rialus whispered details of the preparations Calrach had demanded. Dariel listened, as alarmed as he was amused. Chains? The threat of some blood-rage madness once they were out of the sight of land? He had never heard anything like it. "The Numrek fear the sea? Why?" Dariel asked. "It makes no sense."

Rialus shrugged. "They're strange brutes. If it weren't for the chance to see their beloved homeland again, I doubt they'd ever board an ocean-bound vessel. They say they can't swim. Too heavy, apparently. That could be true, although I've never seen one of them so much as try. Sunning on the beaches of Talay suits them, but they never actually went in the water."

"Anyone can drown, Rialus. Left adrift in the open ocean, everyone does drown. Even you, my friend, but I don't see you shouting to be chained. From all I've seen and heard, the Numrek are fearless. They fight to the death for an afternoon's amusement. What's that game they play where they take turns throwing spears as one of them runs an obstacle course? How can you do that on a whim and yet be afraid of—" The prince paused and studied Rialus. The small man had gasped something and stood clenching the railing, looking queasy. "Are you going to be sick, Rialus?"

"Of course not."

Dariel took a half step to the side, not trusting the man's self-assessment.

The councillor sputtered a moment before finding his voice again. "Who—who can explain another's fears?"

"My sister can," Dariel said wryly. "Or at least she knows how to exploit people's fears." He checked himself and said no more. Why had he even said that? Rialus was still Corinn's trained weasel, likely making notes of any slight uttered about her, even by her brother.

Dariel excused himself. He drifted away without a precise notion of where to go. He knew there were many eyes on him. Ishtat Inspectorate officers stood at silent attention at regular intervals around the deck. Sailors glanced at him as they prepared the ship for departure. A small group of leaguemen stopped their conversation with a pilot and watched him with their expressionless faces. Some even looked down—archers who sat guard in baskets atop the masts.

Dariel would be watched every minute he was aboard. So he would try to get used to it, to ignore it. He could not help taking in the details of the ship, and nobody had yet told him not to. He ran his hand along the railing, feeling the strange yet graspable texture of the white coating. It slid beneath his fingers when he moved them, but with the slightest pressure the stuff gripped his skin. The surface was not entirely easy to walk on, and—noting that many of the crewmen went barefoot—he decided that helped them keep their footing better than shoes. He imagined that water, on the other hand, must slip along the ship's hull without the slightest friction. This ship must be fast, indeed; and it must cut the water with such stealth that the waves might barely note its passing.

It took him a moment to notice the hush, but when he did, he looked up and around. The ship had gone quiet. The workers all paused. The group of leaguemen rushed forward on silent feet and lined the railing. Rialus still stood a way off, his eyes fixed on the docks. Following his gaze, Dariel picked out the only spot of motion among the suddenly stilled throng.

Sire Neen. He was perched in a small chair, an awkward-looking metal contraption in which he sat with his arms draped on the armrests, his chin raised and his eyes above the crowd. Two men bore his weight, one before and one behind him. They were slender but tightly muscled, with haughty looks on their faces. The crowd had parted to let them through. Most stood with their heads downturned. Strange, Dariel thought, but they were league employees. This whole section of the docks was a different world. In it, it seemed, sires were met with, well, with a good deal more deference than a prince!

Not for the first time, Dariel wondered if Corinn had truly ensured his safety. She must have, of course. He was no longer a brigand; the league was no longer allied to an enemy. What's past is past, Corinn had said. In war, crimes are done that must be forgiven during peace. That was simply the way of war and peace. As he watched Sire Neen stand and slowly ascend the gangplank, Dariel hoped the leagueman subscribed to the same doctrine.

Chapter Eight

Corinn had been having the dream for weeks now, long enough that she had begun to fear it would torment her forever. It was always the same. It always trapped her in the same manner, with roughly the same progression of events, the same dreadful realizations.

It began pleasantly enough. Aliver had returned! The palace buzzed with the news of it. He had appeared alive and unscathed. He was ready to help Corinn rule the empire. Her waking mind would have balked at this for many reasons, but her dream self embraced it. Nothing seemed more wonderful than to have Aliver home and let him take burdens from her. She knew that he would forgive her for some things and praise her for others. Together, they would have the power to achieve a truly magnicent rule for everyone.

She thought all these things as she dashed through the halls and across the plazas and up the flights of stairs to reach him. Along the way she diverged into other stories, conversations, travails. She changed her cream dress for her red, or her green for one of purple velvet. These varied from dream to dream, but eventually she walked the final length of hallway, wearing a simple wrap that left one of her breasts bare in the Bethuni manner. She stepped into the room and saw a figure sitting with his back to her. She called his name without speaking, and the man rose and . . . it was not Aliver! The figure that stood and turned toward her was a lean man, golden haired, dressed in a black thalba and snug-fitting trousers. His eyes were an incredible gray, glinting like molten silver, no eyes of a human being and yet they were his. Hanish Mein's. She realized that his lips had been sewn shut on her orders. And she knew that before the needle and thread pulled them tight she had ordered that a ball of twisted fishhooks be placed in his mouth, a rusty mess of a thing. She had wanted him to struggle not to swallow it, knowing that he would eventually have to and that it would rip a bloody path through his insides when he did. She had wanted him to suffer. The idea seemed horrific now. How could she ever have wanted that? At that moment, she wanted nothing more than to throw herself into his arms and forgive him everything.

Though Hanish's face was tranquil as he gazed at her, she ran toward him, thinking to cut the thread, pry his mouth open, and lift out the barbed metal. Her feet would not move her forward. She ran, but the space between them did not lessen. And then she realized the final, dreadful thing. The person was not Hanish either. It was Aaden, and he was clutching his throat as the barbs pierced through and blood gushed. The sight of it, the horror of it, was too much to bear.

She awoke thrashing, alone and tangled in the sheets of her massive bed. For a few seconds she struggled to escape the horror that clung to her, afraid that this time it would not let her go. It always did, though, and then she curled on her side, pulled her legs tight to her chest, and cried. It was a nightly torture she faced alone. She took no one to bed with her—had not done so since the night she awoke beside Hanish Mein and heard him speaking with his long-dead ancestors, promising them her life for their sakes. It was a wonder that she managed to sleep at all.

She made sure all signs of the dream and those raw memories were gone by the time she called her maidens and began her day. Indeed, she hardened herself against whatever hidden import the dream suggested and showed the world a face of utter certainty. That's what a queen was supposed to do. What a mother was supposed to do. She told herself that she was stronger for it. Perhaps she was.

"The longbow is a royal weapon," Corinn said. She nocked an arrow and pinned the shaft to the bow with the crook of her finger. Aaden stood beside her, the two of them behind a marker set out to measure the distance to a target the servants had set up in the grassy area of one of the upper terraces. It was mid-morning on a clear day, the breeze intermittent and gentle, the dream tucked away for the time being.

"I know you like your sword craft, and that's fine. A king, though, rarely fights among the throng. He must know how to take a wider view, to see the entire horizon and all the players. Understand? In the thick of a battlefield you can't see beyond the ranks of soldiers surrounding you. Like that you are vulnerable, as was my brother." She pointed the weapon high into the air, straightened her bow arm, and brought it down to sight, drawing the bowstring back to her cheek as she did so. "You, Aaden, will never be vulnerable in that way."

She opened her fingers. The bow thrummed and the arrow vanished. It was in her hand one moment; then it was gone, only to announce itself the next instant. It stuck fast in the yellow central circle of the wooden target, two finger's breadths away from the ruby heart that marked the exact center.

"You never miss!" Aaden cried. He danced about. "I'd like to see you miss just once. Can you? Just miss once for me. See if you can do it!"

Corinn spoke through a smile. "Don't be foolish. Why would I ever miss what I can hit?"

"To make me feel better."

"That would be a reason, if it worked. But it wouldn't make you feel better, would it? What would, would be if you hit still closer to the jewel. Try now."

Aaden did as instructed, though he took his time about it.

He selected an arrow with deliberation, holding it up before him to gauge its straightness and balance. He ran his fingertips over the fletching, touched the arrow's shaft to his yew bow, and fit the bowstring to the nock. Corinn heard one of the watching servants whisper something to another. Likely, they were commenting on the prince's fastidiousness. She had trained it into him from the start, enough so that he did not seem to conceive of archery without each step of slow preparation. When he finally bent the bow, he strained to hold it still against the draw weight.

"Limit the world," Corinn said. "See the heart. Feel the connection between you and it. Find that. You are not aiming at a distant target. You are laying the arrow on the path already created for it."

His arrow flew, but Corinn knew from the first instant that it was off course. It hit the lower corner of the target at an angle. It twisted and hung limply.

The boy twirled away in childish, smiling exasperation. "What happened? I was looking right at it!"

"You found the wrong path, Aaden." She let that sit for a moment, and then added, "You weren't still when you released. Your arm was swaying. Here, let me show you again."

She fell into instruction, happy with the way Aaden listened, the way he tried to understand her notion of paths. He was earnest in this, even though he did not seem particularly talented as an archer. Watching his form and posture, she tried to remember how skilled she had been at his age, but could not. As far as she could recall she had always known how to see the path to her targets. It had always been there, and, as long as she waited until she found it, she did not miss. When she found it and released, she was as sure of her aim as if the arrow were zipping through a pipe suspended in the air. But when had that begun? She had reached for memories from her childhood, but she never really went further back than the afternoon she first shot targets with Hanish Mein at Calfa

Ven. She must have learned her skills before that, though. She was a young lady by then, not a child. She already had many pains behind her and—

Aaden interrupted her thoughts. "Next time can Devlyn and others shoot with us?"

"Devlyn?"

"He is a good shot, best in his grouping."

"Devlyn." She had heard the name on Aaden's lips several times now. Devlyn. He was from a new Agnate family, she believed. Mainlanders. She would have to look into his ancestry. He might barely be of the upper class at all, considering how many new links the recorders had found to allow previously common families into the aristocracy. Such was the unfortunate necessity since the two wars and Hanish's purges had all but destroyed the old families. It was not the boy's credentials that interested her, though. Rather, it was the tone of admiration in Aaden's voice whenever he mentioned him. She would need to determine whether or not this was a good thing.

"We could have an archery day with them," he continued, "like a small tourney, but just my friends and me. Somebody else might win, but I don't care. It's just for fun. Can we?"

"We'll see," Corinn said. "You know, Aaden, that you are not the same as your friends. You will one day have this empire to rule."

"I know. That is why I should have friends. Companions! Devlyn could be my chancellor. He already said he would be if I asked him."

As the boy was busy setting another arrow, Corinn let her face betray a moment of displeasure. It was gone before he looked up again. "I'll have to meet this Devlyn. It would be a fine thing for you to have companions, but the truth is that when I'm gone you'll have nobody but yourself to rely on. Nobody else—certainly not Devlyn—will have to carry the burden of rule as you do. Understand that?"

121

"There's Mena and Dariel," he said, before bending his bow. "Yes, of course."

But you may not always have them to rely on, she thought. They may fail us. They may oppose us one day. It felt cold to think this, and at first she thought she would say nothing about it. But seeing the concentration wrinkling his brow as he shot, and watching his gray eyes study the results, she felt inclined to push him a little further. His arrow had struck at the edge of the center circle. "That was a fine shot. Let's leave it there for now. Come sit with me."

Aaden reluctantly obliged. The two sat side by side on a stone bench at the edge of the terrace. The balustrade was low, allowing a view out over the sea to the island's west. The nearer waters were dotted with rocky islands that seemed to sink farther and farther as the sea deepened from turquoise to a darker hue. Aaden set his hands in his lap, his knees bouncing with the balls of his feet. He waited, and Corinn, remembering the chattering cacophony that so many children make, was proud again of the son she was raising. A servant brought them two glasses of the berry drink Aaden liked, and then retreated out of earshot.

"I know you are still a boy," Corinn began, "but I have to prepare you for what your future holds. Better you know it now than learn it later. Nobody, not even my siblings, are as important to this nation as you are. You may love them dearly, as do I, but they both have flaws in their characters that you must never let weaken you. Mena is gifted and fierce, but she's afraid of her nature. Her true self is as savage and focused as an eagle. To her enemies she falls like a bolt from the sky, yes? You've heard the tales they tell of her. Her foes can't touch her. She pins them to the ground and rips out their hearts. As she should." She took a sip of the juice. Its tartness puckered her lips. "If that was all there was to Mena's nature, she would be an even better weapon than she already is. She should be all and only an eagle, but there is a dove within her as well. While her beak is carving through her victim's flesh, she starts to cry because of what she's doing. That's a mistake. I would never allow you to be so conflicted. So don't be."

Aaden drew back from his drink and nodded his single, sharp nod. "I understand. Only I don't think I'd like it if Mena was like an eagle. They have cold eyes."

"Better the cold eyes of an eagle than the timid ones of a dove. I've no use for doves." She said this more sharply than she intended. She paused for a moment, wondering why. "As for Dariel . . . I don't know what's happened to him. He used to be fearless, they say, a raider. I didn't know him then, but it's clear he has a natural gift for leading people. I just wish he would use it more. He has no stomach anymore for the hard things. He still smiles and entertains and knows how to show joy, but he carries a weight around in his center. He seems to feel he must make amends with the world and all the people in it. His building projects . . . I don't deny they're useful, but he goes about them for mistaken reasons."

"Is that why you sent him away?"

"I didn't 'send him away.' I sent him on a mission. When it's complete, he'll return better for it. You see, Aaden, I am trying to help them both become stronger, stronger in ways that truly matter, in ways that sharpen them, ways that harden them."

Again, she did not like the edge in her voice. She backed away from it, touched Aaden on his still bouncing knees. He was getting restless. She would have to let him go soon, go and be a boy for a while, free of lessons like these. She wished, not for the first time, that she did not have to say such things to him. Let him just be the boy he wants to be. But if she allowed that, she would be committing all the mistakes her father had made. Dariel had been but a little older than Aaden when he was cast out into the world alone, everything taken from him. Such things had happened before. They could happen again. If they did in his life, Aaden would never be able to fault her for not preparing him.

"Aliver was no better," she said. "You should know that from me, because the tales they tell of him make no mention of it. He may have dreamed fine notions, but what are dreams? They're nothing without the backbone to achieve them. Your uncle did wonderful things, of course, but he died with his work unfinished. He would have left the world in chaos had I not been here to set things right. His flaw, Aaden, was that he let emotion drive him. He let notions take the place of deliberate thought. Akarans have done that for too long. Tinhadin killed his older brother to secure his throne, but he killed his youngest out of fear. Even my father only half governed as he should have, choked as he was by an idealism that made him idle. But not any longer. I am not of that mold, nor will you be. I will teach you better than that. So, what I say is this . . ." She paused until he looked up at her with his full, gray-eyed attention. "Love our family without being weakened by them; honor them as infallible in public while noting their flaws to yourself; demand the most from friends without expecting it; imagine the worst from your enemies so that they cannot surprise you; and rely only on yourself."

Smiling and softening her voice she added, "Yourself and your mother, I should say." She mussed his hair. "All right, Aaden, enough of this talk! I can see you're restless."

"May I go to the Marah hall and train?"

"Yes. Do that. Show me what you've learned later."

Aaden handed his glass to a servant, who took it lightly, bowing and thanking his highness. The prince mumbled his own thanks to the servant, and then stepped close to Corinn and whispered, "Mother, do you ever use your singing to make the arrow . . . hit?"

Corinn slipped her hand around the back of his head and pulled him close. With her lips brushing his ear, she said, "Never."

* * *

An hour later the queen was back in her offices, sitting straight backed and expressionless as Rhrenna introduced Paddel, the head vintner of Prios. He was a jowly man, squeezed unflatteringly into a silken suit that bulged in all the wrong places. He was technically bald, but his scalp had been tattooed a dark blue-black. The ink followed his natural hairline, but the effect was unnervingly peculiar. Paddel seemed quite pleased with it. He regularly touched his scalp with his fingers, as if stroking and repositioning his hair.

Corinn decided to keep this meeting short. She actually knew most of what the vintner could tell her, having received detailed reports from the league for some years now. They had done their work; hopefully Paddel had done his as well.

"How have the trials gone?" she asked.

"Oh, wonderfully! Wonderfully!" The vintner could barely contain himself. He seemed oblivious of the fact that he flung spittle with each excited sentence. "You could not have asked for greater success. All that you wished for, Your Majesty, has been made reality. All of it."

Corinn sat some distance away, behind her desk, but she held her hand out before her chest, a posture half protective and half a threat that she might smack him. He didn't notice this either. "I hope so. Sire Dagon assured me the product would be worth any wait. In order for that to be true, your Prios vintage will have to be a very fine thing."

"My queen, my wine is the balm our thirsty nation needs. You will be delighted."

Corinn doubted delight would play any part in her emotions. She did, however, hide a keen interest behind her intentionally bland façade. She had waited years for this vintage. Balm for the thirsty nation. That would be a useful thing, indeed. It had not taken her long after seizing power to realize that her brother—however he had managed it—had left her gravely handicapped. The people were off mist, and their memories of the nightmares the drug had begun to induce must have been vivid, for none of them returned to the pipe. That was fine in the early days after Hanish's demise. There was work to be done, and more than enough for the people to focus on.

Before long, however, their clear-eyed awareness began to be a problem. They set their sights on her and started to grow disgruntled. First one nation and then another grumbled for independence, complained about being overtaxed, claimed that agents in the night still stole their children, argued Aliver's old pledges as if they were words from some holy book. Corinn was sure that she had to maneuver, cajole, bribe, flatter, and punish at a frenetic rate precisely because the people were no longer drugged. No Akaran monarch since Tinhadin had worked as hard as she had. If she had clamped down on dissent forcefully, it was the people's own fault! The Numrek were hers to deploy, and use them she did.

Initially, she had asked the league to find some way to spread the drug again. After all, it would upset their trade with the Lothan Aklun. Those foreigners still wanted quota. That was why the league had taken over the Outer Isles, to make them into a plantation for raising quota. But the Known World, it seemed, no longer wanted mist in return for it. The league had urged caution, patience. They said that to simply put the people back on mist would be a mistake, even if it were possible. It was too easily recognizable, too much a sign of their old condition. Some might take to a slightly altered variation, yes, but others would chafe and foment against it. All still remembered Aliver and considered him their deliverer from mist. It would not do for Corinn to simply reverse that. They convinced her to wait for a new product to control the people, and in the meantime she accepted payment for the quota in coin and jewel and a variety of other things needed to rebuild the empire. That she couldn't argue with.

It was seven years before they finally came to her saying the new drug had been perfected. It was, they said, made from the same base elements as mist, but they had managed to formulate it in such a way that it could be consumed day or night, without altering one's ability to work, sleep, or procreate. It had proven difficult to contain it in liquid form and in a substance that did not degrade over time. This was important to them, though, as they were convinced the drug should not be smoked. It should seem nothing like mist. This time, they urged, it should be consumed as a beverage, a beverage like . . . wine. Prios had long had a history of wine making. With Corinn's permission, and under league supervision, the operations had been expanded to cover as much of the island as possible. The result, finally, was this Prios vintage, a wine with a measure of the formula mixed in before bottling.

"Watching the test subjects," Paddel said, "one almost wants to throw reason away and join them." He leaned forward, beads of sweat clinging to his tattooed hairline. "The vintage, it isn't grandiose. It isn't unpredictable like mist. It doesn't take one over completely. Instead, from the first drink of it one feels the hum of mild bliss, a constant, happy sense of expectation. On the wine, they are convinced that something wonderful is about to happen. Always *about* to happen. The feeling, when properly dosed, never wears off. They never wonder why this wonderful thing hasn't happened; they only know that it is going to. It's coming. Always coming."

"And yet they still work?"

Vigorous nodding. "They do. Of course they do. Why wouldn't they? They feel wonderful, so what's a few more hours cracking rocks or whatever labor they're at?"

Corinn glanced at Rhrenna, the only other person in the room. Her small features did not do justice to the sharp mind behind them, but Corinn liked that about her. With her freckled Meinish skin and pale blue eyes she could sit within most rooms without drawing any more attention than an average household servant. She was much more, though. She asked, "And when they are deprived of it?"

"That's another bit of brilliance," Paddel said, addressing the queen as if she had asked the question. "If we withhold it, the test subjects feel only a vague unease, like the start of hunger pains or like a chill. And what does one do when hungry?" The vintner paused, grinning. "Eats! What does one do against a chill? Puts on a cloak. Nobody thinks 'Why am I slave to this hunger?' or 'Damn this chill, I'll fight it!' No, they do what comes naturally, Your Majesty. The same is true of the wine. In our trials the patients don't even understand that they crave the vintage. They'll do anything to get it, but they don't even know they want it. And I do mean anything . . ."

Corinn watched him rub his fingertips across his thumbs at some memory of this anything. "What of our military? If our own soldiers drink this stuff, will it make them unwilling to fight? Peaceful?"

"Not at all. They'll rush to battle confident of victory! Understand that the vintage— Oh, how should I say . . ." Paddel squinted his entire face as he searched for the words to explain himself. "They see the world with gilded highlights, yes, but they still see the world. They still walk through the motions of life as before, and honor their responsibilities. They honor them even better, in fact! You, my queen, will rule an empire of happy citizens. They'll do whatever you wish, and they'll never see their lives for what they are—complete and total drudgery!"

"And how do we control it?" Rhrenna asked. "Much of the empire drinks wine. Even children drink it diluted. How do we control who is on it and who is not?"

Paddel responded directly to the queen, grinning through his words. "That is for her majesty to determine, but in my opinion . . . Well, in my opinion, each and every person in the land could drink the stuff. They would all be happier for it, so what's the harm?"

Rhrenna, catching the queen's eye, expressed her loathing with quick pursing of her thin lips. Corinn silently agreed. She had never heard of anything worse, but she did not say so or let any emotion other than vague displeasure show on her face. "Fine. Continue production as you will, then. Store it carefully. Securely."

"Of course. We do. We do. The Ishtat Inspectorate guards the warehouse. When, Your Majesty, might we begin distribution? Sire Dagon said the league are ready and will aid at your pleasure."

"At my pleasure is correct," Corinn replied. "You may go now."

Go he did, ushered out by Rhrenna, although he clearly had to swallow a host of questions and declarations to do so. Once the two left the room, Corinn inhaled deeply, trying to loosen the tension that had built in her as she spoke with the vintner. She smelled him—a sweet, salty scent as if his sweat were some sort of sugared seawater. She would ask Rhrenna to have incense lit when she returned. A soothing scent—that was what she needed. Something to let her think clearly on this.

She loathed the pleasure Paddel seemed to take in the venture. Coming from him the entire project seemed tainted by his vile fingertips. But that should not matter, she knew. It was the result that she cared about; and the results, by all accounts, were as advantageous as she could have hoped. She understood now why the league had been willing to wait to see the formula and the means of distribution perfected. She had only to give the word. The wine would flow through the veins of trade, to markets and taverns, to sit on tables in every corner of the empire. It would wet the lips of laborers and thieves, farmers and merchants, scholars and officials. It would be hard to keep it from the gilded goblets of the aristocracy, but they were as troublesome in their simpering ways as ranting prophets like Barad were among the masses. Let them all be deluded. Let the world rest for a while without strife. Even Aliver could not have objected to that.

The thought of her siblings nagged at her. She would have

to decide what to do about them. Neither seemed to fully understand the dangers of a sober populace. Sometimes she feared that they did not understand their responsibilities. The people could not be trusted! They would forever find fault, make mistakes, and give in to petty jealousies and shortsighted thinking. They would destroy themselves if they were allowed to. That was what Tinhadin had realized; that was why he had grasped all power in his hands and ruled with an iron will.

She would do so as well, and yet she would improve on his model. She would rule with her brain, not her emotions. She would use all the tools she could. She would make the world safe. Nobody would lie to her anymore. Nobody would betray her, steal from her, or abandon her. Nobody would die without her permission. The world would be as she wished it to be. And then she would know peace as well.

Yes, she thought, then I will know peace. If Mena and Dariel could not understand this, she would have to act for them. She loved them dearly, of course. That was why, she knew, they might have to drink the vintage as well. She was not sure yet, but that might be for the best.

Rhrenna returned, lit the incense as Corinn asked, and talked through the remaining matters of business. There was always more. This time it was the merchants of Bocoum who harried her. Their drought had grown dire. Northern Talay— and all the food production and trade it drove—was at the brink of collapse. "Your Majesty," Rhrenna said, "they have really become quite insistent. They beseech you to come and see their plight. They say you will truly understand it only when you see it with your own eyes."

"Fine. I've had enough of these offices anyway. Tell them I will come to them within the fortnight. Tell Aaden as well. He'll be happy for a trip, even a short one."

Chapter Nine

Kelis received the messenger outside his tent. The youth was barefoot and lean, his musculature barely adolescent, though he was likely older than he looked. The light of the setting sun caught twinkles in the dust that coated him, the result of the miles of travel that had brought him to Halaly. Kelis, hearing his message and the coded language he used to demonstrate its authenticity, stood a moment, unsure how to answer. He knew a summons when he heard it. There was no other word for it. Sangae Umae, his chieftain, demanded his presence. Though he was loyal to the Akarans and to Mena's unfinished work, he could not ignore the order. Delay, perhaps, but not ignore.

Speaking Talayan, Kelis said, "Tell Sangae that when I am done here I will come to him in Umae. Tell him I have arrived here with Princess Mena only a week ago. We are to attack the foulthing in the lake, but we still have much to prepare. Once we have killed it, I will meet him in Umae." He began to turn away, but the messenger made a clicking sound with his tongue. Apparently, he was not finished.

The boy's left arm was stunted, half the size of the other. Perhaps this was part of why he was a messenger instead of warrior runner. He did not seem ashamed of it, though, and used the small limb to illustrate his words. "Not Umae," he said. "Sangae awaits you in Bocoum. He is there now and prays your feet do not grow hot on the sand before you reach him."

Bocoum? The bustling city of Bocoum was Talayan controlled, yes, but Sangae rarely visited there. He was a village chieftain, not a merchant prince. Respected as he was for having been Aliver's surrogate father, Sangae had as little use for the rich men of Bocoum as they had for him.

"He is at the coast?"

"Even now," the youth said, one corner of his mouth slightly crooked, as if Kelis were a disappointment for not knowing this already. "He stays in the care of Sinper of the family Ou. Sangae wishes me to take you there. I promised to return with you, as quickly as you can run."

The boy had an attitude of playful condescension. He thought too much of his authority as a messenger—which was no authority at all, really. Kelis decided to ignore this show of self-importance for now. He held to a long silence as he thought. Sinper Ou was his host? That made little sense. The Ous were the most ambitious of the city's merchant families. They were wealthy by any standard, and in the strange way of it, they earned their fortune without ever breaking a sweat. They owned the bulk of the rafts the floating merchants leased and took a considerable percentage of their profits. They also owned great swaths of the coastal farmlands, properties they had acquired piece by piece over the generations and now charged for the use of. They controlled more docks than any other family and imposed tariffs on all the goods that crossed them—both those grown on their land and those transported on their rafts. The Ous were not the type of company Sangae usually kept. None of this sounded right.

"Do you know why he summons me?" Kelis's eyes inadvertently lingered on the youth's stunted arm. "Why he sent you?"

"No, I don't know why he wants you," the youth answered, "but he sent me because I am fast. This arm does not slow my legs. It cuts the wind for me."

"I am sure it does—"

"You will have to work to keep up with me," the boy said.

Kelis smiled but said nothing. The boy had heart, at least. He told the messenger where to find food and drink and shelter for the evening, and he promised that he would run with him as soon as he had helped the princess. If she consented to let him go, that was.

Alone later on the hard pallet on which he slept, Kelis could not stop himself from longing for all the possibilities ended by the point of Maeander's blade. Even without outward reminders, being near Mena meant that memories of Aliver were always close. They lay like objects beneath a thin skin of water, sometimes standing out clearly, other times stirred by the current, shaded by clouds, or reflecting the world above like a moving mirror. Aliver's death had never yet felt real to him. He often daydreamed of the boy he had grown strong with, the man he had loved in his quiet way. He contained within himself images and expressions and bits of recalled conversations that seemed more real than the years separating him from those joyful moments. And in his dreams Aliver lived. He stood before him, ironic, aware that he had escaped death and somehow embarrassed to have done so, beautiful in a way that no other person had ever been in Kelis's eyes.

He always awoke from these dreams confounded. As a boy he had been a dreamer, one of the few who could predict the weather and turns of fortune and make sense of signs brought to him while he slept. His father had despised this gift, for it meant his firstborn son would not be a warrior and would therefore not secure the family's council seat. Kelis's father had managed to beat it out of the young man, jabbing him awake from sleep, making dreaming akin to pain, belittling him as if the gift were a slight to his manhood. Kelis had finally broken when his father adopted another youth to be his firstborn. To his father's delight, Kelis killed the boy, reclaimed his position, and replaced his vision dreams with images of the way he had thrust his spear into his brother's belly and twisted the organs around the point. That is what he had relived for years while sleeping: a nightly punishment.

After Aliver's death, his dreams stopped for a time. He could not remember the moment of the prince's death, either when awake or asleep. It was a blank spot into which he could not see, an emptiness he was reminded of every night, regardless of how filled with life and labor his days were. And when he did begin to dream again—a few months ago—it was of Aliver returned to life. What could that mean? Was there a sign in it that he needed to learn how to read? Might he now become the dreamer that his father—now also dead—had tried to extinguish? Surely, the prince should not be dead. He couldn't be dead! There had been some mistake made, some Meinish treachery that everyone else had been foolish enough to accept.

The night after getting his summons and watching Mena try to comfort the aging chieftain, Kelis did not sleep. Instead, he lay on his mat with his eyes pinned open, imagining journeying south instead of heading north to Bocoum. What if he crossed the great river and sought out the Santoth in the far south? Perhaps Aliver was among them. Maybe that's why he still seemed to live. Or perhaps they could bring him back into life. Maybe they just needed—wanted—to be asked. Aliver had been brave enough to seek the sorcerers out. Perhaps another needed to do the same.

He was thankful when the new day dawned. With the morning breeze and the slant of the sun, the world sprang to life. Mena was a whirlwind of energy, in among the Halaly men like one of them, her voice as loud as theirs and even more in command. She was a sensitive being, Kelis knew, troubled by things she rarely spoke of. But to the world she was at her best when danger neared, all certainty and poise and maybe even a hunger to be face-to-face with peril.

The Halaly had effectively formed a blockade to hem the

beast in. Skimmers and other boats were spaced at even intervals, anchored in place and connected with ropes that made an unbroken line. The early hours were spent shuttling crossbowmen, warriors, fishermen, and others out to the various vessels. A steady wind white-capped the water and buffeted the boats, straining them against their anchors. They had chosen this day for the wind, knowing the rhythm by which the air currents shifted and when they blew strongest.

Once all were as near to being in place as they could be over such bobbing, moving expanse, the signal to lift anchor and unfurl their sails issued from the mouths of Halaly horns. The skimmer that Kelis rode in jumped to grab the wind. The sail snapped as it filled, and he had to hold on as the light vessel surged into motion. The craft—two narrow pontoons with a skin platform between and a simple rudder—had a shallow draft and was built for speed. The water they zipped over was no more than waist deep. He could have rolled into the water and stood half wet, risking only to be cut in two by another skimmer. Indeed, they sailed through reeds and marsh grasses, sliced over lily pads and spreading green muck.

It was an impressive sight, but it seemed suddenly wrong. Why hadn't he considered this before? There are too many of us! How could a hundred ships coordinate an attack on one creature while moving at such speed? They would get tangled and crash into one another as they neared it. He wanted to shout out that the plan of attack was flawed. He wished he were with Mena. Surely she was thinking the same and must be trying to convince the Halaly of this. But he was just one of a few in this skimmer. He did not really even have a role here except to be with the Halaly, to do as they did, and to aid the crossbowmen who would be their main weapon.

The lookout perched at the prow of one of the pontoons shouted. He leaned over the water, his arm outstretched and finger pointing. Kelis tried to follow his direction, but he saw only water and a protrusion in the distance that he took to be a small island. But it was just a round mound of earth atop which reeds and perhaps a few short shrubs grew.

Why, then, did it move? Why did it change shape before his eyes, as if the entire island had rolled over and come up with a new topography? Nobody else seemed as confused as he was. They continued to hurtle toward it at all the wind's speed, shouting to one another, their spray-splashed eyes fixed on their target.

He looked again down the line of moving vessels, having no idea anymore where the princess was, hating the knowledge that she could die here just like any of them, just as her brother had. The formation was ragged now, with some skimmers ahead of others. Kelis's vessel was soon behind a few others, blocking his view of the island that was not an island. He wished—although he knew it was not a true wish but one sprung from the moment—that Mena was content to rule from a safe distance, like Corinn in one of her palaces. A strange thought to have here, and not one that he held for long.

When he next saw the creature it was near enough that he could doubt it no more. It dwarfed any living creature he had ever seen. It was comparable to nothing that walked or swam or squirmed. Its girth was like an outcropping of rock, like a hillside or like the island he had first thought it to be. But it was a flippered, scaled mountain of an undulating semi-aquatic monster, like no fish but with parts of fish in it, like no worm and yet wormlike in the grotesque rolling convulsions that propelled it forward. It bristled with scales that peeled as if it were diseased, no real protection as they opened and closed with its movements, the body beneath them as translucent and spotted and slick as the flesh of a squid. It did not swim at all, for the water was far too shallow. It wriggled away from them with the blubbery determination of a seal made huge. Its speed, though, was nothing compared to that of the skimmers.

The foremost of the vessels reached it. They raced along either side of it, tiny on the nearside and hidden altogether on the other. The first crossbowmen launched their barbed missiles made with a hinged construction designed especially for this task. Strong ropes trailed out behind the missiles. It only took a few moments after firing for the lengths of rope to unfurl behind the swift vessels and yank taut to the cleats secured to the skimmers' prows. The line tugged on the missile, but instead of pulling free, the prongs carved quick trenches through the foulthing's flesh. They sank deeper and stuck fast in a matter of seconds.

The jolt when their boats were jerked to a halt sent several soldiers into the water. Others pitched from the prows when the ropes snapped. In two boats the cleats were ripped out, sending splinters of wood flying.

Kelis saw this all in fragments captured by his darting eyes. By the time Kelis's skimmer neared range, a slightly greater order had been established. More crews were remembering to drop their sails as they set the barbs. Several boats—sails again curved with the wind—now strained as the earth's breath pressed them forward. As more flew past the heaving creature the crossbowmen pierced it and pierced it again. Rope after rope snapped taut. Barb after barb set deep.

Before long the beast was being pulled into the shallows behind fifty skimmers, with more joining every minute. It was even more maddened than before. Its great cavern of a mouth rose out of the muck. It gasped and bared row after row of teeth. It looked as if it wished to roar but was instead more ghastly for its lack of a voice.

Kelis aided his vessel's crossbowman by steadying him as he aimed and by pulling him back into the boat as his missile hissed out. He heard the captain shouting orders to the other crewmembers, and he did what he could to aid them. The next few minutes passed in a blur of confused motion and noise and wind. He was jostled about the boat, had to duck the boom, and nearly toppled into the water. All around them other skimmers cut in and out, colliding in a tangle of ropes and flying bolts, wind slapping cries about. Quite a few lost their lives or broke bones or were otherwise injured; and through most of it Kelis could not tell if their efforts were achieving what they hoped. He knew the water was getting shallower and shallower. He saw that they were cutting through muck now, but it wasn't until the beast itself showed its true fear that Kelis believed they had it.

For some time the foulthing had propelled itself into the shallows, fleeing the skimmers. When it could no longer sink its mouth down to suck from the water, it tried to turn. It heaved and undulated and thrashed about, sending out muddy waves that swamped the nearest boats. It rolled far enough over once that several ships were pulled into the air. Had it kept rolling it could have killed them all.

And still they pulled it on toward the shore, slower now but steady, the wind filling their sails as if it hated the creature as much as they.

When they could go no farther they anchored the ships, jumped into the ankle-deep water and muck, and trudged back toward it, armed with spears and long pikes. Kelis knew that in this—as in most of the day's work—he was but an observer. He stood at a distance and watched as the Halaly took their revenge. The beast was a monster indeed, worse because it had eaten itself and the world around it nearly to death. There was no form to it that could be made sense of, save that the entirety of its bulk seemed built around its great mouth. Ring after ring of teeth pointed inward toward the pink center of the thing. It was, with its voracious appetite, a bringer of destruction, a maker of death by gluttony. It lay gasping, but slowly, slowly it eased toward death. Despite the wounds in it already and the further ones being made by newly cast spears, it was the lack of water to breathe that was to kill it. It was a fish, after all.

Melio came up beside Kelis and shared the spectacle a moment. "If I made you a necklace from one of those teeth," he asked, "would you wear it?"

138

Kelis turned toward him, reminded suddenly that he had forgotten Mena, but calmed already by his friend's joking tone. "Is the princess well?"

"Of course she is."

Melio gestured with his arm, directing Kelis's gaze toward the tail end of the foulthing. There he made out the figure of Mena, who was using the dangling ropes to scramble her way onto the thing's back. She picked her way over the ridges, through the fins and protrusions, and around the embedded hooks. Behind her came a line of shouting Halaly, their joy obvious in their strides, while many others grabbed hold of the ropes on all sides and tried climbing hand over hand to join her.

"You know," Melio said, "I tell her all the time to be careful, but that's just the man in me that says it, that worries for her."

Melio paused when Mena did. High on the creature, she stood with her feet planted wide, the wind stirring her hair and garments. She set her hands on her hips and silently surveyed the masses churning through the mud all around the island of beast.

"In truth, though," Melio said, "I feel she'll outlive us all. She's half a god after all, right?"

That night Kelis took his leave, explaining to Mena that he had to answer his chieftain's call. He would return to her service as soon as he could. She let him go without question, and in the darkness before the dawn he found the messenger waiting for him outside his tent. He had limbered up already, but before he spoke he reached down, straight legged, and pressed his palms to the hard-packed earth.

"What is your name?" he asked as he came upright again.

"Naamen."

Kelis grinned. "Well, Naamen, are you ready to run?"

Chapter Ten

Sire Neen took a perverse pleasure in recalling all the things he knew about the world that the Akarans did not. It was too long a list for him to go through in one sitting, but he often tried. It soothed him. Their ignorance was as much a balm to him as mist was, although combined with the drug's effects it was an even greater balm. Leaguemen had never truly come off mist, not even when Aliver was alive and making the stuff torture people's dreams. For a time, they were plagued by nightmares similar to those of the general populace, but they pushed through them. The drug they used was of much higher quality than what they provided to the masses, and with experimentation they distilled a variation they could again use without torment. For them, the drug was fundamental to every aspect of their lives, as important as water, food, air. Waking or sleeping, for clarity or bliss, to focus or lose oneself completely: mist aided it all.

As he sat in the plush banquet room of the *Ambergris*, the massive ship they had switched to at the Outer Isles, the thought of lecturing Corinn slicked the leagueman's hands with sweat and stiffened him with pent-up desire. He hated her, and he wished her to know it in her final moments, when she gave everything to the league and they destroyed her. If she had accepted the league's offer to meet the Lothan Aklun herself, he would be beside himself with expectation, luxuriating in the surprise he was about to present her with.

Having to settle for Dariel instead was some compensation, and he would do his best to relish what awaited him.

Peppering his hatred was the fact that he also hungered to consume the queen. Often his mist trances were little more than long sessions in which he lectured Queen Corinn Akaran. He stood above her, taking delicious pleasure out of testifying to all the many ways she was not the power she believed. She knelt below him, a slack-mouthed expression of awe on her lovely face, her gestures promises of submission—faithful, subservient, pious submission.

It was no accident that his concubines were chosen for their resemblance to her. They were fine models, really, coiffed and manicured and even altered anatomically at times. He loved it that they were each so alike while also tasting and sounding and smelling and being different. The same and yet different. They were a great pleasure to him. Shame they never lasted long in his service. Shame also that he had opted not to bring one along on this trip. It would not do for Prince Dariel—a whelp he loathed in a different way—to spot her and note the resemblance.

But you should not complain, he thought. Things are about to change completely.

Sire Neen looked around the table in the plush banquet room of the *Ambergris*, happy that his thoughts were trapped within his skull and could not be read by the roomful of people. They were two weeks out from the isles, already well into the Gray Slopes. The ship rocked with the slightest recognition of their waterborne state, but the room itself was as formally decorated and numerously staffed as a palace. A necessity, as few leaguemen really liked the sea.

A little more patience, Sire Neen thought, and all will be made right. Much will be revealed. Old scores settled. Oh, some will be surprised. Some will be shocked. Saddened. But not I! Not I. Nothing will surprise me. I am the surpriser, not the surprised.

"So we are halfway to the Other Lands," he said, lifting his voice so that it carried through the noise of conversation and dining. "What do you make of the trip so far, Your Highness?"

Dariel, sitting across the round table from him, crooked a grin and spoke to the gathered company of leaguemen, naval officers, imperial officials, and concubines. "I'll admit to being impressed," he said. He played with his food for a moment, absently pushing his uneaten morsels around with the point of his knife. "The Range was like nothing I'd ever imagined. To think that the league has sailed through that all these years."

"It is nothing," Sire Neen said. "Nothing for us, at least. We who truly know the sea."

The prince showed no sign he caught the insult. He shook his head in childlike wonder. "And those creatures today—just bizarre. I'll dream of them tonight, I'm sure."

Sire Neen dipped a spoon in his soup, a clear broth filled with soft morsels of white fish. Holding the spoon halfway to his mouth, he said, "If you wake up screaming, Prince, we'll be sure to send someone to comfort you."

The young woman to the prince's left touched a finger to his wrist and drew a line up his arm. "I'd be happy to take care of that," she said. "It wouldn't do for the prince to dream of beasts, not when there are more pleasant things to be haunted by."

Dariel cocked his head toward her with solicitous deference but said nothing.

She returned his gaze with an annoying amount of enthusiasm—from Neen's perspective. He had instructed the concubines to be gracious and generous to the prince in everything. He rather wished they did not perform so willingly. He slipped the soup into his mouth. Feigning rapture at the taste, he closed his eyes. He needed a few moments free of the sight of the prince. By the gods, the boy irritated him. So self-satisfied. Such a pretense of innocence and openness, as if he were not a killer of thousands, as if they would ever forget those who died at the prince's hands on the platforms.

Fortunately, there had been a couple of moments when the prince's naïve composure had been rattled. Both had been pleasant to witness and were some comfort to remember.

When they had first sailed out onto the wave peaks of the Range had been one such moment. In truth, the sight still amazed the leagueman, even though he had witnessed it scores of times. They were not sure what caused them, but the captains believed that some change in the features far below the surface of the water affected the currents above. Nine days out from the Outer Isles, sailing due west with good winds, the *Ambergris*—massive as it was to human eyes—had been but a cork bobbing on a gray-black fathomless ocean. They had been days riding swells of thirty and forty feet, but at that unmarked boundary all had changed.

Far below the bottom dropped, or rose, or undulated for all they knew. Whatever caused it, the result at the surface was that the swells rose into peaks, sheer reaches hundreds of feet high. Riding up them was like grinding over stone, slow and painful. The hull of the ship trembled with the effort, and each time Neen had a momentary fear that the boat would slip backward. It never did, though. Cresting the summit, the heavy bosom of the *Ambergris* thrust far out into the air, spray whipping around those on board like a creature intent on ripping them from the deck. And as the ship tilted onto the slope, the descent switched to a mad acceleration, reaching speeds beyond any seen on land. The *Ambergris* became a careening leviathan at the edge of control, moving so fast the water around them hissed as if being scorched by the hull's passing. They plunged down until the prow dug into the base of the next wave, submerging the fore portions of the deck for several long moments before slowly rising, righting. Then it began all over again. And again.

Sire Neen went on deck only briefly as they entered the Range. He had the pleasure of seeing the expression of awe on

Dariel's face as he looked at the seething immensity of giants rolling toward them, rank after rank for as far as the eye could see. He retreated belowdecks just after, closing his eyes even as he felt his way toward his cabin, keeping the image of the prince's tremulous cheeks and loose lips in his mind.

Yes, that was a pleasure, Neen thought, still chewing that same mouthful of meat, the dinner conversation revolving around him. He heard it, took in most of what was being said at some level, but the focus of his mist-enhanced mind moved elsewhere freely. Today was a pleasure as well. How close, Prince, how close you came to being tipped into the mouths of devils. If only you knew . . .

They had come out of the Range the day before. The sea had returned to its normal swells. Though the waves remained high by most standards, many gathered on deck to marvel at the relative calm of the ocean compared to what they had passed through. The *Ambergris* once more plowed its course in serene control. Sire Neen had stood for a time amusing himself with Rialus Neptos. The adviser was ghostly pale, his cheeks sunken and his voice raw—the result, no doubt, of days of gut-churning seasickness. Neen made a point of speaking about food, with which Neptos still seemed to have a troubled relationship. It was a small amusement, tormenting Neptos, passing the time.

The leagueman had expected the creatures to appear that day, but the moment of their arrival was so sudden it snatched his breath away. He had been standing beside Rialus when the lookouts shouted from the crow's nests. The character of the ocean all around them changed in an instant. As far as the eye could see in any direction the water churned and undulated and writhed. Hundreds of large creatures broke the surface, swimming at speed through the waves like dolphins. But these were not dolphins.

"Are they . . ." Dariel's voice came from behind them, wavering and thin. The prince reached the railing and grasped it.

Sire Neen glanced over at him. "Yes," he said, answering the incomplete question. "Sea wolves. Not truly a fitting name. They're not like wolves at all. They are like nothing really, except themselves."

When he looked back, the creatures were all around the ship. They rose from the depths, quickly taking shape behind the liquid glass of the green water. Their heads were great knotted bulbs of waxy-looking pink flesh, barnacled and gashed and grimed by sea slime. It was hard to gauge their size from the deck. Even from that height it was clear they were larger than any whales seen in the waters around the Known World or even out at the Vumu Archipelago. But they were not whales. They swam with the combined action of flippers that lined their long bodies and an inhaling and exhaling propulsion of water. They swelled and deflated, rose and fell, so close together that it was hard to tell where each individual began and ended.

"Look at them," Dariel said. "I can see why they're feared."

"The Giver never created these!" Rialus said. "They're monsters!"

"Perhaps not," Sire Neen said. "He never did have much imagination. Anyway, there they are, no matter how they came to be." He motioned toward them with his thin wrist, dismissive and casual. "Watch what they do now."

The sea wolves drew in tighter around the brig, so churning the water that it seemed the *Ambergris* plowed through a sea of the creatures. They jockeyed for position along the massive wall of the hull. They caressed it, bumped it, tried to slide up out of the water as if they would climb it. They slapped at it with tentacled arms that peeled away from their bodies and moved with fluid strength. They clearly wished to gain some purchase on the hull. But they could not do so. They slid off the slick white coating. Some propelled themselves out of the water, slammed the hull with the weight of their bodies. These just dropped back into the froth, frustrated.

One creature, marked from the rest by an enormous barnacled protrusion on its head, squirmed in the water just beneath them, keeping pace. It rolled to the side and for a moment seemed to study them with one enormous yellow eye. The pupil contracted, perhaps from the light of the bright sky, but even to Sire Neen it seemed the beast was focusing his attention on him, picking him out from the many gaping faces looking over the rail. The leagueman had the sudden urge to grab the prince and toss him overboard, right toward that eye and waiting mouth. It was a fantasy urge, for he had no physical strength to match Dariel's, but it came to him so strongly he tasted metal on his tongue. But the moment passed. The creature rolled away and vanished.

"There are so many of them," Dariel said. His tone had changed, gone boyish, filled with curiosity. "What do they eat?"

"Your Majesty, how should I know? They don't eat us; that's the important thing."

Rialus's voice wavered as he asked, "We are not in danger, then?"

Sire Neen patted him on the back, nudging him with just enough force to press his torso against the railing. "So long as you don't fall in, Rialus, you're in no danger whatsoever. On occasion an unwary sailor has been snatched from the deck of a clipper, but we're well above their reach here on the *Ambergris*. In the early years, of course, we lost many ships of all sizes. These creatures seem to hate us or hunger for us. Which is perhaps the same thing. They tore ships apart and devoured whole crews. For a time we tried to shoot our way through with ballista mounted around the deck railing. We still lost most of our ships. But that was before we mastered the skin, and this was long ago. We are quite safe now."

"This 'skin,'" Dariel said, "what makes it work? Is it just a paint of sorts?"

"A paint?" Sire Neen showed his disdain for the simplicity

of that concept. "Paint is like a condiment to sea wolves. They eat it with the ship, to improve its flavor. Our skin is no paint, but—forgive me—that is all I can say about it."

"I must know what this skin is," Dariel said. "I'm sure we could put it to use, even in the Inner Sea!"

"There are no sea wolves in the Inner Sea, Your Highness, a fact that you should be glad of. As to skin itself, that's a trade secret. The league must humbly hold that information close. We are only merchants, Prince Dariel, allow us our secrets."

Sire Neen opened his eyes again, realizing that his name had been called, pulling him back from his reverie.

Dariel watched him from across the table, a look of amused curiosity on his face.

"I'm sorry," Sire Neen said, "what was it you asked?"

Dariel said, "I asked if there were any other surprises in store for me, Sire."

The leagueman held back the impulse to run his tongue over the rounded nubs of his teeth. He held the prince's gaze with a smiling visage while several others offered wry remarks. Would it surprise you, he thought, to know that I wake every morning imagining your downfall? Would it surprise you to know that I'm not going to make amends with the Lothan Aklun? Instead, I will destroy them. Would it surprise you to know that you are to be offered up as a gesture of good faith to a people who will eat your soul? As a slave, a toy, a plaything for monsters? Would it surprise you to know that once the Aklun are gone, there will be no greater power in the world than the league? Would it surprise you if I said, right now, "Prepare your knees for bending, Prince. Prepare your knees"?

Eventually, the others quieted and it fell to Sire Neen to answer. He said, "Oh, certainly. If there is one thing I can promise you with certainty, Your Highness, it is that surprises await you."

Chapter Eleven

Barad was picky about the company he kept. He liked honest folk, unselfish and moral and capable of empathy— mothers and fathers who loved, brothers and sisters who cared for each other. He wanted to know that he was listened to when he spoke, and he wanted to believe the words that were spoken to him. He liked people who had known some hardship but who still had the capacity to envision a better future for themselves and others. For all these reasons he tended to avoid royalty. For that matter, he had little use for the upper class in general. In striving for the greater good for many, however, one sometimes had to deal with questionable elements.

That was why Barad had agreed to allow the young Aushenian king, Grae, to attend the first meeting of the Kindred. In his early twenties, Grae was the son of Guldan, a half brother to Igguldan born of the king's second wife. He had been young enough to be spared fighting in the war that took his father and older brothers. He and his younger brother, Ganet, had lived it out in the remote north of Aushenia. He had grown to maturity during Hanish's rule, when Numrek roamed his lands at will, inflicting all sorts of degradations. That must have hurt his heartsore pride.

He had been a fierce leader during the turmoil of Hanish's overthrow. After securing his own lands, he had even marched through the Gradthic Gap and laid siege to Mein Tahalian. He would have won it, too, if Corinn had not sent Mena with

Numrek troops to yank him back. Corinn was content to let him keep his throne for the sake of stability, but she would not allow anyone to redraw national boundaries without her consent. They pushed him back to Aushenia, with permission to rule within his borders as he saw fit—as long as that was in line with the various things the empire required of him.

If Grae was thankful for having lived to call himself king, it did not show on his face or in his demeanor. His haughty blue eyes had an edge of disdain in them. Barad imagined many women would find him quite attractive. He was strong-jawed; his forehead was high and the hair above it strangely disheveled, windblown but in a manner that Barad suspected was in fashion. It troubled Barad that anyone with a title was aware of his objectives, but many people he trusted had vouched for the king's passionate desire to see the Akarans overthrown. And so he now sat opposite the prophet at a large, low table in the back room of a pub in the port town of Denben in northern Talay.

The resistance representatives hailed from all the provinces except Vumu, which was too distant to be a major force. They made for a strange company. Only Grae wore the finery of aristocracy. Otherwise, the men and women dressed as what they were: a merchant from Bocoum, a tribal councilman from Palik, a blacksmith from Elos, a dockworker from Nesreh, a tavern mistress from Senival, an architect from Alecia, a huntsman from Scatevith, and more. Their complexions and features varied with their races, making them a collage of much of the Known World's diversity. Barad himself looked as he always did, more like an aging laborer in coarse clothes than a dissident intent on overthrowing a powerful empire.

None of them, other than Grae, commanded an army, but all of them had been true to the secret objectives they shared. They had protected the coded language through which they corresponded, often sending communications on the lips of travelers who had no idea they were messengers. For most of them, it had been a long road to get here, to sit in nervous expectation, finally meeting face-to-face as one group united in a purpose that stretched across borders, mountains, forests, and seas.

"It is a blessed thing," Barad began in his deep voice, "that we finally can meet this way. It doesn't matter that this room smells of beer and sweat. It doesn't matter that this is a poor man's pub and that soon they'll be singing bawdy songs in the rooms beside this one. None of that matters. Look around you. The faces that you see are faces of the Kindred. We have always been so, but this meeting marks the day we sit together as one family and drink of the same cup. Let us do so twice: now, to begin our partnership and at the end of this meeting, to confirm it."

Motioning with his large hands, he indicated that he meant this literally. On the otherwise bare table before him sat a large silver chalice. It was a simple vessel, not particularly ornate, wide-mouthed and tarnished by age. A dark, rich wine stained the metal as Barad lifted it, held it for the others to see, and then drank. He passed it to the woman beside him. She was dwarfed by his height, but she took the cup reverently, drank from it, then passed it on. The chalice moved around in silence until it reached the far side of the table.

"Forgive me, King Grae, but before you drink let us hear from you. Of all the company, you are the newest to join. Confirm, please, that you are truly one of us," Barad added, smiling to lighten the request. "You see, you could turn us in most readily, whisper it right into Corinn's lovely ear if you wished. Tell us why you would never do that." Barad hid behind his smile the fact that this was unlikely. The Kindred had placed agents in Killintich some years ago. Some of them were quite close to the king, close enough to slit his throat while he slept should it seem like he was going to betray them. But, still, much better that such a thing not be necessary.

It was clear that the monarch, young as he was, was not used to being evaluated. He held the chalice for a moment, rolling the stem in his fingers as if he were considering drinking the whole thing down first, speaking later. He set it down, though, and met the waiting faces. "You'll have me prove my loyalty to you? That's easy, because my loyalty to you is twinned with my loyalty to Aushenia. All that I will ever do will be for my nation's good. And my nation has suffered too long. Have you forgotten this? We suffered throughout our generations of independence, when the Akarans did everything they could to break our resolve, to impoverish us. And yet it was Aushenia that first suffered from the Meinish and Numrek onslaught. We suffered the brunt of their attack. We! The Aushenian people. We were the first wall they smashed against. My brother Igguldan died at Aushenguk Fell while the princes and councillors of Acacia uttered about like upset chickens. We died first—and this was just weeks after offering our soul to Acacia in partnership."

"I know this is true," Barad said. "You were wronged."

"We were wronged!" Grae echoed, his voice higher and louder than the large man's. "Once we were beaten, Hanish Mein gave us over to those beasts. And yet Queen Corinn expects us to forget the past. She'll have us take what scraps she throws our way, even as she stands with her dogs at either hand. The insult of it is more than I can bear. So I will not bear it."

"We are on the same side, then," Barad said. "The suppression of the many by the few insults us all."

Grae drew himself upright and inhaled through his nose before he spoke. He put emphasis on one word, thereby stressing the particularity of his agreement with the statement. "The suppression of the many by the few does insult us all. The Akarans are the suppressors of this world. Aushenia will never forget that. I, as their king, will make sure of that."

The representative from Aos, a man named Hunt, said, "King, your conviction on this is clear, but I hear Dariel is spoken of fondly by your people. Has he not committed himself to benevolent projects in your kingdom? Rebuilding much of what was—"

"The prince's work is nothing to me. I let him drop his sweat on the ground of Aushenia, but I do not love him for it."

"But the people, do they not—"

"My people are not so easily appeased. Remember that we went twenty-two generations outside the Acacian Empire. None of my people has forgotten that. None of them wants things to remain as they are."

Elaz, the warehouse manager who had greeted Barad in Nesreh, asked, "What do they want, then?"

"They want what all of us here want; the end of Acacian rule, the return to the power of independent nations. The world was shaped better before Edifus went mad for power. In Aushenia we have long memories. Children are even taught to read using Queen Elena's Decree. We know in our bones that all the people of the Known World have the right to govern themselves. Let us return to what he destroyed with his Wars of Distribution."

Lady Shenk, a tavern mistress from Senival, asked, "Do you think that the world was paradise then? It was not. It was a mess! The world was a patchwork of feuding tribes led by petty chieftains. Dogs fighting for scraps, they were. Is that what you want to have again?"

"Of course not," Grae snapped. He seemed taken aback by being spoken to thusly by a commoner. He had asked to be here, though, and controlled the temper that flushed his face crimson. "But much has changed since then. We would return to the best of the past and strengthen it with the best of the present. Each nation will have its own king and queen, who will decide what is best for their people, not an outsider sitting in her palace in Acacia deciding for everyone. This is what we all want, right?"

Silence. The others looked about. For a moment they heard

the commotion of the pub through the walls—chatter, a tune sung by a melancholy voice. Their eyes came to rest on Barad, who eventually answered, "You are the only one here who wears a crown. Too much talk of kings and queens does not go down well with this wine. Remember, King Grae, that no monarch can win against Corinn now. No nation can overthrow the Akarans by force. The Mein did it, yes, but the Mein have been vanquished. And the Mein nurtured their plans for years and years before they acted. You surely have not the patience to wait overlong. No, Corinn has a firmer grip on the Known World than her family has had for years. She feeds the nobles of each nation rubies, even as she digs diamonds from their land. She keeps a court made up not just of the best from all the nations but of the most beloved sons and daughters of all the world's kings. Your own sister is among her ladies. Isn't that so? She holds them hostage, the first victims to suffer in the event of any attack. If there is no such attack, all is well. The court is pleasure. The nobles collect their rubies. The kings and queens, Grae, are the only ones in the Known World who aren't suffering like the rest.

"That is why the rising will not be one of massed armies standing behind banners. Instead, it will be a unity of action among the common people. They will rise. They will all put down their tools and demand that the world be remade. That is what the rising will be based on. There will be blood, yes. There will be turmoil. We will be tested. But we will win because we are right, our cause is just, and the world cannot remain blind to it forever. We do not even hate the Akarans. It is Aliver who spoke to me and put this mission inside me. It is possible, when the change has happened, that Corinn will be a part of the new order, if she accepts it. All this may be hard for a king to imagine."

Close lipped, Grae asked, "Do you so doubt me?"

"No. If we did, you would not be here. Many have vouched for you. Hunt has watched Aushenia for years. He believes you are different from most in your class. We question you now only because you must understand our objective. It is not to wipe away corruption and replace it with new corruption."

"So what sort of system do you foresee? When the Akarans are gone, who will rule?"

"The people themselves."

"The people themselves?" Grae checked other faces, apparently wondering if any found that as amusing as he did. "I trust you have a more detailed plan than that."

Barad knew that was a reasonable supposition. He had been asked it many times before, and he had meditated on it quite often. He always returned to the same central conviction: what happened after the rising was not his concern. The people would have to face that themselves, together, in many different ways in all the many nations. He would be one among them, but he had no desire to impose his rule on them or to dictate what they should do with their freedom. His charge—given to him by the Giver and through Aliver's voice—was to break the shackles, to clear minds, to instill a belief in a better future. That was as far as it went. He knew there was danger in thinking thusly, for some men, like this king here, would surely grasp for the reins of power themselves, but this was as it had to be.

He answered as he always did. "The people will do what they will with their freedom. They have earned that right many times over."

"And if someone else tries to take Corinn's throne as his own?"

"The people will make this change happen. They are tired, tired of trading one despot for another. I pity the man—or woman—who tries to reenslave them."

Grae thought about this for a while. He fingered the stem of the chalice. "I was born a prince of Aushenia. It fell to me to become my people's king. I would just as soon it had not and that I still had my brother and father. But this crown is my fate.

It is not my fate, though, to wear any other crown. I do not covet Corinn's empire. I want only Aushenia. My rule of it is a matter between me and my people. Will the Kindred acknowledge that?"

Barad shrugged. "As I said, I will not dictate how people should live. Yes, that can be between you and the people of Aushenia." Nobody said anything, but several nodded curtly. "What of your brother? Might he not wish to be a king?"

"A king of Aushenia, perhaps," Grae said, "but only if I venture to the marshes to hunt with Kralith—"

Lady Shenk interrupted him. "Quit the Aushenian poetry and speak plain. You mean to say only if you die, right?"

"Only then," Grae said curtly. "I swear to you that my brother and I are of one mind on this. How about this, then? I'll pledge you my people's support. Aushenia will join this rising, and when it's accomplished we will demand only our freedom to live as we will, to our benefit."

"I do not acknowledge your right to pledge other people's support," Barad said. "I am already well known to your people. Many are already friends of the Kindred." He let this sit a moment, but not long enough for Grae to respond. "I will, however, welcome your personal support, and I will welcome you using your influence in whatever ways help the people's cause. Do any disagree?"

Nobody did.

"Good," Barad said. "Then there is only one other thing I must ask you. You should know that there is a reason I want you with us. Although the Kindred will not win by war alone, war is to be a part of what's to come. We have some warriors in our ranks, but we need a leader for them. You could be that leader. You have been trained for such things. When Corinn tries to squash us with her Marah, her army, her Numrek, will you lead our military?"

Grae grinned, youthful and arrogant and comfortable in himself again. He asked the room, "The queen would never dream that her fate would be sealed in the back room of a grimy pub in Denben, would she?" To Barad he said, "I would like nothing more than to lead our warriors. All my soldiers will say the same."

"We have an agreement on that, then. I may want even more of you, though. Let's start by traveling together—perhaps with your younger brother as well, if you truly believe he will join our cause. I will show you both some of the world as I see it. Perhaps you will find the view different from the one seen atop a throne."

"You are an odd man, Barad the Lesser. They tell me you were a strong man in your youth. Perhaps you still are. When all this is over, you and I should compete together. Will you run the Killintich race against me?"

"I do not think that's a race I could win, but if you wish . . . Drink now, King, and be one of us."

Barad watched as the young man lifted the chalice and tilted it back. The boy was brash. Perhaps he would be a danger. Or perhaps he would die like his half brother. Barad then let his eyes wander around the rest of the company. He liked what he saw. He did not claim to predict the particulars of the future. But he did know at his very core that a great change was coming. Soon. Soon they would rise. It was, he believed, all coming together. Her highness would be dumbfounded when it hit her.

Chapter Twelve

Dariel had been warned that the isles of the Barrier Ridge—the home of the Lothan Aklun—made a horizon-long barricade of stone, but his imaginings had not prepared him for the actual sight of them. From a distance, and with the changing light of the rising sun slanting from behind the *Ambergris*, the island chain looked like mountains dusted with a cover of snow that clung to the few flat surfaces. He watched them from near the ship's bow. As he stared the peaks grew in height in a manner that seemed unnatural, more motion to it than should be, more, too, than just the lessening of distance. On one hand they were a strange solidity viewed by eyes used to the motion of the ocean waves. Yet for all the gray-stone hardness of them Dariel could not shake the feeling that the entire landmass was moving. It seemed to be ever slicing southward, like the spine of a surfacing whale.

"It's the current that does that."

Dariel pulled his eyes away from the scene long enough to acknowledge Sire Neen, who had just joined him at the railing, Rialus at his shoulder.

"The current flows strongly to the north this time of year. The waves rushing along the coastline make it seem as if the land is moving. But I assure you it's not. It's just a trick of the eye. The angerwall we'll have to cross is very real, however, and a result of the same phenomenon." Sire Neen smiled, showing his rounded teeth. "I imagine that your eyes have not yet seen the islands for what they actually are. Look again more closely. We're near enough now."

Dariel looked back at the coastline. The rocks rose into a vertical blockade, and for most of the ridge's dark expanse there was no sign of habitation. He almost asked why it seemed empty of life. But before he did, he realized that the light areas he had thought snow were actually buildings. He'd had the scale all wrong. The peaks were higher, and the dustings of snow were actually structures several stories tall. Built all along the highest points and thrown loosely about the high cliffs was a spidery lacework, a combination of nature and architectural design.

"Oh." He saw something else. What he had taken to be one solid landmass was in fact many islands. That was why it was so hard to see the scale. Some of the peaks were far beyond the nearer ones. Each was a jagged point thrust directly up from the water. They were not approaching a continent with mountains. They were approaching thousands of separate peaks, massive islands that hid the greater part of their bulk in the black depths.

"Yes, 'Oh,' is right," Sire Neen said.

It was not long before Dariel observed the next surprise. The current rushing to the north got more and more powerful as they drew nearer land. It ripped along the coastline as fast as a river in flood. A ship tossed against the rocks would certainly be smashed to splinters. That was frightening enough, but as they approached a wide gap behind the first of the barrier islands through which they obviously intended to sail, he saw what must be the angerwall Sire Neen had referred to.

Clearing the point of land, the ocean current's interaction was suddenly that of rushing water against the comparatively slack water. Marking the dividing line between the two was a seething wall of water several stories high. The current moved past, while the channel water swirled and roiled, bucking up in great heaving swells, unevenly timed, as if angry creatures were trying to breech but could not break the skin of the water.

"Ah . . ." Rialus said but got no further vocalizing his thoughts than that.

" 'Oh' and 'Ah.' " Sire Neen chuckled. "You make a fine duo."

The *Ambergris* approached at speed, angling across the current and toward the channel. The wind was with them, and they plowed through the rising and falling waves with incredible force, almost as if they wished to crash directly into the island itself. Dariel had done some daring things in his career as a brigand, but now they were traveling at open ocean speed, careening either into a wall of rock or over a wall of water—he wasn't sure which. The lookout called something, as did the captain, and then a bell began to toll. Sire Neen said something, but Dariel did not hear what it was.

He was still staring when a crewman grasped him by the shoulder and pulled him hurriedly toward the center of the deck. He joined Sire Neen, Rialus, and others at the benches that encircled the base of one of the masts. The crewman shoved him down without ceremony and, with a few deft motions, secured a rope around his waist. Tied to the mast, Dariel looked around to see that the others were likewise secured. Many crewmen still dashed about the ship, but when the tolling of the bell increased in rapidity they all scrambled for something to hold.

The bell stopped. For a few moments the only sounds were the wind and the rush of water. And then the bow of the massive ship punched over the current wall and crashed down into the slack water. The prow dove and the stern tilted up into the air, and then the entire ship began to pitch and roll at the same time. The force of it pulled Dariel in one direction and then the next, smacking his head hard on the wooden mast behind him. If he had not been tied down he would certainly have been tossed into the air. Indeed, some of the crewmen were. Dariel saw sailors dangling sideways in the air, holding on to lines for dear life. The hull of the ship groaned and quivered. There was a tearing sound deep in the vessel, and Dariel feared the entire ship would be torn to pieces. And then he feared it would stay whole but conclude this mad maneuver upside down.

The ship corkscrewed to starboard in a manner that shoved Dariel's guts up against his diaphragm, pushing the air from his lungs. The roiling wraith of the agitated water surged up over the railing. The sailors there went completely under water and stayed submerged for some time. The ship balanced on its side, the tips of the masts sunk deep into the water, sails billowing with the current. It seemed an impossibly long moment—a breath held and held and held—before the *Ambergris* finally made up its mind and began the slow roll back upright.

The sailors who had been submerged gasped as they hit the air. Dariel felt just as empty of air as they, just as hungry for breath. A different noise rose from the ship's bowels: shouts of rage from the chained Numrek. He had not seen them the entire voyage, but they made themselves heard now. Dariel had to shade his brow to get his bearings. They were, he concluded, in the lee of the island. Actually, they were even moving forward, away from the current and into the maze of mountain islands before them. He did not try to hide the astonishment on his face.

In answer, Sire Neen offered, "We've found forceful penetration to be the best method of entry." His voice had the same calm tone he used at the council table, and his smile was so incongruous at the moment that the sight of it gave Dariel an instant headache or somehow alerted him to the pounding pain already all around his skull. "There is nothing worse, you see, than getting trapped between the two currents. One has no control at all then. We'll have to explain to the Numrek that we could've had a much rougher ride than that. It's not for the timid, I know, but we of the league are not timid."

Dariel stood with Rialus as the *Ambergris* spent the next hour threading its way through the islands. They progressed at a cautious speed, but it was still strange to watch such a large vessel navigate the narrow channels. Apparently, the peaks dove into the water at the same steep angle as they rose above it, making the waterways clean routes. At times they skimmed so near the submerged slopes that he could see far down through the clear waters. The long-legged crabs on the stones gave the depths perspective, growing smaller and smaller until they faded into blackness. A few times, he thought he saw human forms floating among them, but the water—clear as it was—was deceiving him. Watching the crustaceans gave him a queasy feeling almost like vertigo, as if he might fall from the deck, through the water, and down and down into the depths.

A clipper came out from a harbor as they passed and sliced cleanly through the water toward them. It was a small ship, built for speed, and so dwarfed beside the *Ambergris* that it took Dariel a moment to figure out why the sight of it was so remarkable. It had no sail, nor any oars. It dipped and slipped through the water with no visible indication of how it did so. There was something to it that he was not seeing. Perhaps the league had developed some see-through sailcloth. That would be handy in many ways. But there were no masts either. It was amazing, bizarre, frightening even to see a ship move so unnaturally. Dariel leaned over the railing as the clipper drew up alongside the *Ambergris*. That surprised him as well—that a small vessel could dock with a moving ship—which appeared to be what it was doing.

It did not hold his complete attention. His neck grew sore from craning between the strange craft and the structures perched high and strung across the rock walls. They looked like they had been built by some sort of bird people who were in love with the heights. He thought of Mena—bird-goddess that she was—and wished she were with him to see this. Who were these Lothan Aklun? For that matter, where were they? He had yet to see any signs of life on the islands. They passed several docks, complete with buildings and boats and

161

equipment, but they were all strangely still. He had not seen any boats other than the clipper. That made no sense. The waters should be teeming with vessels moving between the islands.

"I see Aklun architecture impresses you," Sire Neen said. He had been away conferring with the other leagueman. When he rejoined the prince, he seemed to be in uncharacteristically good humor. He even rocked on his toes as he spoke, a childish energy animating him. "It should. Until now, we've never figured out just what material the Lothan Aklun work in. They seem to have been able to shape stone as if it were a liquid."

" 'Until now'?"

Sire Neen shrugged. "Oh, I suspect we will understand it soon. That I'm very condent of."

Dariel found the leagueman's sudden enthusiasm unnerving. He let his eyes roam away. "It's incredible," he said, speaking honestly. "I knew we were coming to it, but it somehow didn't feel real. The Lothan Aklun . . . It's still hard to believe I'll finally set eyes on them."

Sire Neen made a noise that was hard to read, a slight expulsion of air that might have been an indication of amusement. "That much I know to be true. Prince, you might as well know that we were preceded by another league vessel. They should have arrived a fortnight ago, bearing a message of our coming."

"Oh," Dariel said, though his actual thoughts were somewhat more pointed. The leagueman's statement was made casually enough, but the hairs on the back of Dariel's neck bristled. "Why didn't you mention this earlier?"

"League vessels travel back and forth at will. It would not interest you to know all our shipping itineraries, would it?"

With a nod, Dariel conceded that was true enough. "Why mention it now, then?"

"Just to prepare you for the day."

What sort of answer is that? Dariel thought. He was about

to voice the question, but Sire Neen turned his attention to Rialus, who was staring at the league clipper. It had peeled away from the hull as they spoke. It kept perfect pace with them, but still used neither sail nor oar nor any other source of propulsion that Dariel could make out.

"You're wondering what powers that boat, aren't you, Neptos?" Sire Neen asked. "Of course you are. No doubt you've thought the same question, Prince, perhaps feared to ask it . . . I'll tell you. It's powered by souls." He let that sit for a moment in silence, and then looked at the two men, his face a portrait of good humor. "Souls have power, you know. Your Highness should know that as well as anyone. You released more souls at one moment than any other person I've known of. Did you not feel their power?"

There was nothing in his tone or expression to indicate anything other than levity, but Dariel's pulse hammered at his temple, a warning alarm so loud he feared the man might hear it. Leaguemen didn't make jokes. They didn't show emotion. Or they didn't show their true emotions, at least. He knew Sire Neen must be feeling something completely different from his outward appearance. He had to be. If he wasn't, what could possibly have brought on this playful barbed mood?

"You refer to the platforms," Dariel said. And saying it, he remembered the flash of light at his back when the platforms exploded, the fear that the inferno was reaching out for him, the knowledge that the man he thought of as a father was riding those flames up to death. For many, that act of sabotage made him a hero. He had never thought of it that way, though, and the memory filled him with regret. There was power in freeing all those souls from all those bodies, but not the kind of power he wanted to be reminded of.

"I do. I do, Prince. I lost many brothers who were dear to me that horrible day. Do you know that?"

Rialus inhaled a sharp, audible breath. His nervous eyes darted between the two men.

Dariel began, "I—"

"Not just brothers. I lost my wife."

Brothers? Wives? Dariel had never thought of leaguemen's domestic lives. "You—you had a wife?"

Sire Neen flashed a look of disgust. Or did he? The very next moment it was gone, swept away by incredulous mirth. "Of course we have wives, my prince! We are men like other men. How else would we continue our kind? Oh, Prince Dariel Akaran, you amuse me. But tell me, I have often wondered what it would be like to burn alive. My physician tells me that the very horror of it is what makes it bearable. He says the pain of burning all over your body would be so intense that you would be overwhelmed. It would hurt so much that my wife would no longer feel the hurt as hurt. It would become something else, something beyond pain, like death being something beyond life. Does that sound true to you? Surely, you've thought about it, considering that you made that the fate of so many, children even." He shuddered, and as before he looked briefly dismayed, and then instantly at ease again.

Dariel glanced at Rialus, who seemed just as perplexed by the conversation as he was. What were they talking about? Why were they talking about this? Why now? "I don't know," Dariel eventually said. Thinking that sounded feeble, he attempted a tone of greater certainty. "I had not thought about it before. I have tried to put my memory of that day aside. It's not the work I do now."

Sire Neen seemed disappointed. He lifted his chin and studied the prince a moment. "Did you never think to grasp the throne yourself?" he asked. "Acacia's generations have few notable queens. In a time of such turmoil you might readily have stepped into power as your brother's heir. To some it seems odd that you did not. Why defer to gentle Corinn—just a woman, after all?"

"Why would I consider that?" The indignation in Dariel's voice appeared instant and true. It choked his words for a moment and then pushed them out with breath of quick anger. "No, I won't have this conversation with you! What I did at the platforms I did in war against an agent of my family's enemy. Any guilt for it is mine to measure. That's all I'll say. Don't forget yourself and ask about it again."

"No, I don't forget myself," the leagueman said. He reached out and affectionately squeezed Dariel's shoulder. He paused like that, so strangely familiar, and pursed his lips in thought. "All right, Your Highness. No more probing questions. Forgive me if I trod awkwardly." He released Dariel and turned as if to move away. He stopped and turned back, touching a finger to his nose as if a thought had just occurred to him. "One other thing. We won't be stopping in the barrier isles today. There's no reason to. The Lothan Aklun are all dead. Every one of them. You recall how Hanish Mein used a contagion to ravage your people? We've done something similar here. They weren't really so hard to kill. Your Tinhadin had said they were like serpents with a thousand heads. Or something like that. As usual with you Akarans, that was an exaggeration." He chuckled. "So there's no reason to stop. No one to talk to, you see. They're dead and swimming into their rest. So we'll sail on, if you don't mind, and soon we'll dine with the Auldek, our new friends. It's they who matter to us anyway. Like I said, surprises abound, don't they?"

Dariel did not find the words to stop the leagueman as he walked casually away, flanked, the prince saw, by bodyguards who were suddenly more attentive than they had been before. He was too stunned to call out, to move, to demand an explanation. Sire Neen's words jostled in his head. But he had heard him. He had understood him.

Rialus, who had turned to the railing as if he might vomit, stammered something. Dariel didn't make out one word of it, but somehow he knew what he was saying. He just knew. He pulled his gaze away from Sire Neen's back and looked down at the sea. Yes, just as he thought. There were human bodies in the water after all. In fact, there were many floating bodies. Swimming into their rest. The prince felt the presence of soldiers approaching him from behind. He realized then that he had not seen his Marah guards for some time. Many of them had been belowdecks before the angerwall, and those who had been with him were no longer with him. He knew, without turning, that the group gathering behind him was not made up of his soldiers, but he did not rush to look at them. Instead, he kept eyes on the graveyard that was the sea. There were so many bodies in the waves, all of them adrift on the same tide the *Ambergris* rode, all of them being pulled toward the Other Lands.

Chapter Thirteen

A young league apprentice, Noval, sat waiting for Sire Neen among the plush chairs reserved for leaguemen in their council chambers. Several other officials and naval officers stood or sat nearby. With the exception of a few of Neen's assistants, all of them had newly arrived from the sail-less clipper.

"It all went as planned?" Sire Neen asked as he stepped into the room.

"You saw the bodies," Noval said. He motioned toward a porthole with a lazy finger. "Up and down the archipelago it's the same thing."

Noval had not yet joined the higher ranks of the league and earned the title *sire*, but after this he likely would. Noval grinned, leaning back against his chair's cushions as if he might fall blissfully asleep. You'll need to learn to hide emotion like that, Sire Neen thought. He did not really begrudge him his happiness, though. In truth, he could barely contain his own enthusiasm.

"Every Lothan Aklun is a corpse now," said a captain, presumably the one who had piloted the clipper. "A feast for the crabs and sea worms."

Noval nodded and concluded, "Yes, it all went as planned. You, Uncle, are a genius."

Sire Neen pressed his lips together. As much as he wanted a share of the young man's satisfaction, he could not accept it all without a measure of doubt. "Nothing ever goes entirely as planned," he said. "Tell me it all and I'll judge."

Noval proceeded to describe what had transpired on the barrier isles over the last few days. Listening to the report, Sire Neen had to inhale deep breaths. His heart raced as if he were joyously running. Perhaps in the years to come it would be this feeling he relived during mist trances. Certainly, triumph was a sweeter pleasure than anything else he had yet experienced. The Lothan Aklun food for sea worms? Absolutely amazing. Could he truly believe it?

The Lothan Aklun had seemed invulnerable, proud, greedy. They were aloof in a manner most marked by their . . . well, by their simple denial of aloofness. He had met their agents on several occasions. Each time they dressed in loose wraps of white cloth that hung on their leanly muscled frames, always bare of foot. They were slight men and women, healthy look-ing and tanned. Sire Neen had always felt a knot in his abdomen when meeting them. His head tingled in a manner that made him want to flee. Why, it was hard to say.

They smiled and nodded and conducted their business with courteous efficiency. They never invited leaguemen beyond the docks at which they traded their goods, but nothing in their outward appearance indicated threat. They did not even seem to have guards watching over them. This fact alone made Neen's skin crawl as if with a thousand spiders. Who other than people so secure in their power—with unseen weapons ready to unleash—would act as if they gave no thought to it? That the Lothan Aklun had such an effect on him while out-wardly feigning harmlessness had planted in him the first seed of personal animus toward them. This seed had found ready watering in the years since.

And now they were dead. Not so invulnerable after all, it seemed. Now everything that had been theirs belonged to the league. Sire Neen did not know exactly what that meant, but he longed to find out.

"You saw the clipper?" Noval asked. "The captain here has made a quick study of it. He can't explain it in the slightest, but I believe he's rather taken with the vessel. You should see him at the helm."

The captain did not deny it. "There is power in that ship like I've never felt before. It's *inside* the vessel itself, Sire. Truly amazing."

Inside the vessel itself, Sire Neen repeated to himself. *So it's true.* They had long known that the Lothan Aklun stole the life force from chosen quota children with a soul-catching device and then transferred the force into other bodies. But they had heard only rumors that the Lothan also managed to harness the life force to power inanimate objects like their ships. Now they had proof. And if this rumor was true, perhaps the others were as well, but these things could be explored in time. They had other business to see to.

"And have you made contact with the Auldek?" Sire Neen asked.

"Yeesss." Noval dragged the word out. "We have. I can't say that we've communicated all that effectively with them, though. They were somewhat agitated by our arrival. I'll leave it up to you to explain things to them fully. In any event, we've arranged for you to meet their clan leadership tomorrow. We should have the Numrek with us from the start. We mentioned them to the Auldek, but they didn't grasp what we were telling them. Are the Numrek well?"

"The brutes." Sire Neen blew a dismissive burst of air through his lips. "Who knows? I mean, yes, yes, I'm sure they're well. They've been bound in their cabins the entire voyage. They're alive and will likely be overjoyed to set foot on dry land again." He considered taking a seat, but his body tingled with too much energy to sit still. Instead, he paced, amazed at the situation he found himself in. It was all too perfect. He had been too modest in his aspirations; by the end of this he would be chief elder in his later years. The league would own everything that passed across the Gray Slopes, both what went out and what came in. He himself would be a deity while still in the prime of life.

This thought did, in fact, cause him to sit down. "So tomorrow I will broker a new trade agreement with the Auldek. Are they like the Numrek?"

Noval raised his shoulders. Dropped them. "Yes and no. I really can't tell you much about them. They are quite like the Numrek and also not that much like them at all. You should just see for yourself."

A bit casual in his mastery of details, Sire Neen thought. Youth. "Are they rich?"

Smiling, Noval said, "Rich enough. Rich and strange, which together bodes well for us."

"What more do we know about what becomes of the quota?"

"About what they do with them? Nothing. I saw Known Worlders in among the Lothan Aklun. We interrogated the few we captured. Peculiar creatures; they fought like trapped wildcats, though they were body servants, not warriors. Strangely loyal to their masters, they seemed. Quite a few of them died along with the Lothan Aklun, for no reason but blind loyalty. And the ones I saw among the Auldek . . ." He began to illustrate something, his fingers dancing before his face, but he dropped the effort. "Really, Uncle, you should see them for yourself. Don't let me spoil the amusement."

Sire Neen found all this too vague. He was about to say as much, but a commotion at the far door announced new arrivals. Several Ishtat guards jostled their way into the room, all of them focused on a single figure at their center: Prince Dariel. But not Prince Dariel as he had been a few moments ago on deck. The small interval of time between then and now had worked a transformation on him. His lips were swollen and raw. His nose puffy and leaking blood, which smeared across his face. Eyes teary with shock and pain and emotion. And anger. There was plenty of anger, too. He wrenched his body and head about, fighting the Ishtat. But they held him firmly. His hands were bound behind his back. One guard grasped him by a fistful of hair and steadied him. The most ignominious feature was a bit that had been shoved inside the royal mouth and fastened by straps that pressed against his cheeks and wrapped around the back of his head. He could breathe but not talk.

Sire Neen had forgotten the pleasure of running his tongue over his rounded teeth. Seeing Dariel reminded him of it and he indulged. "Oh, that looks most uncomfortable, Prince," he said, grimacing in a show of commiseration. "It looks as though you put up a fight. Commendable, I guess, but futile." He gestured with his fingers. The guards dragged the prince closer. "Look here, Noval, this is Prince Dariel Akaran."

Bowing his head, Noval said, "Honored to meet you, Your Highness."

"I left word for the Ishtat to bring him to us, but it seems he did not come willingly. Perhaps he thought he could fight his way through our entire Ishtat force. He might have thought his Marah would aid him. Alas. They won't." He dropped his voice and added, "We've . . . had to kill them."

Dariel's eyes bulged. He worked his lips and tongue, clearly wanting to speak, but the apparatus let nothing more than grunts and frustrated exhalations escape his mouth—that and the drool that slipped from the corners of his stretched lips. He began thrashing about again. The sight of him was almost too much for Sire Neen to bear with composure. To keep from showing his mirth, he fumbled in his breast pocket for his mist pipe.

He did not look up again until he had lit it and sucked a quick puff of the green smoke. Dariel hung panting, his gaze positively blazing with hatred. "I can see your thoughts," Sire Neen said. Despite the meaning of his words, his voice was syrupy sweet, playful. "They're right there in your eyes. You're thinking, How can he think he can offend an Akaran prince and not regret it later? You never were the brightest of your brood, were you? Aliver would not have trusted me for a moment. Corinn would have figured everything out by now and already be working to undo the damage. Mena, even bound as you are now, would likely have found some way to cut my head from my shoulders. Not you, though. You had a skill at treachery and murder—I'll grant you that—but I've always found you rather dull. You let your sister be master of the world you could have claimed. That lack of ambition mystifies me."

Sire Neen reached out as if to smooth a lock of the prince's hair back into place, but he was not really near enough and did not complete the gesture. For a moment he forgot how much he hated the prince. He felt something like warmth for him. "Should we explain things to you? There's no reason you shouldn't face your future with clear eyes." He gestured for one of his secretaries to vacate his seat. "Let the prince sit."

A kind offer, but one that took the guards a moment to convince the prince to accept. Once he was seated, held in place against the chair's cushions, Sire Neen began a casual discourse, one he punctuated with pauses to sip from his pipe. "As you can imagine," he said, "the league has attempted to gain intelligence about the Lothan Aklun for generations. They were annoyingly secretive, giving nothing, wanting nothing other than to trade mist for quota. That's all they wished of us. No more or less. We sent spies among them, but rarely heard back. Usually, they were lone individuals disguised as child slaves. They had orders—and the means—to kill themselves if discovered."

Neen pursed his lips. "Why did we spy on them? For the same reason that Edifus broke the jaw of any man who raised his voice to him. For the same reason that Tinhadin betrayed Hauchmeinish and exiled the Santoth. Because of the very same impulse that drove your sister Corinn to see Hanish bleed to death upon his ancestral Scatevith stone. Because they were competition, Prince. Because the world, not even the entire stretch of the Gray Slopes, was wide enough to contain our ambition. Why share trade with them when we could own it all ourselves?"

Noval said, "As an Akaran you should understand such thinking well."

Sire Neen slitted his eyes at the young man, not exactly a reprimand but nearly so. He did not yet feel like sharing his discourse. "Yes, well, the league is patient, and because of our patience we learned some time ago that the Lothan Aklun were a ceremonial people. Among their many customs was a yearly ritual, a cleansing ceremony in which every Lothan took part. Each and every one, Prince: you can see how that would interest us. It was some years later, but eventually we gained a sample of the ceremonial purgative that was part of this cleansing from one of the few spies to make it back to us alive. Again, remember that *every* Lothan Aklun takes this purgative on the same day of the year, during the same hour. They, but only they. This gave my grandfather—he was the first architect of this venture—an idea. What, he asked, if we could find a way to poison that purgative in a way that would wipe out the Lothan entirely on a single day?"

He stared at Dariel for a moment. "I see by the way your cheeks are twitching that you acknowledge what a fine idea he had. It proved difficult to orchestrate, though. We simply did not have the agents in place to spread a poison evenly among them. Never would, it seemed. So we tried to find another way. All the time, of course, we kept up the trade. Prospered from it, really. Some of the older leaguemen would have been content to continue like that, but most of us wanted more. What man doesn't really, at some fundamental level, want *more*? More of everything! More riches. More lovers. More power. More revenge.

"Because he remained persistent, my father—who had taken up my grandfather's mission—worked with his physicians until they found a component of the purgative they could separate out. This they made into a poison, a vastly potent one." Here Neen paused and shared a knowing glance around the room, finally returning to Dariel. "Do you see where this is heading yet? Earlier this year—at great expense and risk—we managed to contaminate the purgative. A single agent did it, with a single vial of our poison mixed in with their purgative. It was all manufactured and stored in one place, you see. Security around it was surprisingly lax. A weak spot, indeed."

Dariel had stopped struggling some time ago. His eyes, still red with emotion but calmer than before, remained fixed on Sire Neen. More bewildered now than angry.

"Somebody wipe the boy's chin," Sire Neen said. "It's disturbing to see a grown man drool so." One of the Ishtat actually tried to carry out the order, but Dariel yanked his chin away. Lovely to see the fight in him, Sire Neen thought. I wonder how long he'll manage to keep it up? Out loud he said, "Noval, tell him what you witnessed. Exactly the same as you told me before."

The younger man happily obliged. Sire Neen listened to each detail almost as if he had seen the events and not just heard them reported a short time before. Thus, he envisioned the panorama that was the main harbor of Melith An, the trading port of the Lothan Aklun. He watched as the league schooner, the *Hooktooth*, nosed its way into the harbor. Normally, the harbor was thriving, bustling, alive with boat traffic and commerce. This time, chaos ruled. Neen watched as white-robed Lothans ran shouting along the harbor, chased by their own servants, who were trying to hold them back. But again and again Lothans managed to break free and throw themselves in the water. Some of them even carried others down to the same fate. The waters of the harbor were blocked with corpses and with the dying and with slaves trying either to save their masters or to die beside them.

Once docked and disembarked, Sire Neen imagined himself

running through the streets behind an Ishtat vanguard, trying to find any living Lothan, or capture one of the fool slaves who seemed intent on fighting to the death out of allegiance to them. It was only by piecing together information and by interrogating the few slaves they actually captured that they came to understand the rest. The fever had erupted within hours after the Lothan Aklun had imbibed their ceremonial drinks. They dove in the water because the fever inside made their bodies burn. Those who could not make it to the harbor fell into convulsions on the ground.

"Most of it was over by the time we arrived," Noval concluded, "but still, what we did witness was a sight to see. As far as I can tell, the Lothan Aklun are no more."

Sire Neen let his pleasure curve his lips. "A work of fine planning. Complexity woven in such a way that it made victory terribly simple. And just like that, the balance of the world shifts." He said that directly to Noval, but then he turned and contemplated Dariel.

"Prince, I see the many questions in your eyes. You want to know what's to become of you, don't you? And there's anger there, too. I see it. I see it in the way you tremble and blink rapidly. You want to shout at me with all your Akaran outrage, don't you? How dare we do these things without consulting you! 'Just wait until my sister hears about this!' That's what you'd say, isn't it?"

Sire Neen chuckled. He leaned forward, taking a pull from his pipe before he continued. "The thing is, Prince, more is about to change than just the extermination of the Lothan Aklun. We don't need them, nor do we need Akarans. I had to argue among my own people to make this point clear, but argue it I did. It was time, I said, that the league not simply ride upon the tides of fortune. It was time for us to shape them. The destruction of the Lothan is part of that. Your people will soon wake to the other part. You see, there are traitors at the heart of Acacia, right in the palace, Prince, right in among the royal family. They need only hear confirmation that we have succeeded, and then . . . your family will finally, after all these years, get the type of deaths they deserve."

Chapter Fourteen

It was so much worse than when she had last been here. Even then, two years ago, the northern Talayans had been complaining about the lack of rainfall. Corinn had thought their fears exaggerated. To her eyes the fields looked like . . . well, like fields of growing plants, rows and rows of short trees, fields of golden grasses. She understood that this apparent bounty was achieved only because the staple crops that required the most water had already been replaced by sturdier varieties. Change was not to be feared. The skilled agriculturalists of Talay, she had believed, would adjust.

Not so, as the scene before her eyes now confirmed. It was a vision of devastation, as full of death as any battleground. In the nearest field, withered trees stood naked of leaves or fruit, blackly skeletal and twisted like hundreds of demons captured in gestures of agony. Farther south some grain crop glittered as if the stalks were silvered strings of glass, ready to shatter underfoot. The horizon to the west was choked with smoke. The fires were far distant, but the wind carried the scent of them and dropped flakes of ash from the heavens. The irrigation channels were completely dry, their beds cracked. In several spots across the landscape figures moved, singly or in small groups. They looked more like scavengers than workers. Perhaps they had been workers, Corinn thought, but could do nothing but scavenge now.

The queen took this all in from the earthen embankment

that paralleled Bocoum's southern battlements. She was on horseback, with Aaden at her side, both of them largely silent as a contingent of Bocoum's wealthy estate owners buzzed around them. Each one of these rich men claimed to have suffered more than the others. They detailed the withering of crops, the irrigation and replanting measures they took to adapt, the worsening situation, the bleak possibilities. They even admitted to praying to the Giver and allowing their laborers to call on whatever regional deities they might win favor with. A few had taken to sacrificing pigeons, chickens, even goats. None of it had helped, and the merchants feared the laborers might take even more desperate measures soon.

"We know the Giver forgives, but so far he has ignored us," said Elder Anath. He sat on his horse with straight-backed grace, his bright red robes vibrant against his dark skin. He was the head of the main branch of the Anath clan, the second most powerful of the city's merchant families. It showed in the easy grace of his carriage. Talayans were not natural horsemen, so his ease in the saddle was a product of his class.

"Or he punishes us," Sinper Ou offered wryly. "Some have grown too rich, perhaps, for his liking."

Elder Anath turned to see who had spoken. He studied him a moment and smiled, seemingly content that the man meant to slight him but had not managed it. "One can never grow too rich. The Ous have proved this. Can a lion's mane be too full? Never. But, Queen Corinn, even my fortune—not to mention Ou's—is shriveling under these empty skies."

Corinn knew these men were competitors, but she always suspected much of their repartee was a show for her benefit. They were both rich. They both had married among each other's families. They both had all the rewards of royalty with none of the responsibilities. She spoke crisply, as if the scene before her did not affect her at all. "The Giver abandoned us long ago. He neither rewards nor punishes. That's for me to do.

Come. Lead me to the heart well you spoke of. I will speak with the prince as we ride."

With that, the merchants knew she wished them out of earshot. They started off—even Elder Anath deferring without a word—along the embankment, their assistants and advisers with them. The tall sandstone walls and towers of Bocoum dwarfed them to one side, stark contrast to the flat desolation on the other. Corinn let them ride well away before touching her mare on the neck and urging her forward.

A contingent of Numrek followed them, bare chested and proud, their swords in prominent sheaths, some with axes in hand. They did not ride, since horses were nervous around them and their rhinoceros mounts were suited only for warfare. Their long strides easily kept them in position, though. Corinn had grown as used to them as she was to any servants. They were simply a part of her life.

"What do you think of all this?" Corinn indicated the ruined fields with her chin.

Aaden wrinkled his lips. "It really wasn't like this before?"

"No, you heard how they described it at dinner last night. They exaggerate, but these farmlands are what made Bocoum the city it is. Their crops fed mouths all around the empire. There was a time you could have ridden south from the city for four days before leaving cultivated lands. Acacia's power came as much from Talay's crops as from anything else. An army can bring death, but a farmer can give life. Fortunately, people fear one more than they acknowledge the other."

"Why did it change?"

"I don't know," Corinn answered. "I don't know." She repeated the answer for no reason other than that it felt good to admit it. She could do so only with Aaden, for he had always asked her questions that she could not answer. Why are eggs egg-shaped? Why are sand dunes like ocean waves? Where does wood go when it burns? How does the Giver's tongue work? Nobody else, of course, asked her questions like that, and she loved him for it.

Glancing at him, she said, "I'll have to fix it, though."

"How will you? Will you use—"

"Yes. It's time the world sees some of what I can do."

The boy considered this a moment, his lips pursed and his expression older than his eight years. He eventually answered with a curt nod, his gesture of approval.

The merchants turned off the main thoroughfare and descended a ramp to a south-running road, closer to ground level but still elevated enough to provide a vantage. They worked their way farther from the city, riding on roads and sometimes in the empty irrigation canals. The slow rain of falling ash gave the place a surreal, hellish aspect. It was a wonder that anything had ever grown here.

All of this because of the lack of something so simple: water. Corinn could still scarcely believe it. In Calfa Ven, where she spent as much time as she could, showers appeared out of cloudless skies. The rivers bubbled with water. Floods were the concern, not drought! And a good thing, too, for it was the bounty of that place that had sparked the idea that led her here this afternoon. That and Dariel's charitable work. And, of course, her study of the song. Nothing was more central to her life now than the study of the Giver's tongue.

From the first moment she held *The Song of Elenet* in her hands, on the day that Thaddeus Clegg had brought it to her as a blood gift, she had been changed. It had awakened strength within her, cunning that she had always had but had never used, determination that she knew lay within her but that she spent a lifetime shying away from. It was because of the book that she was able to ally with the league, the Numrek, Rialus Neptos—all of whom she had needed to destroy Hanish Mein. And the song had promised her that more, much more, was to come.

At night, with her servants dismissed and her doors barred,

she had opened the book and fallen again and again into the moving, languid words that were not words. It was a wonder every time; and for the first few years it had been enough just to see the words come alive and to hear them inside her head. When they gave her permission to open her mouth and let them out, she had discovered new joy like nothing she had known before, joy as complete as the moment Aaden had slipped free of her and been laid on her chest.

Aaden was part of the song, in a way. Only he had ever witnessed her singing. She had called up small things for him: glass beads and smooth stones at first, gourds that made rattles, simple toys, and then insects, butterflies, red-breasted birds, and tiny ring-necked snakes. The things she had brought to life were but trinkets, she knew, but singing them into existence exhausted and sometimes frightened her. That last creation had been strangely, benignly terrifying.

When her voice faded that afternoon in her chambers on Acacia, the swirling of sound and shimmering light that had gathered around the object finally dissipated. And there it was, the thing she had spun out of words. A thing that "nobody had ever seen before," as Aaden had requested. The two of them had stared at it in silence. It was a furry creature the size of a six-month-old child, but it did not have legs or arms. It had a trunk but the bulk of it was a head of sorts, vaguely feline, with no sign of ears, no whiskers. Its fur was so fine it swayed in waves at even the slightest motion, changing color as it did so, as if each strand had within it yellows and reds and blues and every shade in between.

For all this, its eyes were its most distinct feature. They were completely round, and when it blinked, some sort of lid passed from one side of the eye to the other, and then back again a few moments later. With each blink, it seemed more and more sentient, as if it understood something new about them each time that membrane slid from one side to the other.

The mother and son stood watching the creature for just a

few short moments. The entire time, it watched them as well, cocking its head and looking from one to the other, waiting. When Corinn began the song to unmake it, she was sure she saw something like disappointment in the creature's eyes. But that may have just been the spell, for within a few breaths the invisible ribbons of sound moved around it, slipping over and through its form and rubbing it from existence.

Aaden's voice had seemed inordinately loud when it broke the silence after the unmaking. "Why can we never show anyone?"

"Because such things are only for you and me to see. This is our great secret, remember? No one else knows; no one else can know. In the song is all the power we will ever need. The knowledge of creation and destruction. In the song is power that the world has not truly seen in uncorrupted glory in twenty-two generations. It's my power. Mine alone, but it will be yours in times to come."

They were far out into the fields when they again drew up to the contingent of Talayan merchants. The city was a prominent but distant barricade to the north. Heat shimmered around them, blurring objects even at middle distances. They had stopped at the edge of a massive square basin. It was elevated above the plains around it, hemmed in by thick earthen walls, and carved down into the earth. There were gates at each of the four sides, with plates that could be raised and lowered. Beyond the gates, irrigation channels stretched off in each direction. It was meant to hold a great body of water, but, like the landscape all around it, it was completely dry.

One of the engineers—several had met the group, along with a few laborers, even some children who stood at a slight distance, nearly naked and silent—explained that a deep spring had once fed the tank. She could see the hole in the center of the square. It had been a steady source of water for hundreds of years. There were a few others like it throughout the fields, but those had run dry much earlier.

Corinn asked, "Water from this tank can be distributed throughout the entire irrigation system?" The engineer began to say that it had never done that, but Corinn cut him off. "Could water from this tank be distributed throughout the entire system? I asked to be brought to a tank that was central to everything. Is this it?"

"As near as there is to that, yes," the engineer said. "Some channels would have to be modified, perhaps embankments reorganized." The man looked to his companions for help. They offered none. "I am not sure, Your Majesty, what you—"

"You have answered me," Corinn said. She slipped down from the saddle and touched the ground. She looked immediately composed, her cream-colored trousers—deceptively cut to look like a dress—as unwrinkled as when she began the ride. She bent and plucked a pebble from the ground, studied it, and then enfolded it in her palm. "I'll have you all wait for me here. No one is to approach me while I'm in the tank no matter what happens. Understand?" She was answered first with silence, and then with a quick barrage of half-formed questions. She cut through them, glancing up at her son as she did so. "Aaden, that means you. Numrek, you stay here as well. I'll be back in a moment." With that, she stepped over the rim and began a careful descent into the tank.

She had to catch herself from falling several times, slamming her palm down against the coarse earth as her feet slipped, careful to keep the pebble trapped in her other hand. It was a deeper pit than she had realized. On reaching the bottom, she glanced up at the figures gathered at the rim. They seemed very far away. Aaden raised his arm to wave at her. She turned and walked on. Again, it took her longer than she expected to reach the center of the tank. She felt the men's eyes on her the entire time.

The heart spring was a scar in the ground just wide enough that she could have leaped into it and fallen to its depths. It was simply a hole with jagged edges that quickly faded to shadow. Looking at it, Corinn had the momentary feeling that it was the puckered maw of some wormlike creature, stuck fast in the rock-hard soil, begging for moisture. She moved up close to it, planted her feet, and sang. She opened her mouth and exhaled the first words that came to her mind.

It was as if the song had been in the air already, and she had joined it midflow the moment she began. She knew the right words, the correct notes, and the tempo and rhythm and duration and inflection at precisely the moment it came into and left her mouth. She did not remember what she had sung once it was past, nor did she anticipate what she was going to sing. There was no linear progression. She was not following the notes or words as written on a page. She was the song, changing with it each moment.

And the song was beautiful. She knew it was. She knew that nothing else since the world's creation had captured beauty so perfectly in sound. She felt her body pulled and swayed with the ribbons of god talk that eddied around her. They caressed her, tugged at her, pulled away bits of her being and floated them on the air and returned them to her, changed. While she did not control the song, she did infuse it with her intentions. She explained—using the words that came to her unbidden—what she wished, what she asked for, what she needed. She sang this into the song, and she could feel understanding between her and the swirling music grow.

At the point that she felt the impulse to, she lifted her arm, opened her hand, and let the pebble fall into the well, singing the entire time. A breath of heated air surged up from the well, as if the worm creature were coughing itself to life. Corinn took a half step back, steadied herself, and sang through it without faltering. A few moments later, the well sputtered, gurgled, coughed again. She felt a spray of vapor rise out of it and evaporate instantly in the sun. She sang on.

The water, when it finally bubbled out of the hole, was thick with soil. It seeped into the thirsty ground. For a few moments it seemed as if the lip of the hole would drink it all. But soon the water began to roll forward, carrying dirt and ash before it, a stain on the ground that the watchers must have seen clearly. It flowed in all directions. Corinn felt it touch her toes and grab at the hem of her trouser skirt. She kept singing. She heard the merchants exclaiming up on the rim. A Numrek shouted her name, but she kept singing.

The water began to gush. It surged a few feet into the air. It splashed the front of her dress and reached up over her ankles, buffeting her feet. She sang on, not feeling where the end of the song might be. She vaguely thought that she might not be able to stop. She might be here still with her mouth open when the water poured inside her and she filled with it. This was not a frightening thought. Nothing was frightening when the song was in her. There was nothing, nothing, nothing to fear.

And then she stopped. Just like that. Her lips paused and nothing more came through them and she knew she was finished. The water continued to flow, growing even stronger. She stepped back from it, awed—now that she could see her work with clear eyes—at the wonder of water in this place. She could taste it in the air. The tang of it was sharp and cold, as if she were standing beside a mountain stream, a rising mountain stream.

She turned around and waded toward the merchants with all the grace she could manage. She was panting hard as she reached the rim, but she did not give them time to study her. "Back away from the edge," she commanded. "Back away! Drop to your knees and bow."

The men looked startled, scared even, but one after another did as she commanded. Several had to dismount, but they did so quickly. Soon the entire company around her—merchants, nobles, laborers, and the ragged children—pressed their knees to the ground, waiting, jittery, caught between obeying her

185

and their desire to watch the water rise. The Numrek contingent stood straight backed, their weapons in hand, looking as if they were ready to attack the merchants, slaughtering them. Not today, Corinn thought.

She stood gathering her breath, holding the moment, using it. Aaden still sat on his horse. She glanced at him long enough to smile away his concern. In a gesture meant only for him, she rolled her eyes, as if acknowledging the silliness of it all. The gesture almost knocked her off balance. She indicated that he should dismount and stand beside her. Then she turned her attention to the bowed heads.

"Are you true to me?" Corinn asked.

"Of course," Elder Anath said.

"Why?"

"You are our queen."

"Are you the only one who thinks so?"

The others spoke then, praising her, talking over one another, some bending forward like worshippers. It was what she wanted, but the sight of them annoyed her also. They were scared now, cowards. "Do not ask how I have done this thing, but see that it was I alone who did it. Tell the truth when you speak of this. The water will rise and rise and never stop as long as this is my wish. It will fill the tank and will replenish itself as you open the gates and feed the fields. This heart spring belongs to all Bocoum. Don't let me learn that any of you have called it your own or deprived others of it. You may look up now."

Corinn's gaze moved from one person to the next, pausing at each one, speaking to them all—old and young, rich and poor—with the same authority. Before, there might have been much to read in the hidden thoughts and emotions behind the various faces. Now, though, they all looked the same. Sinper Ou shared the same slack-mouthed expression as the boy standing a little distance behind him. Elder Anath had a face of wet clay, upon which she could write what she wished.

"I am not just the mother of this child. I am the mother of Acacia. Say that. Say that I am the mother of Acacia."

"You are the mother of Acacia," they intoned raggedly, in different volumes and pitches of voices.

"Say that I am the mother of the empire."

The kneeling group did.

"And remember to pray each day for my health, for should I die, this spring will as well. Betray me," Corinn said, "and your world will dry, shrivel, and burst into flames beneath my sun. This water that I give"—she motioned to the rising body behind her—"I can take away. So say I, and my son." As hard as it was to do, she raised Aaden's arm with hers. For a few moments longer, her eyes moved from person to person, until she was sure that she had made eye contact with them all. Then she smiled and said, soft voiced, "That's the truth, but we are friends here, aren't we? Do not think me angry. I just enjoy speaking the truth. Now drink of this water, friends. It will not cease flowing. Never. Grow your crops, and spread word of the gift I have given Bocoum. I am your queen, and I give this to you."

As the merchants rose and moved toward her, she had to speak over their adulation to announce that she would return to the city now, without the merchant escort. Though they fawned around her until she moved away, it was clear they did not care. They rushed toward the edge of the bubbling tank as soon as she turned her back to them. On her horse again, she rode without looking back. Aaden did, though.

"What are they doing?" she asked.

The boy laughed. "They're acting like children. They are dancing, shouting, and hugging each other. I didn't know you were going to do that! You did magic, Mother, and everyone saw!" He laughed again, and Corinn knew the child in him would have liked to have joined them, to share their giddy enthusiasm, maybe even to jump in and swim. She needed him, though. She could not fall from the saddle. If she did, the

Numrek would carry her back to the city, but that wouldn't do.

She began to reach out to touch him, but just lifting her hand from the pommel made her feel she might fall. She returned it, gripping hard and trying to find the swaying balance she needed. It would not be easy, but she knew she could do it if she kept her focus. For that reason, she rode in silence for several minutes.

"Aaden, ride close to me. Watch me carefully."

"Why?" Serious now, the prince drew up near her.

"Doing such a thing as that tires me very much. I need you beside me."

Chapter Fifteen

If the tales were to be believed, she faced a winged monster. A dragon. A lizard thing of such massive proportions that the beating of its wings snapped trees and blew roofs off houses and sent unfortunate people swirling into the air. It swooped down and grasped cattle two and three at a time, flying loops in the air and tossing its prey like a playful cat. It swallowed cattle whole, in midflight. Its jaws and neck convulsed with the grotesque gluttony of a river crocodile. One farmhouse was destroyed when the thing landed atop it, plunging its claws to snatch at the inhabitants within. High up the southern basin entire herds of goats and their minders had disappeared. It had been spotted as far away as Tabith, which was grave news indeed. If it could travel that far, it might soon discover Bocoum and the bounty of human life all around the Inner Sea, including the isle of Acacia itself.

While Mena had focused her attentions on the tenten creature and on the scourge of the Halaly lake, small bands of Talayan runners had narrowed in on the new creature's lair. They compared one sighting with the next, slowly piecing together when it was on an outbound journey from its lair. It had not been easy to track its movements. The thing was aloft, and it could travel much faster than a person could run.

Still, they managed it, and because of their work Mena was awakened one morning to the news that it had landed a mile away from her new camp. She was up and jogging the distance with her officers immediately. Melio and the rest of her force followed, bearing with them the tools they would need and traveling with stealth. They were in a shallow dale west of Umae, in a land that benefited from the moisture that evaporated from the great lake, blew north on the winds, and then settled nightly to condense among the orchards and pastures that distinguished the country. The marching was easy, the cover good. The Talayan trackers, aided by local farmers and herders, moved them along in the shade of trees, using the lees of hills and the shelter of brush-banked streams.

In no time at all Mena approached the last group of spotters, men and boys with their fingers to their full lips. They indicated with gestures that they were near the top of a hill. Another few paces and she should crawl the last few feet and look over the edge. She did as they advised, awkwardly, with her sword at her side and a waist pack of supplies nestled against the small of her back. She ended elbow to elbow with a herd boy on one side of her and a Talayan tracker on the other.

"Look carefully and you will see it," the Talayan said.

All she saw at first was a wide vale filled with short, rounded, evenly spaced trees. A stream traced a meandering line through the center of it, and here and there she could tell the vegetation had been managed, lanes left open, ponds dug as water catchments. It took her a moment to spot any movement among the tranquillity of the scene, but then a serpentine head moved between two trees. It was there for a second and then gone, and so far away on the other slope of the vale that she was not sure of what she had seen. Squinting, Mena followed it, and was looking in the right spot to see its head rise above the crown of one tree, cock to the side, and, with gingerly precision, nip at the foliage. And then it was hidden again.

Something about what she had just seen sent tingles over her flesh. There was fear in the reaction but a hint of something else also. "What are those trees?" she asked. "How tall are they?"

The local boy whispered an answer in Talayan, two words that Mena repeated. She was quite fluent in the language, but she was constantly being thrown by the Talayan tendency to name things through descriptive use of other words. "Blood . . . heart?" she asked.

The tracker lying on the other side of her cupped his hand to her ear. "You don't call it blood heart. It's *orange* in your language, but orange with red inside. The trees are two men in height, some a little more."

"What's it doing here? Is its lair near here?"

He creased his dark-skinned forehead. "No, I don't think so. It just landed here. We did not expect it."

"Just a coincidence, huh?" Mena muttered. She squirmed forward a few more inches and looked back at the orchard.

When she spotted the creature again, it was somewhat closer. It stepped into a lane and paused, raking its head from side to side and then freezing. It was lean and light on its four feet. In that position it must have been no more than a person's height, but that changed when it reared up on its back legs and took in the orchard—again going still as a statue—from a higher vantage. She could see the reptile in it. It was there in the sinuous lines of its neck and the blue patches along its back and in the long, whiplike expanse of its tail. It was, she thought, akin to the sand lizards that lived right in the huts of Talayan villagers. Its eyes were shaped just like those of the harmless creatures. They were larger by many times, but their size did not completely obscure their origins. She had once thought them curious eyes, innocent, fearful, and yet full of mischief.

There was an avian quality to the creature as well: flares around its neck that seemed like feathers, a crest on its forehead that snapped forward and back with a mind of its own, like the plumage a peacock displayed. When it bobbed its head the motion was comical, like both the tiny lizard it reminded her of and the motion of birds. It moved into the trees again, hunting the juiciest oranges, apparently.

Moments later, down away from the hill, Mena tongue-lashed the trackers for the absurdity of what she had just seen. "Does it not seem strange that the scourge of Talay dines on fruit? That thing is the great dragon people have been speaking of?" The group of men and boys stirred uneasily. "It eats the fruit of trees and walks around bobbing its head as if to a tune. It's as dangerous as a hen! Is that truly the thing we hunt? Look me in the face and tell me that's the last of the great foulthings."

Eventually, several affirmed that it was what they hunted. When Mena pressed them as to whether that exact creature was the one they had seen time and again over the last few weeks, they admitted it was. When she asked them why they had not corrected the rumors about its size and ferociousness they let a long silence sit, before a man answered that it was still dangerous. It was much fiercer than it looked. They had seen it in flight and—

"It flies without wings?" she snapped. "I saw no wings. Did you? Has anyone here fought it? Have any of you seen it take cattle, squash homes, terrorize villages?"

When none of them could explain the discrepancy, she turned from them and walked away a few paces, exasperated. Melio followed her, almost laughing, but she hissed, "This is a farce! Do they know how we've prepared? All the precautions? The worry we've lived with—all because of a giant sand lizard? I should have known: dragons have never lived and never will! What's happened to our reason?"

"Well," Melio said smirking, "you know, I did hear about a group of young men caught poaching near the southern basin. Might be that—"

"Poachers? People have been poaching while we risk our lives to protect them?"

Melio shrugged. "Somebody will always take advantage, Mena. On the day that anything happens in the world without somebody finding a way to cheat a profit out of it I'll dance a jig naked before any who will come and watch. Don't sell tickets, though. I doubt I'll ever be called to make such a show."

Leaning toward him, Mena exhaled a long, fatigued breath. She slipped one hand up around his side, feeling the flare of his back muscles. "Okay," she said, "that lizard is our last monster. It's no dragon, but we still must do something with it. Do we toss fruit at it or kill it? Perhaps we could walk up and put a leash around its neck."

Melio returned her embrace. "You're funny, Princess. Some people—not you, of course, but some sane people—would view this as a boon. Think about it. You woke up this morning ready to risk your life battling a terrifying beast. Instead, we've been given a gift. It's all but over, Mena. We can leave here and get on with our lives. I for one will be very happy to go home and warm your bed for weeks on end. I hope you'll join me. Think of it! We can go home and then you can stop taking those herbs. You'll do that, yes? Stop and be fertile again. I'll plant a child in you and—"

"Don't," Mena said, softly. "Don't talk about that now."

"And we can live our lives," he completed. "Why not now? Now is exactly the time to remember it. I have loved you since the afternoon I saw you striding along the dock in Vumu, bare chested and all, a priestess of Maeben. I loved you then, and I love you now. You are angry you're not going to die today? Put that aside, Mena. Let's go finish this, and then go home."

The preparations took very little time. Her officers had been readying the men and supplies from the first news of the sighting. By the time Mena confirmed they were to proceed, the troops were arriving, weapons in hand. Not wanting missiles to end up zinging willy-nilly through the orchard if the creature bolted, she chose her twenty best crossbowmen and explained to them a variation on the original plan. She sent the trackers and extra soldiers to ring the entire vale to keep the creature hemmed in. With the main group she followed a contingent of excited local boys who led them through a hidden wash and in toward the center of the orchard, low enough to remain unseen by the creature. They crept with increasing stealth, which was no easy task considering the way they were encumbered.

The bowmen walked with their weapons pointed toward the sky, each of them connected by a cord that ran from the bolt and into coils held in their seconds' palms. The line did not stop there, but trailed farther to a third, and sometimes fourth, assistant. These men carried stones cradled to their chests. A few had them in slings over their backs. Some of the rocks were large enough that two men strained to carry them, waddling together, their muscles taut and brows dripping with sweat. Each of these stones had a hole through it. It was this to which the cords from the bows were secured.

Mena kept them all in a tight group, close enough that she could communicate with gestures: a raised palm, a clenched fist, just enough of a beckoning motion with her fingers to move them forward on silent feet. When they reached the final rise that separated them from the grove the creature was feeding in, she made eye contact with them all, touched a finger to her lips, and then turned and led them forward. She drew her sword carefully as she did. She moved into the ordered rows of orange trees, smelling the tang of them, the sickly ripeness of the split fruit that dotted the ground.

Her hand snapped up. Without looking, she heard the group behind her pause, not so much a sound but the sudden absence of whatever sound had been there before to indicate them. She had spotted the foulthing. It was but fifty yards away, on the hillside facing them. It moved casually through the trees, its long neck curving selectively among the branches and leaves. Its back was to them. Mena waved her fingers in the air, and the group moved again, more stealthily now than ever.

As they got nearer, Mena had the hunting party fan out to either side. She slowed the center and let the flanks swing forward, making the group a crescent that half surrounded the foulthing. She knew they could not hope to get much closer, but she moved on light feet, thankful for every inch gained. She could now see that the creature was feathered, a close, tight coating that revealed the muscled contours and bone structure beneath a slick sheen of light plumage.

Without really realizing she was doing it, Mena drew to a halt, staring, curious now instead of angry or excited or frightened. The creature had knobby formations high on its back, and an indication of violet crest feathers running up its long neck. Despite these avian features, it was equally reptilian. Its body stretched long and lizardlike, with a tail that tapered to a thin point. For the first time, Mena realized, she did not feel the stomach-turning nausea the other foulthings had always invoked. She suddenly wanted to watch this one, to study it, to call back the slow-creeping crossbowmen and reconsider. She did not get to.

In the end it was not sound that gave them away. It was the breeze. It shifted. Mena felt it happen, felt a playful arm of the wind reach out and swipe at them and pull their scent and sprinkle it over the creature. The others must have sensed it, too. They stood frozen, breathing hushed, eyes wide.

The beast stopped feeding. Its head sank a few feet, and then it lifted its snout and inhaled through a few silent nostril flares. Without moving its body, it turned its head around and looked over the ridgeline of its back, its neck as supple as a snake. It saw them. Mena knew it saw them both because it looked right at them and because its eyes grew larger.

They were near enough, Mena decided. She lifted her hand to signal the crossbowmen, but realized they might not see her, as focused as they were on the lizard bird. They might not see her, but the creature did. Its gaze snapped to her, met hers, and held her with an intensity that was both animal savage and intelligent. Again, Mena wished she could back away. She could not have said exactly why. This was a foulthing. It was unnatural. It was a threat that did not belong in the world. Before, each time she had looked into one of these mutated beast's eyes, she had seen a perverted malevolence that had to be extinguished. That was not what was looking at her now. She needed time to—

The creature, responding to the motion of several of the crossbowmen, who were setting up to take aim, spun around. Its mouth fell open, hissing, and the plumes along its neck bristled forward, framing its head in a violet, feathered mane. The creature shook its torso savagely, stepping forward as it did so. The knobs on its back cracked away and unfurled to either side. The motion was so rapid and dramatic that it sucked the words of command out of Mena's mouth. Wings! It did have wings! They rolled out as if the bones were joints of a curled whip unfurling. Each short length of bone snapped into place with an audible cracking and popping. It took only a second or two, but in that time the creature was completely transformed. Its wings stretched out above the tree height, enormous and delicate at the same time. The wing bones were finger thin, a skeletal frame that supported a membrane so diaphanous that Mena could see the world through it. It leaped into the air.

"Shoot!" Mena found her voice again. "Stop it from escaping! Shoot it now!"

Crossbow bolts flew up after it, cords trailing behind. Several missed. A few snagged in the trees. One punched through the creature's wing membrane. Two slammed into its belly. One sank deep into the flesh of its thigh. Another nicked its neck. The creature lost its upward momentum. It hovered for a moment, a confused target into which another bolt sank home. The creature arched against the pain. Its mouth gaped as if it were roaring, but no sound came out. It slammed its wings down with force enough to snap branches and send oranges raining down. The one stroke lifted it up, pulling the lines secured to it. The ropes snapped taut, yanking the stones from the ground. The anchors crashed through branches and bounced off tree trunks. One knocked a soldier from his feet. Another smashed an arm that had been upraised against it.

Mena yelled for them to fall back, but most were already diving for cover, running down the hill, hiding behind trees and in hollows to wait for the rock anchors to pull the beast down. That had been the plan: to weight the animal with so many stones that it could not fly, or could not fly far. They could then kill it at leisure, safely. When she thought it wingless, Mena had modified the plan, thinking a less numerous team could get close enough and then essentially capture it the same way.

For a few moments during the wing-flapping chaos Mena thought the plan was working, but with each wingbeat the creature seemed to gain strength and resolve. It strained against the ropes, yanking them through the branches. It would soon clear the trees. She shouted for more bolts to be shot, but the crossbowmen were struggling to reload while keeping their eyes upon the moving beast. She would have taken a shot herself if she had a bow. Something else caught her eye. The creature's tail hung near the ground. It snapped and curled and stretched beneath the flying form, like a living rope looking for a hand to grab it. So that's what Mena did.

She walked forward and grasped it in a clenched fist. She did not exactly plan to. It was so near, so easy to do. She did not think, but some part of her imagined she might hold the creature down. The narrow tip of the tail curled around her wrist, almost playfully, as if it had a mind of its own and would tickle her. She noticed this even amid the motion, even though it lasted only a few seconds.

That's all the time she had before she was yanked into the air. She knew then—as the earth fell away beneath her churning legs—that neither the stones nor her body weight was nearly enough to keep the creature earthbound. It soared upward, taking her with it.

Chapter Sixteen

The messenger sent by Sangae Umae had surprised Kelis every day since they began their overland journey together. Naamen had dashed out of the camp in Halaly at a pace that Kelis was sure he would not be able to hold for long. But he had. Kelis had thought himself still in his prime; but midway through his first day, he had cause to doubt it. The older man kept abreast of the younger only by digging deep into his running memory, finding the rhythm, and searching for the quiet meditative space that he had tapped to help him through his longest runs, like the one he took at Aliver's side in search of the Santoth.

While Aliver had been largely a silent companion, Naamen was inclined to chatter. He made observations on the landscape, talked of random memories, asked questions, and then seemed content to answer them himself. It had frustrated Kelis at first; he suspected that the adolescent was purposefully trying to distract him and to demonstrate that the work did not even wind him. But by the third or fourth day Naamen's voice had become a feature of the journey, inseparable from the pounding of their feet and swing of their arms and the slow unfurling of the land through which they kicked their dusty progress.

Outside the Halaly lake region, the plains baked beneath a dry sun that oppressed the land, as if the heat were a heavy blanket pressing down on the world. Umae, which they passed near, had always been arid, but such heat was unusual this early in the season. Across the flat stretch of land to Denben they found water only in a few wells, the rivers like dry scars cut in the earth by some meandering knife. Along the busy route between Denben and Bocoum it was easier to forget the plains, especially as the roads often took them within sight of the Inner Sea. Still, Kelis knew that things were not right in his homeland. The foulthings were one sign of it but not the only one.

Naamen was just as adept among the urban bustle of Bocoum as he was running across open expanses. Kelis followed the young man as he slipped through the crowd with the fluidity of an eel through a coral reef. The city, sprawling along the coastline for buttressed miles, was technically the seat of government control of the province of Talay, although with the region's tribal variation any central control was loose. More fundamentally, it was the agricultural and commercial hub of Talay. It thronged with merchants and traders and craftsmen; with foodstuffs, warehouses, and luxurious estates. None of these things interested Kelis. He did not really feel at home hemmed in by walls and buildings and crowds, and considered the flaunted wealth of the townsfolk to be obscenely extravagant. In the past, he had always breezed through the city, engaged in some errand or another. He did not intend this trip to be any different.

"Here it is," Naamen said, motioning with his stunted arm.

It took Kelis a moment to sort out what he meant. They had come up one of the high streets of the city center, a busy corridor lined with multistoried buildings. Working their way forward, Kelis picked out the carved image of a lion on a crest above the gatehouse entrance at the end of the lane. It was the Ou lion. It was hardly an original totem animal, but it was distinctive in that the figure stood upright on a body that looked more human than feline. The head, however, was massively maned, the cat's mouth opened in an everlasting roar. It could have been a secondary entrance to an Acacian palace, such was the grandeur of the carved granite archway. Two guards stood at attention at either side, long pikes set on the ground before them and stretching to spear points well above their heads.

"You would think they were royalty," Kelis murmured.

Naamen turned and set his mirthful eyes on him. "Oh, yes, and, believe me, the Ous do think themselves royalty. You need not bow before them, though. Not yet, at least."

The guards held them outside the gate for several minutes, until a secretary met them. He curtly dismissed Naamen, then led Kelis through the elaborate interior gardens, around pools of fish and under palms, between rows of flowering bushes. Inside the main building, the extravagance continued. For Kelis—who had spent most of the last several years in camps, sleeping on mats with bare ground beneath him—the tapestry-hung walls, the incense-heavy air, the rich carpet underfoot, and the dark crimson and gold of so much of the furniture closed in on him like some elaborate trap. He had to breathe deeply to disguise his racing heartbeat and his desire to run away.

The secretary left him in a room filled with couches and ornate chairs, directing him to sit and relax. Kelis eyed a couch, draped with zebra skins. He did not sit. Instead, he moved out onto the balcony and sucked in the salt-tinged air. The Inner Sea stretched out to the horizon, the green waters dotted with sailing vessels of all sizes and shapes. In the distance great trading barges sat on the water, looking like oddly geometric islands. Leaning on the railing, Kelis took in the sweep of the harbor below, the coastline crowded with rank upon rank of white-roofed buildings. The structures were built so tightly together they looked like a throng jostling to tilt themselves into the mirror that was the sea.

How many people lived in this city? Kelis had no idea. Likely, the number would mean little to him anyway. How very different it was from a village like Umae, where he could name every adult, and every child could name him. That was the size of community that felt right to him. He wondered again why Sangae had summoned him here.

"The harbor of Bocoum on a summer's day," a man's voice said, startling Kelis. He turned and saw a man of about his age, richly dressed in an ankle-length blue robe, approaching him. "It is magnificent, don't you think?"

"Yes," Kelis said. It was not exactly a lie but close.

"Good." The man smiled. His face was handsome and broad featured in the way of northern Talayans. He was as tall as Kelis, lean as well, although somewhat more bulkily muscled around the chest and shoulders. He was not a runner. He was fit in a different way and carried himself with confident grace. Seeming to remember formality all at once, he bowed his clean-shaven head. He said, "New friend, the sun shines on you, but the water is sweet."

"The water is cool, new friend, and clear to look upon," Kelis answered. The words came to his lips automatically.

"It would be nice if these words were true, wouldn't it? Sometimes I fear our greetings have mostly to do with what we wish the world was and little to do with how it actually is." Considering the luxury of the building they were in, Kelis wondered what this man had to complain about. "I am Ioma. Sinper Ou is my father. In his name I welcome you, Kelis of Umae. My father and Sangae will be here shortly, along with the one we would have you meet." He gestured toward the tray a servant had just laid on a small table. "Please, drink."

The clear glass pitcher contained a chilled juice, frozen enough that it clunked as the servant poured some into a glass. Kelis held the tumbler in his hand, watching the vapor rise off it. He had no idea how they managed to cool it so. Nor did he wish to ask. He touched it to his lips and sipped. It was too cold, unnaturally so.

"It is a wonderful view, isn't it?" Ioma asked. "Our ancestors looked out upon this harbor for generations before the Acacians planted their first fort on Acacia. Whether or not Acacia chooses to remember this fully is another matter, but we should not forget. That's even more important now. See over there?" The merchant extended his robed arm and pointed.

It only took Kelis a moment to pick out the structures he was indicating. Lower down the cliffs, near the eastern rim of the bay, was a conglomeration of large, richly painted buildings with garish spires like plump, sparkling red bulbs of garlic.

"The King's Academy." Ioma said the official name with disgust. "Should be called the queen's institute for the forgetting."

"You don't care for it, then?"

Ioma nudged him in the shoulder. It was an act of familiarity that would have seemed rude had his host not made it so casually. "Do not joke with me, friend. You know the purpose of that place? It's not education at all. It's limitation. They say they pick the brightest students from each of the provinces. So why is it that those 'brightest' students always happen to be children of prominent families? Why do the children get selected even when the parents have not offered them for consideration? I know you serve the Akarans; I don't wish to make an enemy of you." He paused as if considering how at risk of that he was, and then shrugged and went on. "But you're Talayan as well. That place is a hostage camp. First and foremost, those children are hostages. Second, their minds are scrubbed clean of the truth and filled with the history of the world as Corinn wishes them to know it. Two of my nephews and a niece attend, a cousin also. They tell me all about it. At least it's here in Bocoum. That's something. My family members are hostages only during the day. At night we are free to uneducate them."

Kelis did not say anything, a fact Ioma acknowledged by pursing his lips. "Perhaps I speak too freely. You see, Kelis, I feel already I know you. But I see that I am not as well known to— Oh, here they are now! Prepare yourself for a surprise, my friend."

Three figures approached them through the maze of furniture that cluttered the room. Sangae had been an old man for most of Kelis's life, but he wore his age like an unchanging garment. He was still a slim man—a great runner in his time. His simple garment wrapped his torso and was slung over one of his shoulders.

Sangae embraced him. "It has been too long, my son."

"Yes, Father, but the Giver is kind," Kelis responded. Sangae was not actually his father, but in the village of Umae the terms *son* and *father* had always been used liberally. The other man was clearly Ioma's father, Sinper; they had the same facial structure and physique. The older man wore his hair cropped short around the ears, but it bloomed fuller on top, dusted with gray. Sinper was cordial in greeting him, though he did so with his chin raised and eyes heavy lidded in a manner that made it clear he expected Kelis to offer him the deference usually reserved for chieftains.

Looking over his shoulder as the old man gripped him, Kelis saw that a woman had followed the two men. Seeing her stirred something in him. There were things in her face that he remembered. The wide, smooth forehead; the large eyes separated by the gentle bridge of her nose; her lips full and shapely, held in the pucker that was traditional for Talayan women in formal situations. Part of it, as well, was that her beauty reminded him of an emotion: envy. It was that emotion that marked his realization of who she was: Benabe, one of the many young women who had pursued Aliver as he grew into a man.

"Benabe," Kelis said, "the moon hides in your eyes."

"No," she said, "that is the sun in yours, which simply reflects in mine."

The greeting completed, Ioma took Kelis by the arm and led

him to a couch. They all sat, sipping the chilled drink as servants set a table with small bowls of pickled cabbage and tiny squids, fish eggs on triangles of hard bread. For a while they chatted with no particular direction to the conversation. This was normal enough, really, but Kelis could barely contain his curiosity. He half wondered if he would have to wait until he was alone to find out, and he more than half wondered if the young woman, so quiet as the men spoke, had some role in whatever had brought him here.

Sinper asked Kelis about his battles with the foulthings. He seemed honestly interested in the beasts but also in Mena Akaran. Was she really as fierce in battle as they say? Was it true that she had killed a many-eyed lion beast with her own sword? Could she truly keep pace with Talayan runners when on the hunt? Kelis answered with plainspoken honesty each time.

"So you admire her?" Sinper asked.

"There is much to admire."

"And what of her sister?" Ioma asked.

"Queen Corinn," Kelis said, "I do not know that well."

Ioma grinned. "She doesn't run barefoot beside our men, does she?"

"No," Kelis acknowledged.

Ioma sat back. "That would be something to see. I would pay silver to watch our queen run a footrace. She would have to leave her fine dresses at home, but I wouldn't mind that either."

The comment was made lightly, but for a moment afterward nobody spoke. Sinper looked sourly at his son, but then seemed to accept that a topic of some import had been reached, even if awkwardly so. He cleared his throat. "We are not here for idle chatter. You know that. Nor will we lower ourselves with base jokes about the queen." He slanted his eyes at Ioma, who looked away, contrite as a boy, for a few seconds at least. "No, I will not trivialize her with such things.

204

In truth she is not trivial, is she? In truth she is a woman of power."

Kelis nodded. That fact hardly needed his confirmation.

"Sangae has told me that you have no fondness for her policies. You see her as clearly as we do, and you know—as we do—that she has betrayed Talay. She has betrayed all the people who followed Aliver and defeated Hanish Mein. You agree with all this, don't you?"

This time Kelis did not nod, but neither did he disagree. The old man took this as affirmation. "Why, then, do you serve her?"

"I am at peace with my heart. I don't determine what the queen does. I can only act—or not—as Kelis. That is what—"

"So you claim that you will only ever do noble work for her?" Sinper asked, the slow cadence of his voice becoming faster, sharper. "What of when she asks something else of you? How do you refuse? How do you say no, when you have so long been saying yes, yes, yes?"

"What would you have me do?" Kelis snapped, suddenly angry at the old man. Who was he to lecture, and why did Sangae allow it? "This is a world ruled by lions. To the greatest lion goes the spoils, goes everything that it demands. Right now, Corinn Akaran is that lion."

"Lioness," Sinper corrected.

"Do you never doubt her?" Ioma asked.

"I live with doubt every day."

"I as well," Sangae said softly, drawing Kelis's eyes up to his. "Do not think me a traitor to Aliver because I doubt his sister. The prince was a son to me. You know that. I raised him at his father's request and I loved him as if his blood were mine."

Sinper cut in. "But we do not speak of Aliver. Not yet. Corinn is the one who concerns me. She has broken our noble families and tries to poison the minds of our children against their parents. She didn't stop the league from taking more of our children away. Her crimes or oversights are too numerous

205

to name. She gave us water, yes, but that is not enough, and it was late in coming. My worries about her have become as a tumor lodged in my breast. Any day it might grow to kill me. I would cut it out, but I don't have a knife sharp enough. At least, I did not have such a knife . . ." He dropped his voice at the end of the sentence, leaving it frayed and incomplete.

Ioma, who had stood silent, whispered into the pause. "It may be that we have found that knife."

Kelis stared from him to Sangae, disbelieving his ears. It was not that he disputed that Corinn's rule was flawed. She had inherited a foul system from Hanish Mein, who had taken it from her father, who had perpetuated the crimes of the generations before him. None of them seemed willing to break the old order of the world. Corinn, perhaps, was more like Tinhadin's daughter than Leodan's. She might yet do great harm. But . . . "Why does this burn like treason in my ears?" he asked.

"Treason is a betrayal of one's accepted ruler," Ioma said, "but it is not treason to reject an usurper. In truth, it is a treason to accept a false rule once you know it is false."

Sinper inched forward on his seat, like an anxious youth. He pointed at Benabe. "Kelis, can you confirm that Aliver was intimate with this woman? You were his closest companion. If they were intimate, you surely—"

"Nobody can confirm what another man does in his tent," Kelis said.

"Oh, speak truth!" Benabe said. "I remember quite a bit about what you did—and with whom you did it. We weren't shy back then, were we? You know I lay with Aliver many times."

Benabe had always had a quick tongue. She was as easy with anger as she was with laughter. That ease was part of what had bothered him about her—that and the fact that Aliver had found the same traits so alluring. He heard himself say, "You weren't the only one."

"No, but I did not keep track like you did. If you can name another who was with him, you can likewise name that I was with him."

Kelis wiped at the heat that suddenly flushed through his face. They would think him bitter, jealous. Perhaps they would be right to think so. He controlled his voice as he added, "I cannot know what happened between these two, but if you ask me what I believe, then, yes, they were lovers."

This seemed to satisfy Sinper, though he demonstrated that with an expression more like a grimace than a smile. "So we have a witness."

"Not that we needed one," Ioma said. "Benabe's testimony should not be questioned."

"It will be, though," Sangae said. "It will be."

Benabe stared at Kelis so intently that he had to meet her gaze. "Thank you, Kelis. I know you loved him, too. Aliver knew it as well."

Another flash of heat surged across Kelis's face. Fortunately, his dark skin did not betray it. Yes, Aliver knew it, but he didn't return it—not, at least, in the physical manner Kelis would have welcomed. He had always been careful not to betray the true nature of his feelings for Aliver, and he did not want to now. He spoke as if he had not heard her. "A witness to what? I still don't understand what this is about."

The others exchanged glances.

"Bring the child, then," Sangae eventually said. "Let him see her."

"The child?"

Sangae nodded. "She is a beautiful child, Kelis. She is hope for us all. Call her, Benabe, and let her come on her two feet."

Hope for all of us? Kelis felt his fingertips begin to tingle. Hope for all of us?

Benabe rose and walked to the door at the other side of the room. The four men sat in silence as she spoke to somebody in the hallway. A few moments later she returned, leading a girl of perhaps nine years of age. The tingling in Kelis's fingers became a throb, a heartbeat that moved to the center of his palms.

Benabe said, "This is my daughter. She named herself. She likes us to call her Shen."

The girl walked with her eyes downcast, but as soon as she stopped before them, she raised her head and looked candidly at the four men. Her face was round and gentle, her mouth small, with thinner lips than her mother's. Her skin was a rich brown, but it had been stirred with a cream that lightened it. She looked out at them with remarkably large eyes. Though she said not a word, Kelis could not help but think her quite intelligent. Her features were familiar. They were Benabe's, yes, but that was only one way in which he knew them, had known them since before he ever saw her, before she was ever born. There was no denying it. The girl, Larashen—Shen—was Aliver Akaran's daughter. How could he have lived those years and not known—felt—her living?

"She named herself?" Kelis asked.

Benabe nodded but did not explain.

"Kelis Umae," the girl said. Her voice was clear and high, and the two words on her tongue were neither a greeting nor a question. Just a statement.

"You—you know me?"

"Yes. They've told me about you. You went as far as the river of the southern basin. There you waited, as good as your word."

"These people told you that? Your mother? Sangae?"

"The stones told me." She smiled, and then lowered her gaze, at moments looking no different than a shy girl.

"Stones . . ." He almost framed a question, but let it fade. The fine hairs on his forearms and the back of his neck were bristling. The pulse in his palms was actually painful now. He looked up at Benabe. "Who is this girl's father?"

"You know that already," Benabe said.

"She is a child of two nations," Ioma said. "Look at her,

Kelis. She is our future. She is a trembler, but others have been so."

"Do not call her a trembler," Benabe snapped, and then rubbed her fingers into the girl's shoulders soothingly. "She has visions. She has fits during which she falls on the ground, shaking, insensible, but that is only what we see on the outside. Her mind goes to another place—that is why she trembles. She says that in those moments the stones call her. It is they that possess her body and seek to put things inside her. You know what stones she speaks of. Did not Aliver first see the Santoth as stones? He saw them rise and walk toward him. My daughter sees the same."

Sangae had moved closer to him, leaning in as if he wanted to see her from the same vantage as Kelis. He whispered. "What did I tell you? Nobody told the girl that; she told us of it, just as she told us her name . . . You ask who her father is, but you can see who she is as clearly as I can. What man would not recognize his brother's child? That's who she is. And we think she is in danger."

"Word of her could reach agents of the queen," Ioma said.

Sinper was silent for a moment and then added, not whispering this time, "We should talk of this privately."

"And why does this matter to you?" Kelis said, his voice edged by the unease all this stirred into him. Again, that was not one of the pressing questions he had, but it was what came out.

It was Ioma who answered. "Because, Kelis, Benabe is of the family Ou. Shen is my cousin. Isn't that right?"

"Yes, cousin." The girl nodded. She studied Kelis a moment, then stepped closer. She reached out with one hand and touched her fingertips to his forearm. "I have to go. I would like it if you would go with me. It would be good that way. They will keep me safe. They promised, so long as you take me."

Benabe took the girl away after that. Nobody explained

what the child was referring to and Kelis for some time could not form the words to ask. He moved through the rest of the meeting with an outward appearance of dazed indifference, giving little indication of what he thought. He knew they were talking, vaguely understood the things they were saying, but before he could engage with any of that he had to stare in the face the realization of what Shen's existence meant. Aliver's child! She was the heir to the Acacian throne. Without a legitimate heir to take precedence, rule could have gone to her to be passed down to her line, not Corinn's. She was only a girl, but the eyes of the world would not see her as that. She was enough to set the world at war again, and he, being witness to her, had a role in whatever was to come.

"What did she mean," Kelis asked, breaking back into the conversation that had gone on without him, "about my going with her? With her where?"

"Oh . . ." Sangae let out the word as a long breath. "I thought you would know right away. To the Santoth. She says they are calling her to them."

Chapter Seventeen

The way it happened was strange, Rialus thought. He had lived through it, watching the change in their fortune as it occurred, but it was all so oddly muted. It was sudden, yes—and Dariel had made a fuss—but for all that it was cordial as well. It barely seemed possible that the civil interactions he and the prince had had with Sire Neen and the Ishtat Inspectorate had actually led to him and the prince becoming prisoners.

There was no other word for it. Chains. Manacles. That strange bit shoved in the prince's mouth and strapped tight. They spent a long night together in a cramped cabin, and the new morning found them propelled into motion with nothing explained. Ishtat guards escorted them—with shoves and prods and more threats than the situation called for—down and down into the belly of the ship. Eventually, they emerged through a hatch in the hull near the water level. A gangway descended to what appeared to be a floating platform. It was already crowded with leaguemen and Ishtat, all of whom stood apparently waiting for them. There were several other figures there. Numrek. Rialus had not seen them since the voyage began, but he recognized Calrach and his entourage of ten or so.

Rialus walked down the gangway on careful feet and landed on the strange surface. It was like an enormous slab of gray stone, rectangular and smooth but otherwise featureless.

Initially Rialus thought they were to wait here for whatever vessel was going to ferry them to land. Despite the complete uncertainty of what they were heading toward, he rather wished it would arrive. He disliked the hulking enormity of the ship at his back, so huge it could have squashed them if it shifted. Since he was thinking about that, he nearly fell over when the platform beneath him moved. The entire thing pulled away from the *Ambergris* and slid toward the shore. It was such a strange feeling, for the gray slab did not so much float on the water as drive through it like a solid wedge, unaffected by the swell of waves and tide.

"You look perplexed, Prince," Sire Neen said, "as do you, Neptos. Well you should be. There are a great many things you don't know about the world. Even I am surprised by new things on occasion. How to explain this to you?" Sire Neen searched for the words, clicking his tongue. He ostensibly spoke to the two Acacians, but he pitched his voice loud enough for the amused leaguemen around them to hear.

"Think about the ways that we harness the natural world," he said. "Wind billows against our sails and drives our ships forward. We are familiar with that, but it's no less amazing. We can sit in a cabin while the invisible wind drives us across the globe. A thing we can't see, can't touch—the air itself—can do work that thousands of laborers couldn't accomplish. We can harness the power of flowing water to grind grain or lift loads. We can heat a cold room with fire. Have you never thought how strange that is? Why does wood burn? Why does it make heat? What happens that turns the log into ash? There are so many mysteries, but the league has long pondered such questions. And we have learned some answers.

"But I speak of our own knowledge, not of the Lothan Aklun's magic—which is what powers this vessel. For centuries they told us nothing, gave us nothing, kept all their secrets to themselves." Several of the listening leaguemen grumbled at this. "Recently, though, we had two occasions

212

during which to extract some secrets from them: when we negotiated a contract between them and Hanish, and when we struck new terms between them and your good sister. They gave us a barge like this one. Even as they gave us these things, they withheld the secrets of them. We don't know how to make a vessel like this. It's sorcery, but a very useful sorcery. We will know their secrets soon, of course, since we can now explore their libraries and warehouses and records at will."

Rialus could see that Dariel wished to say something. Sire Neen could, too. He smiled. "I know what you would say, Prince. You'd curse us—the league—as treacherous, devious beasts. And you'd be right! In commerce it's the bold who succeed. The league is bold, and—I'm sure you're starting to see—we have succeeded incredibly. Isn't that right, friends?"

The leaguemen around them agreed. A few of the Ishtat guffawed. Rialus had never seen the company so chipper. It was downright unnerving. He itched to try speaking to Sire Neen again. How to do so, though? What words to catch his interest? He could think of nothing that the leagueman wouldn't squash before he'd even finished his first sentence. He knew more was coming, more news, more revelations, likely more horrors. He did know that Dariel was no longer a person he wished to be too closely associated with. He slid a step away from the prince, as far as he could get before a guard jabbed him.

He set his eyes on the approaching shore—if shore it could be called. There was no sign of actual earth or beach or other natural features. It was a confusion of buildings that together made one continuous barrier several stories high. It was un-decorated, pale hues of tan stone, stained by the sea and by weather, with few windows or anything else to indicate that the inhabitants could look out. It was like the unadorned backs of buildings, like warehouses viewed from a rarely trafficked alleyway.

"Look at those walls," Sire Neen said. "Our spies told of

these, but it was hard to credit them. On one hand they spoke of the Auldek being a military power that no longer fears anyone—neither in the Other Lands nor among the Lothan Aklun—but they swore they built massive walls to hide them from the sea. I think I understand it better now, having listened to the Numrek howls."

"They'd be howling right now," another leagueman added, "if they weren't so ecstatic about seeing Ushen Brae again."

"It may simply be that the Auldek fear the ocean, fear it so much they believe they must hide behind a wall to be safe from it. Isn't that strange?" Sire Neen waited a moment and then turned to Dariel. "All right, Prince, hold your tongue. Keep your eyes open, though. There's going to be plenty to see. But what of you, Rialus? You've barely said a word all day."

Rialus was surprised Neen had noticed. No, he had not spoken for some time. He almost felt his own mouth as stuffed as the prince's, filled with awed questions that bulged his cheeks as much as a mouthful of stones would have. Actually, it was the fact that he had so many questions that kept him quiet. The things his eyes took in, the words he heard bantered about by Sire Neen and the others, the long history of things he had believed to be and had expected always would be and was now being told were no longer all struck him dumb.

Sire Neen waved his fingers toward him, almost flirtatiously. "Say something. Speak. Speak."

"I—I—" Rialus stammered. "I don't know where to begin."

"I'm not surprised. There is nothing harder for a mediocre mind to understand than the fact that the world is ever vulnerable to great change. People like you—and the prince here—believe that the world is. Just is. Some things are. There is an order, you believe, a pattern to things that you never imagine can be changed. You only ever see portions of the way things are. You are like a soldier on a battlefield. You see what is before you. You choose right or left and try desperately to stay alive. That's you, yes? You'll forever be surprised when you

214

realize you have no control over your fate. But the league stands atop a high ridge. We look down and see the entirety of it. With such a view, the world is so much easier to navigate. And to reshape. There are risks, yes. Surprises, surely, but—Look, we've reached our destination!"

The structures that marked the shoreline were but a stone's throw away, the distance narrowing. For a moment, the leagueman's eyes scanned the dock and the heights of bare wall above it. He looked every bit as transfixed by the sight as Rialus felt.

"The league is bold," Sire Neen said, musingly, "and to the bold goes the world, all its riches, all the power. This will be a fine day."

Chapter Eighteen

Dariel kept trying to decide what to do. He kept trying to take control, to act, to assert himself, to say something; but he also kept learning he could do nothing. He could not speak with his mouth stuffed, assert himself with his hands and legs bound, act with the Ishtat guards shouldering him on all sides, or take control while Sire Neen so completely held the reins. He had not felt this powerless since boyhood, since the day his guardian had abandoned him in a broken-down shack in Senival, since that horrible time when everything he knew of the world had been stripped from him. This felt the same.

The barge floated up to a slot in a stone abutment. It slipped into place as if a part of it, like a puzzle piece. Dariel was jostled by the Ishtat, tugged into motion. He tripped on his ankle chains and would have fallen if the guards at his elbow had not held him upright. He tried to spit the bit out of his mouth, to push it with his tongue. He would have yelled for the guards to stop, just pause a moment and let him take in the world. Do him that kindness, at least. Glancing back, he noticed that Calrach and the other Numrek lingered on the barge, staring up at the walls looking stunned.

They were off the barge and trudging toward a gate in the wall. A contingent of others met them, but Dariel was not near enough to make them out in detail. Nor did he have much time to try.

Soon they were all in motion, walking through the gate and

into the city. They marched down wide stone-paved thorough-fares, painted in different shades of green and blue. Stout buildings lined them. They were only two or three stories tall, but they were heavy looking, thick, with rounded contours and painted varying shades of red and orange and maroon. Here and there massive statues stood in the street, forms thirty or so feet in height, in postures of combat, rage, triumph. They were strangely familiar looking, although also totally bizarre. They mixed human and animal forms: a bear's head on a man's body; a standing lizard with two muscled, human arms; a bulbous-eyed frog thing that stood on two legs with its chest inflated; a horned, vaguely feminine form twisted into an acrobatic posture, bent over backward in a sensuous shape trapped in stone.

Dariel was not the only one staring at the statues. Many an Ishtat Inspectorate soldier stared gape mouthed at them. Only the leaguemen managed to seem unimpressed. They walked with their chins raised, faces calm, gestures as languorous as their pace allowed. Occasionally, they spoke to one another in voices meant to be overheard, meant to assure the group that they were in control.

"See this new place with open eyes," Sire Neen advised. "Open eyes but not fearful ones. It takes bold men to act boldly—and to receive the rewards. We come as partners to the Auldek. They will be pleased." Dariel, despite his hatred of the man, found himself hungry to believe him.

Beneath the statues, the streets were as clean swept as any place in the high palace of Acacia, tidier by far than those of other cities like Alecia. And this city—Dariel realized he did not even know its name—was alive with inhabitants engaged in all manner of work. For a time he only partially glimpsed them. There were those tall figures among them, but most were a more normal size, a mixed population like that in any trade-based city. He wanted to see faces, to make eye contact, and to see if he might convey a message to someone, anyone who might help him; but he was surrounded by the Ishtat soldiers and they moved too swiftly.

It was not until they had turned onto a narrower street that he got a true glimpse of this city's residents. His gaze came to rest on a shirtless man's back. He was heavily muscled, bulges that quivered as he heaved sacks into the back of a cart. The first strange thing about him was the uniformly dark gray of his skin. A greater shock came when the man turned to watch the passing strangers. Dariel drew back in horror, momentarily jerking his Ishtat handlers to a halt. The man's face was barely a man's face at all. Instead of eyebrows he had knobby ridges. Long black whiskers ran along his jawline, so stiff and straight they were like metal pins driven into the bone. Worse than that were the golden tusks that protruded from his jaw, just beside the corners of his mouth. They were thick and curved like a boar's. The man betrayed no indication that he considered himself a horror. In fact, his eyes fixed on Dariel's and studied him as if *he* were the oddity.

Perhaps Dariel was, for the next few minutes of stumbling progress through the streets brought one bizarre person after another: a woman whose face, neck, and arms were patterned like a leopard's coat; two boys with jet-black faces and white whiskers jutting from their cheeks; a man whose arms and legs were striped like a zebra's, though his face was that of a normal man, perhaps of Candovian origins. Another man seemed to have a snake coiled around one arm, starting at his palm and wrapping around the forearm, bicep, shoulder, up his neck until the head came to rest on his cheek, its tongue flicking out toward his eye. Dariel was near enough to see that the serpent was an elaborate tattoo. Dariel's eyes shot around to take in others. Again and again, he found more strange patterns and accoutrements. Every human person was tattooed, pierced, or altered. He had seen some odd bodily decorations in his time as a Sea Island brigand, but nothing like this.

They marched through a thronging outdoor food market. The air carried a whirl of scents, sweet mixed with peppery, pungent enough to make his eyes water, with an under-presence of death. Food stuffs both familiar and new crowded the rows of stalls, monkeys hanging beside green-plumed birds, next to fruit he had never seen before and live lizards hung by their tails and writhing. One of the Ishtat overturned a vat of some chunk-filled liquid. The man jumped back from it, retched at what he saw, and hurried to rejoin the procession as one of the leaguemen called him an idiot and a bumbler. Though he tried to, Dariel could not get a glimpse of what the soldier had seen. They moved on too quickly. He was sure of so little and felt himself in a waking nightmare, as if in a dream where he was compelled to specific actions and powerless to change course, to stop, look up, or face the thing that pursued him.

He gasped and fought for breath as the group turned, ascended a stone staircase, and stepped into the great mouth that was a hall opening. They carried on into it, Dariel stumbling even more in the dim interior. When they finally stopped, the prince nearly collapsed. He sucked breaths in through his nose, but seemed to lose the air's effect each time he exhaled. His eyes slowly adjusted to the light, bringing the dimensions of the chamber into perspective. It was a grand rectangular space, high ceilinged, with squares cut into the roof through which shafts of light fell, making a geometric confusion of light and dark. Standing on his toes to peer over the rows of Ishtat around him, Dariel could see a great host in the shadowed areas, hundreds of hulking shapes, all the more menacing because he could not see them clearly. Dark forms, they waited silent and menacing. He blinked furiously to keep the sweat from blurring his vision.

Sire Neen and the other leaguemen stepped forward, following the tall figures toward an illumed square between the two groups. Opposite them, several figures came from the shade into the bright light. They were similar to the Numrek in their size and musculature. They were garbed differently, though, in knee-length leather skirts and sandals with straps that laced up their calves. Most of them wore loose, open-necked shirts that had a look of careful disarray, an effect Dariel had managed in his brigand days.

One of them stepped before the others. He carried a curved long sword, a horror of a blade that Dariel doubted he would even be able to swing properly. A gasp flew through the league contingent. The Ishtat archers behind Sire Neen snapped their free hands back and pinched their arrows, ready to pluck them from their quivers. The Auldek registered them with a flick of his eyes. He took a few more steps. Beyond his loose-limbed strength and size, there was nothing martial in his demeanor. He paused, studied the group a little longer, and then stabbed the sword down into the stone. It was a whip-fast motion, and he had stepped back from it before the archers could even decide if the gesture was a threat. The sword swayed but stayed upright.

Bare chested and powerfully muscled, he planted his hands on his hips, cocked his head, and sniffed the air as he studied the leaguemen. He had long wavy hair like the Numreks', but his was an auburn, gold-flecked shade that Dariel had never seen on them. He seemed in no rush to speak to the new-comers. He turned and said something over his shoulder to the man there. They both laughed, as did several others who heard the comment. The lead man looked back at Sire Neen and said something, a quick barrage of guttural words. To Dariel's surprise—and the Auldek's—Sire Neen responded in kind. He began a steady discourse, punctuated with bows and gestures.

Dariel could not understand a word of it. Spotting Rialus a few guards away, he squirmed toward him. The Ishtat guards barely noticed, intent on the interaction before them. Nudging Rialus with his shoulder, Dariel made sounds low in his throat to get his attention. Rialus looked at him, dazed and seemingly surprised to find him so close. Dariel wrinkled his nose, rolled his eyes about, and gestured toward Sire Neen and the Auldek leader. Rialus seemed to have no idea what Dariel was trying to convey. The prince, seeing this, put his fingers to Rialus's lips, snapped them opened and closed, and then moved them to his own ear.

"Ah," Rialus said, looking back at Sire Neen and the Auldek, "you wish me to translate? It is strangely accented Numrek. Or perhaps Numrek is really Auldek. I don't know. Must I? It's hard enough just making out what they're saying." He exhaled a fatigued breath.

Dariel wished he could smack him.

One of the Ishtat guards grumbled at Rialus's talking, but another shushed him. "Let him speak," he whispered. "Talk, Neptos, just keep it quiet."

Rialus lifted his chin and cocked his head slightly to hear better, but he did not say anything for a while. Dariel jabbed him with an elbow. "Nothing of interest yet," Rialus snapped. "Sire Neen is making formal greetings: that's all. In praise of this and that, honor and the best intentions for mutual enrichment: the usual. The one in the center is called Devoth. The others are Herith, Millwa . . . Oh, I don't know! I can't catch it all. Something about the clan of Snow Lions . . . and antoks."

Rialus went silent for some time, though Sire Neen droned on. Dariel tugged on Rialus's arm. Rialus listened a moment longer and then hurriedly whispered, "Devoth wants to know why Neen is here. Sire Neen says he's come offering them a new arrangement, new opportunities for trade that will benefit them both, and so on."

Devoth turned away from the leagueman and spoke with his companions. Sire Neen folded his hands at his waist and waited, composed. He was a statue compared to the quick, free, and expressive motions of the Auldek representatives. Dariel could see only the back of his egg-shaped head, but he imagined Neen's face was a mask of composure. Where did he get such confidence? Or was it arrogance? It surely helped that there were Ishtat Inspectorate guards and archers just behind him. But so, too, did Devoth have a mass of grumbling shadows behind him. Not to mention the sword still erect in the stones between the two groups.

Devoth turned back. He wiped the back of his hand across his mouth and snapped it outward, as if flicking off moisture. It looked like a ritual gesture, though. Then he fell into a barrage of questions. Rialus picked up immediately this time. " 'Where are the Lothan Aklun?' That's what Devoth asked. 'Where are they? Why are they not here?' He named someone that he wants to speak to. One of the Auldek who led him here started to answer, but Devoth wanted the squashed one to answer. The 'squashed one' is Sire Neen. He's answering . . . Oh, that's rich! Neen says that he is a representative of the greatest power in the Known World—the League of Vessels."

"That's us," one of the Ishtat said, grinning.

"The Lothan Aklun are no more. They are finished, dragged down by their own greed. The league is willing to offer a better trade agreement than the Lothan Aklun ever allowed. I didn't catch what Devoth said to that. He doesn't seem— Oh, Neen's mentioned you. He offers you as a gift. The brother of the so-called queen of Acacia. Those are his words—'so called.' "

Sire Neen turned and pointed toward Dariel. Devoth looked briefly in his direction. Dariel thought the moment might be his chance. He thought of bolting forward through the Ishtat while the attention was on him. Devoth would surely wish to hear from him. He might have the bit removed and then Dariel would turn the tables on Sire Neen and show him for the villain he was. Rialus would speak for him. But in the few seconds it took to think this, the moment passed. Devoth looked away, uninterested, and the leagueman carried on.

"Neen says he understands that the Auldek will have to

learn to trust him, but the league is well known to some from Ushen Brae. He has even brought agents to testify to the league's power and the possibilities for their partnership."

And then, as if on cue, the Numrek arrived. They tramped in, shouting out a chant in their language, a booming percussion of sound like warring drumbeats. Everyone turned to watch them. Even Devoth rose on the balls of his feet, mouth agape as the Numrek approached. They jostled their way through the Ishtat contingent and arrived before Devoth and the other Auldek. They stopped their singing and fell forward, smacking their foreheads on the stones. Devoth and the other Auldek stared at them, their faces stunned, drained of color. The masses behind them edged forward, the front ranks of them stepping into the bright light to see better.

Sire Neen's satisfied voice slithered into the hush, rising above it and, for a few moments, seeming to command the chamber. Before he had gotten far, Calrach snapped to his feet, the others just after him. Calrach glanced at the league-man and silenced Neen with a wave of his hand. Sire Neen sputtered to a halt, clearly surprised. Calrach turned to address Devoth. Rialus murmured a translation, trance-like now, smooth and nearly matched to the speakers themselves.

" 'We who were banished have returned,' " Rialus translated Calrach's voice, which had boomed to reach beyond Devoth into the entire crowd. " 'You may slay me now, if you wish. We give you our souls. If you would hear us, though, we will tell you truths to make you joyful.' "

Devoth considered this for a moment, and then nodded. Sire Neen began to say something, but Calrach spun on him. "Shut your mouth!" he said, speaking Acacian. "Men are speaking. You wait."

Sire Neen stopped.

Speaking in his booming voice, and translated by Rialus's

thin one, Calrach carried on with his address to the Auldek. When they were exiled for their crimes, he said, they followed the banishment as the clans ordered. They did not falter. They did not hesitate. They marched—men, women, children— into the north and out of the realms of the Eight Clans. They wintered in the bitter regions where no plants grow, where white bears hunted them and were hunted by them. They learned to eat seal meat. At times they walked on ice and heard it crack beneath them.

At this claim, a collective gasp went through the Auldek host.

"Yes," Calrach said, "this is all true. We lived years in lands no Numrek was made for, and yet we learned how to live there. We were brave. No one can deny it. We marched north, as you told us to. But we marched so far north that it was no longer north. It became south instead, and we marched down into another land, the land from which the divine children come. We found that place; and we made war there and killed many and took joy in slaughter."

"Why have you returned?" Devoth cut in.

"To give you joy. These fools," Calrach said, waving toward the league contingent, "brought us across the black water. They brought us home, and we came because we can bring you a new world. We can take you there."

"Why should we go there?" another Auldek asked.

"Look, that boy is my son." Dariel could not see the Numrek to whom Calrach pointed, but the effect on the Auldek was considerable. They stepped forward, seemingly awed, many of them talking at once so that Rialus lost the substance of it for a moment. Calrach's voice rose above the din, declaring, "In Acacian lands our women are fertile again. In their lands the curse holds no sway."

Sire Neen chose this moment to pipe up again. Calrach shouted him down furiously and then said, "The leaguemen have killed the Lothan Aklun. Like cowards, they poisoned them all! There cannot be another soul collection. The Aklun are no more."

The grumbling grew. The mass of lanky, long-haired forms crowded forward, many of them yelling angry questions or stamping their feet.

Devoth turned and shouted them down. His voice erupted from his abdomen and shot out with force. Once there was silence, he pointed at Sire Neen. "This one killed the Aklun? I don't believe it, but I don't like him."

"He is an ant." Calrach turned, studied Neen, and then spat at his feet. "He is nothing. Squash him if you wish. His spirit will give you no strength, but if he offends you—" For a moment Rialus stopped translating, but then, as if more afraid of holding the words in than of releasing them, he spoke quickly. "Kill him. We no longer need his kind. Kill him, and we will lead you to a land ready to be reaped. We will have a great hunt."

Devoth did not confirm whether he agreed, but he did draw his sword from the stone. If *draw* was the right word for it. It was as if at one moment his hand was empty and the next it held the massive, curved blade out to his side. Only in the stillness after the action, as Devoth let the onlookers study him, did Dariel's mind register that he had, in fact, watched the entire movement. It was no magic trick. It was just the smoothest, quickest motion he had ever seen. No Marah was that fast. Not even Mena was that quick. No Numrek either.

Sire Neen found his voice again. He dropped his haughty tone and tried a different tack, calming Devoth. Dariel hardly needed the translation now, but Rialus kept at it. "Neen is begging for a moment's patience so that they can communicate fully. They are misunderstanding one another. The Numrek are confusing matters. None of this is as it should be. There have been mistakes made. They should all sit and talk to their mutual benefit."

When Devoth took a step toward him, the leagueman

barked a quick command. The rank of bowmen behind him snapped their weapons up. Devoth paused. Though similar to the Numrek's in so many ways, his face was more expressive, which was why the grin that split it was so disconcerting. Either he did not understand the threat, or he welcomed it. He lifted his blade, held it out to the side, and stepped forward.

A bowman shot. Dariel had seen those arrows up close and knew they were weapons crafted to kill. The steel head of the missile was pronged in a viciously corkscrewed manner, so that the razor-sharp metal would carve a twisting, expanding course inside its target. The single shot fired was perfectly aimed. It slammed into Devoth's chest and buried the shaft to the etching. It must surely have ripped apart his heart and punched right through his back as well. He took the impact standing, but his face contorted in pain. He dropped to one knee and then—as his shouting companions circled him—toppled to his side.

The masses in the shadows roared. The men around Devoth alternately bent to care for him or stood to shout what must have been obscenities at the leaguemen. Sire Neen spoke into the confusion. Ishtat swordsmen closed around him, but he would not let them drag him back. He seemed sure that he could contain this. The archers nocked their arrows, the entire company shifted into combat readiness. Several of the guards near Dariel and Rialus answered commands, ignoring the two prisoners. The Numrek watched it all without comment. Calrach crossed his arms and seemed content to wait.

What happened next sucked what little air Dariel had in his lungs right out of him. It seemed to have the same effect on Sire Neen, who clutched at the guards around him as if he were about to faint.

Devoth rose. He drew great gusts of air into his mouth. His companions helped him gain his feet. Once he had, he roared them away and stood swaying. The Ishtat archers, who had a perfect view of him, let their bows droop. Devoth, before the eyes of all, reached behind him, snapped off the arrowhead protruding from his back, and then tugged the shaft in his chest out with his other hand. He tossed both pieces away.

It was a casual motion, filled with disgust, but immediately afterward he went into convulsions. He managed to stay on his feet, but he shook and jerked and tossed his limbs around. He gibbered, cried, moaned. For a few moments his arms spasmed so frantically that he seemed to Dariel like more than one being, as if there were shadow versions of himself beneath his skin, trying to break free, angry and twisting him with pain as punishment. He seemed so completely driven with anguish that Dariel expected him to drop and die finally from the arrow shot that should have already killed him.

Instead, Devoth came out of the convulsions and moved with the same incredible speed he had shown earlier. Devoth closed the distance to the Ishtat soldiers, swung his mighty sword as if it had no weight to it at all, and cut down the three guards in front of Sire Neen. He dropped to the floor, avoiding the first volley of arrows sent at him; then he spun upward, sweeping his sword diagonally. The blade sliced through Sire Neen's head, starting above the lower jaw and angling up. When the steel cut free, the leagueman's half face twirled in the air above his crumpling body.

Dariel stood as the chamber erupted into chaos. The Ishtat rushed forward. The shadowed masses of Auldek poured into the lighted square, swords drawn. The prince had no idea what to do. His hands were bound. Rialus was no longer beside him. In front of him, the Ishtat and the Auldek fell on one another in a wild confusion of blood and gore.

A hand gripped his shoulder and yanked him around. He thought that it must be an Ishtat soldier or Rialus or a league-man. It was none of these. He spun to see a person with a thin whitish-blue face and a long nose, a woman whose hair sprang from her head like the plumage of some bird. The next instant, someone wrapped an arm around his torso, lifted him off the ground, and began running. It was not the bird person who carried him, however, but rather a gray, muscled bulk of a being.

End of Book One

Book Two

On Love and Dragons

Chapter Nineteen

The Kindred were to meet again at a village west of Danos. Before they did, however, Barad arrived on the Cape of Fallon with King Grae and his brother, Ganet. The trio traveled inland and together explored the region for several days. The area's loamy soil produced bountiful crops of sweet potatoes, carrots, onions, and massive turnips the size of a man's head. Unlike the plantations of northern Talay or the state-run croplands of the Mainland, the region was too rocky to be sectioned off in a grid pattern. The land was irregular, broken by hills and stands of recalcitrant short pines, and not suited to mass labor forces. Instead, small family farmsteads patchworked the area, as they had for centuries. And, as had been the case for centuries, these farmers were forced to pay such a large portion of their crops into the empire's coffers that they little more than subsisted from their labor and their land's bounty.

That was what Barad had wanted the Aushenians to see for themselves. Was it not a crime, he asked as they toured the area on borrowed mules, that these farmers worked their hands into calloused claws? They woke before the sun each morning and labored as long as the orb traversed the sky and sometimes into the night. They were at the mercy of the vagaries of the weather, required to deliver their produce on good and bad years both.

Was it reasonable that after all that labor—over all the years these farming families had worked this land and helped feed the world—that these people's children were rail thin, that their elders died without the care physicians offered the wealthy of Alecia and Manil—not to mention Aos, with its school for training in the healing arts? These farmers shipped away great wagons of foodstuffs, but not one of them grew fat on it. Not one of them acquired any of the luxuries enjoyed by the merchants of Alyth or Bocoum.

Disguised in laborers' rags, the three men pitchforked a wagonload of turnips into a massive storage facility guarded by Acacian soldiers. They added to the mountain of vegetables already collected there. Sitting in the back of the wagon as they jolted away, Barad explained that those stores were for the empire. Such was the way it always had been; such was the way the queen wished it to continue. They walked among the rows of kale and greens, of sugar hearts and blood beets. They saw children thin as waifs, met young men strong about the shoulders, older men slowed with the weight of work, and even older ones stooped by a lifetime of carrying such burdens. As their group rode past the corner of one field, a small girl looked up at them from a muddy trench. Just what she was engaged in was unclear, but it was not play. She was coated in muck, her legs sunk up to the ankles in the stuff, a bucket in one hand and a hooked tool in the other. Barad thought to pause and question her, but changed his mind just before he spoke. She set large, lovely brown eyes on him, framed by a cascade of unkempt curls. She was a small beauty, and he deemed her message one best delivered through her eyes. How would the years treat her? Her eyes asked this silently, so he did not need to speak out loud. He kept the group moving.

None of these sights were unusual to farmhands, but it was not the world most royals ever looked upon. Both Grae and his younger brother took in the scenes with their blue eyes. The younger was nearly a twin of his brother. A little slimmer of build perhaps, but the real difference between them was in his acceptance of deference to his elder. Clearly, the time the two of them spent secluded in the far north of their country—as their older brother and father both died in battle—had made them close. As Grae had said at the last meeting of the Kindred, his brother did seem to share his view of the world.

Throughout it all, Barad studied the young king's face, trying to see the mind behind his words, beneath that handsome visage. He had done this many times in the past few weeks—when he led the Aushenian down into an abandoned Kidnaban mine and asked him to imagine the labor required to dig such a massive wound, as they skirted the wasteland of pig farms along the Tabith Way, even when they toured the slums of Alecia. On first hearing of the latter, the king had asked, "There are slums in Alecia?"

"Aye," Barad had said. "You don't see them from the palaces and government buildings, but they're there, outside what most would think of as the walls of the place. Some of those walls are not a partition that separates inside and out. Some are just barriers between the rich and the poor of the city. You'll never hear the Alecians speak of it. It's like they have one gangrenous hand, but they keep it hidden in a fancy glove, soaked in perfume. You'll see." And the king had seen. Barad made certain of it.

The old slave of the mines knew that one could never be sure when judging another person, but by the end of their weeks of traveling together, he believed Grae had a just heart. The king had never once flinched after seeing what Barad directed him to. He had offered no excuses for the empire, and he had even spoken to several peasants as if they were actual people, something Corinn had never done in her years of rule. There might be true nobility in his blood, something deeper and more full of purpose than the brash young man yet recognized. Barad saw it, though, and it pleased him. The Aushenian would make a fine ally. Used correctly, he could be a tool unlike any he had yet engaged. Ganet seemed just as useful, although in a different way.

On the scheduled meeting day, all the Kindred councillors who could be there gathered in a barn behind a farmhouse on the outskirts of a village. Surrounded by plowed fields, the air around the building was heavy with earth scent. Inside was equally loamy, but stuffy and mildewy as well. Light falling down through spaces in the beams crosshatched the shadows and partially illumed the dark stalls, some of which contained farm animals.

Barad joked that the cattle would overhear them, but in truth he liked the space well enough. The group sat around a wooden table. It was set with a display of fresh vegetables arranged in a colorful pattern, with a pot of stew—mostly tubers—and potato bread. The farmer who owned the place was friendly to their cause. He and his sons carried on with their work outside, and with that cover of normalcy to shield them Barad invited the travelers to eat and talk as friends before getting to business. It wasn't until the conversation eased into a natural lull that he changed the tone.

"What news of the queen?" he eventually asked.

"She lives," Hunt said. His Acacian—with its clipped formality characteristic of the urban residents of Aos— contrasted with the coarse farm laborer's garb he currently wore. He looked almost as out of place in it as King Grae and his brother. "That would be bad enough, but she now charms the people with her good works. The streets of Aos are a-buzz with it. When I sailed from Alyth a troupe of players was acting out her magical deeds. I believe they were paid by the city officials to do it, but, still, people were watching."

"Street performers!" Lady Shenk complained. "They're as fickle as the weather."

"Yes, but they've voiced our message to the people more often than not," Barad said. "Elaz, you were closest to the queen recently. Tell us what you observed."

The former warehouse manager from Nesreh set down his spoon before he spoke. "I did as you asked, Barad. I joined the throng following the queen's caravan. It was a small group at first, sycophants and beggars, but their numbers grew as tales of her deeds spread. She had made her way across northern Talay, and everywhere she went she left miracles in her wake. She made dry wells gush with water."

"Through what trick?" Renold asked. He was a scholar newly defected from the academy at Bocoum.

"I know not. I have seen the water flowing in the Bocoum canals. It's real water. Not a cloud in the sky. The air dry as a desert. And yet she filled them. The landowners were ecstatic. The peasants got drunk on the stuff, jumping and swimming the irrigation canals. I can't explain it, but everything I'm describing I witnessed. If it wasn't the queen's work, I'd think it a great blessing to us all."

"If it wasn't the queen's work, it would be a blessing," Hunt said, "but we know she does nothing without her own purpose. To fatten a pig, a farmer will feed him well. The pig must think his life a paradise, never knowing he gorges himself so that he will be fatter for the knife later on."

"You compare the queen to a pig farmer, then?" Ganet asked.

Hunt shrugged.

"Pig farmer or not," Elaz continued, "she has worked miracles, without a doubt. Children come out to her caravan as it approaches new towns. Even old women with tear-filled eyes call out to her. I've seen this myself. Young girls from the villages threw wildflower petals at her feet. They've taken to calling her 'Mother of Life.'"

"She made the title up herself!" Lady Shenk said. "She's wily, Barad. I'm not sure that you're a match for her after all."

The large man furrowed his brow. "It is not a matter of my being a match for her. It's the will of the people that must best her."

Renold smirked. "All the worse for us. The 'people' are lapping up her gifts. And, in truth, it's no small thing that she can make water flow from a dry well. She works sorcery. Think about that. It can only be that she has discovered Santoth secrets."

"*The Song of Elenet*," Hunt whispered.

The group fell silent. Barad opened his mouth to say something dismissive, but he was unsure of what to say and chose to share the silence. *The Song of Elenet.* Could it be, he wondered for the hundredth time, that such a book exists and that Corinn has it? Throughout most of his life he had considered Santoth lore simply fantasy, stories meant to amuse the masses and feed the Acacians' sense of their past grandeur. But that was before Aliver and the way he dream whispered the masses off mist, before the sorcerers appeared on the fields of Talay to destroy Hanish Mein's army, and before giant beasts began popping up here and there like weeds. Something had changed in the world. There were old powers at work once again, and—if that was true—it might also be true that the queen had found a way to tap into them. That was a dreadful thought, and it was not the only one they had to face.

To change the subject, Barad asked Renold to detail what he had learned about the league's plans. The scholar said that on most things the league was impenetrable and their specific intentions shrouded as if by the mist they once trafficked in. Most who sailed the Gray Slopes believed that the league had burned what remained of their damaged platforms and abandoned the site in exchange for the Outer Isles. League vessels patrolled the archipelago's waters like barracuda seeking prey, boarding any ship that blundered too near, even sinking a few and leaving the crews bobbing in the waters, food for sharks.

It wasn't possible for him to get to the islands, but Renold had found out a few things about their doings through barroom interviews along the Coastal Towns. In Tendor he had spoken to squatters who had been ousted from the islands by Ishtat

Inspectorate officers. Several used spyglasses and had seen league engineers surveying the land; and a few reported having been hired as laborers on compounds of buildings that dotted the island chain. Another man claimed to have shuttled a shipload of wooden dowels and thin boards to Thrain. He had noted the cargo because there were so many of the same objects, with no explanation given as to what they were for. The sailor had speculated that they were to be made into training swords, but Renold had a different idea.

"I realized it when I stopped at my sister's house on my way here," he said. "She has four children, two of them still young enough that they sleep in cribs. The slats that make up the crib's sides are just as the sailor described." Something about this made him uncomfortable enough that his words choked to a halt. The others waited as he took a drink of water, then cleared his throat. He gestured with his hands that he needed a moment to explain. "In the past, the quota was taken regularly from each province. Aushenia avoided this for generations, but I'm sure you've felt the insult of it in recent years." He glanced at Grae, and went to sip again from his wooden cup. It appeared to be empty. "You pay the quota now, just as any other province—"

"Aushenia is not a province," Grae said.

"As you say," Renold demurred. "Regardless, I think a time may come when the league no longer collects quota." Several began to question him, surprised, but he spoke through it. "The isles are to become plantations for the production of one crop: children. That's what they are building. Compounds in which mothers will give birth to children. That's what those dowels are for—for the cribs they will sleep in. Thousands of them."

Hunt said, "As in a factory?"

Renold nodded. "There will be mothers and fathers and children who never know freedom. They will live and die on those islands or in the Other Lands."

"Can this be true?" Elaz asked.

"Monstrous," Hunt said.

"Worse than monstrous," Renold added. "It will look clean to the world. The people won't see it, but it will go on and on."

"They'll see it if we shout about it!" Lady Shenk said.

"Perhaps, but if they cover their ears . . ."

Barad let them argue for a while. Renold had confirmed what he had already expected. It was good that the group hear such things from one another, though. He had always known the league was capable of anything—anything at all—that would ensure their profits. This business on the islands was a logical progression of sorts. Why roam the Known World rounding up children, taking them from parents who then needed to be appeased or quelled? It was inefficient and messy. How much better to control production themselves, to treat the children purely as products, and to do it all far from the sight of the masses? If it proved feasible, the day might indeed come when the queen and the league stopped requiring quota from the provinces. Corinn could declare that she had freed them from the burden, and the Known World wouldn't feel the crime. If that happened, they could shout about it all they wanted. People rarely believe what they cannot see. Not, at least, when seeing is more frightening than not.

"You understand the murky ground we tread on, then," Barad eventually said, cutting in. "If Corinn declares to the masses that she has abolished the quota trade, they will hail her as a savior. She'll put the scholars to work writing new volumes of the Akaran myth. She will tell the people that she has delivered on the Snow King's promises, and the people will eat the lie. They will not believe—or care—unless we could take every one of them to see the place. Obviously, we cannot do that."

Barad let this sit a moment, shifting his eyes from one to another. "That is why time is of such importance. We should announce the uprising before the winter sets in. I proposed we rise at the beginning of the harvest. We spoke of this before. What better time, when the world sees the fruits of a year's labor seized and taxed by Alecia? I mean, we rise at the beginning of this year's harvest, just four months from now. We cannot wait longer, not with the queen spinning magic and the league about to start this slave factory. This is our time. Do any doubt me?"

None seemed to, but Elaz did offer, "There will be many details to see to before then."

"Yes. Yes there will. Let us not fear details. Let us make them our friends instead. For one, there is the issue of the queen and what she is doing. Has she the book of sorcery? If so, what other powers might it give her? And what powers would it rob from her if we took it?"

"Barad, we don't have anyone to answer those questions," Elaz said. "We had an agent within the palace—a maid I had great faith in—but she has gone missing. And we should not forget the blacksmith of the lower town. He was caught outright with an unfortunate document in his hand. He died to keep our secrets. And even they had no real access to the queen. She is not easy to get to, especially not when in spying on her we're always at risk of bumping into the league—who are doing the same with all their considerable resources. At present we are blind—"

Barad interrupted. "What if we send the young king?"

Elaz froze. "Grae?"

The king, who had been considering the selection of carrots before him, snapped to alertness. "Me? You want me to spy on the queen?"

"You are due to visit Acacia, aren't you? Drop in on them now. You would be received as befits your royal status. You can get yourself and your servants into areas of the palace we could not gain. You would arrive with a particular purpose, of course, one that would get you close to the queen."

The young man looked startled for a moment, but then

resumed a calm air. Plucking up a thin carrot, Grae considered it from several angles before he crunched down on the root. He spoke while he chewed. "And what purpose is that?"

He would have us think him calm and collected, Barad mused. He did not fault the young man, but he thought bluntness might crack the façade usefully. As with most things that Barad ever spoke aloud, he had considered what he was about to say carefully. He said, "You arrive on Acacia as a suitor! Flowers in hand, honeyed words on your lips."

Grae spit out the chunk of carrot. "You're joking!"

"It has been a long time since I felt mirth enough to jest." He glanced at Hunt, winked, and looked back at the Aushenian. "I appreciate humor in others—but, no, Grae, I do not joke."

Elaz sucked his teeth, a sure sign his mind was turning over the possibilities rapidly. "There is a movement in the Senate to force the queen to marry," he said. "It's gaining steam, I hear. While she's away making water flow from the dry ground, the talk in Alecia is about who should bed her and how she can be convinced that she needs a man at her side for the benefit of the empire."

Lady Shenk laughed. She slammed the table with one of her large, big-knuckled hands. "For the 'benefit of the empire,' they say? More like for the benefit of some lecher's cock. That's what they're thinking with. It's a mass agitation of ambitious cocks! Believe me, I've seen it before."

"Lady Shenk is not wrong," Renold said, speaking as the scholar he had so recently been, "but the Alecian Senate is not a Senivalian tavern. No, let's not jest too readily about this. Acacian monarchs are bound by the old laws. Among them is the provision that the ruling monarch should be wed. They should endeavor to produce heirs to the throne, as many of them as possible to keep the royal line alive. Corinn has a son, yes, but a single heir is not enough, and Aaden is not the child of a legitimate union.

If the senators push this issue formally, they have a case."

"It's about cock," Lady Shenk repeated. "But you're right about the Senate being no tavern. I'd not let a senator into a tavern of mine. Poor tippers, they are, and always complaining."

Barad placed a hand atop the woman's fleshy arm, to acknowledge her humor while also silencing it. To Grae, he said, "It is rumored that before Hanish's war Corinn—then just a princess—was enamored of your elder brother, Igguldan. Had things been different, they might have married. You might be linked directly to the Akarans already. I know; things are not different. They are what they are, but there is history here to be exploited. I don't just propose this because of Grae's fine jawline and long legs. Those things will help, but what may entice the queen more are the political factors. If I read her correctly, she disdains the Senate. It is a necessary nuisance to her. I doubt that she will wish to marry anyone from that gilded chamber. A union with Aushenia would shut the senators up without giving them any new power. Actually, it would bring her your military might, which would make it even harder for the senators to cause her trouble. I'm sure Corinn will calculate all these things in the time it takes you to bend your knee in greeting. And besides that, the queen is a woman still. She must have womanly needs, just like any other."

"Cock," Lady Shenk said, looking at Grae as if the idea of sending him on this mission no longer seemed quite so absurd.

"Lady Shenk, you have added considerable wisdom to this discourse," Barad said. "Even if the royal cock does not prove sufficiently enticing, Grae will still have the time and resources to uncover whatever secrets he can—including searching for *The Song of Elenet*—if it exists and if Corinn does possess it."

"What if her highness accepts the king's offer?" Lady Shenk asked.

Barad leaned back from the table, inhaling a long breath through his nose. "In that case, friends, we will have to keep a close eye on the young king. The lure of imperial power will be great. Just as the lure of Corinn Akaran's bed will be. I trust, King Grae, that the honor of your ancient line and the righteousness of a free world will shield you against temptations to betray us?"

Grae aimed his blue eyes at Barad and held his gaze a long moment. "If I betray you, it will only be in that I cut the bitch's throat before I deliver her. On all else, though, you may be sure that nothing can tempt me. I carry a hope that generations have been denied. It is bigger than you and bigger than I. I will be true to it."

To this, Barad nodded, a gesture of finality that he would let stand for words. What he did not say was that he would arrange to ensure Grae's loyalty by keeping Ganet close at hand. He would teach the prince things, mentor him, complete his knowledge of the Known World. Or so he would explain it. In truth, the young prince would be insurance. He would be safe and prospering as long as Grae stayed true. If the king somehow fell under Corinn's power, however . . . well, they would face that if they had to.

Chapter Twenty

The morning Corinn was scheduled to meet with the Queen's Council—just a few days since returning from her well-filling tour of Talay—she walked out into the sun of the upper gardens, Rhrenna at her side. Though the day was warm, she wore a long-sleeved dress of Teheen cotton, elaborately embroidered with overlapping animal figures that cavorted across her chest and back. She wore her hair in a tight bun, pierced by decorative combs that looked vaguely martial, as if she could pull them out and toss them as daggers if she grew angry.

She found Aaden swimming in the maze of canals and pools that cut through the gardens. His friend was with him. Devlyn was his name, the one Aaden seemed so fond of. It was unlikely that the pools had been intended for swimming, but Corinn had swum in them when she was young. It warmed her to see Aaden's legs and arms sweeping out in the glass-clear water. He and Devlyn dove among gold, silver, and crimson fish, some as large as a man's arm but all of them harmless. Up until this moment, she was still haunted by her nightly torment. She now banished the memory of the dream. It was a foolishness anyway. Aliver and Hanish were dead; Aaden was alive, and hers, and would be forever.

"Mother!" Aaden called, suddenly discovering he was being watched. He treaded water, losing his rhythm for a moment so that his mouth dipped below the surface. Up an instant later, he spat, then spoke. "Mother, Devlyn saw a hookfish in the pools. As long as a man, he said!"

Corinn stepped to the raised lip of the pool. She gestured for the boys to swim to the edge nearest her. "A hookfish, you say?" Aaden nodded. Devlyn did not, but he swam with a motion somehow more graceful than the prince's. "What's a hookfish?"

"You don't know?" Aaden asked, though he seemed quite pleased to hear it. "It's one of those long, scaly things with barbs down their tails. Like hooks but sharp as Marah swords."

The queen could not help but bend and wipe the light strands of hair back from the panting boy's forehead. Though the very notion of such a fish swimming below her son's feet stirred a flash of unease through her, she knew it was nonsense. The pools had been safe since the sixth king built them for his wife generations ago. Why do boys always wish for monsters? she wondered. Out loud, she said, "Really?"

"Yes! And they have teeth sharp enough to cut to the bone! If they bite you, they don't let go, even if they're taken out of the water. Right, Devlyn?"

The other boy did not immediately meet the queen's gaze. Speaking to the stone rim just in front of him, he said, "Yes. They have green eyes."

"You saw the color of its eyes? That's alarming. Why, then, are you still in the water?"

"To hunt it," Devlyn answered.

Aaden nodded, but Corinn kept her eyes on the other boy. He was handsome enough in his way, with dark eyes and curls of brown hair that glistened with moisture. He would be stunning in a few years, a notion that did not sit altogether comfortably with her. Would he, in olive-skinned beauty, outshine Aaden? "And I suppose you plan to slay the beast yourself?" she asked.

To her surprise, the boy did not miss a beat in responding. "No," he said, his eyes darting up to hers for just a moment, "Aaden will. I'm his second."

Ah, so you do know your place? "And as a second, what do you do for Aaden?"

"Whatever he needs me to. Anything. I have to keep him safe."

"I'll be the king, Mother," Aaden said, sounding older, a bit weary, for a moment. "He knows that. He knows to protect me. That's why—"

Aaden stopped himself, but not before Corinn knew what he had almost said. He had nearly mentioned his wish that Devlyn become his chancellor again. He had stopped, knowing that she would not welcome the conversation in front of the boy. That was wise, although it was obvious from the way both boys' faces went momentarily blank that they had discussed the matter between themselves. That was not as wise.

Or perhaps it was . . . perhaps a prince needed to secure his companions when he was young. Perhaps Aaden would be better off than she, with the pack of ambitious fools she had to contend with. So thinking, she was reminded of the day's meeting. She bade the boys safe hunting and left them again enlivened and shouting excitement to each other.

The Queen's Council was just one of the many panels of advisers she consulted. Unlike the others—who humbly brought her hard facts on the various subjects important to her rule—the members of the Queen's Council tended to inflate their own import. She had accepted that she needed them, but she did not trust them. If they had not been necessary in order to keep up the appearance that she honored traditions, she would have dismissed them and bought advice, entirely with coin, from agents of her choosing.

Early in her rule she had selected some of the ten councillors herself in an effort to create a truly guiding body. She had handpicked Jason, her former tutor. It had not taken her long, however, to realize that most of her choices were just as self-interested as those thrust upon her by tradition. She had stopped trying to make them friends long ago. With the

Council members, her guard was up and senses as alert as they would have been at a meeting of declared enemies. None of this, however, showed on the surface.

"Good councillors," she declared as she entered the chamber that had once been her father's, "do me the service of your knowledge that I may govern with wisdom." It was one of the traditional greetings. She said it with every appearance of sincerity.

As she seated herself, the councillors answered her just as warmly. They could not say enough about the great things they had heard about her trip to Talay. "A triumph!" Sigh Saden declared in his nasally, aristocratic Acacian.

"A voyage of miracles!" Balneaves of the Sharratt family pronounced. In his subdued way, even Sire Dagon seemed impressed. He should be, Corinn thought, impressed and enriched because of it, and more than a little discomfited, too. On the surface they were all praise; beneath, they had to be wondering how she had managed these miracles. They must be stewing over what other powers she might have, a reaction she had intended all along.

Deciding to let them worry a little longer, she indicated that Rhrenna could call the meeting to order.

She did so by invoking the first five Akaran kings, calling on their spirits to infuse the gathering with wisdom. After that grandiose opening, Rhrenna directed their conversation to mundane matters, as Corinn had instructed. Records and accounts, mining production estimates, and even an assessment of the Vumu Archipelago's potential as a source of timber: on such things they passed a long, boring hour.

Turning to military matters, General Andeson, the commander of the Acacian army, admitted that there had been a drop in the overall troop numbers but said it was for the best. He put forth the opinion that the military would better serve as a slightly smaller force than by recruiting less worthy new soldiers. Without a foe to fight, he said, it was dangerous to have too many armed men and women milling about.

"What about security?" asked Talinbeck, a bone-thin engineer with bushy, recalcitrant eyebrows. "My managers swear there's something afoot among the workers—nothing they can put their finger on, but something."

Andeson rubbed his thumb over his close-cropped black beard. "Show me a foe and I'll act, but I can't defend against something nobody can put a finger on."

"I've heard rumors of discontent before," Corinn said. "Are there signs that the dissenters are organizing?"

"No, Your Majesty," Balneaves said. "It's just the low-level grumbling of the masses. That's nothing new. When the mist flowed freely, it was nothing but a murmur. It's still little more than that, but the commoners want to be sedated! That's why they drink. That's why they smoke whatever leaves will blur the world for them. That's why they fornicate and breed and brawl drunkenly in taverns." He could barely keep the scorn off his jowly face. "I say get that new wine to them sooner rather than later. We'll all be happier for it."

Sire Dagon cleared his throat, puckered his lips, and held the room a moment. "The league is ready to distribute when you are, Your Majesty."

Corinn knew they all wanted the empire sloshing in the stuff. Such a course was likely for the best and would commence soon. She told herself that she wasn't delaying. She just needed to know the time was right. "I know," she answered. "And in my time I will allow it."

Baddel, the only Talayan on the Council, went into raptures again. "Your trip was such a success," he said, "that I wonder if you plan another. Talay is big enough. You touched the coastal area, but in the interior—" He stopped, pursing his full lips as if he had not considered that before. His machinations were obvious, but Corinn almost liked him despite it. "Vast, dry mile upon mile. Another hundred wells between Umae and Halaly would do such good. Think what it would mean for the Halaly to have their lake back at full level!"

"By now Mena must have rid the Halaly of the beast in the lake," Rhrenna said.

"I truly hope so," Saden said. "It will refill as it always has. I was wondering about a different matter. The Eilavan Woodlands were sorely taxed by the harvest of timber. First-rate lumber, of course, and invaluable to a nation that needed to rebuild after war. The demand remains high, and the replanting efforts have barely begun. Might you—oh, I don't know—make the trees grow back faster?"

Inwardly, Corinn rolled her eyes. Outwardly, she just looked at him. When had one of these fools ever proposed anything not meant to benefit himself?

Rhrenna spoke for her. "I wonder, Senator Saden, if you are here as the Senate's representative, or as your own? Don't you own an interest in the woodlands' harvest? Your family, if I'm not mistaken, have been harvesting there for a hundred years or more."

"We are one of the many families, yes, but—"

"So you've had more than enough time to learn to manage it properly. The queen does not act to fulfill the personal interests of the few." Rhrenna glanced at Corinn. "Shall we move on to other topics?"

"Forgive us," Talinbeck said. "We just don't know what you're capable of. We don't know how you do the things you do. If you explain it to us, we'll know and—"

Corinn did not like the engineer's earnest tone. The last thing she wanted was for them to start being honest with her now. "Yes, let's move on." She waited a moment. "Are there other topics?" She knew that there was one topic they would likely raise before she dismissed them, but as the silence continued she almost believed she would get away with ending the meeting without facing it.

But then Julian, the Council's most senior member, cleared his throat and motioned that he would speak. He was the only one of the group who had been a member of Leodan's Council. Quite notoriously, he was on record as having doubted that Thasren Mein's attack on King Leodan had really meant Hanish was launching a war. He had been wrong about that, but he had been right in managing to stay alive long enough to see another Akaran rise to rule. It was for that connection with the past that he was a part of the Council.

"I hope you don't mind my mentioning it, Your Majesty," Julian said, his voice tremulous. "I know it's a delicate matter and wholly up to you to consider, but I would be remiss . . . if I didn't bring up the topic of your betrothal. The topic is discussed openly on Alecia. Openly, in truth. Some have even written asking me to speak with you about it."

Yes, Corinn thought, tap old gray-haired Julian for your dirty work, as if I can surely find nothing lascivious in the urgings of such a revered elder. "And what did they bid you say?" she asked, tenting her hands on the granite table and creasing her brow in feigned interest.

Julian blinked. For a moment he looked as if he had forgotten, but then it came back, and he spoke as if surely he had described it all to her before—as, indeed, he had. "Why, they wish you to wed, of course! They've even commissioned a team of scholars to look into the lineages of all the eligible Agnates. There's quite a list, I assure you. Should you be interested, I could have it for you—"

Corinn interrupted. "Is that a list of true Agnates, or does it include the new families?"

"New or old, it makes no difference," Saden answered. "The recent Agnate appointments stand as solidly as the old. All the same now, as it has to be."

"Does that strike you as true, Jason?"

Her former tutor started in his seat. He had not said a word yet other than reading one of the earlier accounting reports, and would probably have been content with that. Whatever things he had seen during his years of hiding during Hanish's rule had crippled him. Creases carved his face and white strands outnumbered the brown in his hair, though he was just past forty. Sometimes, feeling his eyes studying her when she was not looking at him, Corinn felt he viewed her with a certain amount of uneasy astonishment. Perhaps he remembered the shallow girl she had been and could not recognize the person she was now. She rather liked that.

Jason answered, "I don't doubt that the old Agnates will forever remember that they are, in fact, more ancient lines; but in point of fact in the law Senator Saden is correct." His fingers trembled when he gestured with them. "Your list of possible suitors—should you choose to consider it—is larger this way. Easier to find a suitable match, one that none would contest."

"I see." Corinn pressed her lips together as if giving the idea renewed thought. "What I don't see, however, is why I should marry anyone. Do any of you think me incapable of rule? Or is it that you wish to challenge my son's right to the throne? You think him a bastard, perhaps?"

A cacophony of denials. Voices raised in complaint, so ardent that Corinn shared a look with Rhrenna, a look of amusement, although other eyes would not have known it as such. The councilmen's response was answer enough to things she had already believed, so she would go no further with it. There were many reasons men wished to wed her. None of them were advantageous to her. But the issue of Aaden was a concern like no other. If she did marry and had another child by one of these Agnates, and if her husband called himself king and appealed to his class to elevate his own child above a bastard fathered by their hated enemy, well, that was a fight she did not wish to have. Better that she have no other children. Better that her rule stay strong, and that the people come to love Aaden.

Once he reached seventeen, she could step aside and see him crowned king. After that, none would challenge him. A ruling queen always had the option to step aside for a mature son. Corinn had studied the secession laws in detail, and likely knew them better than any senator. She doubted any of them could imagine her to be planning this, but planning it she was. They would be waiting for her death to move against him. She would act before that, though.

The councillors were still squawking when she decided to change the subject once more. Cutting in to the conversation, she said, "I will not discuss this anymore today. If I choose to wed, you'll hear about it promptly, but my marital situation is not to be decided at Council." Several of the councillors looked ready to take exception to that, but she spoke over them. "Here is a thing I wish to speak of: we will bring horse culture back to the center of the empire."

The room fell silent.

Sire Dagon plucked his pipe from the corner of his lips. "Horse culture?"

"Exactly."

"And what horse culture would that be, Your Majesty?"

"Surely, all in this room know of Acacia's ancient traditions of equine excellence. I've been giving it a deal of thought, consulting with knowledgeable individuals, and I've concluded that we should bring the noble practice back into the mainstream of Acacian culture."

The truth was somewhat simpler than that. Aaden had given her the idea while they were riding in Talay. He had observed, quite casually, "One is taller on horseback. I like being taller." Watching him ride away, upright and easy in the saddle, reins held correctly as he had been taught, Corinn had been struck with inspiration. Her people, she decided, had once been horsemen—in some distant past, in the time of the early kings, perhaps. Wasn't Tinhadin famous for his love of his gray mare? Yes, certainly he was. Hadn't Valeeden once had to ride full out from Calfa Ven to Alyth, stopping only long enough to leap upon fresh horses offered by the peasants?

She was vague on the details of these things, but she had not found details very important in convincing people of things they wanted to believe. Acacians had once been horsemen, she decided; they would be so again. One was taller sitting on horseback, just as the future king had said. Let the people feel taller.

"Jason," Corinn said, "tell the Council about our horse culture."

The scholar started again. He set a somewhat pleading look upon her, but when she returned it with an expectant smile, he found words. "Tinhadin was a horseman, it's true. And Edifus kept a great stable of stallions in the Pelos valley. Some here will have practiced the Eighth Form, in which horses play a part. The Akaran royals have always ridden—"

Saden cut in, noticeably annoyed with the change of subject. "The royal family riding does not make for a horse culture. You know that, I'm sure. You know that the reason few people in the empire ride is that the royal family didn't want them to. Simple as that. Your ancestors forbade horses to Talayans outright." He nodded at Baddel, who did not acknowledge the gesture. "Thought riding would cripple them. Turns out it did nothing of the sort. They can run as far and as fast as any horse, farther over a span of days. At least, that's what I've heard. Tinhadin tried to take them from the Mein, but never managed it."

"As I understand it," General Andeson said, "there are laws in the books expressly forbidding commoners to ride. Horses may pull carts or carry packs, yes, but only the military—and the nobles, of course—can ride."

Corinn said, with a tone that suggested she would have said the same thing regardless of what they had said in between, "The past is behind us, and now I look to the future. I don't want my people to always walk the earth like peasants. Not all of them, at least. I believe we'll be stronger if more people know horses. Jason, develop a lore for the horse as well, something to feed the people. Elaborate on what you know and put it in writing. Understand?"

The tutor started to sweep his hand to his chest, knocked his tumbler, caught it, and righted it dexterously. "Your Majesty, develop a—"

"Lore. Develop legends. Heroes on horseback and such things. Seek out some of the old tales in the library. Find stories that include horses. If you can't find them, insert the horses. Plant the seeds. Add another layer to the lore and let it be spoken of in taverns and halls and told to children at night, that sort of thing. Get the people dreaming horses."

Balneaves smiled crookedly. "Noble work, Jason. Go to it with gusto."

"I am glad you think so." Corinn rounded on him. "I have a part in this for you, too." Indeed, she had a part in it for almost everyone here. To different individuals she assigned responsibility for acquiring breeding stock, finding good pasturelands, hiring trainers, contracting architects and builders and blacksmiths. The list of needs was extensive. Corinn spoke with enthusiastic seriousness. Rhrenna duly wrote it all down. The councilmen looked about as if each was hoping another would call the whole thing a joke. But none did, and at the end of the session Baddel walked out mumbling, "As the queen wishes. The stallions shall stud. The mares shall birth. And the people shall ride."

And the councillors shall scurry about like worker ants, she answered, although only within the safe confines of her head.

Later that afternoon, she had one more meeting. This one took place in the privacy of the lower wing of her offices, on an open balcony that looked out over the sea. It was a small space, cut into the rock and hidden from prying eyes from above. She chose it because the man she was to meet could ascend an outer stone staircase unnoticed. It was that type of meeting. Clandestine. It was possible it was even dangerous, but she did not believe so.

Delivegu Lemardine, her agent, was faithful in his own way—faithful to the coin she paid him and to the knowledge that his service might fund a life of whatever vices he enjoyed. He had once aided Rialus in his covert designs, and Rialus had introduced him to her. She did not trust Delivegu, but that was not unusual; she did not trust anybody. Unlike most people, Delivegu had proved useful on more than one occasion.

Senivalians were not known for walking quietly, but in that Delivegu differed from his countrymen. He was up the stairs and but a few feet from Corinn before she knew it. He was dressed showily, as ever, in an open-necked shirt with a brigandlike flare in the sleeves tucked into his snug-fitting trousers; his knee-high black leather boots were laced to shape around his calves. Though he was padded around the belly with a few extra pounds, never had a man looked more comfortable with his body. Indeed, he luxuriated in his size and in what appeared to be natural strength. His face was composed of an unsettling combination of blocky, masculine features and feminine touches, as in the petite pucker of his lips. He was, in his own way, frustratingly attractive.

"Your Majesty," he said, bowing, "I am your servant in everything. In absolutely everything." He held the position a moment, and then rose. "If I may say, you are a vision of—"

"I don't have time for flattery," she snapped. She cupped her hand around a stone resting on the balcony. "Tell me, and then go."

Delivegu smiled. He always smiled. He seemed to find the world and everything in it amusing—insults as much as praise. "The blacksmith was strong. I'll give him that much. Not just in his arms, though those were formidable. For a moment when I first confronted him I thought he might have me. Ever thought you were about to be skewered on a red-hot sword pulled from the flames? Not a pretty—"

"To the point, Delivegu. To the point."

"Yes, well, I lived, as you can see. And I beat the brute to within an inch of his life and then questioned him."

"By what method?"

Delivegu cocked his head, demure, but when she pressed him he detailed his procedure readily enough. The initial beating had been coarse, and for the questioning he chose methods meant to coerce the mind as much as the body. He started by asking his questions gently. Why, he had asked, was the blacksmith's name in a note shot out of the sky by a Marah on night patrol? The man had watched a messenger bird dispatched from the lower town, and rightly guessed it carried some covert correspondence. When the missive was detached from the bird's leg, only one word could be made out on it: his name. The rest of it was coded gibberish.

The blacksmith had shut his lips and focused his loathing through his eyes, refusing to answer.

"He didn't care for me much," Delivegu said, combing his fingers through his black hair.

A monkey came loping up the steps and seemed startled to find them there. It chirruped a greeting and sauntered past them, looking much like a noble out for an evening stroll. It stopped some paces beyond them and stood intently scratching its rump.

The means of coercion had to be improved upon. He had flattened the man's hands in a vise and had driven nails through the finger bones. He had dunked his head in a bucket of water until he passed out, revived him, and did it over and over again. He had stripped the man's brawny body naked and, using a candle, burned the hairs from his body, dripping hot wax on him the entire time. "That was amusing," Delivegu said, "but not effective. Nothing was. I even put a weight on his manhood and promised to make a little cut if he didn't speak true."

Corinn betrayed no discomfort. "And?"

"And . . . begging your royal pardon, but he still didn't speak. I kept my promise and that was that. He died not long after. Who wouldn't? Without a prick the world's a miserable place." He paused a moment, glancing at Corinn.

She was not sure if the amusement in his eyes was from speaking to her with such lurid candor, or if it was his own recognition that she, being a woman, was just as prickless as the blacksmith.

"If he'd had a family, I could have used them, but he was a single man, friends to many but none who seemed right for that purpose—"

"So you learned nothing," Corinn said.

"I wouldn't say I learned nothing. In fact, I did learn something, something quite important."

Corinn rounded on him as if she might hurl a stone at him. "Tell me, then, before I get angry." She had a notion that she could sing something vile, something to undo him right here if she wanted to. He seemed to feel that possibility as well.

Delivegu bowed his head, backed away a step, and took the pleasure out of his voice. "At the beginning he denied any knowledge of any conspiracy. By the end, though, he did not deny that there was a conspiracy, he just refused to tell me anything about it. Indeed, he took his pleasure from spitting his refusal in my face. What I mean, Your Majesty, is that he proved there is some conspiracy afoot. You are not wrong to suspect as much. Quite the contrary."

In annoyance, she flicked her wrist and sent the stone twirling toward the monkey, which had sat down as if it were sharing their conversation. The creature jumped nimbly away, screeching as it did so, contorting its face into an expression very much like human effrontery. It grunted and bared its teeth, but it also withdrew even farther when Corinn bent for another stone. Delivegu watched it all with amusement.

Corinn glared at him. "This is foul news. Why do you take such pleasure in delivering it to me?"

"I take no pleasure in the news itself. If I am enthusiastic about it, it is because I have helped shed light on the presence of rats in the basement. Oh, and I got the bastard's name." He said the last bit as an afterthought but could barely hide his pleasure with himself.

"What name?"

"The blacksmith didn't give it up intentionally. He let it slip once, when he was babbling to himself. Ever heard of Barad the Lesser? He used to foment trouble in Kidnaban. It seems he's expanded his ambitions."

Delivegu grinned again, wider this time. "First the name and then the man. Tell me the truth: I do good work for you, don't I? May that always be true."

Corinn did not have to respond to this. Rhrenna—the only other person who knew whom she met here on the balcony— descended the staircase, one hand lifting her dress so that she could move faster, the other holding a rolled parchment. She glanced at Delivegu for just an instant and then focused on the queen. "A message," she said. "It's about Mena."

Chapter Twenty-one

Mena awoke with a hot hand grasping her skull, searing her where it squeezed. She was on her side, and when she tried to swat the thing she realized through a rush of pain that her left forearm was broken. In the dim light of the predawn hour she stared at the strange droop of the limb, bent where it should have been straight, limp where it should have been firm. It was most definitely broken. Realizing that, she also knew that no physical being held her. It was just the pain from bashing her head on stones in the hillside. The burning on her thigh was from an impact abrasion. The soreness in her shoulder was from when she had dislocated it. She remembered the complete agony of it and the sweetness of relief when the tumbling motion of her fall had reset it. The rawness in her throat was from sleeping in the jumbled position in which she landed, with her mouth open to the dry rasp of a Talayan breeze. She knew a lot of things, but they were so cluttered in her head that she could not grasp the entirety of it.

Instead, she focused on a small thing. The little finger of her left hand had snapped at the base and canted off to the side in defiance of its siblings. It was red and swollen and did not really seem to belong with the others. It was a minor injury in some ways, but the unnatural shape of it captured all Mena's attention, forced her to focus through the pounding bands squeezing her skull. Slowly, she reached out and took the

258

finger in the palm of her other hand. She held it a long moment, awed at how fat it felt. Then she twisted it back into position. As it popped into place she exhaled a jagged curse—not so much at the finger as at the searing splinters of pain that shot up her forearm and into her shoulder and throughout her entire body.

She lay on her back, breathing, holding still so that the pain might forget her and slip away. The gray sky above her was scalloped with high clouds tinted pink by the rising sun. They looked soft. They reminded her of something. As she tried to think what, a few moments passed, and then she raised herself awkwardly. Things to do. She had things to do. Despite and because of her pain, she had things to do.

Over the next hour, Mena limped about, gathering the supplies she would need to splint her arm. There were no trees nearby, and she did not yet want to raise her eyes and look beyond her immediate surroundings. Instead, she found several slim lengths of stone, along with ribbons of mossy turf that she sliced one-handed with her short sword. She was not far from a small stream. Its gentle gurgle called to her, and she hobbled toward it, cringing at the thirsty convulsions of her parched throat.

She stood beside the stream for a longer moment than she wished, unsure whether to drink from it or tend her arm first. Eventually, she did both. She unbuckled her sword belt, let it drop, and contorted her way out of her clothing. She stepped into one of the deeper pools wearing only her eel pendant, the one she had found gripped in a child's withered hand at the base of Maeben's aerie. The water bit her with cold, but that was good. She would be wet all over, but that was good, too, good to wash the filth and sweat and blood from her body. Letting her broken arm float, she scooped fingerfuls of water into her mouth with her right hand. She did so slowly, pausing to breathe between swallows, not rushing.

When she was as numb as she could bear, she crawled from

the stream and—still naked and grateful for the touch of the morning sun—tended her arm. The flesh was not broken, but she could see the misshapen bone beneath her skin, which was bruised in blooms of ugly blue and green and red and yellow. Laying the limb on the ground, she worked around it, a one-armed being caring for a separate entity to which she was bound. She positioned the moss as padding, and lined the stones around it to make a splint. She used a length of string from her waist to bind it tight, a slow, slow process that left her fingers aching, hard as it was to tie with only one hand. She pulled on her left hand as she pressed the splint down with her chin, an attempt at straightening the bone, and then tightened the strings again.

By the time she was finished—dressed again, with the arm in a sling fashioned from the long ribbon of fabric that had been her belt—the sun was high and strong, and she was sweating from her efforts. Was the bone set straight? She could not be sure, but it was the best she could do. She might have looked to her small injuries as well, but that would just be avoidance of the more important thing. She knew these actions were small details, delays before she faced what she had to face. Her body would be bruised and battered for some time, but with the arm splinted she had no reason not to raise her eyes and look for it—for the foulthing.

Climbing up to a ridgeline and trudging along it toward a higher vantage, Mena took in the country around her. It was a temperate landscape of sharp, grass-covered hills. The soil was shallow, and the rocky frames of the slopes protruded here and there. She could not be sure, but she thought they had flown west, into the hills of northern Talay, perhaps not far from Nesreh and the western coast. She remembered glimpsing the sea on the distant horizon. That was before the beast—and she with it—had crashed to the earth in fatigue.

What a strange flight that had been. It had gripped her, hadn't it? Or had she gripped it? Had it wanted her with it, or had she wanted to be with it? She was not sure. She would have thought it a dream if the world around her were not so real and the pains in her body were not so acute. She remembered the moment it yanked her into the air, the way the earth fell away, as if she and the beast were motionless, but everything and everyone below them had suddenly dropped. At least, that's one way she remembered it.

On the other hand, she remembered the incredible, ear-battering sound of it. She had clawed up the tail like it was a rope. Up and before her, the foulthing flew. The beast itself had been silent, but everything else was a confusion of noise and wind, of flapping wings and erratic flight. The swinging weights smashed into her several times before she got her short sword free and managed to cut several of the ropes. This made it easier for the foulthing, she knew, but any one of those stones could have brained her. Besides, the creature did not truly seem to have much life in it. Each wingbeat was a display of power, but between them came long moments in which the wings seemed on the verge of dropping. She clung to the flying creature, sure that they would come crashing down any second, near enough that her troops would never lose sight of her.

The creature was more resilient than she knew, however. The undulating hills of Talay passed far below her, scrolling beneath them as they flew and flew on. Acacia trees became tiny blooms, rivers like lines on a map, her view that of an eagle looking down on a world laid out beneath it. She was not sure how much time passed like that. Hours, perhaps. A few times she believed it was Maeben above her. She thought she heard that great goddess's angry screech. It didn't make sense, not unless she had fallen into a dream. But how could she have done that when she was clinging for her life? Unless the beast really was holding on to her.

The last moments of the flight had brought them into this high country. She thought they were getting lower, but in fact

261

the plateau and the hills upon it rose to meet them. She saw what she took to be the gray bulk of the sea in the distance, and then focused on the hills, the rocks, the pinnacles that grew closer and closer. The creature, it seemed, did not have the strength to rise higher. Its flight grew even more erratic, frantic one moment and slow the next, making them rise and fall. She thought she was going to smash into one rock face, only to be saved when the beast surged above it. Passing over it, Mena touched her feet to the stone in a quick scamper across its surface. She loosened her hand, considering letting go of the tail. Before she did she was airborne again.

The beast had dipped into the next ravine, and as it rose to fight its way over the coming slope, Mena felt her hand slide. Of course she could not hold on forever. Perhaps the beast was letting go of her. The sleek muscles of the tail grew limp in her hand. This time, as the creature just managed to clear the knuckle of rock that topped the ridge, Mena touched her feet to the vertical wall of stone but did not have the strength to hold on. The tail slipped from her grip. For a moment she was held there, her two feet on the stone, her body horizontal to the world, suspended in brief defiance of the earth's pull. Her last sight of the foulthing was from beneath it, as its shadow skimmed across the outcrop of stones and vanished, its tail snapping as it disappeared. She heard Maeben's shrill cry again, and then the earth remembered her. It pulled on her and all was the painful battering of her tumbling fall down the slope. Had she not been so exhausted—her body as limp as a doll's—she might not have survived it.

As she took the last steps up to the summit, a thought rose in her. Perhaps she had been the one crying out, Maeben's fury leaping from her mouth. She did not consider this long, however. She crested the peak and took in a panorama of similar hills stretching out all around her, until her eyes tilted downward and found it. It was there, where she suspected it would be. The beast lay sprawled in the next ravine, its wings flung wide and stained bloody from the many bolt piercings and tears, its body twisted and its tail in looping disarray, tangled among the ropes and weights still knotted around it. It looked broken, dead. Mena felt a knot draw tight in her abdomen. She started down toward it, approaching slowly, trying not to kick stones loose.

As she neared it, she drew her long sword. She wasn't truly afraid; the action was instinctive. In truth, the creature seemed much smaller than she remembered. It was less bulky when contrasted to some of the foulthings she had fought, but it was not a creature whose strength should be measured by its bulk. With its lithe torso and the slim, extended proportions of its tail and the confusion of finger-thin bones and membranes that were its wings, it was hard for her to compare it to anything she had seen before. Such an awkward position it lay in, bent around the stones. Its head was upside down, the soft part of its neck exposed. There was so much to it. It hurt Mena just looking at the wounds, the tears, the places where blood had smeared or pooled. The last of the foulthings. Dead.

"They told me you were a dragon," she said, "but you're no dragon. You're a foulthing . . . but you're not. I'm not sure what you are, but you're no monster."

She had spoken softly, without realizing she was doing so. In the silence afterward she looked around, embarrassed lest she was heard talking to a dead beast. But there was nobody around, not for miles. She thought, for the first time, of Melio and the soldiers who would be frantically searching for her. She knew she should do something to help them: walk back toward the east perhaps, find a settlement or build a signal fire somehow. But looking at the lizard bird, she did not want to. They would find her no matter what she did. She had that faith in them.

Instead, she let her eyes drift over every inch of the creature. It must have been female, she thought. The curves of her neck were sensual, dramatic in her death posture. Mena stepped close and ran her fingers over her. She was soft to the touch, warmed by the heat of the sun. Her coat was close to the skin, something like feathered scales, hued in soft, creamy tones. There was a pattern woven across them, an intricate inter-lacing that Mena could not get her eyes to fully focus on. It seemed to change even as she studied it.

"My sister would have envied this coat," she said. Thinking that, she was saddened that she was the one who would deliver it to her.

Corinn would not have envied the damage done to the creature, though. Each wound turned Mena's stomach. She couldn't stand the sight of them, and suddenly she couldn't stand the thought that the others would see the creature like this, her beauty so fouled by the weapons that Mena herself had called into play. Without really deciding to, Mena began to do what she could to hide the damage. She pulled free the crossbow bolts and flung them away. She untangled the ropes and dragged the stone weights down the ravine. She cradled the creature's tail and let it flow out to its full length.

In particular, she worked to gently arrange the wondrous wings. She remembered them as they had been when they first unfurled, so shocking, amazing in their breadth and their deceptively delicate power. It was hard to twin those images with the ragged things she worked to sort out. The bones that framed the wings hardly seemed capable of what she had witnessed. They were as limp as a thousand broken finger bones slipped inside a thin tube of skin. Mena could pick the wings up and arrange them like tattered sheets. The mem-brane of the wings was just as diaphanous as it appeared, leathery and supple both. It had an oily resin on it. The stuff felt funny on her fingers. It tingled, seemed to course through her fingertips. It smelled faintly of . . . She wasn't sure what it smelled of, but there was something familiar in it, something comforting. It made it slightly easier to stick together the

264

ripped fabric of the membrane and to feel it might just mend, or at least look like it had.

Mena was at this for some time, working one-armed, stumbling because of her own injuries and fatigue. She could not help but speak to the creature. She kept apologizing, commenting on her features, talking as if she were a nurse and the patient simply holding to silence. Perhaps, she said, not all changed creatures should die. Perhaps she should have taken the time to see this one first. She wished she had.

Eventually, she had dealt with everything but the creature's head. Before she turned to it, she thought she would touch it with care. Lift and twist it over, set it right. She could do that. She would. She owed it that. So thinking, she turned and froze at what she saw.

The creature's head—which had been upside down—was now right side up. Her eyes were open. She was watching her.

Chapter Twenty-two

Dariel's eyes snapped open. He went from the nothingness of dreamless sleep to complete alertness. His heart, in its first seconds of wakefulness, banged against the cage of his chest like an animal trying to escape. Where was he? He was sitting upright, held in position by a band wrapped around his chest, hands still bound but his mouth free. He had no memory. He knew, though—as if pierced physically with the knowledge—that the things he had forgotten were huge. His gaze flew about the room, taking in individual things one by one: a water stain on the rough stone of the ceiling, iron rings bolted into the wall, a hanging lantern that cast a peculiarly constant light, the bare back of a heavily muscled, completely gray man sitting on a stool several paces away.

On this his eyes stopped. The man appeared to be eating. He made slight huffing sounds, interspersed with wet noises and an occasional crack, like twigs or bones being broken. He was a giant of a man. He was— Of course! It all came back. He was the one Dariel had seen on the docks of the Other Lands, the one who had lifted him bodily and carried him tucked beneath his arm. He was proof that it had all actually happened: the Lothan Aklun killed, the sea dotted with bodies, the strangeness of the city's inhabitants, Devoth of the Auldek stirred to anger, Sire Neen beheaded.

"Giver return," escaped Dariel's lips, a pious entreaty for aid unusual to him.

The gray man must have heard it. He stopped eating, head cocked, and then slowly eased his bulk around to face Dariel. He let out a low rumble of sound, sinister, bestial. It was hard not to hear it that way, for the man's appearance could not have been more frightening. He was preposterously muscled, with two thick legs, a thin waist, and a torso ridged with neat compartments. His bulk flared up and out from there, chest muscles bulging beneath his gray skin, shoulder joints like two round stones, neck as thick as a boar's. And a boar was what he was. A swine in near-human form.

He approached Dariel, who bucked away from him, straining against the strap that held him fast. He kicked out with his feet, but could neither touch the man nor find purchase enough to move on the slick stone. The man brushed the locks of wavy black hair from his face with the wedge of his hand. He was just as tusked and horrific as Dariel remembered. The golden curves punched straight through his cheeks, just below the corners of his lips. "Ahhh, you awake. Good to see it! Thought you was dead on fright." He followed this with that same low rumble of sound. It took Dariel a moment to identify it: a chuckle. He was laughing. "You got tan skin," the man said in his deep timbre, "but you looking white just now. What, you think I going to eat you?" He reached out and tapped the ball of a large thumb on Dariel's cheek. "Truth is, I more like you than you know just yet."

Hearing Acacian coming from this man's mouth was both welcoming and alarming. His accent was strange. The words were spoken clearly enough, but the inflections he used were kin to no one region of the Known World. Still, Dariel could not help but find some hope. They spoke the same language. That was something to cling to.

The man stepped away, tugged his stool nearer, and returned. He sat down facing Dariel, leaning forward with elbows on his knees and fingers interlaced. "Name Tunnel. Hear it? Tun-nel."

Just when Dariel was getting over the surprise of the man's speaking to him in Acacian, he was shoved back into confusion. Name a tunnel? What tunnel? That couldn't be what he'd said. "What?"

The man smacked a palm against his pectoral muscle. "Tunnel. Name Tunnel." He bared his teeth, seemingly pleased. "Tunnel."

"You mean," Dariel sputtered, "your *name* is Tunnel?"

"He speak proper words! Good to hear it!"

Dariel shook his head. He closed his eyes and opened them and found everything exactly as it had been a moment before. Tunnel stood grinning at him; that, he realized, was what that ferocious-looking baring of teeth actually was. He was smiling. He had gold tusks and wire whiskers, gray skin and muscles that would have put a bull to shame. His name was Tunnel. Simple, really. What was he acting so perplexed about?

With all the feigned calm he could muster, Dariel said, "Hello, Tunnel. Very glad to make your acquaintance. Since you're not going to eat me, would you consider loosening these chains?"

This amused the giant more than anything yet. "Listen that. How pretty you speak! I told her we should keep your tongue in your mouth. Good we did."

Dariel creased his forehead. "I wouldn't disagree with you."

"No, you wouldn't. You be agreeable for sure. Best that way." He inched his stool closer. "Tell me, you really a prince? Akaran for true?"

Had he anything to go on, Dariel would have weighed the pros and cons of answering this question. But he knew nothing about what had happened, what was happening, where he was, or in whose power. Without anything to shape his answer, he shrugged and chose the truth. "Yes."

"What's your name, then?"

"I'm Dariel Akaran. Son of Leodan and Aleera Akaran." Saying the names, Dariel felt a tide of indignation sweep up from his guts. "In Leodan's name I demand you loosen these chains this minute! I'm a prince of Acacia! You cannot—"

"Dariel," the man said, rolling it around his mouth as he pronounced it. "Dariel Akaran. Son of Leodan and Aleera. I know them names, you know? We all know them names, and the ones before. Gridulan, yes?"

"My grandfather."

"That's the one. Tinhadin and them old devils, too. We know them all. Edifus."

Dariel shifted, trying to ease the pressure of the strap around his chest. He already felt his indignation slipping away, though he could not have said why. "You know much of my family, I see. I don't know anything of you or of here, of where I am or—"

"You don't know anything!" Tunnel said this with considerable joy. Clearly, he had suspected as much already, but he appeared pleased that Dariel confirmed it. "Don't know a knuckle's worth and, look, you a prince! Could be you more than that. Could be you Rhuin Fá."

"Rune Fay?"

Tunnel scowled, an expression only slightly more unnerving than his smile. "That's wrong way to say it. Rhuin Fá," he repeated, enunciating with exaggerated lip and tongue motions. "For a long time—I mean a *long* time—we been waiting for Rhuin Fá."

"Rhuin Fá . . . is a person?"

"It's you, maybe. Is the one who will come from the Old Land and flip the world. That's what they say. 'Flip the world.' Can you do that?" Tunnel broke into his horrifying smile again. "Rhuin Fá supposed to come for his children. Take them home. Tell how much he love them. Understand? We been waiting a long time. Generations, you know. Pass, pass, pass." He waved his thick fingers impatiently, indicating these passing generations. "All the time hoping for Rhuin Fá. All the time thinking he coming, knowing he can't go on doing that way forever." He drew back, pursed his lips, and squinted one eye nearly closed. "You know it's wrong, don't you? What they done to all us children. That's why you need to flip it."

Somehow, scattered and vague and incomplete as this was, Dariel knew what crime Tunnel was referring to. "I know it's wrong," he acknowledged. He felt further words running up his throat and out onto his tongue. Explanations. Qualifications. He had been ignorant for so long. He had inherited the quota trade. He had been a child, too. The crime was not his doing, but it had been thrust on him. He could have said a lot of things. It was not as if he hadn't talked it all through with Aliver and Mena and Wren, with everyone close to him except Corinn. With her the subject seemed more dangerous than he had felt ready for. He could have said a great deal. Instead, he bit the words back, aware that he did not know enough yet of this world to say anything with certainty.

"Am I your prisoner? What will you do with me? And the others. What's happened—"

"You not my prisoner. Mór the one. She come talk to you real soon." He answered that much but did not seem interested in opening himself to further questioning. Instead, he said, "I should ask you something. I ask; you answer. Tale says it's that way. Tale says when Rhuin Fá come, you ask him this question. Then you know if he is who he is. So let me ask you. Here's the bridge; you go under it or over it? Which one?"

"A bridge? What kind of bridge?"

Tunnel shrugged. Waited.

Dariel stared blankly for a moment. "Over it. I go over."

"That could be right."

"*Could* be? Don't you know which answer is right?"

"You know," Tunnel said, wrapping his fingers around the curve of one of his tusks and tugging, "tale don't tell. Believe that? Tale don't tell. You may have answered true. I guess we gonna see, soon, too."

Seeing that tusk in his fingers, watching the way Tunnel

pulled on it and the manner with which it seemed to be embedded directly into his lower jaw, Dariel closed his eyes. He had a million questions to ask. Where to start? And could he really ask them of this strange man? What was he, anyway?

Dariel opened his eyes. Tunnel was watching him. For the first time Dariel noted the color of the other man's eyes. Brown. Simple brown. He asked, "You think I am . . . Rhuin Fá?"

"Could be you are. I tell you what, though. Don't matter what I believe." He nodded his head toward the door, from which came the sound of a key sliding home. "She going to be hard to convince." Tunnel rose but paused and turned back. "You know Senival?"

"Yes."

Tunnel studied him a moment, his eyes looking at Dariel but seeing something else. "I—" He hooked a stout finger to his chest. "I Senival. You understand?"

Dariel did. He nodded. The door began to swing open. For some reason, it seemed important that whoever walked in see him already on good terms with the giant. "Tunnel, how did you get your name? Is it just a name, or is it *Tunnel* as in, ah, tunnel. You know . . ."

"I like tunnels," Tunnel said, "always did. Since I was tiny. I like to go through, see? Better than go over. For me that's so." It looked like he might have had more to say, but he shrugged it off, flashed his frightening grin, and left the room.

Since he was tiny? Dariel found that hard to imagine. What had the tiny Tunnel looked like? Was he gray? With baby tusks?

Alone with his chains, Dariel stoked the embers within him back into a blaze. By the Giver, what was the meaning of all this! Each portion of it—the league betrayal, the Lothan Aklun slaughter, being led a prisoner to the Auldek, watching Sire Neen beheaded, being abducted and jailed by a tusked man named Tunnel—was a different coal that burned where it

271

touched him. The fact that it was all confounding and un-explained only made him angrier. When he met this Mór he would spit in her face coolly and make her know the depths of her mistake in treating him so. He would say his name slowly, so that she would hear and realize it and understand that these chains did nothing to change who he was or lessen the wrath he could throw down upon her.

He stirred from daydreams some time later, realizing two people had entered the room. Dariel exhaled a steadying breath. He would make a strong impression. He would be forceful, unafraid, confident. He would ask the questions and manage to do so without revealing his ignorance quite as he had to Tunnel. He told himself all these things, confident that he was already better prepared than he had been a few minutes earlier. He would greet Mór by name. So decided, he turned his head toward the two new arrivals.

One was the white-headed woman he had glimpsed earlier. She was dressed in loose-fitting trousers and a matching shirt, both of them in a sky blue that matched the shading around her eyes and the strange shocks of—well, hair, presumably—that screeched back from her forehead as if she were plummeting through the air at high speed. The skin of her face was eggshell white, and her nose was slightly elongated, pointed to a thin tip that looked almost dangerous.

The other figure was just as striking. More so, perhaps, for she was much more scantily clad, with a tight-fitting wrap around her chest and another around her hips. She was covered from the thighs all the way up with the spotted pattern of a leopard. A cat in human form, she strode toward him on two sinewy legs, as lithe and thin as that animal and looking just as delicately powerful.

Dariel had not known what to expect of his captor, but he would never have imagined this. Still, he recognized the air of command in her posture. He managed a resigned half smile. "You must be Mór."

She strode straight toward him. Without an alteration in her focus—as if the entire walk across the room and what was to follow were all part of a single motion—she drew one hand out, her fingers crooked in tense hooks. She smacked him across the face with all the force she could muster. Not only did she smack him, but she also dragged the stubby clawlike protrusions at her fingertips through his flesh. The sudden pain of the blow snapped his head around and sent him reeling. In the moments after, as he fought to get his breath back, he felt the gouges carved across his cheek and nose and lips bloom with blood.

From just outside the door, Tunnel said, "Oh, not the face!" He sounded more amused than shocked.

Dariel worked his jaw. Things were not going well. But pain is useful, he thought. I'm fully awake now, for example. "Is that what passes for a greeting here? Strange custom. If you'd be kind enough to loosen my wrist chains I'd be happy to return the greeting."

The bird woman said, "Mór, don't—"

But not soon enough. Mór slapped him with her other hand, harder, if that was possible, than the first time.

It took Dariel a moment longer to regain his breath than he would have liked. He kept his voice calm, though, when he said, "It's easy to hit a bound man. Punish me as much as you like, Mór. Get it over with. Then I'd like to—"

"Shut up!" The woman moved so quickly he could not respond at all.

He was about to finish the sentence with "talk," but in the space between the two words, Mór smacked the heel of her palm against his head, driving it back against the stones of the wall. He did not even feel the impact as pain. He just blacked out. The woman's patterned face, from up close, wild with anger, was the last thing he saw.

Chapter Twenty-three

Help yourself. It's good whiskey, isn't it?" Delivegu asked. He leaned back in his chair and lifted his booted feet onto his desk.

"It is that," his guest, a man named Yanzen, said. He did help himself, filling his silver mug for the third or fourth time. "You're not charging this to my debt, are you?"

"No, sir. We're not gaming anymore. This is leisure between friends. Leisure and pleasure. Leisure and pleasure." He pointed at a pipe and the weed pouch on the table. "Have a smoke as well."

Without preamble or apparent provocation, Yanzen said, "You're a bastard."

Delivegu laughed. He did not dispute it or take offense. He was a bastard, after all, the child of a young woman who had been raped by a Senivalian knight one drunken evening. He could not really say the epithet troubled him, especially as he had received from his parents qualities that he was rather thankful for: his father's physical stature and his mother's rejection of anything like a moral compass. Both these things had served him well. Considering his recent interactions with the queen, the traits looked set to help him rise considerably.

They were in the room that Delivegu kept as an office space during the day. With the small cot in the corner it was also a place to sleep after particularly overdoing it in the tavern below. Despite the wear of thirty-nine years of life, his body still enjoyed debauchery with a youthful frequency. Even now, he took notice of the sounds of the evening's revelries that reached them through the floor and walls.

Yanzen picked up the pipe, held it close to his neatly trimmed whiskers, and sniffed. "It's not mist tainted, is it?"

"Such distrust!"

"Who's to say it's distrust? I wouldn't mind a good mist haze every once in a while."

Yanzen opened the weed pouch, pinched out a wad, and jammed it in the pipe. The motions had a coarse quality that was at odds with his neat garments and manicured fingernails and the aquiline grace of his mature features. Yanzen, like many whom Delivegu associated with, had more than one face. He had been in the service of the Saden household since he was a boy of five, first as an errand boy, later tending the family's horses. For a time he trained as second to Sigh Saden's youngest son, before the lad succumbed to a fever. In recent years he had risen to be head of the household servants. It was this position—with the great many intimacies it provided him access to—that made him a person of interest to Delivegu. Something his masters surely did not know was that Yanzen had an affinity for gambling and a considerable appetite for prostitutes. Sharing such vices, Delivegu and Yanzen had been on good terms for some time. The fact that Yanzen owed Delivegu an ever-growing sum of money had not dampened their friendship. Indeed, it seemed to warm both men to each other.

"So," said Yanzen, blowing a cloud of smoke between them, "have you parted the queen's thighs yet? Is she as sweet as she looks, or is it all ice inside her? Opinions differ, you know. Saden boasted the other night that she likes to suck toes. Is that true?"

Nothing in Delivegu's expression betrayed how close he came to reaching across the desk with a fist. He could not have said why he found the comment so infuriating, but the notion that any part of Sigh Saden's body would get near the queen's mouth flushed him with angry heat. It was a lie, of course. Being a man who never had to lie about his conquests, Delivegu despised those who did. That's how he explained it to himself, at least.

He said, "I doubt Saden has anything else that she could suck on. Either that or his toes dwarf his manhood. Just as likely. No, I'm not out to bed her." He paused to let the lie sit a moment, and then continued with something more reasonable sounding. "That way lies madness. I have higher aspirations. I intend to be indispensable to her."

"Do you, now? And what does she think about that?"

"She already calls on me about delicate matters. She has no chancellor, you know, nor does she want one from among her class."

"You fancy yourself in line for the chancellorship, then?"

"In a manner of speaking," Delivegu said. He loosened a few buttons on his shirt. No matter the tailoring he requested, his shirts always cramped his shoulders. "Yes, I know there are matters of birth to be considered, but you let me worry about that. Of course, I'll look kindly on those who aid my endeavors, which are, in truth, the queen's endeavors."

As he finished off his whiskey, Yanzen watched him over his mug. Wiping the foam from the sides of his mouth, he asked, "What can I do for you, then? You want somebody dead in the Saden household? Most anything could be arranged, so long as we price it first."

"No, I hold the entertaining assignments for myself. It's just information I'm after. Your breadth of knowledge interests me. Who, in your mind, is the queen's greatest enemy among the nobles?"

Yanzen shrugged. "Who's to say? Flip any of them over and you'll see a snake's tail coming out his ass. It's the truth. Senator or landowner, estate lord or—male and female both, mind you—they all speak treason when they speak of the queen."

"Do they plot?"

"Plot? Naw, they don't plot. That requires more cunning than most of them have. I can't say that any of them are a danger. Maybe Sigh himself, but he'd as soon marry Corinn as anything else. Drop his old wife in a second, he would. But so many of the Agnates are new blood. They don't know how to be nobles yet. Before Hanish—back then, the court and the Senate were rife not just with snakes but with pit vipers. These new nobles—few of them have any venom in their bites. The hostages, for example. Back before Hanish, sending off noble sons and daughters never meant much. They expected it. Part of their burden. They'd love their heir right enough, but they wouldn't lose sleep when Thaddeus Clegg plucked a child away to stay at court. These new Agnates, though, they worry, wonder what's going on over at that academy, visit whenever they can. They're just not used to their offspring being moved about like game pieces. The bitch played that right." He leaned back, enjoying the smoke and looking ever more at ease. "Anyway, they mostly chew their gums. For the majority, life is better now than it was before Corinn ascended. They don't want to upset that."

Delivegu had flinched slightly at the word *bitch*. It's just a word, he thought, a coarse word that shouldn't be used in relation to Corinn, but nothing to comment on. As for the rest of his friend's counsel, he would have to measure it later, for he was skeptical that the Agnates were as harmless as Yanzen thought. He had been too long in their company, perhaps. Although that was also why he might be right about them.

"And what about the common people?" Delivegu asked.

"Those they all worry about!"

"Does your master ever talk about Barad? Some call him Barad the Lesser, an agitator from Kidnaban."

"Heard the name. Sigh disregards him. A man like him can't see any commoner as a threat."

"Most of them aren't."

Yanzen must have heard some gravity in Delivegu's voice, for he pulled the pipe from his mouth and studied him. "You think Barad might be a threat?"

Delivegu tipped the dregs of the flagon into his mug. "His name has reached my ears. He worries me. He shouldn't be important, and yet I feel he is."

"Methinks you're besotted," Yanzen said. "What was it you said—'indispensable to the queen' or some such? She is a swan that breaks your neck just as you're about to compliment her on the beauty of her wings. Mind me on that. I don't think she's likely to bed you, either. Not even in the comfort of her own compound. From what I hear, she hates it that her brother took up with a commoner. She's going to hate it even more soon. What do you think about the prince's bastard to be?"

Delivegu had been about to drink. He paused, squinting one eye. "What do you mean?"

"You don't know?" When Delivegu did not answer immediately, Yanzen smiled. "You don't, do you? That amuses me. I know something that you don't. Came by it easily as well. Perhaps it's worth something? Some reduction of my debt?"

"Anything is possible, if the information proves sound," Delivegu said. Then he added, in clipped tones, "Tell me."

He had already waited an hour on the staircase balcony when Delivegu finally heard someone descending toward him. As the person rounded the rock wall, he saw that it was Rhrenna, the queen's assistant. Bit of a disappointment. She was not exactly pretty, a little thin lipped and pallid for his tastes. Still, he liked the lines of her neck and the delicate muscles etched there. Perhaps more than anything, he liked that she was such a close confidante of the queen. Sleeping with her might pale in comparison, but he would not turn her away in the right circumstances. He looked her up and down in a manner that conveyed this possibility to her. She showed no sign that she acknowledged it, but he knew better.

"Tell me, Rhrenna, do you ever miss your homeland? It's a shame, don't you think, that Mein Tahalian has been abandoned. Must be caved in and crushed beneath the snow and ice by now. And nearly all Meinish men massacred . . . That must trouble you. So few left to choose from. How is one to maintain racial purity in such circumstances? I trust you've learned by now that men of other races can fill in just—"

Rhrenna cut in, all cold business. "I will hear your message." She kept her chin tilted upward. It was a nice chin, Delivegu decided. He thought about nibbling it, but that must wait for another time.

"Oh, I thought you were just here to make small talk with me," Delivegu said. "I wrote to you saying to get the queen, and saying to make haste." He let his eyes drift down from her face and linger on her bosom and slim waist. "Unless my eyes deceive me, you are not the queen, and I've been kept waiting about as long as I will wait. Get the queen, or you'll be sorry you didn't."

"You don't order me, much less the queen. What is your business? If I deem it merits the queen's attention, I'll speak to her about it."

"Oh, come now. You know the queen meets with me! I'm in her trust."

"I am in her trust," Rhrenna corrected. "You handle certain business for her when she summons you. You do not, however, summon her. If you assumed otherwise, be now corrected."

Delivegu stepped nearer, close enough that he could smell the fragrant oils scenting her neck. "It's no whim, dear girl, that brings me here." Face turned to the side so that he had to study her askance, he whispered, "Likely, when you think of me at night it's as a rogue, a bandit who sneaks into your room, perhaps, and—" Rhrenna jerked her head to turn away. His hand shot up and stopped her at the shoulder. "I wouldn't disavow that. There'll be time later. But right now, I swear to you, my lady, your mistress will want to know what I have to tell her. It's about her family line."

"Tell it to me, then," Corinn said. She came around the corner and down the steps toward them. "And it had better be good. If not, I'll take your impertinence as a sign that business is concluded."

Delivegu stepped away from Rhrenna. He bowed low, holding the position, secure in the knowledge that the muscles of his shoulders and back strained against his thin shirt. He said, "Before you proclaim my doom, Your Majesty, consider my message. I could have shared it with your maid—"

"I am not a maid," Rhrenna snapped.

"But the moment you heard it you'd call for me. Nor would you want it committed to paper, and I'd wager you'd not want to wait until we'd arranged another of those clandestine meetings." He straightened, enjoying the word *clandestine* and drawing it out slightly. "I've only been anticipating your desires." The royal visage remained dangerously annoyed. She was a viper, this one. He got to the point. "The lady your brother shares a bed with, Wren—she's with child."

The queen's face went blank. She looked for a moment as if she were completely devoid of thought: her lovely head empty and his to fill. Delivegu kept his smile from showing.

"I see," he said, "that you're wondering how I come to know so much about the ways of a courtly lady. I can detail that for you."

And he did. He left out any mention of Yanzen, and instead told a tale largely fabricated. His information originated with sources far too low and disreputable for Corinn even to know their names. Through these shifty agents he claimed to have learned of a prostitute—or whore, really, for this one was on the lower end of that profession—who had bragged about having certain knowledge about the prince's consort. Apparently, her cousin worked in the house of a surgeon whose wife served as midwife to some of the wretched in the lower town. "It's a bit complicated—the whole web—but bear with me." How Wren came in contact with such a woman the whore could not say. Sought her out to keep the whole thing secret, he figured, far away from the palace. The whore swore that her cousin was in the very room when the midwife confirmed the girl's pregnancy. In her opinion, the woman looked healthy, and there was no reason to think the child was in any danger at present. But there it was: the prince had a child on the way.

"The girl is thrilled. Wants the pup. Couldn't get enough of rubbing her hands over her belly, even though she doesn't show yet." This last detail he had made up on the spot, but he imagined it wasn't far from true.

Rhrenna was the first to speak. "This is not possible."

"Why not? What makes it impossible?"

The queen turned and placed her hands atop the stone railing. The sun was low on the horizon and orange highlights touched her features. Her face was not blank anymore, but it was as unreadable as it was beautiful. When she spoke, she might have been addressing her assistant more than Delivegu. "Wren is not supposed to be able to get pregnant. A tincture mixed into her tea years ago took the capacity from her. Or so I was told."

"That may yet be true," the secretary said. "Wren has said nothing about this. How can we be sure this whore told the truth?"

Delivegu crossed one arm over his chest and stroked his beard with the fingers of his other hand. "Could be," he said, pitching his voice as thoughtful, as if he were just now thinking it through with her encouragement, "that Wren doesn't want you to know. I don't know why that would be, but women have their reasons. As for the whore, well ... I interrogated her."

"How?" Rhrenna asked.

"You wouldn't like to hear all of it." He almost insisted that be his final answer, but he found himself speaking anyway. Something about shocking them—especially Rhrenna—

excited him. "The end was this: I took her hand and spread it on the table and said that I'd take her fingers off one at a time until she told me the truth, until I believed her."

Corinn asked coolly, "Was it necessary to take her fingers?"

"The threat didn't carry much weight unless I cut her to prove I meant it. I took one, just a wee one, though."

"And did she change her story when you raised the knife again?"

"Well, yeah, she did," he admitted, "but I'd just cut off her finger. She must've figured I didn't want to hear what she was saying, so she changed her story. You can't fault her for that, though. Like I said, she's clever. Anyway, I believed her. I let her keep the other nine digits and we were both happy."

"Barbaric," Corinn said, still looking out at the setting sun, "and flawed. Cutting off fingers is no way to get at truth."

Delivegu could not have disagreed with her more. He did not like the word barbaric, either, or that he was doubted. "I saw the girl myself," he said. It just came out. The lie leaped off his tongue before he had weighed its usage completely.

Rhrenna asked, "You saw Wren?"

"Yes. I wouldn't trust a whore without seeing for myself, of course. So I verified it with my own eyes. She did visit the midwife." To himself, he thought, If that girl lied, losing her fingers will be the least of her concerns.

Corinn said, "Wren was a brigand; it's natural she would seek out low-born assistance. But it may be that Wren suffers some other illness. Your source may be mistaken about the details."

Rhrenna murmured agreement.

"Or it may be that your brother's bedmate has a pup in her." The words came out harsher than he intended, frustration beginning to heat him. "That's what I'd bet on. You don't suppose they just sleep in that bed, do you? Like brother and sister?" He wondered if he had gone too far. For some reason, his normal assurance seemed a flimsy thing when speaking with the queen. It was there, yes, but he always felt as if a breeze could blow it away at any moment. "I beg your pardon, Your Majesty. I don't mean to be coarse—"

"I don't care if you're coarse or not," Corinn said. "I care that you serve me well. That's yet to really be seen. You spoke to the whore, but what of her cousin? Or the midwife herself?"

"I didn't want to stir suspicion before bringing it to you. Best they think you're ignorant of the deceit, for the time being."

"The whore won't run to her cousin straightaway or warn Wren that some brute was asking after her?"

Delivegu frowned. Did she think him a brute? Brutal actions don't make a brute. He'd have to teach her that. "No, I don't think she will," he answered. "Believe me, I know this sort. She cares most about herself and her other nine fingers and other bits after that, as well. You may doubt me all you like, Your Majesty, but it won't change the facts. I simply wanted you to know. I want to be of use to you. I hope you know that."

The queen turned from the now red sun, exhaled, and leaned back against the railing. "You are as helpful to me in your way as Mena or Dariel or Rialus or any other adviser," she said.

The frankness of the statement and the flat manner in which she delivered it caught Delivegu off guard. He tried to respond with some wry quip, but nothing came to him. He wanted other things from her, things not so noble, but he had spoken with unusual honesty when he said he wanted to be of use. Perhaps she was reciprocating that.

"You know, Delivegu, rule is a burden. People believe it a privilege. A gift. A great luxury. None of them know a thing about it."

"I'm sure, Your Majesty, that none is more capable of carrying the burden than you. Tinhadin would have liked you as daughter."

That thought caused her to pause for a moment. She almost seemed amused by it, but whatever melancholy had hold of her now prevailed. "I get a grip on this over here," she continued, showing the area she meant with a tented hand, "only to learn that this over there has gone awry." She brought her other hand into play, and then wiped both away with a flick of her fingers. "I get a grip on that, and two new problems fall from the sky. I deal with those, and then five foul weeds sprout beneath my feet. Why will it never hold still for a moment?"

"That time will come," Rhrenna said, her face tight with concern. She touched the queen on the arm in a manner that suggested it was time for them to go.

She's not happy sharing the queen's confidence with me, Delivegu thought. Get used to it, girl. "It's peace you crave?" he asked.

"We're at peace now, and still nothing is peaceful."

"Your Majesty," Delivegu said, again surprised to find himself speaking honestly, "you set yourself too great a task if you wish to make the entire world peaceful. It has never been that way—or not since the Giver abandoned us. Perhaps chaos is the natural order, to be embraced. Tranquillity might not make you as happy as you imagine. It might seem a bit like death."

"What about bringing peace to my own family, then? That should not be too much for a queen to manage. What, you think we are at peace? Why—because I smile and say I love my siblings and they do the same?"

"Don't you?"

"Of course I do. Only they know me—" She cut her line of thinking with a sharp tick of her head to one side. It must have pained her, for she touched a hand to her forehead as if suddenly struck with a headache. "I didn't ask to be the queen. All my girlhood it was Aliver who was going to rule. That was fine with me."

"What troubles you, your highness?" Delivegu asked. "Tell me and I will find a way to fix it."

"Delivegu, I have powers beyond what you can imagine. I don't boast when I say that. It's the truth. But that was true of

284

Tinhadin, too—he whom you would have be my father. One day I'll explain to you why that's not the compliment you think it is." She fixed her eyes on him and for a moment seemed surprised at what she found. "Why am I talking to you like this? I'll tell you why: because I've just recently learned my sister has been snatched from the world by a dragon. She may live; she may be dead; she may fight the beast still. I don't know. Like anyone else I have to wait to learn of her fate. I want her here with me now. I want Dariel here with me instead of on the other side of the world. I want both those things, yet it's I who sent them away. And I would do it again the moment they returned. You see? I cannot be a sister first and then the queen. It's the other way around. So you tell me that I may be aunt to my brother's child, but I know that I cannot be an aunt—not if the queen forbids it. Not if the queen decides a bastard born to a brigand girl from Candovia will hurt the Akaran name, maybe even threaten the heir. Do you understand me?"

He was not sure he understood all of it, but he believed he caught the relevant thrust. "If Wren's child will cause problems—"

"I will deal with Wren, and you may well have a part in it."

Delivegu nodded, most pious. "The very fact that you say it fills me with joy, with purpose. You tell me what to do and I will do it. Anything—"

"Do nothing right now," Corinn said. She blinked slowly, fatigue on her. "Nothing right now. The queen needs to think it through."

He watched her and Rhrenna as they ascended the staircase and moved out of view as the wall curved away. A short, sweet view it was. One day, he thought, I'll walk those steps beside you both. May that day come soon.

Chapter Twenty-four

Even though he lived every moment of it, Rialus managed to disbelieve the entire ordeal. How could he credit such madness? What in all his years of life would have prepared him for the shoving, blood-spattered, roaring chaos that erupted after Devoth beheaded Sire Neen? The Ishtat soldier beside him lost his arm at the shoulder. His scream was so horrific that Rialus felt like it came from his own mouth. The ailing man drenched Rialus in a spray of blood, which he slipped in as he tried to back away. There, on the floor, he was smeared across the stones, stepped on, and kicked. He swam through bodies and severed limbs and once found his fingers entangled in a leagueman's entrails. He had retched so hard and long he would happily have coughed up his internal organs to end it.

If all that was not bad enough, when he was yanked up off the floor it was an Auldek hand that gripped him; Auldek hands slapped sense into him; Auldek eyes probed his. As they dragged him from the chamber, he saw not one living Acacian. It was hard for him to remember what he saw, but he knew it had to have been a scene of hellish carnage.

When they left him alone, Rialus's thoughts flew away from the details of his present horror. He thought through the pain to recall Gurta. He recalled all the things that had been, that might have been, and that had slipped from his grasp. She had loved him. Really she had. She had said so time and again in her plain, lowborn Acacian. He had seen her love on her soft-featured face and felt it in her caresses and known the truth of it when her body welcomed him each evening—as well as during the morning, afternoon, sometimes in the wee hours of the night. He had planted a child in her. Imagine that! A part of him living within her. Rialus made immortal! A boy child to carry his name and build up his fortune, a child he alone could educate about the world and shape in his image. Better than that, he could shape him in the image of what Rialus dreamed he might have been.

Now that fatherly role was destroyed. It seemed so dim and distant a possibility that Rialus gave himself over to grief. He did not know what was to happen to him, but he knew nothing would ever be the same. He cried, sobbed. He writhed on the floor in physical and emotional anguish, spitting out the blood that pooled in his mouth.

He was in just such throes of self-pity when Calrach found him. The Numrek crouched beneath the low door frame and entered the room. His bulk immediately made the space seem tiny, uncomfortably cramped. He stood a moment, taking Rialus in, and then asked, "What's wrong with you?"

Rialus focused on him and, despite his misery, tried to find a way to answer the question. Nothing he could come up with seemed the right thing to say to the Numrek. Calrach righted a stool that Rialus had overturned and lowered himself onto it. He swept back his black hair with both hands, squeezed it into a tail, and wrapped a leather band around it.

After tying it, he set his big-knuckled hands on his knees and said, "You have a decision to make. In store for you, if you displease the Auldek"—the Numrek rolled back his eyes as he considered the possibilities—"oh, a poker shoved up your ass; that's likely. Also, I've seen times when they bend your shoulder back. Bend it hard, hard like, so you feel the bone is going to jump out of the socket. That's pain. Then they pull a knife red-hot from the fire. A thin, thin, thin sliver of a blade. With it, they just touch your flesh. Tiny touch, no more weight behind it than a feather. But the blade is so red-hot sharp and your skin so taut that that feather touch splits the surface and you'll want to avoid that, too, I think."

"I did nothing."

"You are big stuff now," Calrach said. "Only Acacian they got."

"Dariel?"

"Dead, I suppose. Haven't found his body yet, though. Messy in there, you know. They think you're a leagueman, but no matter. They have questions for you. Just answer them. You'll betray nobody who hasn't already betrayed you. Mein, Akarans, the league: piss on them all. Play it right, Neptos, and you may outlive them."

Rialus stared at him, hating him and completely mystified by him. Piss on them all? Did this imbecile really think Rialus would betray everything in the Known World? Not that he even could, but . . . "What have you done?" His voice was just barely more than a whimper. "And why? Why? Why did you . . . The queen gave you privileges. You lived just as you wanted, servants and cooks and—"

Calrach raised a hand and made a chattering motion with his fingers. "Blah, Blah. Neptos, stop blathering. Those things don't matter! To you maybe, but to us? No. That's no way to live. Not for us. But you won't understand. Why waste words? Enjoy your last days, yeah? Enjoy them, and know that you died for a good cause: the Numrek cause!" He guffawed, crouched forward, and smacked Rialus on the shoulder with a surfeit of force.

Rialus pulled his knees to his chest and lay like an infant on his side. "Vile," he said. "Vile, vile, vile. I hate you."

"Shame. We liked you, Neptos. Remember when we used to make you run and throw spears at you? Oh, you were quick when you needed to be." Again Calrach could barely contain his mirth.

"Vile."

"You think so? Why, because we don't speak like you? Don't eat what you eat? You think you know us, but deceiving you was like telling tales to children. Simple. Boring. Easy. And it was misery; that's what it was, but you never knew us true. Some land? Some servants? Working for that bitch queen? You think we wanted that? Took pride in that? You—who know us better than most Acacians—should have known better. Those years in Acacia: exile, disgrace. You don't care about disgrace, do you? To a Numrek honor is all. That and belonging. We need to belong, understand? Belong." He drew this last word out, making sure Rialus acknowledged it before he would move past it. "We didn't over there in your lands, not without our totem and our people."

Rialus, noting what sounded like melancholy in Calrach's voice—an unfathomably strange emotion for him—looked up. He had thought Numrek faces capable of only a few crude expressions of anger. But he realized he had been wrong. Perhaps he had never looked closely enough, never wanted to settle his eyes on their craggy features for longer than he had to. Right now, though, staring at Calrach, he saw shades of melancholy and regret and shame and ambition all betrayed in the lines of his eyes and forehead and lips and jagged teeth.

"What are you talking about?"

"We could not live as exiles forever. They stripped us of our totem. They made us beasts instead of men and kicked us to the north in shame."

"Who did?" Rialus asked.

"The Auldek, you fool! They are chief among the clans. They—and the others—drove us from Ushen Brae. They called us filth and took our slaves and burned our totem." Calrach seemed at the verge of one of his cursing tirades, but he blew it out of the side of his mouth and kept on. "Did we tell you these things? No. Why should we? The Mein didn't care about the truth when they bought our blades. The Akarans hate the truth, so we gave them lies instead. We let them all think they buy us and order us around. What does it matter what they think?" Tilting his head, Calrach exhaled a long breath. "We have lived wrong for years. Now we wish to live right again."

"What terrible thing did you do to be driven from here in the first place?"

Calrach shot him a dangerous glance. "I'll get the torturer now."

He began to rise, but Rialus blurted, "No, no, don't! Ahh—" He had spoken too forcefully. The pain of it reverberated through him for a few closed-eyed seconds. When he opened his eyes again, Calrach sat watching him. "Don't leave," he said. "You came to tell me things. Please do so."

"I will," Calrach said, after a moment. "Hear these things. I won't tell you twice. In Ushen Brae, no Auldek or Numrek or any other clan—none of us—had given birth to a child in hundreds of years. Not a single birth. No children. You hear? That's right. I am not the youthful man I look. I don't remember my birth year anymore, but believe me, I have lived long, long."

"But, you do have children. I've seen—"

"Don't rush it! Now, I will keep this simple for you. The Lothan Aklun arrived here in their boats. They looked weak. They wanted to lay claim to our barrier isles. They were not warriors, but they were powerful with magic. They trapped us with that magic. They showed us tricks, made flames erupt in the sky, made the ground shake. They even killed with nothing more than whispered words. They said they would pay for the isles with a great gift. They would give us eternal life. You hear me, Rialus? They promised to make us immortal. And they did."

Rialus said, "But you are not immortal. I've seen Numrek die in battle. You fear death like any man."

"More than any man, perhaps. Don't interrupt what I am telling you. They create immortality by taking souls out of one body and putting them inside another. We could contain two, three . . . ten lives within us. This they had the magic to do."

The image of the Auldek leader with an arrow in his chest, twisting and shaking like a thing possessed, popped into Rialus's head. "Devoth—"

"Yeah, you saw that, yeah? You thought Devoth dead from that arrow. Good shot, true, but only one of his souls died because of it. That's why he rose again and—" With the blade of his hand, Calrach imitated a sword slicing through his neck. "No, he has many souls within him. I used to as well. You could call it sorcery. Lothan Aklun sorcery. It's kept us alive all these years, but it came at a price. At the same time as they made us immortal they took away our fertility. We could live forever, but, we learned, we could no longer have children. Quite a trick—giving one kind of immortality, taking another at the same time. They did this to the slaves as well. None of them grow to birth their own young in Ushen Brae. None of them. This is a childless land. All these years we've been childless, except for the souls inside us and for the quota.

"When the Lothan Aklun began to trade through the league we had all the souls we could want coming to us from your lands. But we wanted more. Yes, for their labor, to work for us and take care of our every need. But not just that. Also, they became our children. Slaves, but children too. And because none of us could bear young either, we always needed more. Understand?"

He asked but did not wait for an answer. "I'll tell fast. Listen. The Auldek have many laws. Too many. The Numrek broke one. We were punished. They took our souls from us, burned our totems, exiled us. Made us trek into the ice."

"Burned your totems?" Rialus asked. "Totems?"

Calrach waved his impatience. "Later about that. Stick to the points, Neptos. We marched north, nothing with us but our weapons, clothes. Those were bad times, when we first walked into the north. Many died of the shame of it. Many thought death was the best escape. I felt it myself. Numrek don't kill themselves, but we can wish for it. We can take risks, hunt snow lions, the white bears. You ever kill a walrus with an ax? It's no sure thing, I tell you. Anyway, truth is, I believed the Numrek were doomed to vanish in the ice. Then something happened. You know what?"

Rialus did not have a clue, and his face indicated as much.

"One of our women got a child in her. First in hundreds of years. First one, and then another." He laughed, low and obscene. "And then we screwed like rats. We were having children again, Neptos! You have no child, so you may not know what this means, but it was a wonderful thing. We thought to go back to Ushen Brae, show them the children. But we were exiled. We couldn't. And some said that the birthing only returned because we had passed out of Ushen Brae and had escaped some curse. We did not want to go back and lose the gift again. And then we met the Mein, and got better ideas. You know the rest. Or some of it you know. Is it making more sense now?"

It was starting to, but Rialus still shook his head, which was pounding. He put much effort into speaking clearly. "What of the Numrek back in Acacia, in the palace? And in Teh?"

"They will have it hard, but they are ready for that. As soon as they know we've made it here, they will rise. Kill the bitch. Kill others, you know." He gestured with his fingers that surely Rialus could imagine the possible scenes. "Kill, kill. That sort of thing. And then they'll hole up and wait."

Why did it seem the more he knew, the less it made sense? Wait for what? They were worlds away. They had no ships. The Numrek back in the Known World could cause much bloodshed, but they would eventually be defeated. The league would not tolerate any of this. The Lothan Aklun were no more. And surely their sorcery went with them. The Numrek may not have planned or intended that, but what Calrach described was a confusion, not a situation that should please him so. "I still don't understand."

"Okay," Calrach said, leaning close. "Last thing. I had an idea, yeah? What if I got back to Ushen Brae? Came home and told what we found. Told all the Auldek that a new world awaited them, a world full of humans to hunt, to enslave. A rich world in which all the Auldek could again have children. What if I promised them that and showed them the proof of it? My son. You think, maybe, they would lift the exile? Maybe they would give us our totem back, yeah? Maybe they would march with us across the ice and down into glorious battle, toward the conquest of your Known World?" His grin could not have gotten any wider. "Pretty good idea, huh? I thought so. The league made it even easier by taking me across the Gray Slopes. Hated that, but good news. Devoth and the others like the idea, too. Not my fault the league killed the Lothan Aklun. No blame on me. No, instead, I bring them hope. I bring them a new world."

And that's it, Rialus thought. That's the truth of it. The things that were happening were not just about him and Dariel and Sire Neen. Not even about Corinn. Oh, how she would rage if she knew. But it wasn't about her either. It was about everything. This is about the entire Known World and every-one in it.

"Anyway. There it is. You know. I'll get somebody to torture you now. Fun for you. Fun for him. Everyone's happy."

"No!" Rialus shouted. "No, that won't be necessary."

Crossing his arms, Calrach grimaced, a show of mock confusion that clearly meant he was not confused at all. "No? Why not?"

"What does Devoth want from me?"

Calrach smiled. "I know you, Neptos. I knew I was right! I told them as much. Said, 'Always a weasel, he is. He'll turn.' Is that right? It pleases me that you're so true to your nature. Devoth wants everything you can tell him. Everything he'll need to plan his attack"—the Numrek shook his head at the irony of it—"on your nation. You, Neptos, are an important man. Play it right, and it might be very good for you."

In answer, Rialus curled back into his ball, lying on his side with his knees tight to his chest. He—Rialus Neptos, so often maligned, laughed at, joked with—was in a singular position to affect events. He would find a way to do so, he swore. He would talk with Devoth. He told himself that he would not help destroy his people. He also told himself that he would aim at getting back to Gurta and seeing his child. He did not acknowledge which of these was his greater priority.

Chapter Twenty-five

The play of the sun on the rolling, blond-grassed hills was wonderful. Soothing. Mena sat with the first rays of light and warmth on her skin, taking in the world around her for miles and miles. The land buckled away into the distance in smooth mounds of shadow and gold, spotted with outcroppings of rock that looked like islands. A breeze blew steadily from the south, hot air but not unpleasant. In some ways Mena felt alone in the entire world. She wasn't, though. She most certainly wasn't.

Beside her the lizard bird creature lay in a gentle curve, her tail a river meandering through the grasses. Her head rested on a smooth rock, eyes closed but moving beneath the thin membranes of eyelids. Even in slumber—which she seemed quite fond of—she was never entirely insensible to the world. Her senses seemed to work: nostrils flaring on occasion, the small protrusions that marked the ears adjusting to slight sounds. Mena still could not believe the events of the last few days had actually happened. But there she was, all the feathered, reptilian, delicate beauty of her.

And here she was, sitting beside the creature, inexplicably healed of every injury she had received during her fall. She knew that Melio and the others would be scouring the countryside for her, and she felt bad, knowing they would be desperate, worried. Melio especially. She sometimes spoke his name, wishing that he could hear it on the wind and know she was thinking of him. That sadness was a small feature of her mood. In truth, she was content in a way that she could not explain.

Four days prior, when she realized the creature was alive and awake and watching her ministrations over her body, her heart had hammered so fiercely in her chest she feared it might explode. She could not have said exactly why. It was not fear for her life. She had just examined the animal's shattered form with her own eyes and knew she could be little threat. Nor was she surprised at being watched. Once she realized the beast's eyes were on her, it felt right that they should be, as if she had wished it herself and made it so. There was an element of amazement that the creature could live after Mena had been so certain she was dead. More than anything Mena felt a frantic urgency, a soaring of possibility that had no specific details but that seemed as important as anything in her life.

Mena withdrew a few steps. She sat on a stone and stared at the creature, who looked back at her fixedly. Together they passed the better part of an hour that way. The creature had emerald eyes. The irises sparkled with a metallic sheen. They filled the entirety of the eye sockets. They did not show fear. They did not betray aggression or hunger either. That there was intelligence behind the eyes was palpable, but they were just watching. Mena felt she was being probed as much as she was probing, and she found herself hoping the creature liked what she saw.

They could not remain in this standoff forever, though. When Mena saw the creature's slim tongue taste the air for a moment, she had an idea. Rising slowly, she motioned with her good arm that everything was all right. Stay calm. She whispered, "Stay. I'll be right back. Just stay." She knew she should feel foolish talking to an animal, but she did not. As she hobbled her way back up the slope that she had earlier descended, she wished she had said more. If the lizard bird somehow was not there when she returned, she would curse

296

herself for not having said more, even though she had no idea what that more might have been.

It seemed to take forever to climb down into the other ravine and reach the river again. She was slick with sweat and had to sit for a time, panting, fighting to push back the fatigue and pain pulsing everywhere in her body. Opening her pack and rummaging about in it for something that would hold water made for another pathetic routine. Fortunately, she did find the leather bowl that she used to brew healing teas. She scooped clear water from the river and drank it, then scooped more. Rising without the use of her damaged arm was hard enough, but picking up the floppy bowl was another matter. It took her several tries before she finally had it cupped in her palm, relatively full.

When she peered over the ridge again, the creature was exactly as she had left her, lying in the same shattered posture; but the long neck was bowed as she inspected her wings and torso. A good bit of the water had splashed out of the bowl by the time Mena reached the creature, but she offered what remained. She set the bowl down as best she could, spilling still more, and then she backed away. The creature did not take her eyes off Mena until she had stood some time at a short distance. Then the creature examined the bowl, looked up and considered Mena, head cocked, and then sank the tip of her snout into the water and drank.

And then the staring match began again. They spent most of the afternoon at it. Again, Mena felt inclined to speak. She could not find the words, though, and the creature seemed increasingly content with her presence. That was enough.

Mena slept that night on the slope a little distance away and awoke to find the creature grooming herself, if grooming it could be called. She looked much like a cat licking itself, but she did not use her tongue. Everyplace she might have licked, she instead rubbed with the flat bottom of her snout. She was precise in the motions, careful, especially when tending

297

the shredded membranes of her wings. Just looking at them shot Mena through with regret. That damage was her fault. Hers. She felt it as if in her own body, forgetting as she watched it that she was, in fact, battered and broken herself. From her close observation the day before, she doubted the creature would ever be able to fly again, not with so much of her wings destroyed.

When Mena approached, the creature drew semiupright. She sent waves of tension out through her wing frames, lifting them partially off the ground. The finger-thin bones were still amazing to behold. So flexible, so powerful, and so delicate at the same time. It should have required bulges of muscle tissue and sinew to create the power Mena had felt snatch her from the ground, but instead the creature's wings remained works of thin-lined art.

Mena's eyes drifted over them. The wing membranes did not look as damaged as they had yesterday. Some of the spots that she thought had been pierced clean through had not been, and some of the tears that had looked so ghastly the day before did not seem quite as horrible. She wondered if she had been mistaken.

"You're not as bad off as I thought," she mused. "Well, obviously not; I'd thought you dead before."

Feathered plumes on the creature's neck rose for a moment, and then settled back into position. The creature pushed up on her forelegs, lifted them from the ground, and stood unsteadily on her hind legs, shaking out her wings as she did so. She looked up at the hill that separated them from the river, studied it, and set out walking toward it. Her steps were tentative at first, her body swaying like a drunken person's. She paused and, after a few steadying moments, drew her wings in, first the left, then the right. The curl started at the tips and rolled tight as it neared the body. Somehow the motion tucked the membrane in with it, and in the space of a few seconds she was wingless again, with only two swirled nubs on the shoulders to indicate where the wings now nestled. She loped up the slope and climbed over into the next valley.

She was in the river when Mena joined her. Shivering like a child from the cold, she danced in the small stream, dipped the full length of her neck and tail in. She puffed her plumage so that for seconds at a time she was covered with a bristling coat that then snapped back to smooth in the blink of an eye. The wing nubs flexed a little but did not unfurl.

"You are a bird, aren't you?" Mena said.

She climbed out of the river, turned back to it, and thrust her snout into the water. She drank deep and long, green eyes flicking to Mena occasionally. The creature seemed at ease with her now, not studying her as she had the previous day. Watching her, Mena felt as pleased as a cat lover watching her favorite feline. She wanted to reach out and feel that soft, strangely scaled plumage again.

Before she realized it, she had done just that. Her fingers tingled at the touch, and she drew them back immediately. She touched her nose, smelling the citrus scent of the substance that seemed a part of the plumage. It was not unpleasant, not exactly oily, but it was hard to know how else to describe it. She was aware that the tingling in her fingertips continued, and that she had passed the sensation on to her face. It almost felt like she had inhaled it and now held it in her lungs. She nervously wiped her fingers on her tunic. Still the creature drank, having taken no notice of her touch or reaction to it.

"Sorry that drink yesterday wasn't much. I tried, though. You know that. Now, if we just had something to eat, we'd not be so bad off."

As if in answer, the creature stretched her neck high and opened her nostrils with a few deep inhalations. She rotated and tried the air to the south, seemed to like what she found there, and began to stride away, more energy in her motions than just a moment before. A little way down, she turned and studied Mena, walked on a few steps, and then bent her neck back and met her gaze again.

Mena pressed the fingers of her good hand to her chest. "You want me to follow?" The creature did not answer, of course, but Mena did exactly that.

It was no easy thing, hobbling along over the uneven terrain. Early on, she spent several frantic moments thinking she had lost the creature over a rise or behind a rock outcropping. But each time she was there, waiting, looking back for her. A few times the creature even seemed to respond to sighting her by raising the plumes on her neck, a sign of—of what? Pleasure? Encouragement? So the day passed, they alone on a windblown landscape.

The two were still together that evening. They spent the night in a small cluster of date trees. A tiny ruin showed ancient inhabitation, but whoever lived here had not done so for ages. Mena did not crowd the creature, but she stayed near enough to be able to speak without raising her voice. She told her about Melio and the others who were likely hunting them right now. "They're excellent trackers," she explained. "They'll find us soon. I don't know why, but it seems very important to me that no more harm befalls you. That seems like the most important thing in the world right now: that you be safe. Perhaps I'm just tired of killing. I should be. I didn't mean to harm you, though. I just didn't expect you."

Mena cut herself off. She looked away, shaking her head, and then looked back at the creature. Those eyes were just as intent on her. Her mouth, Mena realized, tilted near the back hinge of the jaw. "Why is it that I want to talk to you so much? You can't understand me. It's absurd. You can't understand me, right?"

The creature stared at her. Stared. Of course she could not understand. Mena exhaled and reached for another date. As she did so the creature nodded, just a tiny dip of the head, but enough to make Mena pause. Was that an affirmation? Had the creature answered that she could understand? Or had she merely followed the motion of Mena's hand? She wanted to ask, but, again, staring into those round, large, innocent eyes, it seemed a complete absurdity.

"Perhaps I bumped my head worse than I remembered."

Mena had that same thought on waking the next morning. Before she knew what she was doing, she moved to push herself up with both arms. Finding one encumbered by her stone splint, she gave the arm a shake, trying to dislodge the thing. Only after she had tugged at the knot in the cord that held it fast did she realize what she was doing. And that snapped her fully awake.

The arm—her formerly broken, battered arm—did not hurt anymore. She flexed her fingers and they moved without pain. There was stiffness. There was a memory of pain still in the tissue, but there was no mistaking it: her arm was nearly healed! She loosened the splint and lifted the limb free and moved it in the air. She sat staring at it, utterly confused, wondering if she had been crazy when she splinted a healthy arm, or if she was crazy now for believing it healed. And then she thought of the creature.

She jumped to her feet, spun around until she found the familiar shape atop a nearby hillock. The creature stood shuffling her feet impatiently, waiting for Mena. She could have remained there disbelieving her sudden healing, but it was as it was. The creature had done it, somehow. Because of her—being with her, touching her, inhaling that citrus scent—Mena had healed just as the creature had come back from the brink of death and now showed only faint scars from the attack. And this same creature wanted Mena's company, just as she wanted to stay longer with her.

And so began another day of travel. She already knew how it would go. They searched for fruit and water, the only two things the creature seemed to consume. Either she knew where the groves of trees grew and what fruit was ripe by memory, or she smelled them on the air and followed her nose. Once, when she scented something that excited her, the creature tried to get Mena to pick up the pace. She ran forward and back, churning up dust, urging her on. Mena's human gait was clearly not sufficient.

The creature bumped Mena's side and lowered her shoulder. Mena understood what she offered and was stunned. She kicked her leg over the creature's spine and slowly slipped on top. For a moment she clung there, spread-eagled on the back. The creature looked at her, amused. Mena tried to find a better arrangement. And there was one: sitting upright, straddling the creature's neck, snug between the nubs of the wings. With her positioned like that, the creature moved forward, falling into a loping, reptilian run that Mena would never forget.

The creature must also have known how to avoid humans, for they saw nobody the entire day. Once they pillaged an apple orchard that showed signs of tending, but evaded what-ever souls might have been about. Atop a bluff on another occasion, Mena spotted a cluster of houses in the distance. She could have walked to them in an hour and named herself and been among people again. Though she was hungry, having eaten only fruit, even light-headed at times, she did not yet want human company.

Indeed, she often scanned the horizon, knowing that searchers were combing the countryside for her, people she cared for and trusted, who had fought beside her many a day. The daily journey she and the creature kept at would be making it hard for the trackers, but she was not sure she wanted to be found even by them, even by Melio. Not yet. Not until she understood this better.

As Mena walked beside the creature on the afternoon of their third day together, she said, "You need a name. I mean, a name for me to call you. I can't think of you as lizard or bird or dragon." Mena stroked the creature's neck. "You're no dragon, anyway. You're gentler than that. You need a real name." She walked on in thought, nibbling her thumbnail as she did so. The creature's head rose and fell beside her, bobbing on the curve of her neck.

"My father once told me a tale about a boy who had a pet lizard. It's a Bethuni tale, I think. The boy called the lizard Elya. He hatched it from an egg. They were together always, though the boy's father did not, at first, like the animal being in his hut. In Bethuni lore orphans of any species are sacred, good luck to those who care for them. But the father was a selfish man who wanted to control all things and didn't like the love his son showed a mere reptile."

Mena cut her eyes over to her companion. "No offense meant. Anyway, he disliked it so much that one night, when the boy was sleeping, he grasped the lizard and carried it out into the night. He tied it to a tree and used a spade to dig a hole. The hole was to be the lizard's grave, and he was going to kill it. Before he finished digging, his shovel struck something. He reached in and pulled out a sack of gold coins. Ancient coins, buried there long ago, coins that nobody had a claim to. And just like that he was a rich and important man. It would never have happened if not for the lizard, and he saw it as a sign from the gods that the creature was special. He didn't kill it after all. Instead, he took it home and woke his village with shouts of joy.

"That's the tale. My father told it better than I, but that's most of it. You know it's a tale and not the truth because the selfish father became generous. I've not seen that happen anywhere but in tales. But I guess we need things to aspire to. What do you think about Elya as a name? I believe it would suit you. If I call you Elya, will you answer to it?"

The creature, perhaps noting the questioning rise in Mena's voice, looked at her.

"Elya," Mena repeated, adding a singsong quality to it. "Elya . . . How do I explain naming to you?"

She tried several ways. She was glad there was no one

303

around to hear, for she knew she would sound a fool or mad or both, but she made a game of it. She touched her nose and said, "Mena" and then touched the creature's snout and pronounced, " El-yaaaa." Nothing. Not that Mena knew what she expected, what would indicate acceptance of the name. She walked off a little distance and, facing away, began calling the name. On turning around and seeing the creature, her face lit with pleasure. "Elya! There you are."

Mena named thing after thing, touching ground and stone and grass and sky and Mena and Elya. The creature narrowed her eyes at this, the first look of suspicion she had made since Mena had found and cleaned her body.

"You think I'm mad," Mena said. "You may be right. Elya. My Elya. Not your Elya, but mine." She found a rhythm in the lines and repeated it singsong. And again, and then she skipped away singing it loud, dancing, her arms swooping like wings. The mirth came upon her complete, like a serious father suddenly playing the fool for a child's amusement. It worked.

The creature bent back her neck, opened her mouth, and coughed a quick barrage. Her neck rolled in jerky undulations so forceful that Mena feared she was choking. But then she stopped and looked back at Mena, relaxed and mirthful. Her eyes twinkled with amusement.

"Does that mean you'll be my Elya? You will. You already are. I feel it—" Mena tapped her chest with her fingers and then moved them to her collarbone and then, as if unsure which spot she meant, up to her head, where she touched a finger to her temple "—inside me. You're here." She tapped again. "How can that be?"

As usual, the creature offered no answer. But Mena did not need one. She knew. Elya was Elya. That night they slept within touching distance of each other, and the next morning was the one on which she awoke beside Elya with that strange feeling of contentment firmly lodged in her heart. She sat, taking in the rising sun to the east. The rest of the human world seemed far off indeed, blissfully so.

On that she was mistaken.

Elya's head snapped to attention, all relaxed slumber gone in an instant. She stared over Mena's head, to the north, head cocked first to one side and then the other as she listened to something. Mena calmed the creature with a few soothing words, with steadying motions of her hands. She asked her to stay put, and then, on impulse, she thought the same instructions. She really did not understand it, but she could not shake the feeling that she could send Elya her thoughts—not words or sentences but the import of a thing. That was what she tried to pass silently to her. Stay.

When it seemed Elya would do so, Mena turned and ran up the slope to get a better view. She crested the hill and, as the undulating landscape on the other side came fully into view, she dropped flat bellied to the ground. She had seen something, shapes where she hoped there would not be shapes. Inching forward, she peeked over the rise more carefully and saw exactly what she feared.

A wide wedge of humanity crawled across the hills. Hundreds of people, spread out far to east and west, many carrying torches that spit clots of slow-rising smoke into the air. From this vantage, they were the main feature of the world, a blight on it. They were also, she knew, her people. Near the center of the front ranks a banner hung limp from a long pole. She knew by its colors that it was the insignia of Acacia, the same one she had seen at Kidnaban years ago. As on that occasion, this sighting filled her with dread. She crawled backward.

When she reached Elya, she nearly said, "Let's go." Part of her wanted to flee and knew that Elya would do so with her. But she did not say those words. Instead, she stroked the creature's neck and rubbed under her chin and brushed the flat of her hand over the flare of her nostrils. "I can't run. It's not fair to them, and it solves nothing, just prolongs it. They're my people, Elya. They love me. You understand? That's why they've come." She cradled the creature's head in the palms of her hands. "Elya, you can leave me. Why don't you do that? Run. Or fly if you can. I'll tell them not to hunt you anymore. No one will hunt you. I promise."

The minute she said this, she knew it was a lie. Even if she could stop the Akaran-led hunting parties, she would never be able to stop others—tribesmen, trophy hunters, any villain looking to make a profit from killing the last of the foulthings. When word got out that Elya was harmless, it would be even worse. Still, Mena said, "You should just go," not believing it but feeling she must say it. She had to offer it, had to make Elya understand that she was free to choose her fate.

Elya moved her head closer, tilted it, and touched the soft flat of her crown to Mena's forehead. That was her answer.

"You should just go."

The creature tapped her head against Mena's several times. Again, her answer.

Relief washed through Mena, suffusing her with warmth from head to toe, even as worry wrapped her chest like iron ribbons trying to squeeze the air from her lungs. "Okay, love," she said. "Let's go introduce you to the world. Let's make an impression."

There was one way, she hoped, to present herself and Elya in a manner that could stun her brave soldiers into the moment of hesitation she would need. That was why she rode toward them with her legs over Elya's shoulders and her thighs clenched tight and her arms wrapped around her neck. For a time she rode blind, letting her mount direct them. She pressed her face against the plumage and loved the touch as greatly as any intimacy she had ever experienced. But when she felt a tremor in the creature's muscles, she drew herself up so that the eyes of everyone they rushed toward would see her. Elya carried right on toward the soldiers as they formed defensive lines and reached for weapons. She did not slow until just before them.

It was hard to tell whether most of the party saw the creature or saw Mena as well. Mena shouted her name, telling them to drop their weapons, but confusion surged through them so thick and loud she was afraid they did not hear. She found Melio's face, locked eyes with him, and saw the frantic intensity there. He could not have looked more perplexed. Still, he shouted for the bowmen to be ready. This Elya did not like at all.

So quickly that Mena could do nothing but gasp as it happened, Elya rose on her hind legs. She unfurled her wings with the speed of two whips cracking. The muscles in her neck stiffened to a steely, flowing hardness. Her chest expanded with a great inhalation of air, and then she smacked her wings down as if to break the earth. They were airborne. The force of it smashed Mena against Elya's back and knocked the wind from her lungs. She clutched the creature's neck and, as they hovered, she fought to draw in enough breath to speak. She saw how close Melio was to ruining everything with a single command. She did not have the breath yet, so she mouthed the first words that came to her and hoped he would see them and understand.

Silently, she said, "I love her."

Chapter Twenty-six

Early one evening in southern Talay, Kelis lay staring at the stars, amazed at how his life had taken this new direction so suddenly. He had lived through the string of events, but he had yet to catch up with them completely in his mind. He had been summoned to Bocoum to meet with Sangae and Sinper Ou. Things had still been normal then. He had enjoyed running to the city beside Naamen. In a vague way that he tried not to think about too clearly, it had reminded him of running with Aliver when they were both young and bursting with vigor. And then he had met Ioma Ou and Benabe and Shen. Aliver's daughter. After that, nothing was the same.

He was still stunned by it. He saw in her features that Aliver went on in living flesh. She was not him, of course. She was Shen. Yet some part of him looked out from her eyes. He could not deny it, nor did he want to. Just a girl, but on meeting her he felt that his purpose in life and all his allegiances were tossed into the air. They still had not yet landed back on the earth.

Nor had he sorted out why the various players had brought her to him. Sangae's motives could not be questioned, but the Ous were different creatures, with different aspirations. Even though he had not opposed the plan in his presence, Kelis had felt that Sinper did not want to let the girl leave his control. Kelis was sure that if it were not for the mythic reverence Talayans felt for the Santoth, Sinper would never have let them leave, would have found some way to claim that Shen would be safer in his compound. And then what? Could he possibly intend to play the girl in a dance for the throne? Why did rich men always crave more?

It would take an army to win Shen the throne, an entire war against Corinn's might. That should have made it seem improbable, destructive, mad, but instead the thought filled him with dread. All of Talay would fight in the name of Aliver's child. Though she be a girl, though she had been born outside of marriage: neither fact would dissuade the people. If they believed Shen was Aliver's child they would fight. They would say she was of Talay, and that her triumph would be their triumph. The madness might begin again. For this reason, Kelis was relieved to get the girl out of the Ous' control.

They left Bocoum the very next day. Ioma had offered a small corps of guards to accompany them, but Kelis had argued for the stealth of small numbers. Sangae wished Naamen to accompany Shen and her mother. When Shen approved of him, the party's number was decided. They shed clothes and jewelry and any accoutrements that would suggest their true identity, dressing instead as a family of migrant laborers.

They walked to a trade depot to the east, and there booked passage on the deck of a fishing boat heading around the Teh Coast in search of yellow fish. They disembarked at Palik, in Balbara territory. Before they left that city they traded their clothes again, looking more like goat herders now. If anyone asked, they were returning from having sold their flock, or were on the way to pick up new stock—depending on the circumstances of who was asking.

Shen seemed to accept all this with equanimity. At times Kelis was nervous in the girl's presence. She was a child! What did he know of children? What did Naamen know? They were two men, both of them childless, who suddenly found them-selves charged with the fate of a nine-year-old girl. He had been less nervous in the company of angry chieftains like

Oubadal. How strange, that he had never imagined what a burden of responsibility caring for a child was. Though in ways he felt Benabe was harsh, always looking for fault, he was glad she was there.

That was what he felt when he stood at a distance and saw only the situation. When he sat beside Shen in the morning, preparing food for her over a tiny fire; when she asked him of animal things or of plants; when she found ways to poke fun at him by mimicking the manner in which he chewed so furiously or the way he held his chin high as he looked into the distance; or when she pulled on her earlobe as he sometimes did in thought—well, then he forgot his apprehension and felt himself a child.

One time, a week's journey into the interior of Talay, they had run into the night to put distance between themselves and the laughing howls of a laryx pack. Kelis had needed to carry the girl. Benabe kept pace with them. Shen was draped around his back and gripped him. He had further tied a wrap around her to help hold her in place. For some time he had been conscious of the weight of her, unnerved by the touch of her skin and innocent intimacy with which her legs wrapped around him, by the friction between their bodies as he ran.

But, again, that was only when he thought about it. Soon he gave himself over to running, watching the land move beneath him, entranced by the motion of his legs over the world, watching the stars hung in the black sky. When the moon rose, it lit the land with bone-white highlights, especially catching in the flowers at bloom on the acacia trees. It was a magnicent country. His legs and arms and lungs and heart were one with it. He forgot completely about Shen and realized he still bore her only when they stopped their flight and Naamen reached to untie the wrap that held her in place.

"That's a lion, isn't it?" Shen asked, the first of them to speak for a long time.

"Yes, child," Benabe whispered.

"Why does she bellow like that?"

"Not she. Only the males roar that way," her mother said. "Who can say why men complain?"

"Bellyache," Naamen said. "Belly too full and dragging on the ground."

Kelis smiled. The embers of a fading fire murmured beside him, crackling and shifting occasionally. He liked listening to it during moments of silence. Those moments never lasted long, though. Shen's lion made sure of that. From the warped, lonely ferocity of its roar, Kelis could tell it was several miles away. In the back of his mind he had been tracking its movements, but in many ways he would rather have ignored it. He had no fondness for lions. He said, "It roars so that all the world knows it exists. Lions are proud, but they are also fearful."

Shen propped herself up on her elbow. She lay on a blanket with her mother. It was unlikely that she had spent many nights sleeping in the bush before, but just three weeks of travel beneath the dome of the Talayan sky and she already seemed at home on the hard-packed earth, in simple clothes, eating the frugal fare Talayan runners survived on out here. "What do they fear?" she asked. "Laryx?"

"Yes, laryx attack lions," Kelis said. "They also fear people, though they don't like to admit it."

Benabe huffed. "They fear us? Then why don't they shut up? Instead, they announce exactly where they are in the world. If I were a hunter, I would set off from here and tell that one"—she paused, pointing in the direction of the most recent blast of sound—"to shut it! That's what I would do." She jabbed her fingers under Shen's arms to punctuate this. The girl writhed a moment, laughing.

"That would be something to fear," Kelis said, "but it's not that sort of fear I mean. Lions hunger for glory. They would die in battle gladly, so long as they took a few with them into the night. They forever worry that they will be forgotten or not honored or laughed at. That is why they spend so much of their lives punishing other creatures. They are petty animals. They steal kills from other hunters. They slay the young of lesser cats and leave the bodies for the mothers to find." Kelis pulled his light robe over his chest, not because he was cold but to fill in the moment when he could have named still more crimes. "They are tyrants. That is why they are such a lure to petty men."

"Sinper Ou has a lion crest," the girl said. "Do you think him petty?"

"Yes," Benabe said, grinning, "tell us, Kelis. Do you think the magnificent, rich Sinper Ou is a petty man?"

Kelis cleared his throat. He was not yet used to the many ways Shen caught him off guard, but he had come to believe she meant no mischief by it. He could not say the same about Benabe, but Shen's questions were asked because she wished to know the answers. She received whatever answer he gave with the same focused interest. In fact, he had already changed the way he spoke to her. He called her "child," but increasingly he did not think of her as kin to others of her age. Are other children like her? he wondered. Have I not noticed, or is she just different? He said, "I do not think Father Ou knows lions as I do."

"Lions were not always the ruffians they are now," Naamen said. He sat cross-legged on the other side of the fire, chewing on peppergrass to clean his teeth. Whatever import hung at the edges of Kelis's interactions with the girl did not seem to affect him at all. He spoke lightly, falling into the heightened delivery of a storyteller. Shen sat up to listen. "When the Giver was yet on earth, lions and laryx and all other animals had peace together. They all knew that—"

"Hush," Kelis said. "She has heard these tales before. She should sleep now."

"No," Shen protested, "tell me. I want to hear it in Naamen's voice."

"Go ahead," Benabe said. "You've got a good voice for tales."

Grinning with triumph, the young man continued. "They were the Giver's creations. They felt his love and knew he shared it equally among them. That was a time of wonder."

He described the wonders in imaginative detail, drawing scenes with both his normal arm and his stunted one. All sorts of animals bounded along in the Giver's wake, singing to praise him. All creatures were newly minted and glistened with the freshness of creation. Everything was just born, and in those first days no creature thought of eating another. Instead, they leaped in the air to pull ripe fruit down from the trees. Shiviths raced with gazelles for the pure joy of it. Elephants fenced with rhinoceroses like playful friends. Eagles lifted mice into the air cupped gently in their talons, so that the small creatures might have the joy of seeing from the heights. Lions wrestled with laryx in brotherly competition.

"Can you see these things?" Naamen asked.

"I can," Shen answered.

"Well, good that you have eyes to imagine it, for it did not last."

Naamen explained that Elenet, the first man, was born into this. For a time he shared in the rejoicing, but soon he learned enough of the Giver's tongue that he became vain. He tried to make his own creations, but because he was not the Giver, nothing he tried came out right. It was always twisted. Wanting to make warmth, he made the sun burn too strongly. Fleeing, he sang to cool himself and froze portions of the world in ice. To warm himself, he made fire, not noticing until later that fire consumes all it touches. To put out the fire, he lifted water from the rivers and created storms. To quell the storms, he blew the sky clean and found he had created deserts.

"You see?" Naamen asked. "Everything he did created chaos; nothing he intended came into being as he intended. Wanting to make himself immortal he opened the door to disease. He created death the moment he thought to fear it and to escape it."

"Nobody had died before that?" Shen asked.

"No," Naamen said, "this is the time of the first generation of everything. There was first nothing, and then there was life. It might always have been so, if Elenet had not acted so wrongly."

But he had acted wrongly, and the Giver lost faith in his creatures. He turned away and abandoned his creations, fearing that any of them might be the next to betray him. In no time at all the world changed. The goodness that was the Giver went with him, and the world was left a different place. Creatures who had been friends began to squabble. Strong ones took to bullying weak ones. And it was not long before some creatures began to feast on the flesh of others. Eagles pressed their talons into the mice that had been their friends. Snakes used their stealth to hunt. Lions ate anything they wished. Fearing that they would all vanish, the hunted creatures learned how to mate and make children, but then the hunters learned these things, too. Painful and dangerous as it was, they had their own young, whom they taught to hunt as well.

Elenet fled from this chaos, though nobody knows to where. In his absence the lions announced that they were supreme of the creatures of the land. The laryx, hearing this, cackled with laughter, for they disdained the lions and thought themselves supreme. That is why lions and laryx still shout at one another today. The lions roar their supremacy; the laryx shout back in hysterics at the lions' foolishness.

"Their blood feud goes on," Naamen said, "and perhaps always will. At least until the Giver returns and sets the world right again."

The storyteller bowed his head, indicating that his tale was concluded. Shen had lain with her head in the crook of her arm. For a moment Kelis suspected she had fallen asleep, but

314

then she said, "I thought the Santoth made the laryx with the touch of their eyes—when they were angry, I mean, because of being banished."

"That is sometimes said," Kelis admitted.

"But Naamen said laryx were there in the first days."

Naamen said, "Sometimes two things are said that don't agree. Which is true? Or are both true? I cannot say. I just speak what was spoken to me."

The girl yawned. "I will have to ask the stones. They will tell me the truth."

Shen said this with childish matter-of-factness, with no hint that any might find the notion fantastic or unlikely or frightening. It returned Kelis to the whirl of his worried thoughts. This was no normal hunting trip or ramble or night camped under the stars to tell old tales. For the second time in his life he was going in search of the banished sorcerers, the God Talkers, the Santoth—the ones Shen referred to as the stones. They were beings he had seen only once, on one furious, horrible afternoon. It was a glorious event in that it marked Hanish Mein's military defeat, but it was wrapped in the emotion of Aliver's death and remembered in scenes so terrible he prayed he would never see their like again.

Even so, he was trying now to find these same sorcerers. Nobody could say why, save that a girl swore it had to be done. He was taking that child, a woman, and a youth with him; and he was doing so covertly, so that the queen he was sworn to serve would not know of the existence of a niece, one who might challenge her own child for the throne.

Benabe's voice interrupted his thoughts. "What do they want with my girl? Can you tell me?" She lay alongside her now-sleeping daughter, propped on an elbow and gazing at Kelis. Her face was lit more by the stars than by the weak glow of the dying fire. Seen thus, in highlight and shadow, she could have been either very old or very young. Either way, she had a beauty that artists would want to capture in stone.

"Me? Cousin, I don't have that wisdom."

Benabe exhaled and looked out at the dark expanse of the plains around them. The lion had stopped its roaring, but in its place a thousand tiny creatures chirped and whirred and rustled and yapped.

"Shen hasn't trembled since we left Bocoum," Benabe said. "Usually, she falls every couple of weeks. I have always hated those moments. It can strike her anywhere, anytime. One moment she is walking; the next she is flailing on the ground, eyes back in her head and mouth sucking, sucking the air. It happens more when she is agitated."

"She doesn't seem agitated," Naamen said.

"No, she doesn't," Benabe said, sounding almost bitter, almost resigned. "We're walking across a continent into a desert to meet sorcerers who should have died two hundred years ago and she's never seemed happier, never healthier. It's like when she wakes up from trembling. Her face goes so calm, peaceful. She smiles and is . . . happy. Me, each time my heart is pounding. Each time I think the fit has destroyed her, but each time it fills her with more joy than I ever have. I should love them for that, but sometimes I hate them instead." She brought her gaze to study Kelis, then Naamen, and then Kelis again. "I don't know if I am doing right to let her go. Kelis, you've seen them. Tell me that they are good."

In answer, he adjusted his cloak, snugging it tighter around his torso. He forced a yawn and held it long, and then adjusted his position as if on the verge of sleeping. "There is nothing to fear," he said, hoping the lie would be enough to end the conversation.

The next afternoon Kelis noticed something strange on the southern horizon. He said nothing about it, not that day or the next. But on the third day Naamen tried to make eye contact with him as they walked. He shot concerned glances that Kelis did not return. Kelis was glad that his companion did not voice his thoughts, for he still hoped he might awake the next morning and find the shapes had been but clouds, mirages, tricks the heated vapors played.

But in the clear air of the fourth morning he could no longer avoid the truth. Near, now, so suddenly near—as if they had crept on their toes forward during the night—stood a horizon-wide wall of mountain peaks. Foothills fronted slanting slabs of granite, behind which dark slopes ramped toward the sky, fading into the haze so that one could only guess their true heights. Rank upon rank of them, shouldering their way around the curve of the world. They were a range like nothing he had seen in the Known World, and they most certainly had not been here the last time he ventured into the far south.

Benabe asked, "I see those, and you see those. We each see those, right? So I ask, why are there mountains before us? Nobody said anything about climbing mountains."

"I do not know these mountains," was all Kelis could say in answer.

"What do you mean?" Benabe asked. "You have been this way before—"

"I have, but the mountains were not there before."

He stared a long time as the others shot questions at him. What did it mean? Were they so lost as that? How can there be mountains so large that they had never heard of them? How could he not have seen them if he had really come this way before? Must they cross them, or go around them, or—

To each he shook his head and repeated, "I do not know these mountains." He glanced at Shen, who was watching him. She was the only one who was unconcerned by the massive barrier facing them. She just cocked her head and smiled, as if untroubled and seemingly ready to carry on.

Chapter Twenty-seven

He had said her name. Mór. It rolled off his tongue like he knew her, like they were old friends or comrades, like he was a master about to chastise her for slack work, as if he had the right to know her name and to shape it in his mouth. She was not sure which of these she most heard when he spoke, but it included all of them. It was a simple thing, but so unexpected that it ignited more anger in her than she had anticipated. The moment she had waited a lifetime for . . . the moment when she would spit in the face of an Akaran prince. A vile, contemptible Akaran! A despot. A criminal. An abomination that deserved to live only until it understood the full extent of the crimes done in its name. She had gone to that chamber ready to revel in finally seeing one of these Akarans, one hated more even than the Auldek or the Lothan Aklun or the league.

Instead, she lost control of herself. And why? Maybe, she thought, as she sat in a windowless room in the maze of tunnels below the capital city, it was his accent. His damned Acacian accent! He spoke as they had all once spoken—all of them in some variation or another—before years in Ushen Brae, speaking Acacian secretly while the official language of the Auldek bent and twisted their pronunciation so that they did not recall how they were supposed to sound anymore. The language of defiance that the People spoke to one another was a sad imitation of the language of the ones who had sold them as slaves. It all held a terrible irony. It was that, now that she thought about it, that had driven her to slash him so forcefully.

Or, well, there was another thing. She hated admitting it, but the cadence of his voice shot her through with the memory of her brother. She would never have expected that. A few seconds in his presence. A few words and the weight of longing for Ravi crashed down upon her. It was not a particular memory, just the entirety of awareness of how much she missed him, how incomplete she was without him. The Akaran bastard! To have brought that on her with just a few words . . . It must have been some sort of Acacian magic. Who could blame her for smashing his head against the wall? He deserved worse. As far as she was concerned, he would receive worse.

She lowered her head farther and tilted the knobby implants that protruded from the tips of her fingers into her scalp, pressing them in until they were painful. She would do better next time she saw him. That was her responsibility. The elders trusted her with this and she would not let them down. Ravi would want better of her; she would not fail him, wherever in Ushen Brae his soul was.

She eased her claws from her scalp, exhaling and drawing herself upright. Her eyes drifted to the small mirror on the table across from her. It was angled away and she could not see her image in it, but she knew what she would see if she turned it toward her: the visage she had come to think of as her own. From her chest and shoulders up across her face and even into her hairline she was spotted like a shivith, ink of black and yellow and shadings in between embedded into her skin, trapped in her living tissue. Shivith. Her current visage would forever be a merging of human features and feline patterning. As with everything in Ushen Brae, the irony was that she could not imagine herself any other way. She did not know herself without the tattoos that defined, placed her, gave her station and marked her as property in this world.

She did remember Ravi as he had been. She had last seen him as a child, unaltered. Everyone had said they wore the same face. So perhaps remembering him was remembering herself as well. His eyes had been deceptively tranquil, with upper eyelids that lay heavy in the Candovian way. Beautiful, she thought. Wise eyes in a wise, rounded face. Ravi . . . How she had clung to him on the ship that ripped them from the Known World and brought them into slavery.

Even in the hull of the league ship, Ravi had chafed at the injustice. His eyes may have looked tranquil, but the mind behind them was sharp and brave. He had whispered schemes of escape in her ears. First one plan and then another, and revised to yet another as each was proven impossible. He sought to win others over. He left her for short periods and spoke to the other captives at night, when the guards left them alone. He tried to stir their fear and anger into something useful. *There had to be a way*, he had claimed. *Had to be! Remember, they were thousands!* Few listened. He had been marked by his outburst on the beach. Though none understood what the leagueman had in store for Ravi, all suspected it was a fate worse than theirs. Hadn't the leagueman said something about being eaten? What monster awaited him, and why let him lead them to a similar fate?

The few who had watched him with nervous eyes, hungry for escape, backed away from him after the leaguemen brought them out of the hold to show them a view of the world that only the league could offer them. The children were led up in groups, gripping one another and afraid of the sea spray and the wind whipping about and the tilting deck. The ship, massive as it was, rose and fell on even more colossal mountains of water. All around them, as far as the eye could see, nothing but the chaos of raging walls of dark gray water, as solid as stone and just as cold. Leaguemen railed at them. They were madmen, perched high up in baskets on the masts. They shouted and flailed their arms and laughed as if nothing in the world was as grand as the fury of the sea. Nothing except their mastery over it. Mór had thought that she would never see a sight more frightening. She was wrong. Horror takes many forms.

It was horror that flowed in her veins when the red-cloaked men returned for them. They came in the morning, striding through the sleeping children spread around belowdecks. They kicked and punched as they went, shouting obscenities and vile threats and finding mirth in every cringing face. They knew where Ravi was, and they came for him. For her. Ravi fought them, but it was not a fight he could win. Watching as he kicked and twisted, and as the soldiers' fists snapped out again and again, Mór wanted to shout. But not just as the vile men. At Ravi, too. *Stop fighting them! Stop doing just what they want you to do!*

The red-cloaked soldiers pulled Mór and Ravi away from the others, hauled them up onto the deck and shoved them here and there, led them down a long, narrow ramp from the middle of the behemoth hull of the ship to a dock. And then the cloaked men with their elongated heads and fragile bodies were beside them. She remembered that one of them had fingernails several inches long, curving things, curling back on themselves. After that they were on the strangest of boats, sleek and white and propelled by some power within it. The vessel cut against the currents and against the wind. Though she had been at sea for weeks, Mór's stomach churned and spat out her insides, splattering foulness down her front. Ravi clenched her hand all the harder, but it didn't help.

The cloaked men—leaguemen, of course—delivered them into the hands of a woman who waited for them on a stone pier. She was the first woman Mór had seen since they boarded the league ship. She walked toward them like some princess. That's what Mór had thought. Like a princess, she wore a sparkling gown, snug on her slim form, a dress that flared out around her ankles and disguised the motion of her legs. She seemed to be propelled toward them as if on wheels. Her features were delicate, pale. Only when she stopped before them did Mór realize that the shapes beside her head that she had assumed were some sort of hat were actually her ears. On both sides they stretched up into points several inches higher than the norm, curving and twisting so that at their peaks they protruded to the side.

Perhaps it was the sight of them—or maybe it was the unnerving sensation of having firm ground under her feet again, or because she had eaten so little and then vomited and was weakened by it—for whichever or all of these reasons, Mór fainted.

She awoke a moment later, with the big-eared woman huddled over her, studying her. In the years to come Mór often thought of her face looking down, the first time she made eye contact with a Lothan Aklun. The woman grinned. "I hear your thoughts," she said, in a language that was not Candovian. It was like Acacian, which Mór understood a little, but different as well. Though she heard the strange words of the language, she also understood their meaning. The Lothan Aklun cocked her head and tugged on one of her elongated ears with a thin finger. "We do this for beauty, and to hear better." It was an almost comforting memory, the woman's voice kind, her words close to whispers. It was the first thing a Lothan Aklun had ever said to her, and it was the last thing she would ever mistakenly believe was kind about them.

Then came another boat ride once the leaguemen had departed, a small vessel but so fast skimming the waves that Mór felt like screaming. It cut between islands, swaying back and forth so that within a few minutes the view behind them became a maze of land and water. They passed for some time along the coastline of one large island, thickly treed and wild looking. Eventually, the boat docked at a small pier near an outcropping of rock. The woman led them out and up a stone staircase cut into the cliff. Ravi still clenched Mór's hand, and, when the woman stopped before a darkened doorway and motioned for them to enter, they stepped inside together, side by side. That was how she entered the chamber that she would remember every day for the rest of her life. That's how she walked on her own two feet into the soul catcher's mouth.

Skylene appeared in the doorway. She stood there a moment, frowning at Mór, her eyes soft even as her thin lips were pursed in judgement. Beneath her pale, sky-blue face were features born of the Eilavan Woodlands of the Known World. It was unlikely that any living in that place would recognize her as their kin, not behind that unnatural hue, not behind a nose stretched by an implant that made it beaklike, not beneath the jagged plumage jutting up like a crown anchored in her hairline. She may have been Mainland born, but now she was marked as a slave of the Kern, the clan that called the southern delta their ancestral homeland and took the blue crane as their totem divinity.

More beautiful than any crane, Mór thought, and then hated the fact that she had thought that once again, just as on so many occasions before. How frustrating that the tortures the Auldek put them through were also changes they grew to love. She looked away from her.

Skylene closed the space between them. She slid her arms around Mór's neck. She pressed her small-breasted body against her lover's back. "You shouldn't have hit him like that," she said.

"I know."

"He may be useful to us. Yoen and the other elders said—"

"Are you here to chastise me?"

Skylene took Mór's chin in her fingers and turned her head around. She leaned in and kissed her full on the mouth. Mór opened to her, hungry for her, thinking, for a few moments, of nothing save the texture of her lover's lips and feel of her teeth. She drove her tongue between them and found the answering luxury beyond.

Too soon, Skylene pulled back. She ran her fingers up her forehead and over the tufts that jutted from her hairline. "No, I'm here to tell you he's awake again, and sensible. I left Tunnel with him. He seems to like talking with him."

"That won't help his recovery any," Mór said wryly. "Did you question him?"

"He tells a strange story. He claims he was betrayed. Claims he came as an envoy from his sister the queen. Says the leaguemen chained him. Says they poisoned the Lothan Aklun somehow and tried to make a new deal with the Auldek. Says the league was going to give him to the Auldek, but then something happened and the Numrek betrayed them all. It does seem to match what I witnessed. And you heard what the spotters said of the waters. They're empty of Aklun ships. Whatever happened—"

"Whatever happened is still a confusion. None of it makes sense yet. The Numrek— What are those vile ones doing back here?"

Skylene did not dispute the point or try to answer the question. "Dariel says that he did not support the quota. Says he was going to find a way to break it, to trade in other things—not slaves."

Mór leaned her head back against Skylene's chest. "You call him by his first name now? Don't tell me you believe him. How many years have they sold us into slavery? How many thousands gone? Generations, and he expects us to believe that the first one of them we catch wished only to deliver us. They lie better than you, Skylene. Don't be fooled by it."

"Tunnel likes him," Skylene said, after a moment of silence. "He already thinks he's Rhuin Fá."

"Based on what facts?"

"Based on the fact that he's been waiting his entire life for it. Just like everybody, Mór. Just like all of us."

"Not me."

Skylene squeezed her shoulder and then stepped away. "So you say. I'm not so sure. Sometimes I think you pray for the Rhuin Fá more than any of us." Before Mór could respond, Skylene clicked her tongue. "Next time you see him, keep your claws to yourself. And you must remember that you are not an elder. You're just their chosen agent. You cannot harm this man without their permission. To do so would doom you as much as him. We're to talk to him. Talk and tell Yoen what we learn. Let him and the others decide what comes from it."

"I'm not a child," Mór said.

"No, you're a brilliant and brave leader, who sometimes forgets her senses."

Mór closed her eyes. I wasn't always like that. I wasn't always.

That day in the soul catcher—whose name and purpose she did not understand until later—she certainly had not been a brave leader. She had been a child who stood against the wall as directed by the large-eared woman. Mór stared wide-eyed around a room she could not comprehend. Lothan Aklun men and women moved about, all dressed in loose-fitting gowns that trailed on the white stone floor. They were uniformly thin. No laborers' bodies, theirs. They were busy with tasks that, for a few moments, Mór thought had nothing to do with Ravi and her. They bustled about, talking and pressing their hands against panels in the stone. At least, she assumed the substance was stone. It was as hard as stone, and it made up the walls; other objects around the room seemed to have been carved from the same material. Toward the center of the oblong room were two raised rectangles like beds, but so flat and cold no one would sleep on them. Some distance above, hanging from the ceiling, were still larger rectangular shapes.

The Lothan Aklun ignored them so completely that for a short space of time she tingled with the notion that they had forgotten all about her. She still held Ravi's hand. Mightn't they both slip away? The door was open. She could feel Ravi thinking the same thing, his excitement making his fingers twitch. It was just there, daylight shining through.

Ravi moved. He clamped his fingers around her hand, painfully tight, and yanked her into motion. Just as she had thought; they ran for the door. They were nearly there in just a few steps. The Lothan Aklun did not notice. The woman who had escorted them had her back to them. Mór did not think about what they would do on the other side of the threshold, other than dash down those steps. Running. Running.

A man's form cut the brilliance of the day. He strode in, his feet heavy on the stone. Both children abruptly stopped. Ravi fell and let go of his sister's hand. Mór had never seen so tall a man, long legged and long armed and with a torso muscled in bulging ridged compartments. Though he wore only a short black skirt and though his hair was long in the manner of Candovian brides, he seemed a warrior about to kill. His fists clenched and released, hungry for the weapons that belonged in them. The strength of him was obscene—that was how she would remember it—and yet she could not look away. A body built for war, designed for no other purpose, suited to no other purpose. An Auldek, she would later learn.

She thought that he had entered just to stop them, but it was clear from the look of casual interest on his face that he was surprised to see the children flailing at his feet. Several more like him in size and bearing followed him, companions chatting as they stepped across the threshold. While she was still stunned and stumbling back, the Lothan Aklun rushed forward, snatched up Ravi, and dragged him, with more strength in them than she had imagined, toward one of the stone slabs. Mór's gaze snapped back and forth from Ravi to the Auldek. Thus, she saw the Lothan Aklun strap Ravi down to a slab. She saw him wrestling to be free. She saw that once he was strapped down, the rectangular box dangling from the ceiling lowered to cover him. She heard him scream her name, just before the stone cover touched the floor and the cry was cut off. The moment passed, and Lothan Aklun hands pulled Mór out of the Auldek's way. Mór was shoved against the wall once more, and there she screamed. Ravi was inside that box. Pale stone. Sharp edges.

The shirtless Auldek exchanged words with the Lothan Aklun. He seemed to want to see under the box that covered Ravi, but they would not let him. Instead, one of them pointed to Mór. He spoke in a guttural tongue she could not understand. Her breath escaped her completely when the Auldek turned and stared at her. He walked closer. His hand came out and touched her chin. She flinched, but his grip pinned her to the spot. He turned her face upward and studied her, even as she stared at him. His visage was a mask for a long moment, creviced and sharp, with eyes as unreadable as a snake's. And then he smiled and said something that stirred laughter in his comrades.

He released her, spun away, and climbed onto the second slab of stone. He slapped the sides with the palms of his hands, as if urging the Lothan Aklun to hurry. The other Auldek moved to the far side of the room and stood in a spot one of the Lothan Aklun gestured them to. The Lothan Aklun busied themselves again. Soon the rectangular cover above the Auldek also lowered, closing around him and cutting off the last few remarks he shouted out.

Mór stood transfixed, her hands clenched together now, working nervously at each other. She remembered the moment, but she could not recall what she had felt. It was a blank space about which the frantic motion of her hands and the things witnessed by her eyes told her little. Ravi was encased in stone. She knew why now, but what had she thought then? It troubled her greatly that she did not remember, and that whatever Ravi went through he faced alone, while she stood, wringing her hands.

And the moment passed. There was no loud noise, no blast of light, no roar or blood or confusion. There might have been a sound that she felt through her feet, something like music, but she was not even sure of this. She watched the cover above the Auldek rise. The Lothan Aklun hurried to him. When they stepped back a moment later, he rolled off the platform. He planted his feet and growled. He pumped his fist in the air, a grin splitting his face. He was the same, save his skin now glowed as if a light burned in his chest and illumed him from the inside out. The other Auldek howled back at him, all of them animated as they swarmed around him, smacking him with their palms. The Lothan Aklun carried on whatever it was they were working at, their backs turned to the Auldek as if they were no longer there.

The other lid—the one that covered Ravi—remained closed. She never saw Ravi's face or knew what was left of him after his soul was pulled from his body and thrust into that Auldek's. For that was what had happened. She would not understand this completely until sometime later, when Yoen explained it all to her in his gentle, honest way. That was why she knew the truth now. That was why her mind had come to accept what her spirit had told her. Ravi was not yet gone; he was a prisoner in another being's flesh.

There was one other thing she did know for sure. She had never forgotten the name of the Auldek who received her brother's soul. She heard it on Lothan Aklun lips and recognized it to be a name, something different from the rest of the foreign words.

Devoth. His name was Devoth. One day she would get to him, find him unprotected. Then she would kill him and let her brother free.

328

Chapter Twenty-eight

Standing in her private chambers as her servants made her up for the Blood Moon banquet, Corinn mulled over the strange letter she had received from her sister. It pleased her to learn that Mena had been found alive and well. Corinn did not, however, care for the flippant tone of mystery in the note Mena had dispatched to Acacia via messenger bird. It said, simply, *I am found, sister. All well. I'm winged! Will fly to you. Look up.* What in the Known World did that mean? Perhaps Mena had suffered an injury after all, one to the head. Even if she remained of sound mind, Corinn did not like the triumphant tone of it. *All well.* Never, in Corinn's experience of rule, was all well. Mena might have dealt with all the foulthings, but there would be something else to occupy them soon enough. She would have to drill this into her sister when she returned.

"Please, mistress," a thin-limbed servant said, "would you lift your arms?"

The queen did so, and the servant wrapped her vest around her and fastened it in place. Technically, the gown was a version of the garment that tradition dictated her to wear at the Blood Moon banquet, which commemorated the fifth king's—Standish's—suppression of the first mine revolt in Crall. A cruel act, though one the histories praised. As with her other clothes, Corinn had had the tailors cut the dress to the contours of her body. This changed the look of the garment considerably. Corinn would hardly be able to eat or drink anything at the banquet, so snug was the fit, but that did not matter. The maroon dress displayed her breasts and the slimness of her torso and the flare of her hips all to startling effect, an unnerving combination of ancient authority and sensuous beauty.

Her sister's were not the only words written by one of her siblings that roiled around in Corinn's head. She had also spent part of the morning with several volumes open on the great wooden tables in the library. She had gone there, as she had several times before, to read in solitude about the ancients: Edifus, like a wolf fighting for dominance among a pack of snarling competitors; his son, Tinhadin, who built upon his father's shaky legacy with a mastery of god talk so complete that he came to fear he might utter it in his sleep and wake to find the world altered; Queen Rabella, four generations after Tinhadin, who rose to power and held it until her death, no king to rule her. She outlived six male consorts, but never agreed to wed. A smart woman, Corinn thought, and a documented argument against the conniving climbers who wished to bed her on their way to the throne.

She read these old texts to try to discern who her ancestors had really been, how they had succeeded, and what they could teach her. Ironic, but increasingly she reached back to those long dead for guidance while shielding her thoughts from those around her. She also read, searching for insights on the Santoth. Though she came across passages about them often, she never felt she understood them any better. They remained shadowy figures, like beings standing at the edge of her peripheral vision.

This morning, though, it had been a newer volume, one on her brother Aliver, that drew her in. Strange to read words that were supposed to be his. The transcripts of his speeches had about them a hint of the same formality that flavored the old texts. Though the book purported to be a transcription of his words, the shaping of scholarly hands was all over them. Rarely did she catch in them any hint of the brother she had known. But, of course, she had not known this adult Aliver, this warrior prince leading an army and stirring the masses to revolt.

And the content? Oh, such dreams. Such morals! He would remake the world as if it were moist clay that he could mold in his hands. Throw out the quota. Sweep away the league. Unclench the Akaran fist and let all nations rise. Free and equal. Partners in the workings of the world. How could he ever think that such idealism could survive a minute in the brawl that was life? It was folly of the highest order. The fact that so many had followed him just served as further proof of that. Fools' folly.

The Snow King, the text called him. Corinn could not help but scoff. She remembered the night Aliver had proclaimed himself that. Did the scholars in their studies and the peasants in their hovels telling tales of the Snow King not realize that Aliver had been but a boy talking about a snowball fight when he spoke those words? Though at times his idealism struck chords within her, she could not forget the reality of things long enough to fall under his spell. There was a difference, she believed, between the words in books and the manner in which the living must move through the world. She had no intention of forgetting this.

When Rhrenna approached her, clicking her tongue in praise of Corinn's appearance, the queen turned her thoughts back to the letter still in her hand. "What do you make of this?"

Rhrenna took the document and scanned it, though she had read it already. "She sounds pleased with herself. It makes me wonder—"

"Mistress, lean forward please."

Corinn did as instructed. Funny that a hairdressing servant at times commanded her in ways that generals and senators and soldiers never could.

"Makes you wonder what?" Corinn asked.

Rhrenna pressed her thin lips together. "I don't know if we should credit it, but Sinper Ou sent a message saying he'd heard Mena had captured the last foulthing instead of killing it."

It took Corinn a moment to answer. She waited for the hairdresser to finish the braid work around her forehead. It was painfully elaborate, but Corinn liked a certain amount of discomfort while at official functions. It kept her from relaxing, which was useful. "Why would she do that?" she asked, once her head was her own again.

Rhrenna shrugged. "I don't know. As I said, there's no reason to credit it. The people like to make up tales about your sister. Given the slightest opportunity, they embellish."

Corinn snorted in agreement. "Maeben on earth, she is."

"Yes, well . . . I came to tell you that King Grae has just arrived."

"Has he?"

"Surprise visit, apparently. He's asked to attend the banquet. Just as an observer, he says. He's content to stand to the side and watch."

"Why has he come?"

"He didn't say. To show off his freckles, perhaps, and the dimple in his chin." Rhrenna grinned. "He's not hard to look at."

Corinn did not recall. She had seen him a few times since she ascended to the throne but had been content to keep him at a distance. She did recall that he favored his brother Igguldan, and something about this had displeased her. "He may attend," she said, "but keep him at a far table. Even a king should provide us fair warning of his arrival."

"As you wish," Rhrenna said, "although I might need to wander over to the far tables myself." Smiling, she nudged aside the servant who had just lifted Corinn's slim crown. She slipped it in place herself. Made of white gold shaped like delicately thorned branches, it had a ruby at the center that was so dark it appeared black. Acacian royals wore crowns on occasion, though they could just as easily demonstrate their rank with necklaces, earrings, or bracelets, even with garments of a style made only for them for centuries now. But Corinn had taken to this piece since the jeweler first presented it to her. There was a rough texture to the gold, and the stone itself seemed to hide secrets within its depths.

"There," Rhrenna said, backing up and studying Corinn as if she had worked the transformation herself. "You're cruel, Corinn. You'll have the men sweaty with lust and the women sick with envy. Most of them, at least. A few might go sick with lust as well."

When Corinn arrived at the crowded outdoor courtyard in which the banquet was already in full swing, she remembered vaguely that she had once thrived on adolescent courtly intrigue. In her early teen years she had cared about nothing so much as the jockeying for status and favor among her peers. Handsome boys, rival girls, older men's lingering gazes and solicitous flattery; who bested whom on the training grounds; who wore the finest garments and how—it had all, for a time, been the very stuff of life. How foreign that girl was to Corinn now. How maddening that her father had let her live in that illusion for as long as he had.

Although what am I truly doing differently? the queen wondered, as she nodded and smiled and accepted the lips pressed to her hand. Again I walk through a maze of illusion, one of my own making. Perhaps some evening just like this one, some raving lunatic from the fringes will strike me down, just as befell my father. Much as befell Aliver. It's a fool's game, but what choice have I? Should I lock Aaden and myself up in the palace or in Calfa Ven? The latter was an appealing idea, but it would not do. Such a course was perhaps more dangerous anyway. No, she thought, better that I see where the snakes lie than that I find myself stepping on them. At least this way I can weed them out.

She moved through the gathered people with a cool detachment, guided by a bevy of maidens who flanked her as persistently as her Numrek guards. Unlike the taciturn guards—who, she noted, had grown more somber in recent weeks, almost as if they were displeased with their work—her maidens were all mirth. The court was a galaxy of many constellations. Corinn was master of them all, but before her floated representatives from around the empire—royal children, rich younger brothers and sisters, tribal princes and princesses—each the sun of some ally's heart, each surrounded by his or her own attendants. And through this patrolled the ambitious and the arrogant: senators and nobles, Agnates and landowners, shipbuilders and leaguemen, mistresses and lovers, guards and escorts. Sycophants all. Liars most. Some loved her, but these she suspected of their own sort of weakness.

Her mind only really engaged when she felt a need to calculate, study, observe particular others to see what they might betray in unguarded moments. She sat in the chair prepared for her, a throne on a dais, a low table laden with food in front of her, a few chairs on either side for the chosen ones fortunate enough to spend some of the evening near her.

As a Vadayan priest mumbled at her ear, Corinn took in the room. It sometimes surprised even her that her understanding of what was really going on around her was so at odds with the appearance of things. On the surface she sat above a party of people, sumptuously dressed, smiling and gay. Torches lit the place. They were sheathed in tall glass tubes that funneled the smoke up above the revelers and cast blue and red and green and yellow light, depending on the tint of the glass. Musicians lined the walls and the railings that hemmed the space, playing tunes that danced from one portion of the courtyard to another, like a chorus of birds at play. Everywhere there were smiling faces, laughter, conversation, flirtation;

between them servants wove with food and drink liberally belched up from the kitchens. In one small area performers enticed the guests to dance. She spotted Aaden at play with his friends. They were like silver fish swimming amid the adults in some complicated game of tag. And above it all the night sky, mild and clear, stars twinkling into being as the sun slipped over the western horizon.

As if all of that were not enough, Corinn had woven a spell from *The Song of Elenet*, a small work of her own creation that would enchant a few hours before fading. It was a mild euphoria let loose in the air of the courtyard, circling unseen, just the thing to make the revelers feel themselves especially attractive, to make jokes sure to succeed, to make the light sparkle a bit brighter, and to make food and drink taste even better than it was. So it was another festive evening in Acacia; what could be more pleasant? It never took her long to spot the things slithering beneath the surface, parasites at work despite the evening's pleasures.

Delivegu was a reminder of it. She spotted him conversing with the party from the Prios Mines. How he had gotten in and what those men thought he was she had no idea, but in a strange way she was glad to have him near at hand. Eyes that lit with smiles when she made contact with them were misleading. She could sense the same eyes go malevolent when she was not looking. She could tell when conversation was amiable, and when the whispered words were unkind to her. She noted small things to examine further later. Senator Saden, while haranguing the woman beside him about something, avoided making eye contact with the newly enriched land speculator from Alyth. The man who passed beside him might have uttered something, but Saden did not acknowledge him until the two were some distance apart. Then he looked back and exchanged a knowing glance. Some petty treachery in the works between them? Likely. She would have Rhrenna look into it later.

Corinn's eyes drifted away from Saden to settle on a young man who stood at the far side of the courtyard, nearly atop the staircase that led to the lower terraces. He was flanked by several men with the firm-jawed look of trained guards. The man's reddish-blond hair was tousled as if an older brother had just mussed it up, yet his face—which Corinn sensed to be handsome even at a distance—took in the crowd with a confident composure.

"Who is that?" Corinn asked, gesturing with her chin.

Her maid answered that this was King Grae of Aushenia. The woman continued to explain that he would have been announced more formally, but he had arrived just a few hours earlier and asked to be in attendance this evening, even if just to watch the court from the—

"I know," she said. "Summon him." She glanced at the priest, smiling. "I'm sure the Vadayan will offer his seat to foreign royalty."

As she sat watching the messenger sent by the maid make his way through the crowd, Corinn wondered why she had done that. The words just came out of her mouth. She had claimed indifference to Grae to Rhrenna earlier; now she called him to her after a glance. The Meinish woman would find ways to poke fun at her for this, she was sure. It was done now, so she sat straight backed and waited, making a point of not watching the messenger interact with the king.

And just like that, before she knew it, a maid announced the monarch with a whisper in her ear. Corinn looked down the steps leading up to the dais and there he was, head bowed. His turbulent hair sported no crown, but that was a reasonable deference here in the heart of the empire. It wasn't that he really looked like Igguldan had, years before when Corinn first met him, but the sight of Grae came bearing more import than she had expected. First love, she thought. That's what it was. Foolishness. So thinking, she cursed herself for asking him over. What emotions would show on her face if she thought of such things here, with all the court's eyes on her? But she could do nothing now but go forward, composed.

The Aushenian straightened. Tall then. His shoulders broad and his form slim beneath them. He wore the loose-fitting shirt his nation favored, open at the collar, partially revealing the lean muscle beneath his coppery chest hairs. "Your Majesty," he said, smiling. "I am honored. I did not wish to disturb you, only to watch this wonderful occasion from the fringes."

Ah, that Aushenian accent. She had heard it often over the years, but it still had a strange effect on her. Its bold tones and clipped edges had poetry in their very nature. She felt her cheeks threatening to flush, but quelled it. "It wouldn't do to have a king sit among the merchant class. There are so few kings of note these days. I couldn't help but ask you to sit beside me. Please do."

"I'm honored." He pressed his lips to the rings of her proffered hand and then took the seat recently vacated by the priest. Grae's face was dangerously reminiscent of Igguldan's, though of slightly more masculine cut, just a little bit heavier in the jaw and bolder in the cheekbones. Even his freckles contributed, as if they had been splashed there playfully, intentionally. He was handsome. Corinn admitted Rhrenna was right about that.

He passed a few moments spouting the usual expressions of respect, and then sat grinning at the gathering before them. "Your Majesty," he said, "I'm ever amazed at the spectacle that is an Acacian banquet. The food alone is amazing. The music entrancing. The guests both dignified and courteous. The women are the most beautiful I've yet discovered in the world."

"Have you made a thorough survey of beauty in the world?"

"I have traveled, and I have eyes."

Certainly you do, Corinn thought. The kind of blue eyes

that adolescent girls swoon over. "Detail your findings for me, then."

Grae laughed and moved to dismiss the subject with a motion of his fingers.

"No, I mean it, sir. Tell me."

She held him to the point until he began an awkward description of the empire's races and descriptions of their women's qualities. He fumbled at first, but picking up on Corinn's projected good humor he soon made a game of it. Halfway through his discourse, Corinn joked that he seemed to have found beauty everywhere he looked. He did not dispute it, but by the end he circled back to where he had begun. He concluded that Acacian beauty is superior because it contained so much of the world within it. "All the virtues of the races, none of the flaws. Your beauty, my queen, is that of the center point of the world."

Corinn's brow wrinkled with skepticism. "Indeed." She took a wineglass offered her by a servant. Grae did the same. "Where's your brother?" she asked. "I heard you two travel together frequently."

"We do," Grae said, "but he's off studying agricultural techniques on the Mainland. He likes to be industrious, my little brother."

"I know the type. You were close to him when you were young?"

They were, Grae agreed. At Corinn's prompting, he told her several tales of their youth, hiding in the far north of Aushenia. Such a wild country, he made it seem, though that might have been because he still imagined it with a frightened child's eyes. She could picture those mountains and thick forests and white bears and snowstorms and swarms of insects as thick as flocks of migrating birds.

"We could not hide forever, though," Grae said. "So I did eventually come back into the world. Only it was a world in which my father and older brother no longer lived. It was a

338

world in which my nation was overrun with foreigners, carved up, a playground for the Numrek. Dire times. Better that they are behind us now."

"You didn't fight for my brother, did you?"

"For Aliver?" Grae looked uneasy, but then regained his composure and answered with what appeared to be simple honesty. "No, I didn't, but I would have. Proudly, I would have. When he was massing to press his battle against Maeander in Talay, I was fighting for the life of my nation. I fought the remnants of the Numrek still on my soil, and I expelled the Mein and closed the Gradthic Gap. It was bloody, and . . . Well, I would argue that Aliver and I were fighting common enemies, even if we did not do so together."

Corinn did not comment on the later statement. "Tell me, when you say that you fought, what does that mean exactly? I mean, I fought Hanish himself, right here in Acacia, but that doesn't mean I actually drew his blood with my own blade. My sister does that sort of thing, not me. But you, when you fight, do you fight yourself, or do you instruct others to fight in your name?"

"My sword is no virgin blade," Grae said. Corinn noted a flare of arrogance held back. "I never sent men into battle. I led them into battle. I will not brag to you, Your Majesty. That would be unseemly. But I invite you to ask others of my character. I think you will find my reputation is sound."

No doubt, Corinn thought. He did look the part of a leader of men.

She could imagine him in armor, sword in hand, inspiring others to acts of bravery. Outwardly, he was the type of man both men and women would follow. She made a note mentally to look into his reputation, as he himself had suggested.

Beneath them the banquet continued. At some point, Wren entered. Corinn followed her with her eyes for some time, believing she could just see the first signs of her pregnancy at her waist, not enough that others would notice, but it was there. Lady Wren, secretly carrying Dariel's child. What did she intend? Delivegu had learned that she planned to announce the child once the prince had returned. Doesn't trust me to react with joy to the news, is that it? Corinn wondered. You may be shrewder than I credit. I'll figure out what to do with you yet.

Different courses came and went from the tables. The musicians played. On several occasions Corinn and Grae had to pause to acknowledge some toast or to chat briefly with those who had the temerity to approach the dais. Once a storyteller told of how King Standish put down the revolt and kept peace in the world, an elaborate tale that Corinn knew had little truth in it. She had enough of the early king's private journals to know how much the official record differed from the confessions of the monarch behind the myth.

She was not listening much, for Grae made for diverting company. Praise for her horse culture plans rolled off his tongue. Aushenians, he said, considered their equine traditions part of what had nurtured their independent spirit. To imagine such a connection with noble beasts near the heart of mighty empire like Acacia excited him greatly. He offered his countrymen's expertise, if Acacia had use for it. Corinn said she likely did, half forgetting that she had started the whole business just to keep her ambitious councillors busy.

Grae was almost too diverting. She sensed something held back in him, an arrogance that hid beneath his genial façade. It wasn't exactly unattractive—especially as he controlled it—but it did make her wonder.

Perhaps she had absorbed too many breaths of her own spell, for she asked, "King Grae, just what is it you're really after?"

Grae jerked his glass of wine away from his lips in midsip, spilling a bit. "My lady?"

Feeling as playful about it as she appeared, she leaned close and, knowing the posture pressed her breasts together and that Grae had to keep his eyes from straying to them, asked, "No man comes to me without wanting something—not even a king. What is it you want?"

"I won't try to hide the truth from you," Grae said, losing his relaxed demeanor for a moment. "I'd fail if I did. I'm an admirer. I always have been, but . . . perhaps I've matured enough to understand it."

"And become brave enough to voice it, at least vaguely."

Grae dipped his head, but kept his eyes on her. "I'll happily get more specific if you—"

"Would like? Well, I would. Indulge me." She stretched out the last sentence, using her lips and the tilt of her head to add allure. She still did not know quite what had gotten into her. When was the last time she had flirted with a man? Ages. Since Hanish, but what sort of flirting was that? Mostly, she had attacked him with her sharp tongue. Strange method of courting. No, she had not batted her eyes at a man since adolescence, since Igguldan. But whereas that had seemed a memory too painful to approach before, Grae seemed a version of the same things she had admired in his brother—a living version, sitting beside her.

"You really wish to know?" he asked. "For me to say it outright? That's not Aushenian style. Normally, I'd have to compose a poem—"

"Which would be very entertaining, I'm sure. Do compose one and recite it for me later. At present, though, be direct."

The king sat a minute looking like a perplexed child, and then he shrugged and regained his charm. "As you wish, Your Majesty. The truth is, I've come in the hope that I might court you, and that if the signs seemed favorable I might offer myself for marriage. With all the respect due your elevated position."

Ah . . . So there it is. At least he speaks plainly. "You want to make me your wife?"

"I'd be content for you to make me your husband, Your Majesty." He leaned toward her. "Look, I am a proud man, content to fight for my honor, to rebuff any insult. And

Aushenia is a proud nation. But I'm also a reasonable man. You, Queen Corinn, are a woman—and ruler—of both grace and immense power. You can't be surprised that I'd wish us and our nations joined. I trust this doesn't offend you. You did ask for me—"

"To be straightforward. No, no, I'm not so easily offended. Certainly not by such reasonable flattery. You do catch me off guard, though. I had no idea my marital status was so much on the mind of Aushenia."

"Oh, it is, believe me. At least in so far as I am Aushenia."

Corinn remembered then that she once professed no fondness for blue eyes. Who wants to look into water? she had teased Rhrenna. She would hardly be able to say that now, with Grae's eyes so intent on her, so refreshing. That's what they were: the promise of a cool drink of water to a thirsty mouth. She almost laughed outright at the metaphor. It was the Aushenians who gamed at poetry. She should leave it to them.

"You know that no such union would be on equal terms," she said, straightening and speaking with the hint of royal detachment. "We would swallow you. I don't say there aren't advantages to that, but we've trod near this path before."

"I know," Grae said, responding with a similarly aloof tone. "And I know you won my brother's heart before mine. But that was not to be. We who remain, however, still have our lives to live. My father and brother both wanted an Acacian-Aushenian union. It is usually the case that great ideas are delayed. The early prophets are slain or maligned. Often we see the full wisdom of visionaries only in retrospect."

"And the retrospective view of your queen Elena? She would not bless this union you propose, would she?"

Corinn did not get the chance to hear his answer. Someone shouted, a rough bark that had no place at a banquet. A second later a scream—high-pitched and feminine—cut through the revelry and left silence in its place. That did not last long, as people began to point and murmur and exclaim.

"What is that about?" Grae asked. He followed the pointing fingers—there were more each moment—and Corinn did the same.

For a few long seconds she did not believe what she saw. And then when she believed that her eyes did see the thing she wondered if it was not some elaborate hoax. And then she knew it was not, just as the crowd knew it and erupted in chaos. What she saw was a winged creature, its wings enormous, lit from underneath by the torchlight and bright against the screen of the night sky behind it, descending toward them. Its body was sinewy and curved, its head that of a reptilian beast, its tail whipping audibly beneath it. Hind legs lashed the air, and for a moment Corinn was certain the monster was going to fall on her.

"A dragon," she whispered, and knew in that instant how quickly death could fall from the sky.

"Archers!" Grae called, on his feet now, shielding Corinn.

There were no archers, though. There never were at banquets. Guests were forbidden weapons, and the only arms allowed inside were those of high-ranked Marah and of her Numrek bodyguards. Both forces peeled away from the walls and pushed toward her, drawing their weapons and shouting for the crowd to make way. They surrounded her, shoving Grae aside. They formed a bristling buttress with their swords pointed skyward. The creature circled a few times above them. In one turn Corinn thought she saw— But that couldn't be.

And then the creature landed. Its feet settled on the court-yard stones with a surprising lightness. With a strange rolling of its shoulders and quick clicking sound, it drew its wings in. Blinking its large, round eyes, it took in the cowering people and the sudden disarray it had caused. The creature held its two thin upper arms delicately before it, claw tips touching and eyes darting about with the nervous energy of a child who

343

suspects she has done something either wonderful or punishable but awaits confirmation of which it is.

In that stillness, Corinn saw the figure on the creature's back. Mena. Her sister had ridden the beast. Now she slid down and hit the stones merrily. She grinned ear to ear and, fixing her eyes on her older sister, asked, as if it were the most natural question in the world, "Did you get my letter?"

Chapter Twenty-nine

Mena had known there were considerable risks, but she thought she and Elya could pull it off. The night sky would provide cover. They would leave Melio and the others in northern Talay and fly high over Bocoum, then low across the Inner Sea. They would approach Acacia from the east, flying over the crags at the back of the palace. She knew the Blood Moon banquet would be in full swing, and that no bows were allowed. There would be no weapons at all among the guests, and the guards were not overnumerous. She had sat through enough of these events herself to know that. Anyway, the guards would rush to protect Corinn before launching any attack. That, she figured, would give her time to make an entrance that would be written down in Acacian official histories.

That was how she had planned it, and that was the way it had played out: a good bit of confusion and shouting and brandished weapons and indignation, yes, but nothing she had not expected. Just why it felt so important to make such an entrance was a complicated thing she had not sorted out in her mind. She did have one answer that justified it, as she explained to her sister early the next morning, when she was summoned to her.

"What was the meaning of that?" Corinn asked, in lieu of a greeting.

When they were apart, Mena had difficulty remembering

Corinn as a child or thinking of her as a sibling. It was only the somewhat distant, somewhat frightening queen whom she recalled. But when they were together, there were moments when Mena saw Corinn as the sister she once knew. Moments when Mena recognized the pursing of Corinn's lips as an insecure gesture made when she felt her beauty was not enough.

Mena chose not to let this official summons become as "official" as Corinn likely wanted. She strode in with a pleasant expression on her face and plopped down on the nearest comfortable seat. She stretched, and in so doing discovered that a yawn resided in her throat and wished to be let free. Corinn watched her, standing with her arms folded and her face wearing a scowl of undisguised annoyance.

"Nice to see you as well, Sister," Mena said, once the long yawn had slipped away. "I can't believe Dariel has truly sailed to the Other Lands. Any word from him?"

"No," Corinn said. "No, there couldn't be. Not yet. No messenger birds fly the Gray Slopes. We won't hear from him until he arrives back at the Outer Isles. Just a few weeks, though, if all has gone well. You will be told about it later. Now, what was the meaning of last night's show?"

"I do wish he were here. I thought about him often while I was hunting, and so looked forward to seeing him." She paused a moment, exhaled, and finally acknowledged Corinn's question, though with no more solemnity than before. "What was the meaning of it? That's a funny question, really. I mean, imagine if some adult said that when we were girls." She put on a gruff voice: " 'What's the meaning of this, young lady?' We would have laughed him out of the room."

"Have you lost your wits?"

"No, not at all," Mena said. "Just the opposite. I've gained some wit. Corinn, I didn't mean to upstage you. I just wanted people to see Elya before they heard tales of her, just see with their own eyes and realize how gentle she is. Word of it is probably halfway around the empire by now, and I'm glad of it. I want her safe. I want every fool with a bow or with delusions of grandeur about dragon slaying to know that she is not a target. She's under the protection of—well, of the queen of Acacia, right? Tell me you don't think she's lovely. You must come and see her. She slept the night in the courtyard off my chambers. It's so funny to see her here, beside household items. You should see how she acted the first time she saw a mirror—"

"You're not making sense." Corinn's anger had slipped just a fraction toward perplexity. "What is that thing?"

"That *thing* is my good friend. No harm can come to her. None at all. You're to put word out to that effect. A royal decree. Let everybody know it." Corinn began to protest, but Mena calmed her with a somber change in her tone. "We've started this from the wrong end. Sit with me. Let me explain it all from the beginning, and then come and meet her with me. Properly, I mean, not with all the confusion of last night."

To Mena's relief, Corinn only held her pressed-lip expression for a few more seconds. Then she called for a pot of tea and sat across from her sister as a servant entered with it. When the servant left them with steaming cups, Mena began her tale.

She told it all just as she remembered. Corinn had heard reports of their progress with the foulthings at every stage, but reports were dry things with no emotion to them. The emotion was what Mena wanted Corinn to understand. She wanted her to know how hard it was for her, seeking out monsters and seeing all their foulness and killing them one by one. She may have been marvelously skilled at it. She may have taken risks and planted fatal blows when others would readily have done so in her place, but none of that meant it was easy, satisfying, enjoyable, thrilling, or any such nonsense. Just the opposite. The fact that she had a natural gift for slaughter was a great burden to her.

"We all have burdens," Corinn said. "You don't doubt the rightness of what you did?"

No, Mena did not. She described the bloated vultures and the foraging creatures, the lion with the eyes down its back, the snakes on legs, the monstrosity that had once been a fish but became a ravening mouth. The tenten beast, she said, had stared at her with malevolence different from a mere animal's. It had been changed not just in size and shape but inside its mind as well.

"The Giver's tongue is a foulness," she said. "All traces of it have to be wiped out."

"You're mistaken," Corinn said. "It's not the Giver's tongue that's foul; it's the corruptions of the Santoth. They were banished for a reason, Mena, and the years in exile have done nothing but make them dangerous ogres. If they made the foulthings, it's because they are foul themselves. Remember, though, if there is truth in any of the Giver's story, it begins with him creating the entire earth and all the many good things in it."

Mena eyed her as she sipped her tea. "You seem surer of this than you were before."

"I know more than I did before. You've been away, but I trust you've heard rumors of the work I performed in Talay."

"I heard tales about you bringing water from the ground wherever you pleased. I didn't know what to make of it."

"Make of it that I've been learning ancient wisdom. Sorcery, if you must call it something, although it's not so exciting as that may sound."

"How? Who is teaching you?"

"I'm teaching myself from some old texts. Don't look so frightened, Mena. I haven't gone mad any more than you have. Nor is it dangerous. Just think of it as—as if I were studying medicine or music. I'm learning things that expand my knowledge in useful ways."

"But to make water come out of—"

"Water comes out of the ground all the time. There's nothing more natural. I just help direct it. But go on with your tale. It's more amusing than my study of ancient spells."

Though she was not sure that was true, Mena did want to get to Elya. She had not said the things she wanted to yet. She described the day she had crept up to the lip of the hill and looked down into that orchard and first seen that reptilian head. Some part of her had known that here was something different, but her mind had not grasped it in time. She told of how they had hunted it, shot it through with crossbow bolts, and tried to weigh it to the ground. They had torn shreds in its marvelous wings. None of it was easy to relive: neither her flight clutching its tail nor the battering she took landing nor the sight of what she thought to be the dead creature when she had climbed down to look upon it.

"I can't believe how close I came to killing her," Mena said. "I ordered her shot at when she had never done anything to anybody. That shames me now."

What joy, then, to learn that the creature was not dead after all! Joy in watching her heal so quickly, in observing her tenderness and her comic ways. Joy in coming to feel a bond with her. That was why Elya was so important. Not only had this creature of such beauty and gentleness chosen her as a friend—her, Mena, the killer of Maeben and so many other creatures. Not only that, but being with her infused Mena with the creature's goodness. She felt that goodness inside her body. She became part of it, and everything about the world seemed better.

"You don't know how much that means to me," Mena said. "You didn't see those foulthings, didn't look them in the eyes the way I had to. For so long I thought of them, of what they were, worrying about what they might become. Corinn, some of them had such raging hatred in them. The tenten beast wasn't just an animal. It hated as only humans can."

"Which is why it was an abomination," Corinn said.

"The abomination is that Santoth sorcery did that to them."

Corinn ignored this statement. "Your creature cannot be trusted. It may change into—"

"No! No, she won't." Mena said this with all the conviction she could muster. She believed it completely, of course, but it was not all she felt. She had dreamed that Elya turned toward her with bloodshot eyes, with that terrible, malevolent intelligence in them. But these were only nightmares, she now believed, the lingering traces of having seen so much in her battles. Nothing more. She meant it when she said, "Elya is what she is, and that's wonderful. She makes me feel good. I haven't felt good in such a long time. I don't remember when I last felt . . . just joyful. Do you?"

She was surprised by the question, making it a full stop instead of only a part of her discourse. She looked at her sister even more deeply, realizing that Corinn had likely been dissatisfied more than she, for longer, in even more ways. She had never quite realized it, but now she was sure.

Corinn did not answer the question directly. "It's preposterous."

Mena smiled. At least Corinn had not said it with malice. "Perhaps, but, if so, I like things preposterous." She leaned back into the comfort of her chair. "What aspect of our lives hasn't been preposterous?"

"What do you intend to do with it?"

"She'll stay with me. As long as she wants to, at least. She's no burden or danger. She eats fruit. Just fruit. Her feet are as light on the ground as a bird's. She'll soon be loved by everyone."

"I don't know that I can allow that," Corinn said. She set down her teacup. "Here in the palace, I mean. There might be an incident. I know you favor this thing, but you should have ended it. Be done with these foulthings forever."

Mena looked at the bowl of apricots on the table beside her and plucked one. That was a topic she did not want to discuss.

In truth, she had begun to suspect that Elya might be pregnant. Nothing definite gave it away, just a feeling of other pulses of life within her. She might be wrong. How could Elya be pregnant if she was the only one of her kind? In any event it was better to keep the possibility to herself for the time being.

"It won't be for long," she said. "I'll fly on her the next time I go to Vumu." She bit into the apricot and managed to speak as she chewed. "I've decided that's what I want to do next: go to Vumu for a time. I'd like to be the priestess again. This time, however, I'll show them Maeben at peace. I'll ask them to look up at the sky without fear. They'll look up and see Elya, and they'll feel safe for once. I'd like to give them that gift, for they gave me so much during my time there. The people will love it; the priests will hate it. Perfect."

"Perfect? Hardly. You may fancy your pet, but remember it's a foul thing. It's distorted. Who knows what—"

"Please, Corinn. She's not foul. I'm the one who hunted down monster after monster. I know foul. Elya has not a drop of bad blood in her. She's beauty, Corinn. Gentleness and humor and beauty. Come. Come right now and see her."

Corinn lagged behind Mena when they entered her quarters. She craned her neck around, clearly nervous. She did not stay that way long, though. Elya—fierce winged creature that sent nobles running and caused guards to fumble for their swords—was marching around the far side of the entrance court under the direction of a child. Aaden sat in the saddle of her shoulders, waving a wooden sword and encouraging the creature to attack. Elya did so, although her attack was rather careful, maneuvering through the chairs and tables of a sitting area. Her neck craned about to make sure she did not brush anything, and her tail carved elaborate circles, occasionally touching objects as if to steady them.

Two maids stood nervously nearby, as did one of the prince's tutors. Clearly, they had been beseeching the boy to come away, but now stood about, curious and worried at the same time.

"I didn't know he was here," Mena said, speaking in a near whisper. "Really, I didn't."

"Not much gets past Aaden. He's as hard to keep track of as Dariel used to be."

"Do you want me to call to her? To get him off?"

Corinn watched awhile before answering. "No. You're right; she's gentle. Even I can see that." Corinn slipped to one side, leaning against a pillar and half hiding herself. Mena joined her and together they watched.

"You say she is easily hurt?" Corinn asked.

"Her wings are paper thin. They're amazing. You can see right through them. If she didn't heal so quickly she'd never have survived. But she does heal amazingly fast. And she made me heal faster, too. I should still be splinted and battered. Instead, I've never felt better."

"You've never looked better either," Corinn admitted. "You look like a maiden in love for the first time."

"Why, thank you, Sister. I was going to say the same about you last night. Sitting next to King Grae. Quite the striking couple you two made."

"You thought that before you dropped from the sky?"

"Exactly," Mena said, a lift in her eyebrows and a slight purse to her lips. "So?"

Corinn did not accept the invitation. "Your Elya, might she have any military purpose?"

"Don't even joke about that. I mean it. Look at her. She's all delicacy. Power, too, but none that I would allow to be endangered. Don't even think about it."

"All right. All right. I had to ask," Corinn said. "She is a songbird, then, not a hunting hawk. That was obvious, actually, in the way she held her hands together and batted her eyelids last night. Preposterous."

Mena stared at her sister, her mouth open and the corners

of her lips uptilted. It had been a long time since Corinn had said something as good-natured as that. She felt awash with affection for her. It was poignant, in a way, for she knew that she had not felt such affection for Corinn in a long time, but what did that matter? Now she was standing with her sister, spying on a child and a dragon. "What better thing?"

"What?" Corinn asked, but Mena did not answer.

When they parted, she embraced her sister for a few breaths longer than formality required. Corinn did not pull away or express any discomfiture. All things considered, it was the finest few hours Mena had spent with her sister since, well, she could not say since when. There must have been a time when they were young and easy with each other, but, if so, she could not remember it anymore. Perhaps they would grow closer now. Why not? The foulthings were gone. Elya was found. Aaden was healthy. Corinn was queen, so confident, in control of so many things. Dariel would be home soon. And when Melio arrived with the rest of the returning hunters she would run her hands down his back and across his backside and ask him to make love to her. And he would, of course, though he would look at her in surprise, smile his crooked grin, and find some way to jest; but she would close his mouth with kisses.

She was almost ready to put down her sword for good. Perhaps the time had come to do as Melio had so long wished. Maybe she was finally ready to be a mother, to raise a child to know peaceful things. Yes, she had not felt this good in a long time.

Chapter Thirty

Delivegu did not much like the tedious work of espionage. It could be quite beneficial, a real boon at times. Certainly, that was all true. But if he were caught during any of its less dignified moments, it would tarnish his image. He went to great pains to ensure that he was always seen at ease, in control, with a drink or cards or a woman at hand: Delivegu, a man with few cares, a man above the petty concerns of others, one who benefited from human folly but never became the butt of it. That was the image of himself he most fancied. He wore a cloak of vice around him as normally as others wore clothing, and he felt just as naked without it.

So the fact that he stood pressed to an alley wall for long, boring stretches of time was not the sort of thing he wanted anybody to know about. It was just the type of action he sometimes needed to take in order to gain useful information. That was why he was doing so one night a fortnight after the Blood Moon banquet. He stood alert as the evening progressed. He kept to the shadows, listening to the footfalls of pedestrians and to the occasional passing carriage and more than once spying passing revelers intoxicated with drink, singing as they went. Ah, the type of activity he should be up to!

Once a dog trailing behind a small group of Talayan dignitaries sniffed him out and stood at the mouth of the alley growling, the ridge of fur along its backbone bristling. Fortunately, the Talayans were too caught up in their conversation to pay the hound much attention. Delivegu stared the dog down, cursing under his breath and illustrating the full extent of his annoyance through the vicious way he jerked his head to the side, an oft-repeated instruction that the creature should move on if it wanted to stay breathing. Eventually, the dog lifted its leg and peed out its opinion of Delivegu on the spot. Only then did it prance away.

If Delivegu managed to become the queen's confidant in the manner he wished, he would make sure to delegate duties like this to others. Not yet, though. Not just yet. First he had to get things right, and he could trust only himself to see that accomplished. This little venture, for instance, might be a dead end. If it was, he would not want anybody else thinking that he cared about it personally, that he spent an entire night standing in an alley.

"Clear your head, man!" Delivegu ran his fingers roughly over his face. "She's just a woman. Nothing to get twisted about."

Yet he was twisted. Things had become personal. That annoyed him. The source, and prime target, of his annoyance? King Grae of Aushenia. That strutting gamecock. He had not liked Grae from the moment he set eyes on him at the Blood Moon banquet, when he watched a servant leave the queen's side, wind through the crowd, and then lead Grae to the queen's dais. A mere courtesy of royalty, he had hoped at first, but then he had another suspicion.

Delivegu knew women, nobles just as readily as tavern girls. He could tell that the queen had been quite taken with the Aushenian. He knew when indifference was feigned, how to read body gestures for the meanings they highlighted or attempted to hide. He did not even need to hear their conversation to know that the queen had toyed with Grae, coy and coquettish. And the lout sat there, tall and self-satisfied, showing his sparkling teeth in a smile and pointing about the room with his square-jawed chin, tossing his auburn hair while the queen ate it all up. Delivegu had wanted to throttle him. It only got worse from there.

The queen continued to entertain the monarch throughout the week that followed, but Delivegu could gain no access to her. Corinn did not call for him. She sent him only one letter stating simply: *Do nothing in regard to the woman and child. She is not your concern anymore.* Not so much as a thank-you, for bringing her the news of Wren's pregnancy in the first place! Nor had his letters—meant to entice her with the suggestion of new intelligence—merited any answer whatsoever. He could not even get a response from Rhrenna. He tried to call on her directly but got no farther than the surly Numrek guards who protected the queen's offices. What strange protectors they made: brutes who looked as if they would just as soon kill a friend as a foe.

Even worse, all the information he could gather from his sources made the palace sound like a marvel of joy and optimism. Princess Mena's spectacular arrival on that creature had set everyone's spirits on high, it seemed. The island flooded with curious nobles wishing to see the beast. Which meant more entertainments, more dances, more banquets: none of which Delivegu was invited to. A barge of entertainers broke off from the floating merchants and docked in Acacia's harbor. They swarmed through the streets, taking impromptu advantage of the festive atmosphere, making it more so. Under normal circumstances, Delivegu would have had a time of it himself, but instead he found himself grinding his teeth in worry that Grae had used all of this cheer to bed the queen. His queen. Maddening.

He knew instinctively that the Aushenian would not like him. Of course he wouldn't. Though the queen probably could not see it beneath his surface charms, Grae was just as much a cock as Delivegu. If the Aushenian strutted his way into Corinn's bed and onto the throne, Delivegu's aspirations—for the chancellorship and more—would be thwarted. That decided things for him.

With nobody else to focus on, he aimed his sights—and a good deal of jealous animus—at King Grae. That was what he had been doing for several days now. He whispered into a few ears, posed questions, offered silver. He spread word among those who had connections with the servants and other staff in the palace or in the foreign district. He was looking for intelligence about the Aushenian king. Anything; romantic liaisons in his past; proclivities that might upset the queen; evidence of cowardice on the battlefield, perhaps. Delivegu had even bribed a clerk with access to the historical library to search the speeches and proclamations issued in the king's name. There had to be something. Grae could not be the faithful admirer that he wanted Corinn to think him.

What did he discover for all his searching? Not much. The king had bedded his share of noblewomen, but that was hardly a secret. Such wasn't even out of keeping with his nation's traditions. He had been known to bathe nude with male companions in the hot springs of the Gradthic mountains, but that wasn't anything he'd be ashamed of either. Northerners did that sort of thing.

His military record was unblemished. Indeed, if his valor in securing his national borders after Hanish's downfall was to be believed, it was amazing he had lived through it. His official proclamations were often critical of the Acacian Empire, of Akaran leaders of the past, and even of the reigning queen, certainly of the quota trade and the League of Vessels' grip on commerce.

But so what? None of these things was enough. Delivegu wrote them out in several draft letters, but in reading each through he saw how petty it all sounded, how insubstantial. Aliver Akaran himself had sought to abolish the quota trade. Dariel Akaran had blown the league platforms to smithereens. Corinn, he feared, would see it for what it was and adjust her opinion of him downward. He needed something more.

This search was what had brought him to the district below the palace, the area reserved for foreign dignitaries. He had been standing in the shadows near King Grae's accommodations long enough that his legs were numb and his head aching from the repetitive tedium of his thoughts. He was so near to slumber that he started when a figure opened the door and slipped into the street. The light was faint, but Delivegu's eyes were accustomed enough to the starlight to make out the young man. He wore a hooded cloak of Aushenian cut. Delivegu had seen such garments before and found them lacking in terms of fashion. Aushenians still fancied themselves hunters of the woods and marshes. Why did cultures always mythologize the past? Silly, really, when what was of more import to them was the ever-oncoming future.

But he shouldn't be distracted. The thing to notice here was that the man wore a cloak when the night was warm. He walked with a nervous gait, looking around as if he feared being discovered. Something clandestine was at hand. Delivegu, quiet as a cat in his fur-soled leather boots, followed the man through the foreign district, out the open gate and down toward the terraces, through the markets, and around the square in which a few early laborers were gathering in the hope of securing work with the dawn. The journey took little more than twenty minutes, but by the time it ended Delivegu scented that his fortunes had shifted.

The hooded man paid an early call on a commoner's messenger service, early enough that he had to pound on the door for some time. He was eventually admitted. Delivegu took up his vantage point a little way down the street. There he waited until the hooded man reappeared, looking just as nervous, and headed back the way he had come. Weighing his options, Delivegu decided to pay his own call instead of following the man farther.

He entered with a casual air, letting the doorbell tinkle his entry merrily. It was a dingy place, crowded with crates and rank with the smell of bird droppings. There were a few cages around the room, large enough to hold messenger birds. Most of them were empty; and the few that were not housed sickly-looking creatures, feather plucked and mangy. Not the type of service a king—or a king's servant, even—would have need to employ.

The proprietor came from the back, looking sleepy and cranky. "I'm not open yet," he said, taking Delivegu in with suspicious eyes. "Door should've been locked. Back yourself out and return in a bit."

"Ah, but you must be open. I saw a customer leave just a moment ago."

"That bastard? He woke me from a pleasant sleep. Nearly bashed his head for it. You move on before I treat you to what I should've given him." The man was shorter than Delivegu, a bit heavy around the middle, and had a limp; but he moved with gruff confidence, coming forward and reaching out to turn the unwelcome arrival around.

"Hold a minute!" Delivegu said, his voice sharp and dripping with threat. "Be careful whom you touch, friend. This could be a good morning for you, or it could be a very unpleasant one."

The man froze. He stood uncomfortably close to Delivegu, as his momentum had taken him a step too far, even as his grasping arm drew back. Craning his eyes upward, he said, "I don't care for threats."

Delivegu smiled and eased back a half step. "Well, then don't hear one in what I said. You need not, if you're reasonable."

"All right, what do you want? Message sent, eh? Can't go out just now. Don't have the bird for it."

Delivegu put on a frown. "Men like you confound me. You're a businessman, but you offer such gruffness to one who, for all you know, has arrived to offer you a fortune in commerce."

"Hah!" the man said. "Been in it awhile and that's never happened. Not waiting for it, either. What's your business?"

"My business, friend, regards the man who was here before me."

The proprietor kept his eyes on Delivegu. He moved backward warily. "That one? What's it to you?" And then, as if he regretted asking the question, he added, "My customer's business is private." He had reached the counter that ran along the back wall. He edged behind it, his fingertips touching the countertop, twitching slightly, betraying more nervousness than his face did.

"You have some weapon back there, don't you?" Delivegu asked. He had come forward as the man backed and stood now with his legs planted firmly, both his arms loose beside his body. "It would be a mistake to reach for it. Don't. Listen to me before you do anything foolish. I need to know what is in that note. You haven't sent it yet, surely." He paused just long enough for the man to protest that there was no note. No protest came. "I won't tell a soul about this. You'll live on just as before. You'll send the note. I'll just know what's in it, and because I know, treachery may well be thwarted. This situation provides you with many opportunities to lose. What I offer is a simple win: two options."

So saying, Delivegu held his arms out. In his left was a small canvas bag, heavy with something. In his right was a delicate dagger. "A sack of coins or a blade. Which do you prefer? And, I assure you, I'm quite skilled with the blade. I was raised badly, you see. Don't look at the blade too closely," he added. "It's sharp enough to cut your eyeball."

"You're mad," the man said, though he did pull his gaze away from the knife. "The note is to his mother. A letter announcing his engagement, that's all. That's what he said."

"If that's true, there's no reason not to show it to me. I'll laugh and you'll laugh, and the note will fly to Mother. No harm done." Nodding at the dagger, he said, "I've nothing against you, but I will gut you like a hog and leave you wrapped in your entrails. Or I'll leave you doubly enriched, and all before normal business hours. Think quickly."

The man did. He valued his life more than his honor. A reasonable way of perceiving the world, Delivegu thought as he took the parchment from the man's fingers, unrolled it, and read.

The note was not an announcement of an engagement, but by this point Delivegu knew it wouldn't be. It was, at first reading, so deceptively simple that one might have wondered why it even needed to be sent. It stated:

B. All is progressing. Will have her confidence soon. G.

Delivegu felt the blood rush through his body, tingling in his fingers and throbbing in his temples and even stirring in his groin. G. He was certain that stood for *Grae*, and just as certain that *she* was Queen Corinn. Who was the B? This was just the sort of evidence he had been looking for, though it meant little by itself. If it could lead to greater evidence . . .

"To whom is this to be sent?" he asked.

The proprietor had no idea. The bird's destination was to be a similar messenger service in Aos, to be picked up by whoever knew to ask for it. Questioned as to whether that arrangement was strange, the man agreed it was but also admitted that he had sent several such notes in the past few weeks. "I don't ask questions, just provide a service, you know." He motioned vaguely with his hand.

Conveniently, the proprietor did not have a bird ready to send the message. It would not leave his shop until the next evening, at the earliest, and this only if his returning bird came back in good health later that day. The ones in the shop were convalescing. This fact had troubled the man who had left the note. The message would be delayed, possibly long enough for an earthbound traveler to beat it to its destination—if the traveler left immediately.

It took Delivegu only a few minutes to draw up his course of action. He returned the missive to the proprietor's hand, weighted it with the sack of coins, and bade him a good day. He did not tell anyone that he was going. He sent no message to the queen, assuming that it was unlikely she would notice his absence anyway.

Late morning he took passage to Alecia, easily enough done, for many boats cut the waters between Acacia and the great city. He sailed through the day, overnight, and disembarked late the next morning. He haunted Alecia's harbor most of the day before jumping aboard a merchant's skiff heading north along the coast. He spent the night aboard that vessel, uncomfortably wet but determined, and the next morning found him leaping the gap onto the stone pier of the harbor in Aos. He had slept little, but he had made good time. He walked along the pier in something of a trance, confident now that he had arrived before the messenger bird could have.

For a time he watched the old men who were using long-necked birds to catch small fish. They sat talking among themselves as their black birds, sleek and dangerous looking, winged their way into the clear water, cutting through the schools of silver fish. Every so often, the men pulled the birds in by strings attached to harnesses on their bodies. The birds protested every time, coming up angry, their throats bulging with living fish, unable to swallow them because of the metal rings around the base of their necks. The old men talked on as they massaged the fish back up and out of the bird's squawking mouths, plopping them into buckets.

Strange the way some people spend their time, Delivegu thought, and finally walked on.

He found the messenger bird shop with surprising ease. He was seated on a bench a little way down from it when it opened its doors. The street was much the same as its counterpart on

Acacia. His stomach was set grumbling by the scent of onions boiling in seasoned oil and water, a soup for the common folk. He clamped a hand over his abdomen and breathed through his mouth. He had not eaten commoners' food in years and did not plan to start again, no matter the lure.

He saw several birds descend toward the coops around the back of the building. One of them, he was certain, carried his message. He watched a few people enter the shop, but none drew his attention until a blond-haired boy strolled on to the scene. He would have ignored him, for he seemed as aimless as any street urchin. Up until the moment he bolted inside the shop. That he did with sudden purpose. When he left a few moments later, he feigned a casual air. Delivegu didn't buy it, and he blended into the crowd in pursuit of the boy. He followed him toward the outskirts of the town, near enough to the farmlands that he could smell the cow and hog dung. He nearly turned back in disgust, fearing he had gotten something terribly wrong even as he continued forward. He was rewarded for staying with his hunch.

The boy met a man who appeared to be nothing but a farmer. The boy handed him something and stood a moment, conversing with him. And then Delivegu understood. B! There he was. There he really was! The infamous Barad the Lesser, the old rabble-rouser of the Kidnaban mines. The sight of him and the recognition of each detail—his bulky, stooped frame; the boulderlike head atop his thick neck; the low grumble of his voice, audible even from this distance—almost caused Delivegu to stumble over his own feet. The good fortune of it was too much to be believed. The man had been wanted for years. There had once been a bounty on his head. That was years ago, but he was still an enemy of the empire, Grae and Barad in secret conspiracy against the queen. Here was the key to all his desires, found walking down a street in a nothing crap hole of a village outside Aos, conversing with a shoeless peasant boy, leading a goat behind him.

363

With a few deft moves, he could capture the empire's most elusive agitator and bring shame on Grae at the same time. These two strokes, he was sure, would strip away the queen's haughty façade, and then there would be nothing between him and the rest of her. Delivegu walked on, his mouth flooded with saliva, a carnivore seeing a kill in reach.

Chapter Thirty-one

It was always small things about his earlier life that Dariel thought of, moments that had otherwise been forgotten. Perhaps it was because they had been forgotten that they had the stealth to slip into his mind unbidden. He thought of the first time he had seen Aaden laugh. His nephew had been but a baby, propped upon a maid's lap one afternoon. As he had done so many times before, Dariel danced about in an attempt to entertain the boy. But this time Aaden did not simply watch him. This time the boy's mouth tilted with mirth, and the strangest barrage of sound escaped him. At first Dariel thought he was coughing, but then Aaden tilted his head back and waved one arm in the air in an unmistakable gesture. He was laughing! Never had that simple act seemed such a revelation of humanity.

Or he remembered a pair of felt slippers he had once bought as a gift for Val and then lost before actually giving them to him. How frustrating! Or he thought of how, as a boy, he had always stared at Aliver when he was not looking. More so than full grown men, the shape of his brother's arms and shoulders and ease with which he handled his training sword had shot Dariel through with admiration.

And instead of remembering Wren in battle aboard the *Ballan*, entwined with him in lovemaking, climbing over the railing of the league warship she helped destroy, or standing beside him during the wind-whipped funeral ceremony for his father and brother, he recalled swimming in the upper garden pools with her one blazingly hot afternoon. Saying she had had enough, she kissed him and rose out of the water and walked away. He watched her body, displayed as it was beneath a thin swimming shift that was somehow more erotic than actual nudity. But once she was out of sight his eyes fell on the line of dark footprints on the pale gray stone. Such perfectly curved imitations of her feet. The footprints had faded so quickly in the sun that he breathlessly watched them disappear.

Such were the things that crept into his mind now during the long hours of caged solitude. Each time he realized that he was daydreaming—and further realized where he was—it was like suddenly remembering something so bad that he could not believe he had forgotten it even for a moment. There really had been an entire sea full of corpses! He could have dived in among them and swum from one to the next to the next and never reached them all, not even if he came up for breath a hundred times. Long had he feared the Lothan Aklun; now he wished desperately that he had gotten the chance to speak with even one of them. Perhaps it was silly, but he could not help feeling they might have had important things to tell him about the world he was now trapped in.

When and how would word of this reach Corinn? Surely the *Ambergris* had sailed with news of the treachery. He did not have her gift for political wrestling, so he knew not how she might choose to respond. A small group sent back to parley with the Auldek? An army prepared to invade? What would the leaguemen tell her? Even if they told the truth, the league did not know what had happened to him. In addition, they had every reason to transform the entire situation into some fanciful version that would suit their needs—whatever those were. Though Dariel worked himself into knots thinking about it, he could not imagine what was happening on the other side of the world. When he thought of Mena or Wren being told that he was dead or missing, it filled him with anguish.

Mór had come to him a second time. She entered, rigid with control, moving deliberately. Tunnel hovered near him, almost seeming like a protector should Mór attack him again. She said something to him in Auldek. The large man responded in the same language, shrugging as he spoke, ending with something that must have been a joke, since he grinned at his own words.

Mór did not acknowledge any humor. Dragging a stool in front of Dariel, she sat down and faced him directly. She switched to Acacian. "If it were up to me alone I'd just as soon feed you to the snow lions."

"Is that an option?" Dariel asked. "Are there lions around here? I'm not saying I'd want to be eaten, but it's possible the lions would treat me better than—"

He flinched when Mór reached for him. She clamped her hand over his mouth and said, "Shut your mouth and let me say what I must. Then I'll go, and you can prattle on in your ignorance. Tunnel will listen. Won't you?"

"He makes good prattle," Tunnel said, tugging on one of his tusks.

"You cannot tell me anything right now," Mór said. "Let me tell you a few things. Will you be quiet?"

Reluctantly, Dariel nodded. He would rather listen to whatever she had to say than have her turn away in anger again.

"Good." She drew her hand from his lips. "I am going to assume that you know nothing. Let's start at that point and nothing will be missed. You are in Ushen Brae, the place you call the Other Lands. We are in the tunnels beneath the city of Avina. I'm not entirely clear what happened when your party met the Auldek, but I can tell you that your people were slaughtered. A handful fled back to the league boats, but not many. You're the only one we have. And who are we? We're not the Auldek. I am Mór of the Free People. You know Tunnel and Skylene. We are all of the People. The 'People' are

367

those you might refer to as quota. We are the slaves you sent here. Many of us are still in bondage. Some of us fight it." She pressed her hand to her chest. "We are those who fight it. The Free People. You may think that this side of the world is just a place where you discard unwanted children. We don't think so. Not anymore. Ushen Brae is the world. It's here we make the future."

"Wait." Dariel tried to gesture with his hands, but as they were bound, he used his shoulders instead, shrugging apologetically. "Just wait a moment. I will stop interrupting. I will, really. I just mean for you to know that I am not your enemy. I'm an Akaran, yes, and . . . you are quota. I know that is a terrible crime of my family, but it's nothing that I started. If anything, I hoped I might stop it. That's why I came—to help." Lest this sound too meek, he raised his chin as he concluded. "You do me wrong by chaining me."

When he stopped, Mór continued as if he had not spoken. "You are a prisoner, Dariel Akaran, of the very children your family sent to slavery. We've grown up. We don't stay children forever. In the coming days, we will decide what to do with you. Some believe you are here to save us. Some know better. But the elders of the Free People are patient and just. You will be tested. Perhaps—though it's not likely—we will find some value in you. But if you can be no use to us, you will feed the earth, and none here will weep. That's all I have to tell you right now."

With that, Mór jumped up from her seat, sending it crashing over behind her. She turned and was halfway out of the room before Dariel spoke.

"Wait!" he said.

Mór froze.

"I'll listen to it all," Dariel continued. "Test me also, if that is my fate. Kill me after that, if you wish, but let me die knowing. You won't understand me, but I know—in more ways than you even consider—that I have walked the world half blind.

That was the way of my people, but it doesn't have to continue. My brother, if he had lived and had met you—would have asked for the same. But he isn't here. I am. So, in his place, tell me everything. Please."

"Your ignorance would take a lifetime to erase."

"I am not the only ignorant one in this room."

Mór snapped her head around. "You resort to insults?"

"Following your example," Dariel quipped. "You were a child when you left—"

"When I was *taken*, not left."

Dariel conceded the point with a curt nod. "When you were taken. That's true of you. That's true of every human living in Ushen Brae. You know nothing of the Known World, nothing more than a child would."

"Generations of People have grown old here, lived, and died."

"Yes, but the People never know more about the Known World than what children of seven or eight can tell them. You may get old and grow wise in your way, yes, but you know little about Acacia."

Mór kicked the stool that was in her way, sending it twirling inches from Dariel's head. It clattered to the floor.

Dariel fought to contain his frustration. "We should be speaking to each other, not attacking each other. I want to know about life here. I want to know what's been done in the Akaran name. I inherited it, too—just as you did. It's the fact that we don't know each other that has allowed this crime to go on."

"How pathetic you are to claim to want to help us now. Now that you're nothing—"

"Mór, I have lived years knowing that there was something foul at the heart of my family's empire. I knew some of it but not all of it. Tell me all of it. Show me. And I will tell you everything I can about the world you came from."

"I know you will," Mór said, threat laced in the words. This time, she turned and left the room before Dariel found the words, or the heart, to stop her.

In the days that followed, his testing began. It was not so much a matter of any one challenge to meet. It was like no other tests he had ever taken. It was a matter of opening himself as completely as possible and giving, giving, giving. The elders, according to Mór, wanted to take him up on his offer to educate them about the Known World. They wanted to know everything they could about the land that had sold them into slavery.

At first he spoke hesitantly, unsure whether or not he was betraying his people. But this was what he himself had asked for. Half of it, at least. Sometimes Mór questioned him, a thing Dariel found both exhilarating and unnerving, but she had other duties that took her away for days at a time. More consistently, Skylene directed the course of his days. She seemed to have more freedom with her time than the others. Most could only steal a few hours every few days away from the chores their masters had for them.

History, religion, mythology, the old tales, geography, nations and races and leaders, bloodlines and feuds and allegiances, the Forms and Hanish Mein and the Santoth and Aliver: they wanted to know it all. Skylene forced him to arrange these various subjects as best he could. Before long, several scribes spent the hours with him, each writing on multiple scrolls, each focused on a different topic. He would jump from one to other as things occurred to him or as Skylene prompted him.

Tunnel visited him regularly also. He did not interrogate him, although Dariel believed he was supposed to. The big man pulled up a chair and sat close to him, near enough that Dariel could smell the fragrant oil that had been worked into his leather skirt and the long laces of his sandals. He would joke with Dariel, smile and laugh at the slightest provocation.

Skylene was fair enough with him, but Tunnel was alone among the People in treating Dariel like a friend returned from a long voyage. They were simply catching up, it seemed.

Dariel would never have imagined that his existence would come to be what it now was. It was peculiar because some part of him felt strangely at ease with it except during those moments of panic and realization. Some part of him had been waiting for this, wanting it. He now hungered for where it might lead.

"Skylene," Dariel asked, as another session of questioning was about to begin, "do you know of any way I could send a message to my country?"

The woman stared at him, her thin lips pursed, wary of the idea. She had just entered the chamber in which he sat waiting, alone. Her appearance was as striking as ever, but her pale blue hue and avian highlights no longer seemed bizarre. To Dariel's eyes, they were now part of her. Strange that he could grow used to her so quickly. She asked, "What kind of message?"

"Just something that tells my people that I'm alive. I don't know what the league might tell them. It could cause all sorts of problems if they think me dead. I don't know what it might lead to. If my sister thinks me dead—or discovers that I'm captive here—she may send an army to avenge me or to war with the Auldek."

"I don't think that's likely," Skylene said.

Dariel studied her. "Why?"

Skylene thought a moment, and then exhaled and shook her head, sadly. "It doesn't matter, Dariel. Whatever will happen, will happen. We cannot change it. Not yet, at least. It's not possible to send any message. We never managed it in twenty-two generations. What makes you think we could do it now?"

"The league then. They may still be along the coast. Can we get—"

"A message to them?" Skylene interjected. "Don't be foolish. The only message your sister will receive will be of their making. Really, Dariel, we have no power where they are concerned. Anyway, Mór would never allow contact with them. They are our enemies, remember? For that matter, you haven't forgotten that they were offering you up to Devoth, have you?"

No, Dariel certainly had not forgotten that. In fact, he had dreamed of that chaotic afternoon more than once. "I had power over the league once, you know."

There was a knock at the door. A moment later the two scribes entered: one with a splash of shivith spots across one side of her face, the other with a crest of black hair jutting from the back of his head.

Skylene motioned for the two new arrivals to take their seats and ready their writing equipment. "I doubt that," she responded.

"I was at war with them once. Killed many."

"That may be, but that doesn't mean they were in your power. You blew up their platforms, I know; you detailed that already. That may have hurt them. Perhaps it made them hate you enough to give you to Devoth, but you can't really believe you had them on their knees. Let me tell you this about the league: they made it clear to each of us that you Akarans are just pawns to them. Once they have us quota aboard their ships and are sailing west, they don't hide the fact that they are the Known World's real power. And the Lothan Aklun, before they were eliminated, likewise dismissed you. You were their customers, but stupid ones, ignorant, addicted, easily fooled and exploited. As for us . . . many among the People hate the Akaran name and hold you responsible for our slavery, but quite a few think your people too pathetic to merit hate. None of us think you accurately understand the way the world has been working."

"And you? How do you feel?"

Skylene answered without the slightest hesitation. "The Kern—my clan—have a saying: 'Truth is a white crane with many heads but only one body.' When they grow agitated, the heads eat one another until only one remains."

"And that one truth prevails?"

"No. The one head can't live by itself, not when it's part of a body that has suffered multiple decapitations. There may be one truth left, but it dies when the body that connected it to the other truths dies."

Dariel's brow ridged with skepticism. "Yours are a dire people."

Shrugging, Skylene said, "The truth overlaps. It contradicts. But in many ways, many things are true. That's why I think a little bit of everything about you and your people."

"If that's true it seems surprising that you're talking to me. If my people are so pathetic, what use are we?"

This did cause her to pause for thought. "The league has used you. The Lothan Aklun have used you. The Auldek have used you. Perhaps we can find a use for you and your information, too. That's what the elders believe. And, anyway, you yourself proposed this."

Feeling a greater import in the question than seemed reasonable, Dariel could not help but ask, "Is it what Mór believes also?"

A smile started to lift the corners of Skylene's lips, but before the expression was complete, she ran a twist through it that made it more like a smirk. "You don't want to know what Mór thinks we should do with you. Trust me on that." Her tone switched, growing crisper and more official. "We've spoken enough. Let's begin. You were going to tell us about the floating merchants."

It seemed such a distant thing to speak about, unreal in this subterranean existence. He started by explaining what he knew of the merchants, about the way the currents flowed around the Inner Sea at different times of the year, how seasonal shifts made it possible for the great barges—cities unto themselves—to sail a circular route that took them all the way to the Vumu Archipelago. They were only marginally governed by the empire. Really, the merchant families of Bocoum held them together within an unofficial government-like arrangement. Though their trade was not rich enough to bring them into competition with the league, they were fundamental to the swirling flow of goods that kept the empire thriving.

As he spoke, images emerged in his mind. At first he thought they were just visualizations to aid his recall of information, but then he realized the images were more personal than that. He had forgotten, but he had first visited the floating merchants when he was a small boy. Of course he had. It was during the spring, when the rafts drifted on the slow current that carved the Mainland's coastline. He must have been six or seven years old, in those long ago days before the world first went mad. He had stepped aboard the rafts—not with his father—but holding Thaddeus Clegg's hand.

With this "uncle" to guide him, he had gazed in awe at the bobbing, flowing, moving creation the thousands of rafts made when lashed together. The population of the rafts was an amazing, polyglot entity, diverse as the entire empire, there before him at once. People of all nations rode the waves, making their lives through trade. With animals in cages and others roaming free, with wares displayed and foodstuffs bubbling and frying and great stores of items piled in ware-houses, with fisheries and clam hangers, cisterns for gathering rainwater and a network of tubing that ran it where needed, it was a grand, salt-tinged, barnacled confusion.

And then he remembered that Aliver had been with them. Tall and older, smart, confident, and a bit arrogant: everything it seemed a man should be. Oh, how Dariel felt tiny in his brother's shadow. That's the feeling that washed over him. Quick behind this flood of feeling came remembrance of the brief relationship they had rekindled as men on the battlefield of Talay. The emotion of it stopped his narration.

"Is something wrong?" Skylene asked.

Dariel fidgeted. "Yes. Many things are wrong. Can I have a break?"

"We've just begun—"

"I know. I'm sorry. I just started telling you about one thing and it brought to mind another."

"We have them only for an hour," Skylene said, gesturing toward the scribes, one of whom sat with pen poised, ready to continue. The other waited her turn, should the subject change to a different scroll. "Then they have to return to their work."

Dariel realized he did not recognize them. Perhaps they had been here before. Likely, they had, but in their silent roles they had no identity to him. Perhaps that was good. Because of it, it was easier for him to say, "I told you before about how my brother fought Maeander Mein. It was his great moment. I believe that, even though he died. Maybe it was great *because* he died. It's hard to explain.

"Everyone who knew him wished he never accepted the challenge. Certainly, the Mein would not have kept Maeander's pledge. In a way, it was a situation in which he could not win. So why do it? Why risk everything for nothing? That's what it seemed like to me at the time, and then when Aliver did die, it was both unbelievable and inevitable. I hated everything at that moment: Maeander and Hanish, the war, every soldier around us. Even Aliver himself. I hated that he had failed and left us. Left me. What I didn't tell you before was what I did in the moments after."

He noticed Skylene nod to the second scribe and knew from the different rhythm of the scratch of her pen that he was being recorded again. Okay, he thought. Let them have this in writing, too.

"Maeander killed my brother with a knife, following the

rules the two of them had agreed upon. I swore—along with Aliver—to abide by the rules and honor the outcome. When I saw Aliver on the ground, and Maeander strolling away, so pleased with himself, I couldn't control myself. I hated him so much nothing else mattered. I said, just loud enough to be heard in the silence. 'Kill him.' When nobody obeyed me I shouted it. 'Kill him!' I ordered. Hear? I *ordered* it done."

He had been looking at his hands for a while but glanced up long enough to make sure Skylene understood him exactly. The scribe's pen scratched a little longer, and then stopped. Her eyes rose to look at him.

"So," he continued, kneading his hands together, "just like that, with a few words, I betrayed the honor my brother modeled for the world. I've always hated myself for that."

"He was an enemy commander," Skylene offered. "You just did what—"

"Aliver would never have done that. Honor is honor. It's not just honor when it suits you. He had agreed to terms, and so had I."

"I'm not sure I understand. Surely, Aliver did not think that the war would be decided between just two men? No matter what, it would have gone on, yes?"

"Yes."

"Then your actions changed nothing, except that you killed one of your enemy's leaders."

Dariel almost laughed. Sadly, he had told himself the same thing many times. Others had said it, too. There was truth in it, but there was also truth in the fact that both he and Aliver believed that people—especially those who led others—should be true to their word. Who knows? Maybe Maeander felt the same. Maybe he would have lived by the outcome of that duel. Dariel would never know because he had betrayed his honor. The irony of it was thick enough to swim in.

It was not just the irony that made him laugh. It was what Skylene had said about the truth having many heads but only one body. "Let's not debate this. We'll end up headless if we do."

The woman ridged her brow for a moment, perplexed, but then registered understanding. "You learn fast, Dariel."

"Not everyone would agree, but I try. And as soon as you start telling me things about Ushen Brae, I will be all ears. Is it time for that yet?"

Skylene thought for a moment. "That's up to Mór."

Chapter Thirty-two

When Rhrenna first brought her the missive, Corinn waved her away. Delivegu had been useful. He would be again, perhaps. And he had a carnal sensuality that parts of her—despite the fact that her intentionally cold façade showed no sign of it—had responded to. But that was before Grae had stepped in and so completely replaced the other man. Grae, with his square-jawed nobility and all the legitimately pleasing possibilities his nuptial overtures offered, a gentleman of noble birth who had proven himself of her class each day of his stay in the palace. Since, Delivegu had seemed even more like an anxious puppy. She had stopped reading his notes. For several weeks now Rhrenna had been discarding them without troubling the queen. If he did not desist, Corinn had decided, his yapping would have to be silenced more forcefully.

Rhrenna needed only to see the queen's expression to know her thoughts. In answer, she said, "Yes, I know. But you should read it just the same. I won't be the one who didn't deliver this to you."

Tiny threads of annoyance flared out from the corners of Corinn's eyes, one of the few places the passing years had begun to stake a claim. She took the note, snapped it open. She remarked at how brief it was, which was unusual for the Candovian.

Your Majesty, I have captured your foe. I have Barad the Lesser and will deliver him to you shortly. Your loyal servant, D.

She let the note drop from her fingers, blowing air through her teeth. How bold-faced of him! She found no reason to believe such a claim. What was he playing at? Last she had heard, Delivegu had been sulking about the lower town's brothels, digging for secrets and doing whatever else pleasured him. Barad the Lesser, on the other hand, had eluded the empire for years, leaving scarcely any leads, a sort of phantom whom she might have doubted altogether if word of him had not been so consistent.

"Delivegu is a fool," Corinn said.

Rhrenna pressed her thin lips together, stern for just a second, before laughing. "We both know that's not true, Your Majesty. He's many things, but a fool is not first among them."

"You credit this, then?"

"Doesn't matter if I do. I'm patient enough to wait until tomorrow morning." She held another folded letter, much the same as the first. "He sent me another, you see. A private message." She displayed both sides of it, as if thinking something through. She was not actually doing so, which was clear from the humor in her eyes. Shrugging, she tossed the note onto the queen's table. "But what's mine is yours, of course. Read it, if it pleases you."

She's gone as giddy as Mena with her lizard bird, Corinn thought. As giddy as me with my suitor . . .

She glanced down, but didn't reach for the letter. Was she growing lax? It had only been a few weeks since Mena and Grae both dropped into her court, but she already suspected she had missed things she would not have before. She had failed to note down a few slights, decided to ignore a suspicion or two so that they did not interfere with her mood. Was that foolish? Or was it time to take some joy in life again?

379

Joy, she thought, might not be the weakness I've believed it to be.

Being with Grae warmed her, and that made her inclined to gentle rule. She found herself flirting with him without the controlled guise that had become part of almost every interaction. That lowering of her guard had loosened the bands of tension that had so long clamped her skull. That was not a bad thing, was it? Grae had taken her hand once as they were sitting on a bench in the high courtyard of the monument to Edifus's first defensive towers. She did not think he knew that his brother Igguldan had once fallen to his knees in awe of the ancients in this spot. Nor did she mention it, for Grae was less and less his brother's shadow, more his own man every day. It was good that she saw him that way, for he was a fine king of his people and might yet be a fit monarch for the Known World.

Once, two days before, she had even set free a small work of sorcery in the gardens: insects of a sort not seen before. Antlike beings with large, diaphanous wings, they seemed to want nothing more than to flit above the onlookers' delighted heads. They seemed almost to sing, as if the flapping of their sparkling wings made music with the air. She was aware that she did this as much to impress Grae as to delight Aaden and his friends, but for once she allowed herself the indulgence. She looked forward to doing so again. Let the people fear her sorcery; let them love it as well.

She had even refused to meet with Sire Nathos, who had come to the island with Paddel, the vintner. Both of them clamored to begin distribution of the new Prios vintage, the mist-infused wine that would glaze the eyes of the populace once more. It was not that she had truly decided against employing it, but she did wonder if it was possible to rule without it. She was loved—or could be. As many tales were spun about her powers and gifts as had been spun about Mena's warrior prowess. Talay was bursting into life again. So much seemed right. But Paddel and Nathos certainly believed in the dangers posed by this Barad. He was the main reason cited to explain the need for the new drug.

"Meet him, then," Corinn told Rhrenna, still without picking up the note. "See for yourself. If what Delivegu says is true, I'll receive him before meeting his prisoner myself. If he's lying, arrange for his death."

The next morning dawned as usual during the Acacian summer: warm but breezy, the sun alone in a blue-white sky, the sea turquoise nearby and a rich blue in the depths. It was almost ridiculous how unrelentingly perfect the weather was on the island. Sitting beside Aaden, Corinn felt a pang of nostalgia for Calfa Ven. They would have to go there again soon, up into the high, damp air, where the nights were chill and mornings mist shrouded and the air always haunted by some animal call, whether it be a wolverbear's roar, a loon's piping, or a stag's trumpeting. Perhaps she would invite Grae along with them. Surely he would love it. She almost asked Aaden if he would like that also, but she was with him for a reason. Best that it be attended to first.

The mother and son sat on stools placed for them to look down through slanting panes of tinted glass. Below them an empty room, one chair at its center. Skylights lit the room brightly, while the viewing area was shaded from the sun by an awning. They could look down without being observed. So placed, they awaited the prisoner's arrival.

"If this man is who my agent claims he is," Corinn said, "he is one of my greatest enemies."

"I know about him," Aaden said, swiping the gold-touched hair back from his forehead. "But how can he be a threat? He doesn't even have an army. My tutor said he goes about riling up the common folk, but that none of them have yet done *anything*, for all his talk. They're tradesmen and blacksmiths and farmers."

"You think tradesmen and blacksmiths and farmers are no

threat to me? Singly they aren't, of course, but Barad makes the many into one. That's dangerous. We rule because the people allow us to rule. They believe we have power, but their belief is the delusion that grants it to us. Don't ever forget that. Nothing you can do with your sword, or with your army, is nearly as important as what you must do with your mind, with your words—"

There was motion in the chamber below them. Four Marah guards entered the room, each with their hands crossed and holding the hilt of both short and long swords, ready to draw. They squared off around the empty chair, facing it. A moment later a giant of a man entered. Hands secured behind his back, he had to dip his head beneath the door frame. He paused just inside the room and stood for a moment taking measure of the space. His clothes hung ragged about him, soiled. One sleeve had torn at the shoulder. After looking around the room for a moment, he raised his head and glanced straight up at the glass through which the mother and son watched.

Corinn spoke a bit hurriedly and perhaps to reassure herself as much as Aaden. "He cannot see us."

The boy said, "He looks like a peasant. A big one, but still a peasant."

Another guard blocked the doorway behind the prisoner. He shoved him forward with a free hand, the other on the hilt of his short sword. The guard directed him to sit in the chair, and then walked around before him and said something the watchers could not hear.

"So, if we assume that this man is a danger to us, what do we do with him?"

Aaden sat silently thinking for a long time. Corinn thought for the millionth time how much she loved this boy. How was it possible to love so completely and to remember it again and again every day?

"Doesn't that depend on how he is a danger? What he is threatening to do and how?" Aaden finally said.

"Yes, those are things to consider. He is a danger because he has a gift for oratory. He is one of the people; and when he speaks to them, he makes them believe that all their grievances are caused by us. They're not, of course. We expect much from our subjects. In return we give them the stability of a prosperous nation. Commoners rarely understand that, and they forget it when a man like this comes into their midst. So his danger is that he blends together a host of grievances and directs it at one target—the Akaran line. At you, Aaden. What is he threatening to do? Destroy us. He believes his peasants could do better at governing the world than we. Or he believes that he will be empowered by our downfall. I'm not sure which. Either way, he would see me deposed. Likely killed after some mockery of a trial. So what do we do with him?"

"We stop him from talking?"

"Perhaps, but that would not undo the things he has said and the emotions he has stirred. What is better than silencing him?"

"If he must talk . . . we should have him say what we want him to, instead of what we don't."

A smile slowly bloomed on Corinn's face. The answer did not surprise her—she had thought of it herself already—but it did please her. She reached out and mussed his hair and said, "Clever boy."

Aaden accepted the praise with a shrug.

"You may go now," Corinn said. "I'll tell you later what this criminal had to say for himself."

But Aaden had more on his mind. "Grae said he would go riding with me tomorrow, all the way out to Haven's Rock. He claims he has a fishing line long enough to reach the water from the top. There's no way that's possible. He must be joking! I can go, can't I?"

"You like Grae, don't you?" Corinn asked, trying to make the question sound light and casual. "You've spent even more time with him than I have."

"He fenced with me. Not like the others but steel to steel. I could've gotten *cut*." The prospect of this seemed to delight the boy.

"Is that so?" Corinn raised an eyebrow. This was not actually news to her. Very little that Aaden did went unreported to her. For that matter, very little that Grae did during the last few weeks escaped her either. She knew what Aaden did not mention about this sparring: that the blades they used were light, with no edge at all. Grae could certainly have hurt him nonetheless, but ten pairs of Marah eyes had been pinned to him the entire time, ready to repay any injury with a quick death. Corinn asked, "Don't you think that's dangerous?"

"No. Not really. He said I was quicker than him. Quicker than he ever was, he said." Almost as an afterthought, he added, "He wouldn't hurt me, anyway. He likes me."

"Of course he wouldn't," Corinn said. "And of course he does."

Aaden's delay in leaving meant that he was still in the hallway when Rhrenna led Delivegu into the viewing area. After the formalities of greeting the queen were seen to, the Candovian said, "Your son looks more like Hanish Mein every day." He motioned toward the corridor to explain the comment's origins.

Corinn eyed him a moment, deciding how severe to be with him. At a glance he was just as elaborately garbed as ever, his shirt brilliantly white, his black breeches tight enough that they seemed to have shrunk to fit his form. The hoops of his gold earrings sparkled, and he wore bracelets on one wrist that clanged together as he moved. But for all the gaudy finery, his face did not betray his usual arrogance. Perhaps his time out of favor had mellowed him.

"You knew Hanish Mein?" Corinn asked.

"To look at, yes. Only to look at. He didn't know me, but he was hard to miss when he had the reins of power. I liked his style." As an afterthought, he added, "Then, I guess you did, too."

Or perhaps it had not mellowed him, Corinn thought. She was unsure as yet. She ordered him to explain his claim and document the identity of the man sitting in the room below them. Delivegu did so readily enough. He explained that he had gained intelligence that led him to a certain commoner's message service. There he had intercepted a message meant for the rascal. He hurriedly transported himself to the message's destination. It was a gamble, a considerable personal expense, but it paid off. He did spot the man. He spied on him long enough to satisfy himself of his identity, and then he decided on a way to capture him.

"How did you do that?"

Delivegu shrugged and looked the closest he could to sheepish. "I'm not proud when it comes to such matters. I came up behind him when he was fumbling with the keys to unlock his rented room. I hit his head with a club."

"Without warning?"

"Of course. How better to do it? And lucky I did, for he didn't go down from that one blow. He turned and reached for me. I needed to hit him twice more before he dropped to his knees. Then he was easier to deal with. A bit, at least."

"How did you know it was Barad?"

"Before I approached him, I questioned an acquaintance of his. A young man with, I daresay, insufficient resilience to resist me."

"This initial information you gained—that which took you to the message service—how was that come by?"

Delivegu cleared his throat. "I have something to report that you may find disturbing." He paused, brow furrowed in an expression of consternation that looked odd. "I wished you to know the other details first, but this part cannot be avoided. You're right to ask. Hear me through, please, before you respond."

Corinn kept her eyes fixed on him as he proceeded. She kept them pinned to his features, focused first on his face as a whole and then on its smaller components: the crook of his nose, the motion of lips, the black hairs of his beard. The focus was necessary, for otherwise she feared she would betray the fact that her heart pounded at twice the rate it had a moment before. She would not even look at Rhrenna, who was hearing the news with her. She knew her face had flushed red, but her expression remained unchanged. Alleys and spying. Following a servant . . . What he was telling her was—

"As you can imagine, I had to be quite rough with Barad. He's a big man, you see, so I had to be careful. Anyway, he was a little bit out of it, and he asked me, 'Did he betray me to her?' I had explained to him that I was in your employ. When he asked, I almost asked him, 'Who?' The word was on my tongue, but I snipped it." Delivegu demonstrated just how precisely he did so by making scissors of his fingers. "Instead, I said, 'Of course, he betrayed you. He's royalty after all. Why would he side with commoners?' I said this to provoke confusion or disagreement or something. But he responded with none of those. He simply accepted it sadly.

"So . . ." Delivegu inhaled a long breath, then said plainly, "There can really be no doubt, Your Majesty. Barad, your enemy among the people, was in a partnership with King Grae. As I traveled with Barad I returned to this subject several times. He didn't give much, so I told him how it was. How King Grae had come to you speaking of a plot they had concocted together. How you and he worked to find a way to capture him. I even said that you and the Aushenian were secretly engaged. It's a skill I have, finding the truth even when the one I'm interrogating doesn't say a thing. There's no question, though. He was in league with Grae, and now he believes Grae betrayed him. I deliver him to you in the hope that you will mete out justice as is right."

Inside Corinn's head a hundred different thoughts assailed

her. On her face she made sure that nothing could be read. Despite the internal turmoil, she heard herself say calmly, "We'll see about all this soon enough. I will speak with him now."

Delivegu straightened like an obedient servant, eager to please and seemingly happy at her reaction—or lack of reaction. Corinn paused at the door and let Delivegu advance ahead of her. Leaning close to Rhrenna, she whispered, "While I am with him, bring Grae to the upper terrace. Let him see to whom I'm speaking. Watch his face. Tell me if he shows signs of recognizing him."

Time must have passed, but she lost track of it. Why it was so hard to concentrate she could not say. Her mind felt sluggish but also touched with a panic that might spread if she were not careful. It was not just thinking of Grae, not just the disbelief that she might have read him so wrongly, not just the gasping knowledge that he had held steel and fenced with Aaden, not even realizing how very close she had come to folly.

In addition to all this, emotions she had not allowed within herself for years rushed in. Memories of her father, of Igguldan, of Hanish: the men who had betrayed her, each in his own way. Was Grae another of these? Was she still the fool she had been at sixteen? More, images of her mother during her illness, the memory of crying and crying and crying on her bedspread as the woman—she who was dying—tried to comfort her. More, there came a bone-deep longing, which she almost never acknowledged, to sit and speak with Aliver, right now, as adults, both of them living.

And then she was striding through the doorway behind Delivegu. She walked into the room and circled around to the front of the chair. The guards followed her with their eyes, and she watched as the prisoner's square profile came into view and then changed as it filled out. She pulled in her attention, blocked out the noise, and concentrated all her being on the exchange she was about to have. It felt necessary to focus her eyes on a single point, while the rest of the world blurred. The man's eyes were brown, spaced wide. Rolling toward her, they looked heavy, as if just moving them would be a monumental task, as if they were stone. She could almost hear the grinding rumble as they shifted.

She said, "Lower your eyes." The man stared at her a moment longer and then obeyed. "How could you think the monarch of one kingdom would betray the monarch of another . . . for peasants? Don't you see how foolish that is? How impossible? And they told me you were bright. Devious. Cunning. Instead, you're none of these things."

Had she really gotten all that out without a hitch or quaver of emotion? She had. The man's steady attention confirmed it. He stared at her feet but said nothing.

"You may speak freely to me," Corinn said, trusting her voice a little more now. "I am not easy to offend. Nor do you frighten me. If your language is coarse, so be it. I have some rough about me as well."

One corner of the man's mouth crooked upward. It looked like a tic, a jerk of his cheek muscles, but the expression held. A lopsided smile.

"Well, speak. That's what you like to do, isn't it? Make up speeches. Exhort. Rant to the masses! Try it on an audience of one."

The man bowed his head, moving that smile out of her view. She watched him gather himself with a series of inhaled breaths. She could have him beaten, she thought. Mutilated. Killed. She could—right now, right here—order his tongue cut out. No more speeches then. And, she realized, part of what was jumbling her mind was the song. It was high in her, roiling about the curve of her skull like liquid flame mixed with sound, hungry to get out. She did not even need to order another to act for her. She could open her mouth and sing him into oblivion.

"You have betrayed your brother's dreams."

She saw the words on his lips, and then she heard them, and then put the two together and understood them.

"Have I? And did my brother detail his dreams to you?"

Barad took a few breaths before answering, but his voice was sure when he did, no hint of deceit or hesitation in it. "Yes. Many nights he spoke to me in dreams." He looked up. "I make up no speeches, Corinn Akaran. I simply recite what I remember, what Aliver wished me to say to the world. You would do well to listen yourself. It is not too late to save yourself from ruin."

Corinn was quicker even than the Marah in responding to this insult. She said nothing. She only opened her mouth slightly and let out the ribbon of song already waiting. It slipped through the air on a whisper, and the thing she had but thought was done. The eyes that had dared to look up at her were eyes no longer. They were stone replicas, frozen in place. Delivegu gasped. One of the guards whispered a curse of amazement. Barad himself did not move at all. His stone eyes stared at her, his expression otherwise unchanged.

She spun away.

In her offices an hour later she recalled the dream she had just that morning. In it, she had arranged to meet Grae in her chambers. She had not explained why, but when he arrived, the room was lit with low lamps, heavy with incense. A single musician in a hidden closet piped a faint tune on a bone whistle. And she stood in a thin shift, a diaphanous garment.

His eyes had widened into two blue saucers when he saw her.

She was naked beneath the dress. She could see by the nervous difficulty Grae had controlling his eyes that he had noticed this. The light from the candle beside her, she knew, would be languid around her curves, and the thought of the power she had just standing there pressed her nipples erect against the thin fabric. He noticed that as well.

"I am no virgin," she had said. "I am no blushing maiden. I have no desire to be in love again. Such things are of my past. I come to you as I am. A queen. A mother. A woman. Those three things may be too much for you to handle, but if you think yourself monarch enough for it, I will have you as a husband. This is me. Consider."

With that, Corinn had slipped loose the knot at her waist and shrugged the silken shift from her shoulders. Corinn let Grae take her in from head to toe. It pleased her to have his eyes adoring her—that prodded her to cut his examination short.

"I'll have your answer now, by the way."

His answer, in the dream, had been to rise and walk toward her, swaying oddly as he did, raising first one arm and then the other. It was a strange ballet that she understood as a custom of his people, a dance of the cranes or some such. She had thought it lovely, and began to return it.

But that was just a dream. In real life, she had not worn that shift. She had not made that offer. Sitting in her office after her encounter with Barad, she checked these facts several times to be sure of them. No, she had shown the Aushenian nothing but gracious hospitality. She had been more generous with her time than normal, perhaps had smiled too readily and spoke to him with unguarded familiarity. But nothing more than that. She was so grateful for this fact that she pressed the tips of her fingernails to her forehead and squeezed, thanking the Giver for her having had at least that much reserve.

When Rhrenna entered, her face as pale and distorted as beeswax grown soft in the sun, Corinn already knew what she would report. The secretary confirmed as much tersely. Grae had nearly swallowed his tongue when he saw Barad. Though Rhrenna spoke to him innocently about what was happening—betraying no suspicion of him—Grae had stammered and even trembled a bit. Sweat had appeared in instant droplets along his forehead, and his attempts at looking casual were clearly forced.

"I cannot believe it was all an act," Rhrenna said, "but there it is. He scorned you—"

"This is not about being scorned," Corinn cut in. The words came before she knew she was to say them, but they were true. Scorn was for lesser people than she. "It's about ruling an empire," she said, and then gave new orders.

Chapter Thirty-three

S he can't climb these mountains," Naamen said. "There's no way."

"I can carry her," Kelis answered.

The younger man plucked the knuckle root he had been sucking on from the corner of his lips, indignant. "So can I! And I will! But still, when we drop from exhaustion she'll be no better off."

Kelis answered this with only a sharp grunt and walked on with his chin high. Inside he feared the same thing. They had trudged toward the peaks for several days, their scale growing as they approached, deceptive, massive in a way that surprised him each time he looked upon them. They seemed to swell when his eyes touched them, as if they inhaled breaths and puffed out their chests to seem larger. Nor did the play of the light as the sun progressed seem to follow the natural order. At times, the upper regions of the mountains were snow dusted. At others, they appeared to have thick vegetation right up to the peaks. On occasion, he stopped, convinced he faced geometries of sheer black rock, unclimbable.

Though he never showed it outwardly, he half hoped Benabe would plant her feet and declare she and Shen would go no farther. If she did, what could he do but acquiesce? In matters of a daughter's welfare a Talayan mother had the final say. Though Shen was a princess, she was also just a young girl.

Even if Aliver had been alive Benabe would have been her foremost guardian.

But Benabe never did shout them to a halt. Her face, in its own way, was as changeable as the strange mountain range. She is strong, Kelis thought more than once. Stronger than she is frightened by the future.

On the evening before they were to enter the mountains, Benabe approached Kelis. She sat beside him and stared up at the range before them, just there, so close she could have thrown a stone and hit the first of the foothills. Her daughter had combed and braided her hair the evening before, and the rows were tight against her scalp, dusted by the dry soil and twinkling here and there with flecks of gold. "I hate these mountains," she said. "They are not right. They are not true."

Kelis prepared a response and then rejected it, thought of another but felt it poor. He cleared his throat but said nothing. Behind them, Naamen and Shen slapped palms together as they played a rhyming game. Occasionally, peals of Shen's laughter flew by them.

"When I was a girl I used to dream of mountains," Benabe said. "A strange thing, yes? I lived in a flat, hot place, but I dreamed of high, cold things. I wanted to see snow. Like the Snow King." She clicked her tongue. "Tell me you had some foolish notion like that yourself, Kelis. Tell me."

I loved a prince in ways different than he loved me, Kelis said, but only to himself. To her, he answered, "It's not foolish to want to see over the horizon. Don't the wise say, 'He who travels farthest best knows his home'?"

"The wise say many things, enough to confuse the rest of us. Ever since I saw these mountains I've felt like I created them. It's those old dreams come back to punish me. Shen says that's not it, though. She says the stones put them here to welcome us. To repel others, yes, but to welcome us. They will guide us through, she says, and on the other side welcome us to safety." She pulled her gaze in and fixed it on Kelis. "Do you believe that?"

"If your daughter believes it"—he paused, but then decided what he had begun to say was the truth—"then I am comforted. She is one of the wise."

"Yes, listen to her. She's wise enough to laugh." Benabe blew air through her nose. Smiled. And the moment of mirth faded as quickly as it had come. "The strange thing is that I'm taking my daughter to find sorcerers who scare me to death, and I'm doing it because the only thing that scares me more is not finding them. Do you know how Shen convinced me? It was after my first meeting with Sinper Ou. He calls Shen his cousin, but there is no kindness in him. He would make her his wife if he could, or marry her to one of his sons. And then he would declare to the world that she lived and as Aliver's daughter was rightful ruler of the Known World."

Kelis felt his pulse quicken. "You really believe he would challenge the queen?"

"If he thought her weakened, yes. But even if he did not, I think he would make a grab for all Talay. The Ous have long thought themselves better than the rest of us. Big lions. Why shouldn't they be kings and queens? I could see these thoughts surging every time Sinper's heart pumped. You see, he would challenge the queen if he could, but I think he would be just as happy breaking the world in two. Talay is rich enough, even for a man like him. All he needs is my daughter standing beside him. He has but to name her Aliver's heir and all Talay will bow to her. Sinper will accept on her behalf. I was sure of this, and sure that he already had a spiderweb around us. I had hidden her all these years because I wanted her safe, unknown. Better a living village girl than the target for wolves. That's what I believed. I still believe it, but secrets are hard to keep. Sangae knew about her long before he approached me. And then he had no choice but to tell the other elders. And what the elders know, the Ous soon learn."

"You could announce her as Aliver's daughter yourself. Take that from Sinper—"

"The minute the world knows of her, she'll have a million enemies, most of them disguised as friends."

"She will have true protectors, too. I would be one of them. I would die so she might live."

Benabe studied him, her large eyes softening with a kindness that made them look fatigued. "Thank you. Shen would not like that. Live for her; don't die. She thinks there is a better way. That's what she told me. She came to me, and she seemed to know all the doubts within me, even though I'd tried to hide them from her. She said that there were a few in the world who could truly protect her. The stones. They promised her that the love they had for Aliver they gave now to her. Only they were stronger than all others combined. Only they could guide her safely through what is to come. She believes them, and I believe they're powerful, but I fear they want more *from* her than they'll ever give *to* her. There are things they're not telling her. I know there are."

The woman leaned forward, got her weight over her feet, and pushed herself upright. She turned to walk back to their simple camp, the moment of confiding at an end. Kelis could not help but ask another question before she went. "You named Sinper Ou's ambitions," he said, "but what are yours? What do you want for your daughter?"

For a moment Benabe's face looked hard, and Kelis thought she might lash out as she had done in their first days of travel. "I want her to live. Live and be happy, and I hate the world for making that hard for her."

"Cousin, your daughter does seem happy. Listen to her laughter."

Benabe did, and then said, "That comforts you, doesn't it?" She did not wait for his answer but stepped away before he could respond.

The next day they began the ascent.

Or they intended to begin the ascent. They looked at the

looming barricade before them and strode toward it. Kelis measured his strides, already trying to use his legs efficiently, knowing that he might soon have Shen's weight to bear. It was there, in the muscles of his thighs, that he first knew something very strange was happening. Though they entered the foothills and soon the mountains, though by midday they could look back and see the plains dropping away behind them, though all around them were inclines above and ravines below and though they went around boulders and over ridges and intentionally sought the easiest passes upward—despite all the physical signs . . .

"Does this feel strange to you?" Kelis whispered to Naamen, drawing him back as Benabe and Shen led the way.

The younger man stood a moment, taking in the terrain, rubbing the elbow of his small arm with the palm of his other. "We're not climbing," he pronounced.

And that was exactly what Kelis had been thinking. His legs, which knew well the burden of carrying his body, were not feeling the strain of ascending. From what they could see, they seemed to have ascended several thousand feet, and yet not even Shen breathed heavily as she skipped forward, chatting with her mother.

"We are looking for sorcerers," Naamen added, shrugging and walking again. "Perhaps finding sorcery is a good sign."

They camped that evening near a small stream beside a copse of acacia trees. Kelis would normally have worried about their dwindling supplies. They had little more than roots and dried fruits and a few twists of oryx meat. But there were more disturbing things to consider—details, small ones but as disturbing as these mountains. How had the air grown so cool and moist? How, in southern Talay, had they come across a shallow stream of clear water rippling over white stones? At first the thickness of the trees was strange enough. From a distance, they were lovely to behold, signs of life and abundance they had left behind miles and miles ago.

But as he sat studying them he noticed other things. The thorns were savagely long. Their leaves had a strange look to them, green on one side, a dull gray on the other, veinless and as blank as paper. Their limbs did not curve with the natural lines of most acacias. Instead they bent like the joints of age-twisted fingers, with bulbous knuckles. Though he had commented on the trees when he first saw them, the more he sat near them, the more he wished to be up and moving. Shen, he felt, should not look too closely at them.

The next day they dropped into a lush valley crowded with trees and long-grassed meadows. Marshy ponds spotted the flat areas, connected by a web of streams. It was an eerily silent place, just the burble of water in the air. That was it. No insects or animal calls, no sign of life at all. Unnatural.

Barely had he formed the thought when Shen called out, as if in direct refutation of it, "Look, birds!"

A flock appeared from behind them, thousands of them, a mass of black darts that cut into the air, rising straight into the sky. They turned as one and carved a rough circle in the air above. They moved faster than any birds Kelis had ever seen, their wings tight at their sides and not, as far as he could tell, flapping at all. They looked to be in a great rush. Soundless save their motion through the air, they cut away and dropped over the far edge of the valley.

"Come on!" Shen called, tugging her mother forward. "We should follow them."

As they walked through the valley and rose at the far end of it, Kelis had the most vivid sensation yet of feeling the mountains move around them. The rate of their strides did not match the speed with which even the distant peaks slipped away behind them. He even paused to look back and still felt the sensation of moving. Just the sensation, not actual evidence of something amiss. He darted his eyes from one area to another, as if he would catch the mountains in the act and shame them. He never quite managed it.

When he rejoined the others, he found them studying something on the ground: a bird, black as a raven but with an insect catcher's small frame and beak, dead—its neck snapped, apparently from impact with the ground. Benabe warned Shen not to touch it, but the girl showed no sign she intended to. They all stood staring for a time. Not too long, for the more they looked, the less the bird seemed like a bird. Kelis was sure its wings had been fixed in position, stiff as the gliders he had carved from wood as a boy. Its eyes were blue, the exact color of sky and so striking against the dead black of its plumage.

It was just the first. As they walked on through that day and then another and then several more, the ground and rocks and slopes all around them grew more and more littered with broken bodies. New flocks rose up behind them every so often and charted their way forward. Each valley brought new displays of the dead, and each morning's flock seemed less numerous or vigorous than the first. They were not true birds, Kelis knew. They were sorcery, like everything in these mountains, beautiful yet malformed.

It may have been the strangeness of the mountain terrain, the fatigue of their daily marches, or the workings of the magic so obviously woven in the world around them, but Kelis found his dreams becoming more vivid, crystal clear in a manner they had not been in many years. Often he relived episodes from recent days, altered in some way. Thus, the walk that took up his days stretched into the sleeping hours. In one dream the crumpled bodies of those birds rose from the ground and tried to fly again, their heads swinging wildly from their broken necks, wings crooked and shattered. They danced, leaping again and again, only to twirl back to earth, tiny bones snapping and feathers littering the ground. Another night he started awake, thrashing his arms and legs as he fought to escape the trees that had suddenly reached out their warped limbs and grabbed him.

And then came a night-long dream of a real evening from years before: the womanhood ceremony he and Aliver had participated in just after earning manhood rights themselves. He relived the entire evening in slow detail. As one of the newly established males, he danced with the other young warriors from all the central villages—Aliver among them—in the slow procession that wound them around and around the circle of admiring young women. The drums beat a steady rhythm, into which darted the plucked metallic bursts of thumb instruments. It was a long ceremony, and it was here again in his dream. He relived each step, each jump, each clap and smile and toss of his head, all done at the same time as the other men. They glistened with sweat, each lean from running and training, all chiseled to the perfection the Giver first sang into being.

Aliver may have been lighter hued, but in the contours of his body and his movements he was the same as any of the Talayans. Kelis knew where he was each moment of the dance. He took pleasure in it, at times feeling like he and Aliver danced for each other. Their eyes met often, both flashing smiles when they did so. He knew that Aliver's joy was in the ceremony itself, in anticipation of what was to come and in joy at so completely belonging, but to Kelis there was more to it. Part of the joy for him was in the awareness that—should Aliver wish it—anything could happen between them. No intimacy would be too much, no pleasure one Kelis would turn away from. It was an attraction he felt for no other man, and yet something about it felt right, full and complete and sublime in a manner different from his attraction to women. It could lead to anything.

But not that night. Nor on any night thereafter. That evening progressed on a tide propelled by the collective will of the village. At some point the music changed tempo, announcing the time of choosing had come. In an instant the new women swarmed in on the men, grabbing them by the wrist, shouting out their choices with voices and laughter. Aliver became the center of a swirling chaos of young beauties. Kelis himself was pulled in two different directions for a time, until one girl won the tugging match by grasping his tuvey band and swirling away with him. Benabe won Aliver, perhaps with the aid of his acquiescence. What a beauty she was then! Kelis could see it as clearly as any man. Aliver was as eager as she was, eager enough that he left the group at her urging, without so much as a glance of leave-taking to Kelis.

Perhaps that was the night Benabe conceived. Perhaps, while he made love to one woman, thinking of a man, that man planted the seed that would be Shen in another woman. Perhaps—if Thaddeus Clegg had not arrived soon after to recall Aliver to the fight that would eventually take his life—Kelis might have watched Aliver and Benabe wed and would have been near them as Shen entered the world and grew. He awoke with this thought, and during the few quiet minutes left before the others stirred he tried to believe he could have lived satisfied with that. And then he had a different thought.

Perhaps Shen is my daughter as well. That would explain why she scared him so, and why he already loved her more than his own life. For that was the truth. What he had said to Benabe was neither a comfort nor a vain boast. Though he had only known the girl a few weeks, it already seemed that protecting her was the single task of meaning in his life.

And then, with an abruptness that meant it took but a few minutes to descend to the plains again, the mountains ended one morning. The four travelers wove through the foothills and trod once more across a flat landscape, one devoid of shade, unpeopled, and as barren as the far south Kelis had first approached with Aliver years before. Even the hardy acacia trees were but stunted, infrequent versions of their normal grandeur. It was there that they came upon the man. Naamen saw him first and indicated it with a grunt. The group of four stopped and stared.

The man stood as still as a statue, garbed in a robe the same sand color as the land around him. He clasped his hands together at his waist and seemed to carry nothing, no supplies, no weapons or staff, not even a skin of water. He was hooded, but the sun reflecting off the sand lit his face from beneath. He stared straight at them, as if he had been waiting for them to arrive at just that spot on the world. Kelis raked his eyes across the landscape, searching for others, for signs that would explain the man. Featureless desolation stretched out in all directions. He focused on the figure again. Was he a mirage they were all seeing, a sign they had journeyed away from sanity?

Shen walked forward. Benabe whispered her name. Kelis half formed a protest himself, but he held it behind his teeth. He strode to keep pace with the girl. As she neared him, the man finally moved. He fell forward onto his knees and into a bow that pressed his forehead to the ground. Once there, with his arms stretched out to either side and his palms flat against the parched earth, the man did nothing more.

Shen glanced back at the others, her expression one of amused perplexity. She knelt and touched her fingertips to the man's shoulder. She intoned the traditional words of Talayan greeting. "Old friend, the sun shines on you, but the water is sweet."

"The water is cool, Your Majesty, and clear to look upon," the man answered, speaking his words to the earth. "You are loved."

In those few words Kelis recognized the speaker's voice.

"I know," Shen said, as if she heard such greetings regularly. "Did the stones send you to tell me so?"

"The stones?" The prostrate man sounded confused for a moment, but then his voice picked up with the rhythms of

401

practiced formality. "The Santoth called you, and you came. That is a blessing. Come with me, Princess. I will take you to them. They have much to tell you."

Before he knew it, the man's name whispered through Kelis's lips. "Leeka Alain?"

The man raised his head, turned, and looked at Kelis. For a moment Kelis thought himself mistaken. The man's face was nothing like the craggy one he remembered on the general. And then it was. And a moment later it was not. His features appeared as fixed and solid as anybody else's, but his face contained more than a single man's features. It was ancient and cracked and eroded with the wear of ages, and yet it was also a face of clear green eyes and a once broken-nose and lips that glistened with moisture when his tongue wet them.

"They don't call me that here," the man said, "but that was my name before."

Chapter Thirty-four

The breakneck speed at which the league clipper careened into Acacia's main harbor would have been reckless even in the light of day. At night, it was madness. But league pilots were nothing if not adept at all things nautical, and the officer at the helm of the *Rayfin* carved a wild course through the anchored vessels, passed the trading floats. He hooked the vessel around the inner watchtower and dropped sails only when momentum alone was more than enough to place it skimming along a fortunately unoccupied section of league-owned pier. He shouted for the messenger to disembark before they had even halted. The man did not need the encouragement. He leaped from a height and ran with all the haste he had been ordered to show.

A scant ten minutes later, Sire Dagon sat bleary eyed, wearing a robe loosely wrapped about his gaunt frame. Mist so clouded his head that his servants had to carry him—against his muted protests—and prop him up in his chair. Even sitting there, with the bay windows thrown open to a chill breeze and lamps on high, he as yet floated on the chorus of angelic voices he conducted during his mist dreams. His head swirled with song, his body light as a silken puppet and able to dance in midair, only now being tugged back down to earth. Blinking, he asked the messenger what could possibly merit the interruption at such a delicate hour.

"I came in haste," the man said.

"So I gather," Sire Dagon said, cocking his head back in a manner that for some reason helped him see middle-distance objects more clearly. The man spoke with clipped Ishtat Inspectorate tones, a fact that registered a spike in the league-man's attention. Ishtats were so highly trained that rarely were they charged with tasks as menial as delivering a message. "What I don't yet know is why, but I trust you are about to tell me. Who sent you?"

"The League Council."

"Why did they not send a messenger bird from Thrain?"

"The news I carry was deemed too grave to be put in care of a pigeon."

"In care of a pigeon?" Sire Dagon found that amusing. Images of officer pigeons with military bearing, cooing orders to a small legion of birds, dancing up from the ground with the aid of the music yet pulsing in his veins . . .

"Sire, you need to listen."

Quite impertinently, the messenger shouted for Sire Dagon's servants. He demanded they bring a sobering concoction to match the leagueman's mist distillation. He needed him back completely, and immediately, he said. He must have said a few other very convincing things as well, because before Dagon could stop it his manservant stuffed an invigorating pill up one of his nostrils. Not pleasant but effective. Within a minute he was more awake than he wished, the burning itch in his nose and at the back of his throat making sure of it.

"Forgive me, Sire," the messenger said, bowing to him now that his orders had been heeded. "I was commanded that I waste not a minute in delivering my message. But you have to be able to hear it and understand it, too. This message is from the Council, without dissent. I wear on my neck this collar, secured with a truth knot that confirms my words are truth."

The man stepped forward, bent, and opened his shirt collar so that Dagon could study the thin rope tied about his neck. Sire Dagon yanked at it, pulling it close. To an untrained eye the knot that closed the circle looked like the confusion a child might create, but in its loops and bunches was an intricacy that was very practiced, indeed. And there could be no mistaking its authenticity. The messenger had been sent by the League Council.

Sire Dagon motioned for the man to step away. Regaining his dignity, he said, "I am listening."

And so he sat hearing about the horror that had emerged from Sire Neen's mistakes. In the space of a few moments everything changed. All their hopes, their plans, all of it would have to wait. Instead, he would have to compose lies faster than ever before. He would have to win the queen's trust, for they would need her armies in the war that was coming.

A few hours later Sire Dagon traversed the terraces and stairways that would lead him to the queen, a messenger himself now. She would not be easy to gain an audience with. Sire Dagon knew the things she had recently occupied herself with. Apparently, she had managed to capture Barad the Lesser. What a stir this had caused among the nobles! All the work of some agent of hers, one Delivegu, a lucky man, and now one officially acknowledged at court. Word of the capture had spread among the common folk, so that whatever benefit there was in it was not immediately obvious. Indeed, a rumor spread that she had mutilated Barad. Cut out his eyes and shoved stones in their places. Still others said she cursed him through sorcery. It was the sort of mad talk that might have sparked the man's rebellion into life, but Corinn had finally ordered the distribution of a new wine. In so doing, she belatedly fulfilled the league's wishes, but that was so often the case. She had also politely but firmly sent King Grae back to his homeland. The leaguemen were not entirely sure what to make of that, but there was something of interest beneath the surface of it surely. With all this happening, Corinn had every right to consider herself tied up in a web of complications. How very simple such things would seem to her by the end of this day!

Just outside the queen's quarters, Sire Dagon stood with his arms outstretched as a Marah searched him for hidden daggers. He tried to keep his gaze forward, his face wrinkled with annoyed tolerance. The last thing he wanted to do was look at any of the Numrek, two of whom stood watching. But his eyes had wills of their own. They flicked over long enough to confirm—damn it—that the guards on either side of the door were looking at him. Was there anything to be read in their craggy features? He was not sure. Stupid! Control yourself, he thought. Without showing it, he breathed deep and slow, steadying himself. Leaguemen controlled their emotions, not the other way around. Before he was waved through, he even resorted to the silent counting regime he had been taught as a boy, arithmetic exercises that he conducted in the back of his mind and that helped render his face expressionless.

"All right," the Marah said, "you may enter. Forgive the formality, sire." He stood to the side and motioned toward the corridor.

Sire Dagon gave him a look meant to indicate that he knew very well where he was going. It is what he would have done in normal circumstances. Again, though, his eyes chose to disobey him. Tremulous, they slid to the side as he passed and, yes, the Numrek to his left was watching him! No mistaking it. The beast had been observing him with more than casual interest.

Once in the corridor, the leagueman quickened his step, trying to walk quietly and listen for any indication that the Numrek was following. He had to pass another two Numrek milling about the anteroom, but he managed it without mishap. Once in the front office proper, he swept in on Rhrenna, tripping on the edge of the carpet and banging his leg against a divan.

The secretary frowned at him. "Sire Dagon . . ."

He did not slacken his strides. Reaching out with one hand,

he clamped his claw around the woman's elbow, wrenching her into motion. She called out in protest, but he shushed her savagely. "Be silent! Your life depends on this!"

The piper sitting in the corner near the queen's actual door did not pay enough attention to look perplexed. He just glanced at the two rushing forward and lifted his flute to announce their presence. He had sounded but a few notes before Sire Dagon opened the queen's door. He swirled in and shoved it closed again a moment later, releasing Rhrenna as he did. It was all an unaccustomed amount of physical activity for the man, enough to leave him panting.

Corinn had been on her balcony. She stepped back into the dimmer light inside, studying the two with an unreadable but certainly not welcoming expression.

"Your Majesty!" Dagon bowed quickly, sucking a few breaths as he did so. "I am here to tell you everything. Everything, without the slightest deception. First, though, have you a secret room? A safe room?"

"What—"

Moving toward her, he said, "You do, of course! I know you do. A room that you can enter from these chambers, that only you have the key to and that you can lock. Where is it?"

"Sire Dagon, I—"

"No!" he said. "Not now. In a safe place. Get us there. Then we talk. Please, Corinn. Your very life is in danger. Please!"

The queen crossed her arms. "I'm in my chambers, with my guards but a shout away. From whom am I in danger? I see only one madman at the moment."

"Oh, you stubborn thing! Fine."

As she watched—now visibly shocked by his outbursts—Sire Dagon brushed past her. He inspected one corner of the room quickly, looking high and low. He measured a few steps to the side, and then grasped the tapestry he found there along its bottom edge. With a flourish, he flung it to the side, sending the needlework depiction of a sunset behind the Senival mountains rippling toward the floor tiles. And there it was! As he knew it would be. Nothing more than two depressions at waist height in the stone, each about the size of the heel of a child's hand. He pressed his against both and pushed. For a moment the wall was as immobile as it looked. He cursed. He heard one of the women whisper something. He cursed again. And then remembered. He pressed harder on the right hand than the left. Of course. A door-sized portion of the wall gave way, suddenly smooth and light before his hands.

"There," he said, turning, panting. "Now you know that we know of this. Would I betray that information without cause? Please, come in with me. I'll tell you everything once we are inside."

The queen glanced at Rhrenna. Sire Dagon knew some message passed between them, but he was too fatigued to riddle it out. Not that he needed to. By the Giver, he had just revealed a secret hundreds of years old, one that by itself changed everything about the trust between the Akarans and the league. He hoped it worked. Of course, if it did not, the queen would likely be dead within the hour.

Without speaking a word or looking him in the face, Corinn moved past him, through the opening. Rhrenna followed, her blue eyes hard on his. Dagon slipped in behind them. He made sure the wall fit snugly back into place, and then he stepped away from it. From this side, the rough-hewn stone, which appeared to be lit from above by an opening to the sky, betrayed no sign of the door. Only at his feet, where a fan of thick dust had been swept aside, was there a sign to confirm he had just passed through the wall. How strange to finally be here. He had known of this place since his early days in his office, but never knew that he would see it himself.

He turned to face the two women. Before he was fully around, Rhrenna had slammed her shoulder into his thin chest, pushing him back against the wall. He felt the prick of a tiny, undoubtedly razor sharp, blade at his neck. The Meinish woman pressed it skillfully, with enough of the flat of the blade that he could feel the pulse of his artery beneath it, and with enough of the edge that he felt his skin on the verge of bursting open around it. Her small face was close to his chin, her teeth bared as if she would bite him as well as cut him. He had expected this, too, but it was savage enough an action to take his breath away again.

"Explain yourself now, Dagon," Corinn said. She stood only a step away, for the chamber was small, more like a fissure in a cave than a manmade room. Lit from above, she was frightening, all highlight or shadow. He had no problem believing her capable of sorcery. She said, "Rhrenna never liked you. She'd slit your throat and bathe in the shower of blood that would bring. Considering that you have shoved us into a secret room—a room that you should know nothing about—I'll happily pardon her and curse the leagueman who challenges me."

A few more breaths. This was so awkward, but to get through it he must get through it. The best way to do that was to hit her so directly she was stunned to silence, and then he would regain some control. "Queen Corinn"—he gasped— "first, you must know that Sire Neen and much of the envoy were killed. Ah—" He inched at a change in the pressure of the knife. He grasped the dolphin pendant hanging from his chest, the symbol of the league, and caressed it between his fingers. "The mission is a failure. We were betrayed in the most foul way. There are traitors within the walls of the palace at this very moment. Please, have the woman draw back her knife."

Corinn did not do so. "My brother?"

"I know not," Sire Dagon admitted.

"Is he alive?"

"I don't know. Perhaps he was captured. He was under our full protection, of course, but was, as I said, betrayed. We think—"

"By whom?"

"The Lothan Aklun. The Auldek. Both. We arrived to find them at war. They both sought to make us pawns. Tricked us. There was a massacre. And, Your Majesty, most important right now: the Numrek have betrayed us."

Corinn stood still. For a long time she looked like some beautiful, bloodless witch, the type of being who might haunt and excite adolescent nightmares. For a few moments, Sire Dagon felt he might have failed. There was too much to say, too much to explain, too many lies to navigate, even as he created more. For a moment, the idea of Rhrenna slicing his life from him did not seem so bad. At least it would end the complications.

"What do you mean the Numrek betrayed us?"

"They— Oh, it's hard to explain with a dagger at my throat."

Corinn shrugged. "Do it anyway."

So he did. As best he could, flinching often, feeling the trickles of blood that oozed out of small nicks made by the knife. He could smell Rhrenna's breath—not unpleasant—and hear the moist coagulation of his blood on her fingers when she flexed them. He told of how the *Ambergris* arrived to find the Lothan Aklun and Auldek in open war with each other.

The Aklun were suffering, nearly defeated; Sire Neen tried to arrange a peace, but he failed. The Auldek met with him under the guise of parley, he said, but Calrach chose the moment to switch sides. The Auldek were their cousins, similar in many ways. Together, they slaughtered the entire delegation party. Only a few from the landing party got back to the *Ambergris*. The vessel stayed a time in Aklun waters, trying to assess the situation. By the time they sailed for home, they believed two things: the Lothan Aklun were all but conquered, and the Numrek were trying to get the Auldek to attack the Known World via the same route they had used.

So he spoke. He did not tell the truth, save for the final

point. As an alternative, though, his version of events was no less credible than the real one.

"You are telling me we're at war? At war with a race I've done nothing to? All because of a league gambit gone wrong? All because you couldn't tell an enemy from a friend?"

Sire Dagon seemed to have difficulty accepting the entirety of the statement, but he could not settle on which part to take issue with. He answered rather sheepishly, "Ah . . . yes. In part." And then, not so sheepishly, "We were not the only ones fooled. But that doesn't matter. Your Majesty, at the moment I pray that we have the leisure for you to berate our stupidity at length. Now is not the time, though. The Numrek have played us all for fools, and they yet stand outside your door. Your Majesty, they must be exterminated. Right now. Today. This very hour. The vessel the messenger arrived in is stuffed with Ishtat. They are armed and ready, and they will take the palace any moment now."

"What?" Corinn somehow made the word sound like a spell of damnation.

"It's all we can do. If the Numrek knew that their brethren have succeeded, they'd begin the slaughter. That's what they've been waiting for, a sign to commence."

"The Marah. They will—"

"Some will die in the confusion. But others we've tried to contact, to explain—"

"You take great liberties!" Rhrenna spoke through teeth that still seemed ready to bite.

"And why should I believe you? The Numrek have never once shown a sign of deceit."

"Oh, yes they have. Majesty, they've written their treachery in blood. In your brother's blood, I fear. You haven't seen it, but must you lay eyes on everything to believe it real? As for you, why would I come to you with this tragedy if it were not true? What fool would make up such misfortune?"

Corinn stared at him for a long moment. "If this is true, how would the Numrek learn what happened? They're not going to pilot a ship back themselves, are they?"

"I . . . I don't know," Sire Dagon sputtered.

"Would one of your people carry the message?"

"No, of course not. They've attacked us. We—"

Rhrenna interrupted. "You're the messenger."

"What?" Sire Dagon grimaced. "No, I'm here to warn you."

"You fool," Rhrenna continued. "If what you've said is true, look at what you've just done. You walked in here sweating, ashen-faced, nervous. You think the Numrek guards wouldn't notice that? Then you push us into a secret room! What more confirmation do they need that something grave has happened? And you're going to attack them? Only a handful of them are on the island. The rest will learn all they need to know because of your actions!"

Sire Dagon was speechless for a moment. He then said, "But we've brought Ishtat. They'll attack any moment. That's why we are safe in here." But even as he said this he felt his logic falling away beneath him. Of course his actions would confirm the betrayal in the Other Lands. The few Numrek on Acacia would die, but they would act as assassins in their last moments. Perhaps his appearance had given them a few extra minutes to kill chosen targets. The rest of the clan, safely on the Teh Coast, would dig in and wait. Who knew what preparations they had made already, what supplies and weapons had been stored?

Corinn, speaking to Rhrenna now, snapped, "How many Numrek are within the palace today?"

When the Meinish woman craned around to answer, Corinn flicked her fingers, indicating she could release him. She did, and Sire Dagon's fingers went immediately to his throat. He touched it gently, as if his fingers could somehow do more damage than the blade had. He realized Rhrenna was answering the queen, but he caught only the end of it.

". . . and there is a handful with Aaden and Mena at the Carmelia Stadium."

The queen let out a gasp of air, as if she had just been punched in the chest. She did it again, forming it into a word this time. "Aaden!"

She stepped for the hidden door, but Sire Dagon dove to block it from her.

"Out of my way!" Corinn hissed this so fiercely that Sire Dagon, despite knowing it was the worst possible action, half stepped to the side. He could not help it, for it suddenly seemed she had the power to crush him in an instant if he did not obey.

Her shoulder brushed him and he watched her from the back as she sought out the contours that would open the door. She had just leaned to push against it when one of the Numrek, Codeth, called for the queen from the other side of the door. The feigned calm of his voice was short-lived. A rush of new voices beat it down, with the clang of steel on steel and the commotion of furniture being overturned.

Nearer, Sire Dagon heard the queen whisper her son's name, barely more than an exhaled breath.

End of Book Two

Book Three
Song of Souls

Chapter Thirty-five

Sitting beside Devoth was the most unnerving experience Rialus had ever lived through. The Auldek had all the brutal physicality of their Numrek cousins. If anything, they had distilled it to its essence and then stirred into it a strange gentility that was all the more incongruous. Something like ferocious anger seethed beneath Devoth's tanned features, but above it lay a veneer of boredom. Rialus could not decide whether Devoth was passionate about life or completely fatigued by it. That was confusing, but even more unsettling was that the Auldek oozed more aristocratic confidence than any Acacian noble Rialus had ever seen—and he had seen many.

Devoth leaned back in his seat, one arm propped at an angle, his knees splayed wide. It was a posture of complete relaxation that also managed to convey that he could spring to his feet at any moment and stride across the world lopping off heads. Devoth now wore a shirt, a thin, somewhat dandyish white cotton garment with crimson satin buttons that matched his trousers. A gold band ringed his thick neck. The tips of his long fingernails had been glazed silver, and his eyes—if Rialus was not mistaken—were lined with black makeup. If Rialus had seen a Numrek so dressed in Acacia he would have laughed at the absurdity of it; here, the effect was almost dashing.

"Rialus Leagueman," Devoth asked, "how do you enjoy being our guest?"

They were sitting with a few others in a private box, beneath an awning of a silken fabric that sheltered them from the strength of the sun. Above and below them stretched a stadium to rival Acacia's Carmelia. The terraced benches surrounding it rose at a steep angle to a dizzying height. Rialus knew that the field was actually dug into the earth; the appearance of height was actually one of depth. But, situated as he was at the midpoint of its height, the view below and the expanse above made him queasy.

"You've no complaints, I hope," Devoth prodded. "Rialus Leagueman?"

Rialus Leagueman! What an annoyance! He had tried several times to make the Auldek understand that he was not part of the league. He hated them, as a matter of fact. They had brought him here as a prisoner! He spat on leaguemen and had nothing in common with them! So he had said, but it never sank in. One guard had even squeezed Rialus's skull and murmured something about the egg shape of it, and then laughed at Rialus's sputtering refutation that there was anything leaguelike about the shape of his head.

Curses and exclamations bounced around in a fury in Rialus's mind, but he had to bite back his complaints and reply, "You've been most . . . kind."

Devoth seemed pleased to hear it. He looked at the other high-ranking Auldek seated nearby, making sure they took note of Rialus's response. They were all of his clan, except Calrach; his son, Allek; and his half brother, Mulat. The fact that they were allowed to sit with Devoth's people was a considerable honor. Allek, in particular, drew stares and whispers wherever he went. If Rialus had not known the reason for their astonishment he would have thought the boy a long-lost prince. He was more than that: he was a miracle to a people who had not seen a child of their race in hundreds of years. Calrach, always more canny than Rialus expected, had known what he was doing when he brought him along.

Allek, who sat in the row in front of Rialus and Devoth, turned around and jabbed Rialus's leg. "Tell the truth, Neptos. Which is the richer people: Acacians or Auldek? I know what I would say, but what about you?"

Rialus had the momentary desire to kick the grinning youth in the face, but he answered the boy calmly. He had actually expected some question like this, considering how much pleasure the Numrek seemed to take in publicly taunting him. "I can't answer that. I've seen most of the Known World, which is wide and rich and wondrous, but I've seen very little of Ushen Brae—as yet only Avina."

"And what do you think of it?" Allek pushed.

"Very impressive," Rialus admitted, "from what I've seen—"

"From what you've seen?" Mulat broke in. He had just bitten a piece of roasted pork taken from the plates of food that occasionally passed from hand to hand. His chewing did not hinder his speaking. "What you've seen is less than nothing. It's but a sliver. Avina stretches along the coast for thirty miles. Thirty miles of city, of palaces and stadiums and monuments: there is nothing to match that in your lands."

Devoth did not seem pleased with the Numrek presumptions. He did not address them, smiling instead at Rialus. "You will see more, Rialus Leagueman. Many grand things. You're our guest, so you'll see the things that make us great. We will always treat you well, now and in the future. You can be sure of it. You believe me?"

He had to push it, didn't he? Rialus thought. They always did. It was one way the Auldek were not so different from their Numrek cousins.

"Yes, of course," Rialus began, but then faltered, unsure how to express his emotions. What was he? Grateful to be alive? Thrilled to have watched everyone he had traveled across the Gray Slopes with be slaughtered? Looking forward to whatever bloody spectacle he was here to watch? Overjoyed to be trapped in a land of brutes who threatened to stick red-hot pokers up his backside? Content to know almost nothing of his fate or what was expected of him? Resigned that if he did ever find his way back to Acacia, the queen would squash him beneath her shapely foot?

"I'm quite comfortable," he managed.

"Good, good." Devoth grinned and tossed his hair around. "It gives me joy to hear it."

The man's hard chin cut the air as he looked about, his eyes lit green by the sun. He kept brushing his hair back from his face, but he also moved in a manner to make sure it fell right back before his eyes a second later. Rialus almost suggested he tie it back with a cord, or perhaps get it trimmed. Not for the first time, Rialus wondered if Devoth was simpleminded. Or if he really might be unaware of the way in which Rialus's life was a misery. He knew neither was likely. Devoth, Rialus feared, was in complete control of everything.

The crowd, which had waited amid a murmur of conversation, erupted in applause and shouts. Rialus kept his gaze on Devoth, who was on his feet, roaring with the rest of them. Lucky, because Rialus would not have managed to hide his animus if Devoth had been paying attention to him. He felt his indignation rising again. It did not get far, because his eyes caught the motion on the field. His mouth opened, silent while those around him cheered.

From six different openings in the wall of the arena, columns of armed soldiers strode onto the field. By their relatively normal stature, Rialus could tell they were not Auldek, but neither did they appear entirely human. One group wore wolf-head helmets. Another was composed entirely of squat, muscled brutes, their naked torsos gray, metal barbs jutting from their cheeks. They bore curved short swords in both hands. Yet another group were slim as acrobats and wore light blue, with plumes on their heads in place of helmets. They carried only slender pikes.

"You understand this, Rialus Leagueman?" Devoth asked.

"Not in the slightest," Rialus admitted.

The Auldek laughed. "Ah, I forget your ignorance. So much to learn."

"Those soldiers, they are not Auldek?"

"Of course not!" someone in the row behind Rialus exclaimed. "Auldek do not draw Auldek blood. What do you think us?"

Devoth explained, "It was agreed that we would not kill our own. That is why our ultimate punishment is banishment, not death. We fight among ourselves, yes." He grinned, making the statement seem an admission of a guilty pleasure. "But in something like this—a matter to be decided in blood—we let our slaves represent us. It is an honor for them. These are special slaves, selected to be divine children. They are elevated above other slaves. Before you are totem warriors of the eight clans of the Auldek. Here. See over there?"

He leaned across Rialus, pointing first toward groups of warriors who had feline facial tattoos, and then the others as he named them. "The Shivith, the spotted cats. Those over there are the Kern, the blue cranes. They look slim, yes? Delicate? Don't be fooled. They're deadly. The Anet clan worships the hooded snake. The Kulish Kra—those with their backs to us—black crows. Those gray ones—Antoks. The wolves represent the Wrathic from beyond the Sky Mount. The Fru Nithexek are brothers of the sky bear, but they are weak, few in number. The Numrek . . . have no totem."

"And there"—Devoth drew back so that Rialus could see past him to the last group—"are the snow lions, the Lvin. Those are mine. My lions. My totem." He timed this announcement perfectly, for the Lvin were the last to enter. Though Rialus had no idea what a snow lion was, there was no mistaking the impact of the slaves so named. They came roaring like some beast of the Talayan plains. Most of them had white faces, sometimes tattooed or painted down across their torsos. In the center were the largest men, several of whom sported tresses as white as snow. As they marched and yelled and smacked life into those around them, their locks danced about them like snakes writhing.

"There are other totems in the land," Devoth continued, his voice low and filled with pride, "but they are small. Ants. These are the eight clans. We are the ones who decide the future; and today, we fight for the honor of being the spear point. None of your race has seen this. None other ever will. Enjoy and feel privileged."

Both enjoyment and feelings of privilege lived somewhere far from Rialus's present state of mind. He had yet to sort out the intricacies of Auldek social and political life. He doubted he would understand it all even if he spent years in Ushen Brae, which he prayed to the Giver that he would not. Over the last few days, Rialus had seen enough of the slaves to know that they were often tattooed, adorned with jewelry, and physically modified. But the changes were minor on the household servants. These warriors were monstrosities. Yet they were the Auldek's own creations. Why do that to them? Why not do it themselves if the Auldek found such things attractive?

Perhaps it was evidence of his compromised mental state, because before he could censor himself, Rialus heard this question escape his lips. "Why is it the slaves who are so adorned?"

The group answered him with incredulous silence.

"I would have thought that—" Rialus stopped, unsure what he might have thought. He changed tack. "I mean, why not yourselves? Since the animals are your totems—"

Mulat murmured a curse under his breath, and then added, "Stupid piss pot of a man. The totems are not animals. They are gods who live in the animals!"

Several Auldek faces continued to stare at him. Words came from his mouth, unbidden. "Very interesting that

422

they—just slaves, I mean—decide this spear-point thing."

"That is what the slaves are for!" Calrach barked over his shoulder. "It is a blood test, you fool!"

"I see," Rialus said. "That explains it, then."

Devoth studied Rialus, making him unsure whether he was about to reach out and smash him across the nose or—

"Have a glass of juice," the Auldek said, motioning that a passing tray should be held for the Acacian's consideration.

Rialus obliged. He took the glass of red liquid in both hands, clenching it tightly to keep his hands from trembling.

"Calrach is correct," Devoth said. "This is the way it is. Our slaves are our children. Their fate is inseparable from ours. The changes to their bodies are called 'belonging.' We don't make all the belonging changes to them ourselves. Some they make themselves. Some things only the Lothan Aklun had the magic for. That, it seems, has come to an end because of the league. We will have to be repaid for this. Very much so."

And that closed the subject. A relief, for Rialus. They turned their attention to the spectacle before them. To begin with, individual warriors from the different groups taunted others into single combat. Listening to the banter they threw around, the way they laughed and swore and taunted, put Rialus in mind of the children who dove for oysters at the docks of Acacia's western harbor. Those suntanned, shirtless youths had the same easy competitive air about them. But the divers did not strike blows that severed a crow woman's arm at the shoulder or split a cat man's head so that the crown down to below the eyes went spinning end over end, or that smashed a lovely crane woman's knee between two war hammers.

Rialus really, really felt he was going to be sick. He motioned as much with the fingers of one hand, vaguely calling for attention. It was the type of gesture that would have brought a servant to his side in Acacia. It was ignored here. A hot sweat broke out on his forehead and spread throughout his body. Saliva surged into his mouth and stayed there, no matter how much he swallowed. What was wrong with these people? Looking about him, he could not match the merriment on their faces with the scenes of carnage that evoked it. Before long he sat with his eyes closed, "watching" only with his ears, which he would have stuffed with wax if he thought he could get away with it and had any.

Thus he passed what seemed like several hours. The clash of weapons, the cheers of pleasure and the boasting and the occasional screams of agony went on interminably. He had begun to think they would never end, and he was rather surprised when they stopped. A great ovation took over the arena for a time, and when it finally died the sound faded to a low murmur of conversation and movement.

Rialus opened his eyes. "Is it . . . over?"

"No, no, not at all," Devoth said. "The cleaners will tend the field for a time, and then we have the mêlée. That is where matters are truly decided."

The cleaners? As quickly as he thought the question he got the answer. Several other doors, different from the ones the slaves had entered by, had also been opened. From them emerged the monsters Rialus knew by description, though he had not seen their work on the plains of Talay. Antoks. There was no mistaking the swinish enormity of them. Nor was there anything hiding the fact that they brought their crosshatched horrors of mouths down on the slain warriors with voracious enthusiasm. Rialus looked away, holding back the convulsions building in his stomach.

Devoth sat back in his seat again, relaxed once more. "So," he said, as if he were asking how he liked the weather or the view, "Rialus Leagueman, will you do as we wish?"

"May I ask what you intend? Just so that I can better answer your question."

Devoth thought about this for a time. He shrugged. Gesturing toward the garish units preparing for the next battle, he said, "See those? They fight for privilege. See how we honor our slaves? At times they decide our futures. The clan that wins here today will lead the invasion. They determine which clan will be the initial spear thrust."

"The invasion?"

"Of your lands. They will beat the winter traveling over the north, Numrek showing the way." He leaned in and whispered, "These honored ones will have the most fun. The rest of the Auldek will follow to complete the work."

"Why?" Rialus asked.

Devoth looked at him.

"I mean . . . that—that it need not be war that comes of this. I could help make a new treaty with Queen Corinn." As he said it, he knew it was true. She would be angry and he would suffer her wrath first, but in the end he would be able to convince her to see reason. They could avoid war. Of course they could. Sometimes great sacrifices needed to be made, but better that than complete destruction. He continued, hope already quickening his speech. "The league could be appeased and the trade continued. I daresay you could win even better terms—"

"Terms?" Devoth said this with an open-mouthed grimace, as if the word were a dead mouse he had just discovered on his tongue.

"Why make total war when you could negotiate peace? The queen wouldn't like it, but you could convince her to give you a toehold in the Known World. The Numrek have had such. I could ask as your—"

Devoth had heard enough. "Nah. You don't know anything, leagueman. We've been too long alive. Too long without real war. We haven't lived as our ancestors did in many, many years. Time that we do.

"The Numrek may have done what you say, but they are the weakest among us. Cowards. Lowborn."

This was certainly said loud enough for Calrach and Mulat to hear, but neither of them turned or acknowledged it.

"We true Auldek know that nothing matters but bravery in battle. We were robbed of this when the Lothan Aklun gave us everlasting life. You think that's a gift? They who gave us life denied us immortality. Made death something to fear. This, Rialus Leagueman, has been our shame. That ends now. The Auldek will go to war. We will die in glorious battle, and our women's wombs will quicken with life. That's immortality, leagueman. To die and live on also. Perhaps you don't understand this, but the outcome doesn't matter. Talk no more of negotiation, of terms. We will take the world, Rialus Leagueman, or we will die with blade bloodied. Either way is joy for me."

And doom for us, Rialus thought. Doom for us.

Devoth leaned back, looking down at the field. "We have asked you many questions already," he said. "You have answered well. Because of you, we trust the tale Calrach tells, we believe in the boy Allek. Because of you, we will embark on this journey. I thank you for that, but now is when your work begins. You will help us shape our plans. You will answer many more questions about your nation. Tell us the geography. Draw us maps. Tell us customs, name the powers, name the people we will meet. You will prepare us so that nothing—nothing—will surprise us. You will find the things that we have overlooked and you will tell us that as well." He paused, tented his fingers before him, and turned to Rialus. "Am I right in saying that you will do these things?"

Rialus recognized that, no matter how plainly it was put to him—the ramifications of his answer were enormous knots upon knots upon knots, all of which should be untied before any answer was arrived at. He knew all that was true, but he also knew he could never untie all those knots. Better just to answer.

So he did.

Chapter Thirty-six

Mór had not seen this vessel messenger before. That made her nervous, no matter how often she told herself it did not matter. It was not him she would be speaking to about the important matters. He was but the vessel, and of course vessels were interchangeable. Only the contents within mattered. But still, she had first to look into a stranger's eyes and search for a loved one. This was not something she had ever grown accustomed to.

They sat across from each other on a hillock in the barren stretch between two walls. Once, the area had been a park, but that was long ago. Now it was abandoned and overgrown with briars, home to rats and other scurrying things. They were alone save for the few guards who stood at a distance, on the lookout for the unlikely patrol of the divine children. They had planned the meeting to avoid this.

"Hello, Mór Avenger," the man said. "It honors me to meet you, as it honors me to carry an elder within and his message from the Free People." He bowed his head as he spoke, showing her the short bristle of a few weeks' hair growth across his crown, the skin visible beneath it and dotted with the heart-shaped imprints of the sky bear. Unusual, for the Fru Nithexek was not a numerous clan.

Mór answered him formally. "The honor is mine. May this vessel never crack."

The man looked up. His wide-spaced eyes were large,

brown, and intense. He smiled. "I have not cracked yet, Mór Avenger. I won't today. You can rest assured of that. Before I begin, tell me, is it true? Do we hold a prince of the Akarans?"

Mór nodded.

"Could he be the Rhuin Fá?"

"Anything could be," she answered, feeling suddenly testy in addition to uneasy. It was inappropriate for him to waste time feeding his own curiosity. "Whether he is or not isn't for me to say."

Pursing his lips, the messenger said, "Nor for me to ask, judging by your tone. Forgive me. For us in the Westlands, though, we are hungry for hope. We hear rumors, but we've heard rumors for hundreds of years. Nothing yet has come of them."

"I didn't take you as that old."

The man smiled again. "You are anxious to begin. I understand. Shall we?"

Despite her impatience, Mór scanned the overgrown walls before answering. She made eye contact with Tunnel, who stood with his arms crossed, leaning against the arch through which they would exit. He acknowledged her with a lift of his chin. Like everything about him, it was a gruff gesture, but it was comforting as well.

"Yes," she said, "do begin."

The messenger cleared his throat. His gaze flicked to Mór, amused just a moment longer, and then his arms went limp in his lap and he seemed to focus his entire consciousness on his breathing. Eyes closed, he inhaled and exhaled. Every so often he let out a low moan. For a time his head dropped forward as if he were asleep. And then it seemed he really was asleep, his moaning nothing but faint snoring. That was how it always was. Mór waited, watching him, curious, as ever, about what was about to happen.

Then, the moaning ceased. The man's breathing stopped. For an uncomfortably long few moments it was as if the sleeping man had passed into death. And then he looked up. He gasped and blinked his eyes open. His now blue eyes—the whites veined with a crimson lacework of age, yellowed and tired—were not the messenger's eyes anymore. Nor was his voice the same.

"Dearest," his mouth said. The voice coming out did not fit the shape or the movement of his lips. A dry voice, slow and patient and heavy with melancholy and love, it was a voice she knew well from her girlhood but had not heard from the actual man in some years. "You are not my little girl, are you?"

Her first impulse was to refute that. Yes! Yes, she was his little girl. Of course she was. That's all she ever would be. It was cruel for him to say otherwise. But she had said that on other occasions, and it did no good. Instead, she swallowed and said, "No, but I am the one who was that little girl. Now I am the woman who remembers that girl and remembers you. Hello, Yoen."

The messenger smiled. His eyes closed for a moment. Opened. Yoen's voice said, "Hello, dearest. I wish my eyes could truly see you, at least once more before I fly. That would do my heart good."

"Let it be so. Let us make it so." A tear welled from Mór's left eye and raced down her cheek. She had not known there was a danger of this. She wiped at it, embarrassed, flooded with memories she rarely allowed to surface. Yoen, the nearest thing to a father she had ever known—more than that, he was father and mother both, and a balm for the loss of a brother. Life was cruel and cruel again, to take everything from her as a child and make her relearn herself under this man's care. And then, later, to ask her to be whole unto herself when he escaped to join the elders in the Westlands, on the Sky Isle. It was too much to bear.

The thing was, she knew that the eyes looking at her, though they appeared to be Yoen's, were not his. They were the messenger's, and it was he who was seeing enough to be able to take part in this conversation. Yoen himself did not see her. He had instilled himself and his words inside this man at least a fortnight ago. They had lived in him, and now the vessel let them out. More than that, he shaped them. He spoke and reacted with Yoen's voice and mind, even though Yoen himself was not part of it. Mór had never understood the process. And she had never liked it.

"What do the elders wish of me?" Mór asked.

"Tell me of the Akaran."

She could tell him things, but whatever responses he made to what she said had to have been embedded in the vessel weeks ago. It made little sense, but few of the things the People had learned from the Lothan Aklun did. She answered as fully as she could, telling Yoen everything that seemed important. She did leave out how she had reacted during her first encounter with Dariel, but that was a detail, not the substance he needed.

"Do you believe he speaks truly?"

With more bitterness than she intended, Mór said, "I don't know what truth means to Acacians."

Yoen's eyes stared at her. Waited.

"He seems to believe himself. He is earnest, but that doesn't mean he's truthful. He may just be foolish."

"We must be careful with him," Yoen's voice said, after considering this for a long moment. "If he is the living prophecy, he must be allowed to find it himself. We cannot thrust it upon him. We can, however, take certain steps. This is what you will do: test him further. Find a true test."

Mór's eyes widened. A true test meant a task to be accomplished in the real world, with real danger. "And if he dies?"

"Then he is not the Rhuin Fá. Mór, my dearest, go with the—"

"Wait," Mór interrupted what she knew to be the beginning of a farewell. "Yoen, how do we know that we don't err by forcing a role upon him? You yourself once told me that the prophecy of the Rhuin Fá might be nothing more than a tale to keep our hopes alive. Perhaps we are giving this Akaran an importance he shouldn't have, putting our faith in someone who may not deserve it."

Though he only had his eyes to express emotion, Mór was sure she could see the look of fatigued love Yoen had so often showered upon her. "Dearest, how do you know that's not how prophecy works?"

That question was still circling through Mór's mind half an hour later, after she had parted with Yoen, bade the vessel farewell, and worked her way back down under Avina. Tunnel led the way. Dariel's cell was changed so often, and she was so distracted with managing the People's myriad concerns, that it was comforting having Tunnel's broad gray back to follow. They arrived at Dariel's new room before she knew it. Tunnel turned and studied her, concern on his face. She had hardly said a word to him as they walked. She realized he had no idea what Yoen had said to her. Considering his obvious affection for Dariel, it was insensitive to hold to her silence.

"It's all right," she said, reaching out and touching the brawny bulk of his forearm. "I have no orders to harm him. He will just be tested further."

Tunnel lifted his chin, a gesture that seemed to have a variety of meanings for him. This time, she thought it indicated relief, acknowledgement of reason, and a slight hint of "See, I told you."

"Yes, Tunnel knows." She touched her palm to his muscled chest, pulled it back quickly. "Go in. Let Skylene know she may proceed as we discussed. She can answer his questions. I will listen from here for a time."

Once she was alone in the cramped passageway, Mór leaned against the stone wall next to the door. As in all these abandoned regions, the door was old and half rotten. It sat slightly ajar, tugging at hinges that probably would not hold much longer. There was enough space that Mór could listen, knowing she was hidden from the speakers inside.

Tunnel's entry stopped whatever they had been talking about. He greeted the prince merrily, like an old friend. He even audibly slapped him on the back. They spoke foolishness for a few minutes, although within it Mór recognized that Tunnel was conveying her permission to finally educate the Akaran. It was time, as she had already discussed with Skylene, to tell him the truth of things.

Mór noted that Skylene and Dariel spoke with an alarming level of familiarity. She did not like it. Were they all so infatuated with the Akaran? Even Skylene, her lover? The thought of it almost drove her into the room, but she was not ready yet, and did not want to enter until she knew what she would say and could do it without hesitation. Anyway, she had agreed that Skylene would be kind to him in ways that she was not willing to be. Perhaps that was all she was doing—playing a role a little too well.

Dariel spoke easily enough. The topic now—his naval battles with the league during the war with Hanish Mein—seemed to fire his oratory. He wants us to think him a hero, Mór thought, and because of it she wanted to doubt his version of events. Still, it was easy to listen to him, easy to forget her skepticism as he told of ships smashing together, of nighttime raids, hidden raider camps, and the great work of sabotage that destroyed much of the league's platforms. Mór remembered that place well, and it was stunning to imagine the scene he described. Flames roaring up into the sky . . .

"Why did you hate them so?" Skylene asked, the scratch of a scribe's stylus right behind her words. "Your family did—and does—partner with them. You came here with them—"

"It was personal back then. There I was, a prince of an overthrown empire, hiding among brigands, fighting the league because they made life hard for the criminals who were my new family . . . Yet I came here, allied with them, more aware than ever of their crimes, but was then betrayed by them to the

432

people who enslave you. And now I'm in your hands. All very amusing." He laughed. "How can I live day after day, trying to make decisions, and yet feel that I've not had one moment of control of any of it?"

"At least you laugh," Tunnel said.

"At some point, what else can I do?"

"You control more than you acknowledge," Skylene's voice said. "I would have loved to have seen the platforms destroyed."

"That didn't come without a price."

"What was the price?"

Dariel took a moment to respond. "I lost a person dear to me, the man who was my second father."

A second father. Mór recalled Yoen's eyes embedded in the vessel's face, but then pushed the image away. It was not the same. Whatever the Akaran had experienced, his loss was nothing compared to what each of the People suffered.

Dariel continued, "And I came to understand later that my actions killed many quota children. I wish that weren't so. It was children like you who died there."

Mór felt like clearing her throat and spitting, or bursting into the room and slapping him again. What right did he have to make those deaths a weight on his conscience? It was an indulgence he didn't deserve. She was pleased by what Skylene said in reply.

"You Akarans dwell on past failures too much. I'm beginning to think that's what made your line so tyrannical: guilt, and hiding it."

"Yes," Dariel said, no indication in his voice that he took offense. Mór imagined him grinning as he propped a leg up on a stool. "But enough of me talking. You give me something now. You said you would."

This was met with a moment of silence, then Skylene cleared her throat. Mór imagined the tight face she was making, the way she would dip her head and sweep her left hand from her forehead up lightly across her plumage. "What do you want to know?" she asked.

"Everything."

"That's a bit too much to tell at one sitting."

"Tell me about the Auldek, then."

And she did. Mór pressed her ear even closer to the gap, for Skylene began speaking softly. Good, she thought. Yes, do give the Akaran truth. Let it be a punishment to that weak side of him that embraces guilt.

Skylene spoke with her usual conciseness, laying out the details in a dispassionate manner that Mór herself could not have pulled off. It was hard to know truth from myth, but some among the divine children had been entrusted with keeping the Auldek's oral history. They passed on what they had learned to the People. The clans of Ushen Brae had once been much more numerous. Theirs had been a warrior culture, rooted for millennia in intertribal strife, a culture in which men lived to die in battle, risking everything to earn a place in the warrior halls of the afterworld. They worshipped a god of war, Bahine, and a pantheon of lesser animal deities, warriors all.

"If they had stayed such," Skylene said, "there would never have been a quota trade."

But things did not stay that way. Though the tribes were rich in fertile land and resources, the constant warring made for feast or famine, triumph or destruction. They might have been strong with swords and axes; when the Lothan Aklun arrived, they thought them hounds fighting over scraps.

"Arrived?" Dariel interrupted. "From where?"

Skylene admitted that she did not know. But they came and, soon after, the league did as well. "It was so long ago that the truth is hard to know for certain, but some believe that the Lothan Aklun and the league were in partnership right from the start, as if the Lothan Aklun discovered Ushen Brae, saw the potential for trade, and called on the league to sail the seas for them.

"The thing is, Dariel," Skylene said, "the Lothan Aklun did not want to trade in ore or spices or oils. Even the mist was important only because the Known World wanted it so. For some reason, they wanted to base their trade of slaves on quota, on souls. They created the soul catcher. It's not a thing. Not a device or tool, exactly. It's the place where the life force is taken from one and given to another. We don't know how it works, or why. There are words written on the floor, they say. Perhaps the spells are written there, or perhaps in some way it focuses the Lothan Aklun's power. With it, they can take the life force from one body and place it into another, on reserve for when it's needed. This is the reason why Devoth didn't die when that arrow burst his heart. He has many lives within his skin. Killing one is anguish, but goes away."

Dariel said, "This is making my head spin. For weeks you tell me nothing. Now, suddenly—"

"Yes, well, your respite is over. Don't faint on me just yet, though. The result of all this is the Ushen Brae of today. The Lothan Aklun traded mist for quota children, and they took them and sold them to the Auldek, who paid great sums for them. The Auldek, in turn, used the slaves to run their world, to build their grand cities and produce a greater flow of wealth than they and the Lothan Aklun could ever have produced themselves. See how it all works?"

"Not really. I mean, I do, but what kind of men would think up such a system?"

And you thought your people were devious, Mór thought. You're children by comparison.

"Everybody in it is exploited," Dariel continued, "except the Lothan Aklun themselves."

"Ah, yes," Skylene cut in. "And now, with them dead, we have a host of new problems to face. Perhaps you should have a drink of water. I have a few more things to say that may make you dizzy."

Chapter Thirty-seven

M ake her fly higher!" Aaden called.

"As high as she can go!" his friend Devlyn added.

"I don't make her," Mena said. "I just ask. She chooses on her own."

"I know, but she should go higher. If I were her, I'd go up and up and up. I wonder how high she could go?"

"As high as she wants, Aaden. As high as she wants." Mena smiled, watching her nephew's upturned, enraptured face. His mouth hung open with the unanswered question. For a moment, Mena was tempted to snatch up one of the grapes left over from their lunch and drop it on his tongue. Instead, she formed the image of rising in her mind and wished it toward the creature.

The aunt, nephew, and his friend sat on a quilted blanket that had been laid out on the short grass of the Carmelia, the massive stadium named in honor of the seventh Akaran king's wife. Around them, the flat field stretched out in all directions, running right up to the walls that hemmed the exhibition grounds. Beyond that, terraced levels of bleachers rose up, enough contoured benches to hold thousands of spectators. They were empty at the moment, though, save a few cleaners working their slow way down the aisle. These Mena barely noticed. The four Numrek guards who stood on watch were more conspicuous, spaced throughout the bleachers in an approximate square around Aaden, their special charge.

Above them, Elya soared through the air. She, of course, was what so captured the boy's attention. Seemingly in answer to Aaden's request and Mena's thought, she steadied her wings and tilted into a slow, circular flight, lifted higher on thermals of warm air.

"You'll get a stitch in your neck if you keep looking up like that," Mena said, winking at one of the three servants that stood attending them. The young woman smiled back.

Aaden showed no sign of having heard her.

Eventually, Elya was but a speck in the sky.

"She's going to disappear," Devlyn said. He was a handsome boy, slightly taller than Aaden, dark haired but with features that did not clearly mark his ethnicity.

"She won't, will she?" Aaden asked, his enthusiasm exchanged for concern. And then, as if something had just occurred to him, "Tell her to come down now."

"But you just told me to send her up! She's barely gotten started."

Mena joked with them for a time, playing with their growing anxiety. When both boys began to look truly troubled, she set an arm on Aaden's shoulder and did as he requested. She was no surer now how the communication between her and the creature worked than she had been at first. There were no rules to it, no way to explain or quantify it. She simply thought to Elya, and Elya responded. It was not words Mena used but visual images. As now: she saw the world from high above and imagined plummeting down, the contours beneath her taking shape, the outline of Acacia amid the shimmering cobalt sea, the terraced palace and the lower town and the spit of land upon which the Carmelia lay, three people waiting on a square of woven fabric. She imagined all this and knew that Elya would both think it and understand what Mena meant by it.

That was just how it seemed to work, with images and also with emotions. Elya could pick up Mena's frame of mind readily. Sometimes Mena realized what she was feeling only because of something Elya did in response to it. When Mena grew pensive, thinking about Corinn or concerned about Dariel on his mission far away, Elya might make faces at her, invite her to fly, or simply draw near and let joy radiate between, like heat from her body.

At other times Elya knew when to withdraw. When Mena and Melio were intimate, for example, Elya acted as silly as any maid making a show of embarrassment for having caught them entwined in the bedsheets. She backed away with her head low, stepping lightly on the balls of her feet. Had her skin not been hidden beneath her soft plumage, Mena reckoned she would have seen her blush. Yes, between them there was no other word for it than what she had shouted to Melio back in Talay: love. Elya had brought a new level of love into the palace. Much needed.

As the avian and reptilian and wholly unique winged being plummeted down the last few hundred feet in a headlong dive, Mena greeted her with thoughts of affection, of admiration for her beauty, and thanks for the many ways she kept Aaden enthralled. Elya fell toward them with her wings close to her body, her head stretched forward and tail straight as an arrow behind her.

Only when Aaden and Devlyn raised their arms in alarm and the three servants dove for the ground did Elya snap her wings out. The effect was immediate. The membranes of her wings billowed back, stretched taut, and filled with air. Her wings caught hold of the air so completely that all of that incredible speed vanished. She hung above them for a few seconds, and then retracted her wings, that rapid clicking as they curled and shrank to nothing but small protrusions on her back. The air within them escaped and she touched down lightly on the grass.

Aaden rushed toward her. He threw his arms around her neck and pressed his face against her plumage. For a time the boy was lost in speaking with her, a tumbling stream of words that Mena could not follow. Elya, though, cocked her head, blinked her eyes, and wrinkled her nose as if she understood everything the boy was saying and found it all most engaging.

"It's too bad Grae isn't here," Aaden said, wrenching himself away for a moment. "He would love this. If he was, would you let him fly with Elya?"

"Remember what I said. I don't command her. She could let him ride if she chose, but . . . I think she is very choosy." As is your mother, she almost added. She leaned toward him and nipped his nose between her fingers. "You should feel honored. You're special, and not just because you're the prince. That means nothing to her, and she likes you for what's truly inside you."

The boy took this praise as he took all praise, as if it were his due and as if it were as light as the words themselves. He climbed upon Elya and called for a servant to fetch his bow and blunted arrows. With his quiver slung over his back and the flash weapon in hand, he urged Elya into something faster than a walk. The creature was careful with him. Mena could tell by the awkward way she moved, taking care to keep him steady on her back, even though it required extra contortions of her limbs. Devlyn knew better than to ask to ride himself. He fetched his own bow and made a show of circling, an instant hunting party. Aaden shouted for Mena to join them, but she declined. She was content to sit on the blanket and watch them, to smell the salt-tinged air and hear the rhythmic concussion of the waves on the base of the seaside wall of the stadium.

Small ruminants, about the size of dogs and looking much like lanky potbellied hares, munched on the grass a little distance away. They had been brought in after Corinn chose to seed the field several years ago. They kept the grass trim, and their droppings made for a pleasantly fragrant fertilizer. At first sighting Elya they had fled in awkward, loping fright. Now they hardly took notice of her at all. At Aaden's urging, Elya pressed her body low to the ground, intent as a carnivore stalking. The grazing animals were no more afraid than hens are with a toddler in their midst. They did not love being shot with the blunted arrows, though, and Devlyn seemed particularly good at stinging their backsides.

How strange to think that just a few weeks ago Elya was not even a part of her life. That seemed impossible now. She was family. Even Corinn saw it! And, like family, Elya had affection for the boy that went beyond his personal traits. Perhaps she smelled the bond between him and Mena and offered herself to him because of it. Or maybe he was special. Mena warmed to the thought. Maybe he was. Surely, he managed to balance both his childish nature and a calm acceptance of his heredity and the role it meant lay before him. She tried to imagine Aliver having been that at ease, but he never had been. What, she wondered, did this contrast between them mean? What might the reign of King Aaden amount to?

Motion on the stairs caught her eye. Two more Numrek had arrived. They emerged from one of the tunnel mouths at a brisk pace, stopped, and scanned the field and then the bleachers. Seeing the other guards, one headed toward the chief of the guard detail, and the other walked to the other nearest Numrek. Mena watched them speak for a moment, and then she looked at Aaden and Elya, who were at the far edge of the stadium now.

There was another reason for her good mood, a secret she and Elya shared. Three days earlier, in the private courtyard that had become Elya's domain, the creature had shown Mena a clutch of four eggs. They nestled within a blanket, tucked in a basin that caught the rays of the afternoon sun and preserved the warmth in the stone. They were like no eggs Mena had ever seen before—as large as dinner plates, tapered from one thicker side down to the other, only faintly oblong, and colored by pale orange swirls against a creamy background—but there was no mistaking them.

Nor could she doubt the nervous, hovering concern in Elya's demeanor. Mena looked up from the eggs, with moisture gathering on the rims of her eyelids, to find the creature standing behind her, waiting. In the look was a mixture of so many questions. It was hopeful, proud, frightened, seeking approval, but also defiant, ready to react should anger need to be a part of her response. In her eyes were the hopes of a mother faced with the enormity of what it meant to create life. How Elya could have been pregnant or how the eggs could be fertile Mena could not explain, but she did not want to. She just welcomed it.

Or perhaps Mena saw the things she imagined she would have felt faced with evidence of her own unborn children. Either way, she formed thoughts of warmth and pride and comfort and joy in her mind and floated them toward Elya. Even now, she still felt the pulsing intimacy of the moment. She knew that the first thing she would do back in her quarters would be to return to the eggs and whisper kind things to them.

She had said nothing about it to Corinn or Aaden or anybody else except the four maids who lived and worked in her private quarters. Them she could keep nothing from, but they were loyal to her and just as smitten with Elya. They would do nothing to endanger her, which is how Mena had explained the need for secrecy. "People are quick to fear," she had said, speaking to the four young women as they huddled around the nest the evening she learned of the eggs. "Even my sister might think nightmares will be born of these eggs. Foulthings. But we who know Elya best know that there is nothing but goodness in her." She had waited for eye contact with each of the women before continuing. "These babies will be beauties. They will be blessings on the empire, if only we are brave enough to see them born into safety." They had agreed, as she knew they would.

Even so, the eggs made her think even more about

journeying to Vumu. Perhaps she should take the eggs, Elya, and Melio to the archipelago. She could raise Elya's offspring there in greater seclusion. Melio would go with her. Of course he would, especially when she told him she was ready and willing to grow his child within her. She and Elya would be mothers together. And then what? Perhaps she could start the other project she had been thinking of recently: an academy of the martial arts. It would not be the same as the Marah training. She would make it something else, less about killing and more about honing the body and the mind and finding peace through mastery of skills. She would have to achieve this herself first, but she increasingly felt she might be able to, now that the wars were over and the foulthings no more.

"Princess," one of the servants asked, "will Prince Aaden be eating anything else? Or needing anything more from us?"

Mena said, "No, I don't think so. You may go back to the palace. We'll be along soon as well."

She used the impetus of the exchange to rise and stretch her legs. The newly arrived Numrek and the chief guard left their post and proceeded toward the other group of two with their long strides. Likely, Corinn was checking up on them, Mena thought. She did that often, even within the royal confines and other protected areas. Mena began to walk toward her nephew and Elya.

I'm sorry to keep secrets from you, Mena thought, but you'll see. You'll thank me later, and we really will find ways to be better, to do something with this rule of ours. Not that she thought it all through in reasoned terms, but Mena half believed that Elya could warm Corinn's heart. By the Giver, she needed that! Something had to melt that icy barrier she maintained between herself and the world. Mena had thought Grae could do it, but Corinn had rebuffed him and sent him away without explanation. Afraid, Mena thought. She's still afraid to love. It did not make much sense, but she could not help feeling that Elya, with time, would change that.

Aaden had dismounted, his stalking game seemingly forgotten. It looked, from a distance, that the two boys were performing an arm-waving drama, with an audience of one rapt creature. Without deciding to, Mena knew that sooner or later she would mention the eggs to Aaden—a slip of the tongue, perhaps, an inadvertent hint dropped in such a way that he, inquisitive as he was, would not let it go unchallenged. It would happen, and she would shrug and they would keep the secret for a time. Eventually Corinn would find out as well. She would purse her lips and ask sharp questions and fume about the dangers and then . . . well, then it would be fine. How wonderful it would be to have smaller versions of her flying above the island! What tales the people would tell then. A new age dawning, new creatures to announce it.

Mena was still some distance away from the trio. Glancing back, she saw that two of the Numrek had climbed onto the field and were following her. A tingling of unease climbed up her spine. She never liked having people at her back, especially not armed ones. That was nothing unusual. She brushed her fingers along the belt that snugged her tunic at the waist. Just a strip of leather. No weapon on it. That realization was another unnerving jolt, but just as quickly she brushed it away. Of course she was unarmed. She had made a point of putting down her sword when she returned to Acacia. It had been hard to do, but important because of that. Who wanted to live with a sword always in hand like another limb? Not she. She quickened her pace briefly, skipping ahead in a manner meant to keep her mirthful mood physically alive.

Elya—apparently at a signal from the prince—leaped into the air. Her wings rolled out and beat hard enough to keep her aloft a moment. Aaden lifted his bow, nocked an arrow, and drew. For a moment, it looked as if he planned to shoot her. But then he snapped around and loosed the arrow toward the sea. Elya snapped her wings down hard and bolted after it. A game of fetch, then. Watching them, Mena dropped back into a walk again.

She approached the boys from one side as four Numrek came down the stairs and approached them from the other side, and as two others closed the gap behind her. The guard in the front beckoned Aaden toward him with a hand. "Prince," he said, his Acacian thickly accented, "your mother wishes for you to come to her. Please come. I will escort you." He kept moving forward as he spoke, the others close behind him.

"Wait!" Mena called, but she was not sure why the word shot from her mouth. She was only twenty or so strides away. She had only to hurry forward and she could leave with them. Something was wrong. The guard had just done something Numrek never did. Her hand automatically went to where her sword hilt would have been. There was still no real reason to feel threatened by the prince's guards. And yet threatened was exactly what she did feel. She asked, "What are you doing? I will take them. Draw back and—"

"Please, Princess, the queen wants me to—"

That was as much as she heard. Two things happened at the same time. She realized it was that "please" that had sent her pulse racing. Numrek never were polite like that, even when serving the queen. Then a shout turned all their heads. Looking up into the heights of the stadium, a figure she recognized as Melio dashed up from one of the tunnels, armed and followed by a river of Marah, their swords unsheathed. They ran along the landing and hit the stairs at a tumbling run, leaping four and five at a time.

Mena grabbed for her sword again, and again clutched only the air. She looked back at her nephew, who was standing beside Devlyn, perplexed, his hands on his hips as if in grown-up disapproval of the Marah's strange urgency. Mena cried, "Aaden!"

He turned his head.

The chief Numrek turned back to the prince. He stepped toward him, grim faced but unhurried, a dagger slithering from his sleeve and into his hand. The motion was so muted, so in line with the matter-of-fact manner that the Numrek usually kept up around the prince, that Mena did not believe what her eyes told her. Casually, the Numrek reached down and drove the blade into Aaden's belly. He twisted it, studying the boy's face as he did, and then yanked the blade out and jabbed it into Devlyn's abdomen. The Numrek twisted the blade, then ripped it down. Devlyn's intestines tumbled onto the grass, the boy collapsing at almost the same instant.

Mena had started to run forward the moment she saw Aaden stabbed. Her strides ate up the remaining distance so that when she vaulted over Aaden and toward the Numrek she was in full sprint. The Numrek, surprised and still stooped forward with his dagger blade spilling Devlyn's insides, snapped his eyes up. The muscles in his back and shoulders and arms tensed, and had Mena been any slower, he would have caught her with an upswing of the dagger.

But such abrupt, complete Maeben fury drove her actions that she was a blur of deliberate motion. As she flew forward, she kicked her legs out to one side. She caught the Numrek's head to her chest, clamped her talons around it, and held tight as the momentum in her legs swung her around, horizontal to the ground. She felt two moments of resistance. First, the muscle of the Numrek's late reaction, and then the catch as the vertebrae in his neck reached the limit to which they could turn. They snapped.

His body was so heavy, legs planted so firmly, that Mena swung all the way around with the now dead head clutched to her chest. She let go and landed on her feet. She caught the dagger that was just then falling from the Numrek's suddenly limp grip. With her left arm she shoved him in the chest, needing to use all her force to make sure his body, with the wobbling head still attached, fell backward away from

Aaden, who was now a knot on the ground, unconscious.

The others were upon her now, two with swords drawn, another swinging an ax before him, intent on killing her quickly. Mena moved faster than thought. She ducked beneath the hissing arc of the ax that was swept around by the first of them to reach her. She stooped under him and sliced the tendons at the back of his knee. The man fell roaring to one side, knocking one of his companions down and entangling another in his writhing agony. The few seconds this allowed was enough for her to scoop Aaden up with one arm, half dragging, half carrying him as she scrambled backward. He was warm and slick with blood, heavy and so very fragile at the same time. He said something, a moan or single word or a hope that Mena could not make out, but that was all.

The two Numrek shoved the wounded man away and came at her, their massive strides eating up the distance quicker than she fed it out. The one approaching from nearest the oncoming Marah said something to the others, but they stayed fixed on her. Mena changed the direction of her retreat to keep him in view as well. She did not look, but in the periphery of her vision she registered that Melio and the others were about to reach the field level. Near, but not near enough.

She feared she would have to put the boy down again to fight, but then something behind her caused the Numrek to slow. They hesitated, weapons raised defensively. Their eyes widened. One of them pointed, as if the others might not be seeing what he saw.

Then Mena understood. And she knew what to do. She dropped one shoulder and twisted her body around, throwing all her weight behind the other shoulder, which came up and around, lifting Aaden off the ground. She swung him in the crook of her arm, which she snapped taut at the exact moment to hurl him into the air. It was an awkward move, her force not entirely controlled. The boy somersaulted in the air. Only then did Mena see Elya.

She had landed at a run and was closing the last few strides with her head low to the ground. She moved with a frightening, reptilian rapidity, all sinewy snapping and writhing, her feather plumes erect and trembling, her mouth open in a rasping hiss. Her head stretched out, neck reached to receive the tumbling boy. He slid down her length and his torso smacked against her back, cradled between the nubs Mena used as a saddle. And then Elya leaped over Mena, wings snapping out and smashing down, shooting her and the prince up into the waiting sky.

Chapter Thirty-eight

T his place is eating itself," Skylene said. "That's what's wrong with the Auldek. They thought they had bargained for a blessing; instead they got an everlasting curse. They live on, bodies the same, souls more and more twisted. That's the curse of the soul catcher."

She poured water from a small stone pitcher into two beakers of the same marbled material. One she pushed across the table to Dariel, the other she held up for Tunnel, who shook his head. She sipped from it herself. "Think of it. On one hand you live on year after year. You die every now and then, only to rise again. Wonderful, yes?"

Dariel rolled the stone beaker between his palms, enjoying the smooth texture of it, the coolness against his skin. His wrists had been unbound only a few days before. He was still relearning mobility. A short length of chain still hobbled his legs and chafed his ankles, but he was making progress, earning their trust. That was what this sudden discourse was about, wasn't it? Something had changed. He could hear it in Skylene's voice and see a hint of something tickling the edges of Tunnel's bizarre features. He said, "I don't think that immortality is so great a gift, not if it keeps you forever separated from loved ones who have died before you."

"True. And what if you can never have children? You cannot see yourself in generations that will continue after you. For some, this doesn't matter; for others, it drives them crazy."

"Is that why they started to"—Dariel hesitated, glancing between the two of them, one looking like a bird woman, the other like some muscle-sculpted boar man—"make these changes to you?"

"That's not what I mean," Skylene said. "What they do to us, we call 'belonging.' They did it as a way to maintain a connection with the animal deities, so that they did not give them up entirely. It is painful at times, but pain passes. We grow used to the changes. Sometimes proud of them."

"How is it even possible?"

Skylene smiled. "Tattoos are tattoos. We do much of that ourselves. There were some chosen by the Auldek to make other changes to, but anything truly difficult was done by the Lothan Aklun. Tunnel's tusks. They are metal, but they are also part of him, fused right into the bones of his skull. The Lothan Aklun can—or could—do many strange things.

"No, what I referred to were greater corruptions. There have been two clans punished for unpardonable perversions. The first, the white-eyed snake clan, is called the Fumel. Their crime? Guess it."

Dariel stared at her, his face blank. He had no idea, and it seemed a waste of time to even try to guess.

"The Fumel broke the first restriction. They started to raise the humans as their own children. They pretended they were their own blood. Some among them tried to make their slaves look like Fumel! Imagine that. They had these slaves in Fumel guise subjugate the other slaves.

"When the other Auldek heard of it, they punished the Fumel, demanding that they turn over all the altered children to be exterminated. They would not. The other clans united to attack them, but the Fumel fought. By the time it was over too few of them were left, and upon those, the crimes done against the other clans were too great. The Fumel were wiped out. If you journey to the south to what used to be their lands you may someday see the Bleeding Road. It's where the

Fumel corpses still adorn the stakes they were impaled upon. They once had a city built on a hill surrounded by a network of shallow canals. When the other clans were done there, the hill was a hole in the earth, filled with water. The Bleeding Road leads for miles across their lands and ends at that lake. It's symbolic, you see?"

I imagine so, Dariel thought. It sounded like the kind of punishment Tinhadin might have meted out.

"That was three hundred years ago. Since then, Auldek have not killed one another. There was another clan more recently that did another forbidden thing." She paused. She glanced at Tunnel, then at the silent scribe who sat listening.

"What did they do?" Dariel asked.

As if she needed the prompting, Skylene sighed and said, "They ate them. It may have been a madness that took hold of them. It may have been because they believed it was the easiest way to acquire their souls. It may have been, as some argue, that they believed by eating young flesh they would become fertile again. They may have done other things as well. We don't know all of it. We know that it was disgusting. The other Auldek took all this clan's slaves and put them to death."

"The slaves?"

"There is no prohibition on killing the People, just on eating them or adopting them. This time, the Auldek didn't kill the clan as well. After the Fumel, they vowed they would not do that again. Their lives—even if they were tainted by crimes—were too valuable to waste now that there were so few Auldek left. Instead, the clan was banished. Sent from Ushen Brae and cursed never to return."

"The Numrek," Dariel whispered.

"Exactly right," Skylene said. "Your traveling companions. The other Auldek killed the souls within them, so that they had but their one mortal life, and then drove them into the north. During that time they were not heard from. Exile meant

450

death in all likelihood, but not as a certainty. That distinction was enough for the Auldek to accept it as just punishment."

"The Numrek ate people in the Known World, too," he said. "Mostly when they had just arrived, but at other times as well. Corinn forbade it when she took them into her service. I've not heard that they ate human flesh since then."

"They would not," Skylene said, "not if they had their sights set on returning to Ushen Brae."

Dariel's head swam with questions. "What does it mean . . . that they've come back? It's all with a purpose?"

"A purpose, yes." Skylene hooked her foot around a stool and pulled it out from under the table. She sat and leaned forward, her elbows on her knees. Not for the first time, Dariel noticed how slimly athletic she was, feminine, but in a way that had a coiled physical danger to it. She said, "Think about what's happened. The Auldek didn't punish them when they returned. By their own decree, they should cut off Calrach's head and set it beside that leagueman's. They didn't. And they haven't banished them again. To put it plainly, they've been talking with them. Your friend Calrach returned with an offer. They have been discussing it ever since. They haven't been this excited for centuries."

"What offer?"

"That I don't have permission to tell you."

"You'll tell me half a thing?"

Skylene smiled. "When does anybody tell all of a thing? I've told you what I can."

Her words had finality, but her posture—leaning toward him, knees apart, face close to his—sent different signals. He wasn't sure how to read them.

"Ask me something else," she said.

Heat rushed across Dariel's cheeks. He very much wished that Tunnel and the scribe weren't in the room. He felt a sudden urge to reach across and touch her sky-blue skin. It was not an entirely new desire. Alone so often, his thoughts of

Wren had grown increasingly blurred, intermingled with Skylene's sharp avian features and Mór's feline grace. More than once, he had woken from dreams of coupling in ways he had never imagined in life. But such thoughts had no place here. He pushed them away.

"Why don't you revolt?" Dariel asked. "The People. With their skills and their numbers they could slaughter the Auldek."

Skylene mulled the question over, something that was both a smile and an expression of grief residing on her features. "The league, the Lothan Aklun, and the Auldek have had hundreds of years to perfect their institutions. They know our minds. When we first arrived, the Lothan Aklun kept us on an isle called Lithram Len. They tested us there, asked us things, watched us; and for a time they let us struggle among ourselves. They observed who shared; who fought; who showed compassion; and who was cold inside, calculating, greedy, savage. They learned our individual weaknesses and strengths, though they saw both as traits to be exploited. Eventually, they sent us to the role that suited each best. The meek went to their work. The savage to theirs. The devious to theirs. Those with the most rebellion in them become spirit children."

"The ones who get eaten?"

Skylene nodded.

"But still, you all know where you came from. You're more the same than different. Obviously, you haven't forgotten—"

"Dariel, our lives here have many faces." She placed one of her fine-boned hands on his knee, her fingers light. "There are many who work in the fields to harvest mist. The generous seeds they are called. They labor. They don't know they're laboring, because the oil from the leaves of the plants numbs their minds. They walk dazed, seeing a world different from ours. They're only in this world enough to be sent to work, to follow instructions."

Dariel asked, "Mist comes from a plant? Harvested in a field?"

. "Yes. The very thing that helps buy the children from your land is worked by slaves in this one. That is the system the Lothan Aklun and the Auldek set up. It perpetuates itself while they live mostly at ease." She let this sit with him a moment. "But not everyone is drugged like that. We can't all be. There are many who work the myriad tasks that sustain the Auldek. Every job imaginable is done, somewhere, by the People, but not necessarily by Free People. Some hate us. Ones called the golden eyes handle commerce. They trade and live lives of some plenty, though they are not free. Others, like the divine children . . . kill. They are warriors almost to match the Auldek. They thrive in palaces, with slaves of their own. They live like nobles until the moment the Auldek call for them to fight, and then they do that with joy as well. Some even forget that they are not free, forget that their individual desires could be any different from the orders given to them. That Lvin you saw in the arena a few days back—he was chosen because the Lothan Aklun knew what he might become. I don't know how, but they see things in us that we don't see ourselves."

The Lvin in the arena. Dariel wished he had dreamed that as well. It had been the only time since his captivity began that he had seen the light of day. Tunnel, who had watch duty over him that day, explained that he had something he wished to show him. Dariel had followed him through the passageways, stumbling on legs stiff from disuse. Tunnel had taken off his ankle chains for the walk. Hobbling along behind the man, it was obvious to both of them that Dariel was no flight risk.

They met several other slaves in a cramped bend in a corridor, a few Dariel recognized, a few he did not. Together, they crowded around slots in the wall that looked out upon some sort of exhibition ground. Dariel's view was partly cut off by beams, but it was enough. He soon understood—by the sights of carnage he witnessed and by the roars of adulation and by the tremors driven down into the stone around him—

that he was somewhere within the foundations of a massive structure, a stadium of some sort.

On the field below him, a mass of warriors butchered one another with a speed and furious precision Dariel had never witnessed before. The figures—lightly armored or not armored at all—were clearly human. At least, they were the human-animal merging that he knew marked the People. Tattooed in the various totem patterns, adorned with tusks or feathered plumes or what looked like scaly protrusions enhancing their backbones. They fought in clan groups, each group standing against all the rest. They leaped and spun, slashed and ducked and kicked and even snapped out somersaults. It could have been some mad, frenzied acrobatics exhibition, except that they worked with weapons: swords and axes, long spears and jointed staffs that whirled about at bone-breaking velocity. Death blows were announced by gouts of blood. Limbs wheeled through the air. Heads were sliced from shoulders and kicked beneath the churning legs.

The battle was short-lived. By the time Dariel understood that one band of warriors—marked by white tattoos and dangling hair locks—had gained the advantage, the fighting was all but over. The soldiers of the prevailing group relaxed, straightened, and let the blood and bits of tissue drip from their bodies. There were several opponents left before them, survivors from among the other clan groups. The chanting in the crowd and the thrum of what must have been thousands of feet on the stone indicated that the action was not concluded yet.

Still, it was a moment before one of the winning band stepped out before the others. The lone warrior was massive. A man muscled like Tunnel but as tall as a Numrek. He carried wide-bladed axes in both hands. His skin was white from midway up his torso, over his shoulders and arms and face. As grand as any lion's, his mane framed his head with a bulk of knotted hair and swaying locks, nearly white but with a slightly gold tint. Dariel would have stared at him for a long time, but he was still only long enough for his remaining opponents to line up across from him. Once they did, he stepped toward them.

"You see him? The chief warrior among the Lvin?"

Dariel whispered, "Yeah, I see him. How could I not see him?"

Tunnel said, "Good. Good that you see. He is sublime motion, the most honored class of divine children."

As if to demonstrate the definition of this, the Lvin chief unleashed a long-limbed choreography of slaughter that had touched each of the four opponents before the first one had even dropped to the ground, falling from the height of his severed legs. It was like a single movement that they did not even try to fight. The last Dariel saw of the Lvin was when he threw his arms out and yanked back his head, mouth open. He might have roared. Surely he roared, but if so it was drowned out by the booming applause of the unseen crowd.

"Saw," Dariel said, correcting Skylene's last statement. "The Lothan Aklun saw your traits. They don't see anything anymore."

Skylene brushed this aside. "That Lvin—Menteus Nemré is his name—lives in a palace with his own slaves, his own women, whatever he wants. He has all of that as long as he fights when the Auldek tell him to. You see? We're not so different here from your people over there. One man—one child, even—will sell out another just so quick." She snapped her fingers. "Considering all these things, the fact that the People have survived so long in defiance is a wonder."

"Whom do you mean when you say 'the People'? Those in rebellion, or all the slaves?"

"Both. It depends on the context in which it's used. We fight for all the quota slaves, even those who harm us, and especially those too numb and beaten down to understand their plight. Privileged or shackled, it doesn't matter. We are all the People, and none of us are free. 'Divine children' is an Auldek title. When we are free, we will put that name away and just be people instead.

"But you see, Prince of the Akarans, the People can't gather an Acacian army by issuing a summons. The Auldek are not easily killed. You saw Devoth take that arrow through his heart. He pulled it out and chopped off the leagueman's head. They could have shot him full of arrows. He would have risen again and again. You've never seen the Auldek fight."

"I've seen Numrek."

Skylene conceded that was something by cocking her head, then righting it. "The Numrek were always lesser fighters among the Auldek. Some say acknowledgment of that is what drove them to their crime in the first place."

"But with the Lothan Aklun gone," Dariel said, "the Auldek can't steal more souls. They have only so many lives, right? So if they are attacked they'll be weakened. They could be beaten eventually."

"Those slaying those spirit souls would suffer. Would you volunteer to die so that the twentieth warrior behind you might finally slay the Auldek you died killing?" She let the question sit just long enough for Dariel to think he would have to answer it, and then she went on. "And even that is only assuming the soul catcher will not be used again. It's out there you, know, still on Lithram Len."

"You think it's a thing? A thing to be used?"

"It is a tool of their sorcery. I do not say it would be easy for anyone to master it, but neither can I say it's impossible."

"Who would use it? Would the Auldek?"

"They know where it is. The Lothan Aklun made them travel to the island to get their souls. It's a short trip, but it was punishment of sorts, since the Auldek hate to be at sea."

"Just like the Numrek," Dariel said. "Why is that? They are fearless about so many things. Why this terror of water?"

"Because," a different voice said. They all started, surprised, as the wooden door swung open and Mór swept in, suddenly changing the atmosphere, crowding the room with her presence. "Because the Auldek, no matter how strong, cannot swim. They've tried, but the same density of muscle and bone that makes them warriors also makes them dead weight in the water. They sink." She folded her arms and stood, defiant, as if expecting to be refuted.

Dariel was not about to. "Ah, all right—"

"That's why they never voyage across the Gray Slopes themselves," Skylene added. "And it's why the Auldek were so shocked that the Numrek did. It could only mean they had something important to tell them." The last words came out hesitantly, her eyes on Mór the entire time.

"You've said that before," Dariel said. He let the statement hang, inflected at the end like a question, one obviously meant for Mór.

She did not answer it, but she did say, "Here is something we haven't told you. It's not just the Auldek who cannot bear young. The same is true of the People. We live and die, but we do not continue ourselves. That's another curse you Akarans arranged for us."

Mór's eyes cut toward Skylene, but then snapped back. "You've learned enough for just now. I have a task for you. Accomplish it, and we will hold nothing back from you."

Dariel was still facing the enormity of the revelation Mór had just made. It explained so much, and seemed awful in a way that he could not take in all at once. He wanted to. It felt important to do so, but Mór had asked him a question. She likely thought he was hesitating because he was considering the answer. In truth, he did not need to consider it at all. He had been waiting, listening, hiding long enough.

Dariel said, "Tell me."

Chapter Thirty-nine

Corinn had never run so fast in her life. She had never felt more frustrated and frantic, filled with an awful urgency that made her want to burst out of her skin and fly. She held the skirt of her gown in both hands, pulled high so that her legs were free to move. Marah crowded her on all sides. They would have preferred to have held still in a defensive circle around her, a human wall with halberds and swords jutting out like the spines of a porcupine. It took all the queen's effort to keep them in motion. She propelled them against their will by shoving them forward and spewing curses and threats at them. Aaden was in danger. Aaden might be dead.

She had stepped out of the secret room into an office strewn with bodies, blood, and organs—both human and Numrek. Though Sire Dagon begged her not to go, she strode away. She had to find Aaden. Hopeful one second; near tears the next; boiling with white-hot anger just after, when interrupted by scenes of violence, people confused, stunned, getting in her way. She hated when they got in her way! Standing about stupid-faced, gaping. Nobles or peasants, old or young: it did not matter. They worked their jaws in meaningless chatter. She had never hated them more. Several times she roared at them, and each time they peeled away before her, like sheep before a wolf, terrified. If they prevented her from reaching Aaden in time, she would kill them.

Coming off a ramp and up a short flight of steps, she trod on the hem of her gown and fell against the men in front of her. Arms pulled her back up. Hands touched her with an intimacy that would have doomed the owner of them an hour ago. One guard whispered respectfully that perhaps they should turn back, get her to safety in the upper palace. His voice trembled and she recognized him as one of her Marah, alive after the battle with her Numrek guards in her offices. "We'll keep you safe there, Your Majesty, until—"

In answer she reached for his waist and pulled free the slim dagger sheathed there. "Are you a coward?" she asked. Judging by the way the man's face froze, he must have thought she was about to slit his throat. She let him think so for a second, and then sawed at the skirts of her gown. The razor-sharp blade ribboned the light layers of fabric. She tore it all free by the fistful. She moved so viciously that she cut the flesh of her thigh. She did not notice until a few seconds afterward, when the warmth of her blood filled the gash and overflowed.

By the time she reached the tunnel that led into the Carmelia, dashed through it, and came out in the open air midway up the stadium's ranks, she was as sweaty, blood-stained, and panting as if she had been at the butchery of battle herself. She froze as the view rose up before her, her eyes searching for her son even as she saw Mena and Melio and clusters of Marah soldiers, all fighting a few Numrek. There were many dead Marah already, and three of the Numrek lay as broken corpses on the eld. The remaining three were bellowing whirlwinds. Their curved swords scorched the air around them, long hair flying as they wrenched their heads around from one foe to another.

Where was Aaden? She didn't see Aaden. He had to be here. He had to be—and then she spotted a child's small form lying facedown on the grass. Her breath left her in one long ahhh. He was so tiny. Like a doll.

Oh, Aaden.

As she said his name in her head she knew it was not right.

The name did not fit the body. It was not Aaden. The figure was a little longer of limb than Aaden. Dark haired while Aaden was fair. It was *Devlyn*.

She shouted, "Find the prince! Find him, now!" The command came from something tapped into the urgency of life, something far greater than she.

As the guards dashed down the stairs and ran to either side, calling for the prince, searching for him among the rows of seats, Corinn turned her gaze to the ongoing battle. Her sister was there, tiny beside the Numrek she faced—Greduc, who had so often walked behind her. Greduc, who had once held his arm out, Aaden dangling from it, standing as tall and still as a tree, grinning as the boy's legs kicked in the air. Corinn pressed her palm to her chest, realizing she was frightened now from all the moments Greduc had had her and Aaden in his power. At any time he could have killed them both.

I am a fool! she thought.

Two Marah worked with Mena, making a triangle around Greduc, but he always turned to keep the princess before him. Mena held a curved Numrek sword in a two-handed grip. Mena never knew her limits, Corinn thought, and then was appalled. What a vile thought, tainted as it was by an adolescent desire to see her sister punished for the arrogance. She had to get control of her thoughts. Defeat him, Mena. Kill him, my sister! Make him die and die and die!

Mena yelled something at Greduc that Corinn could not hear. The Numrek responded, and whatever he said caused Mena to hesitate. Her sword drooped slightly. One of her hands rose, sketching her confusion with a motion of her upturned palm. The Numrek jerked his chin upward and spat. That ended the intermission.

The attackers drew closer to the Numrek, who roared into motion, battling the Marah but always driving toward Mena. She somehow managed to parry, duck, slip to the side. She stumbled then righted herself and swung the heavy blade around, nearly taking off Greduc's head—except that he managed to block and, stepping back, twirled into a surprise attack that caught the Marah behind him and took his arm off at the shoulder.

Corinn pitched forward and vomited. Strong hands grasped her, steadying her. What was wrong with her? Her mind was so scattered, cluttered, random. Aaden! Where was Aaden? She scanned the bleachers. Her guards were racing through them, bending to check under seats, dashing along other rows. They were looking, but she knew that if he was in the stadium she would feel him. Perhaps Mena had hidden him. Yes, that was it. Hidden him someplace safe. Corinn stepped forward, thinking she would descend toward the chaos and—

"No, Your Majesty," a voice behind her said.

Delivegu strode the last few steps to reach her, behind him several more Marah, all of whom rushed past her to join the fight. Rhrenna followed them as well, carrying her dagger. "You shouldn't even be this close," Delivegu said. "If one of them sees you, he may charge. Come. Draw back with me so that you can't be seen."

"I cannot find Aaden," Corinn said. "He was here."

Delivegu set his hand on her shoulder and scanned the stadium, his face grave. He looked at Corinn, took her other shoulder in hand. "We'll find him. He's not here."

Exactly, she thought. He's not here! Now that seemed a good thing. Aaden was somewhere else, which had to be better than being here.

"He's probably safe."

Exactly, Corinn echoed. He's probably safe.

Rhrenna stood beside her now. "The palace is secure," she said. "Balneaves Sharratt is checking the records to determine how many Numrek were on the island. There's fighting still in the lower town, as some of them were trying to flee the island. They won't get off. And General Andeson is already committed to sail for the Teh Coast, to blockade the—"

"Good," Delivegu said. "Good!" He was not responding to Rhrenna.

Corinn followed his eyes back to the field. One of the Numrek had fallen. The Marah who had killed him worried his back with jab after jab of their swords, and then ran to aid the others. Corinn remained aware that one of Delivegu's hands still rested on her shoulder. She reached out and found Rhrenna's hand and clasped it. Together they watched the tide of the fighting turn.

The next to die got caught dealing with too many foes. Melio hacked him in the side with a two-handed diagonal swing. His blade bit into the Numrek's side, cut him to the spine, and then stuck fast like an ax driven too deep into a tree trunk. The Numrek fell onto his knees, yanking the sword from Melio's grip. Two Marah swept in, the first with a downward strike that sliced off a portion of the Numrek's face. The second leaped into a twirling attack that first cut through the arm the Numrek raised to block it and then sliced halfway through the side of his skull.

Now only one remained. As the rest of the Marah circled him, their weapons before them, he seemed to come to terms with the situation. He let his sword droop a moment, turning slowly to take them all in. It looked like he might be surrendering, but then he roared and ran toward Mena, his sword raised high in a two-handed grip. He looked undefeatable, unstoppable. The Marah closed on him with their own furious intent, slicing and stabbing, then making sure the fallen Numrek would not rise again. Corinn lost sight of Mena, and did not spot her again until the soldiers began to stumble away from the body. Some fell to their knees. A few sprawled on the grass. Still others dropped their swords and moved among the injured, aiding them. It was over.

Corinn saw Mena standing a surprising distance away, panting, her arms limp at her sides and her body curved with fatigue. She had dropped the Numrek sword and stooped before it, as if unsure of what it was. She looked like she might fall to her knees at any moment. Instead, she glanced up and met Corinn's eyes. She stepped forward, unsteadily. She stumbled from the field and mounted the steps toward Corinn. She seemed to regain some of her abnormal stamina as she climbed. Corinn shouted her question. "Where is Aaden?"

When Mena reached Corinn she grabbed her by the wrist and pulled her into motion. "Come," she said. "Elya has him."

Elya has him! Of all the things she feared or hoped to hear this caught her completely off guard. The lizard has him?

"You look a mess, sister," Mena added. "Rhrenna, tell me what has happened."

The Meinish woman began recounting the details she had begun to give Corinn a few minutes earlier. Mena peppered her with questions. She answered. Delivegu and several Marah followed as well, silent for the time being. Listening to the two women talk helped Corinn through the moments of waiting, as they retraced their path back to the palace. She tried to concentrate on their voices that talked through the crisis like veterans of such things. Corinn knew she should join them, but she couldn't. Not until she knew.

They found Elya and Aaden in the central gardens of the queen's palace. Arriving, they had to push through the throng of nervous servants. In the center, within the open area of benches and chairs, in the middle of the mosaic of the Akaran family symbol, lay Aaden. He was on his side, one leg crossed over the other, his arm cradling his belly. Asleep. Or dead? Corinn could not tell. The lizard stood off a few paces. It stood propped on its hind legs, its forearms held together and its slim paws pressed one against the other.

Corinn moved forward, somehow more patient now that she actually saw her son. The emotion that had driven her to the Carmelia had drained out of her. She just wanted to know. That was all. She just had to know. And so she walked calmly across the tiles, the hushed crowd watching her. Reaching her son, she knelt and whispered his name. She sat down and slid her hands under his head and shoulders and drew him onto her lap. There was a strange, tangy citrus scent on him that was pleasant to inhale. But there was also blood on him, yes, soaking his clothes all around his mid-section. "Oh, Aaden," she said, drawing him still closer. So much blood. He was warm. Limp as he was, she knew that he was yet alive. Leaning over him, she felt breath pass through his lips, faint, oh, but there. He breathed, but it was fading.

She heard Mena call for the royal physicians and bark other orders. Reasonable things, things she should be saying herself. All she could do was hold Aaden in her arms and feel grief and fear opening around her like the maw of the toothed worm that lives in the center of the earth. She felt it rising, hungry, enraged. The worm was death. *Death!* It wanted to swallow Aaden. She had never known what death was, but now she did. It was a worm in the center of the earth. A hungry beast of a thing that wanted her son.

But she would not give him her son. Why should I have to? I've given so much already. Why can I not have this one thing—a son to love? Why? She realized she was talking to the beast inside her head, but it did not care. It began before her and would go on after her and never, never would care for words like that. If she held on to Aaden the worm would swallow her as well, gulp them both down into the fetid abyss that was its belly. She and Aaden, Mena and the servants. The entire palace. No, the island Acacia itself. If she held on to her son and denied the worm, its jaws would rise from the sea and clamp shut around them and drag everything into the deep, unless . . . unless she sang.

I have to sing!

Thinking it, she realized she had known it all along. The worm was ancient, and since she had first read from *The Song of Elenet* she had felt it stir. She had not admitted it, but she had felt it roll and flex beneath the earth. It had welcomed her song. It wanted it. It fed on it. Why had she not understood this until now?

Mena leaned over her, saying something, but Corinn ignored her and everyone around her. It did not even matter if they heard her. Nothing mattered except that she sing for Aaden before the worm ate them all. They knew nothing about it, the fools! Corinn had done nothing useful the entire day, but she would now.

With her lips brushing the soft flesh of Aaden's neck, she opened her mouth and breathed out the song. It came to her willingly, those mysterious words and the notes they rode upon. She did not form it. She just released it, aware that if she did it would heal the damage inside Aaden. And that would appease the worm. It was a promise of some sort, a deal she was making with things unknown.

She sang.

In the seas surrounding the isle of Acacia, Corinn was certain that the jaws of the beast paused just below the surface, halting the great swell of momentum that had driven it. It paused because she sang. It listened. It heard, and then the worm sang with her, a great bass rumble that was beautiful, and horrible, to hear.

Chapter Forty

Leeka Alain. It really was the old general. Several days after encountering the man, Kelis still found himself reliving his surprise. He watched him askance whenever he could, relearning his sun-browned features and trying to order the details of the man's life in a way that might explain his presence here in the arid expanse of southern Talay. Here was the man who had commanded the Northern Guard in Hanish Mein's time. He was the first to face the Numrek, the first to kill one of those giants. They had called him the rhino rider, for he had descended the Methalian Rim into the Mainland atop one of the Numrek's woolly beasts. He had been too late with his news of the coming invaders. Though he fought hard and long on many fronts, he had not been able to repel Hanish's multipronged attack. Leeka had been lost to the world after that, only to appear years later to rally Aliver's troops against Maeander on the Taneh Plains of northern Talay. And then he had disappeared during the chaos unleashed by the Santoth.

Now it was nine years later and again the veteran general had rejoined the living. He was no longer simply a hard-bitten soldier. He was something else now, but just what that something was Kelis could not say. Leeka did not look a day older than when Kelis had last seen him. Yes, at first his features had seemed to shift and reshape themselves, but that had stopped after a few hours. His face took on a normal solidity, his jaw square, mouth wide, cheekbones high.

His eyes, Kelis remembered, had been penetrating, those of a commander of soldiers who dealt with the world with a hawklike sharpness. Now his eyes seemed to absorb the world, as if he were hungry for everything he saw.

"Walk with me," Leeka had said, "and your questions will be answered." That was all he had bidden them do. Benabe balked and Naamen questioned and Kelis felt the weight of that simple request like a stone in his gut. He felt he had no control over their fate, no leadership to offer except the authority to place them in the hands of forces he did not understand. Forces he had reason to fear.

Shen, though, smiled and asked, "Is it far?" Leeka assured her that it wasn't, although they should travel slowly and with patience.

And that was what they did. They trudged farther south, through a featureless landscape, no motion upon it save the rippling dance of heat, no living creatures save their group of five. With Leeka's nod of assent, they sat out the hottest hours of the day huddled beneath small geometries of shade cast by sheets draped over thin stakes they drove into the ground. Leeka himself stood at a slight distance, hooded and so still that Kelis sometimes felt the old general had slipped out of this world and left a scarecrow in his place.

The four sipped their water sparingly, all of them aware of how little they had and how devoid of moisture the landscape was. They could not even find the tubers or cacti that years of training had taught them existed in even the deepest desert. Kelis felt himself going dry from the inside out. His flesh became a strange leather that shrank to wrap his muscles and tendons and thinning blood vessels. He sometimes pretended to drink from the waterskin, to spare the precious liquid for Shen. Though they never said anything about it, he suspected Benabe and Naamen were doing the same.

Leeka never drank. He did not sleep. He never showed fatigue or seemed to feel the heat.

As the sun slanted westward each evening, they rose and, with a few terse words of encouragement from Leeka, began their trek again. Shen walked beside the hooded man often. She was the only one who seemed at ease with him and also unaffected by fatigue or thirst. By the way he inclined his head toward her, and the way she tugged on his arm and looked up at him, one would have thought they were conversing—an uncle out with a favorite niece, perhaps.

But, as far as Kelis could ascertain, very few words passed between them. On several occasions when they seemed in animated discourse he crept up behind them, close enough to make out the intricate pattern of braids tight against Shen's skull, close enough to hear the clicking of the beads fastened to the ends of them. But that and the scuffing of their feet and their slow breathing of the always hot air and Leeka swallowing were the only sounds he ever heard.

"He is insane," Benabe said one evening, "and he is teaching my daughter the trick of it. I do not like that man." She had made this clear from the first sighting of the hooded man standing alone in a desert expanse. During the passing days, she had not tired of reminding Kelis of her opinion. Several times she proposed that they break from Leeka and turn north or toward the coast to the east. They could return later, she said, with the help of others. Her lips were cracked, her skin dusty, her features gaunt. She had to speak slowly, between careful breaths, but she was no less the fiery, protective mother.

"You think a man who stands in the desert by himself is sane?" she asked. "You think he should lead us anywhere? He's lost, and we're following him. What's that make us? I'll tell you—bigger fools."

"Shen says that—"

"Shen is a child! She may be something more as well, but she is a young girl first. She dreams. She trembles and hears voices."

"Before, you said that—"

"I know what I said. But what did I know? Sitting in a mansion in Bocoum . . ." She shook the thought of it away. She was silent a moment, and then said, "I want to say that I will die if he harms her. But when people say that, they don't really mean it. But I am simply stating the truth: I will die." She jabbed him with an elbow. "You will too. I'll see to it before I go."

Though not as constant as Benabe, it was obvious Naamen, too, had his doubts. He approached Kelis after she drifted away. He walked silently beside him for some time, and then said, "After today we will have no water."

"I know," Kelis said.

"So you also know that we are walking dead. Benabe is right: we should not have come."

"Do not let a coward wear your skin," Kelis answered, all the more harshly because he was wrestling with the same thoughts. "When you are called to a quest, you go. You trust. We must trust Leeka."

In an answer of sorts, Naamen had exhaled and took in the desolation around them. What more need he say when the entire curve of the world was nothing but sand cracked by the sun, so parched that the ground looked to have never known a drop of water?

Naamen said, "He may be a gatherer of the dead. He is taking us to—"

"Have faith! In Shen, if not in Leeka. She is the only one among us who matters. Aliver's daughter, remember? He leads us through her."

"I never knew the prince."

"Know his daughter, then, and feel privileged."

Kelis did not waste any more breath trying to convince him. Naamen and Benabe could base their thoughts only on the world they knew and the things they had seen. Neither had seen the Santoth. Kelis had. Neither had ever seen Leeka before. Kelis had, and because of it, he was sure that they had no choice but to follow him. Kelis did not truly feel the certainty he tried to project, yet what choice had he but to face with dignity whatever came?

They did not walk as late into the night as usual. They made camp on a plain dotted with oblong boulders, like slim eggs balanced upright, each taller than a man. Kelis had not seen the boulders until they were among them—strange, for his eyes had been searching for anything to break the monotony. But there they were. The group stood within a cluster of them, the others showing unease behind their fatigue.

Leeka kept moving. He scooped out a bowl shape in the sand and sparked a strange blue fire into it. He had not poured any substance into the bowl. Nor had he struck flint and tinder. Nevertheless, a flame roiled around the depression like a liquid, brightening to a greenish glow, then settling to a turquoise illumination that touched all the watching faces and made the world behind them fade.

With the fire burning but nothing being consumed, Leeka looked at the group. He bade them sit. Once they had, he said, "Touch the fire. It will not burn you."

"Touch it?" Naamen asked.

"Yes." Leeka demonstrated, drawing back a sleeve and pushing his outstretched hand into the substance. It rippled at his touch, licked up his forearm. He showed no discomfort, and when he withdrew his hand it was unharmed.

"Why?" Naamen asked. "Why should we touch it?"

"You should do as your friend suggests. Trust."

Naamen glanced at Kelis, at Shen and Benabe. For a moment he looked like a child caught out by an elder, but then he pressed his lips together and looked at the liquid flame. He shot his fingers into it quickly, straight and close together, then drew them back, stared at them, and then eased them in again. Astonishment loosened his features. "It's not hot," he said. "It's . . . like cool water."

"Like water," Leeka said, "it will refresh you. Touch and drink of it. It will sustain you until you return to your lands."

Just like that, Kelis's thirst—which had faded to so deep within him that he was no longer aware of it—returned. Nothing had ever seemed more enticing than that fiery liquid. His hand scooped into it and came up dripping flame. Naamen was right. It was cool to the touch. He brought his hand to his lips. It was delicious and like liquid life as it slid down his throat. He felt it reach the center of him and begin to slip out as if into the veins of his body. Just one handful, then he sat back on his haunches, head tilted to the sky, eyes closed, completely filled. For a time he forgot everything, understanding vaguely that the others had done the same.

"The Santoth are here," Leeka said. "They thank you for bringing the heir to them. She is loved. They will answer your questions now."

Remembering the sorcerers as he had seen them on the plains that day, Kelis opened his eyes and looked around. The five of them were alone. "They will?"

"My teachers will speak through me, yes."

"Now you'll answer our questions?" Benabe asked. The euphoria of having drunk the flame had filled her features, but her voice still had its edge. "Now that we walked through the desert with you for three days—now we can ask you questions?"

"Mother," Shen said.

Leeka said, "Perhaps I should begin with what they think you should know. You should know that the Santoth are protecting you. They have been for some time already. They feel your fear and they understand, but you are safe here. When you leave, you will find your way safely back to the world of people. They promise you that."

"What do they want with my daughter?"

"They want her to be safe."

"Safe from what?"

Leeka was silent a moment, his eyes focused somewhere else. Eventually he said, "They wish me to explain. Shen knows these things. She and I have discussed them. Time that you know as well, mother of Shen. Understand without doubt that the Santoth have been in communion with the girl her entire life. We know you know this, and yet we feel the doubt in you. Don't doubt."

Benabe sat with her daughter at her side. The mother's face wore an expression like hurt, as if the man had touched an old wound. Shen must have seen it, for she took Benabe's hand and rubbed it.

"For many generations of the living world the Santoth knew no hope. They suffered their banishment, undying. They knew much of what transpired in the world, but they were not part of it. They remembered so much, and yet their grasp of the Giver's tongue slipped from them. It eroded, grew tainted. It became a dreadful thing even to them. You cannot understand how they suffered."

"You do?" Naamen asked.

"They have let me experience it with them," Leeka answered. "It is a gift to me, but I would not wish this knowledge on you. But then Aliver came to them. As you did, but he came unbidden. He stirred hope in them again. He reminded them that their banishment could be lifted. He could have done it, being a firstborn of a generation of Tinhadin's line. There had been others, of course, many others. But none of them had sought the Santoth. None of them came so close to releasing the Santoth to do good in the world again. Aliver said he would. That's why his death tormented the Santoth. They journeyed to find him, and they did; and in the disappointment following, they let themselves release their rage." Here he looked at Kelis. "But you know that. You were there."

Kelis looked down. He rubbed the knuckles of one hand with the fingers of the other. He did not wish the others to see the horror of that day on his face, but he was sure it would be there for all to see. Why, they might ask, had he brought them here to those who had unleashed abominations on the world? He wouldn't be able to answer.

"My teachers feared that their exile would continue long and long. They feared that, but when they listened and waited, they realized Aliver was not completely gone. He lived on in the one we call Shen. The bond they had with Aliver continued with her. That is why they have been able to speak with her all her life, even from when she was in the womb."

Benabe did not look at Shen this time, but again the girl rubbed her mother's hand, comforting. There was apology in the motion, and yet her young face was eager, waiting for Leeka's words.

"You asked what the Santoth wish of Shen," Leeka said. "They wish only what she wants to give, only what her father had tried to give. Only she can call them back to the world. Not the queen. Not the queen's child. Only the firstborn of a generation of Tinhadin's line. Aliver was such a son. Shen is such a daughter, and she has agreed."

This caused Benabe to break her silence. "I don't know what you think she agreed to, but I have agreed to nothing. I'm her mother."

"She told you of the stones," Leeka said, "for years she told you of them."

Benabe did not deny it. "Shen is a child. She knows nothing about—"

Leeka raised his hand. "She knows a great deal. Mother, without insult, understand that you are the one who knows nothing about these things."

For a moment Kelis thought Benabe was going to hit the old soldier. Like any Talayan tribal girl, she had been trained in fisting, a martial art that, ironically, used elbows and knees more than fists. She could have driven his nose into his skull before his instincts pulled his head back.

473

If Leeka felt threatened, he gave no sign. "A great conflict is coming, war on a scale never seen before."

"War with who?" Benabe snapped. "The Mein were thoroughly beaten. Aushenia wishes Acacia no harm. Talayans have their own issues, too. There is no one to war with. The queen grips the world in her fist!"

"Her fist is not that large," Leeka answered. "The Santoth can see farther than you or I. They see a coming war on a scale never seen before, against a new enemy. Preparations have already begun."

The glow from the fire bowl was stronger now. By its light Kelis saw the faces of his companions as they absorbed that news, weighed it. But that was not all he saw. Behind them hulked the oblong shadows of the stones. He glanced over his shoulder. Surely, they had not been that near before. He began to comment on it, but found the words stuck on his tongue.

"The Santoth," Leeka continued, "would aid the Known World in the struggle to come, if the queen would share *The Song of Elenet* with them. She has it. My teachers know that. They feel it every time she reads from it, every time she sings. They could explain it to her better than she can learn it on her own. They could help her, and help all the people of the Known World."

Benabe was on her knees now, leaning toward Leeka, in an even better position to strike. "Tinhadin, who was the greatest of the Santoth, came to fear sorcery and drove it from the world. Why should we want it back? Forgive my asking, but who does that serve other than them?"

Kelis's eyes flicked between her and the stones. They crowded so near now that he imagined he could reach back and touch the rock behind him. Naamen saw them also. His mouth opened and remained that way.

"Is it a good thing to survive the coming slaughter?" Leeka asked. "Without the Santoth, you won't. Without the Santoth, the Known World will learn chaos of a kind it's never

474

experienced before. Without the Santoth, Corinn Akaran will not learn the dangers of her sorcery. We know that she does not understand fundamental things. God talk does not create things anew. The Giver could, but when humans sing, we can only steal, rearrange, and often corrupt. There is always a consequence. Alone, the queen will not be able to see the consequences until it is too late. She needs the Santoth much more than she knows."

"So you wish us to believe," Benabe said. "You still haven't explained what role my daughter plays in this."

"She will stay here, with us," Leeka said. "We will hide her and protect her and commune with her and ready her for—"

"No." Benabe said the word with firm matter-of-factness. "No, I will not allow that."

"The decision is not yours to make. It's Shen's. She has made it already."

"Mother?" Shen asked softly. Like Naamen, her attention had drifted out past the ring of people to the stones surrounding them. She cocked her head slightly, listening to something beyond the argument about her fate.

Benabe ignored her. "I will stay with her, then," she said.

Leeka's eyes might have softened as he answered her—might have, Kelis was not sure. "That is not possible."

"It must be. I will not hand her over to you, no matter what she says."

"Mother," Shen said.

"If you wish to help," Leeka said, glancing up to include Kelis as well, "take the Santoth's message to Queen Corinn. Make her to know that the Santoth must have the book. They will have it, whether she consents to it or not."

Shen stood up. "Mother, the stones have come. They are speaking. They want to—"

She got no further. Her head snapped back. Her teeth gnashed at the air and her arms flew out. She looked like she had been pierced in the chest by something that wanted to lift her into the air. Benabe leaped to her feet and reached to catch her daughter, but the stone behind her suddenly moved. It turned into a cloud of sand, a moving pillar that had something like a human form at its center. It sped past Benabe and surged around Shen's trembling body and caught her as she began to fall backward. Benabe screamed. The other stones surged in on the group, spinning together and roaring like an angry wind.

"They mean no harm," Leeka shouted over the noise. "They will protect her from all harm until the time is right."

Benabe's voice rose louder still. "Grab her!"

Kelis tried, but the moment he stepped toward the girl, he lost sight of her. The swirling sand pressed against him. He could barely move, no matter how he tried to kick or lean or twist his way through it. A few times he saw Shen—her face, her legs, her supine form—revealed in quick glimpses, never in the same place twice.

Leeka said, "And if the time is right, she will let them free. She will lead them back into the world. If what we fear does come . . ."

As quickly as it began, it ended. The pressure holding Kelis in place vanished. He crashed to the ground, bumping against Naamen, who had also fallen. Silence. Stillness. The fire was out. Kelis blinked quickly. Soon he could see the stars and low moon outlining the people around him. He rose, counting the figures, scanning the featureless plain around them. He saw Benabe, Naamen, but no one else.

"They're gone," Naamen said.

In answer, Benabe let loose an ancient-sounding wail, long held, unending. Her daughter was taken.

476

Chapter Forty-one

Rialus perched on a west-facing windowsill in his quarters, several stories above ground level, with a view out across the seemingly endless city of Avina. Buildings spread out in all directions, mazelike. Many had been glazed in sparkling hues of crimson and orange. More than one tower floated flags that announced their clan affiliation. Here and there trees rose between the structures, tall, lean poles that exploded in circular plumes at their highest points. Above, flocks of pigeons swooped in great swaths of motion. Starlings darted through the air. Higher up, tiny black pinpricks hung in the sky, watchers. Occasionally gulls flew on patrol, an air of ownership and condescension in their every motion and in each harsh cry.

A hundred different columns of smoke billowed dark clouds into the air, mixed in among five hundred thinner plumes of gray. Even more small white puffs belched out of pipes and chimneys. The columns were not so much a symptom of the contaminants of the air—as they often seemed to be in large Acacian cities like Alecia—as they were reminders of the thousands and thousands of lives being lived in those countless buildings, in workshops and at hearths, around public cooking pits and in great halls filled with revelers. Or so Rialus imagined.

Despite the smoke, the air tasted fresh enough. It carried the salty tinge of the sea, the only reminder—other than the gulls—that it was so near. The edge of the Gray Slopes lay just to the east over a barricade that, through some trick of its architecture, replicated a receding cityscape. The inhabitants of the city had turned their backs on the shore and seemed to willfully ignore their coastal location. If they did glance east, they saw the illusion of the continuation of the city, nothing else.

Even knowing that a portion of the view was an illusion, Rialus still marveled at the size of what he could see and at the way it seemed to go on far beyond the reach of his eyes. How large was the population? As with everything here in Ushen Brae—he no longer thought of this place as the Other Lands—Rialus could not make sense of it. He heard the Auldek bemoan their long centuries of infertility. And he mentally marked down each mention of the rare occasions when an Auldek did die. It only made sense that their numbers had dwindled over time. The fact that they would plan such a massive war in the hope that it would return their fertility attested to this. As did the awe in which they held Allek, the annoying Numrek whelp. On the other hand, the expanse around him indicated a thronging population.

He had put the question to Devoth once. They had been speaking together during a long session in which Rialus was forced to write down every member of the Akaran royal line that he could remember, from Edifus onward. The subject enthralled the Auldek. Rialus suspected it was the chronicle of deaths that held a morbid fascination for him, so he made a point of detailing how each monarch had succumbed. He even made up a few ghastly ends. Why not? Who could call him a liar?

As the meeting ended, and feeling that the Auldek leader was in good spirits, Rialus began, "How—I mean, how—"

"Speak it, leagueman," Devoth said. "You know you're going to, so why not do so without the stammering? Do all your people speak that way?"

478

Rialus inhaled, thinking, I would speak it if you and the Numrek didn't love to interrupt me at every chance. He made sure to enunciate. "How many of you are there? How many Auldek, I mean, in Ushen Brae?"

Devoth drew his head back thoughtfully, creased the corners of his eyes as if surprised and somewhat suspicious of the question. "There are enough of us," he finally answered, "and there will be more soon. That's what this is all about. That, Rialus Leagueman, is what this is truly about."

With that, he had turned abruptly away, leaving Rialus uneasy as well as curious. On that occasion, and on this one as he recalled it, he had to remind himself that he was not the traitor Devoth believed him to be. Though he had spent hours now divulging information that, on the surface, made him look like the most loose-tongued betrayer, he told himself this was all a ruse, a way to buy time. He would find some way out of this situation, but he needed to survive in the meantime, even if that meant he needed to appear to have betrayed his people.

As Rialus sat on the windowsill telling himself this, his servant, Fingel, approached him. The backless sandals she wore audibly smacked the bottoms of her feet with each step. The sound had annoyed him at first, until he understood it was the only sound she ever willingly made. She never spoke a word unless it was required, a silent servant who announced her presence only with the sound of her feet. She was lovely to look upon. At first he thought her beautiful despite the fact that she had wire whiskers in her cheeks and tattooed bands under her light eyebrows, but before long he began to suspect these things added to her beauty, strange as that seemed to him. She looked to be Meinish by birth, had that race's pale skin and straw-blond hair. Thin featured, delicate, with a slightly upturned nose and a slim body that nevertheless drew his eyes back again and again to the contours beneath her simple shift: she was nothing like his top-heavy Gurta, but that made it easier to admire her without being pricked by conscience or memory. She was quite distracting, really, all the more so for being so cold and detached.

Speaking in her usual dead tones, Fingel said, "His magnificence, Devoth of the Lvin, summons you." She held out the small marker of carved silver that proved it.

"Does he?" Rialus took the marker and rubbed his finger across the Lvin emblem embossed on it. "What do you think would happen if I didn't go? Told him I was busy?"

Fingel stood, no expression animating her features, as if her mind were blank and she had not heard him speak. It was her customary expression. She had looked at him directly only once. Early on, he inadvertently spoke to her in the Meinish tongue. It just happened, a flashback to his years spent in Cathgergen, brought on by the racial purity of her features. She raised her gray eyes and studied him, the look on her face the sad, sympathetic expression one might fix upon a child with a damaged mind. And that was it. She turned away and never, as far as Rialus could remember, looked him in the face again. Her constant silence prompted him only to blather more than usual.

"Am I important enough to him now that he would tolerate insolence?" he asked. "I should be. Where would he be without me? I'm his expert on the Known World. Perhaps," he added, offering a faint invitation to conspiracy with his tone and grin, "we should tell him I'm not well. A headache perhaps. What think you of that?"

The girl could have been asleep with her eyes open.

Even a beauty like you can get tiresome, Rialus said silently, though he did not mean it. Aloud, he acquiesced, "Fine. I'll meet with his magnificence."

Fingel pivoted. He followed her, his eyes incapable of looking away from her figure. He almost detoured to the toilet chamber before he left. There, in the near privacy, he regularly used mental images of Fingel as he pleasured himself. He knew he could have physically taken her anytime he wanted to. She was a slave in his complete power. Devoth had made that clear. For that matter, he had bedded servants back in Acacia who he knew were not terribly willing. Just a part of the privilege of his office, it had seemed. But here he was not so sure he could face Fingel's reaction.

She deposited Rialus in the care of four of Devoth's slave soldiers. They were young men, thick about the chest and as haughty as newly appointed Marah, though sullen as well. Two of them had the Lvin clan's white facial tattooing. The third had whiskers. None of them were a match in appearance to the victor of the mêlée, but few men would be. Like Fingel, they spared no words for Rialus. As they trudged through the city streets, Rialus framed by the square of them, they occasionally talked among themselves. When Rialus offered a thought or question, however, stone silence. They acted as if they were waiting for an excuse to ram their rather horrific-looking pikes through his guts.

Nothing new. All the slaves he had interacted with in Ushen Brae made it clear that they held him in complete disdain. Total lack of interest. He could make no sense of it. Shouldn't they look to him as a connection with their homeland? Anger or hope. Either emotion would have made more sense to him. They gave him nothing. Despite his strangely privileged position, this troubled Rialus. Might he find no allies here? Nobody to turn toward to help him nd the means to defy his captors? Though he could not define the shape of his eventual defiance, he was sure it must come. Must, if he could find the way to achieve it. But he was no closer now, weeks later. He still knew nothing, it seemed, of this land or people.

If he could slip away on his own for a bit, explore where he wanted to, probe around . . . Devoth had promised him that he would learn about Ushen Brae. What had he said? *You'll see many grand things. You're our guest, so you'll see the things that make us great.* So much for that. He had never left the environs of his own quarters except for excursions of a mile or so to meet with other Auldek officials, escorted always by slave guards. Would that he could see what they were hiding from him.

Although, having thought that, maybe being by himself would not be a good idea either. There were things living in Avina that he had no interest in coming upon by accident. Once, while following Devoth through a long hallway, past doors that opened onto different gymnasium chambers, he had seen a creature that made him stop abruptly. It had caught his eye because of its size, which was like that of no other creature he had ever seen. Like one of the foulthings, perhaps, but he had never set eyes on one of those.

This thing stood to the height of three or four men; and even that was not an accurate measurement, for it squatted on long, bent legs. It was winged as well—large, black, jointed wings, membranous and foul, awkwardly held out as it waddled. It looked like some sort of bat, made gigantic. It was furred on the chest and around its long-jawed, canine face. Horrible, and somehow made more so by the sight of an Auldek high on its back, fastened there in a harness. The creature leaped about at the Auldek's direction, its wings aiding it. The Auldek held a spear in one hand and had several more quivered beside him.

"Nice, huh? That's a kwedeir," Devoth had said, having stepped back to see what Rialus was gaping at. "You don't want to go in there. It's near feeding time."

As Devoth said this, Rialus noticed a slave being led in and then pushed against his will toward the creature. "You don't mean it's going to—"

"Eat that man? Yes, I do. Strange, the way they eat. They like to stalk their food. Even when it's presented to them, they stalk it, and then leap and bite it around its head and then pause. Every time they do the same. They pause and listen as the unfortunate one screams. And then they bite down and rip the head off while the body still flails about beneath. Do you want to watch?"

His eyes seemed inclined to do just that, but Rialus snapped up a hand to block the view. "By the Giver, no!"

Devoth rumbled out his mirth, but he nudged Rialus to get him moving down the corridor. A few steps farther on and a high-pitched scream cut through the air, an anguished cry of terror. Devoth did not so much as flinch. He did, however, grunt and say, "We use them to catch runaways. Good sport."

On reaching Devoth's estate, his escorts put Rialus in the care of the household servants and then turned away without a word. And what then? Was he rushed right in to an audience with his magnificence? Hardly. Instead, as he expected, he was told to wait in the inner courtyard. It was a beautiful enough space, partially open to the air, with pillars of marble that supported trellises thick with flowering vines. A pool in the floor gurgled, home to eel-like fish that cocked their heads and followed Rialus's every move. It would have been a pleasant enough area to wait in, if there had been something to sit on. What kind of waiting area did not provide a place to sit?

Typical Auldek, he thought, display luxury while making one uncomfortable at the same time.

Standing, he wondered what Devoth wanted to talk about this time. He feared he had exhausted his knowledge of usable information. Their last meeting, actually, had a note of finality to it, as if everything had been decided. Devoth had summed up the entire plan of attack. It was to be one great march of virtually the entire Auldek population, all except those unfit for the journey. Many of the divine children would accompany them, warriors and servants both. The Auldek did not seem to fear to return the quota to their homeland, at least not the ones they were planning on taking with them.

"It will be a misery," Devoth said, "but we must begin the journey in the winter. We will spend the first month trudging into the arctic, getting colder each day. We'll stay all along the coastline, frozen stiff, no doubt, thinking ourselves insane for leaving Avina, On this schedule, spring will start to warm the land at about the time we must leave the coast. Here." He pierced the map with one of his long fingers. "But then when we turn inland, it will grow cold again. We'll return to winter. That's what Calrach swears, and he says it should be that way, because for a time we travel only upon ice, on some inland sea. We must be fast, though. For if we are too late getting there, the ice will thin. We might fall through. Calrach lost several of his tribe to that fate." Devoth spoke this with an air of solemnity Rialus had never observed on him. "At least," he added, "they had but one life to die through."

Strange, Rialus thought, to imagine an existence in which a single death was an oddity. He wondered if such a perspective was a strength, or if it might be a weakness somehow. "I've said it before, your magnificence, but, please, allow me to express my concern . . ."

Devoth scowled but did not otherwise dissuade him.

"It will not be the same as with the Numrek. The league will certainly warn the empire."

"You chirp like a cricket," Devoth said. "Listen, chirp no more. This war will happen. It will be a wonder. You can't imagine! You don't know how we go to battle. We haven't done so in hundreds of years—not since the early days, when we were drunk with the soul catcher's gift. Few of us even remember those times. But I do. In the past we warred with one another and almost destroyed our race. Ironic, no? We win the gift of immortality and become so high with it that we slaughtered one another like never before. You have no idea. This time, the clans will all join in one massive force. We'll roll across the land, marching, riding haired rhinoceros and kwedeirs and fréketes. You haven't seen a frékete yet, have you? Oh, but you will."

The image of the winged, jointed monstrosity that was the kwedeir flashed in Rialus's mind. The bunched muscle beneath the gray skin, the swaying movement, the enormity of it as scaled by the Auldek riding its back. And that was what he had seen. What might fréketes be? He could not help himself. He shuddered.

"Exactly," Devoth said. He grinned with one side of his mouth. "Snow lions hunting for us and antoks clearing the way. Behind us, still other slaves will push weapons of war. We'll ride singing, Rialus Leagueman, chanting, joyful. The Numrek tell me they had a mighty slaughter when they fell upon your lands. This, though, will be like nothing your people have ever seen. Be glad you'll get to watch it from our side instead of from the ground as we trample you. Leagueman, try to understand, we've been dead in our living bodies for years now. We are ready to live again, to battle, to risk everything, to make children, and even to die. It will be wonderful. For us, at least. Not so much for your people."

A male servant finally came and got Rialus, a good hour after he had arrived. A short time later, the servant paused and pointed to a figure in the center of a large, labyrinthine inner garden. "He is there, master. Can you find your way from here, or should I walk farther with you?"

"No," Rialus said, more sharply than he expected. He was quite capable of finding his way forward now. I can see him, he thought. In the Giver's name, I'm not a complete idiot! He had the impulse to wiggle his fingers in the servant's face dismissively, but he knew the man would not so much as deign to respond if he did. Rialus would be left looking silly. "I'm fine," he said. A few steps forward, however, and he was not sure of that.

A snow lion stepped out onto the path some twenty feet in front of him. It was a massive thing that moved with slow, heavy menace. For a moment Rialus thought it would cross the path, but, sensing the Acacian, the feline paused. It turned its head and set its gray eyes on him, moving as if its head and wild mane were as heavy as stone. Its tongue lolled out a moment, wagging, and then was slurped back in. Rialus cried out, "Eyyaaahhhh." His fingers twitched. The summons fell from his hand and clattered, all too loud, on the marble tiles.

The cat lowered its head, the muscles along its back and forelegs rippling beneath its white coat. Its tail flicked, one quick movement that was enough to make Rialus start. He was sure the beast would leap on him, knew that it could cover the distance in one bound, knew its large paws hid claws that would grasp him as mercilessly as an alley cat does a mouse. Indeed, the lion seemed to be speaking to him. Did he realize, the beast asked, that it could crack Rialus's head between his jaws and slop out his brains with his tongue?

Rialus peed. He did not feel it coming. It just happened, the warm flow starting at his groin and trickling down both his legs. He would never be sure—but he had his suspicions—that the act of releasing his bladder saved his life. The lion's nostrils flared. It obviously smelled the urine. Its upper lip drew back from its teeth and trembled for a moment—a look of derision if Rialus had ever seen one. It raised its head, turned away in disgust, and carried on across the path, leaving Rialus the sight of its swaying genitalia as a lingering image.

He considered backing out, running to his quarters, and changing his clothes, but there was not time for that. He picked up the summons and carried on, walking awkwardly, for the urine was already cool, hoping his robe would hide any stains.

As he walked, he noticed something strange in the air around Devoth, things darting and hovering as he stood still. A swarm of insects? Perhaps the beetles performing some strange act of Auldek hygiene? He could not make out what it was until he drew quite near. Then he saw more clearly.

Not flying insects at all, but hummingbirds! Ten or more of them zipped through the air above Devoth, flashing scarlet and metallic green and yellow. They darted, swirled, chased one another, and then hovered. They were beautiful, all motion and grace and . . . they returned again to Devoth. He even held one on the palm of his outstretched hand. They had no fear of him. Indeed, they seemed to be competing for his attention.

Noticing Rialus, Devoth turned to face him. He smiled as the tiny bird flitted up from his hand and then settled again. "Ah, there's my leagueman. Do you like my birds? They like to dance with me. They love me, as you can tell. And I love them."

Staring at them, Rialus did not know how to answer. He opened his mouth, but only a breath of indecision escaped him. He might never understand these people. He wished to think them foul and base and ugly, but nothing as beautiful as a hummingbird had ever loved Rialus. Fast behind this thought came another, completely unbidden and without warning. What, he thought, if the world is not meant for Acacians after all? What if the Auldek deserve it more than we?

As if in answer, Devoth grinned. For the few seconds that he held the grin, Rialus was certain the Auldek could read his thoughts. "You know, leagueman, if you hold still like that for long enough, one of my birds may nest in your mouth. That would do neither of us any good. Come, we have things to discuss. We'll begin the march within a fortnight." With that, he bobbed his upraised hand, and the tiny bird whirred into flight once more.

Chapter Forty-two

Mena would never forget the strange song that Corinn whispered to Aaden as he lay unconscious and bleeding that horrible afternoon. She could not remember the words of it. She was not even sure there were words. It had a shape that might have been language but that was vague and hidden beneath a melody that defied description. It was sound and breath and notes. It contained more voices than just Corinn's, mixed with music and exhalation and sobbing and a thousand promises. It mystified her.

And the others as well. One of the servants asked if they should pull the queen away from the boy, but Mena shook her head. Whatever was happening—whether the song was a funeral dirge or a sorcerer's spell—it was Corinn's right to sing it. A mother's right. Perhaps a queen's right.

When finally Corinn drew back and let them attend the prince, the physicians gasped in amazement. Aaden's abdomen had healed. There was blood aplenty, but try as they might they could not find any cuts in the boy's flesh. Bruises, yes, a swollen line above his groin that looked like a long-healed wound, abrasions. But the boy simply was not suffering from the dagger wound they had come running to attend. He was no more hurt than if he had been through a rough patch of sword training. He slept, breathing steadily, his face as peaceful as that of any child deep in the dreamworld.

"He will sleep until he wakes," the queen said.

"But," one of the physicians began, "how did—"

"The Giver has helped me heal him," she said, inflecting the god's name in the manner that gave its feminine form. "Let us praise her and be thankful."

After verifying Aaden's lack of injury with her own eyes, Mena had sought out her sister. Corinn had already turned her back on the scene and was striding away, Rhrenna rushing to keep up with her. Mena caught her in the hallway, but Corinn would not even look her in the face. She mumbled something about washing the blood off. That was all. She left Mena standing in the hallway, caked in grime.

Corinn had not even looked at Elya, and that was cruel, for the creature was trembling with worry, obviously afraid that she had not done well enough. Mena returned to her and assured her, through whispered words and caresses, that she had done very well. Wonderfully well. She was a beauty. She had saved Aaden, and Corinn would thank her for it once she recovered from the shock.

Believing this to be true, Mena could not have been more surprised with how quickly her sister had—well, *recovered* seemed the proper word. Proper, but not the right one. Several days later, Aaden still remained asleep, but Corinn had put her grief and fear behind her. She emerged from her chambers as poised and controlled as ever, washed clean and seeming all the more forceful in her beauty. Her face was leaner, perhaps, just slightly more angular and perhaps several years older, though this may just have been because of the tight-lipped expression she took on.

She summoned the Queen's Council and demanded that the Senate in Alecia send representatives to witness what had happened firsthand and to hear Sire Dagon's testimony. She met in various sessions all day long, leaving one military briefing to receive ambassadors, after which she left for still more meetings. She even agreed to go to Alecia herself, to address the largest audience of senators and representatives from around the empire possible all at once.

She had time for everyone, it seemed, except her sister. Mena could not secure a moment alone with her. When they did speak, it was only on official matters in the company of others. The queen assigned Mena the duty of briefing all incoming soldiers on the best manner to fight the Numrek, even demanding she hold mock battles in the Carmelia. Mena could not help but think this cruel, for the stadium brought to mind again and again the horrible moment when the Numrek had sunk his blade into Aaden's belly, and then into Devlyn's—the poor boy. She fulfilled her role with Melio at her side. He was a comfort, but it was Corinn she needed. Like Elya in her simple way, Mena, too, craved Corinn's absolution. Her sister managed to deny her, without ever overtly saying that she was doing so.

Once, when Mena asked for a word alone with her, Corinn looked at her as if she were a slightly slow child. "Of course we can talk," she said. "Would you like me to have the merchants of Bocoum wait until we're done? They've only sailed across to promise their financial assistance and the invaluable use of their barges to transport troops and goods. They've come to offer their aid to the nation at a desperate time, but if you would like me to have them wait, I will. The other option is that we speak later. Which do you prefer?"

It was no real question, obviously. Mena bowed in answer and withdrew without complaint. How could she argue? What she wanted was intangible, emotional, a sense of connection Corinn might be incapable of providing. While, on the other hand, Corinn seemed a monarch with a hundred hands now, each of them was juggling different aspects of this new crisis.

Fortunately, Corinn allowed Mena access to Aaden whenever she wished. She went there often, as she did one afternoon after a long day of fighting and lecturing on the hot field of the Carmelia. She wanted to see him before returning to her own quarters. He slept on as before, but she still felt it necessary to visit him, thinking that somewhere in his core he might be aware of the world, might crave comfort even if he was incapable of asking for it.

There was a touch of perfume in the air, a musky scent that she had smelled before but could not place now. Some noble, perhaps, come recently to pay his respects and offer gifts. Indeed, quite a few had done that. Corinn had permitted only Agnates the honor, and only if they promised to enter quietly, view the prince from a distance, and leave whatever present they had in the space cleared to display them. A pile of them now crowded the corner.

"Oh, my lovely boy," Mena said, lowering herself gently to the edge of his bed. He lay on his side, head resting on his two hands in a posture that looked almost deliberate, as if he had taken it just to model sleeping, childish innocence. She ran her fingers over his hair, pulling a few strands back from his forehead, and then sat taking him in. There was much of Corinn in his features, which meant much of their mother. But there was no mistaking signs of the boy's gray-eyed father as well. She did not see it as much when he was awake. Now, though, with the leisure to gaze at his features, she could see how much Aaden was a child of two nations. She wondered if Corinn acknowledged it, too.

Mena had never seen Hanish Mein in person. Strange that a man who had affected so much of her life—and still did—had never been in the same room as she. She had met his brother Maeander. She had turned herself in to him in Vumu, and used him to transport her back to the world all those years ago, just after she had hunted and killed the god Maeben. When she looked close at the parts of Aaden that were not Akaran, it was Maeander she saw in her head. So sharp featured and tall; handsome, yes, but in a high-chinned, arrogant manner. Fortunate, then, that whatever Meinish traits Aaden showed had been softened by Corinn's round-edged beauty.

She did not doubt that the boy would wake just as Corinn said. Whatever had been in that song, part of it was power, the sorcery Corinn had been studying. But would he wake remembering the moment the Numrek betrayed him? Would he see that knife thrusting toward him, or would he be spared it? For that matter, had he seen what happened to Devlyn? Mena hoped not, for she could not bear the thought that he would live with that brutal image in his mind, with the responsibility he might feel for his friend's death.

"Don't remember it," she said. "None of it was your fault. The guilt all rests on others. Devlyn was a brave boy; think of him as dying to save you. That's what he wanted. That's why he will be remembered as a warrior. A hero. I'll make sure it's so. And you will, too, when you wake.

"Oh, Aaden, how beautiful Elya was when she rescued you. So fierce and full of love for you. You wanted to fly with her, didn't you? Well, you did. She loved you so much, she swept in and lifted you into the air and carried you away from all that evil. See, I told you that she thought you a special boy. There's the proof!"

And then she did something she had not planned to. She paused a moment, until she was sure she wanted him to hear this news. Perhaps it would give joy to his sleeping mind, be a comfort to him until he awoke. She began, "I have something to tell you about Elya . . ."

On her return to her quarters, she found Melio waiting for her. He stood on the balcony, leaning out to take in the view of the harbor. He had set a glass carafe of lemon liqueur on the stone balustrade, two glasses beside it, one of which was half full. "Any change?" he asked, his eyes soft on her as she approached.

"No. He sleeps on."

"Perhaps it's better that way. I've hardly managed to sleep since battling the Numrek. Too much to worry about."

Mena watched him pour for her and then took the glass he

492

offered. "You've slept more than you're aware," she said wryly. "Either that or you've perfected your imitation of a drunken man snoring."

"Be nice," he said, looking affronted. He reached to muss her hair, but she cocked her head just sharply enough to indicate that she was not really in a playful mood. Melio took the hint. He set both elbows on the weathered stone and scanned the sea. "It's been busy. The harbor. More boats in and out than I've ever seen. The harbor patrol has been keeping them anchored far out, controlling the flow." He glanced at her, inviting a response.

"Hmm," Mena said. She looked at him as well, though she was still thinking about Aaden.

"Mena, Corinn gave me orders today. I can tell you haven't heard."

"What orders?"

"She's sending the Elite to support General Andeson in Teh. I'll have to go meet with his officers shortly. They have the coastline blockaded, but it's the Teheen Hills they're really worried about. If the Numrek get there, they'll be hard to track. They could stay alive for months, us spending our resources chasing them while the Auldek start out on their march—if that's truly going to happen."

"Is it?" Mena hated the question, but she had to ask it. She had heard so much talk the last few days, so many rumors, but it was still hard to believe that a people so far away were somehow a threat to them.

"The queen seems to think so. That's what the league reports, and they were the ones who brought the news. Hard to refute them right now. They're adamant that it's happening, and that the Auldek have no interest in negotiating. That's what they were doing when everything went mad."

Melio finished the sentence hesitantly, reacting to the way Mena cut her eyes down from his face. He knew her well, and because of it, she knew that he understood her to have thought

493

of Dariel. Dariel had been at that attempt at negotiation. Whatever went wrong happened to him, before his eyes, perhaps to his body.

Drumming his fingertips on the stone balustrade, Melio resumed. "Anyway, it's a sound plan. About Teh, I mean. The Numrek are here already. They are our enemy again. There's really nothing but for us to destroy them. The Elite should be a part of it. As their captain I—"

"She's punishing me for not taking better care of Aaden," Mena said.

"No, she's not. Don't say that. You know your sister," he began, but then waved that away and began again. "You know how she functions. She is wrapped up in details. Those come first. I doubt very much, Mena, that she thinks any ill of you. She's just not one to remember small things like feelings."

For the first time, she sipped the lemon liqueur. Sipped it once, and then tilted it back and poured the entire drink down her throat. Wiping her mouth with her hand, she spoke as if she had not heard Melio at all. "She thinks I allowed Aaden to be stabbed. And she's right. I did. I watched it happen."

"Stop, Mena!" He set his glass down and turned her to face him, with a hand at her shoulder that then slid up to cradle her head and neck. "I'm only going to say this one more time. Nobody blames you. Not even Corinn. She may think she does. She may even act on it, but in truth she blames herself. It's she who made the Numrek her personal guards. It's she who put her son's safety in the hands of brute enemies. Tell me you didn't always know that it was wrong to think them our allies. They ate human flesh! What was she thinking, trusting them? She was thinking about how much she liked it that her guards put the fear of death in everyone else. She liked it that she was different and didn't have to call on anybody, even her family, for protection. Don't pull away. You know what I say is true. She knows it as well. But you, Mena, kept Aaden alive. Corinn knows that, too. Don't expect her to thank you for it anytime soon, but she knows it deep down."

Melio drew his hand away from her neck but only so that he could use both his hands to grasp hers. "Now, there's something else we should talk about."

"No." She knew exactly what it was. She knew because she had been thinking about it, too. He had been patient, and she had known that in the joyful times after he had arrived back on the island and Elya was working her magic, he had been on the verge of opening the topic again. If he had asked a few days ago, she would have agreed. Things were different now.

"Let us make a child," he said. "Stop using that root powder and let's be parents to a new generation."

"Not now. Look at what's—"

"Yes, now! We've waited long enough. Do you really want to let me leave to face the Numrek without even trying? What if I don't come back? Will you wash your hands of my memory?" Mena started to object, but he spoke over her. "Why shouldn't I think that? You already do it. I hate the way you wash me out of you! Like there's something wrong with me. Like you don't want any remnants of me inside you. Every time we make love, you kill that part of me that wants to make life with you."

He dropped her hands, a gesture of disgust to match what he was accusing her of. His face—so perfect when he smiled—became a mask of creases, disdain, frustration. It was horrible to see. As he backed away, Mena stepped toward him. "You just told me not to say foolish things. You don't either. I always want you inside me. Always. You are here already. Right here, in my center." She showed the spot by making a blade of her hand stabbing it in her chest.

"Don't tell me the world is going mad again," Melio said. He did not hide the spite in his voice, a twisted sort of malice that coiled with vulnerability and love—hard to separate one from the other. "You always have a reason. You wanted to wait until

Aaden was older, to make sure he lived and was healthy. Nice of you not to compete with your sister. But he did live. He's healthy and he'll wake up soon, better than ever. He's the heir. She can't possibly worry about your having children. Just tell her that. Then, it was that you couldn't be with child and fight the foulthings. Fine. That's done. And now you're going to say that the world is in chaos again. Too dangerous, right? Not right now. Afterward. Excuses, excuses, Mena!"

He said that harshly, then seemed to regret his tone. More softly, he said, "There always needs to be a new generation, no matter the circumstances of the moment. We can never know what the future holds. But I know what's true right now. Right now I love you and you love me. That love is a gift from the Giver, and you should thank him for it by making something of it."

"No," Mena said, but then hated the word and knew it was what she meant. It was she who drew closer to Melio now, one arm pulling his torso against hers, her other hand wrapping around the back of his head and pinching his hair between her fingers. "Not now, but after whatever is coming—with the Auldek, I mean—is over we can try."

"Me-naaaa!" He drew the name out, exasperated. "These things of life—love between two people, the quickening of new beings—they don't stop when events ask them to. They are life, much more so than the wars we make, the monsters we slay."

Tugging his hair, she cut in, "Listen. I will swear an oath to you. My promise to you and to the Giver. When the Numrek and the Auldek are dealt with, we'll make a child together. I swear it. But, Melio, I can't not fight if we are to have war. It's the only gift I really have to offer. It's what I'm good at. I'm Maeben on earth. I can't pretend otherwise."

"It's not the only thing you have to offer," Melio began, but did not explain further. He considered her skeptically for a moment. "Make children together. Not just one. We have years of delay to make up for."

"Yes, that's right." She pulled him closer and pressed her cheek against his collarbone. He let her stay like that a moment, but then pulled back.

"Look me in the eyes," he said. "Do you swear by Maeben as well?"

"Yes." And saying so she realized she did mean it. She was going to fight like she never had before. She was going to give everything she had, because the dream she had conjured of a peaceful life remained a thing to fight for. Just one more war. Just one, and surely the Giver would let her rest. "You are my Vaharinda," she said. "You will give me many children, enough to people the world."

He finally released the wonder that was his smile. All the components of his face shifted into joyful arrangement. "Okay, Mena," he said, "I just hope you get to keep this promise."

So do I, she thought, moving her mouth to meet his. So do I.

Chapter Forty-three

A fine morning a week after all the chaos with the Numrek, Delivegu walked past the Marah guarding the entrance to the queen's compound, his chin raised, haughty and disdainful of their fixed stares. He quite enjoyed it. How quickly the talented rise. When he reached Rhrenna's offices in the anteroom, however, he made himself more personable. "Secretary," he said, showing his perfect teeth, "I have need of an audience with the queen."

"I know," Rhrenna said. "You told me as much. That's why I gave permission for you to come this far. I'll need to know why you wish to speak to her before you go any farther."

Why indeed, Delivegu thought, smiling. Why indeed? "Oh, it's a small thing, but I think she'd like to know it."

Delivegu's recent capture of Barad the Lesser had won him more than a few privileges. He now, officially, had a post in Rialus Neptos's staff. It would have annoyed him if Neptos—ratlike creature that he was—had actually been around, but he was away indefinitely, if not dead. Corinn kept her plans so close to her lovely chest that very little came through the offices of the councillor. What little did, the upper-level staff seemed intent on keeping from him. The first days in his post he took to calling himself—privately, of course—"Acting Chancellor Delivegu Lemardine." Time would remove the "Acting," and then, finally, all would be right in the world.

Perhaps he would eventually achieve "Chancellor and Queen's Consort Delivegu Lemardine, he of the mighty erection." That last part was true, of course, and the rest . . . Well, one could always dream.

In keeping with his new role, he was granted office space in one of the outer buildings of the palace's governmental wings—not the most distinguished sector of the grounds. Documents brought to him from the councillor's office had to travel from those rarified regions down several staircases, along a back alley, through a few underpasses, and up a ramp most often trafficked by laborers and their animals. The stink of the beasts drifted through his open window. He would have kept it closed, except the room, shadowed as it was for much of the day behind a high archway, was damp almost to the point of being chilly.

Something similar could be said about the secretary who came with the office. She was not exactly disfigured—nobody who worked within the palace displayed any of the physical ailments one might see regularly among the common people—but there was something unnervingly masculine about her: shoulders wider than normal, hips narrower. Her jaw was square as any Aushenian dockworker's, her voice just as gruff. He was being unkind, perhaps. She filled her position efficiently enough, with barely a wasted word or action. He would rather have employed a dim-witted, pretty girl that he could have slathered across his desk when the spirit moved him. The fact that this woman did not entice him seemed a personal affront. Even worse, he had dreamed about her several times, dreams of a sexual nature that left him squirming when he awoke. He tried to avoid looking at her, not an easy task in a small office space.

Though the palace was abuzz, he did not have much official business arrive at his desk. Fortunately, wearing the badge of his new rank allowed him free rein to wander much of the palace. The queen's office wing remained barred to him, as did the Akaran family's private quarters, that small city unto itself. Those he needed special permission to access. No matter. Strolling along the upper courtyard gardens, chatting with the guards who seemed a fixture at each gateway, watching the gape-mouthed fish hunt minnows in the pools, striding through corridors past senators and league officials and rich merchants kept him entertained. They all wore such grave faces. Concern hung about their shoulders, worry over the fate of the empire. Delivegu viewed the turmoil as an opportunity, but not one that should spoil his appreciation of his sudden rise in stature.

He flirted with noblewomen when opportunities arose. He did his best to orchestrate chance encounters, especially as one particular girl from Manil positively entranced him, such a small bud of mouth on her, and young enough that he knew, just knew, he would amaze her with his carnal knowledge. Even climbing all the way up to old Edifus's ancient ruins amused him. Good exercise for the legs and lungs and, by the Giver, what a view! The Inner Sea all around, glistening like colored glass lit from below. The tales said the first king was a suspicious, paranoid man. That was why he perched here so high above the sea, with views in all directions. Delivegu doubted that contained all his character. Surely, a man could not choose a spot in the world such as this without an eye for the splendor of it. Edifus, he was sure, had an eye for beauty.

Still, though, the nation faced a crisis. A grave threat. A new enemy and all that. Considering this, he sequestered himself in his offices for at least a few hours each day. He did his best to keep apprised of the workings in the higher reaches of the councillor's offices, sending frequent missives to them, cajoling information out of their tight fists. For his efforts he soon found himself deluged with documents that he was expected—no— not to consider and offer his sage opinion on, but to sort, to stack, to arrange, as if he were a lower order of office employee. He suspected the crates of dusty paper were actually long meant for disposal. He nearly made the mistake of storming into Rialus's office and accosting the staff, but then realized that was likely what they had wanted him to do. Make a fool of himself. Prove that he was not one of the elite, become a laughing-stock. Clearly, his promotion did not sit well with some of his new peers. He held his tongue, and perused the piles for something helpful to his advancement.

Late one afternoon Delivegu came across some sort of diagram or architectural survey. He would have tossed it, if his eyes had not touched upon a few words written at the top corner. He recognized the handwriting immediately: Rialus Neptos's. He would have known the crimped writing anywhere. He thought it indicative of the character of the man, which was why Delivegu himself always wrote with bold, strong strokes meant to own the page.

He would have tossed the diagram away right then, except that his secretary stepped in to ask if he needed anything more from her for the day. Not wanting to fully curdle his already dubious mood by looking at her, he sank his head toward the document, murmuring that, no, he did not need her anymore. She asked if he wanted the pile of papers on the floor disposed of. He said that could wait for the morrow. She spoke on a bit longer; Delivegu resolutely kept his eyes on the paper. By the time she left, he realized he might actually have something of interest in his hands.

It was a diagram of buildings viewed as if from above. The longer he stared, the more he believed he saw something familiar in it, something about the shape of the exterior walls and the indication of a jutting portion . . . Yes, it was the royal palace, the residence areas! As soon as he thought that, he noticed the same words, palace residence, penned in Rialus's hand. Had he read that, or had he figured it out himself? No matter.

He pulled a lamp closer, as his offices were already well in shadow and growing dimmer by the minute, and he made a careful study of the lines and shapes. Equations and architects' notes about materials and descriptions of renovation projects apparently done over the many years crowded the page. Little of it meant much to Delivegu. He did, however, tingle with the suspicion that Rialus's cryptic scribblings had been written after all the rest and had some other import. Half sentences and signs and arrows that could have been meant only as notes to himself, for they confused the diagram more than explained anything. To make it worse, much of what Rialus had written he had later crossed out.

"He makes no sense," Delivegu complained. "A waste of my time . . ."

Once again, he nearly tossed the diagram onto the pile of papers rising beside his desk. But if it was a waste of time, why had it occupied Rialus so long? He bent and studied it further. It was a map of secret passageways. Of course it was! That was what the broken lines drawn within the walls were! Yes, it did appear that many of the passageways were no longer usable. Some of them Rialus had scratched out with positively angry motions. Had Rialus kept this document at the queen's orders or secretly? That Delivegu could not discern, but it did seem clear that the queen had taken pains to eliminate these passages.

"Suspecting some deceit, were you, Your Majesty?" he asked. "Where's your trust, your faith in your loyal servants?"

If she had suspected treachery, it looked like she had been very effective in sealing the place up. Each time he tried to trace his way in with a finger, he invariably reached a dead end. At least, that was the case until . . .

"Now, that's interesting," Delivegu said. "That's quite interesting."

Outside, he stood beside the wall in a quiet area of the palace grounds. He would not be able to say later whether the secret entrance had been missed or whether Corinn had allowed it to stay open. Nor could he ask, of course. He suspected that the tunnel had been effectively sealed off for a time, but it appeared to have come open again when a new door was knocked into a once-closed storage space. Perhaps the queen never knew the change was made. But this was conjecture. What he did know was that it existed. Just as the diagram indicated, there was a narrow slit in the southern buttress of the royal quarters, a fissure between two walls just large enough for a person to slip through. It was the strangest thing, for one could stand a few feet away from it and not see the opening for what it was. Even when he did stick his head in, a facing wall met him, making it seem like the opening led nowhere. That was an illusion of the architecture.

Tricky this, Delivegu thought, admiring. He moved farther in.

He had not planned on going far. He just wanted to look, to verify that the tunnel really took him inside. If so, he would retreat and consider how this new information might prove useful. That was his intention, but curiosity kept him moving just a little farther, first into that storage room, then through it down a passage, and still little farther after that. The stones sweated; the air felt musty and close, terribly quiet.

When he stepped out into an ornate hallway, complete with wall hangings and carpets and life-sized statues spaced at intervals, he knew he had accomplished all he needed to for an evening. He strolled a few steps forward just to feel the soft give of the carpet underfoot, inhaling air lightly scented with a citrus incense. Oh, that's nice! This could really suit me. And the statues looked so very real. It made his skin crawl, how textured like real flesh they were, clothed as ancient warriors from around the empire. He could not help but marvel at the work, play at staring these wooden warriors down. He even challenged one to a duel.

When he heard the voices, he did not initially panic. They were not in his hallway but were approaching from around the corner, chatting. All he had to do was retrace his steps and slip back into the wall. The crack through which he had come was just . . . here? No, not there. Solid wall there. Down here a little farther beyond that table? No, not there either. The voices came from two women, growing nearer. Here? No, nothing but stone! He could not for the life of him find his way back into the passageway. Certain that the women were about to step around the corner, he yanked open the nearest door and dove inside.

As he strode across the room he was aware of a bed and a sleeping form in it. Still moving, he turned to confirm the person did not awaken. What he saw caused him to halt. He swung back toward the bed, tiptoeing, and looked more closely.

The prince!

For a moment his skin crawled. If he got caught in the prince's bedroom . . . If the boy opened his eyes and shouted . . .

The two voices grew louder. Delivegu set his sights on what he needed to find: a place to hide. He ran across the room and slipped behind the curtains that covered one of the floor-to-ceiling windows. There was plenty of room for him to stand unseen.

The door opened and two maids entered, discussing something that somebody had done. Delivegu did not have time to make sense of it, for they did something near the bed, said a few words directly—presumably—to the sleeping prince, and then someone else arrived. They greeted the new arrival with deference. For the next few moments he tracked the maids by sounds they made, tending to details of the prince's bedding, perhaps. Quick work. He heard them whisper a farewell. The door opened and they apparently stepped out. Whoever had entered after them, however, remained in the room.

"Oh, my lovely boy," a female voice said.

It was not the queen's, though it was familiar. He had heard it before. But where? She did not provide him another opportunity to figure it out for some time. She stayed silent. At first Delivegu stood stiff and breathed carefully and barely moved at all, but as the minutes passed he relaxed.

She'll leave soon. She'll leave soon.

Later still, he thought, I hope she doesn't fall asleep.

She did not. Every now and then, he could hear just enough faint noise to indicate movement, a creak of weight on the bed, breath inhaled through the nose and expelled as a gust through the mouth. He imagined her stroking the boy's hand, gazing down into his face, concerned. Reasonable enough. He still wished he knew who the woman was. A suitor, perhaps? Did a boy so young have suitors?

Well, he is a prince, Delivegu mused. Probably has a gaggle of suitors. The lad is handsome, as well. Prince, I hope you know how to use those good looks in the years to come. Had I your title . . . Oh, the damage I'd have done to the nation's virgins. Hardly bears thinking about . . .

The woman spoke. He heard her clearly enough, and lost interest just as quickly. She was saying emotional, womanly things about how good the boy was and how the dragon creature had loved him. He listened with half his attention, until she said something that pulled him back.

"I have something to tell you about Elya."

With that he placed the voice. Princess Mena, she who had ridden in on that dragon creature, slipped off, and spoken so casually to the queen.

"You can't tell anybody. You have to promise. I mean it. Promise."

Silence for a moment. Delivegu had half a mind to step out from behind the curtain and point out that the boy was unconscious. If you wait for a response, you might be there awhile, Princess.

"Okay. Since you promise . . ." A few more words slipped by without taking shape, and then, "You can't even tell your mother."

Delivegu perked up.

"She wouldn't understand. She—well, it's not easy bearing her responsibilities. It makes one hard, skeptical, always looking for the ill that hides beneath any good. Sometimes I think that the more you look, the more you find. The more you look, the more you create the things you most fear."

The princess said something else under her breath. She must have looked down and cursed into her hand, not liking the direction of her own words. Delivegu was already calculating the value of what he had heard. A bit of criticism spoken to an unconscious boy? Value: naught. Give us something more, he thought.

"This is only for you to know," Mena said. "Elya has laid eggs. Four of them. Oh, you would so love to hold them. And you will. Once you're better, you'll come to my quarters and I'll show you them."

That was the chance event that brought Delivegu to the queen's offices and had him standing before Rhrenna, so pleased with himself that he felt no need to rush to answer her. He would not be describing the circumstances of the encounter in detail, nor discussing the rather troublesome time he had had escaping the royal quarters later that night. He would, however, offer information he would claim to have gleaned from his ever-reliable "sources." It would be easy enough to lay the information on one of Mena's maids, someone who might have chanced upon the eggs, and might have told someone else, who might have told . . . that sort of thing.

"For what reason do you want an audience with the queen?" Rhrenna asked, repeating the question for a third time. She kept her voice clipped and her gray Meinish eyes cold, but Delivegu knew better.

His smile was an unwavering crescent, and his talent for talking through it long practiced. "Rhrenna, now that I'm a man in high standing I feel inclined to boldness. When, my darling, will you consent to get to know me better? Privately, I mean. Just you and me. Wine perhaps. Good food and a place of comfort to retire to? That sort of thing."

Rhrenna studied him a moment before answering. "Don't you mean that question for the queen?"

"Ah—" He had not expected that. It set him back a moment, wondering if the fact that she asked it indicated the queen had spoken to her about it, or that she intuited the queen would be receptive. "Ah . . . what man could fail to find her highness a great beauty? I'm no different. But the queen would have no interest in me, certainly." Though the sentence was declarative, he left it dangling, loose ended, and rather sounding like a question. Rhrenna's answer was franker than he wished for.

"You don't stand a chance," she said. "Enjoy your lecherous thoughts of her in private, Delivegu. That's the only way you'll find satisfaction. I mean no insult, though. I'm of the opinion that no man except Aaden—when he becomes a man—will ever get near the queen's heart."

"And what of you, then? Would you ever try me?"

"Try you?" Rhrenna laughed. "Oh, you're a charmer, Delivegu. Try you . . ." She spun away and resumed perusing the papers on her desk.

Well, that didn't go that well, he thought. He was preparing a witty remark, something to brush her off and indicate no acknowledged harm to his sensualist's casual demeanor, when she continued.

"Yes, I imagine I would try you," she admitted. Her eyes rose to meet his. "I think you smell rather good."

Never had the mention of his bodily odor been such an invigorating kick in the groin. She did not let him linger on it at present, though. "Again," she said, her voice resuming its official curtness, "for what reason do you wish an audience with the queen? If you don't answer me now, you'll have to leave."

507

She likes changing gears, this one. Fine. I won't complain. In fact, Delivegu felt like purring, such was the pleasure of his position. "Once again, I have intelligence for her," he said, "news that she may find very, very interesting. I have word that something important is about to . . . hatch. Four things, in fact. Four things that someone has kept hidden from her."

Chapter Forty-four

I t was a delicate instrument, thin and artful, a slight curve in the handle, with one end weighted and shaped into a hand-grip. The tip ended in a blackened needle point. Dariel knew what it was from the moment he laid eyes on it. He had spent the last few days studying crude maps of Ushen Brae's coast-line, in exercising his body and explaining nautical concepts and terms to Tunnel and Skylene and the others who were to be his crew, but this last thing marked the final stage of preparation. After this, his mission began.

"So . . . you're serious about this? You want to tattoo me?"

Looking over the device, Mór narrowed her eyes. "Without markings you stand out like a freak among the People."

Dariel, head cocked, prepared to take exception to this.

Mór looked at him straight-faced, no trace of humor on her feline features. "Like a freak, I say. Or a degenerate. Others who see you will think you a child who has done nothing in his life. Unworthy. Without signs of belonging, nothing you say would change their opinion. Besides, that plain face of yours will forever announce your Akaran blood. It could be the death of you among the People."

"How about just drawing some spots or something? Stylus and ink. That sort of thing."

"It's been explained to you already, I'm sure. Should the divine children question you, any 'stylus and ink' work would be readily discovered. No, your fate has brought you here—just as mine brought me here. The tattoos must be real."

"Why do I think you'll enjoy doing it?" Dariel asked, smiling wryly.

"Because it hurts, you mean?" she asked, playfully innocent in a way Dariel had never seen before. "Dariel Akaran, when I wish to cause you pain, it won't be with this. I'll find a real tool for it. Believe me."

I don't doubt you, Dariel thought. I don't doubt you at all. I still have the marks from our first meeting, remember? As she spoke on, he had to tell himself to lower the edges of his grin. He should not be so pleased about this. The tattooing was going to hurt, and it was going to be permanent. What would Corinn think when she saw him again? If she ever saw him again . . . She would never understand or approve of something like this. It would seem an act of surrender, of lessening himself and his stature as an Acacian prince. She would expect him to command them all to do his bidding. The thought nearly made him laugh. He had, of course, commanded many people in various roles—both as an Akaran and as a Sea Isle raider—but this was different, perhaps in a way that Corinn would never understand.

Increasingly, the Known World seemed far, far away, not just in leagues but in its hold on his thoughts. Sitting and talking with Tunnel and Skylene and some of the others, caught up in the horror and largeness that was Ushen Brae, Dariel had to wrest his focus back to his homeland again and again. It was in danger, he knew, of attack from the Auldek. He remained vague on how great that threat was, but he tried to remember it and to think of Corinn and Mena and Wren and all his companions from his raiding days and the common people he had come to know and care for while working on his rebuilding projects. They mattered. And he had to get back to them.

"It will be your temporary pass," Mór said, "although the mark itself will not be temporary. You may still fail us, Prince Dariel, but I've been told to give you the time and freedom to be among us. It's a chance not to fail." After a pause, she added, "I hope you don't."

Dariel nodded. Never a skilled liar, it was the best he could do to express his resolve. In truth, he had accepted the mission Mór offered him for reasons of his own. Yes, he would be part of a small team sent to steal a Lothan Aklun boat, a soul vessel. One had been found tied up at the southern end of the warehouse district. The league had not yet noticed it, probably because a series of skerries—small, rocky islands—blocked the area from the open ocean. Dariel would prove he was the raider he claimed to have been. He would captain the vessel. He would pilot it south to a marsh area called Sumerled, where they would ground the boat and set fire to it, thereby denying it to the league and—even more important—freeing the souls that had been bound to power it.

Dariel had agreed to all of this readily enough. To himself, he swore that if he got the chance, he would flee in the cutter. He had no idea if he could really make the Lothan Aklun ship work, and he realized the People themselves knew so little about the sea that they assumed things about his knowledge that they shouldn't have. But so be it. He would try. He would pilot across the Gray Slopes in it if he had to or follow the coastline north and pick his way through the Ice Fields. He would work out the details later, but this might be his best chance at getting home. He had to grasp it if he could.

"What totem would you take?" Mór asked, sorting through the instruments on a small table.

"I will take what you feel I deserve," he said.

"I don't know what you deserve."

"If it was my choice I would wear the face of the Shivith. Spots, like yours."

"You jest," she said, glancing up at him.

"No." Dariel said. He knew it sounded strange, and he knew people would stare at him back in the Known World, but this he could answer truthfully. "I find the effect quite pleasing. I'm not ready for whiskers just yet, thanks. Some spots, though—

if they look similar to yours—might be interesting. But, as I said, if that offends you, choose another totem. Or . . . someone else could do this."

Instead of looking at him, Mór closed her eyes and absorbed his choice within herself. "As you wish. And, no, I'll do it." She lifted the tattooing needle like a stylus in one hand and turned to face him, a tiny bowl of black ash ink pinched in the fingers of her other hand. "This will hurt, but pain is transitory. Only our legacy endures. Come, sit here before me. This will take a while."

Dariel did as she asked. She was right, of course. It did hurt. And it did take a long time. But every painful moment of it was tempered by the nearness of Mór's body, by the scent of her and the fleeting moments when her elbow or wrist, hip or breast brushed against him. He tried to remember Wren, but it was hard. When he pictured Wren's face, he saw it overlaid with tattoos, indistinguishable from Mór's. They were both from northern Candovia, after all. By the Giver, he could not tell them apart anymore.

"I'm sorry," he whispered as she worked, "about . . . the People not being able to have children. I didn't know. We should have asked. I'm so sorry we didn't. If we had, I swear to you things would have been different."

By the way she paused it was clear to Dariel that Mór was considering what he said. Her only answer, though, was to continue piercing his flesh.

"There," she eventually said. She picked up the blood-stained towel she had used throughout the procedure, wet it in some liquid, and used it to clean his face. Despite himself, Dariel flinched at each touch: the liquid stung. She stepped back from him, setting down the needle of torture and contemplating her work. She smiled.

"So you're amused?" he asked.

She laughed into the back of her hand, trying to squelch it. Holding up a mirror, she said, "Perhaps you should see yourself.

See how you look, now and forever."

Dariel reached out and accepted the mirror. He turned it toward his face. He expected to see a stranger staring back at him. A beast, perhaps. Something strange and perhaps frightening. He expected—despite the curious anticipation he felt—to be frightened by what he saw and sickened by the permanence of it. He was not. In fact . . .

"What are you thinking, Akaran?" Mór asked.

"That I make a fine Shivith," he said, speaking his thought aloud.

Mór made a sound low in her throat. "We'll see."

Late the next afternoon, he moved as one of a group of ten. Unbound completely now, he followed Skylene's slim form through the maze of subterranean passageways that had been his home for weeks. This time he was not being shifted to another cell. This time they came to a door, opened it, and stepped outside.

At first his eyes shot across the field beside them. It had been a long time since he had taken in the open world from ground level. The sky hung ominously huge above them. Rows of strange vegetables—bushes about a man's height that bristled with long arms, each ending in a fist-sized bud of some sort—seemed to be marching toward him in military lines. Blinking, it took him a moment to confirm that they were, in fact, stationary, but a moment after that he detected movement coming from another quadrant.

The wall above him was alive with a sickening, slithering, unnatural motion. The first sight of it made Dariel's skin crawl. He stopped and stared up at— Well, it was hard for him to say at what. The entirety of the long, high structure seethed with limbs. They were thorny tentacles, many ten or fifteen feet long, looking like the underbellies of a thousand giant octopuses, reaching out with arms lit greenish orange by the dying day's light. For a breathless moment

513

Dariel thought them creatures that might rush down toward him, snatch him up, and tear him to pieces.

"What are those?" Dariel asked.

Tunnel followed his eyes and took in the wall, unimpressed. "Plants," he said. "You don't have plants over there?"

"Not like those," Dariel said.

"Don't worry." Tunnel nudged him on the shoulder. "They won't eat you. Plants in the inland . . . *they* may eat you, but not these ones. Come."

They moved on along the wall, undisturbed by the writhing limbs. Dariel stayed close, trying to match the other's composure. Failing at it.

They cut around buildings and ran through fields and climbed, for a time, over rooftops. Dariel had to keep his focus on his progress, on the placement of his feet and hands and on keeping up with the others, but he took in the panorama that was Avina in quick glimpses. Enormous. Never ending, it seemed. Buildings jutting up into the distance.

Tunnel had sworn to him that Ushen Brae was a land of mountains that rose up straight out of great lakes, of jungles that stretched from horizon to horizon, with insects the size of antoks and flightless birds that hunted the Free People in packs like wolves, of arctic regions thronging with snow lions and white bears. There were creatures out there so fierce that the Auldek feared them, beasts with massive jaws or stinging parts that could drain life after life out of them. These animals, he claimed, were the reason that the Auldek built coastal cities even though they turned their back to the sea. Tunnel admitted he had never seen any of these wonders or horrors himself, but he hoped to one day.

Dariel thought it sounded exciting, dangerous in all the ways that set his boy's fancy tingling.

Twice, the group had to split up to navigate crowded streets. Dariel walked beside Tunnel on one occasion; behind a young Wrathic named Birké on the other. Birké had no tattoo work

514

that Dariel could see, but he did demonstrate the wolflike qualities of his clan totem with thick facial hair that covered his cheeks and forehead. He also sported canine teeth so large they showed in bulges against his lips even when his mouth was closed. They looked completely natural, in a strange, unnatural way. When he smiled—which he did first on seeing Dariel's new facial tattoos and then again after they had walked through a crowded thoroughfare and rejoined the group in the shadows of an alley—he was simultaneously terrifying and hilarious. Dariel thought he might quite like the young man as a friend, should he be provided the leisure of friendship again.

The sun had fully set and the sky had settled in to early evening dark by the time the group gathered in the corner of a warehouse. Dariel could smell the sea. It was so near, just a wall away, he thought. It smelled like freedom to him. Skylene sent Birké and another man to check the last bit of the route to the destination. The rest waited. Dariel found himself standing beside Skylene. She pressed closed to him, closer than seemed necessary. He knew why. She was staring at his freshly tattooed face.

"I can't get used to seeing you like that," Skylene said. "You look like one of us, but I sat talking to you so long I know you're not one of—"

"Perhaps I'm becoming one of you," Dariel cut in. His face was still sore, and he could not help but feel the touch of her eyes as a physical pain. "Give me the chance at it, at least."

Skylene kept looking at him. "Mór must have enjoyed doing that work. Did she make it hurt?"

"What do you mean? Of course it hurt."

Smiling, Skylene said, "It doesn't if you chew kenvu root. It deadens the sensations on the skin." She touched a spot on his face with a fingertip. "Makes the markings painless. She didn't mention that?"

"No, she didn't mention it," Dariel snapped. "What's wrong

with her, anyway? Does she just enjoy hurting me? Slapping me. Sticking me with needles. Insulting me every chance she gets. Is she like that always? With others?"

"Mór has been one of the Free People for many years," Skylene said. "Her problem is not cruelty. It's that she loves too much, cares too much. She's missing half her—" Skylene stopped, shook away whatever she was going to say. Instead, she lightened her tone. "Anyway, she doesn't enjoy hurting anyone. I think she likes you, actually."

"Tell him," Tunnel said, staying her. "Give it."

Skylene looked at him sharply. "We'll talk later."

"Please," Dariel said, "tell me. What don't I know about her?"

"Ah . . . Mór wants nothing for herself, except one thing." Though she had committed, it still took Skylene a moment to continue. "She had a brother. A twin named Ravi. They were taken together but were separated when they arrived in Ushen Brae."

"So, what . . . she's looking for him?"

"In a manner of speaking, yes. He didn't become a slave. He was eaten. His soul was taken from him and given to an Auldek. Mór wants to find him. I don't know what she thinks she can do. I don't think she even knows. But they were twins. Understand? They were in the womb together. They are two halves of a whole. She can feel that he goes on somewhere. Even though he lives in an Auldek's body, she wants to face him . . . perhaps to release him. Now, let's stop wasting time. Let's go. There's Birké. Let's be quick."

She pointed at the shadowy figure who had just reappeared at the far side of the warehouse. He waved, indicating that the area was free, at least temporarily, of divine children. Dariel asked no more questions. He fell in step behind Skylene, with Tunnel and the others behind him. The rest of the journey was brief. They walked for a time through a dark corridor, then wove through another jumbled warehouse, and finally stepped out onto a seaside dock. The salt air off the water was wonderful. Dariel sucked it in, loving the moist touch of the sea breeze on his face. It instantly reminded him of Val, the man he met as a feeder of the palace furnace, who later saved him from death in a lonely hovel and raised him to be a raider, to love the sea. His second father.

Out beyond the edge of concrete pier, the sea moved, black and shimmering. He caught the hulking, jagged shapes of outcroppings of rock near shore through which water sieved. Jets of white foam burst up at regular intervals, ghostly in the darkness, frightening and full of danger. Perfect, Dariel told himself. Just as I like it. Just as Val would like it. Wild.

"Dariel!" Tunnel called to him from the edge of the pier. "Come. See it."

He jogged forward and looked down, for the water was well below the level of the pier. There, tethered to a lower platform at water level, was the boat. A very peculiar boat, similar to the sailless craft he saw slicing the water beside the *Ambergris* out in the barrier islands. Walking down the ramp toward it, his eyes took in every line and shape of it. It was so sleek, low to the water, covered all over with that white coating particular to league ships. It ran more than a hundred feet long, but was narrower than any seagoing vessel he had seen before. A water arrow. The steering wheel was in a raised, semi-enclosed structure near the back.

The others waited for him, standing uneasily beside the rocking vessel, seemingly at a loss. This, after all, was where Dariel's expertise was supposed to take command. As yet, he had no idea how to make the thing work, but that was a small detail, certainly. Spratling could sail any vessel, even one, he hoped, without a sail.

Dariel inhaled a deep breath, filled his chest with it, and leaped across the narrow gap. What began as a graceful move, however, did not conclude as one. The slick surface of the deck shed the leather soles of his sandals so completely that he spent a few frantic seconds dancing as if unexpectedly thrown onto ice, his arms wheeling. He just managed to get down to his hands and knees, where he paused, breathing heavily.

The others watched him, perplexed and more than a bit concerned.

"It's slippery," he explained.

Skylene squinted one eye, raising the brow of the other.

Dariel had felt the slippery surfaces of league ships before, on Sire Fen's league warship, the *Rayfin*, and most recently the *Ambergris*. This one felt even slicker. It may not have been so, but he needed to keep his feet under him now more than ever. Remembering that some of the sailors on the *Ambergris* had worked barefoot, he sat and unlaced his sandals. Barefoot, he rose to stand again. It helped. His skin clung to the coating in a way leather did not. He almost felt he could squeeze the deck with his toes.

Looking at the Free People watching him, he said, as if impatient, "Come on. Take 'em off and climb aboard."

Inside the steering cabin a few moments later, Dariel gripped the wheel and said, "What powers this?"

Birké stood next to him, wolf like, waiting, and then confused. "What do you mean?"

"What— With the boats I know, we use the sails and the wind to push the vessel across the water. Or we use oars at times. Understand? There has to be something to provide the power, but here is nothing but—but the wheel." He stared at it, as if his explanation made him even more confused about the situation.

"Wind?" Birké asked. His lip curled back, exposing his canines. He seemed to find the idea barbaric. He waved until he got Tunnel's attention. "You use wind? The power is in the boat. Just think it to do what you wish."

"Think it? Be serious!"

"What?" Tunnel appeared, fresh from organizing the others, positioning them to best cast the boat off. Birké answered him, speaking in Auldek, gesturing toward Dariel. Tunnel brushed past him and grabbed Dariel by the wrists. He slammed his hands onto the wheel. "You brigand, yes? Act like it! Hold the wheel. Drive the boat." Dariel began a sputtering protest, but Tunnel spoke over him. "I know you'll do it." He added the last sentence casually. As he turned away, he pulled Birké with him.

Alone, seeing the motion on the deck below him, feeling the rocking of the boat, Dariel realized that the prow had already been cast off. It floated free of the dock. These people know nothing of boats! They think a boat moves because the pilot thinks it into motion? This is a fool's mission, and I'm captain of it.

"How about waiting for captain's orders?" he shouted.

A few of the crew looked up, perplexed. Dariel waved them away. This, apparently, was read as a sign to cast off the other lines. Before he could stop them, the entire vessel was loose and pulled by the outgoing tide. Looking over his shoulder, he saw the jagged teeth of the nearby skerries, no longer exciting. Terrifying instead. He cursed to himself and then out loud to everyone. They were about to be dashed against stone, end of the mission and end of his hopes. How had that happened so quickly?

"I never said to cast off!" he yelled, though it was futile. The "crew" had all they could handle keeping themselves from sliding off the deck, especially as it began to roll more in the growing chop.

Just think! Drive the boat by thinking? He still gripped the wheel, tugging it as if he would rip it off. And then he realized how strange his hands felt on the wheel. The material, whatever it was, hummed against his palms. He half pulled back, but his hands did not want to leave the thing. It held him. He could have jerked them away. He knew that. It was a gentle pull, filled with energy. It was waiting for him.

"By the Giver," he mumbled. The ship was waiting for him!

Whatever was going to drive it was not in the motion of the air, nor in the pull of oars against water. It was in the vessel itself! He felt it so clearly it was almost as if the boat spoke as much to him.

Tunnel, standing on the heaving deck, drenched by the waves sending spray high into the air, his arms outstretched for balance or in threat or both, roared, "Daarrriiiieeeeelllll! Drive it!"

It was the prod the prince needed. Without loosening his grip on the wheel, he craned his head around. They were nearly upon the rocks. They rode on the pull of water being sucked out to sea so forcefully that within a few seconds the stern would crash against the rocks with shattering force. Dariel imagined the prow of the ship slicing through the water. His head flew back, pulled by the force of the vessel being wrenched forward. For a split second he believed it was the force of impact, but in the next moment he realized there had been no impact. The boat flew away from the rocks with a speed that amazed him.

He yanked his body back into position just in time to wrench the wheel to starboard so that the boat would not slam back into the pier. The crew tumbled and slid about the deck, grasping for holds; all except Tunnel, who still managed to stand upright, grinning and laughing and roaring with glee, "Daarrriiiieeeeelllll! Rhuin Fà! Rhuin Fà!"

The next few minutes of his life were as hair-raising as any he had yet lived. The boat was a wonder, yes, but he had so little control of it. It responded to his thoughts, but it was hard to remember to think constantly. He would let his attention wander for a moment, only to realize they were about to smash up against some rocks. He would start to shout commands before realizing he had all the command he needed in his hands. It should have been easy, but he brought the vessel near to destruction a dozen times before they slipped out of the fingers of reaching stones and found deeper, open water.

There he pressed the vessel forward. They sped through the night, the prow of the boat slapping down each time they came to a wave crest, sending up spray. Had he ever sailed as fast as this? He was not sure, could not truly tell with the night so dark around them. He did believe he could go even faster, and longed to do so in the light of day, with no fear of crashing into some outcropping of rock.

By the Giver this is a ship! This is a ship!

How could they destroy it? It seemed a mad idea. The power of it! The things he could do with a vessel like this! He could be Spratling again, but a Spratling like the world had never seen before. He would run rings around the league, around anyone!

"Don't enjoy it too much," Skylene said. He had not noticed her come up beside him. "Remember why we're here."

"You can't still want to destroy this," Dariel said. "Feel it. This is a wonder. Do you know what I could—"

"We must destroy it."

"Why?" Dariel asked.

"Because it is evil." She leaned near him, brushing his shoulder, and spoke loud enough for only him to hear. "You believe it's so wonderful because of the power within it. But it's what makes the power in it that is so horrible. Ships like this one . . . they run on souls, Dariel. The essence of children. Quota children. That's what's trapped within them. They burn souls. Think of a child sent into slavery. Think of that child tossed into the furnace of this boat, firing it from the inside. That's what this is. I know it's enticing. Evil often is." She paused and then said, "You might want to slow."

He had been watching her profile as she looked forward. He swung his head around and eased back. As the prow dropped and some of the exhilaration of speed left him, he saw what had prompted her. For some time the long shadow of an island to the east had crept closer as they sped along it toward the south. Now, from an inlet of the island, came a blaze of light and motion. It must have had a deep anchorage, for a league brig nestled close to the shore, lit up with blazing pitch lanterns. Small vessels ferried supplies and people ashore. Men worked on the docks, unloading supplies. Even as they watched, new lights flared in windows of buildings all along the shore. The league, it appeared, was taking the place over.

"What island is this?" Dariel asked.

"Lithram Len," Skylene said. "They must have just found it."

"Where the soul catcher is?"

She nodded. "Go slowly and pull us back nearer the mainland coast. We should not be seen, especially now. The People need to know the league has found the island."

Dariel sailed as she instructed. He managed to cut behind a slim barrier reef that hid them for some time. Beyond it, he increased speed as the glow receded behind them. It was only then, when he thought about something other than piloting the boat, that he chewed over what he had just seen. The league were on Lithram Len. The soul catcher was on Lithram Len. No, he had never seen the thing himself, but he had seen Devoth shake off one death—pull an arrow from his heart and live on. That was enough to make him believe in the device.

If they find the soul catcher chamber itself, he thought, and learn how to use it . . .

Dariel drew up, his face glazed by a thought so sudden that he forgot to see through his eyes or animate his features for a moment. The vessel, sensing the waning of his focus, lost forward momentum. The bow drooped and the stern rose and the rocking of the waves took them in its rhythm.

"What is it?" Skylene asked.

"Wait a minute," Dariel managed to say. But that was as far as he got. He had to think through the idea that had just gripped him. It was a mad idea. Dangerous. An idea that would have him dealing with forces he did not yet understand. Neither Mór nor the elders had asked it of him, and if he proposed it, he would be asking the crew—these friends so new to him—to risk their lives as well. He should just drive his energy down into the boat and feel it surge forward, continue this escape, find a way to get the others ashore, and then sail away without them. Go home.

Tunnel bounded up from belowdecks. "Why have we stopped?"

Why even think what you're thinking? Dariel asked himself. When did their fight become yours? He tightened his grip on the wheel and intended to answer Tunnel by pushing the boat back into motion. Though he thought that, his will was not behind it. The boat continued to rock, dead in the water. Others gathered near, talking among themselves as they approached, and then joining the hush of those waiting for him.

It had been so long since he had thought of a venture like this. He could not help but think of Val. What had he said, one of the last things he told Dariel before sacrificing himself to destroy the league platforms? "I've been waiting to understand how best to say good-bye to the world. Now I've found it." That's exactly it. Dariel felt something similar now. Not that he needed to say good-bye. It was not death he felt near him, but life. Real life! A purpose that began here and might lead who knows where?

"What if . . ." he began. "What if we don't take this boat to Sumerled? Not just yet, I mean. What if instead we go to Lithram Len? What if we destroy the soul catcher ourselves, even if we have to fight the league to do it?"

"Dariel," Skylene said, "there are only ten of us."

"A perfect number. Who would expect it? We'll catch them unaware."

"You want war with the league," a voice—he could not pinpoint whose—said.

"Haven't you known that was happening all along?" Dariel asked. "They've never done anything but make war on us, on both sides of the ocean—we've just been too dull to see it. War with the league! That's exactly what I want. I fought them before, but I didn't finish it." With this acknowledgement, he felt a sudden need to laugh. Mirth spilled out of him, unexpected, all consuming, wonderful. "Let's strike them first." That seemed such a wonderful notion, so very right. It felt like the challenge he had been waiting for. It was business unfinished, and, he was sure, it was the start of the path to his fate. He had never, ever, felt that so clearly.

"What do you think? Let's fight them, starting here and now. We'll find a way. I didn't plan this, but we've seen what we've seen. We have to do something about it."

The crew remained quiet, all of them looking at one another, considering. Dariel could not read them. Their altered, tattooed, and adorned faces seemed as expressionless as he had ever seen them. Even Skylene gave him nothing. Tunnel did, though.

He slapped one of his thick arms down on Dariel's shoulders. Pointing at Skylene, he said, "What did I tell you? Rhuin Fá. That's what Tunnel said. Dariel Rhuin Fá!"

Chapter Forty-five

Corinn would have to reach all the way around the curve of the world and touch a mind that did not expect it, but this should be within her powers. Dream travel. She had witnessed it before. She knew it could be done. Lying in bed beside Hanish Mein, she had listened as he spoke across great distances—even through the barrier between life and death—with his ancestors. The Tunishnevre had been a spiteful coven of the undead, with their own source of power, one that came from the curse that had denied them true death. And that curse had come from Tinhadin. Santoth sorcery. As such, it should be within her power as well. After all, the Tunishnevre, when speaking to Hanish, had demanded he murder her. They had failed. They went to the real afterdeath instead, as did Hanish. Corinn still lived and ruled and had a son. Who, then, was more powerful?

This was but one of the myriad things that she held in her mind after the Numrek uprising and the League of Vessels declaration that a war was coming once more across the Ice Fields. She had, in a surprising way, found a sort of pitching, tumultuous equilibrium. Once she knew that Aaden was safe—and she did know that with enough certainty to put worry for him behind her—she rode the noise and confusion of unfolding events with a calm certainty.

Much of this came from her realization that she had known something like this was coming all along. She had known not to lower her guard. She might have been tempted to forget it briefly, lured by Mena's enthusiasm and Grae's attentions, drawn even to notions of higher nobility in her rule, thinking she might leave the people free of sedation and find ways to bring some of Aliver's high ideals to life. As much as she had held power grasped in one hand, she had tried to loosen the clenched fist of her other hand. That had been a mistake. Even the flexion of her fingers in considering the possibilities became an invitation to disaster. That was why she had not been ready and had not seen the treachery standing right behind her for so long. That's why Aaden had nearly died.

Unforgivable.

When faced with violence right before her eyes she did nothing but watch. She was completely unprepared in that moment. While Mena fought, Corinn stood and stared. That could never happen again. She had been lax in her study. Spending time summoning furry creatures for Aaden? Casting euphoria spells at banquets and creating flying insects? Foolishness! Even the water she fed into northern Talay was done for the wrong reasons. It was needed, yes, but she had enjoyed the approbation of the masses too much. She had delighted in hearing herself called mother of the empire. And what was that but a title she had commanded her people to use? No, the truth was she had been wasting time, wasting power.

Such neglect was completely and utterly unforgivable. She swore that she would never be that weak again. It amazed her that she had let slip so much of the strength that had helped her grasp power and steer the Known World out of Aliver's war and back toward prosperity. She had now to remember the person who had climbed to the throne nine years ago. She had to be that person again, tempered by experience, mother to a child whom she would never, never let come to harm.

Part of this included determining the real extent of the threat coming toward them. Trust the league's version of events? Hardly. Sire Dagon could profess his complete and utter honesty until he went hoarse; she needed to hear from other sources before she could decide how to act. Dream travel seemed the only possible way. It was, at least, worth a try.

The first time she planned to attempt it, she dismissed her servants and prepared her room herself. She dimmed the lamps. She lit sticks of incense and set a mixture of soothing herbs bubbling in fragrant, citrus-infused oil. She put on a formal dinner dress of dark green velvet, with a high neckline and full sleeves. Lying on her back atop her bedspread, she smoothed the folds of her dress out around her, feeling unnervingly silly. Did one dream travel in one's garments, naked, or without a body at all? She did not know if any of her preparations were necessary, but she needed some sense of ritual, something to occupy her as she gradually drew nearer the moment.

And what to do in that moment was another riddle she had yet to solve. However Hanish had dream traveled, he managed it without true knowledge of the Giver's tongue. Perhaps he used some fragment of it. Or perhaps his success had a different explanation. Corinn had consulted *The Song of Elenet* with this question in mind. As ever, the words and music of the book had surged up to engulf her. As ever, she closed it, knowing she had learned from it but incapable of putting her finger on the knowledge and examining it.

She slept for a time, a fitful slumber in which she counted the passing hours. Eventually, awake again, she just lay, calming her heartbeat, letting her body go limp against the bedding. She allowed herself to drift toward sleep again. She focused her attention on her breathing. No, on the awareness that her thoughts were a thing different from her body. Housed in it, yes, but not contained. Not trapped. She imagined her true essence floating up from her body and—

Ah! That did not work. She lifted her fist and smashed it against the mattress in exasperation. She sat up. This was not the way. It felt like something a fortune reader would instruct her to do. Some nonsense, like when she pretended to be able to read symbols in her girlfriend's mind as a child.

Use the song, she thought. It all begins with the song.

She fell back against the bed, inhaled, called up the swirling music that was the Giver's tongue, and, very softly, sang. She did not entirely understand the notes and words and shapes of sound that came from her mouth, but she knew the intent was right. She wove them in with her hopes, with the preparations she had already made. Trying to shape them even as she felt shaped by the song escaping her, she lost herself in the effort.

At some point, she realized the song was not on her lips anymore. It was in her. It was her and would travel with her. She pushed her spirit up and out of her body, floating free above the bed and then through the ceiling and beyond. For a time she swam through air above the palace. Such a strange feeling. She had an awareness of her physical form, but she also knew how very incorporeal it was. Part of her lashed at the air with limbs that were not entirely there but that were not entirely absent. Ultimately, it was thought, not physical effort, that moved her through space. More than thought, it was thought propelled by force of will.

For some time she flew from point to point above the palace, slowly learning to feel the presence of souls, sleeping and awake. She found she could draw herself to some individuals simply by settling thoughts of them in her mind and then driving toward them. Thus, she felt Rhrenna's sleeping presence and Aaden's. She knew the bed in which Delivegu slumbered, not alone. Any of these she could have stirred awake, but they were not her objective. She aimed for a person much, much farther away: Dariel.

She conjured every memory she had of him. She held her thoughts of him until she had them within her, contained like the seething balls of creation from which she built the creatures she summoned for Aaden's amusement. The song helped her. It gave shape to what she wished to do. She took that swirling embodiment of memories and thoughts and images and emotions that to her were Dariel, and then she hurled them forward.

It was like tossing a great ball of energy, a thing that hungered to be released. She sped behind, hooked to it, shooting forward across the Inner Sea. Oh, it felt good! Such speed. She watched Acacia recede as she passed between Kidnaban and the Cape of Fallon. Before long, the mountains of Senival rumbled beneath her, as if they were a herd of stampeding creatures. Wonderful. Such power and freedom. She raced across the coast and farther until . . .

She forgot what she was doing. Her progress slowed. For a few moments she felt the force that had been pulling her casting about in one and then another direction. Then it simply stopped. In a spirit form, immune to the cold or fear, Corinn hung in the air high above the Gray Slopes. Below her, the ocean moved in unending undulation. Watching it, she knew the waves gave life to all the earth. She knew, looking down, that there could be no more horrible thing than a dead sea. It meant a dead earth.

But why am I thinking that? I'm here for a reason. I'm searching for—

Her eyes snapped open. She gasped a breath so loud she thought for a moment that she screamed it out. Sitting up on her bed, in her gown, the air heavy with incense smoke, she realized she had failed. Dariel! She had been flying toward Dariel, driven by her thoughts of him, scorching toward whatever place or fate in the world identified him . . . but then the energy that propelled her realized it did not know where to go. She should have been able to find him, but there was no scent, no trail, not even an intuitive feeling for where to head. At some point, there was nothing. That was why she had stopped somewhere out above the Slopes. If her brother was out there, she had no power to find him.

"Dariel," she said. In speaking his name she felt a strange, dread certainty that she would never see him again, neither in life nor through the song.

The following day passed much the same as the one that preceded it. One appointment after another. One function before another. Her last official meeting that afternoon was with Paddel, the head vintner of Prios. She kept it short, not wanting to look too long at his heavily jowled, red-cheeked face. He sat at the far end of the table from her, as unattractive as ever, squeezed into a black jacket that was so tight he could barely move his chubby arms. She did not sit through all of his fawning, praise-laden greeting.

"Since last we spoke, have the trials of the vintage continued to go well?"

"Yes, of course! Better than well. See here, the reports—" He fumbled with his papers, rising to bring them to her.

"Just tell me this," Corinn said. She signaled with disdainful fingers that he should stay seated. "It works as efficiently as you thought before? It lifts their spirits, gives them a feeling of bliss, and yet does not dull minds?"

"Quite so. One might almost say it sharpens—"

"And once they taste it, they will forever crave it?" The man nodded vigorously. "What happens if they are deprived of it?"

"There's no reason that they should be deprived of it. We have vast stockpiles of the raw ingredients. We have enough to last us until we win or lose the coming struggle."

"That's good. But, again, what happens when they are deprived of it? You said before that they will do anything to get it—but if they cannot get it, what happens to them? How long until they recover?"

The nodding stopped. Paddel's mouth puckered, a stupid expression that Corinn wanted to slap away. "I don't know. We didn't deprive any indefinitely. They were so"—he grinned and lifted his shoulders, a gesture meant to indicate that surely she understood this point—"insistent and so pleased when they had access to it again. Why deprive them?"

The scowl on Corinn's face stayed constant. That annoys me, Paddel, she said to herself. *You should have researched this area instead of taking so much personal pleasure from it.* It was too late now to conduct more tests. She had waited too long already. Let it be done.

"Send word to your people," she said. "Release the vintage."

"Yes?" he asked, excited, his mouth now like that of a dog panting in expectation. "Do you mean it?"

"I just said it, so obviously I mean it. How quickly can you distribute it?"

"Oh, quickly indeed. The main warehouse is in Prios, of course, but in preparation for your order we've shifted stock to Danos, Alecia, Bocoum. We even had a storage facility in Denben. We can send word by messenger bird and have crates riding south toward interior Talay by tomorrow evening. And across west to Tabith, which will give us the entire Slopes coastline!" The possibilities took his breath away. He stammered on for a time, and then, realizing something, looked at Corinn with new admiration. "You are so wise to have arranged this, Your Majesty."

She showed no pleasure in the compliment. Instead, she flicked her fingers to indicate that he should leave. Before he reached the door, she stopped him. "One final thing. Do conduct the test. When one is addicted and is deprived indefinitely, what happens? Find out."

Later, in her offices with Rhrenna, Corinn closed out the day's business. The Meinish woman read from the meticulous notes she kept, detailing a variety of points achieved and yet to be faced on the morrow. Listening to her voice soothed Corinn. Much of what she said, conversely, did not. "Wren has petitioned for an audience with you. I told her the timing was ill but said I would put the request to you."

"Wren . . ." Corinn exhaled. Dariel's concubine. Pregnant

and growing plumper every day. Though Corinn avoided speaking to her, she caught glimpses of the girl often enough. Her narrow eyes always seemed to be waiting for Corinn, fixed on her before she had realized they were going to make eye contact. She was pretty, indeed. A northern Candovian. One of those slim, athletic women upon whom a baby is but a shapely bump that adds to her attractiveness, a moon to be caressed. "I can't see her now. She'd likely ask me to acknowledge her child as Dariel's."

"It is Dariel's."

"Yes, but I'm not at all sure that I want to declare that right now. Tell her I'm too busy. If she likes, she could retire to Calfa Ven. I'll send physicians. She could have the baby there, in peaceful seclusion."

"I already felt her out about that, Your Majesty. She would rather be here in the palace."

"Fine," Corinn said a little coldly, as she wanted to close the subject, "but she'll have to wait for an audience."

Rhrenna nodded and noted this on her documents. Watching her down-tilted face, Corinn remembered that she once thought Meinish women uniformly bland of appearance. Too pale, thin-skinned, with finely drawn features that had a coldness in keeping with their frigid nation. At the time she had thought it ironic considering that the men of the same race had been striking, especially Hanish . . . Looking at Rhrenna now, she realized that her feelings about Meinish women had never been accurate. Yes, their features were as described, but they had their own style of beauty. What had kept her from seeing it was jealousy. Fear that Hanish might one day choose one of his own over her.

Forgetting the annoyance of a moment before, Corinn acknowledged a very different emotion instead. "Rhrenna, I'm sorry."

The secretary looked up and studied her. "For what?"

Was this folly? To admit a crime and wish it otherwise?

No, she did not think so. "For what I did to your people."

"Oh." Rhrenna cleared her throat, looked back at the documents. "We weren't innocents."

"I know. You knew all the time, didn't you? All the time that we rode together and I showed you the ways of court and we were young together—all through that time you knew that Hanish might one day sacrifice me to the Tunishnevre."

Rhrenna drew in on herself. She pulled her gaze in, head down as she stared at the papers on her lap. Her blond hair fell around her. "I never wanted that to happen."

"But you knew it might. I'm not chastising you. You are closer to me now than my sister is. Perhaps I love the blood you share with Hanish. Maybe that's why I feel so close to you. For some reason, I know that the fact that you would have betrayed me then means that you won't now. Or ever again. Am I right?"

The young woman's head bobbed. "You are right."

"I know it," Corinn said. She folded her hands in her lap and inhaled a long breath. Something about doing so made her feel she had sucked in Rhrenna's promise and owned it. "When this is over and we're at peace again, I will lift the ban on entering Mein Tahalian. There's no reason it shouldn't be opened again, lived in again. There's every reason it should, actually. If I did that, would it please you?"

Rhrenna sat as if she were still studying the pages before her, but her gaze had drifted off slightly, unfocused. "I don't think I could live there again. Maybe if I lived to old age I'd return, but I'm not sure. I think some others would, though. I know some want that very much. It wouldn't be the same, of course. There are too few of us left, but I know some Mein who would take their families back to Tahalian. Even their mixed families. They'd pry off the beams that seal it, open the steam valves, and heat the place. It could never be the same, but it would be good for life to fill the place again. I would like to believe that an entire culture can't just be forgotten."

This time it was Corinn who took a while to respond. Though she had begun the conversation, it surprised Corinn to realize that Rhrenna had truly thought about this before. She had even spoken to other Mein about it. A culture forgotten? What a strange idea. To Corinn it had always been the opposite. She had feared the world would remember the Mein too well, feared that they might yet have some power, some way to shape the world. Hanish so often haunted her thoughts. How could he not when he so clearly lived on in Aaden? The Mein—in her own mind, at least—were far from being forgotten. That had seemed a problem before. Now, however, she sometimes wished she had not ordered Hanish killed. Perhaps there could have been some way for them to live together. What a powerful pair they would have been! Rulers for the ages.

Outside, a bone whistle announced the advancing hour. Other flutists and pipers picked up the melody and spread it down from the palace toward the lower town. Corinn listened until the music faded into the distance, reminded by it just how tired she was. "Rhrenna," she said, "I am not going to destroy it all. You believe that, don't you?"

The answer came back to her with welcome speed. "Yes, Your Majesty, I believe that."

That night, after visiting Aaden and singing healing into his sleeping form, Corinn tried to dream travel again. She waited even later than the night previous, and she aimed for a different target this time. Dariel might not be reachable. Maybe dead, or perhaps the connection would never snap tight between them. She tried not to think too much about it. *Think only until you know what to do. Then act.* This time, when her spirit lifted and pulled free of the shell of her body and began the long flight through the dark night, it was another man's name she screamed out before her, racing behind it. This one, surprisingly easily, she found.

Her feet did not exactly touch the floor in the room, but she did reach stillness at the foot of a sleeping man's bed. His face was hidden beneath a cushion, his arms thrown wide. He looked like a man recently suffocated, but the nasal grinding of his breathing testified to his continued life.

"Wake," she said.

A form rolled in the sheets and then settled, still again. Nothing more.

"Wake!"

Corinn instilled all her will in the command, and this time a shape pulled away from the physical form hidden beneath the blankets. She could not have said whether the image was clothed or naked—no more than she could have detailed the same about herself. He simply was as he was. Many details of his form blurred, were unsteady, or translucent. At the same time, other identifying features showed clear. Thin shoulders. Bewildered. Muffled and ill at ease in a way that would have been expressed by disheveled hair on a physical body but was now a part of the impression of the spirit. His face, droopy and dull eyed, was just as she remembered, just as gape mouthed. How bizarre that she could reach around the world in spirit form and still find Rialus Neptos to be . . . well, Rialus Neptos.

"Queen Corinn?" he asked.

She did not answer. She looked around the room. She could not have said what she would have expected, but a grand bed was not part of it. Nor a chamber with finely constructed furniture, wall hangings, rugs so thick they must suck at the toes of one walking across them. Rialus had no finer quarters in Acacia!

Her eyes settled back on him. "This I find very strange," she said.

His head snapped around from side to side, taking in the same sights she just had at double the speed. "This is—ah— difficult to explain."

Corinn wanted to ask him to do so, but she knew her

connection with him could not last long. She already felt the fatigue of being so far from her body. Felt the pull back toward it, and knew that it would grow stronger with each passing moment. And she knew somehow that she was in danger like this. If anything—or anybody—snipped the long thread that connected her to her corporeal self, she could be lost forever. Dead, even if her body lived for a time in a long sleep.

"Rialus Neptos," she said, cutting into his stammering explanation, wanting to be direct and calm so that he would be as well, "is Dariel alive?"

"Dariel? Ah—"

"Just answer each question I ask you. Do no more or less. Just answer. Is Dariel alive?"

"I don't know." Rialus thought for a moment. "I—don't think so. There was a terrible battle at—"

"You can tell me nothing of him?"

"No. I wish I could, but—"

Corinn flared with impatience. She realized from Rialus's expression and from how the room snapped into greater focus that the intensity of her emotions showed. She had his attention again, waiting. "Are the Auldek planning to attack the Known World?"

"How did you know that?"

"Answer!"

"Yes," Rialus said. "Yes. They're brutes, Your Majesty. Not like the Numrek. I mean, not really. They're more . . . dignified. Do you know they keep beasts like white lions in their palaces? Just let them walk around like they own—"

"Rialus, in the Giver's name, do no more than answer my questions!" She gave him a moment of staring intensity to come to terms with this, and then asked, "How great a threat are they?"

"Very, I'd say."

"They have a large army?"

"Yes, but it's not just size that matters. They have some terrible creatures. Antoks and things worse. And the Auldek cannot be killed."

"Cannot be killed?"

"Well, not exactly 'cannot.'" He fumbled for a way to explain it, and then seemed puzzled that he was even doing so. Looking at her anew, he asked, "Am I really talking to you? This is so odd."

Corinn flared brighter than ever. "Let me see their army."

"What do you mean?"

"Think it. Make a picture of the things you have seen and things you imagine you will see. Make all those things in your mind's eye and I will take them from you."

He did, and she did. The images were blurry, shadowed, overlapping, and without context or explanation. But she saw vast numbers of soldiers in animal guise. She saw beings similar to Numrek being chopped down and then rising again and again, as if impervious to mortal injury. She saw the ranks of an army of men and creatures, giants and winged things. She saw tramping feet and hulking forms unlike anything in the Known World. She heard the bellowing of angry beasts and rhythmic chants of war songs. So many of them that they faded into shadow in the distance, like a never-ending parade of demons finally escaped from entrapment and hungry for plunder. It was all that she needed to see.

"One more thing, Rialus Neptos," she said, once she had drawn back and could speak again. "Have you betrayed us?"

The man could hardly have conveyed as much shocked indignation with his real body as he did with contortions of his spirit face. "No! Never!"

"You must prove the truth of that. If you have any honor, Rialus Neptos, you will find a way to serve me. If you wish to see your wife again, you will find a way to serve me. Understand?" Corinn asked the question, but she did not manage to stay long enough to hear his answer. She could no longer resist the call back to her body.

Early the next morning, Corinn summoned her secretary. She instructed her to have Rialus's wife, Gurta, sent to Calfa Ven for the duration of the coming conflict. "Put her under my royal protection."

"Ah, so she's a prisoner," Rhrenna said. "She is heavily pregnant, you know, but I'll arrange for her every comfort."

Corinn then called in a bevy of scribes and told them to prepare a dispatch for transport by bird. She spoke a message to be sent to the governors and chief officials of each province, to the Senate in Alecia, and to a host of other important figures who needed to hear the news first. She confirmed the truth of the league's claim. An enemy—the Auldek—did march against them, bringing with them horrible creatures and an army in the tens of thousands. Among them were many quota children—warriors now and with hearts hardened against Acacia. They were the greatest threat the Known World had ever faced. If they did not unite and defeat them, all would perish. Battle against the Numrek was, in comparison, just a diversion.

"Prepare your people." She paused, looking over the bent heads of the scribes, listening to the scratch of so many styluses against parchment.

A few of them completed writing and lifted their tools. Rhrenna asked, "Is that all of it?"

Corinn shook her head, waited until all the scribes were ready for more. "Tell your people," she said, "that the Law of Quota, which has been in effect since Tinhadin's time, is now revoked. As of today, no more children of the Known World will be sent to the Other Lands. Let the people know this. Invite them to drink the vintage of Prios in celebration. Hear me again. The quota is abolished."

Chapter Forty-six

Kelis kept thinking he should dig for knuckle root. His eyes scanned the dry land for the tiny shrubs that marked them. Surely, they needed to suck the moisture from knuckle root. How else could they survive? He stood in the mornings, sniffing the moving air for moisture, for any indication that water lay more in one direction than another. Nor could he help but tilt his head and listen to any animal sound, a call at night, a scurrying nearby. Several times, he caught mice with his hand net. Only as he looked into their trembling, frantic eyes, did he realize he had no desire, no need, to eat them. Once, he went so far as to skin a sand snake, dry the meat with the heat of the sun. And then he sat disgusted by it, knowing that neither he, Naamen, nor Benabe could stomach such fare.

This must be Santoth magic, he thought. Nothing else explains it.

Almost four weeks since Shen and Leeka had disappeared. He knew because he had counted the days. He had, right? He had scratched the growing number on the dry skin of the back of his hand. Twenty-eight days, but it felt much longer. It might have been an entire lifetime. He might be ancient now. Everything in the Known World might have changed, be unrecognizable. Or, for that matter, he and the two souls with him might be the only people left on the curve of creation. Everything else seemed so distant and clouded by time and blurred, unreal. Even events he knew himself to have been a part of struck him as mythic. Hunting foulthings with Princess Mena Akaran? Watching Aliver Akaran dance to his death with Maeander Mein? Standing in awe as sorcerers screamed rents into the land, dropped worms from the sky, and blasted men into vapor?

"Kelis?" A hand gripped his shoulder and shook him. Naamen leaning down before him, looking close into his face, his kindly eyes so tired now. "Are you with us?" He did not wait for an answer. "We should not let Benabe sit alone too long. She speaks to herself."

"Ah . . ." She speaks to herself. He had heard those words before. Naamen had said them before this, and he had responded to them in a certain way. It was a game between them, a way to keep sane by joking about insanity. What had he said? "So do you."

Naamen smiled. That was what he wanted to hear. "No, I speak to the winged goat and the boy with cat eyes and my long-dead mother. That's different."

"Of course," Kelis said, rising to his feet. "My error." He draped an arm around the other man's shoulder and together they walked toward the woman who had become the center of their lives.

Right after Shen disappeared, Benabe had been frantic. Her wail became a scream of rage and loss. She ran into the space that the swirling shapes had occupied, her arms flailing as if she had hooks on them that she was desperate to sink into flesh. For a moment, as she lashed the air, Kelis almost believed the power of her fury could tear through into whatever realm the shapes had escaped to. But she did not, and the moment passed, and eventually Benabe lowered her arms and stood panting.

Kelis called her. Her eyes, when she looked at him, were burning with anger. The hatred she had just directed at the air she turned on him. She battered him back and then down to one knee, asking him over and over why he had brought them here? Why hadn't he protected Shen? Why had he let that madman take her daughter? Why? She would have hurt him if Naamen had not gripped her—with strong and weak arm both—and pulled her away.

By the next day, however, Benabe made use of her anger. Instead of directing it at Kelis, she organized the manner in which they were to search for Shen. The first week they took turns marching in daylong treks. One of them always stayed at the exact site from which Shen had disappeared, while the other two walked out in different directions, calling her name into the dead, silent expanse around them. Though Kelis had lived in Talay almost all his life and had explored much of the dry expanse of the continent, he had never seen a land so empty of life before. Yes, there were beings out there, hiding, like the few small animals he caught, but the effect of the place was to highlight how vast—and how vastly empty—it was.

He knew that there was an end to the southern reaches of Talay. Of course there was. Ships sailed the turbulent waters below it and came back north. Dariel had done that; league vessels made the journey regularly. He knew this, but standing on the flat expanse, staring south, Kelis saw nothing, nothing, nothing, but a parched skin stretching to the horizon and promising more of the same beyond. If the Santoth had her, they had taken her to a place he could not see or hear or reach. He tried to remember the things Aliver had told him of the ancient sorcerers, but he could recall so little.

Sometime in the second week Benabe's grief shifted form. Instead of driving her to action, it exhausted her. She sat still throughout much of the day, staring into the empty space before her with glazed eyes. On occasion she shot to her feet, casting about, asking whoever was with her if he had heard Shen. Had they heard her? She ran out in one direction, calling Shen, only to turn back a moment later and run the other way, tracing loop after loop until Kelis or Naamen grabbed her.

Then she dropped back to the ground, sobbing, mumbling that she had heard her daughter's voice.

Kelis and Naamen took turns sitting with her as the other continued searching. Neither found any sign of the girl at all. Their own footprints crosshatched the sand for miles around them, testifying to their efforts. Never did they find a print of anyone else.

In the third week Benabe began speaking to herself. She had very little to say to her two companions, but she held long discourses. She spoke in words, yes, in sentences. But they did not add one on to another to form anything that he could make sense of.

About the only time he did understand her was when he stepped too close and she said, "Move your shadow," as she did on the morning that Naamen woke him from his own circular knot of thoughts.

Kelis, realizing he had broken one of the rules of their scant interaction, sidestepped so that his shadow did not fall across any part of her body. At least this had not changed. At least she remained aware enough of the world to notice the change in the light caused by his presence. That was something.

"Should we take her north?" Naamen asked a little later. The two men stood a short distance from her, whispering. "We can't stay here, can we? We'll die here. I want Shen back, too, but nothing that we've done shows that we can find her. We don't have the power. We should get Benabe back to Bocoum before she loses her mind completely."

"It's her decision to make," Kelis said. "We can't take her against her will. If she wishes, it's her right to die here."

The man rubbed his stunted arm with the palm of his normal one. "What of my rights?" he asked but then hurried to explain away anything callous in the question. "I don't wish her ill. I so badly want to have Shen back, to have Benabe back as she was. I would do anything to make that happen, but days and days pass and we're powerless."

"The Santoth would not have taken her without a reason."

"And what if that reason is evil? How can we know they didn't lure her here just to—"

"Don't," Kelis cautioned. "Say those words and Benabe will hear them." Both men looked at her, sitting as she had been before, mouth moving. "Naamen, there's no reason for you to stay. Go north. Tell Sangae what's happened."

Naamen wrinkled his lips and said, with a resignation touched by humor, "I don't think so. If you're staying, I'm staying. I want to make sure you get through this. You promised a good race after all this is over. I'm going to hold you to it."

So the two stayed on into a fourth week, passing the days much as before. They did not range quite so far anymore, but they waited and kept their shadows from falling on Benabe. And waited some more.

And then came the morning when Kelis's eyes fluttered open to take in a predawn sky. The heavens were a dark shade just the purple side of black, alive with stars to the west, slightly yellowed by the coming sun to the east. Lovely. And quiet. No hyenas cackling or lizards scurrying, no bird or insect calls, certainly not a sound from another human being. Just a sublime, forgiving stillness. He lay like that for some time, watching, feeling more relaxed than he had in days and days. Only very, very gradually did he realize that the touch of small hands on his was part of what was soothing him. And, after that realization, some moments more passed before it occurred to him to wonder how this could be. Who was holding his hand? He turned to look.

A young girl sat beside him, watching him, his hand clasped in her lap. "Hi," the girl said. She smiled. Shen.

"What's happening? Tell me I'm not dreaming."

"You're not dreaming," the girl said.

And, no, he wasn't. That became clear. He had not felt so

543

clearheaded in weeks. He stared at the girl, studying her features. Her skin right there before him, her round face and thoughtful eyes. "It was kind of you to wait here," she said. Her words were alive in the air between them, clear as they ever had been during their long march down into the far south. He felt the breath of them on his face, as he felt the warmth of her hands, the moisture where their skin touched. "I thought we might have to search for you."

"Your mother would not leave," he heard himself say. "She said you would return, and if she was not here for you, she would not forgive herself."

Shen smiled again. "I tried to speak to her sometimes, but it didn't work well. I think I just made her upset. I didn't mean to, though. She's a good mother. I told the Santoth that, didn't I, Leeka?"

As soon as the name was out, Kelis saw a shape standing a little distance away, a lurking shadow that made him quickly sit up. It had not been there a second before. Shen stopped him from rising farther, and in the pause he realized it was Leeka Alain, clothed just as before, head cloaked and just as eerily still. Had she called him into existence just by saying his name?

The hooded figure nodded, his voice a whisper that came from the blackness where his face should be. "You did."

"Kelis, don't be frightened of him. It's just Leeka. He only looks scary." Shen patted his hand. "How long has it been? How long have you been waiting?"

"A few weeks. No, a month. One month today."

The girl nodded, face grave suddenly. "We must hurry, then. Time is short. I should explain to you, so that you'll know and not be frightened, and so that you can help me explain to my mother, so that she won't be frightened. Naamen, too. He will come with us also. I want you to hear first, though. All right?"

Kelis nodded.

"Good. Are you ready? Don't be afraid. The Santoth are

here with me. Look." She cocked her head just enough to indicate a vague area over her left shoulder.

Just as with Leeka, the beings she named snapped into existence. Kelis did not see them materialize: they were just there when they had not been a moment before. The figures stood bunched together: hooded, vague shapes that the rising sun cast in highlight and shadow. Seeing them, Kelis felt his heart pound. They looked like an army of assassins, standing immobile and yet shifting even in their stillness, not entirely of this world. He tried to number them, but he lost count each time. Numbers did not seem to stick to them. Not so many; not so few. Oh, why did they just stand there? He would have said they were waiting for something, but waiting was not the right word. They were eating each moment, impatient. They pulsed with energy contained through force of will. They were hungry, and—Kelis knew—they would not wait long.

"What do they want?" he asked.

Shen stared at them as well, though her expression was calm, lips puckered in an almost wistful expression. "They asked me to release them from exile," she said. "And I did."

"You . . . could do that?"

The girl smiled. "Yes, silly. They asked me the same thing. They thought I had to be a boy to do it, but they were wrong."

"Shen, what do they want? They are danger, Shen. They were exiled for horrible—"

"I know. They showed me. I saw it all. Those things that happened long ago—with Tinhadin—it wasn't like the old tales say. I saw it and it's . . . different." She frowned, exhaled through her nose, looking so very adult and so childlike at the same time. The words to continue seemed hard for her to find. Touching her fingers to her forehead, she said, "They put the knowledge in my head. I can't explain it all to you right now, but the important thing is that we need them back in the world. You know *The Song of Elenet*? The Santoth know when it's being read. They can feel it. For many, many lifetimes it went unread. It was silent to them. They feared it was lost. Even my father could not find it. But that was before. It's been found, Kelis. Someone has been reading it, studying it, for the last few years. For all the years of my life. You know who, yes? My aunt, Queen Corinn."

"I saw the canals she filled with water in Bocoum. Heard tales of the things."

"Yes, that's part of the problem. She is doing things without understanding the consequences."

"Consequences?" The word—and the yawning things it might mean—seemed too big for her small mouth. "What consequences? Like the foulthings?"

Looking slightly impatient, Shen glanced back at the Santoth, signed to them with her hands, then turned back to Kelis. "They want us to start moving. They know how slow we are. I can't tell it all to you. Some things I don't have words for. Yes, the foulthings are part of it. The Santoth made those themselves, and they regret it. But they say the beasts are nothing compared to the curses Corinn could unleash. Every time she takes from one place and puts in another place, she leaves a scar between the two. Others of the song can use those scars to enter the living world."

"Others of the song?"

"Kelis," Shen said, placing a hand on his shoulder like a mother might to a child, "the Santoth weren't the only sorcerers ever thrown down or banished. There were others. There were evil ones like the Five Disciples of Reelos. There were early mistakes of Elenet. There are sorcerers from other worlds the Giver created. Some of them—especially if they put their ears to the scars—can hear Corinn's singing, too. Some of them have already begun speaking to her, gaining strength from her. She may not even know it, but the Santoth believe she has opened doors. It is only a matter of time before things step through those doors into this world. That's why we must go to Acacia, speak to my aunt, let the Santoth study the book, and prepare to face whatever is coming."

Shen exhaled. "I think that's enough for now. Are you ready? It's a long walk."

Kelis could not imagine what to say. Better that he be practical. "We should wake your mother and Naamen."

"She's not going to like this," Shen said, speaking through a crooked grin. She pushed herself to her feet, looking over at her mother's form, wrapped tight in a blanket. "I'll wake her with a kiss. That will be nice, won't it?"

He nodded and watched the girl walk away, again revealing herself to be the child she was, light on her feet and small, so small. But what was in store for her?

A little distance away, Leeka stood immobile, face hidden, though his body turned to follow the child. And a little farther, when Kelis swung his gaze toward them, were the sorcerers, immobile and yet seething with motion, watching them all. Impatient.

Chapter Forty-seven

Mena found the note beside her on the bed when she awoke. Seeing the square of paper, she knew exactly what it was, and the knowledge twisted her heart. Melio . . . It meant he was gone, probably afloat already on one of the early transports sailing from Acacia for the Teh Coast. A cruel trick, for he had given no sign that he would leave her like this when they spoke last night, nor when they made love just hours ago. He had said not a word when she yet again washed herself clean of his seed. Or perhaps he had.

The night before, naked against him, still breathing hard from the conclusion of their lovemaking, she spoke as if it were just another night. True, she did touch on the bizarre realities of their life, but these were topics they turned over many times.

"All this that we're doing," she had said, "in so many ways, it feels unreal. I live it, yes. I do it. I slay monsters and ride a winged lizard and lead armies to battle . . . It's strange, though, when I step back and imagine how others will hear this story. That's what it is, you know? It's a tale from the distant past. It's Edifus and Tinhadin. It's Hauchmeinish. It's the Forms before they were Forms. How is my killing Maeben or slaying the foulthings any more probable than the Priest of Adaval slaying the wolf-headed guards of the rebellious cult of Andar?"

"There were twenty wolf-headed guards, for one thing. You had much safer odds."

Mena nudged him. "Be serious."

"Even if people forget the Priest of Adaval, they will not forget Mena Akaran. Not Maeben. Not the slayer who flies with beauty. Not the warrior princess who beat back the savage Numrek. Such things can't be forgotten."

Had they said more? Yes, she believed they had. Strange, though, that they had managed to speak of mundane things. She had described a dream she had had in her childhood, one in which she and a girl had tried to catch fish with nets. He had claimed he never dreamed, saying life was strange enough for him by far. They had talked nonsense about which were worse, the bites from mosquitoes in Senival or those of the black flies of the Aushenian spring.

At some point, Mena had rolled away from him and, without thought, out of habit, really, went to perform the brief ritual of cleaning her sex and washing away his seed with the herb mixture he so hated. Perhaps it was at that moment that he parted with her. For, when she slipped back into bed, he turned away without comment or protest. His breathing had been steady, though not yet that of sleep, and she had chosen to wrap an arm around him and hook her ankle over his and share the silence. That silence, though, may have been different to him than it was to her.

The note she held pinched between the fingers of her two hands testified to that.

M,
You were right about everything, of course.
I was slow to learn, but I know it now,
M.

She knew the words by heart, for she had written them to Melio almost ten years earlier. It was the note she had written him. And below it, the same postscript:

549

I love you.
If ever the world allows it I'll prove it to you.

Exactly what she had written just after returning from killing Maeben on Uvumal and just before she gave herself up to Maeander Mein. On that occasion, she could not face saying good-bye to Melio. There was too much uncertainty before her, everything in the world at risk, and she had not been sure that she would be able to face it if he asked her not to. She penned the letter and set it beside him and snuck away on silent feet. Cowardly in many ways. Hurtful in others. And yet the things she wrote to him were completely true. He had been right; she had been slow; she did love him and wanted to prove it someday.

How to interpret this newer version of the same? Was he making the same promises to her? No, because he had no need to prove himself. He had never failed her in any way. Or was he reminding her of the things she once promised and had failed, thus far, to deliver? Yes, she thought so. There was only one thing more she could have done to prove her love to him, and she had held off doing it year after year after year. She deserved to be reminded of it. If it really was meant to remind her of her note to him, she understood; and if the world allowed her another chance, she would not fail to give her all to him. She would prove her faith in him, if not in the goodness of the world.

If that was her refrain for the morning, by the afternoon she had taken on another. *She's only my sister*, Mena told herself time and time again. *I don't fear my sister.*

The fact that she repeated this a hundred times as she walked to answer Corinn's summons rather belied the assertion. When Mena entered her office, Corinn stood behind the chart table, studying the array of maps and documents displayed there. She looked up, distracted for a moment, and then calmed her features. "Mena, I'm sorry that

Melio has had to leave. I know that must be hard for you."

Mena cleared her throat, finding the opening kindness somewhat disconcerting. "Thank you," she said.

"We are coming to times of great sacrifice," Corinn said. "Much will be asked of all of us. Much taken from each of us. You may believe, though, that Melio will be in my prayers just as much as you are, Sister, just as much as Dariel is." Corinn did not give Mena time to fumble through a response to that. She came around the table, but instead of approaching Mena she moved off to the side slightly, stopping beside another table. "I want you to have this. The King's Trust. It is your blade now. No one deserves it more than you."

The King's Trust? She did not know whether she wanted that blade. Too ancient. Too much history tempered in blood. If the legends of it were true, Tinhadin himself had infused it with Santoth sorcery, making it a blade that learned from each contest it fought and took something from each person it killed. Hadn't Tinhadin's grandson used it to execute prisoners? Something he wished to do personally and with only this sword.

"I have a blade," Mena said.

"Your Marah sword is special to you, I know," Corinn acknowledged. "I know well the tale of how you crawled out of the sea with it strapped to your wrist and became that bird god of yours, Maeben. And, true, perhaps the blade is a blessing to you. You've certainly accomplished much with it. But this"— she motioned as if to direct Mena's attention to the ancient sword, something she did not need to do because her eyes were already fixed on it—"this is the very blade that Edifus wielded with his own hand at Carni. It's stained with his blood. Look there on the hilt. That blackened area: that is the blood of the king's hand. I'm sure you know the details better than I—how he almost lost his hand when he caught a foe's blade pinched in his grip."

Mena's fingers itched. A real physical sensation. Of their

own accord, they wanted to wrap around the stained hilt and slip the blade free. That's what her body cried to do. She held back. She put one hand to her chest, felt for the eel pendant beneath the fabric of her shirt. She pressed it. There must be awful power in this sword, for the look of it was nothing special. Old, battered, within a simple scabbard with few ornaments, and yet something in her so wanted to pull the blade free.

The last time she had touched that blade was in the hours after Aliver's death. She had picked it up only long enough to wrap it in a burlap cloth and stow it snugly with the king's possessions. When next she spoke of it, she gave other soldiers instructions on how to care for it and return it to Acacia safely. Since then, she had had no wish to handle it again.

"Why do you stand there gaping at it?" Corinn asked, a touch of annoyance in her voice. "It's a great gift. It's mine to give, and I offer it to you as a demonstration of my faith in you. You are worthy of it. Pick it up."

This last was an order, no other way to interpret the tone. Despite herself, Mena grasped the scabbard midway down the hilt and lifted it, horizontal, before her.

"Do you accept it?"

"Yes," Mena said, and then specified, "for now. I'll take it into safekeeping, and use it if I must. One day, though, I'll return it to you, so that you can give it to Aaden. It's rightfully his."

That seemed to please Corinn. "Good. Yes, good on both counts." She nodded.

With that confirmation, Mena laid the sword down again.

"Now," Corinn said, sharpening the edge on her voice, "I give you this sword for a reason. You have a mission, Mena. I can trust it only to you. Even if our brother were with us, this task would go to you. You, more than Dariel, are the wrath that drives the Akaran sword hand. You will soon have to make use of it." She paused, looking frankly at Mena. "I would have used this language no matter what, but since seeing you fighting the Numrek I mean it with much more sincere certainty. Thank you for what you did, Mena. I had only heard of your feats. I believed in them, but I didn't understand them. Now I think I do, a little, at least."

Of all the many persons—generals and foot soldiers, Marah and warriors from around the provinces—who had praised her martial abilities, none had ever touched her with quite the sense of pride Corinn just did.

"I have received firsthand intelligence that the Auldek will begin their march during their own winter. They're timing it that way, so that even if they suffer in the early weeks they'll still have solid ice on which to cross the frozen seas above the Ice Fields. Comparing that with league reconnaissance, we estimate that if they are unchallenged they could arrive on the Mein Plateau by midsummer."

"That's so soon," Mena said.

"Yes. Too soon. Look at these charts with me." She motioned Mena nearer. When they stood side by side, Corinn drew her finger up along the western coast of the Known World, from the Lakelands north, along the Ice Fields, and beyond the boundary that had normally bordered Acacian maps. "I proposed a way to delay them. A small force could hold them for some time along the pass through which they will likely traverse from their lands into ours. It's a narrow strip of land, all of it mountainous. If they would sail, they could bypass it, but the Auldek fear the sea. So they'll have to thread their entire force through a series of narrow passes. It wouldn't be easy in any event, but I plan for us to make it very much harder indeed."

She is sending me to my death, Mena thought. For a moment she pondered whether that should offend her. Was it a bigger crime to send a sibling to her death, or did it show a sort of valor on her part?

"Perhaps you'll even repel them. Perhaps you'll decide the war right there in the far north. That would give the singers something to bray about, wouldn't it?"

Mena nodded. That's what her sister wanted her to do. That's what her queen expected of her, and—though she still didn't entirely understand—she felt powerless to deny her. What else could she do in the face of Corinn's certainty?

"We'll arrange a meeting tomorrow with all those on Acacia who can advise you, but you'll need to leave soon. Very soon. I've arranged a sloop for you leaving three days hence, to carry you first to Denben; then you'll go by land along the Tabith way. By the time you arrive there, your main generals will have gathered, and soon you'll head north. Your troops will mostly be Candovian, though I'm putting out a call for volunteers, with the promise of considerable rewards for those who accept. Maybe some of Dariel's raiders will join you. They're supposed to like a good fight, aren't they?" She smiled. "These are just sketches of the details. Tomorrow, you can ask all the specific questions you like and have them answered. I know how much I ask, but whom can I ask but she whom I trust most? Mena—Sister—Akaran, do you accept this mission?"

"Of course," Mena said. You've left me no choice, really, Corinn—Sister—Akaran.

"Wonderful!" Corinn said, smiling radiantly. "Make the brutes regret they ever left home. I know you will." She rounded the desk again, her fingers trailing over the papers there as she did. Thinking the meeting over, Mena turned to leave.

"By the way," Corinn asked, in a matter-of-fact tone, "what will you do with Elya while you are gone?"

"I don't know. As I said before, she is not built for war. I—"

Corinn interrupted her. "That's become clear to me. I hope you know that she is welcome to stay here. Nothing would make me happier, in fact."

Really? That Mena had not expected. "Really?"

"Of course." Corinn stepped around the desk and extended her hand, fingers beckoning. Unsure, Mena lifted one of her hands and let her sister grasp it. "She did save Aaden's life, after all. Mena, I was wary of her. The way you arrived—quite frightening, really. I thought she might hide some corruption just below the surface, but I've seen no sign of it at all. And she more than proved herself by what she did for Aaden. I may just grow to love her as you do. And Aaden, you know how he adores her. It would do him so much good to have her here to greet him when he awakes. One fine thing within all this madness. Do say that you'll let her stay here. She may reside in your courtyards, just as she has been doing."

Mena tried to think quickly through the possible implications of this. What about the eggs? She suspected they would not hatch for some time. She did not know this, but it felt that way. The eggs gave off an air of contentment, of peace, as Elya had when she stood watching, wide-eyed and trusting, as Mena gazed at them. She felt they would hatch when the time to hatch was right. Considering that, might it not be better to keep them secret longer? Corinn may have been struck with sudden fondness for her, but it was, as yet, a new fondness. Better that it grow more substantial. And it would. It will. If she lived weeks with Elya and saw her become more and more important to Aaden, well, then she would know for sure, and the eggs—or the hatchlings—would be welcomed as the blessings they would be.

Perhaps I'll even be back to see it happen. Let the Giver make that so.

"That sounds like it's for the best," Mena said. "Elya may follow me for a while when I first sail. She won't fully understand, but I'll explain what I can to her. I'm confident she will choose to stay in the palace."

A thought flickered across Corinn's face, but it disappeared so fast Mena could not read it. The queen said, "That would be perfect. That all sounds just perfect."

Chapter Forty-eight

Sire Dagon met the others of the League Council in a darkened chamber of the league compound in Alecia. A light distillation of green mist clouded the air, moving in ghostly swirls on the air currents. The first rank of leaguemen sat in a tight circle, each of them leaning back in an intricate reclining chair. Beyond the first ring there was a second, and a third, and beyond that the nonspeakers huddled close, listening. At meetings like this only the first three circles could speak freely, and they all did so without really seeing the others. It could take a long time between the asking of a question and an answer, especially as the group's mist-drenched state meant that they shared a certain linkage of thought. Their minds hummed like tuning forks that spread the same note among them. They had separate minds, yes, but it was—in the council chamber—impossible for any of them to deceive the others.

"Events did not proceed as we expected," Sire Dagon admitted. "Our intelligence about the Auldek was . . . partial. Flawed, I'm afraid."

An answering rumble of voices reverberated in the dim chamber of the League Council.

"You speak in understatement." Sire Grau's voice had an unusual clarity to it, a cadence untroubled by the tremulous effects of his advanced years. Dagon recognized what powered it: flames of anger stirred up from the slow embers that usually fueled him. "Neen saw what he wished to see, not the actual truth! He acted on what he wanted to believe, driven by emotion, blind to the flaws of his actions. Rarely has a leagueman made such grave mistakes."

Sire Grau sat beside Dagon in the first circle. Neither man looked at the other. Usually, the mist had a calming effect, enough so that they conducted all council business—no matter how fractious—with heavy-lidded calm. On this occasion Dagon felt an increased level of clarity in his own mind, calmed not at all by the unease surging through the chamber in waves. It had been many, many years since they met to discuss so many events not entirely in their control. For the younger among them, this marked the first such time.

Sire Faleen, though below Grau in authority, calmed them. As the Council Speaker, it fell to him to shape the direction of the meeting. Dagon did not mind at all that he turned it first toward Sire Neen's fiasco in Ushen Brae. He shared among them all he knew of what had happened, which was a great deal. They had probed the minds of the few Ishtat to return alive from the meeting with Devoth. No leagueman had made it out of that butcher's chamber, but the Ishtat minds housed images of the gore and at least fragments of the conversation preceding Neen's abrupt beheading. All agreed that he should have seen that coming. Devoth had betrayed his intentions by the way he moved his body and in the way his eyes darted about. Neen had been too flushed with dubious victory over the Lothan Aklun to see, too sure he held the world's wealth in his hand.

"Fool," more than one voice declared.

Faleen did not dispute the label. "Sire Neen made grave mistakes. He cost us dearly."

"Awkward the way he mishandled things," a voice in the second row said. "Should he be forgotten?"

A murmur of approval greeted this suggestion. "Yes. Yes. Let him be forgotten," several voices said at once.

The greatest enthusiasm was in the outer rows. Neen's demise would allow one of them quicker access to the inner circle. Dagon craned his head around just slightly and let his eyes cant farther from there, searching for the man who had proposed the forgetting. He spotted him. Lean faced, although with wide-set eyes that tilted downward at the outer edges. His name? Lethel. Sire Lethel. He was Neen's second cousin. So much for familial loyalty. Among the league, though, none would fault him for it. In truth, they all shared similar blood.

Sire El said, "He may be forgotten, but his errors should not be."

Grunts of affirmation. "Forget the man; remember the folly so as not to repeat it."

Dagon was not entirely sure how one could repeat the specifics of Neen's folly, but he let a low rumble build in his throat, his consent to the proposal.

"He is forgotten, then," Faleen said some time later, once it was clear that nobody objected.

That small measure passed quickly. What to do with Ushen Brae now that so much had changed took somewhat longer to work through. They turned the issue over for some time, exploring the possibilities, the problems, the likelihood of salvaging something of the once so very prosperous trade. The Auldek were abandoning Ushen Brae as they spoke. They would leave the continent peopled with many of their former—and infertile—slaves. Do they find a way to return to the old order? Or must they create a new one? Let the quota in Ushen Brae die out? Or offer them trade instead? Perhaps they would like slaves of their own. So many questions.

The same in regard to the Known World. Would the Auldek conquer? Likely so. Many of them walked with a hundred souls beneath their skin. A hundred deaths at their disposal. How could weak Acacians stand before them? The fragile coalition of the Akaran Empire would shatter when such a threat approached.

"The bitch with her plan to end the quota," Sire Revek said. "Does she really mean it?"

There were moments that Dagon disliked the shared communion of the council. One could not lie. The others could even have measured the beating of his heart or felt the sweat on his palms if they wished. They would sense that he did not like calling Queen Corinn "the bitch," but they would also forgive him. After all, he did the work few of them did, out among the peasants, so much of his life in service to them all. Considering that leaguemen never told peasants the truth about anything, their complete openness with one another had an ironic quality.

"Yes, Chairman, she likely does mean it at the moment," Dagon answered. "She is an Akaran, after all. She remains victim of notions of glory and benevolence, especially during times of stress. Not the substance of benevolence, of course— the show. That's what pumps her blood. She may abolish the quota now, resume it later. She may see that the trade is simply no longer viable. In a great many ways she is right about that."

"She has no creativity," a voice in the third row said. "There is always a way to exploit for gain."

"We see that, yes," Grau said. "The peasant folk rarely do."

Many voices climbed over one another in anxious agreement with the chief elder.

"But the bitch has finally consented to release the vintage," Revek said.

"Within a few weeks the entire Known World will be addicted to it. Will that not unite them?"

"It will. It will," Sire Nathos said, speaking about his area of expertise, "but I don't think that it matters. United they may just fall faster. Let them line up to get cut down. Better that than that they splinter and hide in the various provinces. Either way, I would not bet on their chances. And we need not. If the Auldek prevail, who is to say we can't do business with them? When the Known World is populated with Auldek and their newborn children—babies for the first time in hundreds of years—what will the Auldek wish for?"

"Peace."

"Stability."

Nathos nodded. "They'll begin to fear death again. They'll want sedate, docile servants with no rebellion in them. They'll want to grow rich as they dream of their children's lives. We will have them in our power just as much as we had the Acacians."

Faleen asked, "And if, by some strange turn of events, the bitch beats them back?"

"I rather hope she doesn't," Nathos admitted. "That seems . . . boring. But if that happens, she'll have a newly addicted, certainly battered, nation to rebuild. She has no idea how completely we own her."

"And she still does not know what happens when one stops drinking the vintage?"

"No. No, she let that go untested."

Sire Grau chuckled. "So we have them forever. Oh, my brothers, isn't commerce wonderful? My mood is rising. What else have we to consider?"

Sire El reiterated an idea he had proposed before. Perhaps the time when they need fear their own military might was behind them. They should enlarge the Ishtat Inspectorate. If they could not sell quota slaves as regularly, they could train them instead. They were already doing this on a small scale, and the first young soldiers bred on the Outer Isles had successfully joined the ranks of the Ishtat, without mishap.

Several from the inner circle, including Faleen, grumbled against this. "We should be wary lest we make ourselves like the peasants," Faleen said. "I want no army to rebel against us, no kings or queens or senators."

"I did not propose kings or queens or senators," El snapped. "I propose that we make use of a means of production we have gone to great expense to establish. The plantations exist. They produce souls, bodies. We must find something to do with the product, lest it all go to rot."

"Either the bitch or the Auldek or the quota slaves in Ushen Brae may one day turn against us," Sire Lethel said, speaking with unusual boldness from the second circle. "Who knows what the future holds? It may be that we don't just need to protect our products and wealth. Who is to say we won't need to fight for our very existence?"

They lay pondering this for a time, and then slowly, one by one, they gave their consent. The conversation continued. Eventually, as the entire group slowed with shared fatigue, Faleen, with Grau's approval, recounted the consensus. Sire El could build his army. On one of the small isles, another league-man would oversee the production of concubines, quality ones who would be as much spies and assassins as they were lovers. Still others would follow the Auldek's progress, corresponding with them just enough to let them understand the league might yet be their friend.

And finally they came to where they began. The confusion that was Ushen Brae. Sire Faleen himself would journey across to oversee the exploitation of the Aklun relics, which some were already searching for. Another should venture farther, right across to the mainland itself. The slaves being abandoned there could not be allowed to run amok.

"Who will take up this responsibility?"

The response was immediate, uncharacteristically swift. "I will." Again, that voice from the second row.

"Sire Lethel?" Faleen asked. "These are affairs of the real world, you understand? Among the peasants. There is risk—"

"And there is joy in taking risk," Lethel said. "My cousin enjoyed risk. I do as well."

"Will you err as your cousin did?"

"No," Lethel said. "I will not. I believe he should be forgotten, but I would not have my family forgotten. I will succeed where he did not. I swear it. If I cannot, I will arrange to have my own head set rolling."

"Do any object?" Faleen asked.

For a time a murmur of discussion swept around the rings, but it was not true objection. Few would want the task, Dagon knew. Why should they? Few of these men are like me, Dagon thought, or like Neen. Perhaps this Lethel is a person of promise. He let these thoughts slip away almost as quickly as he formed them.

Still, it alarmed him when El spoke his name. "Dagon, you must return swiftly."

Reminded of it, fatigue wrung his body anew. He had arrived just an hour before the meeting. Now, likely, they would turn him back toward Acacia in the morn. He felt a hard elbow of annoyance press his ribs, but he breathed through it and asked, "Have we any particular message for the queen?"

Grau cleared his throat harshly, as if he had something caught in it that he wished to expel. His voice calmed when he spoke. "Use whatever words you like. Just make her know the league understands that the changing situation means we must all adapt. Let her know the league has only ever wished to facilitate trade that was in the best interests of the empire. This is no time to trade in quota. Tell her she has our full support and no malice whatsoever."

"You mean lie on every count?"

"Of course," Faleen said. "What other way is there to do business?"

"None that I have yet found to be better than our own methods," Dagon said. Despite his fatigue, he felt rather better now than he had when he began. He should have known that would be the case. The future always looked brighter when joined with the hazy wisdom of this peers.

Grau must have picked up his thoughts. He said, "On some things we change with the situations of the world. But in other ways we stay true to the fundamentals that have always served us. Yes?" The answering affirmation filled the chamber with echoing, raucous enthusiasm—muted, of course, by the mist, but thunderous by Council terms.

Once it quieted down, the chief elder added, infusing his words with the certainty they all craved, "The League of Vessels will ride out this storm as ever we have. This is what has always made us great. It's why we will prosper now, just as we prospered during Hanish Mein's short rule, and as we thrived all the years since Tinhadin's foolish actions. Who but our ancestors would have had the vision to partner with the Lothan Aklun, sorcerer fugitives from Tinhadin's wrath, blood relatives to that madman? Who but we would grab the opportunity to help them punish the Known World year after year? We grew to hate them, but it was a beneficial partnership. Who but we could so long keep it secret that the trade that fueled the world was a product of old hatreds between kinsmen?"

Grau chuckled. "Before long, the seas will calm. The sun will burn away the clouds. And we will yet be masters of the world. Masters of whom is yet to be seen, trading what it is yet to be determined, but it hardly matters. We have many options. So, what we have is a change of everything and a change of nothing at all. On all counts we will profit. And don't forget, brothers, our people are yet searching for this soul catcher we have heard so much about. When they find it—and other Lothan Aklun relics—I'm inclined to believe our losses will be no worse than pinpricks on a rhino's hide. Don't you agree?"

They did.

Chapter Forty-nine

He is designed for war. How else to describe it? Look at him! Just look at him . . .

So Rialus thought as he scurried to stay just behind the headman of the Lvin, the chieftain of the entire Auldek nation, and—as of today—the commander of an invading army: Devoth. His strides each doubled Rialus's. His shoulders punched forward and back as he walked, squared and higher on his frame than those of normal men, as if he wore sculpted armor draped over them. But the sculpting was nothing more than his natural contours; the bulk measured only in the striated cords of his own muscles. He went bare armed, shoulder joints rounded knobs, bulging at the biceps. His back—wrapped in tight-fitting leather—started wide and tapered toward his waist, where it met his buttocks and the swinging tree trunks he called legs.

Rialus kept his eyes above this part of the Auldek's anatomy, feeling the same unease he experienced around thoroughbred animals. Any creatures designed for violence and latent with sexual strength troubled him. He doubted there was even one individual in the Known World to match Devoth's physical stature. Certainly no Acacian ever had and likely no Mein either; no Halaly or Candovian; not even a freak, straw-haired Aushenian from the Gradthic Range was likely to reach the Lvin's height of eight savagely proportioned feet.

The benefits of four hundred and some years spent doing

nothing but training for war, Rialus mused. That and teaching hummingbirds to sip sweet water from your mouth; raising pet lions; running endurance races over twenty-, thirty-, and fifty-mile courses; practicing archery; singing epic poems, and painting with a brush and ink. Yes, Rialus had continued to learn more about the Auldek with each passing day. None of the newfound knowledge, however, made anything about them make better sense to him. None of it balanced the knowledge that the entire nation was ravenous for war, rushing toward it with a breathless anticipation that seemed almost childlike. Though he had a considerable part in the planning stages of the coming invasion, this day had reared up before him suddenly. Things, it seemed, were moving as fast as the Auldek's massive strides.

Thus, Devoth, Rialus, and their small party went out from the Lvin area of Avina at a brisk pace. They walked atop an elevated network that took them from rooftop to rooftop through a district Rialus had not yet visited. Dropping to street level, they strode for a time down a thoroughfare that swarmed with onlookers, slaves mostly, but all caught up in the excitement of the moment. They yelled encouragement and clapped. Some banged cymbals together. The youngest tossed folded bits of paper shaped like birds and insects, yet another Auldek pastime. The light crafts looped in the air above them. Were they happy to know the Auldek were departing? It did not seem so. The enthusiasm seemed sincere enough, and the tears in the eyes of some held both joy and sadness. Rialus would never understand slaves.

Slick with sweat before long, Rialus welcomed the coolness as they dropped into an underground passageway. The Auldek to either side of Devoth talked as they moved, but Rialus did not follow what they were saying. It was enough just to keep up.

And then they emerged into the sun again. Devoth led them across a rectangle of pink marble. He began the ascent of a wide staircase. Above it, nothing but the sky, bright blue, streaked by high clouds and promising a fine day. Only as he reached the halfway point did he slow his pace. He inhaled a breath, head back slightly. Rialus did the same and he imagined he smelled the scent and essence of many, many souls.

Devoth paused. He did not turn fully around, but he twisted his head enough for Rialus to see his sharp profile. His long hair tumbled over his shoulders in auburn waves. "Are you ready to be stunned, Rialus Leagueman? I think this will be a sight you have never seen the like of before."

Actually, Rialus thought, I'm rather tired of being stunned. This entire journey: the waves of the Barrier Ridge and the sea wolves of the Gray Slopes, punching through the angerwall and gazing up at the heights of the barrier isles, the floating dead in the sea and the chaos after Sire Neen's beheading and . . . the list went on and on, and by the look of things it would do so endlessly. He would just as soon live the rest of his days without such excitement. But as he mounted the last steps and the field below them came into view, Rialus beheld the army that Devoth and the other Auldek had gathered for their invasion.

It was enormous. Countless bodies crowded a massive rectangular clearing that stretched toward the horizon. In the near distance, separated into rectangular units by their clan affiliation, marked by different-colored armor and garments, stood the Auldek themselves. Rialus knew enough to separate them at a glance now: Lvin and Kern and Kulish Kra nearest, Anet and Antoks and Wrathic just behind them, the Shivith along the left side. The Fru Nithexek, a clan he knew little about, were a thin line at the rear of the Auldek ranks, and the few Numrek stood in the right corner near the front. The totem clans of the Auldek.

Rialus tried to find some way to number them but ended up feeling he was guessing. There might be twenty or thirty thousand of them. Not so many to represent an entire race, really. But they were only a portion of the gathered host.

Behind them, stretching back toward the rim of the horizon, went the divine children. They were likewise sectioned off by the clans that claimed them, garishly clothed, many of them altered to physically resemble their clans' totem animals. How strange to see human wolves howling, white-faced lion men baring their teeth, cranelike people snapping their heads from side to side, others pretending to hiss like venomous snakes . . . Madness, on a massive scale. Those farther back lost shape and individual detail. They blended into a moving mass. They looked like ants swarming, piled on top of one another and intertwined so that it was impossible to tell where one ended and another began.

Lining the far edges of the mass of soldiers were the beasts that would also attack Acacia. Kwedeirs—those batlike monstrosities with riders strapped to their backs—shuffled uneasily, their awkwardly bent wings rustling, seemingly eager to fly. The kwedeir was not a totem animal as far as Rialus knew, but the clans aligned with animals fierce enough for battle had representatives also. Antoks were spaced out in ranks receding into the distance. They wore intricate harnesses with pockets in which soldiers perched, seven or eight for each creature. There were white-maned snow lions and shivith cats, lean and restless, ready to bolt; wrathic wolves the size of horses, with long muzzles that quivered as they growled; and even a few sky bears, bulky carnivores the color of dirty snow that—judging by what he could see—chose to stand on their hind legs when agitated. Above it all the crows of the Kulish Kra swarmed in excited flocks. Certainly, though, they were trained pets. Certainly, they were anticipating the slaughter that such a mass commotion must lead to. When had the world ever seen such a bizarre, murderous throng of man and beast and man-beast?

And all this, Rialus knew, was a gathering of just a portion of the army. A supply train had already been sent out along the route to prepare the way—to stash food supplies and gear, to construct makeshift outposts to aid the coming army. Devoth had explained that hunters and laborers would travel before the main column, and that a never-ending convoy of slaves would follow it, shuttling the supplies to keep them alive in the northern regions. To hear him describe it, they would drain Ushen Brae of its population and send a river of new life flooding into the Known World.

Just before he stepped away from him to address the crowd, Devoth turned to Rialus. He pointed one of his long, thick-jointed fingers at him. "You are a witness. Watch and listen."

He turned away before Rialus could answer, leaving him with the disquieting feeling that he might be tested afterward on what transpired.

"This will be the greatest work of your lives!" Devoth shouted to the crowd, once they had settled down to allow him to speak. He spoke slowly, and for a moment Rialus found the cadence strange, especially as the sentiments themselves were impassioned. "You know why you're here. For war!"

The crowd affirmed that they did, indeed, know that was why they were gathered. It took a while for the approbation to die down, since the commander's words needed to be repeated for the farther reaches to hear. Cheers came back at him, delayed by the distance.

"This war was hundreds of years in the making," Devoth claimed. "Hundreds of years. Think how fortunate you are! You will be remembered for it—whether you live or die. You will be remembered and envied for the things you are going to see and deeds you are going to do. You will be legends. Do you doubt it? Who but the heroes of legend would dare to march into the great north? Who but legends would kick white bears and ice maidens out of their paths and tread across frozen water, walk above a fathomless sea, through biting wind and snow, across tundra and over mountains? Who but conquerors would dare face all that just to reach their enemies? Tell me that doesn't sound like legend!"

Judging by the shout that answered his prompt, they rather liked the notion.

He knows how to work a crowd, Rialus thought.

"Yes." Devoth paced back and forth across the platform, hand cupped beside his ear, pulling the cacophony in as if it were personal praise, eating it with his grin. "Yes."

For a time, Rialus lost the flow of Devoth's discourse. It was hard not to just gape at the throng of warriors and beasts: antoks pawing the ground; kwedeirs rolling their shoulders, cracking their jaws as if they might snatch up a snack from all the morsels around them; the masses rolling back their enthusiasm in delayed waves. The passing moments made none of it less horrifying. When the cheering suddenly faded, however, Rialus knew he had better listen more carefully.

"So how could we not offer you a great reward? Divine children, could we not honor you? Tell me, what would you like to have most in the world?"

Devoth leaned forward, awaiting a response. Only, there was no answering sound. The enormous army stood hushed. Even the antoks cocked their massive heads and listened to the eerie silence of thousands of breathing beings. The Auldek smiled and nudged one another knowingly, but the masses behind them seemed genuinely baffled.

What exactly is going on? Rialus wondered.

"You don't know?" Devoth asked. "Let me suggest something, then. I know you will come on this journey and fight this war with us because you are loyal and you are proud and this, more than anything in your lives yet, is what you were created for. But if you help us gain this—when we conquer the Acacians like the warriors we once were; when we of the Auldek race are fertile again and can make our own children; when we give up the souls inside us and live only the span of a single life once more; when we are mortal again; when we have all these things that we most want—then we will free you."

The hush that remained was more shocking than sound would have been.

"You will be free to do whatever you wish. Slay the Acacians, if you will. Enslave them, if you care to. Make war or peace as suits your souls. We will not hinder you." Devoth grinned. He curved his arm back, bicep bulging, and tapped his fingers against his chest. "If it pleases you, mass an army and make war on us. That would be great fun, yes?"

Still the crowd held its breath. The divine children stared up at Devoth, rapt, so many faces stunned and disbelieving. This made Devoth laugh.

"Lvin, Kulish Kra, Shivith, Kern, Anet—all Auldek clans, lend me your voices. Let them know what I say is true."

From one section of the Auldek ranks and then another, shouts rose in affirmation. Each group called its name, testifying, confirming. Senior members turned and nodded, pointing at Devoth to verify that he spoke for them all.

"Now, hear me once more and answer me!" Devoth bellowed above them. "Do you want freedom? If so, you have only to say so and then to fight for it. Answer me!"

It took a moment, but this time the masses did. They cried for their freedom.

"Good. I am glad you do not disappoint. I knew you wouldn't. I know this also: for this battle we take everything with us. For this battle, we fly as we haven't for centuries. We call upon old friends, mounts that have not allowed riders for years now. Mounts that we have promised carnage." He turned and shouted back the way they had approached. "Old friends, come to me!"

Rialus snapped around, not knowing what to expect but ready to be surprised again. He was. He did not hear the flapping of wings, though he would dream that he did for many nights to come. He saw them first as moving forms that were almost ghostly against the light blue of the sky. They rose up. One and then two more and then others. Winged, they flew. They flew fast, taking on size as they grew nearer, slicing in and out among one another, at times dark crescents of motion, in other instances slivers of shapes almost invisible.

At least, that was true until they landed. Some dropped onto columns beside the army. Some fell right among the crowd, which fled, leaving landing areas for them. A few flanked Devoth on the platform. One alit on the steps in front of him, between him and the ranked masses. This one landed on all fours. It stayed like that for a moment, as if adjusting the burden of its own muscular weight, and then it reared up, wings outstretched, massive, larger even than the kwedeirs, built differently. The creature was hairless and slick, its musculature more humanoid than those batlike creatures, more like a being meant to walk upright. Its back and upper wings were a blue so dark it neared black, but its belly, face, and the front half of its legs were a smoky white. Its head was like a hairless ape's, with a protruding jaw full of visible teeth and large eyes that took in the scene with a confident, intelligent malevolence.

Rialus forgot to breathe. When he recognized the burning in his chest for what it was, he tried to inhale and could not remember how.

Devoth turned and glanced at Rialus, blinked. "I mentioned fréketes, didn't I? I see you are impressed. Watch this."

With that, he bounded down the stone steps toward the winged creature. The beast turned and followed his progress, eyes dilating, nostrils flaring with an audible inhalation of air. Its jaws opened, and for a moment Rialus was certain the creature was going to devour him. Instead, it tossed its head back and roared, an incredible sound that shredded the air.

Rialus slammed his hands against his ears. The beast half turned away from Devoth. It moved one of its wings and offered him a bulging thigh that Devoth leaped on. With a few deft movements the Auldek had climbed onto its back and slammed his feet into the stirrups of the slight frame wrapped around its body.

He had barely grasped hold of the straps when the creature surged up into the air, Devoth clinging tightly. As it reached the height of its leap, the frékete beat its wings and skimmed away over the awed heads of the throng. People ducked as it passed, flattening themselves on the ground. Then they rose with bellowing and shouting, a cacophony to which the antoks and kwedeirs and the other fréketes added. A great noise. An army announcing itself.

Rialus pulled his hands away from his ears and instead placed a finger to his lips. He whispered, with no faith that he would be answered, "Giver protect us."

Chapter Fifty

They had to work fast. They had a day or two to accomplish their objective, Dariel figured. No longer. That was why he pushed the Lothan Aklun vessel to such amazing speeds. It smacked, smacked, smacked against the green swells, sparkling beneath the light of a mid-morning sun. The prow cut the waves around the rocky southern tip of Lithram Len and then turned back to race up its ragged eastern shoreline. They might be spotted, yes, but delay was not something they could afford.

It was true that the league had been struck a blow when Calrach rebuffed them. Sire Neen—Dariel could not help but chuckle thinking about him. The memory seemed more manageable now that he was free in the world. Tunnel and several others clinging to the rocking deck nearby looked quizzically at the prince as he laughed. That just made him guffaw all the more. "Rather changed your view of the world didn't it?" he shouted. "Getting your head lopped off, I mean." The others just stared.

The fresh air and the motion of waves beneath him and a ship's wheel in his hands did a great deal for his humor. He felt a vibrant energy at his center that he had not really felt since his days as a brigand captain.

He let the energy feed him from the inside, and he let the urgency pressed on him by the outside world drive him forward. Knowing the league as he did, Dariel knew they would not spend much time mourning Sire Neen. Nor would they be

573

deterred from whatever it was they intended in Ushen Brae. The activity on the west side of Lithram Len proved as much. It could only be a matter of days before they began exploring the other side of the island, where Skylene told him the soul catcher was. She was the only one of the party to have information about it, and that came only from the things Mór had told her. Even this information came largely from a child's memories, but Dariel knew such things could have surprising accuracy.

A little way into their northern turn, Skylene called for him to slow the boat. They would have to study the coastline carefully not to miss entrance to the soul catcher. It was hidden in plain sight, Skylene said.

Trees of a type that Dariel had never seen crowded the shore. Slender trunked, they were as tall as any pine in the high forest of Calfa Ven. The trees exploded near the crown with branches that shot out in every direction. They looked top-heavy, but the branches entwined with their neighbors and those joined the many into a single, linked partnership.

Rocky outcroppings interrupted the trees now and then. It was for a particular one of these that they searched, riding the waves now, nosing along more slowly. Dariel made sure to scan the sea horizon often for any other vessel, but he also watched for submerged rocks and could not help but stare for long moments at the shore.

"On the mainland there are vast forests filled with creatures." Skylene had come up beside him. The breeze off the water stirred the tufts of feathers at her hairline. "They say there are creatures on Ushen Brae—squirrels and flying rats and howling monkeys—that live their entire lives in the tree canopy. Imagine that: having no need of the ground beneath you. The world is odd, isn't it?"

"That's what keeps it interesting," Dariel said.

"Well, yes. And this island is interesting, too. As lush as those trees are, as thick, no animals live here. Listen, you'll hear no calls. Not even birds. They say it has always been that way on Lithram Len."

Indeed, now that she mentioned it, the place did have an eerie stillness. It was hard to imagine the island not crawling with animal life, but he saw no motion save the leaves stirred by the wind. Staring at the trees they did seem almost as if they glared back, like their entwined embrace was not so much an act of mutual support as it was preparation for aggression.

Just after midday, Birké, with his Wrathic hunter's eyes, was the first to see something. His arm shot out, pointing. At first Dariel saw nothing but another bulge of rock that pushed through the trees and overhung the water. He moved the vessel closer, willing it to ride calm on the swells, angling so that he could see into the water more clearly. There were rocks there, rippling and near, under the glassy green tint of the water. It was not until he swung the boat all the way around and backed into the shelter of a natural quay that he realized he had navigated a route that brought him to rest at a pier, a carefully hidden structure just beneath the rock outcropping.

The others had the boat secured in a few moments, and Dariel leaped onto the dock even as Birké started to ascend a stone staircase cut into the buttress. The steps were invisible from the sea but obvious from this angle, a curving ascent that kept to the natural contours of the wall. Dariel followed.

It was a quick climb, and soon he stepped through a darkened opening, as if into the mouth of a cave, breathing heavily from the exertion. The others crowded the room and he had to slide between them. As his eyes adjusted, he realized the chamber was not truly cavelike. It was sculpted, oblong and sleek. The stone had a light within it, a faint illumination that seemed to grow the longer they stood there. No one talked, but they walked slowly around the chamber.

Tunnel said, "This is truly it?"

Skylene nodded, her sky-blue face grave and beautiful in the soft light. "It's as Mór described. Exactly." She pointed to the bedlike stone platforms. "Ravi—I mean, the child to be sacrificed lies on one of those. Whoever is to receive his soul takes the other. Covers come down from above." She looked upward. Indeed, rectangular structures hung there. "And whatever happens is hidden from view. The Lothan Aklun do things. That's all she could say."

"Who were these people?" Dariel asked.

"Some believe that the Lothan Aklun came from your land. Sorcerers who fled persecution"—she ran her hand gently over one of the panels, not actually touching it but as close as she could come to doing so—"and became persecutors in this one."

From my lands, Dariel thought. How could they have come from Acacia? "I've heard no tales of that."

"Not all tales get told," someone said.

"These sorcerers, they put their magic into things," Skylene continued. "Like they put souls in the boat. Like this chamber. This is the place. It's all as Mór described. It may be incomprehensible to us, but the league might not find it so. They are so near, they may find it any day. They may have texts to show them its use. I don't know—"

"If the league has any idea what this can do, they'll search for it," Dariel said. "They'll find it. They'll use it. I know that much about them."

"Destroy it," Birké said. "Let's not wait a minute more."

Another man, Tam, answered this with motion. He unclipped the mace that hung at his belt, gripped it, and tested its weight as he decided where to strike. Dariel understood him to have escaped from the Fru Nithexek, though the only marks of the sky bear on him were dark, circular tattoos around his eyes. He picked his target, a slanting compartment in the wall with hand-shaped, raised impressions on it. Those near him stepped back.

Dariel began, "Somehow I don't think—"

Tam swung the mace. The iron head of it bounced back

576

from the panel so forcefully the young man's arm was flung over his head. He lost his grip on the mace and several had to duck out of the way to avoid being hit. Tam cried out, and for a cold second Dariel thought he might drop dead, cursed or something. But, no, it was just the pain in his shoulder and hand that caused him to cry. He stood, rubbing his shoulder, looking hurt and embarrassed at the same time.

Dariel took a moment, and then finished the sentence he had begun. "That we can just bash the place to pieces."

"Tam," Skylene said in a voice that made the statement the commendation she intended, "thank you for demonstrating what won't work. We have to find another way."

Dariel listened as the group talked, but he had his own idea and it held most of his attention. He circled it, unsure he wanted to offer it. It might fail for so many different reasons. There were risks. Perhaps as much as anything, it meant pushing through a wall of memories he did not relish facing. Or should he? Didn't he have to? Those memories were tied up with the same children who were brought here. They included the same people he was now working against. He had unfinished business with the league. This could be a part of that.

"I think I know a way," Dariel finally said. The others stopped talking and turned toward him. "I did something like this before. We blow it to bits—explosions, flame, and smoke."

Tunnel nodded gravely. "Good idea." A moment later, he added, "How will we do this thing?"

"We'll need an explosive, of course," Dariel said. "I think I know where to find one."

They used the cover of darkness to hide them, sailing back around to the west side of Lithram Len. The moon was just a sliver, but the stars were bright and Dariel seemed to have no trouble feeling the contours of the shore and sensing the dangers beneath the black and silvered water. The others were quiet. Dariel could sense their fear rise to a trembling pitch when the glow of the league vessel-crowded harbor illumed the night sky. They were close enough to the shoreline that they saw it first as a hazy smoldering above the dark silhouette of the trees.

As they got nearer, the sky took on a reddish aspect, seeming lower and choked with smoke. Dariel inched the boat around the last headland. The bustling harbor, with its maze of dock works, and the city behind it came into view. It hummed with life just as when they had first seen it.

The moment they were in view, Dariel knew how much they stood out, bright white vessel that they were. Fortunately, the league had already commandeered many Lothan Aklun ships. He saw several moving in the harbor now, even more at dock. Coming around into the light, they were now on display for any eyes that chose to see them. Instead of retreating, the prince willed the boat forward, toward the burning torches and hundreds of workers, each of them an enemy.

"Best to hide in plain sight, right?" Dariel offered. "We still agree on that, don't we?"

No one answered. No one objected either. This was as they had planned, debated, and argued about all afternoon. From what they had observed the first time, there was no way they could get near the harbor without being seen. The night they had passed it during what should have been the dead hours, it was lit too well, was thronging with laborers and Ishtat guards and leaguemen busy making the island theirs, so clearly the time of the day or night would not aid them. In the end they all agreed. They would do just what they were doing now: sail in as if they belonged, as if they knew what they were about and were as intent on their work as any of the others.

It was no perfect plan. It might work. It might not. They could easily be discovered. If they were, they would likely die. But they could not sail away from it without trying. Dariel half wondered why he himself felt such resolution, but only half. He knew how much this was an opportunity to relieve some small portion of the guilt owned by his family. How could he do anything but try to make that happen? Beyond that, it just felt good. Captain of a ship again. With a crew who jumped at his orders, even if he had to explain his needs each time. And they trusted him. They would not let him pilot them into the enemy's mouth otherwise. Skylene had even given him a dagger, a small, straight blade that he had shoved through his belt. Yes, he was one of them for the time being.

Working the ship closer to the docks, he darted his eyes about, searching at the same time he checked for danger. He knew the barrels would be here somewhere. The league never went far without their flaming weapon. It would be stored off the ships if possible, somewhere removed from the center of activity.

There! Yes, there on the far side of the harbor, at the end of a long arm of pier, sat stacks of drums. He knew them by their color: bright red. Hundreds of them. There was activity at the pier next to it, but the area around the barrels was deserted. Calmly, trying to think slower than the pulse beating in his throat, Dariel steered across the harbor, turned and angled in, coming to the docks on the far side, so that they would be sheltered somewhat from view.

Once docked and tied secure, Dariel turned to the waiting crew. "This is it. The pitch in these barrels makes an unholy fire. It'll blast that soul catcher to pieces and leave a fire that'll burn for days there. The more barrels we can get, the better. Let's go, quickly but calmly."

They could not be sure that the league used the people as laborers yet. Since slaves kept by the Lothan Aklun weren't necessarily adorned in the same ways, those with the most noticeable signs of "belonging" stayed hidden. Skylene, Tunnel, the two others of the Kern clan, and Birké crouched on the far side of the deck. Under Dariel's direction, the others began the work of shifting the barrels from the pier to the boat.

The next pier over seemed to be closer each time Dariel

glanced at it. Fortunately, the boat moored there was on the far side, and the attention was thus directed away from them. A group of Ishtat Inspectorate guards stepped off the vessel and stood for a time talking beside it. Dariel kept up the motions of loading and securing, but he watched them every chance he got. He just caught the scent of the mist pipe one of them was smoking. Enjoy it, he thought. Just relax and enjoy the pipe and don't turn around.

The barrels were heavy enough that they had to be tilted and rolled along on their rims, and then carefully leaned from the dock into the hands on board the ship waiting for them. This last move in particular needed to be done slowly, as demonstrated when Tam let a drum loose too soon. It crashed down on the edge of the deck and teetered a moment. Then it fell back against the pier and splashed into the harbor's gray waters.

"Forget it," Dariel said. "Keep going."

"I'm sorry," Tam said. "I thought—"

"It's floating," another observed.

Dariel cursed. There was no retrieving it, as it bobbed under the pier, just out of reach. "Leave it," he said, hoping it would stay trapped among the pier's many pylons. Tam continued to apologize, but Dariel cut him off, not as kindly as Skylene had been with him earlier. "Just keep working. Try to look like you know what you're doing."

A few minutes more, and Tunnel had had enough of waiting. He crammed himself into Birké's shirt, though he could not button it and his bulk threatened to burst the seams of the shoulders. He went to work, and Dariel was glad he did. Where the rest struggled to carry one barrel between them, Tunnel somehow got his arms around two at a time, carrying one under each arm. With this help, the stacked rows on the boat's main deck grew quickly. Dariel kept busy making sure they were properly secured. A few more minutes and they could—

"Dariel?" It was Skylene. Just one word, but the tone in

which she spoke it told him everything. Instead of looking at her, he scanned the docks. He spotted the problem quickly.

An Ishtat guard stood at the end of their pier, watching them. Dariel turned to Skylene and, with a motion of his eyes, reminded her to stay hidden. By the time he had turned around again, the guard had started toward them.

"We're going to have company," Dariel said, just loud enough for those hefting the barrels to hear him. "Keep working. Except you, Tunnel—get out of sight."

The Ishtat strode toward them now, eyes flexed. He wore the cloak of his order, bright white and trailing behind him as he walked. A thin sword hung at his side, and one gloved hand rested on its hilt. "Hey!" he called. "What are you doing? You think you can just drop barrels of league pitch to float away? Look!" He pointed toward the water on the other side of the pier. The barrel had floated free. "Get out there and fetch that!"

Dariel bowed his head and motioned his apology with his hands. He called the others and acted as if he would just pull out and pick up the floater. The man carried on toward them, however. As he got closer his steps slowed. And when he was near enough to make out individuals, he squinted, for a moment so perplexed he could manage nothing else. And then he said, "Who are you? You aren't one of ours."

Dariel smiled. "I?" He leaped from the deck to the pier and walked toward the Ishtat, holding an amiable expression. "Who am I?" He laughed and cocked his head in a manner that suggested he had a story to tell, one that would explain all this, one that would make them both laugh, even if the tale did not make the teller seem entirely free of guilt.

He tried to convey all this in the few steps it took him to reach the man, and it must have worked. Instead of drawing his sword or signaling an alarm, the guard had his chin raised and his hands planted on his hips. "Yes. Who are you, and what do you—"

Dariel swept his hand up, bringing with it the dagger. He

slammed the blade in the soft center of the guard's neck. The man's face registered shock. His arms hung limp, and this may have fed his terror. His eyes cast about as if demanding that his body do things that it refused.

The prince said, "My name is Dariel Akaran, if you must know." He yanked the blade to the side, and pushed the guard's body over, so that the spray of crimson jetted away from him. Moving with the body's momentum, he kicked the guard from the pier. As the body splashed into the water, Dariel cast his eyes over the harbor, the deck of the nearest ship, portholes in its side, and the street leading away from the water. Nothing. No one seemed to have noticed. Not yet, at least.

He spun and said, "Last of the barrels in, lads, and then let's go!"

The others, Skylene included, stared at him. Birké's jaw dropped, exposing his canine teeth. Tam was so wide-eyed it looked like he feared for his own life. Even Tunnel looked uneasy.

"What?" Dariel asked, leaping back on the boat. "You think this could be bloodless? Gape at me later. Now let's keep moving or there'll be a lot more blood in the water. Quickly now, quickly."

The last barrels went on the deck. The ropes were untied. Dariel steered the boat away from the pier and turned it toward the open water. This was the part he had feared most. To be so close to success but needing moment after moment after moment in clear view of anyone watching. Work on the docks might not draw much attention, but a ship outbound in the middle of the night was a different matter. Dariel felt a hundred eyes drilling into the back of his head. He fought the urge to turn around as much as he held back from surging forward at full speed.

Steady, he told himself. *Just steady forward. Off to make a delivery, that's all. Nothing suspicious here.*

Right there before him, bobbing for anyone to see, floated

the loose barrel. He wanted to ram the thing and fly, but if anybody saw him sail by it without retrieving it . . . He angled the boat toward it, pulled up until it bumped the side, and then instructed the crew to pull it aboard. Seconds passed as they grasped for it, but it slipped out of reach.

Skylene appeared beside him, looking back where he would not. "The body is in plain sight now," she whispered.

For the first time that night, sweat beaded on his forehead and ran down over his temples. He had to wipe it from the corners of his eyes. Still he did not turn around. He slid the boat toward the barrel, gently. Tam appeared with a boat hook. With it, they got the barrel secured against the side at the stern. Finally, they hauled it up.

Steady forward.

"They've seen it," Skylene said.

Dariel cursed. He tried to find something else to say, but nothing came.

"One guard is motioning to some others. He's pointing at the water."

"Giver!" Dariel ground through his teeth, watching as the headland crept closer. It might have been a plea, but it sounded more like a threat. Skylene glanced at him a moment, and then looked away.

"They converged on it," she reported. "It looks like they're preparing to launch a boat."

Steady forward.

As they neared the spit of land that would take them out of the harbor's sight line, he asked, "Well?"

Her elbow brushed his as the hull crossed into the deeper current coming around the headland, changing the boat's rocking. She did not answer until they fell into shadow. "I don't think they picked us out, but perhaps we should make haste."

And so they did. Dariel pushed the vessel even faster than before. They sped under the light of the stars, and then turned and ran around the bottom of the island as the eastern horizon warmed their faces with the coming sun. They were back at the soul catcher in no time.

If Tunnel had been impressive on the docks, he was a wonder now, stripped shirtless, muscles glistening with sweat as he heaved barrels onto his shoulders and ran up the steps. And though Tam had bumbled twice in as many days, he worked all the harder to make amends for it now. Dariel almost told him to slacken his pace, but the young one was working so hard he did not have the heart to dissuade him. Of course, they feared a league ship would arrive at any moment, but the hours passed without anyone showing. Before the noon hour they had the chamber stuffed with all but one of the pitch barrels, and soon after they had soaked a length of rope in pitch to create a wick.

All told, they had searched, debated, planned, sailed, loaded, run, and hauled throughout an entire day, a night, and into the next day. Still, when the work was complete and the others cleared the chamber to wait at the boat and Dariel stood alone with a torch burning in his hand, it seemed the moment had come too quickly. All he had to do was finish it.

Standing with the torch clouding the air of the chamber with black smoke, he pushed himself forward. One step and then another, and then he bent and brought the flame close to the pitch-soaked rope. Even then it was hard. He had to tell himself that this was not the same as on the platforms. He was not Val, going to his death. Nor was he Spratling, a child being orphaned for a second time. He would live through this act, and no souls would be lost by it. Just the opposite. This would save lives. Save souls. Perhaps even his own.

The wick took the flame and bloomed to life. Dariel watched it long enough to verify that it was good, and then he turned and dashed out and down the stone stairs, glad to feel the sea air on his face, unreasoningly gleeful that a vessel full of friends awaited him.

Years before, as he had raced away from the exploding platforms on the black-sailed *Ballan*, he had not looked back. He had feared whatever demon was rising there, all the rage roaring up into the heavens, the hands reaching out toward him. He could not have defined just what frightened him so, for it was many things overlapping, some submerged in memory but no less powerful. This time, he turned. He held the wheel as the prow cut the sea, but he twisted around and watched. The others around him clapped and cheered each explosion, for there were many. Hands grasped and patted joy to him, and he returned it.

What he saw was a plume of white smoke that rose slowly above the concussions of flaming rage. It tilted like a giant, like an enormous tree of ash unfurling into life. It looked wonderful. Peaceful. Thankful.

Three days later he beached the Lothan Aklun vessel on a sandspit in a shallow marsh area of Sumerled, just up the throat of a river that the People called Sheeven Lek. He watched as Tunnel directed the others to uncap the last barrel of pitch and let it pour out into the hull of the vessel. They lit it, and it went up fast, with a great whoosh that was a monster inhaling and then a burst of warmth that tilted Dariel back on his heels. He did not say a word of protest. No matter how beautiful the lines of the boat and how incredible the power within it, that was stolen power, trapped unwillingly. Enslaved. It could never be his and should be freed. So it was, and he almost felt he could hear the relief of the souls escaping.

And two days after that he met Mór and a small group of the People at the edge of the wilderness. Skylene presented him to her, all of them gathered on a stone slab elevated above the tamed woodlands to the east and the wilds stretching off to the west as far as the eye could see. The wilderness looked like it went on forever. Granite stones ran north to south in great undulating, weather-round ridges, like the crests of waves. At first, Dariel was not sure where to set his eyes: on the abundance of nature or on Mór, beautiful in the full light of the sun. He chose Mór.

Skylene briefed her on all that had happened: the stealing of the boat, the plan to destroy the soul catcher and the success at doing so, and then their destruction of the boat. It was an official report. Dariel knew that Mór would have heard the details already. Still, they all waited through it, Dariel searching for any signs of thoughts behind Mór's eyes. He could not read her at all. Just looking was a pleasure of sorts, though. Was it because of who she was, or because beneath the shivith spots he saw Wren in the shape of her eyelids and the roundness of her face and the way her cheekbones rose to prominence? Was it Mór he loved looking at, or the lover Mór reminded him of? He really wasn't sure.

If Mór received the news of the soul catcher's destruction with any personal emotion she did not show it. She did, however, take Dariel's hand in hers. She pulled him forward a half step and placed his palm against the center of her chest. "The People praise you," she said, "and thank you. You have done for us something we had not managed to do in all our years here. You arrived with knowledge we do not possess and used it to aid us. Likely, you cannot know the good you have done, but still I praise you for it."

Her expression while she said this was as firm as a nanny's measuring out a disobedient child's punishment, but after a short pause the corners of her lips—first the right and then the left—and then her cheeks as well tilted into a grin. "It's a start, at least. We won't kill you . . . yet. Come look at this with me."

The two moved away from the others, climbing the sloping stone, which was coarse underfoot, with granules that crackled and popped free beneath their weight. A flock of long, slim birds flew toward them over the hillocks to the northwest. They were black silhouettes against the reddening sky, until they dropped into shadow and stood out white against the deep green of the trees.

"Beyond here, the land is wild," Mór said. "The Westlands. It is not unpeopled. Just wild. Beautiful beyond measure. Before the Lothan Aklun arrived, the Auldek tribes had settled portions of it, but their inland cities are ruins now, their cultivated fields reclaimed by forest and jungle." Her voice had grown conversational in a way it had never been with him before. "The Auldek like to hunt us on their kwedeirs, but there are regions of Ushen Brae that even the hunting parties have never reached. The Auldek are powerful in their way, but they live only on a thin sliver of coastline, afraid of the sea on one side, with a wall against the continent on the other. They were satisfied with that."

"But you are not?"

"No. Never could be. I want what is here. To make use of this land in ways the Auldek have long forgotten. If this land were ours to do with what we wanted, we would build a paradise like nothing the world has yet seen. Of course we would. Who better than slaves to know the value of free life?"

A nation of orphans, Dariel thought. None of whom can have children. What kind of future is that?

Mór turned her face toward him. "Think of it. We would know how to build a just society. That's a thing the world has never seen."

The sun shone warm on her features. Her skin looked so soft. Dariel wanted to run his fingertips across her cheek and down toward her lips, wondering if he would feel the shivith spots if he closed his eyes.

When Mór spoke, it seemed she had taken some portion of his own thoughts and woven them into something different and pressed it back toward him. "Though I set the marks on you myself, I don't fully recognize the face I made. I'll have to get used to you slowly, Dariel Akaran. I should tell you that it's certain the Auldek are marching to attack your nation. I don't know all the details, but they take an army like none they have mustered in years. They take war beasts and many of the sublime motion. I can't say how this will change Ushen Brae or how it will change your land. You have helped us, though. Yoen wants to meet you, but I told him that first I would offer you release. If you want to go now and somehow aid your people, I will not stop you."

He would have jumped at such an offer a fortnight ago. Now, though, he heard it coolly. It wasn't that he cared any less about the Known World, about his family, or about Wren. But the truth was twofold. On his own, he would never get back home. On his own, he was but one man who would have to shout for anyone to notice him, and the only ones who would notice would be his enemies. On his own, he would be running a fool's errand—one of the heart, yes, but not informed by the mind. And, too, he felt a different purpose. It had gripped him on the Lothan Aklun vessel and had not left him yet. Perhaps spirits had entered him when his hands held the steering wheel. Something had happened, for he was different, and in being different he felt a step closer to being more completely himself.

He said, "I would like to meet Yoen."

"You really want to know us?" Mór asked. "Us and these lands?"

Dariel said, "Yes."

"You know that I have not forgiven you anything. It may be that you are truly to have a role in the People's future, but that will only be decided over many, many more tests."

"I know."

"And you know that there is no easy road back to your land from here."

"I know."

Mór stared directly into his eyes for a long time, long enough that it grew hard for him to return her gaze. Dariel felt his eyes moisten, but he did not blink or break the exchange.

"It may be that you and I are both realists. Dreamers, too, I think. But realists as well. You cannot go to your land right now. I cannot accomplish the single greatest thing I hope to right now either. I'll tell you this, though. If the day comes that our work here is done, I will go with you to your lands. I will hunt until each and every Auldek is dead. And if I have my way, I'll be able to look into my brother's eyes before he fades from life. That's a dream of mine."

She broke the stare as if it were nothing. "Come then," the woman said matter-of-factly. She showed him her back, and began to descend the granite slope.

Dariel watched her go for a moment, and then lifted his gaze and looked toward the setting sun, across the crowns of trees, verdant green, gilded beneath a flaming sky. He had the impulse to turn and look back over the route they had traveled, or make eye contact with Tunnel or Skylene, but for some reason he felt the need to look only forward. He began walking, feeling the slope of the stone under his feet. He followed Mór in search of her beautiful land, populated by wild things and free people.

Chapter Fifty-one

The night before she rose to attempt the greatest works of sorcery she had ever tried, Corinn had a dream. She awoke feeling it heavy with import, dripping with guilt. She had relived an afternoon earlier that spring, when she and Aaden had ridden together in a carriage bringing them down from Calfa Ven. The boy, as often happened, became sick from the jostling of the wheels over the rough stones. His face went pale and he sat for a time, percolating the stew that, as if on cue, erupted from him as they started down one particularly steep section of switchbacks.

Corinn hated the scent of vomit. It filled her nostrils like a taint of something poisonous. She had never been able to deal with this type of sickness, and she had not on the day she dreamed of. Instead, she got out of the carriage at the first opportunity, leaving maids to care for her son as she walked for a while in the mountain air, clearing her lungs.

That much of the dream was just a version of events that actually had happened, a small and inconsequential event one afternoon in the mountains. What happened next had not happened in actual life. It couldn't. The players had not all been alive on that day.

As she walked, taking in the mountain view—the green and blue of the peaks before her, slowly receding as they dropped in altitude—a man appeared on her left side and took in the landscape with her. Corinn looked over at him, knowing who he was before her eyes touched him: her brother, Aliver.

He said nothing, just smiled at her, shook his head, motioned back toward the carriage in which Aaden sat, likely still green with his illness. He was saying that he understood her and that he loved the boy. Such a good boy. He was saying that the boy would be the king he never got to be. He was saying that he understood Corinn's actions and she had no need to explain herself, even now, as she walked in the fresh air while maids swabbed the vomit from the corners of her son's mouth.

"I'm not a bad mother," Corinn had said, though Aliver had said nothing to suggest he thought she was. "You don't know how much I love him."

"No, of course not," a voice said. Not Aliver's but the man on her right side, walking with them as well. She turned toward him. Hanish Mein. His clean, crisp features. His blond hair shone around his face and draped his shoulders. His gray eyes glowed. She wanted to press her lips against them and pull in the gentle calm of them.

Before she could, Hanish dipped his head forward. He threw his body after it, jumping into a somersault. Before he had turned one circle, his body became one large, orange leaf. It danced on a sudden breeze. Aliver did the same, and the two men, who were now leaves, twirled and dipped and rose on currents in the air. Watching them, Corinn began to whistle.

Though there was joy in the final moments, she awoke with the memory of the dream—and of the actual day that began it—imbedded in her abdomen as a physical pain, a knot that remained within her even after she joined the flow of the living day. She swore to herself that if she ever, ever, got the chance to pull Aaden close and kiss and caress him in illness like that she would do it with all her heart, holding nothing back. But this was not something she could see to today. She set it aside and continued with the course she had decided on.

First, she surprised a guard by arriving outside the cell that housed the prisoner Barad the Lesser. The soldier stood nearly asleep on his feet and did not seem to register Corinn as a real person until she stood right before him. "Soldier," she said, "open the door."

The man shot fully awake at the sound of her voice. Suddenly terrified, he turned and fumbled a long time with the keys to the door, apologizing the entire time, dropping them twice and cursing himself and then apologizing more. His terror of her seemed out of all proportion to the circumstances, but on entering the cell Corinn recalled that any guard of this prisoner had reason to fear her.

Barad sat on a cot against the far wall, the bed tiny beneath him, like a child's. She wondered if he ever lay on it, for surely his legs and arms would have hung down to the stone floor. Thinner already than when last she had seen him, angles and joints measured his bulk. His legs rose unnaturally long, bent at knees on which he had set his crossed arms and rested his forehead. A single wrist chain attached him to an iron ring in the wall. On hearing her enter, Barad lifted his head and rolled his sightless stone eyes in her direction.

Yes, she thought, there is reason to fear me. She turned and gestured for the guard to leave them alone. He did so gladly.

"You don't smell like a Marah," the prisoner said, after a few moments of silence. His voice carried the same grave timbre she remembered from before. It held a weight and substance at odds with the lanky, emaciated form that produced it.

"Do they feed you?" Corinn asked.

The man squinted. She knew he could not see her, but a lifetime of habits still ruled his mannerisms. "The queen? So the queen pays a visit to a blind prisoner? And to ask after the quality of his meals? The world yet offers surprises. Yes, they bring me food. I have little appetite, though."

"You must regain it, then," Corinn said. "If I wished you dead I would have killed you. I do not wish you to starve."

Barad tilted his head back in a motion that became an

openmouthed yawn, audible in the enclosed room. When he was finished with it, he rubbed his nose with his manacled hand. The chains clinked dully. "Kind of you."

"No, not really. I don't have much use for kindness anymore. Not for its own sake, at least." Corinn looked about the cell for a moment, though there was nothing in it to catch an eye. "Do you know that my son almost died?"

Barad crooked one eyebrow, another gesture made like a sighted man. "I heard something about that," he said. "I am sorry. Innocents should not be victims of our wicked dance."

"Traitors tried to kill him, Barad. Traitors who would kill you as well and enslave or butcher all the people you so love. Those traitors showed themselves by trying to kill my son and me. You see? This is something you haven't acknowledged. The Akarans represent the people you love to the world. When first an enemy aims to harm them, they aim at an Akaran heart. Think of my father."

The prisoner considered her words for a respectful length of time, and then said, "That's not quite how I see it."

"Yes," Corinn snapped, "but you don't see it any other way either. You don't see! You never did."

"And you've made sure I never will again." He said this sadly, inhaling as he did so. "I did like looking upon the world. I truly did. You don't know how it is not to see but to move your eyes and hear stone grinding inside your head."

"Before Aliver's war against Hanish, you claimed to have dreamed he would return. Back when nobody knew if he even lived, you boasted that he spoke to you in your dreams. Is that true, or was it a self-serving lie?"

"I was not boasting," Barad said, "and it was the truth as I understood it."

"How do you explain it, then?"

"I don't."

"Do you hear his voice now?"

Under a ridged, skeptical forehead, he said, "Aliver is dead, Your Majesty. I've never spoken with the dead."

No, but perhaps you will, she thought. Perhaps very soon. "Tell me, was my brother wise?"

"He was."

"And were you committed to him completely?"

"Of course. We all were. In the brief span that was Aliver's war, nobody—not one single person—betrayed him."

The thought of that almost took Corinn's words away. She wanted to spit that it could not be true. Somebody, somewhere said ill of him. Some soldier deserted camp at night. Some officer coveted his status. Somebody . . .

"Your Majesty, I think I understand you better now. What's wrong with you is that you feel you are alone. Isn't that it? You are alone, and it frightens you. But you don't have to—"

"I am not alone! Millions—millions—" She said the number, but was not sure how to complete the thought she began it with. Nor did it matter. A blind fool! "You will use all your gifts of oratory in my service."

"No," Barad said. "I will not."

"You will. You will bring to the people word that in my presence and through long conversation with me you have learned that you were wrong. You maligned me mistakenly. The truth—"

"Is not yours to create."

"—is that I am the last and only hope for the Known World."

"No."

"You know nothing! I have looked across the world and seen the coming enemy in my own mind. In my head!" She gestured savagely at her temple, as if she would jab her finger through it. "I've seen them, and they bring beasts and hunger and vengeance—"

"They will pay you back for the Akaran sins."

Corinn could not help but use her body to express herself.

"No, that's where you're wrong. The Auldek will kill us all. They want to make our lands theirs. And—and the quota children returning with them hate all of us. Not just me. You, too. Will you explain to them that you are not the villain who sent them away? Do you really think they'll stop long enough to hear you? The difference between us is nothing—nothing!—if we're both dead. We will be, unless all the Known World unites behind me as fully as they did behind my brother."

"That cannot—"

Corinn held up a finger as he began to interrupt. Oddly, something stopped him. He himself did not seem to know what, and his stone eyes did not move at all. But he paused, and she continued. "You will tell everybody, and have them speak, so that my words are spoken by a million tongues. I don't trust many people. I have no allies who would not abandon me. The few who would be true to me—Mena, Dariel—doubt me. It pains me that this is true, but it is. I love them, though. They don't know it, but I even need them. I need them to be the people they are."

She had not thought to say that earlier, but now that she did, she knew it was true. It really was true. For a moment, the emotion of it choked her. And then she wanted to say more.

"Mena, the goddess of rage who is also so kind, with her sword and wings . . . how can I not love her and want her free to be who she is? And Dariel. I don't know what's become of him, but I love him, and I wouldn't want him to be anything other than what he is either. Even Aliver, if he were still among us, I'd welcome with all his ideals and plans. I might have to fight with him, but they are my family. My blood."

She thought of Hanish for a moment, but not in the way she wanted to. She pushed it back and calmed her voice and said, "You're not my blood. So I don't care what is in your heart. I care what comes out of your mouth, and I think only of how it will help me protect the Known World. You, Barad, are going to be one of my staunchest allies."

"Never."

Corinn launched herself at him. Big, gangly as he was, she smashed into him, grasping his head in her arms. "Your mind is mine!" The man fought against her for a moment. He drew back a mallet of a fist, cocked, and began to bring it forward, until she slipped her thumbs around and pressed them against his stone eyes. The fist froze. His body went limp, as if she held the center of him and he could do nothing.

"Your mind is mine," Corinn repeated. "Listen, and don't deny it."

Early that evening Corinn went to the gardens of Mena's region of the palace. Though she felt the fatigue of the song she had sung for Barad, Corinn knew there was more left in her. And there were two more things she had to do before she rested. Tonight was the night for it. She felt full of resolve, powered by a measure of certainty, and she planned to see it through.

She walked cautiously, her eyes often flicking up to the bluing sky. Elya was far away, flying behind Mena, and though she had many guards looking up at the sky to spot the creature's returning and pipe a warning, Corinn still moved fast. She wove her way through the tables and benches and chairs that seemed to absurdly crowd Mena's balcony.

Delivegu had given her no specific information on where the eggs might be. In the gardens, yes, but it was no small space. It could take hours to find them; and this assumed they were real, which was not something she could be sure of. The night was crisp, the moon lighting the stones and plants and furniture well enough. She had dismissed Mena's staff, but still, still she felt a tingling urgency to—

And there they were. Corinn realized she had expected something grander than what she found, but that suddenly seemed silly. This was no foul nest like Mena's stories of Maeben. It was not elaborate. It did not smell of death, nor was it gilded. Four eggs nestled in a curl of fabric. They were strangely shaped, oblong and flatish, with swirls of color set into a creamy base. Warm to the touch, they gave her a certain joy. It came right through her fingertips, a welcome.

Corinn looked around. She held still for a long moment, sure that she would hear and feel if anybody was observing her. Nobody was. She slipped her hands down into the basin, grasped the cloth in her hands; and pulled the entirety of it out, the eggs snug inside. She sat down on a stone bench a little distance away, cradling the bundle to her chest. She could feel the life pulsing within them. Wonderful, powerful, fierce: that's what they would be.

She whispered the notes of the song that had been building in her head. She would sing to these children. Sing to them in the Giver's tongue, so that when they emerged into the world they would do so in a form shaped to her needs. She could not have Elya, but she would have her children. Yes, they were lovely already. Full of goodness, but it was not goodness that she would need in future days. Before then, she would need weapons like none the Known World had ever seen. These babies would not be feathered, timorous protectors. They would be her warriors. She sang all this into them, and she knew they heard and liked what she was telling them. They shifted inside their eggs, shouldering and stretching the shells, already eager to hatch.

And then the final thing. Her last work for that night. Late now, in her room, the lights dim and all her servants sent away. The largest of the spells she had planned. It would exhaust her, she knew, but she did not want to wait for another day. There was strength in doing, she realized. There was power in using the song. There were voices happy to aid her. Voices who, in more and more tangible ways, urged her on.

What choice did she have? they asked. Everything was in danger. She had to be able to trust someone completely, someone whom the people would love and rally behind, someone who would take part of the burden from her and carry it with her, someone who had held the world in his hands already. Someone who loved her and would be truly by her side. Someone who would thank her for forgiving him.

Barad, the agitator from the mines of Kidnaban, a rebel, a seditious, treasonous, poisonous barb in her side—a blind fool—was right. She was alone. She had been for years. Maybe she had been since the day she saw herself in the fingers of her dying mother's hands so many years ago, when she was but a girl, when first she learned how callous the world was. That was then.

The things to come she could not do alone. She did not face the future for herself and she did not want to face it by herself. She did not have to. She just had to take from one place and give to another. In this case, she had to take from her family's blood. She understood that better now. The voices helped her. The song made more sense now. The worm had a beauty as it turned and it helped her gain control. She was not a child anymore: awkward with her motions, clumsy, seeing a blurred world. Her hands were her own now. Each digit, each contour and wrinkle and blemish. They were her hands!

Confident in this, reassured by whispers from far away, she opened her mouth and let out the song that would make for her what she wished. Death was not so great a barrier. She had spent her life thinking it was the final, the absolute, the end, the horrible curse. But that was only part of it. The voices helped her understand this.

As she sang it just seemed more and more obvious. She had found a truth that escaped those with no knowledge of the Giver's tongue. As she sang, she peeled back the barriers between life and death. As she sang, she searched among the vague forms on the other side of what she had believed to be life—though she knew the barrier was not the simple thing she had feared.

And there she found one of the ones she sought. At first he was as diffuse as a scent lofting on a breeze, spread thin and in communion with so much of the world. She drew the traces of him in. She sang, and the farflung essence of him could not deny her invocation. For a time it was like her words were hands and the one she sought was sand draining through her fingers. But she sang the harder for it. She pulled him toward her, so forcefully that eventually . . .

He stood before her. He was there, upright, diaphanous, luminous at moments, but also tangibly physical. It was a he, and she knew him, though the details of his face moved and rippled and would not settle. Not yet.

"What have you done?" he rasped, like an aged man stirred from a dream of youth.

For a horrible moment, Corinn thought the figure was questioning every decision she had made since they had last seen each other. She could never explain it all! Life had placed before her a thousand challenges, each with a million barbed entanglements and dangers. Decisions had to be made and they fell upon nobody but her. She had made them as best she could. None could fault her. None could understand her. None could know what it meant to rule an empire. None, except perhaps the very one who had posed the question.

She realized time was passing and she had not answered. The man's eyes bored into her. He asked again, "What have you done?"

This time she heard the question differently, or chose to. "I have pulled you back to life."

"Why?"

How could she answer? She could say that she was afraid of the threat marching toward the Known World. She mistrusted herself now more than ever before and could no longer tell whether the things she did were for good or for ill. She could explain that all the power she had amassed was nothing if she was blind to those who would harm her son. She had so nearly lost Aaden! If that could happen, what other horrors might yet await her? She could have admitted that each weapon she held—her allies the league, who lied to her with every other word; the wine with which she would make a nation of obedient servants; the song that even now danced out over the world, stirring a worm deep in the bowels of the earth as it did so—was a two-faced treachery waiting to strike. She should swear that she hated sending Mena and Dariel out as unwilling agents, loathed that she seemed incapable of opening herself fully to them. She might declare that she wanted none of these things to be so. She needed him to help her remedy it all. It was all too much to carry on a single pair of shoulders; and if he would help her, perhaps together they could chart a surer course together than either of them could alone. She could have said that she doubted every high ideal that had ever escaped his lips but admitted that a part of her very much wanted to believe.

All this she might have said, but she did not. Though she meant it all, she also knew that she still clung to each writhing portion of the things she hated; she was herself the two-faced treachery that she feared and that she wished he might save her from. She was, even now, just a breath away from wishing she had summoned a different person altogether. So instead of confessing everything, she said, "Because the world needs you. Things are not complete. We need you in life, not darkness."

"Darkness?" the figure asked. He closed his eyes as if remembering the meaning of the word. "No, death is not darkness. Nor have I forgotten life. Each moment brings new souls into the afterdeath. They bring news of the living, though it fades from them fast. But I have not been dead to life." He opened his eyes again. "I know of you and the things you have done."

Corinn had not expected to say what she did then. She had not even known she thought it. But it was true, and it felt very important to say it now. "Then you know that only you can save me. Please."

As she waited for the answer, the figure before her became that much more tangible, just a little more solid, not quite so transparent, even though he remained vague and half formed. The man held up a hand. He nodded, not in affirmation but to indicate that he would answer her. It was an offer that deserved consideration, and he was not so at peace with death that he would fail to think it through. He just needed a few moments. Then he would answer her.

Queen Corinn Akaran folded her hands in her lap and sat as straight backed as she could in her fatigue, awaiting the spirit's answer, ready—if he should accept—to whisper his name and complete the spell and bring him truly back into the world. *Aliver Akaran*, she would say, and mean every word, *life needs you still. I need you still. Come back. Fight the coming war at my side. Complete the work you left undone . . .*

Acknowledgements

Gudrun reads everything first, which is lucky for us all. I thank her for that; readers should, too. I'd also like to thank Jamie Johnston (aka Dariel) for giving this novel the once-over. Hannah Strom-Martin was a wonder with an editorial pen, and this novel is better for her efforts. As ever, I'm so pleased and lucky to be able to work with my editor, Gerry Howard, and to have the guidance of my agent, Sloan Harris. I'd also like to welcome the widening family of editors and readers coming to my work around the world, in tongues I don't yet speak. Thank you.

HANNIBAL
PRIDE OF CARTHAGE

By David Anthony Durham

In a time before Caesar, before Augustus or Constantine, before the Gallic Wars or the conquest of Britain, in a time before Rome's place in the history of the western world was assured, the nascent empire had first to survive a devastating assault by its most formidable foe. A man celebrated and feared like few figures from history, his name was Hannibal Barca, and the bitter conflict between his people and the Roman Republic shaped the destiny of nations…

Capturing the panoramic scope of what would become known as the Second Punic War (218-202BC) – from Hannibal's famous elephant-mounted crossing of the Alps to the savagery of battles like Trasimene and Zama – this epic novel chronicles a titanic struggle through the actions of individual characters: Hannibal, his nemesis Publius Scipio, their princes, generals and foot soldiers, friends, lovers and wives. In these pages, ancient history is brought to brilliant, thrilling and unforgettable life.

'An extraordinary achievement: Durham puts flesh on the bones of Carthage in a way that no novelist has done since Flaubert'
Tom Holland, author of *Rubicon*

'Wonderful…not only deeply evocative of time and place, character and situation, but also lyrically written, compellingly composed… a masterpiece'
Jeffrey Lent, author of *Lost Nation*

'Vividly captures the frenzy of ancient warfare… a skilfully structured and gripping novel'
New York Times

9780553814910

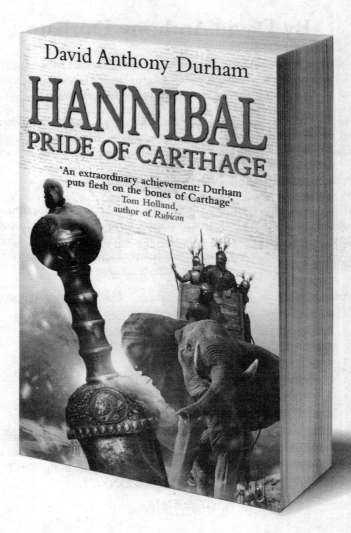

David Anthony Durham

HANNIBAL
PRIDE OF CARTHAGE

'An extraordinary achievement: Durham
puts flesh on the bones of Carthage'
Tom Holland,
author of *Rubicon*

ACACIA

BOOK ONE: THE WAR WITH THE MEIN

By David Anthony Durham

Presiding over Acacia, an empire named after the idyllic island
from which he rules, Leodan Akaran has inherited a peace
and prosperity won long ago by his ancestors.

He's an intelligent man, a widower who dotes on his four children,
and so hides from them a terrible knowledge – that Acacia's prosperity
is founded on the trafficking of drugs and human lives. He is also a man
of integrity and determines to end this vile trade.
But powerful forces stand in his way.

Then an assassin, sent from the Mein – a race exiled long ago to an
ice-locked stronghold in the frozen north – strikes, and the Mein unleash
surprise attacks against their old oppressor. Mortally wounded, Leodan
puts into play a plan to enable his children to escape,
to survive and to fulfil their destinies.

And so begins an epic quest – to avenge a father's death and restore
an empire, *this* time on the basis of universal freedom.

'Demonstrates that he is a master of the fantasy epic'
Washington Post

'Entertaining and engaging… If *The War with the Mein*
is an indication of what is to come in this epic saga,
Durham could be making a very big name for himself'
SFFWORLD

'Vastly entertaining… Will good win out over evil? In Durham's
morally ambiguous world, the uncertainty is part of the thrill'
STRANGEHORIZONS

9780553819670

DAVID ANTHONY DURHAM

ACACIA

THE ACCLAIMED NEW FANTASY

'Demonstrates that he is a master of the fantasy epic.'
WASHINGTON POST